TIMEWAVE!

The popping of the time bubbles and the roar of the froth shut out all other noise, even the sound of Hubert's straining engines. Several buildings of the TAC were now encased in bubbles; I even felt some temporal droplets falling and watched as my skin began to dissolve where the droplets touched it. No time to compose a poem.

"Hubert!" I screamed into my phone. "Now or never!"

The vehicle finished his lap and roared up to me in a shower of temporal droplets; his hull was spattered with corrosion from the droplets.

The door to his cockpit popped open and I sprang inside with Nick-Nick, my weapons and my bag of artificial money.

Hubert was shaking with fear and still pouring every ounce of energy into forcibly waking up the full power of his interdimensional faculties. But the roar of the timewave drowned out the noise of Hubert's engines and of the whole world.

Then we saw it, shimmering and bearing down upon us like the grapes of wrath, nonexistence in its wake. I thought of seeing myself dissolve into nonexistence an hour ago in that time bubble and I decided I'd had enough of that shit.

"Now, Hubert! Get us out of here!"

Hubert didn't need to be told twice. He began to vibrate with the activation of his interdimensional drive, and as that great wave of non-existence overtook us we slipped into that interdimensional space that serves as the doorway to the past.

Before the door closed, I glanced once more at the world we'd left behind. It looked like a very cold and lonely place.

APOLLO STARMULE

Apollo Polyhistor Starmule was born and raised near a swamp in West Tennessee. His family owns a part of this swamp, and the young Starmule spent many relatively happy hours skirting around the edge of the swamp with his dog and fowling piece. He attended University in the Obion River country of West Tennessee, and graduated without honors from the University of Tennessee at Martin with a degree in journalism and a minor in military science. He worked as an Infantry officer for the Reserve Components of the Army during Reagan's Golden Reign, and also worked many exciting and challenging jobs that enabled him to experience the lifestyle of America's working poor.

Starmule's spiritual path was always the primary component of his life, and at the age of ten he began secretly developing and following a subversive spiritual method. The method was subversive because its objective was Truth, and this Principle was actively discouraged in the community and in the country as a whole. He did not know that there were others working along spiritual lines until he reached college and was exposed to the work of Alan Watts, a fellow drunkard. Mr. Watts' exposition of Zen helped bump student Starmule out of the agnosticism into which he had briefly fallen into a more integrated approach to his own spirituality.

During the Nineties, the furnace of spiritual refinement made it impractical for Mr. Starmule to continue trying to merge with an impure culture, so he left his home in Austin, Texas and withdrew into the wilderness of Northern California. His quest led him into certain interdimensional activities that were devoted to erasing evil from the experience of this earth. He helped "clean up" a sacred mountain that had temporarily fallen to the naughty ones, but the experience left him 'way beyond mere exhaustion, and in the end his penis had to be pulled out of the fire by a Tibetan Lama and a Native American Shaman. Though not that large, his penis also required for its extraction the assistance of a group of Tibetan Buddhist monks.

Today Mr. Starmule is holed up somewhere in the mountains of North Carolina. He is a fornicator. He has no wives and no known offspring in this part of the timeline.

Books by Apollo Starmule

UNDO THE WINTER: The Odyssey
of Sonny-Bob Culpepper

And Coming Soon:

AH, MAN! A Slim Volume of Poetry

SCARLET SCHOOLGIRL AND OTHER POEMS

BELTANE'S CHILD

This Goode Booke Published By

SATYA YUGA BOOKS
Asheville Weaverville Nacogdoches Tokyo

This Extraordinary Product Is Printed And Distributed Simultaneously
In The United States And Across The Pond In The United Kingdom.
So We See There Has Been A Reconciliation Between The Colonies And
The Crown.

The Compact Book Visual Literary System Offers The Highest
Attainment In The Production Of Letters, Words And Sentences
In A Small, Easy To Carry Format That Will Soon Render
Stone Tablets Obsolete.

The Book's Remarkable Performance Is Due
To The Invention Of Paper, The Printing Press, And To The Cunning
Binding Of Many Printed Sheets Together
Into A Single Continuum Of Messaging. Nothing Will Ever Beat It.

Statement of Artistic Derivation

All characters in this fine literary product
are either archetypes or sub-archetypes, or
secular or religious or historical celebrities.
Nobody in this book is based on anyone
you know--unless you know archetypes or
sub-archetypes, or secular or religious or
historical celebrities. And the perceptive person
may conclude that sometimes these categories
may overlap. A person of still greater
ability at contemplative observation may
perceive how there are no categories at all,
only points of expression of particular forces
which continually cycle about one another.
This person is a candidate for either sainthood
or for admission to a mental institution.
Or both.

Cover Illustration

*THE CHYMICAL WEDDING OF LUCILLE THE PROPHETESS WITH
CAPTAIN SONNY-BOB CULPEPPER*

By
Jacinda Sedgley

Cover Design By Angela Donelle Underwood

Dedicated to Those Free Souls in Austin,
The Capital of The People's Republic of Texas,
Who Introduced Me to the Ways of the Goddess
Including, But Not Limited to,
the Young Woman Who Got Me Out of My Clothes
For My First Expression of Public Nudity

"I'm not like other women."

--Mark Twain

INTRODUCTION TO THE NINETY-FOURTH EDITION OF UNDO THE WINTER

Never in the history of literature was there such a close relationship between a writer's voice and readers' response as there was between Apollo Starmule's books and the people--particularly the Indigo People-- of the early twenty-first century. Starmule burst on the scene in the middle of a social stagnation with no underlying spiritual fire to burn away the dross . . . and became a one-man Roman Candle, penning nearly forty books that lit the people's souls with a new Vision of their own capacity for spiritual Achievement, and led them to break up and burn the ancient forms of the past and recombine the elements of their own psyche to better reflect their new Vision.

Heady, heady stuff . . . Starmule's books grabbed his audience by the balls and kicked their ass halfway to the moon . . . and made them laugh practically every centimeter of the way. We take it for granted today that spiritual and moral Achievement involve getting down and dirty with the shadow side, purifying it of glamour and illusion, but Apollo Starmule faced a world where the principles of true, deep spiritual Work were practically unknown. And the people, despite their reluctance to deal with their shadow (actually, because of that very reluctance) were actually ruled by their shadow side. Apollo Starmule tricked them into facing the truth about themselves and pointed the way to their redemption by melding spiritual Vision with the shadow of the people in such a way that the spiritual energy began transmuting the perversions out of that shadow thru the illuminating application of Cosmic Fire, and revealing that you give up nothing except glamour and illusion, and gain everything when you create a genuine, fiery spiritual Path for yourself. Then the people thus inspired went out and created a new world . . . our world, baby.

Those of us who were assigned to the first decade of the twenty-first century will never forget Apollo Starmule's detonation of the Cosmic Fire of his Truth Pattern in bookstores worldwide with the publication of his groundbreaking novel *UNDO THE WINTER: The Odyssey of Sonny-Bob Culpepper.* In contrast to the milksop new-age cotton candy in vogue at the time, *UNDO THE WINTER* cast a clear, no-holds-barred light on human perversions, and revealed the keys to human redemption in an updated form of the ancient language of the human psyche. The genius of this kind of work is that you don't have to study it; the ancient language just sort of seeps into your awareness with a pulsing rhythm as you page thru the book enjoying the wild tale of Captain Culpepper and chuckling like a mad fool at his bizarre adventures. By the end of the book, you realize that an alchemical change has occurred in your perceptions, tho' you may be at a loss to describe the nature of this change.

UNDO THE WINTER is such a clear and humorous presentation of the human subconscious by an author whose subconscious mind was also his everyday conscious mind that it became the first true print-on-demand bestseller. The novel eclipsed every other work of fiction of the day in the degree of interest it generated, and today ranks as the number one bestseller of all time, having sold more copies than the *Holy Bible* and Hugh Hefner's *Memoirs* combined.

And the people who allowed their perceptions to be changed by Starmule's Work went out and created a New World. Our World. And because Starmule's perceptions were born on Our World, they rhythm and resonate today with as much force and vigor -- and humor -- as they did in the first few years of the twenty-first century. Ain't no trendiness here; this Work was born in the high-up hills and carried like a pine-knot Torch into the valleys, setting afire the dead wood of preconceptions so a new green forest of Truth might rise to replace the tired sentimentality and exploitation of the so-called "new age", and the stagnant savagery of the controllers of society.

The Book stands in a class of its own. Some are calling it Speculative Mythology, though real Mythology involves little speculation. Apollo Starmule invites us to live as mythical beings, not just think or jabber about it. To live the Myth, you have to be willing to drop the illusion of objectivity and learn to *feel*, and learn to quit lying about your feelings. In your feelings lies the truth of your own nature and your ability to consciously connect with the Universal Pattern of Metaphor in which we all dwell. Those who guide themselves by intellect cannot feel the guidance of the Great Pattern, and so completely miss the nature of Reality. Thus world tragedy is brewed by the mere intellectual, while those who allow themselves to chivalrously feel the Pattern merge themselves with all the true Visions of humankind. Valor leads to the Pattern.

When a dog or a cat or a deer or a musk ox sees you, he sees a metaphor for something in his religion, something in his "world consciousness". He sees a character from out of his mythology, he sees a legendary being. Many generations of his ancestors have known you and told stories about you. He doesn't dissect you like the so-called scientists of the twentieth century in an effort to find what you are *not*, he accepts you whole and interacts with you as metaphor. Perhaps you are a frost giant to the musk ox, for with your .30-06 rifle you may appear to be an invincible force of nature to him as you stalk the frozen wastelands where he resides. Obviously, you are a god to your dog and a slave to your cat. To the deer, you are a part of the Pattern which demands a cyclical sacrifice from his people, perhaps in return for furnishing them with corn and soybeans, and then leaves his tribe in peace for the rest of the year.

In this sense, the dog or cat or deer or musk ox consciousness is similar to the wizard's consciousness, except that the wizard consciously moves throughout more levels of the Pattern and there are more dimensions to the metaphors he perceives and interacts with. So the wizard serves to organize more varied communities of energies than do the critters whose religion is similar to his. The wizard is more fluid and has more dimensions to his consciousness, thus he is more whole and is a more able administrator than the dog or the cat.

Nature spirits communicate in metaphors; for instance, if they speak of unrolling a carpet, they probably mean they are about to unroll the etheric pattern for the new carpet of grass that is to be pulled up thru the soil by that pattern in the springtime. This fact must always be remembered if any of our communication with nature spirits is to be useful, for even if they sometimes seem to speak the King's English, they most certainly do not share the King's thoughtforms. When they seem to speak your language, they most probably are merely reflecting your language back upon you; most certainly, it is not their native tongue unless perhaps you yourself are an elf or gnome or somesuch.

If you are a woman who has Achieved a high level of sparkling gracefulness, you may have realized that the male cannot help but conceive of you as a goddess. It is written across his psyche and in his cells. It is written in the quickening of his aura when you approach. There is no objectification in this experience if the man is a gentleman, only a deep appreciation and possibility of emotional connection. There is no cure for this condition, so have compassion and understanding for the effect you have on your male neighbor. For in his holy madness lies the reflection of the Beauty of your own female nature.

The "Human Being" is a metaphor for a collection of relatively intelligent energies that stalks the earth in a certain fairly predictable fashion, interacting with the various kingdoms in nature and perceived by each kingdom thru the unique lens of its own understanding. Thus each species or variation within each kingdom knows humanity thru both the lens of its own nature and thru the nature of the unique interaction it shares with Humanity. No kingdom in nature perceives some objective "truth" regarding any other kingdom, but each kingdom regards the others thru the lens of mutual relationship born of distinctions between the kingdoms which allow those kingdoms to share a planet in a mutually nourishing fashion, each Achieving some goal in service to the whole. The idea that there is competition in nature is false, and those who subscribe to this illusion have restricted their own consciousness away from intelligent interaction with the Pattern. Thus they cannot be nourished. They are always trying to "get", with the result that they can never allow themselves to receive. Hence their agitation. That which is divorced from its own nature cannot avoid distress. If religion is about anything, it is about coordinating energies which are at once distinct from one another and complementary to each other. In other words, it is about *sharing*.

And so we see the soul's willingness to share with the outer form that cloaks it. We have spoken of metaphor as the Pattern, but really it might be more appropriate to say that metaphor is the cloak of many colors that serves to give form to the Force of Life that resides within the Pattern. Let us call that Force God, knowing that all our souls reside within that Great Force as indivisible jewels that give sparkle to the Great Force, and let us say that each of our bodies and personalities is our own personal thread in the Pattern of Metaphor. When our outer form has mastered the process of sharing, it will be a pure, refined reflection of our souls. This is how the Pattern of Metaphor comes alive. When the threads begin to scintillate with the knowingness of Self and the fusion with Self, the whole Pattern glows in love supernal. Of course we are made in the image of God! God is love, and God's nature is the nature of sharing. Love is the nature of sharing.

And we see the religion of the Goddess return, for such religion is based upon the growth, nurturing and sharing of the Beauty of the human soul thru the medium of the body and appropriately cultured personality. The gentlewoman is the Leader of the future world.

A legend, or myth, is an area of the Pattern where the symbols relate to one another in an organized, intelligent, rhythmic fashion. The energy sent forth from these legends stimulates the brains and nervous systems of all living beings near that area of the Pattern, moving those beings to take up residence in a legend, or in a particular part of a legend, thus allowing the legend to outwork in their own lives as they influence the lives of their neighbors toward a new legendary consciousness by their own newly-enriched vibrations. The wizard is the master of this outworking; other beings play a complementary role in the weaving. And all the weavers themselves become a part of the new Pattern. Separation is an illusion; there is one vast and starry carpet of Being composed of many interwoven threads. But only the wizard can bend and mend the legends, making them more appropriate to an evolving Pattern when this intelligent Pattern decides it is ready for a new movement, a new evolution. Thus the wizard is the master of Time and Perception, who sit upon his shoulders like two diligent ravens which may be sent into the ruins of decay to find that one spot which must be quickened at the appropriate moment to console the Pattern into birthing itself into a reorganization of fresh new livingness with new qualities unfolding, as previously developed qualities support, nurture and complement the new.

The wizard can only be seen when he wants to be seen, wearing whatever particular garments seem most appropriate to the new movement within the Pattern. When the Pattern has become frayed and wants to arrange itself into a fresh new beautiful Harmony, the call goes out and the wizard is drawn forth from the bowels of Time and Destiny to perform a new weave. Hopefully, he'll be sober when he shows up for duty.

But let us not digress too far from Apollo Starmule's novel. The extraordinary Book you hold in your hands is a dish of raw meat, reflecting a mad delirium that can never be understood by the scholar, but only by those deep-feeling ones who are ready to undertake the discipline of their own soul's lust for purification. So Starmule's Work lacks the sophisticated naiveté of the "new age" material and the manipulativeness of everything else, but it does contain that multilayered rhythm that all sacred writings have always held. The direct, honest people contain the keys to human evolution, and always have.

The rhythms of the psyche belong to the meek, not to the sophisticated assholes.

Ephraim Blavatsky
Field Agent Supervisor
Cultural Beginnings Section
Year 2482 of the Common Era

UNDO THE WINTER

THE ODYSSEY OF SONNY-BOB CULPEPPER

INSPIRED BY ACTUAL EVENTS

TO: Freya Hatfield
    Special Correspondent
    Goddess News Network

FROM: The Tibetan
      Spiritual Advisor
      Temporal Adjustment Corps

SUBJECT: Official Report On Attempt To Save The Timeline

DATE: 4 Sept. 2175

1. Enclosed is the official record of Captain Sonny-Bob Culpepper's attempt to save the timeline. Due to the nature of the adjustment he attempted, CAPT. Culpepper is the only human being who knows what actually happened. Hubert, his interdimensional vehicle, has verified CAPT. Culpepper's official version of events. However, we at the Temporal Adjustment Corps have our doubts.

2. CAPT. Culpepper's official report is full of self-serving imaginational constructs. That's the polite way of putting it. Some of these situations are, shall we say, highly improbable, even for the individual CAPT. Culpepper refers to as "Hemingway".

3. You can make of this report what you will. As you prepare for your broadcast, I do encourage you to consider your reputation.

Your Obedient Servant,
The Tibetan
Spiritual Advisor
Temporal Adjustment Corps

P.S.: Are we still on for Saturday?

PART ONE

ENKIDU THE MECHANIC

PROLOGUE

It had been a long month, and I was tired of drinking mare's milk and eating practically nothing. My buddy Genghis pooted-- lactose intolerant -- then suggested we go steal a goat from the village we'd been reconnoitering.

"Why not?" I shrugged. "Red meat is high in iron, and we still have a long way to go." Our bodies needed that iron.

Two weeks later we rode down from the hills and I watched as my friend Genghis and his Mongolian warriors slaughtered relatively innocent civilians -- men and children -- then raped the women. No biggie. I'd seen it all before and in many timezones. The ancient Hebrews were just as bad, maybe worse. But you can't force civilization on hogs; I wasn't there to interfere, but to gather material for my documentary. I cheerfully filmed as my hogs butchered the other hogs.

Their fires sputtered from the dripping grease as they tore at the meat of their slain enemies. They beckoned me to join them, but I replied that I was happy with mare's milk. A lie, but I wasn't going to turn cannibal unless it was really necessary.

I filmed as they again raped the wives and daughters of their new food supply, sometimes offering them a bite from one of their relatives. They usually refused, but were left no choice in the matter of the rapes. And it wouldn't be too many more days before those wives and daughters themselves were food.

I'm tired of mare's milk, I thought glumly, then stole a glance at one of the fires.

CHAPTER ONE

The intercom chirped. "Lieutenant Culpepper report to The Tibetan, please."

I looked up. After six pots of coffee and another all-nighter, I was nearly through editing my documentary about the Mongols. Soon it would become a standard text at the Academy, and maybe even help to get me on a promotion list before too much longer. I'd been a lieutenant with the Temporal Adjustment Corps (TAC) for thirty-three years and was chomping at the bit to make captain.

I shut down the computer and stood up at my desk. I nearly fell over backward; those last two pots of coffee had been Irish coffee. Then my bladder cramped and jerked me forward, restoring my equilibrium. I tottered to the latrine and relieved myself, then spat on my palms and slicked back my hair. I noted my beauty in the mirror. I was a handsome operative nearly six feet in length, with green eyes and hair that would have been blonde if it had been washed recently. The normal pallor was beginning to return to my skin, as it had been several weeks since I'd been riding out in the sun with my Mongol friends. I kept my biological age at thirty-five years (not so young as to seem immature, but not old enough for a swollen prostate), though my actual age was seventy-two. I was an old coot by the standards of previous centuries, but now that we had Practical Immortality there was no telling how old a human being could grow in subjective years while remaining young biologically. My generation was the first to receive the full benefits of Practical Immortality; I was born in the year 2100 and might live until hell froze over, for all anyone knew. I smiled. It was great to be alive, immortal, and working in Gaffney, South Carolina.

I turned away from the mirror; even Adonis must get tired of admiring himself occasionally. But Adonis, I reminded myself, would never forget to shave. It had been several days since I'd last scraped off the stubble. Well, maybe no one would notice. I buttoned up my uniform shirt, made sure I had my belt on, and proceeded to The Tibetan's office. He ran things around here.

* * *

When the TAC was founded it was believed that its work should flow from a spiritual impulse to prevent contamination of the space-time continuum by those whose motives might be less than pure. Its primary mission was to maintain the integrity of the timeline by making whatever adjustments were necessary to insure that things in the past stayed pretty much as they'd always been. This was considered desirable because people of my time lived in a pretty good world, and by Goddess we weren't going to allow some doofus to go back into history and change something -- such a procedure might have negative consequences for our time, or even (shudder) cause our world to disappear entirely.

Anyhow, the NSA agents and Delta Force operatives who founded the TAC felt they needed divine guidance regarding the management of history, so they procured a Tibetan lama to command the organization. They knew they would have to make adjustments in the past to insure that our world kept rolling along. Nobody knew how many alternate timelines had been wiped out already by some fool cultural anthropologist with time travel technology, or by an inquisitive adolescent who'd figured out how to "time hack" on her own. Well by God (or by Buddha, if you are The Tibetan) our timeline would be the one that stayed. We'd win the "Survival of the Fittest Olympics" for timelines. Nothing less than a gold medal would do.

"Announce me to The Tibetan," I told his door.

"Okay," the door replied. I heard its muffled tones coming from the other side, then it said formally, "The Tibetan will receive you now. And don't forget to remove your shoes!"

I took my shoes off and placed them on the mat beside the door. "Damn Buddhist customs," I mumbled irritably.

"I heard that!" the door shouted.

I stepped forward and the door slid back to reveal a sparsely furnished room. Incense hung in the air, and I thought I detected the odor of hashish--or perhaps it was just the aroma of The Tibetan's potpourri.

A wizened little man with closely cropped white hair sat across the way on a mat, smiling beatifically. He'd arranged the lighting to produce a halo effect around his head.

"Lieutenant Sonny-Bob Culpepper," the door intoned, "is here to receive your orders, O Holy One."

The Tibetan beckoned to me. "Come closer, Sonny-Bob. Come closer and sit."

I was reluctant to get too close to him for fear of his chewing tobacco. Sometimes when he'd get enthused about something and began jabbering wildly in Tibetan the slobber would fly all over the place. It was a danger to anyone concerned about his hygiene--but then, I reflected, I had the weekend off, and with the documentary finished I would probably take time to bathe. There was no problem, then.

I paused halfway across the room to admire a life-sized nude sculpture of country music legend Dolly Parton. Her dimensions were right up my alley and I said as much to The Tibetan.

"Yes," he said with a dreamy, far away look in his eyes, "she is delicious. And I should know, for once I traveled back to the 1970's to meet her and we became the chest--I mean, the **best**--of friends. We spent several weeks in the Smokey Mountains making love every day, or at least every two or three days between visits to the trout pond. Those hatchery raised trout weren't very much sport, but Dolly was. She drained every drop of love from my loins and then went on tour with Kenny Rogers or somebody.

"So I headed back to the Fifties to meet Patsy Cline, but was intercepted and dragged back here by Internal Affairs. They watched me for a long time thereafter, which put a damper on **my** affairs. But it was worth it to flaunt the rules and be with Dolly for those few weeks. Love always wins over rules, Sonny-Bob. If ever you have to choose between rules and love while working for me, I want you to choose love. Understand? Choose love."

"Okay, sir."

I sat down in front of him as he spat; an amber glob sailed across the room and nailed a horsefly on the wing. *That must be the kind of control they teach you in lama school*, I reflected.

"How's your documentary on the Mongols coming?"

"Almost finished, sir. And I hope it's at least a century before I have to drink any more mare's milk."

"That shit's good," The Tibetan said, smacking his lips. "I wish I had some right now."

Well, what can you expect from an old boy raised in Tibet?

The door spoke. "Miss Lewinsky to see you, sir."

"Show her in."

I rose to my feet as an angel of love and beauty wafted across the room and into the arms of The Tibetan, who planted a wet and juicy one on her willing mouth.

She wiped the tobacco juice off her lips as The Tibetan released her. "Monica, I want you to meet Lieutenant Sonny-Bob Culpepper, the agent I've told you so much about."

She sauntered over to me, hand extended, and her hand was not the only thing that was extended in that room. "Hello, Sonny-Bob," she said huskily.

"Hello, ma'am," I managed to croak, all the while aware of my acutely throbbing rudder, and somehow I knew she was aware of it, too. "How do you do?"

"I do fine, Sonny-Bob," she whispered wetly. "I do just fine."

"Monica is one of our best undercover operatives," I heard The Tibetan say, as though from a great distance. "She's just back from assignment in the Twentieth."

"Yes. . . . ," she said, licking her lips, and there was something about that pink tongue flicking at the corners of her mouth that made my knees nearly buckle, and I sensed that her knees were about to give way as well.

She moved closer as I collapsed; I fainted and might have died right there if I'd hit my heads on something, but Monica caught me, and as consciousness departed I was aware only of her tongue, her pink flicking tongue . . .

I awoke some hours later, and my first conscious thought was of Monica. Then I felt a certain sensation in my trousers, and knew that I'd had a nocturnal emission--in broad daylight, no less.

I heard voices whispering together, then The Tibetan's wild giggle, and I knew I must still be in the Boss' office. I propped myself up on an elbow and looked around.

I was lying on a little pallet that had been assembled just for me; it was composed of a couple of The Tibetan's Persian rugs and a snow leopard hide. My head had been resting on a Bible, King James Version, words of Jesus in red.

The Tibetan was lying with his head in Monica Lewinsky's lap as she gently poked grapes down his throat, her sweet fingers sliding in and out of his puckered mouth. They wore only light cotton kimonos--suitable attire if you've just been fornicating.

One of Monica's nipples--and I swear it was big as a bass lure--had worked its way free from her loosely tied garment. She glanced over at me. "Baby's awake."

The Tibetan chewed the last of his grapes and sat up. He reached for his tobacco pouch. "Welcome back to the land of the living, Sonny-

Bob."

I was feeling cross. I had been so busy all week working on that damned documentary that I hadn't had a chance to get laid. How long had it been? Seven or eight days, at least. And now I had expended my wad in my own trousers, instead of in a woman's warm vault. *"Well,"* I thought philosophically, *"that's what happens when you let it build up that way."* But then I glanced again at Monica, and was cheered by the thought that with this one, I could go four or five times without a break. She had it in her, she did, and I wondered at the historical roles such a beauty might have played--Cleopatra, no doubt, and Nefertiti, and perhaps Pauline Bonaparte . . . there was just no telling without reading her files, but I knew she had it in her to play the greatest womanly roles that could be played. She was a woman to topple empires, this one was . . . she must have been Helen of Troy . . .

"Sonny-Bob!" The Tibetan cawed. "Snap out of it!"

"Yes, sir," I said, sitting up slowly. I had to sit up slowly, as my telescoping rod, my own sweet root, was beginning to make itself known again. "Yes, sir. I'm all here."

"You certainly are," Monica laughed.

I blushed for the first time in forty years.

"Monica's here to brief you, Sonny-Bob, if you can just stay awake long enough. And if you can't, we'll have to have you neutered. I've got an important mission for you, and for once you've got to pay attention. Understand?"

"Yes, sir," I said contritely. "I'll pay attention. To the briefing."

"Brief him, Monica."

Lewinsky was suddenly all business. She stood up, went to a closet and pulled out a uniform. The garment showed a lieutenant colonel's rank. She dropped the kimono and stepped into the trousers, and I saw her bush, her sweet precious bush, as big a bush as I have ever beheld, big as an adult porcupine . . .

"Sonny-Bob! Don't you go away again," the Tibetan warned, wagging a stern forefinger.

I remembered what he'd said about me having, uh, an **operation,** and averted my eyes at once. After about five minutes my pulse slowed, my blood pressure began to return to normal, and my flag fell to half-mast.

I peeked around cautiously, and saw that my sweet Monica--no, mustn't think of her as sweet, might get hard again--I saw that Lieutenant Colonel Monica Lewinsky, Temporal Adjustment Corps, was standing a few feet in front of me, poised with businesslike certainty. Her attitude had completely changed; the pouty seduction was gone and she was no longer sexy. *How'd she do that*, I wondered. A chameleon, this one was. Better watch her.

"Lieutenant Culpepper," she said, "we have a timewave."

CHAPTER TWO

"A timewave!" I gasped, as the blood drained from my face and my member went completely limp. "A timewave?"

She nodded. "A timewave. We've been able to establish that the wave originated in October, 1983 . . ."

"Just in time for Halloween," I muttered. "How fitting."

" . . . and everything we know of history between that date and the present is rapidly being demolished. *Everything's* gone, Lieutenant-- everything! I want you to be aware of the magnitude of this."

I was trembling. If the wave destroyed **everything** . . . why, then I myself would have no existence when it flooded the present moment. I was on the verge of tears, but didn't want to be seen crying by a woman, particularly one I might want to fuck one day . . . if one day even existed. So I bit my lip and didn't cry, but couldn't help saying, "I'm scared."

"I'm scared too, Sonny-Bob," the colonel said, her tone softening. "We all are scared, particularly the agents we've already sent back to deal with the catastrophe--they don't exist anymore."

This time a tear did trickle down my cheek, followed by another and another . . . if they'd already sent agents back who had failed, and who had ceased to exist, why now it must be my turn. And I didn't want to go. I almost said as much, but then remembered my manhood, the cockiness of knowing that every mission I'd ever been assigned had been completed successfully . . . more or less. I steeled myself, then allowed the warm cockiness to flood my belly and my attitude. I'd learned all this in yoga class.

Colonel Lewinsky was watching me closely. "That's better. I was beginning to worry about your psychological state."

"My psychological state is just fine," I told her, knowing I could have a breakdown, if needed, after I got back to my office. There was my stuffed elephant, Nick-Nick, who resided in a bottom drawer of my desk. I'd had him since I was three or four years old, and he was always a comfort in times of distress. I'd even carried him on a few missions.

"Nick-Nick," I accidentally croaked.

"Say again?"

"Nick-Nick is his stuffed elephant," The Tibetan sighed wearily. "He always turns to him in a crisis."

Monica--I mean, Colonel Lewinsky--began slapping her swagger stick against her palm. "Lobsang," (only The Tibetan's sexual partners were allowed to call him by his name) "Lobsang, I think we should send someone else."

"Honey, there **is** no one else, you know that. Sonny-Bob's the last of the best. Hell, if he'd just kiss the general's asses like all the other field agents, he might've been the first we'd have sent. But the generals don't like him and always give him shit assignments. He's never even been allowed to save a continent. But he **has** always achieved total success with the missions he has been given."

It was true. The generals were prejudiced against me. I'd saved a few nations, but never a continent, and certainly not an entire timeline.

Yes, my buddy The Tibetan **mostly** ran things; he decided which missions needed our attention based upon his mighty spiritual understanding of All That Is. But then, as per the organizational structure set up by the Founders, he had to assign the missions to the Council of Generals, who picked the agents and developed the strategies for those missions. The fact that The Tibetan and Lewinsky were briefing me was odd in itself . . . I had a sudden suspicion. "Where are the generals?"

The Tibetan and Lewinsky glanced at each other. "Gone," The Tibetan said softly.

"Gone," Lewinsky whispered.

Just as I thought: the feebleminded generals had each gone to stop the catastrophe themselves, instead of assigning it to their best agent--me--and they had each drowned in the timewave.

"I'm not interested in this mission anymore," I sniffed. "Let the generals drown."

"Lieutenant Culpepper," Colonel Lewinsky said in measured tones, "we're **all** going to drown unless you undo this timewave. **You** are going to drown, and so is that stuffed elephant of yours--what's his name?--Nick-Nick."

She was watching my body language closely. "Yes, that's right. If you can't stop this timewave, Nick-Nick will vanish--poof!--will never have existed, in fact."

I gulped. There was nothing I could do; my fate was sealed. I **had** to go on this mission. Had to save the timeline for Nick-Nick.

"For Nick-Nick," I muttered. Then, a committed yell: "For Nick-Nick!"

"That's better, Lieutenant. I knew we could count on you." But the way she glanced at The Tibetan revealed the fact that she thought we all were doomed.

I stood, hitching up my pants. "I'm off to 1983, goodbye."

"Just a minute, Culpepper. We're not through with your briefing, and you haven't been dismissed yet. I'm beginning to believe you've forgotten every custom, courtesy and protocol you learned at the Academy. If I were Lobsang--no offense, Lobsang honey--I would make damn sure you knew some customs and courtesies, beginning with shaving, bathing and wearing a clean uniform."

"I've spent a lot of time with Mongols lately," I said defensively. "And it's been thirty-three years since I graduated the Academy. They've kept me a lieutenant all that time; if they'd promoted me and given me extra classes I probably wouldn't be so offensive to you."

"Well, Lieutenant," and here a trace of the sexy Monica reemerged, "I'm not saying you're offensive to Monica Lewinsky, though you're a complete dirtbag as far as Colonel Lewinsky is concerned. When I'm Monica, and it's just the two of us alone sometime, I'll show you what I mean. I--I mean my Monica self--has done some things that left her gagging with disgust for days, such as my activities during my last mission to the Twentieth. There I--I mean she--or us--oh, never mind. What I mean to say is that during my last assignment I had to create a scandal with an official who disgusted me beyond all measure. It was a backdoor attempt to throw some negative publicity upon his administration, as we knew that some of that negative press would be reflected onto his executive officer. We figured that our work would help defeat the election of the executive officer when it was his turn to campaign for his bosses' office, and we were right. He had to be defeated, because he would have led first America, then the rest of the world down the path to totalitarianism.

"But what we didn't figure on was that the guy who won the election, a troll-like little fellow named Bush, would be just as bad, if not worse than the guy we helped him defeat. Bush reinstated the Crusades of the Middle Ages, the only difference being that in the Middle Ages his kind were intent on proving the supposed superiority of Christianity, while the Burning Bush, as he came to be known, was intent on proving the superiority of democracy. He used the military to pursue a personal agenda, rather than limiting the use of organized violence to the defense of the country and the principles of liberty and non-initiation of force it was founded on. Just as his predecessors believed Christians could be created at the point of a sword, the Burning Bush believed democrats could be created at the point of a bayonet. An oxymoronic belief in both cases, and contrary both to the originating impulse of Christianity and of democracy.

"The Burning Bush and his staff of devils were good at one thing, though: infringing on the free choice and right to privacy of their countrymen. With their so-called Patriot Act--which on the instinctual and emotional levels implies that you're a patriot only if you support fascism and colonialism--they began the process of usurping an insistence on freedom from the hearts of their countrymen and restoring them to the forelock-pulling subservience of their forebears who never left England.

"So we solved one problem, only to find that with the election of the troll Bush we'd created another problem which placed the timeline back in jeopardy.

"We knew we had to restore the timeline to its original strength and integrity, so we dispatched a team of scouts to discover what had gone wrong earlier in the life of the Burning Bush to turn him into such an incompetent, treasonous, fascist jerk.

"Our scouts reported that in his young adulthood, Bush had severely altered his mental capacities through the use of cocaine, pot and alcohol, and later thru wallowing in fundamentalist religion. What longing does a fundamentalist of any religion secretly carry in his heart? Why, to make war upon infidels, of course! His vision of Paradise, or Heaven, or Asgard, or wherever he imagines his final resting place to be is always bound up with committing acts of violence against other faiths, or against those who have no faith at all. And somehow Bush and his kind had gotten the origins of democracy mixed up with their fundie religion, conveniently forgetting that democracy actually originated among the Pagan Greeks and was implemented in America by our friend Jefferson and his band of deist cronies. Democracy is one of many Pagan innovations the imperialist Christians have appropriated and tried to hog the credit for. Our friend Washington publicly stated that the United States was not a Christian nation, but don't try to tell the drug-and-religion altered minds of the fundies that in twentieth century America.

"So really, Bush's Crusaders were fighting for a blend of religion and democracy, and not for true democracy. They wanted a pinch of theocracy to take the place of the lines of cocaine many of them snorted in their youths."

I raised my hand. "Yes, Sonny-Bob?" Colonel Lewinsky inquired impatiently.

"Some of my friends among the Sacred Prostitutes have explained in some detail the mood-altering effects of fundamentalist religion," I said. "If Bush and his gang were fundies, they would have either believed or pretended to believe in the denial of the flesh, and this course inevitably incites a burning rage in the breast of the fundie, whether he frankly admits this to himself or not. Putting off natural pleasure to an afterlife which may or may not exist causes him to cultivate unnatural lusts, which rage against and sabotage the very beliefs that created them, thereby creating his hypocrisy.

"And some of these unnatural lusts are geared toward trying to introduce some measure of suffering into the rest of the world, whether this be through the obvious means of bombs and guns, or through the more subtle means of trying to make the laws of the land over into the image of his religion, then insisting that everyone else be bound by those laws.

"The laws some primitive societies have against public nudity is only one example of fundamentalist contempt for the natural world, and of their fear-based contempt for those who would prefer to live in harmony with nature, and with their own natures. It's much easier to lust after a person who has some degree of clothing than a totally nude person, so with the anti-nudity laws the fundamentalist is insisting that even people who prefer the innocent playfulness of Eden descend into the same self-created hell of lust that the fundamentalist occupies.

"And since the fundamentalist cannot publicly direct his passions into natural activities, he directs these twisted passions into creating unnecessary wars. Those passions *will* break to the surface sooner or later, typically in state-mandated violence. The fundamentalist is always the one who screams loudest for patriotism, and wraps his lusts in the flag of his country and delivers them in the form of bombs to whatever object he has attached his sentimental old lusts to, his hatred to. And he's usually the one who prays most fervently for the execution of criminals . . . the pain of his fundamentalist self-denial has turned him into vengeance incarnate, while in his hypocrisy he continues to preach the virtues of the gentle Lamb. And his twisted mind usually finds ways that don't involve facing his own lusts to justify his devolution. He returns again and again to the fundamentals of an unnatural and inaccurate religion created by ignorant and intolerant desert-dwellers thousands of years ago, rather than introducing his hate-filled mind to the fundamentals of a natural god of love and beauty.

"The fundamentalist of any religion has cast himself out of Eden, and he won't rest until he's destroyed Eden."

I sat back out of breath. Monica Lewinsky's sermonizing was

contagious.

She smiled. "Well, Lieutenant, your Sacred Prostitutes have given you some mighty and wholesome spiritual insights. And that ties right in to the end of the story of the Burning Bush.

"Between the drugs and the religion, Bush had become a lust-swollen factor of unstable self-righteousness and arrogance. He pushed the timeline out of integration. Sheepishly, we set to work to correct the matter.

"We sent a couple of Temple Prostitutes back to console the young Bush away from drugs and fundamentalism. They saved his brain, and his heart. Instead of becoming a fiendish slow-witted troll, Bush remained relatively innocent and became a Celtic Pagan Priest. He also owned a baseball team called the Dallas Druids.

"Finally, he was elected president just as scheduled, becoming the first Pagan President of the United States, and also the first president to admit to having two wives at the same time.

"His vice-president, a fellow named Cheney, took his boss' example of honesty and forthrightness to heart and left the closet, becoming the first openly gay vice-president. He also was the first vice-president to wear an evening gown to the State of the Union Address.

"And at the beginning of his second term, President Bush became the first president to openly break the hymen of a young virgin at Beltane, restoring the ancient fertility rites before the nation and the world upon a great bed that had been placed in front of the Capitol. But since he wasn't a fundamentalist Pagan, nobody had to participate in Beltane if they didn't want to or watch the President's gleeful activities.

"President Bush's sly and shame-faced predecessor had brought dishonor and untruth to the sexual act, profaning it before the world and illustrating the 'principles' in action of a degenerate Christianity. But instead of hiding his sexual activities behind closed doors and then lying about it as his predecessor had done, Mr. Bush helped restore the sexual act to a place of honor and sacredness within the minds and hearts of his countrymen.

"So our Temple Prostitutes supplied Bush with a lot of bush, and it got him back on track. 'Like cures like.' "

"History's hard," I muttered, "just like geometry."

"History *is* geometry, Lieutenant. Always remember that."

"Yes, ma'am."

"Anyway, Lieutenant, before I got sidetracked by the tale of the Burning Bush and his restoration to normalcy, I was trying to tell you about the scandal I created to defeat the election of the screaming, infringing nutcase called Gore. That work disgusted me more than anything else I've ever done, and I worked in a New Orleans brothel for six years in the 1800's. But this guy I had to suck and fuck--Slick Willie they called him, and he was perfectly named--was more disgusting than any john I ever serviced as a nineteenth century whore. I'm in Heavy Therapy right now, trying to get his slimy energy off me. Compared to him you're a shining angel of valor with perfect hygiene.

"Anyhow, Sonny-Bob, you seem a little kinky." And here that wet pink tongue touched her lips again. "And if you stop this timewave, I'll reward you with the best piece you've ever had, six ways from Sunday, my place, your place, or anyplace. You won't even have to bathe; if you want to be a wild Mongol I'll joyfully go down on your sword.

"Mongols aren't nasty, Sonny-Bob." She shuddered violently. "You don't know what filth and slime are until you've done Slick Willie."

"Then I won't do Slick Willie," I solemnly promised. In fact, with this creature Slick Willie on the loose in the 1990's, I vowed silently never to visit that decade.

Then she was all business again, and it seemed almost as if she were using her military discipline to shut out the memory of the foul creature she'd just told me about. For the first time I pitied her. Then compassion flooded my heart and I moved beyond pity and only wanted to comfort her.

I stepped forward with my arms outstretched, and she almost fell into them, but then she stepped back and held up a restraining hand. "No, Sonny-Bob . . . no, Lieutenant, there isn't time. I appreciate the gesture, but it will have to wait until you return. We're both going to be very busy for the couple of years before the timewave reaches us; we've got to get you retrained, and I'm . . ." A tear trickled down her cheek. "I'm entering a convent at 2100 hours this evening. I'm going to become a nun of the Christian faith. If I'm well--if I've fully recovered from my experience in the Twentieth when you get back, then I'll leave the nunhood and we can visit. But not before." She straightened herself up and wiped a hand across her eyes, then repeated firmly, "Not before."

I decided to wait until I got back to tell her how much I like nuns.

The Tibetan had his hand on the Colonel's shoulder. "Finish the briefing," he said tenderly, and from the look in his eyes I figured that when I returned--if I returned--from my mission, that if Colonel Lewinsky had divorced Jesus and left the convent, she would probably be remarried to The Tibetan. *She has a thing for religious figures,* I observed.

And The Tibetan has always had a thing for slutty colonels.

Colonel Lewinsky cleared her throat and stepped away from The Tibetan. "What you need to know, Lieutenant, is that this timewave is in the form of a nuclear winter. It originated in a nuclear exchange between the United States and the Soviet Union, and as I said earlier we traced the catastrophe back to October, 1983."

I felt a little indignant. What did those godless communist deviants think they were doing? In the history I'd studied the President of the United States of America, Sir Ronald Reagan, had inaugurated a military buildup in an attempt to bankrupt the Soviets, knowing they couldn't match the huge sums the U.S. was spending on defense. Sure, Sir Reagan was perfectly willing to nuke them, but he never had to. His plan worked; the morally bankrupt Soviet system also became financially bankrupt and fell into the dustbin of history. No nuclear exchange was needed, no nuclear exchange had occurred.

For defeating one of history's great tyrannies, Sir Ronald Reagan is honored to the present day. To some degree, we owe our civilization to him, we couldn't do without him. The winds of freedom he introduced to the world eventually brought us nanotechnology and time travel, and confirmed our right to keep and bear arms and to worship our Goddess in a sexually explicit fashion.

A giant stone idol of Sir Ronald Reagan stands in front of the TAC Central Command to this day. He is our patron saint.

"So what went wrong?"

"That's what you'll have to find out, Lieutenant. All we've learned is that the timewave originated in this nuclear exchange and that the resultant nuclear winter is expected to last a century. Right now the timewave is at about 2050, and the winter is still going strong. And--" She paused significantly. "And there are no discernable lifeforms left upon the earth by 2045, not even a damn cockroach. It's gone, all of it, everything that makes a planet habitable--no flora, no fauna, no humans. Only a few strains of bacteria are left, and they won't amount to anything for a few billion years. The earth is dead, Sonny-Bob. The earth is dead."

I felt myself getting riled at those Soviets. It seemed to me that the best thing would be to go back to 1945 and nuke them with just a few strategically placed warheads--not enough to imbalance the planet, but enough to destroy the alleged Soviet civilization before they developed The Bomb. Then they would never be a threat.

"Lieutenant, I can see your wheels turning. Our first thought also was to destroy the Soviets before they had their own nukes. But--" And here she grew a little pale, as though she couldn't quite come to terms with the horror of what she was about to reveal. "But, Lieutenant Culpepper, it wasn't the Soviets who began this nuclear war. They were merely responding to an all-out nuclear strike by the United States . . . a strike ordered by Sir Ronald Reagan."

She tried to sit down heavily in a nearby chair, but missed and as the chair went flying, she fell to the floor like a sack of potatoes.

As for myself, I could only stare in horror at the words seared across my brain, the words that said Sir Ronald Reagan, the Savior of our race, had somehow been convinced to destroy our very timeline. For my people are very religious and are a spiritually polarized race, and Sir Ronald Reagan is one of the top beings in our pantheon, second only to the Great Goddess of Love Herself, Paphian Kythereia, The Cyprian, the Goddess Aphrodite. My bowels broke loose and I fell on my face.

I was only out for a few minutes, and when I came to a very solemn Tibetan was injecting me with nanos, those little submicroscopic machines our civilization depends on. The Tibetan was servicing me with medical nanos, which can rebuild any organ or restore any limb, right before your eyes. They rely primarily upon the glucose in your blood for their fuel and construction materials, and can rearrange the atoms of one substance to create any other substance.

"Eat this bottle of glucose tablets," The Tibetan said, and I complied. I could feel the nanos working in the cartilage of my nose, a nose which was throbbing with pain and dripping blood everywhere.

"Next time fall onto a pillow," The Tibetan advised. "Your nose will be better than new in another minute or two."

The Tibetan spoke the truth. I'd seen nanos rebuild organs and limbs many times in the field; no injury was too great to be healed if the nanos were injected quickly enough. Unfortunately, the nanos were indiscriminate in their repair work. I could also feel them rebuilding my foreskin. Now I'd have to get circumcised again.

"Lieutenant," I heard Lewinsky weakly moan. I turned in the direction of her voice. There she sat, ass on the floor and propped up against the wall. A wet cloth consoled her forehead, and both her uniform jacket and blouse were partially unbuttoned. One breast was hanging out, but somehow it was unattractive.

"Lieutenant . . . you may have to insure that The Pirate Jimmy Carter wins the 1980 election."

"NO!" I screamed, and it was a scream of defiance and rage at Lewinsky, at The Pirate Jimmy Carter, at The Tibetan, the TAC, nanos, everything; it was a scream of defiance at ALL THAT IS. ALL THAT IS . . . except for the Divine President, Sir Ronald Reagan. In Him had I always believed, in Him I would always believe, timeline or no timeline. Sir Reagan was the only certainty in eternity.

I slowly and deliberately extracted my Kel-Tec pocket pistol and pointed it at Lewinsky's face. "Now you die," I told her, but before I could squeeze the trigger The Tibetan had shattered my elbow and knocked my weapon across the room. He knows Kung-Fu.

"Be still and let the nanos rebuild your elbow," he said. I complied, still seething with rage, but unable to do anything in the presence of The Tibetan's vast martial knowledge.

Lewinsky looked at me thru clouded, far-away eyes. "I wish you'd pulled that trigger. I wish I'd stayed in the Twentieth and let that timewave roll right over me.

"Lieutenant, no one knows what will happen if The Pirate Jimmy Carter snatches the presidency from Sir Reagan. But whatever happens, it will be better than what's happening now with this damned timewave. At least Pirate Carter is unlikely to order a first strike against the Soviets."

She coughed, and I fancied I saw blood on her lips. Bleeding ulcer combined with acid reflux, I noted clinically. She took a roll of Maalox tablets out of her pocket and ate the whole thing. Then she just stared off into space for a while, and at first The Tibetan and I didn't realize she was dead.

CHAPTER THREE

The Tibetan wept. He wept at the funeral, he wept on her grave. He'd begun weeping that day in his office and hadn't stopped. It was clear to me now that Monica Lewinsky had been much more to him than just another slutty colonel.

Maybe they were soul mates.

We were walking back to his office after the funeral; Monica had been interred about three-quarters of a mile away at TAC's Cemetery of the Knowns. It was called that because when we lost an agent, we frequently didn't know how he'd died and were unable to recover the body. We all took comfort from the fact that these lost agents were out there somewhere, fertilizing the soil of the future--our future--with their holy remains. But it was even more comforting when we had a recognizable body and could give it a proper burial. We got closure that way. Hence, The Cemetery of the Knowns.

The Tibetan leaned on my arm. He wore his saffron lama's robe, and for the first time in two decades I chose to wear my dress uniform. I was glad it hadn't faded much.

"She'd been a priestess, Sonny-Bob, a priestess of the Great Goddess Aphrodite. Did that work for almost as long as you've been a lieutenant."

I glared at him, then remembered the occasion and my gaze softened.

There were three great religions in the land in these modern times: the religion of the Neo-Cyprians, which of course was the worship of the Goddess Aphrodite; also the Christians were still around, though in dwindling numbers as many of their members, particularly among the young, found the sexual religion of Aphrodite much more satisfying than the orgy of blood and vengeance Jehovah demanded. Finally, there were the Tibetan Buddhists, good folks and not at all bloodthirsty or vengeful. They were growing in numbers and had surpassed the Christians, who frankly were regarded as atavists by most of our increasingly uninhibited and loving society. The Buddhists and Neo-Cyprians mixed freely and flowed together as smoothly as spring water upon the face of a rounded pebble, for both had foresworn vengeance and adopted the energy of love as the highest manifestation possible.

The only really disharmonious element in our society was the perpetually raging Christian one, still blistering in the hell of their own materialistic delusions, still too frightened to turn around and face their own shadows and undergo the intense spiritual discipline necessary to evolve out of fear and into love. Jehovah was as pissed off as he ever was, the giant screaming slobbering bully who rode on a thundercloud and damned all who ignored him . . . or who chose to laugh at him. Well, he wouldn't be around much longer. Aphrodite was kicking his ass. I guess that made him madder than ever.

I used to wonder why the Christians always refused to make any serious effort to follow the teachings of Jesus, a being as superior to Jehovah as a dog is to the tick that rides in its ear. Finally, I quit wasting my time with such thoughts. There is no telling what an atavism will do. But there's one thing that all atavists have in common. They all prefer fear to love.

Anyway, all the prophesies, as well as predictions by the sociologists, indicated that the Christians wouldn't be able to swim against the flow of love much longer and would finally give up and let love's current, and the current of their own sexuality, carry them along on the glorious expansion of love and sex.

Frankly, most had already given up. Oh, they might attend Sunday morning services in their own church, but many also chose to spend Sunday evening embraced by the Goddess. This really gave the Christian ministers fits.

"I didn't know she was a Neo-Cyprian, sir. When she spoke of entering a Christian convent, I naturally assumed that was her religion."

The Tibetan stumbled, but I caught him. He steadied himself and we proceeded at a slower pace.

"She was mentally ill, Sonny-Bob. After that last mission to the Twentieth she wasn't the same woman. She brushed her teeth fifteen or twenty times a day and drank Listerine at every meal."

The Tibetan jerked away from me and his hand went to where his sidearm would have been if he'd been wearing one. His face was a mask of savagery. "I swear to you, Sonny-Bob, if you save this timeline, I'm going back to the Twentieth and kill this Slick Willie before he has the chance to destroy my Monica. I swear it!"

It distressed me to see a highly respected religious figure display this thirst for vengeance. But I felt sure it was a temporary aberration. I knew--well, I hoped--that soon he'd settle down to the spiritual task of processing and releasing the grief and rage from his heart, and letting the love flow back into it. I felt sure that's what Monica would want for him, and it was certainly what I wanted. For if The Tibetan couldn't exist in a luminous spiritual state, what chance did I have?

Anyway, I had a theory that should help to restore his equilibrium. "Sir," I said gently, "if I save this timeline, there's a chance we won't lose Monica."

"Huh?" The Tibetan stared at me uncomprehendingly.

"Think about it, sir. Monica had held herself together--more or less-- for the few weeks she'd been back from the Twentieth. She was in therapy, and you told me she'd been making progress. If this situation with Sir Ronald Reagan hadn't come up, she might have made it. The shock of knowing we might have to prevent the election of one of our Gods is what pushed her into oblivion. **That** was the huge sack of cement that broke the camel's back. Between the therapy and that infernal Christian convent, she probably would have survived, if it had not been for this last great shock. Although she certainly wouldn't have been normal after her exposure to Christianity, those people do have a certain repressive discipline that she might well have been able to turn to her advantage.

"Sir, I really do believe she might have survived if not for this thing with the Deity Reagan."

He wanted to believe, would clutch at any straw of hope, and now the light of hope shone in his eyes. His lips began working, but no sound came out. Then finally he said, "You've got to save her, Sonny-Bob. You've **got** to."

"I'll do my best to save the timeline, sir. I can't do anything directly for Monica because if I occupied myself with trying to save her we'd lose the timeline. It's the timeline I've got to focus on. But if this timeline **is** saved, then Monica's salvation may be an indirect effect of that, especially since I don't plan to prevent the election of Lord Reagan. He's our God, sir, the consort of the Goddess, and I won't cross him. If the timeline is saved, it must be saved with the presidency of our Lord intact. Sir Reagan's influence on history--on our culture--must be preserved.

"But sir--whether Monica lives or not, you've got to promise me you won't go back and whack this Slick Willie creature. To do so would just create another crisis for us to solve; we'd have to go back and prevent you from killing the creature, then you'd be locked away for at least a century by Internal Affairs. Fucking Dolly Parton is one thing, whacking Slick Willie is something else."

He was silent for a moment. Then he said, "I promise."

"You promise what, sir?"

"I promise I won't go back and whack Slick Willie, whether Monica lives or not."

"That's good sir, that's what I wanted to hear. But please repeat the promise and let me see your hands."

He looked startled, then looked as though I'd hurt his dignity. "You don't miss a trick, Sonny-Bob, do you?"

"Not if I can help it." I grinned. "The Mongols have a saying: 'Beware of men in saffron robes who won't show you their hands.'"

He saw he'd been defeated, so he tiredly held his hands out. "You were right, Sonny-Bob. I had my fingers crossed. But here they are now, perfectly uncrossed, and since I'm wearing sandals I know I can't cross my toes. With you staring at me I can't even cross my eyes. You're a good agent, Sonny-Bob, a fine agent. You should've been promoted long ago."

I wished the Council of Generals felt the same way. Only they could promote an officer. Although The Tibetan couldn't promote me, he'd recommended me for promotion numerous times. The generals would consider his recommendation--theoretically--and then make a decision. But I had it on good authority that they'd never actually considered the promotion, despite The Tibetan's best efforts. I'd been told they always took my letters of recommendation and ran them through the document shredder or put them in their private latrine when they were running short of shitpaper.

Anyhow, I was the only field agent who never got promoted and I guess it really was, as The Tibetan had stated, all because I refused to kiss the general's asses like a good little agent. All the other little agents puckered up for the generals so they could be promoted one day and become Great Big Agents, but not little Sonny-Bob. Oh, I did kiss General Louise Sheffield's ass from time to time, but only because I liked the taste of it.

One result of everyone being promoted except me was the fact that all my classmates from the Academy who had stayed with the service were either full-bird colonels or generals. Hell, six of the twelve slots on the Council of Generals were occupied by my classmates.

"Just try not to screw up too much and remember to brownnose the generals and you'll get promoted," I muttered.

Oh, there was Johnson, who was only a lieutenant colonel--he'd flubbed a mission to Atlantis. We think Atlantis was unaffected, but don't know for sure because the continent sank before a verification team could be sent back to check on Johnson's work. So because of this slight element of uncertainty, Johnson received a letter of reprimand and was promoted more slowly than the rest--except for me.

My thoughts returned to the present and I saw that The Tibetan was looking at me strangely. "Sonny-Bob," he said slowly, "I'll see what I can do about that long overdue promotion. You deserve it; you're almost the only agent who hasn't screwed up a mission. At least, not yet."

"Thank you, sir," I answered, with no real hope that he could do anything for me. Those damned generals! If I saved this timeline I was going to kick their ass.

The Tibetan was starting to look more energized; a trace of his old self was re-emerging. I'd given him hope, and hope is the medicine a grieving man needs. "I promise not to kill Slick Willie," he said strongly, "whether Monica lives or not." His fingers, toes and eyes were uncrossed.

He slapped me on the butt and we trotted back to his office.

"Sorry for your loss, sir," The Tibetan's door said respectfully. "I know there'll never be another Monica."

"We'll see about that. Sonny-Bob thinks that if he can save the timeline, Monica may just pop back into the land of the living."

"Interesting," said the door. "I wouldn't have thought it possible." Then the damned thing burst into a guffaw. "I know that with Lieutenant Culpepper's talents we all sleep better at night. Hee hee! And now he can raise the dead."

"Kiss my ass, door," I said.

"I don't want to get my lips dirty!"

"Break it up, you two! There's work to do. Now Open Sesame!" The Tibetan stamped his foot impatiently. "Open Sesame, I say!"

The door slid open a little unsteadily, still giggling about some manifestation of humor in its own private world.

We entered the office and The Tibetan gestured to a chair, which then floated over and positioned itself under his buttocks. He let himself sink into the butt-cuddling comfort of the cushion and sighed heavily. I got us a couple of beers from the fridge behind his little bar and tossed him one. But the arc of the flying beer was a little outside his grasp and the bottle smashed itself to pieces on the door, which yowled in indignation. I threw another and another, which also smashed onto the door. The door was dripping with beer and rage.

"If you keep cussing like that," I told it, "I'm going to write you out of the timeline. It wouldn't be too hard, and no one would miss you."

I walked over and handed The Tibetan his beer as the door shuddered amid muffled sobs. "You really shouldn't have been so hard on it, Sonny-Bob. It doesn't know any better."

"I'd say it's beginning to learn, sir."

"Well, never mind that now. I've had your new orders cut," here he handed me a disk, "and you'll see you are to report to the Twentieth Century Tactics Class over at the Academy. This class is two years long, and we've got just over two years before that timewave floods the present moment and eliminates us. So there's time to get you trained.

"I know you've never been exposed to anyplace like the twentieth century, and I'd say you're in for a wild ride. All our operatives who have worked the Twentieth feel that all the people there are stark raving mad. Some of our agents can't take the insanity and have to be hospitalized. In fact, uh . . ." He cleared his throat uncomfortably. "In fact, Sonny-Bob, the instructors who'll be responsible for your training are all currently patients in a mental institution. You see, we sent the regular instructors back to stop the timewave, so of course they don't exist anymore. But we have several fine agents who, uh, developed problems after working in the Twentieth , and they'll be your instructors. The hospital administrator has assured me they've come far enough in their recovery to be treated on a semi-outpatient basis, so they'll spend their days at the Academy with you, and each evening they'll return to the institution. We feel this will be a satisfactory arrangement for everyone involved."

Somewhere in there The Tibetan had broken eye contact with me. I wondered why. I was sure I could deal with these instructors, though I might have to drink more than usual.

The Tibetan glanced at me coyly and saw I was unperturbed. He brightened a little. "So study hard, don't just sit around with your thumbs up your ass. You're our last hope, son. You've got to know what you're doing before you leave for the Twentieth."

It was true that I'd never been exposed to anyplace as out of touch with reality as the twentieth century was rumored to be. The closest I'd come to the Twentieth were two missions to the North American frontier during the early 1800's; once to give Jim Bridger a clue as to how to "discover" the Great Salt Lake, and another time to save Kit Carson's scalp from the Comanches (I gave the warriors several synthetic wigs and they let my friend Kit leave with me).

Anyhow, after those two missions it seemed to me that people were becoming steadily more imbalanced, so I swore a mighty oath upon the beard of Sir Ronald Reagan that I would avoid the next two centuries with their creeping deviant madnesses, if at all possible. Of course, now that the timewave was on its way all bets were off. But I knew the Deity Reagan would forgive me.

Still, I didn't want The Tibetan to worry about my abilities to cope with the Twentieth. "I've seen crucifixions and witch burnings, plagues and genocides. Once I trailed Moses and the Israelites around and filmed their genocidal wars against people of different ethnic backgrounds. I believe you saw my video. Anyhow, I should be able to handle the relatively minor atrocities of the Twentieth."

But despite my bravado, my pucker factor had increased tenfold just in the last minute or two. I had to admit it: I was afraid. The Twentieth was outside my area of interest. I was going to have to study hard in that class just to learn enough not to be attacked by the police forces of that era. The twentieth century was the home of the police state, with a cop on every corner who had practically unlimited authority. And I knew from the videos I'd seen of the Twentieth that citizens were not permitted to resist the brutal attacks of these primitive policemen. I knew what Hitler's Gestapo had done; I'd watched the video of Field Marshall Reno's forces burning alive the members of a minority religion at a place whose name echoes to this day: Waco. And all the cops and their leaders had to do to remain in power after they'd committed an atrocity was to say how sorry they were. As long as they were sorry--or said they were--they got off scot-free.

In most previous timezones such conduct would have caused grumblings among the public at large, or even been condemned outright. In some timezones the public would have risen up to throw off their chains. But the people of the Twentieth--known as "The Simple People" by natives of future timezones--were exceptionally easy to manipulate and deceive. The authorities even had special physicians, known as "spin doctors", who raised lying to a high science. Their purpose, unlike that of a traditional physician whose job was to heal, was to make the people mentally and emotionally unstable so they would be easier to manipulate and control. If they could get the people to ignore facts, the spin doctors had done their job.

So most of the people didn't even object to these atrocities, feeling that it couldn't happen to them--though sometimes it did. Karma--if you don't recognize injustice, then eventually you'll be knocked in the head with it. The Lords of Karma want us to wake up . . . anyway, that's what the priests and priestesses of Aphrodite and Reagan say.

The Tibetan reached up and stroked my cheek. I firmly removed his hand and said, "None of that. You aren't finished grieving for Monica yet; at least try to discipline yourself to wait a decent length of time.

And I've told you time and again I don't like chewing tobacco and don't want to be directly exposed to it, but you've got it dribbling all over your chin. Why are you still chewing that stuff? I don't know how Monica puts--did put--up with it."

The Tibetan sniffed. "She chews too. Or she did chew, and she'll chew again if she pops back into the timeline the way you speculate. So off with you, Sonny-Bob. Off with you to the Academy so you can learn to survive in the unstable Twentieth, and maybe save the timeline."

I headed toward the door as The Tibetan stood up. "Go with Reagan, Sonny-Bob. Go with Aphrodite."

I tried to salute and could barely remember how. Then I marched out the door.

INTERLUDE: A BUBBLE IN SPACETIME

I stepped into the hallway and . . . things began to change. I had a curious sensation of weightlessness; the building began to flicker and grow a little translucent.

I shrugged. So it was here. The timewave was on its way and the building was trapped in one of the bubbles on the leading edge of the wave's froth. In a minute, or an hour, the building would be fully dissolved as the main body of the wave caught up to its little bubble.

Had I failed? Had I been swallowed alive by the Twentieth like so many other agents, was I locked away in some twentieth century mental hospital--was I even alive, Back There?

Who knew?

So this is what it's like to drown in a timewave, I thought. I sat down on the floor to compose a poem.

A bubble advances

the wave stands tall

dissolving the moment

into a deep trough.

I thought it was pretty good. I titled it "Changes" and put away my notepad. I supposed it would be considered a treasonous poem by the TAC, as our very purpose was to prevent such alterations. But under the circumstances, who gave a rat's ass?

I stood up and as the building flickered I noticed an officer, smartly dressed, coming down the hallway toward me. *What the hell*, I thought, *maybe one of the generals didn't go to the Twentieth and I can enjoy watching him dissolve.*

I began walking to meet him, and . . . I met myself. I'd been promoted, I was happy to see, and was now a captain. I saluted myself, and myself returned the salute. We paused and surveyed ourself.

"You need to shine those shoes, Lieutenant," my captain self said. I ignored him.

After a moment I asked, "Did I succeed?"

My captain self shrugged. "I don't know, I haven't been to the Twentieth yet. I just got my certificate of completion from the Twentieth Century Tactics Class and wanted to drop by to pay my respects to The Tibetan before I disappeared into the Twentieth."

He grinned. "But it looks like you're about to disappear right now!"

I felt myself fading and I knew he was right. One more gasp--I pointed to his trousers--"Your fly is unzipped, sir!"

Then I was gone, and everything around me was gone, and I was nothingness, and there was peace . . . peace . .

There was peace.

CHAPTER FOUR

It had been a long two years, and I'd never studied so hard in my life.

I had never enjoyed "book learning"; I was always better at picking things up in the moment. On the job training, you know. But even I had to agree that it was best for me to learn all I could about that savage time before going to the Twentieth. Otherwise, those primitive police forces were sure to descend on me.

My computer had just given the alarm to awaken me, and I lay in bed studying my erection. *This thing comes every morning*, I observed, *yet it never wakes me. How can it be so stealthy?*

There was a sacred Temple of the Goddess just down the block; I supposed I might have time to stop in for a quickie. There was usually someone on duty at this hour, and my erection and I frequently paid a visit to whatever comely representative of the Goddess was available. They let me pretend to be Sir Ronald Reagan as we lay together in the early morning sunlight.

Like all civilizations, ours had a creation myth. In ours the Great Goddess Aphrodite and her consort, Father Ronald Reagan, lay together and knew each other Biblically. And they were together forty days and forty nights. Then when they rose from their bed of stars and showered in the light of the sun, Aphrodite fell into the pangs of labor and shot the earth out from between her legs and it assumed its orbit around the sun (**everyone** knows the earth revolves around the sun). And Aphrodite and Ronald Reagan saw their divine offspring, and they knew that it was good. As you might expect, only a few people took this story literally. But there are fundamentalists in all religions, I guess.

But no, there could be no temple visit today. That timewave was due to hit sometime this afternoon and last night when I clicked into the Goddess News Network I saw that already there were scattered reports of time bubbles. Our civilization was beginning to dissolve, but for the most part would be around for a few more hours.

Anyway, sometimes when I get really enthused it takes me ten or twelve hours to finish my orgasms, and the timeline wouldn't be around that long. No, today could not be a day of worship. Not if there was to be a tomorrow.

I rose from my nest and showered (after two years of retraining I was getting pretty good at this). I took pains not to linger over my member, knowing that if I did it would propel me down the street and into the temple. That's how it frequently happened, you know: before my cornflakes, before anything, if I began to massage ol' Hemingway he would send me dancing nude and soapy down to the temple. I wagged a solemn forefinger at him. "Not today, Hemingway. The timeline depends on us." I fancied I saw him nod in understanding, then he fell to half-mast. "Good boy," I said.

After performing the major elements of my personal hygiene routine I poured myself a whiskey and sat down to my cornflakes. Each of these products was manufactured by a fine old company. The whiskey came from a place called The Jack Daniel Distillery in Lynchburg, Tennessee and the cornflakes were built by the Kellogg Company of Battle Creek, Michigan. I say they were built because I suspected Kellogg's manufactured some of their flakes with nanos. I guess they figured no one would notice, and in truth nano-produced food was practically indistinguishable from food grown in the dirt. But sometimes the Kellogg flakes were so clean and pleasing to the eye that they just had to be artificial. I ate them anyway, enjoying every bite. When you're drunk it doesn't matter.*

I finished breakfast and stood up, and ol' Hemingway was finally as limp as he needed to be for me to put my underwear on. I pulled out a well-worn brief that sported a tag depicting fruit, then rejected it as being disrespectful to the timeline. On this day of all days I wanted my underwear to be fresh, sweet and clean and without holes, rips, or railroad tracks.

Finally I stood in full dress uniform before my mirror, and I saw that I was splendid. My Mongol friends would never have recognized me. Indeed, I looked so tasty they might have been tempted to turn me into a casserole.

The Tibetan had somehow managed to circumvent regulations and promote me. I was the only agent in TAC's history that had been promoted without the approval of the generals. I smiled. "Won't they be surprised when they pop back into the timeline and see you," I told my

---

* Historical Note: Here in the late twenty-second century, the Jack Daniel product is made exactly as it was during the nineteenth. No nanos are involved in its production.

splendid self, wondering if the doddering old fools would try to demote me back to lieutenant. "I wouldn't be surprised; they're an ungrateful lot."

I turned from my mirror and grabbed a fresh bottle of Jack Daniel's. "Time to go to work," I told my computer. "Goodbye."

"Goodbye honey," she said. "I hope you have a good mission."

"If you're still here when I get back, my mission will be complete."

"That's sweet."

So with my Jack Daniel's in hand and a case of beer under my arm I sauntered down to my landing flat and greeted my car. "Hello, Bluebird."

"I've been waiting for you," she said. "I was afraid you'd been caught in a time bubble and I'd never see you again."

I smiled. "Lightening doesn't strike twice in the same place, dear."

"Well, I don't know what that means; all I know is I'm glad you're ready to travel. With this timeline disappearing the way it is, we're all depending on you, Sonny-Bob."

She shivered. "We're all depending on you."

I slid into her cockpit after tossing my beverages into the backseat. "You people have made me feel like Atlas, bearing the whole timeline upon my shoulders."

"Sonny-Bob, you *are* Atlas, you're our Atlas."

I was starting to get irritated, the way I so often did these days. I reached for a beer and popped the top. "That's why I'm drinking so much now. I used to be satisfied with one shot of whiskey in the morning to open my eyes, then only a twelve-pack each evening after my last temple visit of the day. But now I drink all day long, even during the classes I've had at the Academy."

I snorted. "Those fool instructors have even tried to force me into an alcohol and drug rehab program. I told them if they didn't back off they could kiss their goddamn timeline goodbye."

"Did they back off, Sonny-Bob?"

"Yes."

I finished the beer, reached for another. I was drinking a fine beechwood-aged product. "Take to the skies," I told the Bluebird, and she leapt into the air as nimbly as a seagull.

"Straight to Gaffney, Boss?"

"No, I want to fly over Lake Hendersonville first."

Asheville, North Carolina's cultural center, fell away beneath us as the Bluebird gained her altitude, then pointed her nose south.

"Boss, you aren't going to go fishing again, are you?" the Bluebird asked anxiously. "There isn't time."

"Maybe I am and maybe I'm not," I replied somewhat venomously. "You'll see when we get there. I don't tell you how to fly, you stop telling me how to do my job."

"But Boss, you do tell me *when* to fly--"

"Silence!" I roared, and the Bluebird was so startled she rolled over onto her side and lost some altitude. I waited for her to straighten up and fly right, and after a minute she did.

"Bluebird," I said pretty gently, considering the mood I was in, "Bluebird, would you say you are a logical being?"

"Of course!" I could almost feel her draw herself up proudly. "Of course I'm logical, Boss! I'm a computer, and logic is the first thing we learn."

"You're much more than just a computer, honey, but I'm glad you consider yourself a logical being. Now tell me, my logical Bluebird: Would it be logical for you to interfere with my mission? You do want this timeline to succeed, don't you? Without this timeline you would never have been created."

"Of course I want the timeline to succeed, Boss! What kind of question is that?"

"It's the kind of question you need to ask yourself, sweetheart, because whenever you hassle me about this mission you become a distraction. I don't need to be distracted by you, I need your support-- yours and everyone else's. That's why I get so cranky sometimes.

"I need your support. My alcoholism is enough of a distraction."

The Bluebird suppressed a sniffle. "I was only trying to help, I . . . you know I support you, Sonny-Bob." I could almost feel her blush. "I . . . I . . . I . . . *appreciate* you, Boss. I do!"

"I know you do sweetheart, and I appreciate you, too. You're the finest car I've ever had; I wouldn't trade you for a whole fleet of Rolls Royces.

"And all I'm asking is for you to use a little logic, a field you're well-trained in, as you've noted. Now: is it logical for you to distract me from my mission?"

"No, my drunken Boss, it is not," she said, with just a hint of contrition.

"And Bluebird, would it be logical for you to alter your behavior and speech patterns in such a way that I can feel your warm support?"

"Yes, Sonny-Bob. My conduct will be altered."

I could tell she was beginning to weary of the conversation so I let the matter drop. "Thank you, Bluebird."

"You're welcome, Boss. You've given me much to ponder."

Shortly we were over Lake Hendersonville. "Take us down to two-hundred meters, Bluebird."

This lake was the finest in southwestern North Carolina. It was formed in 2049 when a meteor hit what was then the city of Hendersonville. Nothing was left of the city; all that remained was a great hole. But soon the hole filled with water and became a lake. The game and fish people stocked it with trout and other delicacies, but the lake was mostly known for the purity and texture of its catfish. These waters held both blue and channel cat, and both varieties were white and flaky and pleasing to the palate.

I first learned of the goodness of the Hendersonville catfish when I was on an escape and evasion exercise. For six long weeks my classmates and I had to avoid a pack of instructors costumed as Vikings. They carried Viking weapons, and while they might rough us up a bit if they caught one of us, they were forbidden to kill or torture us. But they got around this rule by occasionally importing real Vikings--not a lot of them, but just enough to keep us on our toes.

We didn't worry too much about the instructors, but you could never tell what real Vikings would do. But then we discovered that you could usually tell a real Viking by his odor, and our noses helped us avoid capture by the genuine Norsemen.

Then to make a difficult situation worse, our scumbag instructors began cheating and sprayed themselves with artificial Viking fragrance. Now we were really confused.

Finally, some of us located their command post and spied on them a bit, trying to catalogue who was an instructor and who was a real Viking. This helped us some; we all pooled our resources and knowledge when we encountered one another in the field. Camaraderie, teamwork . . . oh for the days before my classmates turned into generals! Now they weren't worth a damn.

There were a few new instructors during this cycle of the escape and evasion course, and you could always tell who they were because when they sprayed on the Viking fragrance they would go into convulsions and vomit, while the other instructors and any real Vikings that might be present would be standing around pointing and jeering. The Norseman is cruel.

Anyhow, in the end they all stank. I guess we did too, though I suppose most of us bathed in creeks or lakes when we had the opportunity. I know I did.

So when Cadet Sonny-Bob Culpepper found himself standing on the shores of Lake Hendersonville, he immediately disrobed and plunged into the water, all the while keeping a wary eye out for Vikings. Then, as he was happily bathing, a fish bit his dick. It was a small fish and didn't do any real damage, but it gave young Sonny-Bob an idea: he need starve no more, he would eat the cousins of the fish that had tried to eat him.

So he activated his predatory instincts and stole some fishing tackle from an unwary camper . . .

The Bluebird's voice broke my drunken reverie. "Sonny-Bob," she said timidly, "the morning is getting away from us."

I started. If the morning was getting away from us, then so was the timeline. I tossed my half-empty beer can out the window, hoping to hit a water-skier, but I lost sight of the can and don't know if it struck its target or not. Anyhow, the skier continued on, seemingly unperturbed.

"Bluebird honey, let's go check my trotline."

Without a word, the Bluebird zoomed into the inlet where I kept my trotline. One end was tied to a tree, the other weighted with an anchor and dropped into the middle of the inlet. There were about nine hundred hooks on it.

"We don't have time to check the whole line," Bluebird said, again speaking rather timidly.

I said nothing, for I knew that she was right. I figured I'd get two or three big cats off the line to give to The Tibetan--anybody who likes Yak's meat is bound to enjoy eating a decent animal product--and then we'd go.

I leaned out of the Bluebird with a gaff and pulled up the line. I extracted a four pound channel cat and a six pound blue. *That's enough,* I thought, *these will feed The Tibetan for a while.* I was about to let go of the line when I felt something heavy pulling back. I put some elbow grease into it and tried to wrestle the thing to the surface. "Whatever this thing is, Bluebird, it's huge. Probably a world record blue cat."

Bluebird was silent. She knew I wasn't going to let go of a world record, timewave or no timewave.

"Honey, what's that lake where they have the Loch Ness Monster?"

Bluebird cleared her throat. "That would be Loch Ness, Sonny-Bob."

I finally got the thing to the surface, but it was neither a great fish nor the Loch Ness Monster. It was a huge sign, similar to the one that hung over the TAC's Central Command--the sign you couldn't see from most angles because of the overpowering presence of the huge stone idol of Lord Reagan. Grunting, I disengaged it from the sixty or so catfish hooks that were lodged in it, then instructed Bluebird to back up slowly towards the bank.

"Yes Boss, but be careful. Remember that time you fell out of me trying to catch that eel."

She needn't have reminded me; I got over forty hooks in me. HUGE hooks designed to catch huge catfish. If Bluebird hadn't been so resourceful I probably would have drowned tangled up in that trotline. She extended one of her gliding wings (she seldom uses those; relies mostly on her anti-gravs) and propped my chin up above the water so I could breathe as I rather painfully removed the hooks. Afterwards, she'd comforted me with kinder words than I'd deserved as I lay up on the bank getting drunk and shooting up medical nanos.

No, I wasn't going to fall out of my Bluebird again.

My breath was coming in heavy gasps by the time we got the sign up onto the bank. I was sweating and getting sober fast. I sprang out of the Bluebird to have a look at the thing as the car also turned her sensors on it.

"What's it say, Bluebird?" I asked, knowing she was programmed with most human languages. "I figured the damn thing would be in English."

"It *is* in English, Sonny-Bob," she responded mildly. "It's upside down."

"Oh." I grunted some more and got the thing correctly oriented. It said:

Appalachian Mall
A Total Shopping Experience
For Smart People

I wondered what an Appalachian Mall was. I wasn't sure they had any of those in any of the timezones I'd visited. "Must be a place where people went to deceive one another with commerce."

I'd seen deception houses before, from ancient Babylon right up to the trading posts of the Hudson's Bay Company. "Yes, that's what it must've been, Bluebird. A deception house."

By the twenty-second century commerce was unknown. Nanotechnology had given us a world where everyone's physical needs were instantly met; ergo, there was no need for commerce. Oh, we still had a few fine old companies that lingered; some people made cornflakes and liquor for the sheer joy of it, then freely gave the stuff away. But since you could program nanos to make **anything,** most of any individual's worldly possessions were nano-made. I'd made the

Bluebird with nanos from a design furnished by a website descended from a company called Mercedes-Benz. Sure, I'd made a few alterations, customized her to my taste . . .

My taste. I'm surprised she turned out so well.

Anyhow, nanotechnology had brought us a world that wildly exceeded the dreams of even the most ardent communists and anarchists. No more famines; if your crops fail life will go on as usual because you'll program your nanos to build a stack of pancakes, or whatever it is that you prefer. Just put something into your Nano Production Device (NPD) for the nanos to use as fuel and construction material (a stick will do) and out comes a piping hot stack of Mama's homemade pancakes, without any of the blemishes or inconsistencies usually found in a dish prepared with human hands.

Unless you program the nanos to create blemishes, of course.

"Bluebird, we'll leave this sign right here and come back and get it after I've saved the timeline. We'll donate it to the North Carolina Museum of Unnatural History in Raleigh."

I stumbled back into my automobile. "Go," I said.

The Bluebird launched herself into the air with evangelical fervor, heading swiftly for the border with South Carolina and the TAC's Central Command at Gaffney. She didn't want to dissolve into nonexistence; she wanted to shove me back into the Twentieth as rapidly as possible in the desperate hope that somehow I, Sonny-Bob Culpepper, the black goat of the Temporal Adjustment Corps, could somehow save the timeline. I chuckled. The public had aggravated me to death ever since GNN had broken the story about the timewave, but the public suffered, too. They were scared shitless.

"What's so funny, Boss?"

"All of you!" I chortled with alcoholic glee. "All of you! You all find out that I'm the Chosen One, specially selected to save your goddamn timeline, and you start bending over backward to please me. Except for you, Bluebird--you don't try any harder than usual to please me--but everyone else does. I used to be considered about equal to a bird dropping, but now everyone treats me as if I'm Sir Reagan himself.

"And it's **hard** to be the world's hero, Bluebird. I can't visit a bordello without little kids lining up for my autograph. I feel like that early astronaut--what's his name? John Glenn. I feel like John Glenn, with everyone trying to pour Goddess-sanctified temple oil on my head for a blessing and harassing me to pose for their video diary.

"The only good to come of all this is that I can't turn around without getting laid. But the flip side of that is I'm usually so drunk I don't know who I've gone to bed with until the next day. Some of them are quite frightening."

"The Tibetan should have had you quarantined, Sonny-Bob," the Bluebird said somberly.

"Not unless he'd quarantined me with prostitutes," I countered.

The Gaffney Obelisk lay in the distance, rising hundreds of feet into the air like a great glistening marble penis.

"I want to drive."

"But Boss, you're still too drunk to drive."

"I want to drive."

She reluctantly turned the controls over to me and I headed on toward the Obelisk, knowing I could get my bearings from there and be at the TAC in a jiffy.

I saw the Obelisk as though in a tunnel, then suddenly the Obelisk was on my right, then on my left . . . hell, I couldn't tell where the goddamn Obelisk was.

Then suddenly it loomed up in front of me like some huge unearthly Titan's penis, and I slammed on the retros and yanked the joystick to my left, skidding off the surface of the Obelisk. Then as I swung around I hit a goose.

"Take the controls, Bluebird. Land us in the vicinity of that goose, I want to save him for Thanksgiving dinner. You were right, I'm still a little too tipsy to drive."

I could almost feel her smugness as she circled around the Obelisk and landed at the foot of it. At least she didn't say, "I told you so-- asshole." The Bluebird is a precious angel, and doesn't take after her drunken father.

I sprang out and collected my goose, then turned around as I heard a deranged scream. The Keeper of the Obelisk was running at me with his baton raised high. "I saw that! You'll pay for defacing the Obelisk! I want blood, you unchristian deviant!"

Uh-oh. The Keeper was a Christian, and so believed in fire and blood and vengeance. I'd pulled off my uniform when we went fishing and wore only my underwear and shoes, so he couldn't tell I was a warrior. I unfastened my badge and identification card from the front of my underwear and held them high. I shoved them into his face as he came screeching up. I noticed he wore one of those Christian bondage rings (only Christians believed marriage was bondage, everyone else celebrated marriage as love and freedom) so I said easily, "How's the family? Are you sure they still exist? Did they ever exist?"

Instead of detonating, he fizzled. The air went out of his balloon, so to speak.

"I'm sorry, sir, I didn't know you were a warrior. Say, according to that card you're the Warrior Culpepper! You've come to save our timeline!"

And here the damned fool fell at my feet, grabbed me around the knees and bathed my shoes in his tears. I was afraid he was going to vomit the way he was choking, so I told him to stand up. He staggered to his feet, then stood there humbly, hat in his hands, unable to look me in the eye. His baton lay in the grass several meters away.

"Yes, I'm going to save the timeline," I told him gently. "But every hero needs the folks back home to support him, he needs to know the people are on his side. Can I count on your support? Do you want to be a member of my Home Guard?"

"Yes, Warrior Culpepper. Thank you, Warrior Culpepper. I'll be a member of your Home Guard."

Then I had a wicked thought. "Every member of my Home Guard has sworn a mighty oath to lie with a representative of the Most Holy Goddess Aphrodite on this most fateful of days. I command you to go to the Temple of the Goddess, procure a sacred prostitute, and lie with her, all the while praying for the success of my mission."

"Warrior Culpepper, I am but an humble Christian, unschooled in matters of love. But now that you've sanctioned it, I will go get my wife and we both shall go to the Temple and lie with a representative of the Goddess. I swear it!"

This was rich. The old buzzard had waited for who knew how many decades for someone he'd deified to give him permission to properly and joyfully use his tallywhacker. And I had just done so. So now he could go violate those perverse Christian wedding vows of his with a clear conscience. It appeared that he and his wife had just been waiting for an excuse, and now I'd given them the best excuse in the world. Through the sanctified lovemaking in the temple they could support my mission and help save humanity. Good deal, Lucille.

"Well, I've got to go now." I patted him on the head. "Timeline to save and all that. Maybe I'll see you in Temple one day."

I took my goose and got back in the Bluebird and she headed for the TAC. When I looked back towards the Obelisk I saw the Keeper running in the general direction of the Gaffney Grand Temple.

I smiled, looked up at the heavens. "You owe me one, Aphrodite. You owe me one."

The Bluebird landed in the TAC's executive parking lot and I stumbled out of her pulling my uniform on. I turned and kissed her. It was the first time I'd ever done that.

"Goodbye, my Bluebird--I mean, so long."

The Bluebird was sniffling. If she'd had tear ducts, I know she would have rusted herself.

"Boss I ... I ..."

"Yes, honey?"

"Boss, I *love* you! I *love* you, Boss, yes I do!"

"I know that, Bluebird. I love you too, sweetheart."

I kissed her cockpit again, this time lingering a moment.

She was crying. "Boss . . . come back to me, Boss . . . promise me you'll come back."

"I'll be back in a jiffy, sweetheart. I'll just go restore this old timeline, come right back to you, and we'll go catfishing for a week. How's that sound?"

"It sounds good, Sonny-Bob. It sounds good . . . maybe too good to be true, with all that's happening."

"Bosh! The other agents screwed this mission up because they rely on regulations to tell them how to proceed. You know I don't have that problem. And the generals screwed up because they're politically correct idiots."

I drew myself up. "Never trust a politically correct person to do a man's job, Bluebird. Never trust a politically correct person to do anything . . . except to bite you on the ass when you're not looking."

My tone softened again. "I'll be back, Bluebird honey. Promise you'll wait for me."

"You *know* I'll wait for you, Sonny-Bob! I'll wait for you 'till the timeline freezes over a million times! I'll wait for you . . . I love you, Sonny-Bob Culpepper. I love you."

"I love you, my Bluebird," I said, kissing her tenderly for the last time. "And I'll see you soon."

I walked away quickly then, her muffled sobs ringing in my ears. Once I'd rounded the corner of the headquarters building I leaned against the wall and released the grunts and sobs I'd held back in Bluebird's presence. I'd never known until just now how much that car meant to me, but I swore that if I made it back alive I'd never take her for granted again.

After a few minutes I wrung out my handkerchief and put it away, hoping that no one would notice the redness of my eyes, or that if they did they would conclude I'd been using drugs.

I picked the goose and the catfish up from the ground where I'd dropped them--the catfish were still alive, and flopping around madly--

and went around to the front entrance to the headquarters building. A young female lieutenant saluted, then opened the top two buttons on her jacket and blouse and what I saw there made me return the salute, in more ways than one . . .

I steeled myself. "Not now, Hemingway," I gasped hoarsely, "we've a timeline to save." I nodded at the young lady, then hobbled around to the statue of Sir Ronald Wilson Reagan, where I waited for Hemingway to subside.

In the shadow of this man of greatness I gazed skyward, up into those gaping stone nostrils thousands of meters above the ground. And I was glad that stone men do not drop boogers.

I shook my head sadly, wondering how Sir Ronald Reagan could have found it within himself to anoint us with this timewave. The Father of our Culture, trying to abort us and replace us with . . . what? A nuclear winter? It made no sense. I knew that the All-Seeing Eye of Lord Reagan peers throughout time and space, that there was rhyme and purpose to all his glorious activities. But surely, just this once, he had needed a monocle.

Hemingway, in a spirit of cooperation, had fallen to softness and I stepped out from the shadow of the great man and skipped up the steps into HQ.

The staff duty officer was prancing around and wringing her hands nervously.

"Good afternoon, Major Williams," I smiled. "How've you been?"

"Lieutenant . . . I mean **Captain** Culpepper! Thank Goddess you're here! We've all been worried sick, afraid you weren't going to make it. The Tibetan even wet his robe."

She pointed an accusing finger at me. "Don't you know there are time bubbles popping up everywhere?"

"I know a thing or two about time bubbles," I assured her. "And lightening doesn't strike twice in the same place."

"What do you mean . . . you *couldn't* mean you've already been in a time bubble . . . could you? No one could survive such a thing! You would have been dissolved . . . wouldn't you?"

A queer sort of hope and fear mingled in her eyes. "Wouldn't you?"

"Yes, I was dissolved. But I wrote a poem." I scribbled out my poem "Changes" and handed it to her.

A bubble advances

the wave stands tall

dissolving the moment

into a deep trough.

She screamed, then tore at her hair and began laughing hysterically. *This officer needs to take a poetry appreciation class*, I mused. I called for a medic, then went into the break room and deposited my catfish and goose in the freezer. Then I poured myself a cup of coffee and sat down.

I had a problem. I knew I'd met myself on this day. Thing was, I didn't want to meet the son of a bitch. Why couldn't Lieutenant Culpepper stay in the past where he belonged, instead of riding that damned time bubble into **my** Now? The dipshit. If I could remember what time it had been when I'd met the earlier version of myself I could wait a couple minutes until the lieutenant had gone into nothingness before walking down that hallway to The Tibetan's office.

But no, I had no idea what the time had been when I'd met myself. So I was flying blind, and when you fly blind time usually wins. I sighed and gave in to the inevitable. I would saunter in looking sharp, all spit and polish, and give that earlier version of myself a look at the officer and gentleman he could become if he would just work hard and try to leave off some of his more disgusting habits. And he had. I was the result.

But the Academy tends to have that effect on people, and now that I was free again I expected to shortly revert to my previous condition. Nevertheless, I would pause to briefly inspire my earlier self--then I'd shuck the uniform and change into sandals and loincloth as soon as possible after he'd faded away.

So I spit all over my shoes, then yanked the cloth off the table where I was sitting and buffed them to a high sheen. "Let's go get this over with," I muttered, then stood and made for the break room door.

But wait: Lieutenant Sonny-Bob had cackled something about my fly being unzipped just as he faded away . . . there was no reason to disappoint the little beggar, so I tugged at my zipper . . .

It was stuck. I yanked on it hard, and was still yanking on it when Colonel Jefferson came in, escorting Major Hemings on his arm.

"Sonny-Bob's been doing that ever since we were at the Academy together," Jefferson laughed. Major Hemings just blushed and turned her head away.

"You're just jealous, Tommy Boy, because you don't have what it takes to be a field agent anymore," I grunted, still tugging, still tugging.

Jefferson reddened. I could see I'd hit him where he lived, but he'd had it coming. After his last mission he'd had a breakdown and had to be confined to a mental rehabilitation hospital for a number of years. When he got out he was still sort of unbalanced and couldn't go back to field work, so the generals had assigned him to Administrative Affairs. I'd heard he was pretty good at riding a swivel chair.

Finally my zipper came loose and Hemingway almost flopped out, but I got him contained in time. No use making Jefferson more jealous than he already was.

I exited the break room smirking at Jefferson. "Chairborne!" I yelled, and then I was gone.

INTERLUDE: A BUBBLE IN SPACETIME

I stepped into the hallway and . . . things began to change. The building began to flicker and grow a little translucent, but somehow I felt heavier, like I'd gained twenty or thirty pounds.

I shrugged. So it was here. The time bubble from hell had just arrived.

I felt heavy enough to fall right through the gently pulsing floor, but somehow I didn't. I tippy-toed down the hall towards The Tibetan's office.

I saw the fool lieutenant sitting on the floor and putting his notepad away. He stood up when he saw me and began walking to meet me, as I knew he would.

Lieutenant Culpepper saluted and Captain Culpepper returned the salute. We paused and surveyed ourself. There was a certain gleam in his eye that said he was happy he was going to be promoted . . . or maybe he was just glad he'd written a good poem.

"You need to shine those shoes, Lieutenant," I said. He ignored me and I restrained an impulse to slap him.

After a moment he asked, "Did I succeed?"

I shrugged. "I don't know, I haven't been to the Twentieth yet. I just got my certificate of completion from the Twentieth Century Tactics Class and wanted to drop by to pay my respects to The Tibetan before I disappeared into the Twentieth."

He began to waver, pulsing back and forth between Now and No Thing. I grinned. "But it looks like you're about to disappear right now!"

He pointed to my trousers. "Your fly is unzipped, sir!"

Then he was gone, and the building solidified into its usual level of static density and I felt about twenty or thirty pounds lighter.

I zipped up my fly.

CHAPTER FIVE

"Announce me to The Tibetan," I told his door.

"Okay, sir," the door whispered. It had behaved in a subdued fashion with me ever since I'd covered it with beer, then threatened to write it out of the timeline.

The door slid open and The Tibetan himself stood there, his Buddhist patience one of the first casualties of the disappearing timeline. He grabbed me and yanked me into the room without even demanding that I remove my shoes.

"I expected you hours ago," the saint said peevishly. "Don't you know today is the day we all disappear?"

"I stopped at the lake to check my trotline, sir. I left you a couple of big catfish in the freezer in the break room."

The Tibetan looked as though he couldn't believe his ears. "Sonny-Bob," he said slowly and deliberately, as though trying to hold himself together against some great force, "my existence is **not** worth a couple of catfish."

"Also, sir, there's a goose, but that's mine. I'm saving it for Thanksgiving."

This time The Tibetan exploded and tobacco spit went everywhere, including onto my uniform. "You stopped in the middle of a commute to go goose hunting! On this day of all days! Sonny-Bob, I'm wondering if I should revoke your promotion."

"I don't see any reason for that, sir. If I save the timeline I'll have proven my worth to you. And if I fail none of us will ever have existed to begin with, so I will never have been promoted, so there's no problem."

The Tibetan waved a weary hand. "Your logic is irrefutable, Sonny-Bob. But we only have about an hour before the timewave hits with full force. So get out of here **now** and get your ass to the Twentieth--

"And why didn't you go yesterday, for Buddha's sake, instead of waiting 'till the last minute? You finished your classes a week ago. No, don't tell me. You were laid up drunk again at the Temple of the Goddess, fucking the brains out of one of her whores."

"Sir!" I gasped, shocked to the core. I had never heard The Tibetan speak ill of women before, and certainly not the sacred temple prostitutes. "Please don't speak that way about the prostitutes. We want their blessing on this mission."

"Alright, goddammit, Sonny-Bob. I'll pray to the Goddess and burn incense to Her after you're gone.

"Now GO!" he thundered, and I went.

As I ran down the hallway, I heard him call, "Go with Reagan!"

I pounded on my office door. "LET ME IN!"

"Not until you've remembered the password," my door said for the fourteenth time.

"You thick-paneled son of a bitch! Don't you realize that in a few minutes we'll all be history . . . we'll be *less* than history, because we'll never have existed. That timewave is about to strike and I've got to stop it. But I'm not going without Nick-Nick! Now let me in!"

"Nick-Nick . . . hmmm." The door pretended to think. "Nick-Nick . . . yes, I do believe that's the correct response. You may enter, sir."

Well, at least I had a door that was creative enough to cheat in a crisis. I hadn't used Nick-Nick as a password for nearly three decades.

The door slid open. "Good door," I said.

"Thank you, sir," the door responded primly.

I ran to my desk and opened the drawer that contained my icon. The stuffed elephant lay there, cradled in his bed of fine Mongolian horsehair, waiting for his next assignment.

"Nick-Nick, we've got trouble. I'm going to need all your strength and resources to persevere this time."

No, Nick-Nick wasn't a technologically sophisticated icon, he couldn't speak back--not in so many words. But we communicated on a different level, and I knew he understood my moods as I understood his. We had been together for seven decades.

Nick-Nick had been with me in the cradle, and had been watching the first time I made love to anyone besides myself. He'd followed me through journalism school, then had trekked with me around the solar system when I worked as a correspondent for GNN.

Then, after I'd had to leave that job, Nick-Nick had been with me through those lean and desolate days working as a stringer for various online journals. And he'd been with me when I finally found my way into a prestigious position at the University of Ottawa as an associate professor of yellow journalism.

After the scandals at the University had subsided and I'd been driven away, Nick-Nick returned home with me to the Carolinas, where I'd finally found my calling and enrolled as a cadet at TAC's Academy, with a view towards becoming a field agent with the TAC.

Someone had come calling that day as I lay satisfied in my bed in Asheville with a fourteen year old prostitute-in-training and her auntie, who ran the Asheville Diocese. I'd been back in the Carolinas less than a week, and already I had two good friends.

"Arise, Lord Culpepper," my computer intoned. "Arise, and greet thy guests."

I padded to the door, my girls were still asleep. I told the door to open just a crack, and when it did I saw a strange little man in a saffron robe flanked by two warriors in TAC uniforms. One of them was female; she might have been Aphrodite Herself if she'd been nude, or if she'd been sexily attired. She was the reason I opened the door a few more inches.

"The lady can come in," I whispered, so as not to wake my prostitutes. "But I'm not interested in you two."

The Tibetan glanced at the beautiful female warrior. "I knew we'd have to bring you to get him to listen to the proposition."

Captain Jo Stonehenge smiled, and it was such a beautiful, radiant and sexy smile that my knees turned to jelly and I fell against the doorjamb.

"I used to be a Jehovah's Goddess," she whispered wetly, and my knees shook so hard I nearly hit the floor.

The Jehovah's Goddesses were descendents of a primitive religious sect that existed two or three centuries ago. It was said that this group visited door to door, handing out religious pamphlets that forecast the end of the world. But when the end of the world consistently failed to materialize, this tribe grew weary of itself and its depraved Christian dogma and converted itself into a Neo-Pagan religion. They threw away their Judeo-Christian pamphlets of separation and fear and depraved emotionally-fluctuating egotism and took a leaf from Aphrodite's book.

Now there was a Loving Hall of the Jehovah's Goddesses in practically every town. You could visit them in their Loving Hall, but I liked it best when they went door to door rather loosely attired and willing to drop their robes for anyone with a winning smile. They still handed out pamphlets, but instead of forecasting gloom and doom like other followers of Jehovah, they predicted a continuing expansion of love throughout the universe.

They also handed out condoms and gave medical nanos to those with sexually transmitted diseases. In short, they had gone from being devils of the distant past to being angels and goddesses of the present day. When I was a kid my favorite visitors were always the Jehovah's Goddesses. *They* were the ones who had introduced me . . .

"Mr. Culpepper! Mr. Culpepper! Snap out of it!" It was the first time The Tibetan had spoken to me that way, but it certainly was not the last.

I blinked and looked at him. "How do you know my name?"

He smiled, and I caught a whiff of his tobacco breath. "Oh, I've had my eye on you for a long time."

I stiffened. "I'm not queer, and even if I was your breath stinks."

His smile vanished. "Mr. Culpepper, I'll come to the point. We've heard about your misfortune in Canada and we want to offer you a job. Now let us in so we can talk or we'll just forget we ever heard of you and you can continue being useless."

I considered. I didn't particularly **mind** being useless; in our nano-based culture no one had to work for a living and it was my Constitutional right to work for pleasure or not at all. Still, if these people wanted to hire me and give me a uniform I'd probably get laid a lot more often--not that I ever had any problems with the women, mind you, but it would be nice to be able to visit with regular women occasionally instead of always relying on the prostitutes, whose sacred duty it was to fuck me half to death in holy ecstasy.

No, the sacred prostitutes wouldn't refuse helping me get in touch with my feminine side thru the wild and judicious use of their bodies, as long as I maintained the proper and respectful attitude towards the Great Goddess Aphrodite and towards the prostitutes themselves. However, I must admit there were times when, uh, regular, non-sacred women didn't quite appreciate my unmitigated beauty. Just a couple of nights before, for instance, I had propositioned a young teenybopper at a skating rink and she'd pulled a gun on me. That kind of shit had to cease, and if I had a uniform, maybe it would.

"Come in," I said.

The door slid open and those people from the TAC slid through, and I figured it would be best if I waited 'till I had my uniform before trying to grasp Captain Jo Stonehenge's titty.

I offered my guests chairs around the kitchen table. "It's awfully early, my friends. Have you had breakfast yet? Let me get you some cornflakes and liquor."

We sat there munching our cornflakes and looking warily at one another at first, but after a couple of drinks we all began to mellow out a little. The Tibetan pulled out his pouch and stuck a wad of Beechnut chewing tobacco in his jaw and an expression of bliss overcame his face. After a minute he spat an amber liquid into his shot glass and he radiated such bliss and contentment that I briefly considered converting to Buddhism.

"Mr. Culpepper . . ."

"Call me Sonny-Bob."

"Very well, Sonny-Bob. And you may call me--" He puffed himself up a little, "The Tibetan."

Captain Jo Stonehenge smiled. "And you may call me Jo," she said softly.

"And you may call me Ross," the other TAC officer belched, a cornflake on his chin.

"Well," I said, "now that we know what to call one another, I believe you were going to give me a uniform."

"Mr. . . . Sonny-Bob, we weren't going to **give** you a uniform, we were going to offer you the privilege of **earning** it."

Damn and Blast! I was afraid of something like this.

"Go on," I said weakly.

"As I said earlier, I've had my eye on you for some time--" A look of alarm must've crossed my face, for he held up a reassuring hand and continued, "but not for homosexual purposes.

"We in the TAC are privy to certain classified--one might even say esoteric--information. This information comes not only from the past, but occasionally bits of it flow down the timeline from the future. You do know something about time travel, don't you, Sonny-Bob?"

"Nope," I replied honestly. "I never had any use for it. Once when I worked for GNN I had the opportunity to do a feature on you people, but when they told me I'd have to travel backwards through time a few years as part of my research, I said, 'To hell with that noise.' I've heard about some of the accidents you people have had."

The Tibetan looked at me impatiently. "Old prostitutes' tales, mostly. I get a little tired of defending our record. Oh, there were quite a few accidents in the early days, from the first timejumps in 2090 until the technology was finally perfected with the development of the particle recondenser in 2117. All the bugs were worked out that year and we haven't had a failure of the technology since."

"Well, if I'd known that I would have accepted the assignment, and I'd have accepted it anyway if I had known you have such lovely goddesses working for you." I smiled at Jo, and she smiled back.

"Anyhow," The Tibetan continued, "a while back a bit of information flowed down to us from the future that indicated you might be of some use eventually. The information was not detailed and since it came from a couple centuries up the timeline we couldn't go ask for clarification, as our regulations, while giving us unlimited access to the past, prohibit us from going more than fifty years into the future. We figure the future TAC can take care of its own timezone."

I sniffed. "I don't like regulations."

"Yes," The Tibetan cleared his throat. "We've noticed that about you. And the scrap of information that was handed to us from the future indicated that perhaps that was why we should try to recruit you."

"I just want a uniform. I don't care anything about scraps of information."

"Well, that's all the information we have, anyway. I must admit, every officer of the TAC who has looked at your case is mystified as to why we should offer *you* a job. We didn't get any specifics from the future explaining that, and frankly none of us can come up with an explanation.

"Sonny-Bob Culpepper, I tell you plainly: you are simply not TAC material. It would never have occurred to us to recruit you or anyone like you, if there is anyone else like you. But if we can't trust the future, then what can we trust? Those rare times we've had contact with our counterparts from the future have led us to believe their judgment is sound.

"Though in your case--well, let's just say a little agnosticism is called for."

I was hurt and wanted these people to leave so I could find solace in Nick-Nick.

"I'm as good as you are!" I blurted, as the blood rushed to my face and tears began to form.

Jo patted my hand. "I'm sure you are, Honey-Bob. May I call you that . . . Honey-Bob?"

"Yes," I blubbered, and as the tears began to flow she scooted her chair up alongside mine and pressed my face into her ample breasts. She comforted me, nursing my face, patting my back, stroking my hair. I quickly began to feel better, but forced myself to make mournful noises, as I didn't want to leave this newfound haven, this sanctuary of Jo Stonehenge.

When I finally did look up I saw that Jo and I were alone. "Where are The Tibetan and Ross?"

"The Tibetan said I should comfort you for as long as you needed it, and he and Ross escorted your prostitutes back to their temple. He said you could respond to the job offer at your convenience."

"Jo?"

"Yes, Honey-Bob?"

"I may need comforting for a long time."

And so it was. We spent the rest of the day together, Jo Stonehenge and I, talking and laughing over bourbon and branch water and eating popcorn. And when evening fell we grilled tofu together and ate in the light of the shining stars, the shining stars. And the moon rose, all luminous and ecstatic, and with the bliss of Jo's touch and the warming radiance of her heart, and of the bourbon too, I knew whose face was in the moon, and it was Jo's.

And forever after I would see Jo's face in the moon, sweetest satellite in the heavens.

Jo became my lunar goddess.

The night burned itself away in the all-consuming glow of our hearts as we lay together like Madonna and child, I with my face pressed into her ample motherhood--or whatever it was--and she stroking my hair, caressing me and softly cooing, softly cooing. Not a slip of the tongue occurred, and no entrance of the good ship Hemingway into a safe harbor. The prostitutes had drained Hemingway's batteries, anyway.

And when morning's sun had dissolved the lunar glow I felt refreshed, happy and somehow lightened. The whole world glowed with promise, and I had never felt the glow of promise before. I took Jo's hand and we stood on the balcony together, sharing a cup of Red Zinger.

"I love you, Jo."

"I know you do, Honey-Bob. I love you too." She pressed herself against me and her natural body fragrance was more exalting than the finest perfume. Lilacs and honey, and watermelons, too. Plus a fair amount of animality.

No, we hadn't made love that night, nor have we ever made love to this day, yet we love one another and share a bond profound.

I turned to Jo. "I'm accepting the job."

"I know you are, Honey-Bob."

I quickly fastened Nick-Nick's badge around his neck with a little collar. Had to make him feel official so he could access his power.

Then I shucked the uniform, which had The Tibetan's tobacco spit all over it, and stood there naked, looking for my loincloth. I couldn't find it but figured they would have an extra down at the Tactical Devices Section. That was my next stop, anyway. I grabbed Nick-Nick and took off on the run; the clock was ticking. If I could just slip into the past before the timewave hit I knew I could accomplish great things. Between Nick-Nick and Hemingway I could do anything!

Hemingway flopped around in protest as I sprinted, bouncing off my knees as I ran past Colonel Jefferson and Major Hemings. The Major's mouth flew open and her eyes bulged out, almost as though she'd never seen anyone of Hemingway's stature.

"Off to save the timeline . . ." I grunted.

"Call me!" the Major yelled. Jefferson did not look amused.

I sprinted all the way to the Tactical Devices Section, running through the door dragging a bruised and surly Hemingway.

"Quick!" I panted to a lab tech. "Get me a loincloth!"

She stared at me, but it wasn't me she was staring at. It was Hemingway. Hemingway gets all the attention no matter where I go.

"Now!" I snapped. "I need that loincloth now! I'm off to save the timeline."

She blinked and shook her head. "Yes, sir!" She then scurried away.

I saw Roger Bacon across the way and Hemingway and I ran to meet him.

Roger was a rather fussy old man with a bit of a British accent. In his job as a field researcher he'd spent more time in the past than anyone else in the TAC before becoming the head of Tactical Devices. Indeed, he'd spent so much time in the past that it was speculated his personal timeline extended well beyond seven hundred years, which must have been some kind of record, if true. Certainly he was on a different operating schedule than the rest of us. If he left to spend fifty years in the past, he'd return to the TAC a little later on the same day he'd left. We youthful peons, on the other hand, would adjust our personal timelines to be congruent with what they would have been if we'd never visited the past. In other words, if I left on 15 JAN 2172 to spend three months with the Mongols I would return on 15 April 2172. My personal timeline was congruent with the flow of history.

But Roger Bacon's personal timeline wasn't congruent with anything, as far as I could tell. Although he was born a couple years later than me his vast realms of experience exceeded mine and Hemingway's combined. Known throughout the timeline for his wisdom and sagacity, it was said he'd served as some sort of advisor to King Arthur and had been the inspiration for one of the characters "created" by some British author named Fleming. Also, he knew Shakespeare. Claimed to have been his grammar school teacher, in fact.

"Hi Roger," I said. "How's tricks?"

He looked up at me dourly from his workstation, his long white beard rippling slightly from some vagrant breeze.

"It's you." He said it with a certain finality. "I've worked to save the British Isles for centuries with my research, but all the research in the world won't save us now.

"I need--the timeline needs--a real field agent, and they've sent you. Sonny-Bob Culpepper, yellow journalist and textbook author and a royal pain in the timeline's ass.

"And now you stand naked before me, that penis of yours bruised and troubled, and I'm supposed to give you a couple of tactical devices, pat you on the back and send you on your way to save the timeline. And somehow everything's supposed to work out all right.

"Great Goddess, we are doomed. Our modern Camelot will fade away even more thoroughly than the last one did.

"We are doomed."

"Well, thanks for your support," I said crossly. "But I'm the last field agent, and therefore the only option the timeline has left. It takes five years to train a new field agent, and this mission requires an additional two years of specialized training in twentieth century tactics, which I've just completed at the hands of a cadre of insane instructors. There wasn't time to recruit and train anyone else. The timewave would have interrupted the training. No, there was only enough time to get me, Captain Sonny-Bob Culpepper, certified on the twentieth century. And I'm pleased to report I graduated without honors, which means I didn't let those fool instructors interfere with my basic instincts and creativity."

I sniffed. "But you wouldn't understand, Roger Bacon. You're a bookworm."

"And you're a drunken and naked journalist, son. But I guess you're right. If the best agents have already failed, then the best agents did something wrong. Maybe, in spite of your ignorance, you have something going for you that will give you a chance.

"But not if you enter the twentieth century with your dick hanging out. Those taboo-ridden people back there wouldn't know what to think of your Hemingway and would lock up both of you.

"Most people back there would view a man as being criminally insane if he should stand up publicly and declare he has a dick."

"I know," I said somberly. "It's a police state back there. Damned few warriors, but tons of police.

"And they're all insane. The Pagan Spirituality Movement of the twenty-first century with its cleansing, healing, taboo-breaking energy hasn't happened yet, so those people are programmed with the same non-information their ancestors were programmed with. They don't seem to realize--hell, they don't *want* to realize--that programmed information degrades over time. They won't see that information which may have been valid at one time will have eroded and been corrupted over the course of centuries.

"The original information might have been true, but with the loss of data and the substitution of false data that occurs, the programming doesn't mean shit anymore.

"Plus, changing times call for a conscious change in programming. The programming should be properly expressive of the energy of the moment. But the Simple People of the Twentieth don't understand. They are frightened; they don't want to understand."

"Well, Sonny-Bob, at least we agree on this aspect of history," Roger said, thoughtfully stroking his beard.

Then he glanced at Hemingway. "I've been to the Twentieth a time or two and I have to tell you, Sonny-Bob, that if you avoid the penitentiary back there it will be the most unlikely thing that has ever happened on this green, moist earth.

"For instance, in the United States, where you're going, their taboos forbid a man of a certain age from making love to a woman of a certain age. If their alleged authorities captured a man of, say, twenty-one years who had made love to a young woman of fifteen years, they'd lock him up and throw away the key in many jurisdictions. Surprisingly--or perhaps not so surprisingly if you've studied primitive humans--these "age of consent laws" were not based upon science or nature but upon Christian fundamentalism, and they varied from state to state. With a primitive irrationality, they would pretend it was permissible to screw a thirteen year old in New Mexico, but a crime against nature to screw an eighteen-year old in Wyoming. You and I can see it's absurd to pretend that sexuality is governed by artificial boundaries drawn on a map, but we're logical. These primitive humans were irrational.

"And with their typical hypocrisy they employed a double standard. More was expected of men under these age of consent laws than women. With men the laws were frequently enforced, unless the male "offender" was wealthy or a celebrity. But these laws were seldom enforced against women. For example, if a twenty-one year old woman--or a hundred year old woman, for that matter--was apprehended making love to a thirteen or fourteen year old man, in most cases the woman would be allowed to go free--much to the delight, of course, of her younger lover.

"The schoolteacher, however, was a frequent exception to this rule. If a female schoolteacher in twentieth century America was apprehended making love to one of her students, either male or female, she would most likely be treated as harshly by the authorities as the older man in the first example."

"No!" I said, shocked. "That's impossible. Not in a century so close to our own! Sexuality is one of the most important subjects taught in any school. During my Advanced Sexuality Class at Nina Hartley High many of us got to make love to the instructors, sometimes publicly during the after school programs where we were permitted to show the members of the community how far we'd come in our understanding of nature, and of our own natures. This was especially true around the Beltane season. All this was good training and has served me well.

"No, Roger, no. Schoolteachers serve as vessels of the Goddess, as well as instructing students in other important matters such as rifle and handgun safety and marksmanship, massage therapy, and martial arts. I know the Twentieth is primitive, but I just cannot believe it would be illegal for a teacher back there to display a deep affection for her students."

"Then you must have slept through some of your recent classes or been too drunk to pay attention, Culpepper. Anyone who has either studied or visited the Twentieth knows how scared these people were. They were scared of everything, nuclear holocaust--"

"With good reason," I interjected.

"--air pollution, hostile contact from space aliens. And history has shown that all these concerns were based on reality. But their biggest fear had nothing to do with reality, for they were afraid of one of the gentlest, sweetest aspects of themselves. Yes, as incredible as it seems to us, their own sexuality scared them more than anything, at least in the dominant Judeo-Christian culture.

"The people in the Twentieth--particularly in the United States of America, where you're going--were the most sex-obsessed people the world has ever seen. You can see it in the media of the time; everything they did had a sexual connotation. They couldn't sell carbonated sugar water without linking it to titties and sexually expressive flicks of the tongue. Combine their sexual obsessions with the repressions they'd inherited from the past and you have an explosive situation. That's why these people were so habitually cruel. 'Repression Creates Perversion--' that's the most obvious principle every schoolchild recites in his or her litany. A child today can't graduate from third grade without understanding this principle, and no genuine human civilization can arise without this understanding.

"But there *were* no genuine human civilizations in the Twentieth, Sonny-Bob. And if it weren't for the Divine President, Sir Ronald

Reagan, and the impulse of freedom he grounded in the earth, coupled with the energy of Aphrodite's love and passion, there would be no free and compassionate societies today."

"Well, at least they had some sort of family unit in the Twentieth," I commented. "Didn't they?"

"Not really. They had something called a 'nuclear family' that existed in several slight variations including, if you can believe it, something called a 'single parent' home. But unlike our group archetypal marriages where every member brings specific energies to the union and every child has several parents, there was virtually no such thing as compassion manifesting consistently through a family. Oh, there were scattered occurrences of familial compassion, but these were the exception. Just flashes in the pan, so to speak. And even if one of these compassionate flashes occurred on Thursday, by Friday the family would be back to manipulating and exploiting its members.

"I suppose this must've been the reason for the incest taboo. If these people habitually exploited each other, and they certainly did, and if they were habitually cruel to one another, and they certainly were, then this cruel exploitation would have carried over into the sacred arena of sex, and it certainly did. So if a family actually practiced intra-familial sex in those days, it would have been manipulative and hurtful by definition.

"As hard as it is for a civilized person to understand, the incest taboo may have actually--to a slight extent--reduced suffering within the families of these primitives."

I considered. For a society to be so degenerate as to need a taboo against incest was unthinkable to me. It was just another soul killing rule and seemed to be among the worst of them. True, I'd encountered the incest taboo in many timezones and among many cultures, but despite their goddamned taboos, relatives fucked one another anyway. Then guilt was created, which led to shame, which led to even more secretive and cruel behavior. It seemed to me that this taboo was more trouble than it was worth. Certainly, the happiest cultures I'd ever visited were those that had few or no taboos regarding sex. Polynesians, that's the ticket . . . or ancient Thailanders . . . hell, even the Vikings were far more civilized than these twentieth century people; they were much more open with their displays of sexuality, and therefore happier.

When a society criminalizes voluntary sexual conduct among human beings in any form, that society is repressed, perverse, and doomed. Everyone knows that.

I started. Roger Bacon was looking at me strangely. "Are you all right?" he whispered gently. "I know they said you'd been rehabilitated . . ."

"I'm okay," I said shortly. "I've been okay for years."

That wasn't quite true. I'd been captured once by the Spanish Inquisition, and our current discussion regarding the lack of compassionate sexual conduct among primitives had caused some old memories of that harsh time to resurface.

They'd branded my scrotum and tried to teach me that Hemingway was bad. He spat on them in contempt. Those infidels had tried to reprogram me according to their own lack of compassionate standards, but I resisted and my resolve won the day.

I'd managed to inject myself with some long-term medical nanos (they'd last for weeks, instead of the usual twenty-four hours) when it became clear that my capture was imminent. Then I'd swallowed a whole jar of glucose tablets. So every physical wound they inflicted on me was almost immediately repaired.

They accused me of being in league with the devil, but I said no, I was in league with the Goddess, and with Ronald Reagan.

"Where can we find this Ronald Reagan?" they asked in their broken Spanish. Or maybe it was just that I wasn't well versed in that particular language.

"He is a God, whose holy name shall echo down the centuries, ringing in freedom for all humanity . . ."

That was enough to set their blood boiling; you could tell they weren't Republicans.

They hauled me out the next day, had an alleged priest pray for my immortal soul (but he didn't mention Hemingway's) and then they tied me to a post and set fire to me.

Well, that hurt. I'd rather not discuss the agonizing details. But as the flames ate away my flesh the nanos built it back, and by and by the ropes that held me in place burned through. I staggered and stumbled out of that flaming woodpile, the nanos still rebuilding my flesh, rebuilding my flesh.

But the nanos had depleted the glucose in my blood and I was as weak as a flaming cat. I staggered up to a woman who was selling apples. "I'm hungry," I said.

She ran away screaming, and as the flames fizzled out I fell into her little wagon, tipping it over and swimming in a sea of apples. I began munching apples as fast as I could. I lay there naked and burned, munching apples, munching apples.

I noticed the priest was making signs and passes in the air and seemed to be praying. Well, whatever he was praying for, it couldn't be to my benefit. So I rose to my feet and threw an apple and hit him in the head, and as he collapsed the crowd broke and ran.

"What, do you have taboos against burning men eating apples!" I snarled, throwing several apples into the crowd, each apple striking one of the godless Christians. Then I realized I was throwing my source of glucose away and stopped myself. I began munching apples again, munching apples.

And when my need for glucose had been thoroughly satisfied and the nanos had rebuilt me, I walked to the cowering priest and stood over him. "Your god cannot defeat Aphrodite," I told him, finishing off the last few bites of an apple.

"Aphrodite gives me love and Ronald Reagan gives me strength. You have neither love nor strength. Your god is dead."

I walked away from him then, leaving the pitiful sanctified felon wallowing in the dust like an ancient hog. I found my way back to my own time, forgetting about the instructional video I'd been there to produce.

But after I was released from the emotional rehab facility I was an acknowledged expert on the traits of sexually repressed cultures. I lectured on the subject for a couple years at the Academy before they let me go back to fieldwork.

Roger was stroking my hand. "It may take decades for your to forget, son. I know, I've been persecuted by sexually repressed cultures, too."

Then he stood, and suddenly we were together. Our lips found common purchase and Hemingway began to awake from his slumber. As I spat out a mouthful of Roger's beard, Hemingway began to bob and weave in a strange kind of Morse Code, almost as though to ask, "What are you doing, Sonny-Bob? I thought we only liked girls!"

I pulled away from Roger. "I can't do this, Hemingway's right. I only like women sexually. Roger, I'm . . . I'm . . . I'm homophobic! Always have been."

Roger released me. "We'll wait 'till another day, Sonny-Bob. The time's not right, what with the world ending and all.

"But I respect your homophobia. It takes courage to be homophobic in a sexually enlightened culture."

I thought I was off the hook and could now shake a leg and go back to the Twentieth without further erections. But no, as I stepped back from Roger, that cute little lab tech came running up with my loincloth.

"Here you are, sir," she panted. "I had them sew a pouch inside for your . . . uh . . ."

"His name's Hemingway," I said smoothly. "And he likes you."

It was true. Loch Ness might be in Scotland, but the Loch Ness Monster was right here before us and he was becoming aroused. I noticed the young lady, who had been wearing a lab coat when I entered the facility, was now standing before me topless. Her nipples were pierced and a golden chain charted the path between them. There was a quest in her blue eyes and a suggestion on her pink tongue. I shuddered as Hemingway came to full arousal.

"Roger," I gasped, "what time is it?"

"Quarter 'till three," Roger reported calmly and without jealousy.

I shuddered again as I felt a delightful tongue begin to massage the underside of my Hemingway, and then he was fully embraced by the warm welcome wagon of her smacking lips. "Timewave's supposed to hit at 2:58. We've only got --" I shuddered, bucked and groaned as Hemingway relieved himself, discharging his essence into the willing vault of oral love he'd been presented with. I knew he'd gone several hours without relief and so did not chastise him. And like a vacuum cleaner the lab tech continued on, slurping my Hemingway and tickling my balls . . . my, she was hungry!

"Donna, I think that's enough," Roger said firmly, pulling the young Pagan away from my Maypole. "If that timewave hits at 2:58, Sonny-Bob's only got thirteen minutes to step into the past, and if he doesn't make it we're all history."

She stood then and looked me in the eye. She hadn't been able to contain all of Hemingway's passion, but then no woman can. Drops of his essence lay thick across her breasts and found purchase in her hair.

She dimpled. "Call me!"

"You know I will, honey."

Then she scampered away, bursting with pride and enthusiasm as the last woman to milk the warrior Sonny-Bob Culpepper before he departed to save the timeline.

"Hemingway," I spoke aloud, "if you let that happen again before we leave for the Twentieth, the timeline will be destroyed--and that means no more pussy for you!"

Hemingway fell a little, he was *trying* to be compliant . . .

But he needed my help. With yogic discipline I channeled all excess blood out of Hemingway's veins and coiled him up neatly as I stepped into my new loincloth. I rolled Hemingway into the pouch, which was about the right size--that lab tech Donna had a good eye for detail--and he knew enough to remain quiescent as long as he was in the pouch, as an inflation at this point would only produce discomfort. He slept fitfully, no doubt dreaming about the timewave and wondering if he would ever be the subject of a woman's devotions again. Yes, I had to save the timeline for all of humanity, but I had to save it for Hemingway, too.

"Twelve minutes, Sonny-Bob."

"Well, what do you have for me, Roger?"

"Not much, your vehicle will produce most of what you'll need. But here is a standard bag of medical nanos," he grinned, "just in case Hemingway gets cut by a sharp tooth.

"Also, I see you're not wearing any weapons. Don't you usually carry weapons?"

"Yes, but I must have left them in the Bluebird. I was drunk and emotionally strained when we said our goodbyes, so my weapons must still be in her cockpit, along with my fishing gaff."

"It's wise to be sober when you're handling weapons, Sonny-Bob."

"I know, but you can't have everything. Carrying weapons is part of my job and alcohol is my medicine. You can't deny an operative his medication; I think it's in the rules."

"Whatever. Here's a pocket pistol for you, fully charged. Easy to conceal, yet far more powerful than any handgun of the twentieth century.

"And here's an extra powerpack."

"Thank you."

"One more weapon for you . . . I know you may not want it, as chaste as you are with respect to your anal cavity . . ."

"Oh, no," I groaned.

"Oh, yes. Suppository gun, one each, maximum effective range four-hundred meters. A virgin gun, never been used."

Never been used. At least that was something.

"Roger, I . . ."

"No time to argue, Sonny-Bob. Now bend over."

"Hell no, Roger! I can put it in myself."

"Then do it. Eleven minutes remaining in the timeline."

He handed me the slender, golden tube. It fired an energy beam, like all our weapons, and to keep it from turning an operative's intestines into fried chitterlings it boasted several unique safety features. For example, its sensors knew the temperature range and moisture level of the human anal cavity and the gun would refuse to fire when lodged within any anus. This was only one of the many outstanding safety features of this fine weapon.

Still, I had never used one. As Roger said, I'm a little tight-assed, maybe a little too concerned with the chastity of my waste disposal unit.

Roger held out a jar and I dipped my fingers into the petroleum jelly, then slicked up the surface of the firearm. The loincloth was loose enough that I could pull the fabric back from my anal cavity, and . . .

I took a deep breath. Here goes . . .

The thing slid inside me and I gasped, and the gasp was not one of ecstasy. Since I'd never carried a suppository gun before, I was tight, tight. Plus, the thing was cold. Well, that would soon change.

I slid it up further inside me, further into my hitherto unexplored chamber until only the looped cord hung out. Pulling on this cord is how you get the gun out of your ass . . . they say it pops right out . . .

Oh, I believe . . . yes, that's the prostate. That wasn't altogether unpleasant . . . let's move the gun around a little more . . .

"Sonny-Bob! Here's a Handi-Wipe; you've got the gun installed, so quit fooling with your ass."

I looked at Roger shyly, beginning to see that maybe these homosexuals knew something I didn't. I accepted the Handi-Wipe and in a few seconds my fingers sparkled once more.

"I've got one other item of equipment for you, but this is one you won't fully understand. I don't understand it myself and I've been studying it for centuries."

I knew at once to what he was referring. Money.

Money.

The god of all degenerate human cultures.

Roger walked over to a worktable that had stacks of artificial money piled up all over it. I knew that this huge pile of money would cause the people of previous timezones to go into multiple orgasms, but those of us brought up in this first genuine human culture could never understand how this inanimate thing, which had no intrinsic value, could create such passion. Lust, really.

Roger handed me a sort of purse. "This is a wallet, sometimes referred to as a billfold. You'll carry artificial money in it and you'll carry the wallet itself in your pants, once you get some pants."

Then he swept a great mass of the artificial money off the table and into a huge bag. He handed it to me. "This money should pass as real where you're going, but if it doesn't you may find yourself in hot water."

Well, better than being boiled in oil, I guess.

"Nine minutes left in the timeline, Sonny-Bob. You'd best scoot on over to the motor pool, sign for your vehicle, and get the hell out of Dodge."

"Yes, Roger. And Roger . . ." I felt myself glance shyly at him once more, " . . . if I manage to save the timeline, I'd like to talk to you some more about . . . uh . . . about the gay lifestyle." I felt Hemingway twitch, but wasn't sure if it was a twitch of alarm or of desire.

"Of course, Sonny-Bob. I'll be glad to help you with that." He took me by the shoulders and turned me toward the door. "Go with Reagan, Sonny-Bob. Go with Aphrodite." He swatted me on my bum and I headed for the door gathering a full head of steam.

It was several hundred meters to the motor pool and I had to run a gauntlet of titties to get there. All the female lab techs and staff officers had come to see me off and were lined up baring their breasts and licking their lips, many were playing with their nipples. The line of bare-breasted females extended all down the hallway and out the door across the grounds for a hundred meters. I ran like hell but Hemingway, in spite of his confinement, began to swell a little, so my sprint at length became a hobble.

"Don't these ladies know they're all in mortal danger?" I grunted. Yet here they were, flashing me with their tits when every second counted. If I didn't leave for the past quickly enough I would never leave at all, and everyone here would never have existed. "I'll never understand women . . . but at least these are a hell of a lot more civilized than the ones where I'm going."

I made it to the motor pool and Hemingway began to subside almost immediately.

I glanced at the cuckoo clock as I stumbled through the door. Four minutes left.

The motor sergeant--only this one was a motor corporal--was precariously balanced on the rear legs of a chair, his back against the wall. He was snoring as if there were no tomorrow. I looked around the motor pool and couldn't believe my eyes. Every booth I could see that should have held a TITTY (Tactical Interdimensional Time Traveling Yacht) was empty. Empty! Without a TITTY I couldn't go anywhere. With a squeal of anguish I charged the motor corporal and knocked the chair out from under him. He awoke with a squeal of rage, which became a penitent squeal when he saw who I was.

I yanked him up by the scruff of his neck. "Cocksucker! Four minutes 'till the timewave hits! Where's my TITTY?"

"S . . . S . . . Sir! There's only two TITTIES left!"

"Then where are they, boy! I don't see any damned TITTIES."

"Follow me, sir." He stumbled down the center of the motor pool, then began to run. We ran for over fifty meters before we reached the last two booths. On one side of the aisle was an ancient and cranky TITTY we called Grandma Moses, and on the other side was a gruff and frequently non-compliant TITTY named Hubert.

"Which one do you want me to activate, sir?" the corporal panted.

"Which one! Which one! What the hell happened to all the good TITTIES!? Where are they?"

"All the other agents took them, sir."

"Then why didn't you make some more goddamn vehicles? You've had two years; you could've made scores of vehicles by now."

"Nobody told me to, sir."

"Nobody told you!!! Where's your goddamn motor sergeant? I want him on the carpet right now!"

"He's gone, sir. The Tibetan sent him into the past to try to stop the timewave after all the other agents and generals failed."

Well, I'll be a monkey's next door neighbor. The damn Tibetan thought more of a motor sergeant's abilities than he did mine and gave him a chance to stop the timewave before summoning me. For the first time in my career I was growing tired of this meddlesome Oriental.

Well, I had no choice. It was either Grandma Moses or Hubert. Einey meeiny miney mo, catch a TITTY by the toe.

I heard time bubbles plopping all around outside, we'd be lucky not to get swallowed by the froth before the main body of the wave hit.

Grandma Moses, one of the earliest of our vehicles, was old and arthritic. I was sure she wouldn't be able to warm up in time, so that left only Hubert. Nobody wanted to work with him because of his attitude, but now there was no choice.

"Wake up Hubert!"

"Yes, sir!"

The corporal plugged a cord into Hubert's stimulus port and flipped a wall switch, and the battered and dingy vehicle coughed and came to life. He yawned. "What time is it?"

"Time's running out, Hubert. Timewave on the way, two and a half minutes 'till it hits. Set your coordinates for Fairfax, Virginia on August first, nineteen eighty-two. We're the only ones left, Hubert. The only ones who can stop the timewave. Everyone else failed."

The vehicle turned his sensors on me in bewilderment. "Sonny-Bob Culpepper? Oh my Goddess, this can't be true. **You're** the one who has to save the timeline . . . oh sweet Jesus . . ."

I was growing tired of this response every time I announced myself as the Savior. "Not just me," I snapped, "**us**! Us, Hubert, me and you, like Butch and Sundance, like Gilligan and the Skipper. It's up to **us** to save the timeline and now we're the only ones who can do it. So set your coordinates, we have two minutes three seconds!"

Hubert was getting control of himself. "Coordinates set, Sonny-Bob. But it takes me at least three and a half minutes to warm up--otherwise I can't summon the power to open the interdimensional doorway."

"You'll have to do it in less than two this time. If you can't, none of us will ever have existed."

Hubert yanked himself away from the power cord and backed out of his booth. He began lumbering down the hallway. "Meet me outside, Sonny-Bob!" Then he was gone with a roar and I ran after him, hoping against hope that Hubert could somehow pull a rabbit out of his hood.

I exited the building and saw Hubert racing around the test track like mad, he was wild, he was wild. I glanced up at the vital stats board and saw he was approaching . . . no, he'd reached four hundred miles per hour and was still accelerating. Well, about a minute left. I had time for a phone call.

I flipped open my phone. "Culpepper to The Tibetan."

"Sonny-Bob! You haven't left yet! Now it's too late, too late! Less than a minute--"

"I know what time it is, Tibetan. And I haven't left because you sent the motor sergeant back to do my job, and as a result there was no one here qualified to run a motor pool. Instead of building new vehicles the motor corporal just sat around with his thumbs up his ass. So I had only two vehicles to choose from, Grandma Moses and Hubert, and I chose Hubert, since I figured he'd warm up faster. He's warming up now, but he's already said there's not enough time. So I just wanted you to know that if the timeline vanishes, you're to blame. Goodbye."

I left him with that thought and glanced at my watch. Forty-five seconds left. I began programming my phone to connect with Hubert.

The popping of the time bubbles and the roar of the froth shut out all other noise, even the sound of Hubert's straining engines. Several buildings of the TAC were now encased in bubbles; I even felt some temporal droplets falling and watched as my skin began to dissolve where the droplets touched it. No time to compose a poem.

"Hubert!" I screamed into my phone. "Now or never!"

The vehicle finished his lap and roared up to me in a shower of temporal droplets; his hull was spattered with corrosion from the droplets.

The door to his cockpit popped open and I sprang inside with Nick-Nick, my weapons and my bag of artificial money.

Hubert was shaking with fear and still pouring every ounce of energy into forcibly waking up the full power of his interdimensional faculties. But the roar of the timewave drowned out the noise of Hubert's engines and of the whole world.

Then we saw it, shimmering and bearing down upon us like the grapes of wrath, nonexistence in its wake. I thought of seeing myself dissolve into nonexistence an hour ago in that time bubble and I decided I'd had enough of that shit.

"Now, Hubert! Get us out of here!"

Hubert didn't need to be told twice. He began to vibrate with the activation of his interdimensional drive, and as that great wave of nonexistence overtook us we slipped into that interdimensional space that serves as the doorway to the past.

Before the door closed, I glanced once more at the world we'd left behind. It looked like a very cold and lonely place.

CHAPTER SIX

Blackness for a while, then--

It was snowing! I'd told Hubert to take us to August, nineteen eighty-two, but wherever this was it clearly didn't match the coordinates I'd given him. It should have been hotter than a high school virgin here, but we'd materialized in a snow bank. Damn and Blast! I'd never heard of a TITTY popping into interdimensionality, then popping right back out after a timewave had struck, but maybe that's what had happened. Maybe this was the long-running nuclear winter I'd been sent to stop . . .

Hubert groaned; the lights on his control panel flickered and grew dim. "Sonny-Bob?" he rasped.

"I'm here, Hubert."

"F... Fucked up, Sonny-Bob. Couldn't get myself up to full power, wasn't enough time. Looks like we landed in the Twilight Zone."

He whimpered. "A dead world, all my fault, all my fault . . ."

"Hubert! Snap out of it. Where--and when--are we, exactly?"

"Don't know," he blubbered. "My navigational array is off line, interdimensional drive is cracked and the parts fused. Anti-gravs functional, but just barely. Weak . . . weak . . . that premature jump took all my strength . . ."

"Okay, okay, Hubert. So we're up shit creek without a paddle in the middle of a blizzard. Don't worry about it. I'll do any worrying that has to be done. All I want you to focus on is getting your navigational systems up and running and on recharging yourself. Will you do that for me?"

"Yes, Sonny-Bob." His voice was a little more stable, and perhaps a little stronger. "I'll work on my navigational array. I'll send some nanos in to repair it, should take only an hour or two. But it'll take weeks--maybe months--before I can rebuild my interdimensional drive. That's the most sensitive piece of equipment we have--"

"I know, I know. If you screw that up we'll wind up with our molecules scattered to infinity. But don't worry about that now. Just work on your nav systems and let me know when and where we are as soon as you've got it figured out."

"Yes, sir."

"And Hubert," I said, clutching Nick-Nick to my breast for warmth, "I know you're low on energy but please try to keep the cockpit a little warmer. I'm wearing only a loincloth and my dick is cold and shriveled."

"Okay."

I was in the early stages of hypothermia when Hubert announced, "I've got it! I know when and where we are, Sonny-Bob!"

"Wh-what? Oh, good. Let's have it, Hubert."

And I hoped to Goddess that whenever we were, we were **not** caught in the nuclear winter. Yet by now Hubert was completely covered with snow . . .

"We're near Lincoln, Nebraska on December 15, 1982--"

"Praise the Goddess! You're a genius, Hubert! A genius!"

"I . . . I am?" the vehicle responded timidly.

"Yes, you are!" And I kissed his control panel. He shuddered, but said nothing.

"Hubert my pal, we've still got time to save the timeline. The timewave doesn't hit until October, 1983--"

"Whew!" Hubert gushed. "When I saw we'd landed four and a half months *later* than the coordinates you'd given me, I figured the timewave had hit the fan. October 1983, you say . . ."

"Yep. The timewave hits in October '83. I wanted you to land early so we'd have over a year to stop the thing. As it is, we've got nine or ten months. Beautiful! Let's have a drink."

"I'm programmed to produce a variety of teas and coffees, also wheatgrass juice and mineral water. Also some delicious boiled custards . . ."

"Hubert," I said impatiently, "what about alcohol? I need booze."

"I don't know what booze is, Sonny-Bob. And what do you want alcohol for? Surely not to drink."

Then I remembered. The motor sergeant, who was currently lost in nonexistence, was one of the tiny minority of tee-totaling Christians in the TAC's employ. He'd wiped the memories of all our TITTIES clean of any data pertaining to alcoholic indulgences. So Hubert didn't even know what an alcoholic beverage was, let alone how to produce one. Well, I'd have to further his education once we climbed out of this snow drift and found our way to what passed for civilization in this timezone.

"I'll have a custard," I said wearily, "and a glass of water."

"Coming right up, Sonny-Bob." His nano production device whirred and a moment later the glove compartment popped open and the tray that held my beverages was extended.

I slurped the custard noisily. "That's good, Hubert. The best custard I've had in years." A lie, it tasted more like grease than custard, but I wanted to shore up his confidence in case he had any doubts about himself after the navigation snafu. I needed him to be fully present, not lost in self-doubt.

"I aim to please," Hubert said. "Now, what is the exact nature of this timewave we've got to stop? You didn't have time to tell me before we left."

I told him and he shuddered so hard his joints creaked. "If I had known it was a nuclear winter I'd have gone right to pieces when we materialized in this snow. People don't realize it, but I'm very sensitive."

"I'm sure you are, Hubert. Now, how are we going to get out of here? You say you've got anti-gravs?"

"Only a little. We won't be able to get very far if we leave now. But I'm recharging my energy, having the nanos convert some of the snow for me, and I'll be fully repaired and recharged in about ten hours. Except for my interdimensional drive, of course."

"Of course. Well, go ahead and fix everything and recharge yourself. Wake me up when you're through. And try to raise the cockpit temperature at least to sixty degrees. I've got hypothermia and my nipples are frozen solid."

"Okay."

Hemingway and I slept fitfully, shivering with cold. Our dreams were of a soft nest and a young girl, plus two or three older women, but even so it was too cold for Hemingway to arise even to one-quarter mast. He lay there in the loincloth, discouraged and blue and fearing the frostbite that might interfere with his sensitivity.

But then we dreamed of Monica Lewinsky. We dreamed of her wicked smile, her pouty lips, her heart-stopping flicks of the tongue, her more than ample breasts with their playful protruding nipples. And in the end, I feel it was this dream that saved us, that brought enough warmth to my body for Hemingway and me to survive the night. For awake or asleep, we knew a Goddess when we met one and in the dream, at least, the Goddess Lewinsky also knew us. We dreamed she was a connoisseur of fine cigars, and when she lit the match and touched it to the cigar my body was also aflame with desire for this most pristine of sacred women.

Yes, once she'd been a priestess of Aphrodite, then a lieutenant colonel with the TAC, and finally had intended to become a nun of Christ when the emotional strain she was under caused her spirit to depart. But her spirit lived. It lived in my dreams.

"Sonny-Bob! Sonny-Bob! Wake up! It's me, Hubert. You're not dead, are you? Have you frozen to death? WAKE UP!!"

It was the first time in a generation I'd woken without an erection, though Hemingway was on the verge of having one as a result of being invited to walk down Monica's sacred corridor of love in the dream . . . it lay right before him, he could and did touch it, he touched the wiry bristly bush that guarded the entrance to the sacred site, and then he knocked on the beloved pinkness of this Goddess, and she opened wider still and finally some blood found its way to Hemingway after all, and he'd just begun to rise . . .

"Sonny-Bob! WAKE UP!!!"

"Wh--what? Hubert, is that you? What time is it?"

The barely expanding Hemingway dropped all the way back down into a shriveled pile of blue flesh. This was the first time in a generation he'd been that small.

"It's 0500 hours, Sonny-Bob. I'm glad you're alive."

"Me, too. Turn the heat up to about eighty, will you? I'm just *barely* alive, and if I'm to undergo a full resurrection I have to be warm. And make me a coffee while you're at it."

"Cream and sugar?"

"No, black . . . the same way I like my women."

"Coming right up, L.T."

"And don't call me L.T. I've been promoted, Hubert. I'm now a captain."

Hubert's nanos were whirring, the glove compartment popped open and extended a coffee to me.

"Cappy Culpepper. Who'd have ever thought you'd get promoted?"

"Dreams can come true, my fine feathered TITTY. Dreams can come true."

I drank my coffee in silence for a while and Hubert was content to let me sit there and warm up. After a while I said, "That's good, Hubert. You've got me warm, my blood's beginning to flow again. You say we're near Lincoln, Nebraska? Good. We'll go there first and get me some clothes. I have a bag of artificial money I can buy them with. But first we have to find a disguise for you."

"I've been thinking about that, Sonny-Bob. There are no automobiles here that resemble me and none that use anti-gravs. Their primitive vehicles still use wheels--ugh! I wouldn't want to be limited in that fashion, but I guess it's necessary that I pretend to be one of them."

"Yes it is, Hubert. We both have to pretend in order to save the timeline. Do you have any of these primitive automobiles in your files?"

"Sure do. I've got plenty. I kind of like the phallic nature of a bus--" He displayed one on his viewscreen, "or the manly lines of a pickup truck. I think one of these would be a wise choice."

"Okay, Hubert. 'An ye harm none, do as ye will.' But I like the pickup truck best."

"A pickup it is, then." Hubert began to vibrate and as his nanos whirred his skin rippled. All our TITTIES are shape-shifters, have to be so they can fit into any culture. The untold trillions of tiny little nanos embedded into their skin make it easy for them to become anything they want, at least superficially. But they can still fly and swoop through the various dimensions.

We sat there for a while as Hubert changed. He made me another cup of java which I appreciated, and offered me another custard, which I declined.

At length his nanos stopped whirring and his skin stopped rippling, and the shifting cushions beneath my buttocks grew firm once more . . . too bad, Hemingway and I were beginning to enjoy that . . .

"What do you think, Cappy Culpepper?"

"You look fine, Hubert. I'm sure we're so well camouflaged now that no one in this culture will be tempted to regard us as a deviation from the norm." I could feel his glow of pride as I patted his control panel.

"That's called a dashboard, Sonny-Bob. And if anyone asks what kind of vehicle you drive tell them you drive a Dodge Ram pickup truck."

"Okay, Hubert." I didn't tell him how silly this terminology sounded to me. I didn't know what it meant; it didn't convey any information to my ears. Still, if Hubert liked it, that's all that mattered.

A TITTY has to feel good about itself.

A fence was down in the north forty and several cowboys were headed out to repair it. Their horses, chest deep in the snow but plowing onward, had been growing steadily more skittish for the past few minutes. They snorted with wild-eyed apprehension and started pulling in the other direction as the cowboys tried to urge them towards a strange looking drift.

Suddenly, the drift exploded. A purple Dodge Ram burst from the snow and leapt into the sky. The horses reared, screaming in horse language and pawing at the heavens. Two of the four cowboys were unseated, the other two held on for their lives.

"Hubert, looks like those guys are in trouble. Let's go back and check on them."

Hubert sailed back over the cowboys and this time the other two lost their seats as their horses fled the scene. I leaned out the door, looking down at these twentieth century humans. "Are you dudes okay?" They said nothing, but stared dumbfounded at us.

"Hubert," I said irritably, "I thought you told me this truck wouldn't stand out."

"It's the anti-gravs, Sonny-Bob. Remember, they don't have them here, their cars can't fly. But once I find a road to set down on, I'll be indistinguishable from any other purple Dodge Ram."

"Oh. Well, they seem to be okay."

One of them pulled a six-shooter, and I slammed Hubert's door as bullets "pinged" off his hull. "Glad you're bulletproof, Hubert."

This place wasn't so different from home after all, at least not in terms of people taking potshots at me.

"Shall we travel, Sonny-Bob?"

"Let's."

Thirty minutes later we were parked outside a deception facility in Lincoln. The facility was designated as:

WAL-MART
Guaranteed Quality At Discount Prices

"It says they have discount prices, Hubert. So I won't need this whole bag of artificial money." I'd tossed the wallet, or billfold, that Roger had given me into the bag along with the money, so I groped around until I found it. I stuffed it full of the artificial bills, then checked to insure my badge was still clipped to the front of my loincloth. I knew that some of the locals might consider my skimpy costume a little odd in this cold weather, so I figured that if they saw my badge they would conclude I worked for one of the police forces of the twentieth century and leave me alone.

"Stay here, Hubert, and don't get in any trouble. I won't be long."

The parking lot had been mostly cleared of snow, yet there was an icy glaze underfoot as I approached this imposing facility. My dick was growing cold again, and I just wanted to get inside.

I tried to get in, but the door was securely fastened. I began to pound on it, hoping the merchants inside would take pity on me. Finally, one of them approached and opened the door a crack. "We won't be open for another ten minutes, sir."

"I am cold. Take pity on me."

"Sir, you really shouldn't be dressed like that in this cold weather."

"I know that, female merchant. That's why I'm here. I have a whole wallet full of arti-- I have a wallet full of money--and I'm going to use it to buy clothes. I don't want to spend another night like last night. I nearly froze my penis off."

She just looked at me, an unfathomable expression on her face. She started to back away and let the door close, but I got my fingers inside and yanked it open. She looked like she was going to scream, as females so often do when I'm around. Probably their sexual circuits are overloaded by my presence.

"Take some of this money. I give it to you in a spirit of friendship. Now will you let me proceed?"

She was staring at the bill I dangled in front of her face. Instead of screaming, she now seemed to be stricken speechless.

"Is that enough, Miss?"

She slowly nodded, then gingerly took the bill from my fingers. Then she held the inner door open for me and I stepped through confidently, as though I'd dealt with these merchants a thousand times. I grabbed one of their shopping carts--they'd showed me how to use these at the Academy --and glanced at my benefactress again. She was still staring wide-eyed at that bill. Then suddenly she ran off somewhere.

I really needed to wear trousers if I was going to deal with these twentieth century people, so my first object was to locate the trouser section. I found it without too much difficulty and began examining some blue jeans I'd found. This jean was a sturdy trouser, well-suited for a TAC field operative, so I dropped my loincloth and tried several pairs on until I found my size. Then I put about a dozen pairs in the shopping cart. I suddenly had that uncanny prickly-skin feeling you get when you feel you're being watched, so I slowly put my loincloth back on and pretended to be absorbed in my shopping. But I had all my senses on high alert. If these people were spying on me I wanted to catch them at it.

Now that I had my trousers I thought it prudent to obtain some underwear. I turned and caught an attractive young servant girl in a blue Wal-Mart apron staring at me. "Excuse me, Miss. I don't have any underwear. If you will direct me to the appropriate section I will purchase several pairs of drawers."

She turned and headed off at a fast pace through the many racks of clothing and I followed her. She periodically checked over her shoulder to make sure I was still there.

Shortly we began passing artificial titties with some sort of slingshot device strapped over them. I realized we must be in the sporting goods section and figured that some of these people must hunt rabbits and squirrels with slingshots. This sport was not unknown in my own time.

"Miss? Miss!" She stopped in her tracks. "How does this slingshot device work?" I was fumbling with the thing and finally found there was a safety clip in the back. I got the slingshot loose and waved it above my head. "Let's see," I mumbled, "you must put handfuls of gravel in these big conical holders." Suddenly I felt a sunny smile break out on my face. "This is more than just a slingshot," I cried, "this is a sling shotgun!" For the first time I admired the ingenuity of these twentieth century people.

I approached the servant girl, still waving the slingshot device above my head. "Where do you store your ammunition? I want to buy this thing, and I'll need lots of ammo." I didn't want to go to the trouble of quarrying the gravel myself. I stamped my foot impatiently. "I want some ammo!"

The girl broke and ran, and I had to stop myself from chasing her down. Although only a servant girl, I realized that it could be risky to pursue her because these people had so many bizarre taboos. The rulers of this Wal-Mart facility might think ill of a customer in a loincloth chasing down one of their servants while waving a double-barreled slingshot. The Vikings wouldn't have cared.

I tossed the slingshot in my buggy and continued on. I thought of buying the artificial tits as well, but didn't want to clutter Hubert's cockpit up with non-essentials. If the slingshot couldn't hold its shape, why then I'd just have to eventually buy another.

A bit later I learned that these "slingshots" were really prisons for the titties. Such contraptions are unknown in my time, where women are free.

A manservant approached me. He had a wary, strange look in his eye and I began to feel it might be only a matter of time before one of these odd people snapped. I had to finish my business and get out of here.

"May I help you, sir?" the manservant said. He carried himself with a certain authority, so I knew he must be some kind of overseer, perhaps even a eunuch. It was almost like having a taste of Old Babylonia.

"I need underwear."

"Follow me, sir."

The eunuch led me to the underwear section and I tipped him with a bill. I understood it was the custom to tip these people when you were pleased, and I wanted to make sure I followed all these odd customs so as not to attract attention to myself.

The eunuch's eyes bulged out and his jaw dropped. I knew I'd made a mistake but I couldn't pinpoint where. He looked wild; I was wishing I had my gun. The slingshot would have to do.

"Sir . . . sir! Are you sure you want to give me this?"

"Yesss . . ." I said slowly, fearing my conformity to custom had a flaw.

"But sir! This bill has four zeros!"

So that was it. He wanted more zeros.

"Take another," I said, opening my wallet to him. "Any one of your choice."

He was staring at me more bug-eyed than ever, a little drool hung at the corner of his mouth. But now I was confident I was in conformity to custom. There could only be one answer to the eunuch's conduct; he didn't even recognize the customs of his own century. Therefore, he had a drug problem. I had studied all about the drug problem of the Twentieth, about how sexual repression and economic deprivation led people to try to escape through drugs.

I placed a consoling hand on his shoulder. He flinched, but said nothing. He was trembling under my fingers, I knew it must almost be time for his next "fix".

"Don't worry, son," I said in what I hoped was a tender voice. "You may not believe it, but I drink too much. I know how it is."

I took two more bills out of the wallet and inspected each to make sure it had at least four zeros. I stuffed them into his pocket. "Now go get some help," I said.

A great sob escaped him and he began choking and weeping as though he'd swallowed his tongue or something. I held him and patted him on the back, trying to console the poor dope fiend. "Look what this century has done to you," I whispered softly.

But I had to go, because from what I'd seen I believed all the servants in this deception facility had a hand in the same vault of drugs this one did and I didn't want to pay for all of them to get rehabilitated. I had to make that artificial money last.

I held him by the shoulders as he convulsed with sobs. "Go with Aphrodite, my son. Go with Reagan."

Then I dropped my loincloth and began trying on underwear. You had to tear open these little plastic bags to get to it. I wondered why they made it so difficult.

When next I looked for the poor unfortunate eunuch, he was gone.

I quickly found my size and chose a number of fine underwear with tags depicting fruit, similar to the ones I wear in my own timezone. It gave me a sense of nostalgia to buy the underwear with the tags depicting fruit.

(Of course, I always have to go to extra trouble to insure that Hemingway is fully housed, such as folding him and putting him in a special pouch like the one the lab tech Donna had sewn into the loincloth. But here I figured I could make do without a pouch just by running Hemingway down alongside my leg--the jeans were loose enough to accommodate him. I hoped.)

Then I bought shirts in a wide variety, socks and shoes came next. Finally I was done, and looked forward to getting out of that place before these drug addicts flipped out and descended on me. As I pushed my buggy towards the exit I had a sudden thought. I'd seen some overalls back there; the overalls were looser than the jeans and would be ideal if Hemingway was too large for the jeans. With the overalls I would have the option of either running Hemingway down the leg or pulling him up and letting him rest on my chest. Excitedly, I ran back to the trouser section and procured two pairs of overalls. Now I was satisfied.

I pushed my buggy towards the doorway marked "EXIT". I'd forgotten already I had to pay for these clothes, even though I'd already given money to some of the servants. When you've been brought up in a moneyless culture, you're used to responding as if everything is free. And in my timezone, it is.

But not here. "Sir!" A dull growl came from behind me. "Them clothes ain't free."

I turned and beheld an oldish fellow, probably in his sixties. Almost as old as me, but this primitive didn't have the advantage of Practical Immortality and the maintenance of youthful beauty that comes with it. He wore a gun and a blue shirt with a badge. I recognized him as being some sort of cop. There was a black cord tied around his neck, and I saw at once I could use this cord to strangle him, if it came to that.

What sort of cop walks around with a strangle-cord tied around his neck? A cop on drugs, obviously. This freak was just like the rest of them.

"I know these clothes aren't free, sir," I said pleasantly. "I was just testing you."

His hand moved to the butt of his gun. It rested there. "Pay for them clothes, or leave 'em behind."

"Of course, officer. And may I commend you on your diligence and warriorship."

I trotted to one of the moneychangers. "I have a buggy full of clothes over there. How much do I owe you?"

She dimpled, and Hemingway began to grow hard at once. I have to deal with this problem every day. Sometimes I wonder if it's worth it, but upon reflection I always conclude it is.

Anyhow, the front of my loincloth began to throb and surge as Hemingway sought to unwind himself. She dimpled again, and her blush excited Hemingway all the more.

The girl was naturally pale and I grew faint over her alabaster beauty. Her hair was flaming red, and I of course wondered if that more important patch of hair was also red. I could feel the energy between us, and I knew her pussy had to be distended and moist. As Hemingway tried to reach out from the confines of his loincloth, so too was her pussy trying to reach out from its undergarments. Her pussy, her sweet wet pussy . . .

Hemingway surged . . .

"Sir? Are you all right?"

I groaned. "I have this problem. At least, sometimes I think it's a problem. I have this penis, you see, who has a mind of his own and pretty much directs my actions. His name's Hemingway, and if you would just . . ."

"Sir! I will not. And if I wasn't amused by you I'd call security right now. I think you'd better pay for your selections and leave."

Well, at least she was too mature to run away screaming. She was older than a lot of the women Hemingway responded to; must've been at least twenty. But then Hemingway had never been overly selective, and had known women of all ages in the Biblical sense ever since Biblical times.

I held out a wad of artificial money. "Here, my dear," I said weakly, trying to keep Hemingway under control. I was fighting the Battle of the Bulge and I was losing. Any moment Hemingway might burst out of the loincloth, I was sure he was going to.

"Forgive me if I've violated any of your taboos," I gasped. "I hope that's enough money. Goodbye."

She stared at that wad of money, then got that strange look in her eyes they all had. The ancient texts were right when they claimed this century had a drug problem. Dope fiends were all around me.

I hobbled away, trusting I'd given her enough cash, when she came after me. I was confused; Hemingway was so damn hard now and in such an agony of confinement I couldn't think clearly. But it's frightening to be chased by a dope fiend no matter how beautiful she is.

Because of Hemingway I had no chance to outrun her, could only stagger and stumble. She caught me by the arm and I turned and cringed, hoping she wasn't wielding a knife or axe. The ancient texts warned of such behavior.

As it turned out I needn't have worried. I learned that this woman, this youthful bursting beauty, was perhaps the only sane and sober one among all these moneychanger types.

"Sir!" She looked me in the eye, and out came that lovely pink tongue of hers, flicking suggestively around her gleaming teeth, the way women's tongues always do when they want what I want. "I said a moment ago that I would not. I was wrong. I hope you'll forgive me. Now I say that I will! I will! Yes, I most certainly will."

Endorphins flooded Hemingway as he heard that announcement. "Thank you, Miss. If you will I will."

"But--" I glanced nervously at the glowering cop, "did I pay you enough?"

"You certainly did, honey. I'm quitting this shit factory today and going back to school. Mama and Daddy will be proud."

I couldn't quite grasp what she was talking about, but if she was happy I was happy. She hooked her arm through mine and together we pushed that buggy into the searing cold of Nebraska, and since Hemingway was about to explode at that moment I think the cold is all that kept him in his dormitory. He withdrew a little.

The grouchy old cop followed us. "Hey Lucille? That freak pay for all that stuff?"

"Fuck you, Leroy! Of course he paid for it, and it looks like he makes more money in an hour than you do in a decade." She extended her middle finger and waved her hand at Leroy, and Hemingway felt himself quicken again as he--or as I--or maybe as both of us glimpsed the polished nail of that finger. It was red.

"And fuck you, commerce! I'm going to major in philosophy."

Apparently I had inspired this Lucille, somehow.

Together we walked to Hubert, and with the wind blowing briskly my nipples were frozen again. Lucille had grabbed a jacket, a fuzzy furry thing, and shucked her servant's apron when she left her position at the moneychanger's table and joined me. So I was pretty sure her nipples were still pliable.

I rapped on Hubert's hull. "Open up, Hubert."

His door opened and he said, "Glad you're back, Sonny-Bob. Dogs have been pissing on me."

Lucille gave a start. "Your truck talks!"

"Um, yes he does. I made him myself, raised him up from a tin can. I installed some special circuits in him."

"A tin can's ass," rasped Hubert. "I was created over forty years ago by a motor sergeant. And I'm tired of being pissed on."

I gave Lucille what I fear was a rather sickly smile. "He has an attitude problem, my dear."

She looked at the "truck" and ran her fingers along his surface, and I could see his skin ripple to her touch.

If her touch can make a truck's skin ripple, imagine what it will do for Hemingway.

Hubert sighed, and I feared he was going to roll over onto his back so she could scratch his belly. That certainly wouldn't do. Not in a public place.

"Lucille, would you like to join me inside?" I gestured gallantly into Hubert's cockpit--I mean his cab, as I believe they called the cockpits of these pickup trucks--and Lucille smiled, smacked her lips and climbed inside. I started to join her, but suddenly Hubert tried to slam his door. I grabbed it before it could shut and wrestled with him. "Hubert! My nipples are frozen! Open up for my frozen futuristic ass!"

I was fighting with my TITTY and not making any progress when I heard Lucille speak. "Uh . . . Hubert, why don't you let Sonny-Bob come inside? That is what you called him, isn't it? Sonny-Bob?"

Hubert relaxed at once; she certainly had this old TITTY in the palm of her hand.

I sprang into the truck and slammed the door, leaving my new clothes outside. I could get them later. Right now this lady was more important. "I'm sorry it had to be Hubert who introduced us, Lucille. I was so concerned about being surrounded by dope fiends all I could think of was getting out of that deception facility. I didn't think to introduce myself."

"That's all right, Sonny-Bob. This has been the most interesting day I've had in a long time. First you pay for my college, then you introduce me to a talking truck. And now I'm going to introduce you," she removed her jacket, "to Miss Lucille."

She leaned over to me, and I grabbed the emergency kill switch that could be used to shut Hubert down, even against his will. All TAC's vehicles were required to keep this switch, no matter how they might otherwise be disguised. And I was determined that Hubert was not going to use Lucille and me as material for his childish sexual fantasies.

"Sonny-Bob! Don't you dare! I won't look . . .Stop!" Hubert was anguished. "Stop!"

"Some things should go unnoticed by a truck, Hubert, and this is one of them. Goodnight. Enjoy your nap."

I yanked the switch and Hubert gave a startled gasp, then his control panel--I mean his dashboard--grew dim and extinguished itself.

I smiled at Lucille. "Now I have you all to myself, honey."

She'd placed her fingers behind my neck as I faced her; now she pulled me to her. "Now you're mine," she said, and for a moment all I could see were green eyes and red lips and a gently questing tongue . . . then a blackness full of exploding stars as our lips joined. This was love at first fuck . . . actually, it was only lust.   But the endorphins produced were of a very high quality.

After being immersed in one another for a long time we paused to catch our breath. "Whew!" said Lucille. "I've never had a kiss like that."

"I've had lots of practice, sweetheart. I've had several wives."

"They were fools to let you go."

"Maybe . . ."

She was on me again, this time passionately, fiercely, with an open writhing mouth and an ardor I'd seldom experienced, breathing herself into me like a goddess/slut of ancient times. Then with surging breasts she bit my lips and sucked my tongue into the frenzied whirlpool of desire that carried us into oblivion.

But then Hemingway popped out and tried to come between us.

She looked at him, shocked. "Oh, my . . ."

I said nothing, waiting for the inevitable actions that always follow the shock when a woman first meets Hemingway.

After a moment she started to get command of her faculties. "I guess this is the powerful penis you tried to tell me about in the store."

"Yes it is, honey," I whispered softly. "And he likes you."

Then she went down on me and a shudder of pleasure coursed throughout Hemingway, then rippled through my entire nervous system.

After tasting the fruit of my passion she looked up. "Let's get rid of this diaper."

She ripped the loincloth off me and I was as naked as a Nebraska jaybird. I reached down and fondled her titties, and she quickly removed her blouse, losing a few buttons in the process.

And then I saw it. "You're wearing a slingshot!" I gasped.

I reached down again and fondled her titties in spite of that slingshot, and she just smiled as I popped her breasts out of those gravel holders. She reached behind herself and undid the safety hook and shrugged out of the slingshot. She tossed it away.

Then she removed her shoes and her red toenails glistened, making my mouth water. She slid out of her jeans and flicked off her undergarment. "Time for a panty raid," she laughed.

She put the panty on my head--**my** head, not Hemingway's--and left it there as though it were a cap. It smelled good, full of the sweet musk of WOMAN.

Then she went down on Hemingway again. Before she'd only licked him, but this time she tried to ingest my splendid lovesicle.

She coughed around him and her eyes bulged out as she deep throated a portion of my Hemingway. This was not unexpected; many women respond to Hemingway with bulging eyes.

I grabbed her head gently, careful not to shove too much Hemingway into her just yet; that old dick takes a lot of getting used to. After a time she surfaced and began climbing up my body, a kiss here, a lick there. She moaned in excitement, I guess she was looking forward to the penetrational challenge of welcoming me into her sweet pussy, which by now I felt must be the sweetest pussy in Nebraska.

She lingered over my nipples, spitting on them and rubbing the spit in with her fingers as though it were massage oil. It felt good. Then she licked and sucked on them for a while before working her way up to my neck. She lay stretched out on me then, head on my chest and rubbing Hemingway vigorously with her leg, and I realized she was taller than she'd appeared in that little Wal-Mart apron. She was about as tall as me. She was well padded, but it was evenly distributed. She had a nice shape. With her flaming red hair she was a beautiful Goddess, one of the finest I'd encountered. I'd had no idea the twentieth century could boast such women.

"Honey, you must be exhausted after climbing up my dick. You can relax for a while on your back and I'll do some of the work."

She smiled and rolled off me. We were fortunate that Hubert was sporting something called a king cab, which basically meant there was more room to fuck than in an ordinary truck. Plus, Hubert had designed his seats a little differently from most trucks so I could sleep in him. There was no back seat in his king cab at all, just empty space where I stored my moneybag, and you could fold down the backs of both front bucket seats to sleep on.

Or to fuck.

My sweetheart lay supine upon the extended seat on the passenger's side, which had suddenly become a golden couch of passion. I marveled at her. This was an extraordinary woman, she had more of the Goddess in her than any other primitive woman I had ever known. If I could have taken her with me I would have, but this was impossible as I had to go find Ronald Reagan later that day, and also a liquor store.

She had been so focused on Hemingway earlier that she hadn't had a chance to weigh my balls, my hefty balls, she'd only licked my scrotum a few times and kissed it once. So the first thing I did when I had her on her back was to straddle her face, my great balls resting one on each of her cheeks, with the great Hemingway lifting turgidly above her nose and running 'way off into the distance somewhere. I was a little surprised he hadn't come after she'd first licked him, considering the pressures he'd experienced earlier, but I probably shouldn't have been. Hemingway, for all his faults, is a compassionate dick and he usually puts the pleasure and welfare of women first, particularly those who have good hearts and lusty loins. He wanted to come and by and by he would, but first he wanted to fuck her silly, as he knew she wanted him to do. He could have sprayed his spunk all over her pretty body, but he really wanted to give it to her harddddddd, he wanted to slither and hump himself up inside her before exploding with love. He'd rather discharge his essence **in** her than **on** her . . . at least this first time.

So my balls were resting on her face, one on each cheek. They were a *huge* compliment to Hemingway. In kindergarten the other kids, particularly the females, had called me "Mule Dick" and "Basket Balls", and this was even before I'd learned to really use this equipment in service to my Goddess. Ah, if those other kids could only see me now!

I felt her kissing my basket balls, licking them, fondling them with her red-nailed fingers. I thought I heard her praying to them. I was pretty sure I heard a prayer.

She opened her mouth as wide as she could and tried to swallow my left nut, the biggest left nut in the universe, and she managed to do a pretty good job; she got it almost halfway into her beautiful scarlet-lipped mouth. She kept it there a while, licking it, munching on it, caressing it, nurturing it. And when it had become fully relaxed, she went to work on my right basket ball. It must sound unbelievable, but the work she did on my basket balls actually relaxed them so much that my entire reproductive system lost the urgency of self-expression and even Hemingway relaxed, nodding off, nodding off, though he never quite went into slumber.

I suspected Lucille of using Shiatsu on my balls.

Anyway, once my right ball had been licked and massaged into complete relaxation, I was just sitting there more or less on her face in the complete peace of perfect composure, just like in yoga class. Hemingway lay draped lazily across her face as she took his measure; she kept running her hands up and down his length, kneading him and worshipping him, then scratching him slightly with those red nails. She kissed or licked him from time to time and he would twitch in acknowledgement, but didn't seem inclined to stir more than that. I sighed peacefully. I hadn't been so relaxed and at one with myself since before I'd learned the timewave was coming. And I hadn't even spurted my wad yet.

"Lucille, I thank my Goddess for you," I whispered huskily, tears in my eyes. "I thank the Great Goddess Aphrodite for making you in her image and sending you to me."

I slid down her body a few meters, just enough so the head of my lovesicle touched her lips again, its shaft running down her body between her breasts until it ended in my pelvic region. She just smiled and said, "I love you too, Sonny-Bob." Then as she began to lick his sensitive head Hemingway came to life once more, throbbing with the natural rhythms of the timeline and crying out for justice. And I know there must've been some pre-come oozing out his head because she commented on it. "You've been eating your greens, Sonny-Bob." It was true. I'd had Hubert make me a glass of wheatgrass juice en route to this Wal-Mart.

She took Hemingway's great head in both hands, her red nails--those red nails!--twitching as Hemingway throbbed. She kissed him again and he nearly spat, his color had changed from a fleshy pink to a bluish purple; there was more pre-come, this time a strand of the nutritious stuff stuck to her sweet scarlet lips as she smiled at me. Then the strand broke at my end and the comestring lay across her chin, and also a glob of it was still on her lips. She reached up with her middle finger as I gasped and collected the strand of jism and stroked her lips with it. Then that perfect pink tongue appeared and greedily flicked at the come until it was gone. She swallowed in an obvious way, and I knew she wanted more. She was still sucking her middle finger and staring at me when I shuddered, it was all I could do to keep from spraying my spunk into her face and hair.

I knew now I would have no chance to get to her pussy before I exploded, so I decided to make the most of it. "Lucille honey, see how much you can swallow. I'll give it all to you . . . ohhhh . . . I'm going to explode before I can fuck you, but you can swallow all you want."

She gave a little tittering laugh that thrilled me all the more and made

Hemingway heavy with love, a tear in his lone eye. "Sonny-Bob, I want it all. I'm going to swallow every ounce of your juice I can."

That did it. Now that I knew she wanted it in her face I gave Hemingway permission to proceed. The wild stallion was no longer reined in so he began to throb like a seesaw, bouncing off her lips and nose, pummeling her with his desire. I just sat back and watched.

She got some more pre-come on her lips as she fought the monster, wrestling him with both hands and trying to find a more permanent purchase for her lips. For just an instant, then, his head was in the right position and her mouth went down on it like a vegetarian's on a giant mushroom-headed carrot.

My lovely penis throbbed wildly, but she had him in her mouth; a few inches, anyway, and she wasn't about to let him go until he'd been milked. His great blue veins formed ridges that lost themselves in the wilderness of her desperately distended lips, a wilderness that was rapidly being charted. My scrotum bounced around merrily as she held on to the thrashing Hemingway for dear life, the balls within the scrotum not quite clinking, but still obviously present.

She gagged, yes she did; all women gag on Hemingway but some are exceptionally dedicated, and Lucille was one of those. She fixed her eyes on me with love and a certain innocence I was surprised to see in a woman with a big dick in her mouth. Her head bobbed up and down on my root vegetable, her hunger insatiable. She was able to keep the meat in place now, she'd learned his rhythms, and her red-tipped fingers moved farther down his shaft as she imparted justice to the universe in her own sweet way. She bobbed as Hemingway weaved.

Suddenly, Armageddon! Hemingway coughed and Lucille's eyes grew wider still, then he charged, driving himself deep into her throat, I couldn't stop him. She fell back gagging but still valiantly holding on, keeping him in her mouth, and he exploded with a conscienceless treachery, not caring who got hurt, for he was hard and he was hotly spurting. He used her.

Lucille was crying, but I never knew whether a woman was crying with pleasure or pain; only Hemingway was close enough to her to know, and he didn't care. He never cared.

She had taken all the come she could ingest in that first split-second of his detonation, then she released him and the force of his explosion drove him out of her mouth. He was slapping her in a traitorous rhythm as she clutched at him desperately, trying to regain a connection that had been lost in his brutality.

Come was everywhere. Lucille had a mouthful of it and was fighting to swallow it; it was on her face, in her hair and it tracked my passion down her slick and naked young body. **My** passion, for I cannot blame everything on Hemingway.

The fluid of my life sprayed around the king cab and I knew Hubert would give me hell about that. Hemingway convulsed and spat for two or three minutes; Lucille had managed to grab him again and licked some dribbling jism off his shaft, which stimulated him again and made him spit a little more.

Finally, it was over. Lucille lay back, bruised and exhausted, and in an attack of conscience I wished I had some vitamins to give her. My sex juice was all over her and she was still vainly trying to swallow the last of it she'd collected. She was a slick Goddess of Love who had sacrificed herself upon the cross of my desire.

I suddenly felt my relations with women needed improvement somehow.

But I put on a brave face for Lucille . . . or maybe for myself. "How'd you like your meal, darling? Semen is full of nutrients; I'll bet you won't be hungry for a while."

She nodded weakly, still wiping the moist goo off her face and licking her fingers clean of it. "That was the third interesting experience of my day, Sonny-Bob. But I don't have the stamina to repeat it."

I nodded sympathetically. "Many women don't have the fortitude to complete even once such experience. You're among those Goddess Amazons who have fellated me to completion. You're a warrior."

She smiled, and for a moment I stretched myself out on her and kissed her cheek, my nearly flaccid member sliding against her slick body. But the slick friction began to stimulate him again and he began to grow. "Lucille honey, I promise I **will** get to your pussy. And this time I really **will** do most of the work. You've done far more than your share and I thank you. You just lie back and relax and I'll give you a foot massage."

She nodded weakly, her eyes half closed. I realized that if this was going to be a really good experience for Lucille, as I wanted it to be, she would have to emerge unbruised, unbroken and unstretched. Such an outcome now appeared unlikely, except for one thing: I had nanos. Medical nanos.

I surreptitiously pulled out my bag of medical nanos from under the seat. Lucille was breathing hoarsely, then a strange rattling noise started in her throat. She appeared "out of it", so I figured she wouldn't even notice a nano injection. I jabbed her toe--the first digit after the big toe-- with the injector. In just a few minutes she'd be fine.

The indicator light on the injector lit up, telling me that all the nanos had been delivered. I removed the disposable device and put it in the litter bag, then licked the drop of blood off Lucille's toe. I squatted at her feet and waited for her strength to return.

CHAPTER SEVEN

"Mama, Daddy I had the strangest dream. A wild man with a huge dick and two basket balls paid for my college, then fucked my face in his talking truck . . . Oh. I see it wasn't a dream."

I was still squatting on the floorboard about eye level with her pussy and staring up the length of her body. "No sweetheart, it wasn't a dream."

We looked at each other a while then, she from her perch upon the seat and I from my position on the floorboard, glancing occasionally at her foxhole.

"I feel good, Sonny-Bob! In fact, I feel great! Better than I've ever felt. I'm young and juicy and ready to go again. I had no idea you could make a woman feel this way."

Of course, it was the nanos that made her feel that way, not me. But I didn't tell her that. These nanos would last for a little over twenty-four hours, eliminating any disease-causing microorganisms and repairing any injury. So she would feel better than she ever had for at least another day, after which the nanos would dissolve in her bloodstream.

I looked at that alabaster skin, the skin I'd accidentally bruised black and blue, and it was bruised no more. The nanos had healed the bruises and her skin was purer and whiter than an Alaska snowfall. The white chicks always get to me.

Of course, so do the black ones!

I felt behind me and activated Hubert's nano production device. This thing can be activated independent of the vehicle's consciousness, because sometimes an agent just wanted to sip a cup of coffee in silence and not be distracted by his TITTY.

"Custard or coffee?"

"What?"

"Would you like custard or coffee?"

"Um, I'll have a custard."

"Excellent choice, miss. And thank you for dining with me."

Hubert's NPD whirred, then the glove compartment popped open and extended two custards. I sipped one experimentally, tasting for grease. But Hubert had perfected his technique; this one was outstanding.

"This one passes muster." I handed the cup to Lucille. I took the other custard and sniffed it, then tried a sip and found it too was clear of grease. "Mighty fine," I said, smacking my lips. "Mighty fine."

Lucille was just sitting there, looking from me to the glove compartment and back again. "You have the most unusual truck I've ever sucked cock in, Sonny-Bob. Your truck talks and it makes custard. Just like in a James Bond movie."

"My truck will make you an omelet if you want one, sweetheart."

"No thanks, uh . . . I'm full, as you should know. This custard is just a sweet ending to the main course."

"Sweets for my sweet," I smiled, feeling my heart chakra finally activate.

In my timezone, the Sacred Prostitutes of Aphrodite, as well as Her priests and priestesses and the psychologists and sociologists, all teach that the heart chakra is the primary organ of humanity and that living in your heart is the only good. Even the penis and the pussy take a back seat to the heart; our shrinks and religious figures teach us to coordinate these aspects of ourselves so that the heart's energy flows through the raging loins, and lust becomes transmuted into loving passion.

Of course, it doesn't work every time. The Sacred Prostitutes of Aphrodite had been working diligently with me for decades, trying to teach me to join my loving heart with my raging member. The accomplishment eluded me for a long time, but once I finally felt it I wanted to remain in that state forever. Hemingway gave up nothing, yet received everything.

But I lost my heart consciousness time and again, leaving me with an undisciplined, undignified raging bull between my legs. The prostitutes said this was normal, it takes any man a long time to learn to live in his heart and to coordinate his heart with his dick. Even the sacred prostitutes and psychotherapists I'd fucked said it took them a long time to activate their hearts, then coordinate their hearts with their pussies.

In fact, a prostitute couldn't receive her[*] second degree initiation until she'd had her heart and pussy coordinated for three years, radiating unconditional love and purified passion to all the world. The prostitutes teach that this is actually the norm for humanity, and that in an ancient Golden Age everyone lived this way. They tell us that in the twenty-

---

[*] There are male prostitutes too, but I don't pay any attention to them.

second century we are returning to our spiritual birthright, we are learning to join the human with the divine. And we are all Aphrodite's children. She will be patient with us.

Well, I'd never seen any Golden Age, but I'd only been back as far as some of the last of the Atlantean cultures, right before the Great Flood. Those cultures were degenerate, and with their lack of respect for individual liberty and for spirituality they should have been washed away. But you know, there has always been a rumor floating around the TAC that millions of years ago a Golden Age really existed and that they had time travel, too. Some operatives even believed their "TAC" had contact with the founders of our TAC and that our TAC was the reemergence of an ancient lineage that existed long before even Atlantis. It was held by some that a few time-traveling operatives from that ancient Golden Age survived--and quite possibly caused--the ancient catastrophic alterations to the timeline and went underground, forming secret schools that carried the ancient flame of spiritual enlightenment down through the ages. Of course, by the nineteenth or twentieth century these schools themselves were degenerate and didn't amount to a wart on an Atlantean's ass. Their form had lost the spirit; many of these schools actually preached various forms of sexual repression such as monogamy, thus encouraging the perversion that automatically goes along with sexual repression. In the words of my friend Roger Bacon: "By the twentieth century these schools had all become 'Mickey Mouse'. They would accept **anyone** for membership; some even advertised openly in tabloids such as the *National Enquirer*. They practiced social promotion, which meant that as long as you paid your dues they would continue initiating you into ever higher degrees, whether you understood your lessons or not, and regardless of whether you even did your homework. It wasn't like the old days, when you had to swim through a pool of crocodiles to get initiated."*

Anyhow, the sacred prostitutes had taught me to love, though I couldn't do it all the time. I was in awe of the ability of the senior prostitutes to radiate unconditional love while fucking me with as much enthusiasm as a recently de-virginized adolescent.

The lesson here is plain: you **have** to be a highly sexual being to become a highly spiritual being. The loins fuel the heart, then the heart purifies and nourishes the loins. It's the most pleasant and beneficial of

---

* From *Mystery Schools Throughout The Ages: A Text By Roger Bacon* © 2164 by Bacon And Eggs Press.

natural cycles. I was surprised the people in the twentieth century hadn't noticed.

Lucille was looking at me . . . yes, she was looking at me strangely, the way everyone does from time to time.

"I love you, Lucille," I said. And I meant it.

As the expanding radiance filled my breast and enveloped me, Lucille scooted forward on the seat and raised the back of it to its usual position. She took my face in her hands as I knelt before her, but I quickly looked back down, unable to gaze upon her splendor. For she was shining with a radiance I'd never imagined and I suddenly became aware that this woman, whom I already knew was unusual, was much more unusual than I had at first perceived. A power radiated from her, a charisma of rubies and gold. Lucille was the most unusual person I'd ever met.

I began to understand what I had found in her. Somehow, Goddess knows why or how, I had stumbled upon a woman who intuitively had the compassion and strength of character to channel Aphrodite's golden energy, the energy of love, the healing energy of love through sex. And I was ashamed to have come unto one such as she without burning the offerings of rose and myrrh and humbling myself in her presence. But she was Aphrodite. She would forgive.

"I love you too, Sonny-Bob," she whispered.

"I know you do, Lucille. You are Aphrodite, and Aphrodite *is* love. You're an incarnation of unconditional love, as well as a sexual powerhouse."

Her fingers were stroking my hair. "Let's make love, Sonny-Bob. Make love to me."

"I can't," I whispered. "I'm not worthy."

She laughed. "That didn't stop you from beating me half to death with your Hemingway, sweetheart."

"I didn't recognize you then."

"I forgive you. And I pardon Hemingway."

Hemingway had been unobtrusively curled up on the floorboard, ashamed at having been so rough with this Goddess. He twitched when she pardoned him, but he knew he wasn't worthy to face her. He couldn't face her.

Hemingway and I had learned something from this encounter, and I marveled that we hadn't learned it before. Treat every woman as a Goddess, at least until she proves otherwise. Because somewhere, some day when you're least expecting it, you *will* meet a Goddess and you want to treat her with the respect and love she deserves.

I knelt--groveled, really--before Aphrodite, she of the flaming red hair and golden heart. I knelt before those precious feet and kissed each one in its turn, pledging myself to the service of the Goddess. And I silently thanked her for showing me the Way.

My lips brushed her knees; to me they were more than flesh and bone and cartilage. My kisses found their way to her quadriceps.

She bent over and pulled me to her. I lifted her legs and slid myself under her, supporting her weight as we sat facing each other. For once, Hemingway was not a distraction. We looked into one another's eyes for a long time and I knew she could teach me everything I needed to know. Hers was the voice I'd been waiting all my life to hear.

Then our lips met, our teeth clacked, and our tongues began. Amid the smacking and the clacking, our hearts joined.

The birds have no notion of this, nor do the bees. That is a twentieth century old inhibited wives' tale. For the inhibited never come to love. Not true love.

Then we stayed joined, tongue to tongue and heart to heart, for a long, long time. We breathed our souls into one another's bodies. And when we finished this kiss of eternity and looked back into one another's eyes I said, "Lucille, Goddess Aphrodite to whom I declare my heart, I want to do something for you." She just smiled with wisdom and love.

She had elevated me to her level, but now I traced the route of descent, humbling myself before her. I worked my way to her breasts and they were breasts indeed; the breasts of a goddess are never just titties. I slobbered on them with a desperate love and with fingers and tongue I knew their rigid nipples, her nipples of love and fire; they were as red as her hair.

My tongue found her navel, then the top of her beautiful burning bush of fire and joy. Her pussy, pink and distended and juicily glistening was framed by her red-nailed fingers, and there was a golden ring through her outer labia. I gently removed those sweet fingers and licked and sucked the fluid of self-love off them as she softly moaned, her beautiful body lost in small convulsions. Her fingers tightened in my hair.

I smiled. "For my Goddess," I whispered. "I offer myself to you in worship."

A soft prayer came from my lips as I prepared myself. I was going to try to serve this woman the same way I served the temple ladies, with tongue and heart and soul. Yet Lucille was not just any sacred woman; I saw her now as WOMAN, and as WOMAN strong and purified, embodying all the virtues of WOMAN from ancient times into the far future, but purified and cleansed of all frailties. There was no pettiness, fear or manipulation about her. She didn't want to control me or dominate me, she wanted to set me free. She wanted me to fly as a winged heart.

I gazed into the Vault of Heaven.

I pulled her clitoral hood back and marveled at the shining jewel underneath, the star that would guide those of sufficient wisdom and heart to her Holy Manger of exultant joy. I stroked this fine jewel and made ready to deliver it from melancholy.

I raised up my hands to her glistening breasts with their pert red nipples and I stroked the undersides of those nipples as my face went down to praise her.

As I sucked her swollen clit up through the gap in my front teeth, I realized I could do without alcohol if I could drink deeply of this lady every day. She must have been well-nourished, for unless I was hallucinating her flavor was the flavor of ripe peaches, plus some deep secret flavor of womanhood that had eternity in it. Her flavor glowed in my mouth; my lips met her pussy lips in holy ecstasy. For the period of our togetherness our life was a prayer.

I was bathed in the Holy Spirit of Love and elevated to a Mt. Olympus of Goddess understanding. I saw the world and the cosmos as a unity, and the timeline wasn't straight, it was a golden sea of circles. I saw Jesus resurrected by Aphrodite. I saw my destiny. I was just one tiny spark in Aphrodite's flaming heart, but I was a part of her and she permeated me. For the first time in a long time I felt clean.

I came to myself . . . Hemingway was in her, but he was relaxed and satisfied, at peace with the earth and with his own nature. I didn't know how he'd gotten there; all I remembered was being drawn to her clit, then breathing softly upon the gate of her sweet pussy and a taste better than magnolias and ripe peaches. All I remembered after that was God . . . the divinity of this woman, the divinity of myself, the divinity inherent in all things.

I don't know where my personality had gone. I don't remember it being there. Just the tunnel, then a great Light.

She stirred and moaned softly, then opened her eyes and looked at me, and what I saw there was a soft brilliance beyond imagining. She belonged in a temple, that was her natural home. Yet I had found her in a Wal-Mart.

"You are my friend," I said to her, and she placed her hand alongside my face and we shared the glow for a long time. A vague memory came to me then . . . I remembered falling through the Gate of Heaven, weeping without end, a sense of loss profound. Then had come the fullness and restoration of this woman and I savored a peace I had been apart from for what seemed a thousand years.

I'd come home.

Well, of course I wanted to take her with me, but that was impossible. I was seventy-four years old and this former Wal-Mart servant girl was the most powerful and loving person I'd known in all my years, but I had to go contact Ronald Reagan and that would be dangerous. I couldn't expose Lucille to that kind of risk. I'd probably have to get through his centurions just to talk to him.

Or--and I didn't much like this thought; it seemed sacrilegious--I might have to kidnap him and hold him for a while to try to convince him not to nuke the Soviets. Well, he might get mad about that, but Aphrodite loved me and Aphrodite wears the pants in the Reagan family.

Lucille had languidly dressed herself; I was still naked. But now her breasts swayed freely beneath the fabric of her blouse and I realized she'd neglected her slingshot.

"Honey, you've forgotten your slingshot."

She chuckled, eyes twinkling with merriment. "I thought I'd leave it with you for a souvenir, Big Boy. Panties too, they should hold my odor for a while. I don't want you to forget." As if I could!

I was touched. In my timezone women usually didn't leave their underwear with me. But then, they had no slingshots and frequently didn't wear panties, either.

In any case, I appreciated Lucille's thoughtful gesture. I plucked my loincloth off the floor. "Honey, here's an article of clothing that smells just like me. I want you to have it."

At this I thought her sweet smile became a little strained . . . but no, it was just my imagination.

I held Nick-Nick up for her to kiss. "He wants to say goodbye, Lucille. Nick-Nick and I will both miss you. We've learned a lot from you."

She kissed him softly, then again. A tear came to her eye, for we had been conscious of eternity together, and my stuffed elephant had been a part of that. "Goodbye, Nick-Nick honey. Take care of Sonny-Bob for me, will you?"

Then with both arms straining, she lifted Hemingway off the floor. "So long, Hemingway. I'll miss you." She kissed him, then couldn't stop herself and licked the length of his bald head.

Hemingway nodded, and also began to fill with blood. I grow faint whenever that happens. Lucille dropped him.

"And now you, Sonny-Bob Culpepper, the hugely endowed wild man who paid for my education . . . the James Bond who has a talking truck that also makes custard . . . I'll *really* miss you, honey sweetheart. I'll really miss you."

She placed her torso in my arms and hugged me to her, stroking my back and running her fingers down my neck. I reciprocated, and as I felt those nipples grow hard and those breasts jiggling against me I was just about ready to write the timeline off and stay with Lucille . . .

Tears were trickling down my neck, and they were hers. But I confess I dropped a couple of tears, too.

We stayed like that for a long minute, then she released me and pulled back, dabbing at her eyes.

"I wish I could go with you, Sonny-Bob, but now that I have the money for school I'm going back to the University of Nebraska to finish my degree in philosophy. I have a calling."

"I know you do, sweetheart. I've felt the magnetic energy of your calling today. If I could I'd stay here with you and clean your house and wash your dishes while you're at school, then love you with everything I've got in the evenings. But I have a calling, too. I've got to find Ronald Reagan."

She looked at me then, but didn't ask why I had to find the President. I guess she figured I was Secret Service.

One quick kiss on my cheek, then she handed me a piece of paper she'd scribbled something on. "Call me if you're ever back in Nebraska, Sonny-Bob Culpepper. Call me."

"You know I will, honey."

With that she was gone, stepping nimbly out of Hubert and vanishing into a day that had turned clear and begun to warm up.

I looked at the paper she'd given me. There was a number on it that I took to be a telephone number, but what really got my attention was her name: Lucille Hicks. A name every schoolchild knows.

I don't know why I hadn't put it together before. Lucille . . . Nebraska . . . philosophy . . . radiance and charisma.

Dr. Lucille Hicks was the woman who had anchored the energy of Aphrodite in our world with her body and loving heart at the first of her temples in Lincoln. And she'd formulated the doctrines of Sir Ronald Reagan into a coherent structure with her brilliant mind and disciplined will. She'd kept the wheel of progress turning on the axle of time.

This woman was Lucille The Prophetess! I'd made love to the Lynchpin of History.

CHAPTER EIGHT

Hubert was in a foul mood. We were cruising down something called an interstate and Hubert bore a grudge at me for not letting him spend more time with Lucille.

"You got to talk to Lucille The Prophetess!"

"You did too, Hubert."

"Yes, but only for a minute. You shut me down. And then you fucked her. I wanted to be there for that."

"I didn't fuck her, Hubert," I said gently. "I made love to her. The second time, anyway."

Hubert grunted, then was silent for a long time. I'd had the devil's own time getting him to leave that parking lot. And he'd been on the verge of physically acting out his displeasure.

When Lucille had gone I'd opened the door and stepped naked into Nebraska. I saw that my shopping buggy full of clothes had rolled across the parking lot so I went to get it. As I wheeled it back to my "truck" I noticed that grouchy old cop Leroy standing just outside the Wal-Mart facility glowering at me. His hand was still on his gun. I figured he was just jealous of my huge ungainly penis and of the fact that Lucille's lips and body had found it.

I waved at him. "Bet Lucille's never sucked your dick, eh Leroy?"

He turned and went inside.

Well, I could just load the clothes into Hubert and ride naked for a while, but when I thought about Hubert's temperament I realized the weather might not be the only chilly thing I'd have to face. So I got dressed. Warmly dressed.

When I activated Hubert he yawned, then backfired, which I guess is the truck equivalent of a fart.

Suddenly a pair of eyes appeared on Hubert's viewscreen, the viewscreen that was disguised as a windshield. They were glowering at me.

"Sonny-Bob, you ungrateful . . ."

"Now before you get angry let me explain. When a boy and a girl get together . . ."

I paused as a blinking light appeared on the dashboard. It indicated Hubert had activated his weapons systems.

I gulped. "Hubert, what's up, buddy?"

The glowering eyes had shifted away from me for a moment. Now they snapped back. "I'll deal with you later, Sonny-Bob."

Whew! Apparently I was in no immediate danger. But I couldn't have Hubert taking out his wrath on innocent civilians.

I cleared my throat and decided to be straightforward. "Hubert, why have you activated your weapons systems?"

"Dogs, Sonny-Bob, dogs. A whole pack of 'em headed our way. They pissed on me the whole time you were in that Wal-Mart, howling with laughter. But they won't piss on me again. I've had enough."

"Be careful, Hubert. We can't afford for you to be seen discharging your advanced weaponry in this timezone. It would startle the natives."

"I don't care anymore, Sonny-Bob. You got laid and I got pissed on. Someone's going to pay."

"Hubert! Remember the Ninth Principle Of Ronald Reagan: 'Thou shalt not do murder unless it is morally justified'."

Hubert revved his engine. I could tell he was in a moral quandary.

"They only pissed on you. Think for a minute! Is what you intend to do to them morally justified? How will you feel about yourself tomorrow? Think, Hubert, think!"

His engine sputtered and nearly stalled, then he said, "Aw, I'm not going to murder them, Sonny-Bob. I'm just going to hit them with my stunbeams. They're just dogs and I am a compassionate vehicle."

"That's my TITTY," I said, stroking his dashboard. "But the fact remains, if that cop in that Wal-Mart sees even your stunbeams flashing he'll call for the police forces of the twentieth century to descend on us.

"We'll get you laid someday, but right now we need to unass this area and find Ronald Reagan."

His thirst for vengeance struggled with his conscience and good sense for a moment, then his engine revved and we began rolling across the parking lot.

"Thanks, Hubert."

"Don't mention it . . . asshole."

I judged we were several states short of arriving in Fairfax, Virginia and as slow as these twentieth century vehicles were it might be days before we got there. This was nearly intolerable. Hubert could simply have leapt into the great sky of the West and floated us to Fairfax in a jiffy. But we were trying to fit in.

I did notice that practically every other vehicle on the interstate was passing us, so some time after the sun had set I finally asked Hubert to speed up, hoping his wrath at me had abated and that he'd be in a better humor. He was silent for a minute, then explained to me that we were driving the speed limit and that everyone else was breaking the law. "You don't want us to get pulled over by the twentieth century police forces, do you Sonny-Bob?"

I allowed that I did not and thanked Hubert for looking out for my welfare by keeping his conduct legal. But I wondered how all these other cars got away with their banditry. They were never pulled over by the police. Maybe they knew something we didn't. Anyhow, we'd have to play it safe. And I was glad that Hubert and I appeared to be on better terms.

His eyes appeared in the windshield as he said, "I forgive you, Sonny-Bob. You're only human. And in your case you have the liability of being a slave to your reproductive organs. Your conduct in this regard is inevitable."

There was some truth in what he said. The Prostitutes of Aphrodite had been trying for years to teach me to master my lust and transmute it into loving passion, and I'd come pretty close a number of times, at least temporarily. And today with Lucille I'd come closer than ever. I wondered how long it would last.

"Thank you for your understanding, Hubert. And don't worry, someday your ship will come in and you'll have a lady, too."

"Sometimes I wonder."

"You've had ladies before, Hubert."

"Yes, but it never lasts. They lose interest quickly and then vanish. Sometimes I wonder if there's something missing from my personality, some chunk of programming I didn't receive that all the other TITTIES got."

"You just haven't met the right lady, Hubert, that's all. But I'm sure there's one out there for you somewhere."

We rolled along for another minute or two, then Hubert said, "What're we going to do in Fairfax?"

"We'll use the branch station there as a base of operations to spy on Ronald Reagan. D.C. is just across the river from Fairfax. Once I've determined how best to contact him I will proceed."

Our branch office in Fairfax was in the basement of the headquarters of the National Rifle Association. The NRA let us maintain this operation in exchange for certain technologies they could use to fight the Democrats. Indeed, it was speculated by some of our junior officers that the TAC generals had founded the NRA themselves, 'way back in 1871, in preparation for the battles to preserve liberty in the twentieth century. But we had no proof, and I didn't much care one way or the other. I was just glad they were on our side.

The operation was nothing fancy, just an information specialist (glorified clerk) and a couple of his wives. It was considered too risky for him to pursue poon-tang among the natives, and since most of my people refused to do without lovin' for any length of time our support personnel were frequently allowed to bring some of their spouses or lovers with them. They hid down there for months at a time, dodging Democrats and the liberal news media, who would've blown their cover if they'd found out about them.

Some of the NRA officers and employees would provide the specialist with the information he needed regarding developments in this timezone, and if anything happened we didn't like our guy could summon a field agent in nothing flat.

This tale tells a part of the story as to how liberty was finally preserved from the machinations of the Democrats, who by the late twentieth century had undertaken a political and propaganda campaign to convince the populace that they were weak and helpless and needed the Democrats to make personal decisions for them--in other words, to control them.

And it is a sad commentary on what passed for twentieth century womanhood that so many of them cast their votes based upon their sexual desires, allowing their emotions to be manipulated by the spin doctors of this degenerate political party. (Maybe I'm a sex addict, but even I have enough sense not to vote with my dick.)

If Dr. Lucille Hicks of the University of Nebraska had not risen up early in the twenty-first century to unify emotion, love, and logic, thereby restoring the heart and common sense of Americans and serving as a shining example of the powerful and loving beings women could be if they worked on themselves, the country probably would have eventually fallen to the Democrats and you'd have to get a license every time you went to piss--or applied for a job, or went to buy a gun (except that guns wouldn't have been legal for very long after the Democrats took control). You'd have had to get the Democrats' permission every time you wanted to fuck . . . and don't apply on weekends, the Democratic Office Of Fucking Services is open only on weekdays.

The Democrats and their allies in the twentieth century news media and in Hollywood are famous in my time for their hypocrisy. That's about the only thing they are famous for in my time. For example, the Democratic elitists held a gathering that was sponsored by wealthy entertainment personalities, though it was billed as a grassroots effort. It was called the Million Mom March and there wasn't a grass root anywhere among the organizers. (Also, they fell far short of their goal of a million moms, though they might not have if the grassroots of America had genuinely been involved.) Anyhow, this Million Mom March was an attempt to lower the consciousness of Americans as to their own self-worth by making them question the validity of self-defense, and to make them feel guilty if they owned guns. The ultimate object of the March was to eliminate guns.

One of the featured speakers at this March was a "lady" named Barbara Graham. What she didn't reveal in her speech, and what the Million Moms' friends in the mass media mostly failed to report, was that she had used a handgun five months earlier in an attempt to murder a young man. The twenty-two year old man was left paralyzed; she'd shot him in the spine. The cops found four illegal handguns in her house and car. The Million Moms backed this criminal when she went to trial. The would-be murderess was sent to prison for aggravated assault with intent to kill and eight other charges.

Another speaker, a person named Rosie, wanted everyone who owns a gun sent to jail. This despite the fact she'd taken money as a spokeswoman for a retail store chain that was one of America's largest gun dealers. You'd have thought she'd have a credibility problem, but the mass media of the time held her up as an idol of moral rectum-tude (excuse me, I mean rectitude) so the public continued to take her more or less seriously.

This Rosie also provided a bodyguard for her family and supported his attempts to get a permit to carry a concealed weapon. But this was typical of the liberal hypocrites of the time. They considered themselves elites and acted the part, supporting restrictions for everyone but themselves and their liberal elitist friends. And the "soccer moms" that supported and allowed themselves to be manipulated by this Rosie and her elitist friends apparently didn't realize that Rosie and company would not reciprocate. Rosie and company didn't give a damn about soccer moms or anyone else except their own circle of wealthy liberal elites. If Rosie had her way, the soccer moms would have lost their rights along with everyone else who didn't belong to the class of Liberal Masters.

Ho-hum. Really, this story has been going on for thousands of years. I've seen it up and down the timeline. The same control-freak people reincarnate time after time, caught up in their own patterns of control and manipulation and trying to take the rights away from the rest of us. We don't take such people seriously in my time, but in the twentieth century most people hadn't learned their own worth and were afraid of the elites. They didn't want to be scorned by the elites.

I could go on and on. There was the senator named Frankenstein . . . no, I believe her name was Feinstein. Another one who was trying to take the guns away from other Americans while she carried a handgun in her purse and bragged about how she was going to "take out" anyone who tried to harm her. She could get a permit to carry a concealed weapon in her home state of California because she belonged to the class of liberal elites. Joe and Josephine Citizen, regardless of party affiliation, wouldn't have had a chance to get a permit in the primitive California of the twentieth century. But the wealthy liberal elites always provided themselves with ways around the restrictions they forced down the throats of other Americans.

So the late twentieth and early twenty-first century Democrats had sold every ounce of honor they ever had and understood only control and manipulation. They were spearheaded in their efforts to crush the will of Americans by trial lawyers and were no longer the party of the people. The Democrats were the party of control and repression, ruled by people who thought of themselves as superior to others and who acted like it, exempting themselves and their friends from laws and principles everyone else was subject to, particularly the anti-self defense laws. The liberal elites wanted to protect themselves and their families, and privately made arrangements to do precisely that, while publicly feigning ignorance of this motive as they tried to strip non-elite citizens of their Goddess-given, Constitutionally affirmed rights.

These deceivers were so tricky and cunning they almost stole the 2000 presidential election. They nearly pulled off what would have been a coup. To be so tricky you can pull off a coup without a military force-- now **that** is tricky.

I was forced to learn all these things in my Twentieth Century Tactics Class in preparation for this mission. It made me sick; I threw up several times and wept bitterly. So did the instructors. But righteousness, love and freedom eventually won; the Democratic devils were driven out and America's spirit and her honor prevailed. She evolved into a compassionate society.

Reasonableness disappeared (the reasonable person is one who sets a priority on other people's illusions in the hope that they'll support some of his own cherished illusions) and logic was transmuted into a tool for pursuing justice in a manner consonant with compassion.

Ultimately, it was a coalition of Republicans and Anarchists[*] who, under the spiritual and moral guidance of Lucille Hicks, started our country on the highroad to love, freedom, and justice. Those lowroad Democrats[**] just sort of dried up and blew away in the winds of productive change.

My stomach had been growling, so Hubert said, "Sonny-Bob? Let me make you dinner. Or if you want a home cooked meal, we can stop at a diner somewhere."

"I don't know if food would be a good idea right now, Hubert. I've been thinking about the last decade of the Twentieth. I'm nauseous."

"Sonny-Bob, you haven't eaten all day, just had some custard and wheatgrass juice. When was the last time you ate?"

"Well, subjectively speaking, it was yesterday morning. I had Kellogg's cornflakes."

"Then you have to eat," Hubert said decisively. "They say that natural food is better for people than nano generated food, so I'm going to stop at a restaurant and you're going to eat. End of story."

I said nothing, but felt a warm glow spread from my belly to my heart. Hubert cared! It was nice to work with a TITTY who was concerned for my welfare.

---

[*] Naturally, the alleged news media always failed to report the true nature of Anarchy. They wanted to program the public to equate Anarchy with chaos, and the public cheerfully let them do it. The truth is that Anarchy is the most peaceable and harmonious condition humanity could find itself in. Anarchy is about compassionate cooperation and the movement to love. Since laws get in the way of love, laws are discarded under Anarchy. Those who introduce chaos are not Anarchists, and Anarchy is in no way related to chaos. It is worth emphasizing that the news media of this primitive culture almost always mischaracterized any group or individual who supported freedom and love, because freedom and love run directly counter to the illusion of self-importance that burdened those who worked in news organizations, and because the planetwide growth of freedom and love would mean the end of the schemes practiced by the major news organizations to introduce the illusion of fear and separation in their constant, daily attempts to manipulate the people of the earth.

[**] It is very worth our while to note that the originating impulse for the Democratic Party is the same impulse that manifests as Anarchy in a civilized society. But in the late twentieth century the Democrats moved away from their originating impulse, an energy which manifests as the color green and vibrates to the sweet hymn of nature and equality.

Those eyes appeared on the windshield again. "Don't take it personally. I'm only looking out for the safety of the timeline."

"Of course you are, Hubert."

Hubert got off at the next exit and crossed the overpass. There was a restaurant there designated as Shoney's Big Boy. The facility sported an icon of a giant obese toddler. The proud toddler hoisted a plate above his head that had a sandwich on it. It looked good.

Hubert parked himself there. "Go in and eat."

"Okay."

I climbed out of Hubert and strode to the entrance of this facility. I was not unaware of the fragrance emanating from me. It was the fragrance of the juices of sweet Lucille; I hadn't had a chance to bathe yet and was still picking those red hairs out of my teeth.

Lucille had left a taste of springtime in my mouth; springtime trout, the most fragrant of all fish.

I entered and all heads turned to survey me. "Hello friends," I called, waving to everyone, trying desperately to fit into this strange new century. "I've come to eat."

An elderly man on his way out spat into a flower pot and looked at me. "Smells like you've already had a big dinner, son." He left shaking his head. Another twentieth century male jealous of my free sexual expression. They could really use some sacred bordellos in this timezone. Where I'm from lots of candidates can't handle the challenges of sacred prostitute training, so they drop out and some of them open bordellos dedicated to pleasure and the Goddess. Not as much healing occurs at these bordellos as at the temples, but the fucking's really grand. Sometimes you just want to rut with the Goddess watching and lending her blessing to the process. If you need some really deep healing, you can always go to the temple the next day.

Anyway, if this tight-assed timezone would just loosen up a bit no one would have any reason to be jealous of me.

A servant boy led me to a table. I sat there gazing at the menu. They had catfish, grilled or fried, and a tear of nostalgia ran down my nose and plopped into the glass of water the servant had given me.

In the far-flung future I hailed from, there was no Lake Hendersonville now and no catfish. Worst of all there was no Bluebird. A lump rose in my throat and I could barely breathe. I was dizzy and on the verge of having a crying spell. I'd try to hold it in 'till I could find solace in Nick-Nick. Oh, I missed my Bluebird so!

"What'll ye have, honey?"

I looked up. A buxom middle-aged woman stood before me, blonde haired and pink nailed. The hair seemed to be artificially colored. She chewed gum, as so many people did in this century, but I wasn't too disgusted. Her eyes were a faded blue, her lips a cross shade between red and the pinkness of her nails. She was beautiful; she reminded me of Jo Stonehenge. Here was another beautiful twentieth century goddess who'd been forced by the heartlessness of economics to work for a living, instead of serving in the temple where she belonged. I loved her at once and wanted to reach out to her, but I knew I couldn't sample every goddess I came across and still have enough energy to save the timeline.

My mouth began to water as I wondered whether her toenails were pink . . .

"Honey, if you're not ready to order I can give you another minute."

I felt myself smile wistfully. "No ma'am, I'll order. I'll have whatever you think is good."

"Sweetie, you don't want to know what I think is good . . ." she looked at me closely, "on second thought, maybe you do. But I'm not allowed to solicit on these premises. I'm not allowed to solicit at all anymore; if I get caught breaking my probation . . ." This time a tear trickled down her nose.

"You are beautiful," I said.

She turned crimson and suddenly her whole face was wet. "I've had lots of men say that to me, honey. But I think you're one of the few that means it."

"Men don't respect women much in this timezone, ma'am. They don't know how to honor them and serve them as representatives of the Goddess. Men need to learn that when they honor WOMAN, they honor themselves."

She was choked up. "I'll get you a nice dinner, sweetheart." She walked quickly away, dabbing at her eyes.

There was another pretty lady sitting at a nearby table. She smiled at me and I smiled back, as another of Lucille's hairs tickled my gums. She must've been around eighty, but looked pretty healthy. She belonged in a temple, too. So many beautiful women in this century, and so few aware of their own divinity. I wanted to weep for them and would when I was alone. I also would pray for them.

A young fat child waddled up to the beautiful older lady. I looked closely, but didn't think he was the model for the toddler icon outside.

"I'm done Grandma, but I couldn't get it to flush."

"That's all right, darling. Someone else will flush it."

"Can we go see Grandpa tomorrow?"

"If it's not snowing again we'll drive out to the cemetery. Grandpa will be glad to see us."

"I love you, Grandma."

"I love you too, honey."

The beautiful older goddess hugged him tightly for a moment, then stood and they left the table. We smiled again and said hello as she passed, and I caught the glimpse of a bondage ring on her finger. I guess it was the ring her late husband had given her. These people didn't know any better; they degraded themselves and their relationships by enforcing a code intended to regulate love, and love is the one thing you absolutely **cannot** regulate. Where regulation is, love is not. Where love is, regulation cannot be.

But these people hadn't yet begun to recognize the nature of love. They thought of it as an emotional fluctuation rather than experiencing its true nature, which is the nature of the Godforce, and therefore of themselves. For each human heart is a tiny spark from the heart of God. And that force within the heart is not an emotion and cannot be described, only experienced. Anyway, that's what the prostitutes say.

I turned slightly in my chair and watched the beautiful silver haired lady who didn't know her own glory, her movements yet reflecting that on some primal level she knew a part of herself. There was a spark of youthful passion riding subdued within her, and if this society had been a free one she could have been happy and fulfilled in so many ways. In my time she would have been loved and she would have been loved . . . she had her grandson, true, but in my time she would have been allowed to serve as a vehicle of worship and express many aspects of herself. Here in this one-dimensional society, she was only allowed to express one dimension. Yet she was a goddess capable of giving and receiving such pleasure. And such love.

She paid for their meal and left with her grandson and I felt the energy from my heart chakra commingle with the watery fluid of my emotional centers. I was sexually aroused again, but I wasn't starting out with lust this time. I was feeling a loving passion, and felt myself full of vivid life.

These people are why I'm in business, I thought, feeling my heart swell with love. *I'm here to help them along.* All I'd ever wanted out of life up until now was a little pussy and booze and a stuffed elephant and a car that loved me. But now I wanted to serve someone besides myself. *Everything of mine belongs to humanity. And that's fine. Humanity is my vocation.*

My meal arrived as my goddess-waitress sort of bustled around with the bravado of one who presently doesn't want to process emotions. I loved her and felt for her, but didn't see anything I could do for her except to try not to create any incidents.

"Here's a seafood platter, honey. Fish and clams. Crabs, too--but don't tell anybody I gave you crabs. Bad for business." She chuckled and I was happy to see her smile.

I patted her hand. "You can give me crabs anytime you want."

Along with my meal she left an urn of coffee and a pitcher of water, which I drank greedily, suddenly feeling the full effects of Hemingway's activities earlier in the day. He'd dehydrated me.

A fellow came in and was shown to a table within spitting distance and immediately my nose twitched. I smelled cop. He reeked of rules and regulations. Had to be either a cop or a damn preacher. He looked at me and as our eyes met I tried not to snarl. His nose was also twitching; I guess he smelled something on me. He looked back down at his menu.

Well, no twentieth century cop was going to ruin my meal. I focused on my crabs. I plowed through the meal in nothing flat, and when I finished I became aware of a goddess presence beside me. I belched and looked up. My goddess-waitress was gazing tenderly at me and I knew she had come to bless me.

"How was the meal, sweetheart?"

"Nutritious and delicious, darling. I want to come home with you."

Uh-oh. I'd said it before I had a chance to think. A sex addict gets easily distracted in any century.

She was beginning to grow red again. She put her hand on the chair opposite me to steady herself. I felt with a sensitivity I didn't know I had that here was a woman who deeply needed healing love. It seemed to me that my friend Lucille had prompted me to evolve, somehow. I felt Lucille's presence nearby.

The beautiful waitress-goddess was trying to think of something to say. Sometimes people want to talk when all that's called for is a silent embrace.

"I . . . I . . . was going to offer you desert."

"Thank you, ma'am. I'd like to have desert, as long as it's at your place."

What was going on?! I couldn't control my tongue, and this time Hemingway wasn't the cause of the disorder. He slumbered peacefully, dreamlessly under the table.

It was Lucille Hicks, Lucille The Prophetess. I could see now why she was known as The Lynchpin of History. Every fiber of my being now resonated to her vibration. She and I had accomplished something together, something I hadn't even consciously known I'd been working on.

A tear tracked its way down my cheek as I understood, or at least thought I did. My earliest desire in life was not to be a warrior, but to join the sacred prostitutes in the temple and become one of them, to smile with them, to love with them. Yet I never felt I was worthy of that sacred trust, never felt I had the strength of character to be able to summon the discipline to join this sacred circle of healers. So I'd repressed this dream, pushed it back, forgotten about it. Yet now it had sprung up in my face when I'd least expected it, as repressed dreams always do. Lucille had pulled it out of me and now I knew the dream would never die, would always be a major part of me. If I did somehow save this timeline I was going to have to apply to the temple when I got home. The head of the Asheville Diocese was my friend, but she was a strictly disciplined woman and never played favorites. I had no idea if she would be willing to accept me as a Probationer, but now I knew I had to try. I might not make it, but by Goddess I had to try to become a prostitute. **If** I made it back home and **if** home was there when I arrived.

. . . yes, a sex addict gets easily distracted in any century, but this wasn't sex addiction. My dick wasn't even hard, and my sacral center, root chakra and belly were burning with a disciplined zeal that flowed from my heart. It was the flame of loving passion, not the undisciplined wildfire of mere animal lust. And I somehow knew that at the appointed time my dick would still inflate. All was well.

The force of Aphrodite's love was guiding me now and its reins were in the hands of the radiant soul humanity would one day call Lucille The Prophetess. The lust was gone and there was no egotism at all, just an empty awareness of this woman's need to be served and a sudden filling up of that awareness with the force of Aphrodite's love and passion.

My heart was on fire.

I knew I had a purpose in life.

"I . . . I get off at eleven. But I can leave a little early if you meant what you said." She was gazing wistfully at me.

"I always mean what I say, sweetheart. And you are a star whose radiance fills my eyes."

Her hand found my cheek, her eyes were moist. "I'll get you a piece of pie and I'll be ready to go in a few minutes." She bustled off.

I took a sip of coffee and fished out my wallet of artificial money. I hoped one bill with four zeros would be enough to pay for the meal. I placed the bill on the table and waited.

My sixth, seventh and eighth senses kicked in and immediately my eyes turned to the cop/preacher man at the next table. He was staring at the bill I'd placed on the table.

He looked at me. "I haven't seen one of those for a long time."

"Paper currency is common in this century," I told him, remembering my lectures on the subject at the Academy. "It is legal tender for all debts public and private."

"Yes, but I'm talking about the denomination. Back in '69 the Treasury Department decided to stop distributing currency in that denomination. They also stopped distributing $500, $1000, and $5000 bills. True, some of all those are still in circulation, but the Federal Reserve Banks destroy them as they are received."

Damn and Blast! Roger Bacon had flubbed his research. My bag of artificial money contained bills with many different levels of zeros. I had all the denominations the cop mentioned, plus others that I was beginning to suspect had never existed. I might be in deep shit here.

The copper rattled on. "Uncle Sam used to produce a $100,000 Gold Certificate, but this note was only for official transactions. I'd say you've got a pretty rare piece of currency there. Mind if I take a closer look?"

"Go ahead," I said, perhaps a little sullenly. I handed the bill to him.

He perused it thoroughly. "I'd say you've got the real thing here, but don't expect to pay for your dinner with it. They won't be able to change it."

Change it? What the hell could that mean? Change it into what?

"Uh, do you think they could . . . change a bill with two zeros on it?"

He had a strange look on his face. His nose was twitching. "They might be able to change a bill with two zeros if the zeros were prefaced by a one. If you happen to have one of those rare, discontinued $500 notes, they won't be able to change that."

I had both of the above. I opened my fat wallet and searched for a bill that had a one and two zeros. I found one and lifted it triumphantly. "I will pay with this."

"Good," he said. He handed the bill with the four zeros back to me. "You must be as rich as Croesus to be hauling around that much cash."

"Yes, I am rich."

The copper plucked a french fried potato off his plate and began to munch it absently. "I've spent the last four years chasing counterfeiters, so I know all about currency. Good thing that $10,000 note of yours is real, otherwise I'd have to haul you in. And I don't want to get distracted that way. I have a new job now."

My pie arrived. My waitress-lover bustled off, but I was barely aware of her jiggling.

"What is your new job? Do you . . . uh . . . pursue smugglers?"

"Nope. I've worked various assignments for the last eighteen years with the Secret Service, but this is the first time I've been assigned to guard a president. I'm headed out to President Reagan's ranch in Santa Barbara and I'll spend the next few years looking out for his welfare. After that I'll probably retire. I can't imagine ever getting an assignment that would top working directly for President Ronald Reagan. Reagan is God."

"I agree with you there," I said, my mind working furiously. If President Reagan was in Santa Barbara, then Hubert and I had been traveling towards the wrong coast. More time wasted, in a timeline that was running out of time.

Every person in my timezone knows about President Reagan's ranch in Santa Barbara. I'd been there several times, walking in his holy footsteps, trying to think the same thoughts he must've thought, and wishing I had a nuclear arsenal--not for anything special, just for kicks.

Reagan's Ranch had been visited by almost the entire population of the earth in my timezone at least once, and many of us made regular pilgrimages. As Mecca and Rome began to lose their significance to the people of the earth, Reagan's Ranch arose to fill the void.

The copper was smacking his lips over his iced tea. "This'll be the best Christmas I've ever spent. This is the reason I joined the Secret Service."

"Guarding President Ronald Wilson Reagan is the highest of blessings," I agreed, mentally kicking my own ass. I should've remembered that every Christmas presidents migrate to farms and ranches to recharge their souls with love and compassion for the universe and for the humanity which they serve. (This changed in the alleged presidency of the 90's when exploitation and deceit took the place of service, but in December '82, where I was now, the clarion call of presidential service still sounded and was embodied by the Divine President, Ronald Reagan.)

"Well," the copper continued, "the President is due to arrive at his ranch tomorrow and I'm scheduled to arrive the day after. I guess I'd better drive fast."

He stood up to go as I absently twirled a fork in my pie. He wasn't such a bad fellow, after all. At least he wasn't a preacher.

"Godspeed," I told him sincerely. "May Aphrodite smile upon your journey."

I watched as the protector of the Divine President went to pay for his meal. He looked several times over his shoulder at me.

I was going to have to break the news to Hubert that we'd been going the wrong way. He'd probably blame me, and maybe he should. I was familiar enough with presidential habits to know they migrated this time of year. It was less than ten days 'till Yule, the holiday that people in this century referred to as Christmas. The Christians--who actually had no idea of the date of Jesus' birth--had stolen this holiday from my ancient Pagan ancestors, though in my civilized time we Pagans had stolen it back. We celebrate Yule as a genuinely holy day, though these twentieth century Christians, in keeping with their materialistic religion, had turned this once sacred day into an orgy of material vices. They might not fuck (or at least pretend not to) so their sexual energy found perverse expression in glamour and rampant materialistic greed. This is the way they raised their children. It's a miracle of Reagan and Aphrodite that these people ever got out of the twentieth century . . .

Only they didn't, I reminded myself. I had to fix that.

My new lady came up to me. She wore a coat over her frock. "I'm ready to go now," she said. Then she saw my money on the table. "Don't worry about paying, honey. I already took care of it."

She was generous as well as beautiful.

I stood, and arm in arm we walked out of that dining facility, past the fat toddler icon and into the parking lot. I saw Hubert's headlights arch up in a "Not again!" fashion.

"Just drive down that road--that's Chimney Road--about five and a half miles, then turn right onto Long Branch Road. Drive up Long Branch until it dead-ends and you'll be at my house."

She kissed me on the cheek. "I'll be waiting."

Then she left, without trying to coax me into following her. I guess she was leaving me an "out" in case I'd been less than sincere with her. She could not know--at least not yet--that I was under the influence of my heart and of the saint Lucille Hicks. But she would find out soon enough.

I approached Hubert and got inside. "For a minute I was afraid you were going to spend the next few hours fucking, Sonny-Bob."

"I am, my fine feathered TITTY. I'm going to fuck the woman you just saw me with and I can't wait. She's a beautiful goddess more brilliant than the sun and my heart wants her with a profound passion.

"That lady is in need of healing, Hubert, and I'm going to help her. This society has devastated her, the way it has so many of its goddesses. But I'm going to restore her if I can. I've got to try.

"And Hubert, I know you won't believe me, but I feel like a sacred prostitute. My heart is aflame with love for that woman and for all humanity. I love them all, Hubert! And my love directs me to serve, so that is what I will do."

I patted his dashboard. "Right now I even love you, you big tin can."

Hubert was moved. His eyes had been watching me again; now they blinked rapidly and he said hoarsely, "I'll go along with you, Sonny-Bob. I can see you've changed; you're not a scumbag right now. It was Lucille The Prophetess, wasn't it? She changed you, didn't she?"

"Yes, Hubert, she did. I don't know how long the effect will last, but Lucille got me to a higher plane than any of the sacred prostitutes I've ever fucked, and while my heart is on fire I'm going to make the most of it. I'm going to serve that woman. She needs to experience love, and I adore her."

"Let's go then," said Hubert, revving himself up. "Where to?"

I gave him the directions and away we cruised. I was thankful I had a TITTY who would support me. Maybe Hubert didn't fully deserve his unsavory reputation with the TAC.

Along the way I filled him in on the subject of Presidential Migration, and how we had to turn around and go back the way we'd come. "So if it's all right with you, Hubert, we'll just hang around here until after sunset tomorrow, then fly to Santa Barbara. I'm really tired of this slow-assed road, anyway."

"Suits," he said.

We pulled into the driveway of the temple of my newfound goddess. Hubert's tires crunched on the gravel. "You don't think she has any dogs, do you, Sonny-Bob?"

"I wouldn't be surprised. Single people in the country usually keep dogs and shotguns."

"I'll defend myself, Sonny-Bob, if it comes to that."

"I'd expect you to, Hubert. Just don't use deadly force, that's all. Just send a little electric shock up their stream of urine and they won't bother you again."

"Wilco, Sonny-Bob. Ten-four. Have a good night. I know you will."

"Thanks, buddy. Same to you. I'll see you tomorrow."

Hubert shut himself down and lapsed into slumber. There was a goddess waiting for me on the porch.

CHAPTER NINE

In a dream once I'd followed a silver stream of light to a temple. A Lady of Violet waited for me inside. Her eyes, lips and nails were violet, and somehow her skin, though pale, seemed to shimmer lightly with the energy of violet.

Her eyes were the most intelligent eyes I had ever seen. And she knew me.

She took my hand and led me to a soft pallet. Then she dropped her robe and stood before me naked. "This," her fingers framed her clit and pussy, already glistening and making me happy, "this is the seat of passion." She smiled. "You are already familiar with this."

Then she placed my hand between her breasts. "This is the heart chakra and it is the seat of love. It is the seat of your Self, for you are love. It is the seat of the soul." She moved closer to me as a desperate whimper escaped me, the very first whimper of the unity of all my selves. She breathed on me.

"No person can become whole until they purify themselves and unify their heart with their passion. No person can be healed until they live fully in the heart and allow their heart to rule the purified and integrated outer form."

I wanted to look back down at her pussy, but her eyes held me. They shifted to blue, then green, then gold. Finally they were violet again. I marveled at her.

Then she gestured to the pallet. "There is the easy way. You and I can lie together and I'll fuck you with a passion you've never seen, and then you can get up tomorrow and leave. You'll be fully satiated. It will be the fuck of your life.

"Or," she gently stroked my hand as it absorbed something of her, lying between those perfect breasts, "you may truly have me. I will help you become a more loving being if you so choose, and will help you purify and integrate yourself.

"Decide!" Her voice echoed like a clap of thunder.

I had not been able to look away from those violet eyes. They knew me, and they held me. I longed for her, and for I knew not what, but I knew she held the Key.

As the tears welled and began to spill from me I said, "I want you and I want you to show me my Self."

"That is good," she whispered, pulling me to her. "Let us merge."

The Lady of Violet held me in her energy for what seemed like centuries. My tears were like the great flood that submerged Atlantis. My heart was both exalted and swollen with grief. I knew pain, but I was held by love. I knew agony as the Lady exposed me to my cruel selves, yet this was the beginning of the touch of Redemption. I welcomed it.

Finally, after a very long time, something happened. My heart grew calm and I was both empty and flooded with radiance at the same time.

My whole body was flooded with radiance, some from my own heart and some from the Lady of Violet. I felt her energy purify and console me, and I knew that above all things she was Love.

I felt a unity between all my faculties, between all my selves, that I'd never felt before. I was a crystal of many facets that was being flooded by the violet, and as my selves began to accept one another I knew that one day I would be clear and pure.

My sex was the sex of love; I was neither female nor male, though I contained both these possibilities within myself. Yet my loins began to throb with a more powerful presence than they ever had before.

I wanted to physically make love, but could also stand in that loving integration the Lady of Violet had brought me to and be making love with everyone and everything in the cosmos. No action was necessary as I radiated the love. I was making love to the universe. I was the universe making love to itself.

Then the Lady released me and we were joined in love as we gazed into one another's eyes. "You have chosen the more powerful path, Sonny-Bob. One day you will be able to serve another as I have served you. We will meet again in the Spirit of Love."

Then there was a flaming violet light all around me, permeating my being, penetrating my soul . . . then a bright flash of white light and I woke up.

I'd forgotten about that dream until just now. I guess I'd been too drunk to remember in recent years. But now the words of the Lady of Violet came back to me: "One day you will be able to serve another as I have served you."

I knew that day had come.

"We will meet again in the Spirit of Love."

I approached the porch, looking up as my newfound queen floated her gaze down to me. Life was meant to be like this.

I climbed the steps and we went inside. It was a small house, but warm.

I had been feeling a presence all around me, a red presence alternating with a violet presence. Then the energy resolved itself into two distinct signatures, one of Lucille and one of the Lady of Violet.

"Your name is Amber," I said, reading her name tag from the Shoney's Big Boy dining facility. "And I am Sonny-Bob."

She said nothing; there was an energy about her that was bursting for expression. She trembled. I took her hands in mine and led her to the center of the room. I gazed softly and with much love into those faded blue eyes. We just held hands for awhile as we began to share ourselves.

After a bit I moved closer to her and kissed her softly. A tear ran down her cheek and I brushed it away, feeling the sting of her agony. I loved her so. I placed my hands upon her shoulders, then let them fall to her waist like rose petals. We looked into one another's eyes.

I knew Aphrodite was here to help me redeem her sister. I felt Aphrodite's flaming golden heart giving sustenance to my own.

I pulled this woman, this Amber of Shoney's, to my breast and served her with my gentle heart. And by and by the radiance of my heart flowed to my sexual center and permeated this most expressive of faculties.

Hemingway arose and was exalted.

As stubborn as an ox's penis, Hemingway had always insisted on getting his own way. But now he only wanted to serve this beautiful goddess and see her healed. Flooded with love he arose, and began to survey his kingdom from a new perspective.

My right hand found her breast as my lips found her mouth. We kissed gently at first, we kissed sweetly.

Then my lover was seized with an urgency of expression and she drove her tongue into me like a writhing javelin. I sucked it greedily, feeling it glide over my own tongue and slip off the surface of the slick teeth.

Her leg was pressing against my cock and her breast lay revealed before my hand. I bowed and praised it with lips and fingers, making the nipple glow with rigid excitement.

Then suddenly my hand was in her panties, her pussy straining against it, begging for it, bursting with an ecstasy of need. I found her sweet clit and licked my lips; the clit was engorged and her pussy was ready to be served by tongue or cock.

I smelled the odor of her womanhood and it drove me wild and I forgot myself and all things except this goddess of earthly scents and pleasures.

My other hand began working its way around to her ass as the hand I'd had on her pussy found its way to my lips; I tasted and breathed her from my own hand, I was drunk with her.

She trembled and thrashed in my arms, crying with the need of her passion, dry humping her hotly flaming womanhood against the rigid cock of my desire.

"Sonny-Bob . . . oh! Got to have you in me . . . got to have you in me . . .." We tore off each other's clothes.

Her eyes grew wide as she saw the size of my erection, but she wanted it and would not be intimidated by it. She knelt and kissed it.

She stood, and her bare clit lay throbbing against my fingers. I traced a little circle around it as she shuddered and moaned. "Oh, honey, honey yesss . . ." She was touching herself as I sucked her breasts and played with her clit. I knew I was going to place myself inside her before eating her, but I wanted an early taste, so I pulled her pussy-wet fingers to me and sucked them thoroughly one by one as she bucked and cried . . .

She was crying with need. She thought she needed a good fuck, and she did, but she needed a lot more than that. She needed a good *loving* fuck, not a good standard fuck. The energy of love had to be the signature of this moment. She had to be celebrated, not abased. She had to touch her godhood. That is why I was there. Her need had to be replaced by a positive expression of love and desire.

I guided her to the wall and placed her against it, the fingers of both our hands intertwined. I placed my mouth upon her begging lips and pushed them apart with my tongue; I opened her up. Then I filled her with my breath, just breathing into her to share my soul with this most beautiful of women.

As I breathed myself into Amber I prayed silently to Aphrodite, Lucille and the Lady of Violet to help me serve this woman and anoint her with the Love of the Kingdom of Heaven.

I placed my right hand against my lover's heart chakra, feeling myself embraced and guided by a violet energy. My emotional centers flowed together with the energy of my heart and I felt refreshingly purified, and I shared this with my lovely Amber, whose spirit I could see flying through eternity on her own winged heart. My erection pushed against her.

"Amber, I love and serve a Goddess who made you in Her image.

She loves you and so do I. For when a man loves the Goddess, he loves all her sisters. Sweetheart, this is not going to be just a fucking, it is an anointing. If you open your heart to the energy of Aphrodite's love you will be healed."

She didn't fully understand, but there was a deep hope in her eyes, a hope given substance by the energy we'd shared thus far. "Why me?" she whispered through tears. "Why me?"

"Because you need to be healed, sweetheart, and love is the only way. Love is always available to all of us if we can just release the blocks we have to it. If we can accept love, we will be immersed in it.

"Do you accept love, Amber honey?"

"Yes," she whispered. "I accept love. I love you, Sonny-Bob."

"Sweetheart, it's important that you love yourself before you love me. None of us can love anyone else unless we learn to love ourself first.

"And I want you to know that I'm not the cause of any healing that occurs here tonight. The Force of Love, which permeates the universe, is all that can heal you or me or anybody. Love will be both the cause and result of your healing, and **you** are the cause of it, because you've decided to accept all the love the universe has for you into your life and heart. And that love is infinite, Amber. It is infinite. And **you** are infinite, my friend Amber. For you are love."

"I accept the Force of Love, Sonny-Bob." She stared with that deep hope into my face. "I accept the Force of Love."

"Thank you, darling. I feel your acceptance of God, and of the loving goddess which you are. And I want you to know you are surrounded by all the love the universe has to give tonight. It is yours, all of it, now and forever. As long as you continue to accept it, it will always be yours."

I kissed her deeply and slowly, and our souls knew each other through the touch of our breath. As I drew back from her I saw that her terrible need had been replaced by a calm acceptance of her destiny. And her destiny was the destiny that belongs to each human being. Her destiny was to learn to reflect the love of her own heart, and therefore of the universe to which she belonged.

More to the point, considering the circumstances, I felt her begin to glow with some positive loving desire. As I felt the first awakenings of her heart, I also felt it joyfully share its energy with her sex. My soul rejoiced and I was elevated into an experience of the Light.

"We're surrounded by angels whose hearts are on fire, beautiful Lady Amber. And there are two women here who love you even as I do. One of these women is a Force of Red, the other is a Lady of Violet. Both are governed by love, both kneel before the Altar of Love.

"They are here to serve you and cleanse you of all repression and perversion, for these two things always go together. If you accept the Light of their service, you will be cleansed, you will start to become integrated, and you will begin to learn to allow your awakening, loving heart to rule your personal will."

She looked at me wistfully. "I don't think I understand, but I feel it. I feel the Love."

"I know you do, sweetheart. You're starting to glow with it. And you don't have to understand now. Just feel the love, you don't have to do anything but feel the love. You belong here on this earth, you belong here in this universe. You have a right to be here and be unmolested. You are loved, and you are Love."

As the tears flowed from both our eyes and as the cleansing love filled up the room, I returned to the physical act which, when it is done in the energy of a heart centered love, is a most splendid sharing.

The healing energy Lucille had transmitted to me now glowed in my heart and governed my actions. As I raised this woman's leg off the floor and pushed my cock into her, the sex per se was the least of what was going on. A cleansing energy of violet permeated us, an image of a fair golden goddess appeared in my mind and I knew at once the radiance that was Aphrodite. A golden radiating heart pulsed out from her breast and I saw the Resurrection and the Life, the transformation of this decadent repressed culture into the glory it would one day become. And as the beautiful woman in my arms wept and moaned, I felt and saw her programming washed away in the baptism of the love within her, and her inner beauty began to revolve out of the dark recesses of cruel and ignorant repression, for to repress the darkness is also to repress the light. Up, up she went into the center of her heart, which expanded and glowed with a light profound. I almost had to shield my eyes against it.

I grew excited from the energy, excited on every level. I pushed my hotly throbbing cock deep, deep into her and she bucked around him moaning and weeping, then screaming. I felt her cunt ripple along my wand of love and magic as I shoved and withdrew, shoved and withdrew, hammering out a path of loving passion in a profound loving violence.

She orgasmed repeatedly, screaming, screaming, and releasing emotional blockages that served her no more. The blocks were whisked away by the energy of the Lady of Violet as the energy of Lucille The Prophetess urged me deeper, deeper into this woman, deeper into the fucking of her.

I drove the full length of Hemingway into her, something I had not expected to be able to do. But she accepted me and even screamed for more, thrashing wildly against the wall. I humped her with a fury then, a fury of the flaming passion of my desire for her, I fucked her and I fucked her.

Both her legs were off the floor and wrapped around me as I shoved her against the wall, trying desperately to sink deeper into her. She cried and whimpered, then moaned and moaned as I took her, over and over I took her, Hemingway was doing his job.

The miracle of the flesh built towards the explosion of the edifice it had created; Hemingway was wild all throughout the length of him, his huge balls swinging wildly, then tightening up . . . he thrust and he thrust . . .

And then I was gone. A flooding explosion of all that I was poured out of me and I heard myself screaming . . . but then there was nothing, just a soft and gentle blackness embracing me, caressing me, welcoming me home . . .

Then the stars began to glow in that blackness and I felt myself falling, falling . . .

The world resolved itself around me in a pink pulsating energy and I found myself embraced by a beautiful woman, a beautiful woman of sweat and love who held me to her and who wept with me. Amber had begun to know herself.

CHAPTER TEN

"Breakfast in bed, Sonny-Bob. I'll bet you don't get that too often."

"The only breakfast I'm interested in is you, Amber. Still, I do have to keep up my strength so I won't let you down."

"You couldn't let me down, honey, *not ever*." She kissed me.

After our activities of the previous night Amber and I had taken a long, slow bath together, exploring one another's bodies with the enjoyment of being human. And continuing to breathe our souls into one another with deep, deep kissing.

She lay on the bed beside me as I munched my bacon and sipped my juice, pinkie extended daintily. *I must not give the impression I don't have any manners.*

"I love me, Sonny-Bob," she giggled.

"I know you do, sweetheart. I love me, too."

After I finished my breakfast (Amber ate the oatmeal) we lay with one another again, savoring each other's bodies and touching one another's souls. Hemingway slipped easily into her; she could take him more easily than any other woman I'd ever been privileged to meet.

And the morning fled before the sun. Around noon we showered, again appreciating one another fully with exploration and hugs and deep, deep kissing.

Afterward, Amber looked at me shyly. "I love you, Sonny-Bob," she said softly. "And you were right, I had to learn to love myself first.

"I don't understand everything you said last night, but I'm beginning to understand Love. And I thank you."

"Thank **you**, sweetheart, for giving me the opportunity to serve. And I love you too, and really love is all any of us has to understand. That's all there is, really. Everything good flows from love.

"Intelligence, will, sexual passion--when these forces are purified, we find they all flow from Love. Love is the source of ALL. Love **is** ALL, Amber. There really is nothing but love."

I wondered what had happened to me. I'd never talked like this before. I was a drunk, fer Chrissake, and a pussy-chasing drunk at that.

I'd chased pussy all over the timeline. Other than journalism and warriorship, the only things I'd ever cared about were pussy and alcohol and my car and toy elephant.

What had come over me?

Amber's hand lay gently on my cheek. She stared up into my eyes filled with the love of her own heart. "I had a dream last night, Sonny-Bob. There was a message for you in it. Do you believe messages can come in dreams?"

"Yes, sweetheart, I do."

"I sat on the top steps of a great big courthouse; it looked like one of those old Greek buildings they show on Public TV. I was wearing a seamless white robe and a golden ornament on a golden chain lay upon my breast. There was a golden cord tied around my waist and from it hung another shining ornament that lay upon my vulva. And for the first time in my life I really appreciated my vulva. I appreciated being born a woman. I felt a radiant glow of love for myself, and it ran from my heart to my pussy. And it permeated my womb.

"You may not understand this, dear, being a man, but for the first time ever I loved myself as a woman and I loved my beautiful, fragrant pussy!"

"I understand," I said. "I love your pussy, too. And I love you as a woman, and I'm glad you're a woman, and I'll praise the Goddess forever for allowing us to meet. I love you, WOMAN."

She smiled, eyes twinkling. She continued, "Suddenly there were two women sitting at my feet, touching my feet, kneading my feet. One had flaming red hair and nipples and nails and was naked, and she had a pussy so succulent that even I wanted to suck it. There was a gold ring in her labia, and I grew excited by this woman . . . you should have seen those pussy lips!"

Amber sighed, flushed and beginning to sweat. She was almost touching herself again. Well, I knew exactly what she was talking about. Lucille's pussy lips would make a nun's mouth water and would give the pope a stiffie. If he were heterosexual, that is.

Amber pulled herself together and cleared her throat. She took a deep breath and continued. "The other beautiful lady wore a purple robe and her lips and nails were also purple. But her eyes! Sonny-Bob, I don't know if you've ever looked into purple eyes before, but those eyes looked right through me. They were brilliant and calm and shining, and this woman knew me, Sonny-Bob! She knew me! I felt the depth of her, and when I did I felt the depth of myself. And all parts of myself began to shine and come alive under her touch. I saw parts of myself I didn't like and had never wanted to look at and some parts of myself I had even tried to kill, but I felt this lady's calm deep love and I knew all would be well if I trusted this process.

"Then the purple lady said to me, 'You are wise, Amber, for trusting this process. For you **are** this process, and by trusting the process you are trusting yourself. You are a spark from the heart of God, and the spark must always trust the flame.'

"And so I just sat there for awhile as they smiled at me and massaged my feet, looking up at me with love beyond love. They washed my feet with a warm water that smelled like roses, then poured a scented oil on my feet and did a deep, deep massage. My feet had never been alive before, but while these ladies were massaging them my feet were on fire with life and I knew I could walk anywhere and do anything. My feet were glowing and throbbing with life! Until last night I had always felt off balance, somehow, I had always felt ungrounded and unsure of myself. But for the first time I began to feel balanced and powerful. I felt the power of my feet and I felt the love and the power of my sex. The love flowed from my heart throughout my vulva and into my feet, even as the sexual energy flowed from my feet to my vulva, then up to my heart. It was a great unending cycle of purification and love and rejoicing in the experience of being human. I began to realize that all God had ever wanted was to be human."

I looked at Amber with a new respect. As always, a woman was outpacing me again. How do they do that, I wondered. As soon as the first spark of genuine love is ignited in them they are off and running, while I'm stumbling along in the background somewhere with my thumbs up my ass. Still, I guess I do okay for a damn wino.

Amber smiled at me, and I realized I really was faced with a goddess. My hand went to my heart, and she placed her hand over mine and shared the gentleness of herself with me. Then we kissed, and she shared her breath with me, the breath of my life and of the life of all creation. She was my source, and all I ever wanted was to return to Her. And now, in some small measure, I had.

We shared the breath for a long moment, with the gentle biting of the lips that accompanies such a rejoicing, and we shared with the touching of the tongues, and all my sadness began to stir. For I knew it would take time for my redemption to be complete. Still, I took Amber's face into my hands and knew her as fully as I could, lightly sucking on her tongue as she shared a taste of forever with me. I wished so much for an eternal unity.

We were both kind of breathless as we released each other. We smiled shyly at each other. For we knew one another's secrets.

After a moment Amber tossed back her hair and I felt a wave of relaxation and acceptance of self flow off her. She undid her blouse and took off that slingshot thing, the device these people called a brassier. Somehow, she reminded me of an eighteen year old. Then she sort of shrugged, and stood and tossed away the rest of her clothing and stood before me naked and grand and beautiful, and still she reminded me of an eighteen year old. Only, I had never seen an eighteen year old who was so beautiful. I felt Aphrodite's presence in the room. My heart was spinning.

Time and again have I found myself in the presence of Divinity. And Divinity is always a Woman.

She sat back down on the sofa, on the far end this time, and smiled at me and I swear she was thirty or forty years younger than she had been a moment before. She was shining and glowing with the love of herself, and she extended some of that self-love to me. She reclined against some pillows and languidly surveyed me. She put her feet in my lap and gave me the privilege of serving Her through gently and lovingly touching her feet. To touch the feet of a goddess is to be truly exalted.

After a time she smiled. "I guess I should tell you the rest of the dream, Beloved."

"If you will, my Lady."

"Well, I was enjoying being served by these two ladies, just as I am enjoying being served by you now, Sonny-Bob. Only, there's one difference. Last night in the dream I was soaking up love like a sponge, but today I have so much love to give it's flowing off me and onto you. You may serve me, but you are not less than me. We are equal sparks from the heart of God. I bless you with my love and my sex, and you reciprocate. We are equal, we hold each other up. One of us could not exist without the other. And I would never have come to the experience of my own True Self without you. I bless you forever, my darling, and I accept your service and your love. We do sustain one another. We always have."

I was growing sexually aroused again, but I was held up in such an energy of love that love was all there was. Maybe it would be appropriate for us to physically make love again, or maybe the timing wasn't right and we'd done all we needed to do on that level for now. It didn't matter. Love is all that mattered, love is all that ever matters. I was so honored and privileged that Amber and Lucille and the Lady of Violet had included me in their circle, their Holy Circuit of Love, and Sex, and Compassion. Obviously, I meant something to them. But I knew with a dark foreboding that I couldn't hold this level of expansion forever. I wasn't like the women I knew, who could expand and expand and expand, seemingly forever. Oh, they might have minor contractions, but essentially the expansion into their hearts, into their True Selves, seemed to be an easy thing for them, at least compared to me. No matter how high into the consciousness of my Self I arose, I always fell off the ladder and landed on my fat ass. Well, at least I was dedicated enough to always try again.

" . . . massaging my ankles, then working the oil into my calves," Amber was saying, "and it felt soooo good I can't tell you!

"This dream was the first time I've ever had a woman touch me with genuine love and passion, Sonny-Bob. But--" she laughed, "I doubt if it'll be the last! They both smiled at me and continued the massage, but said nothing. When they had finished my calves, they let the hem of my robe drop back to my ankles and gently stroked my entire body through the fabric of my robe. When they touched my vulva and stroked my breasts I nearly died! My nipples were hard as diamonds and I was about to explode, and then I **did** explode, and my robe was soaked with the evidence of my passion. My friends laughed sweetly and massaged my juices back into me and I exploded again and again . . . finally, my entire awareness of self rose back up to my heart and I expanded and expanded and I touched myself forever and ever and ever . . . I can't tell you!

"Then I came back to myself, back to the part of myself that calls herself Amber, and I was centered in the glowing whirlpool of love that radiates from my breast. I became my Self, then that Self came back down to Amber! I glowed with the honey of my Self.

"My two new friends were glowing just like I was, and we all laughed together. Then they showered me with rose petals and knelt back down at my feet again, and with the sweetness of their essence they attached some of the rose petals to my feet. Then, very lovingly and very sweetly, they kissed my feet. I was completely relaxed and radiating my essence, which is Love.

"Then the two women spoke to me in unison: 'Woman, you have borne much. Let the cross fall away into splinters that burn when they touch the ground. Only after the ground has been scorched and the fire has died may you walk on it again, and where you walk the green grass will grow and the Rose of Love will prevail.

" 'Let suffering burn itself out and come to an end: the day of the cross is over, the day of the Rose has begun.' "

Well, now. That was a pretty fair representation of what had actually happened before we had this timewave to contend with.   The old

Christian/Moslem/Jewish/Atheist repression **had** burned itself out; people were sick with the materialistic suffering they'd brought upon themselves. They burned themselves out through many lifetimes with egotism and repression, until finally nothing was left but the charred ground, the lifeless shell of their egotism.

Then the Goddess had arisen and her Springtime had come, and the inner life of humanity had grown juicy again, and this was reflected in the outer life.

Of course, some might interpret Amber's dream as a forecast of the nuclear war, but I didn't think that was the case. The nuclear winter that followed that war had dispensed with both humanity and the Goddess once and for all--there was no springtime ever again after that happened.

So I knew Amber's dream was a history I'd actually studied in school, and which with the help of an always loving and forgiving Goddess I had to restore.

Some cops enforce laws. I enforce history.

Amber continued: "Then the kneeling ladies bowed to me, and again they kissed my feet. 'We honor you for your suffering and exalt you into the Light,' they said. 'Be thou redeemed, and know that you are loved, and you are loved, and you are loved forever. The Chalice is full of wine; when you are ready offer the baptism of your heart to humanity. Let the Race grow in Love. So Mote It Be!' "

Tears flooded both our cheeks. Amber had scooted over to me and I faced her, this woman who I now knew would always shimmer and glow for me, and for all who could accept her. I took Amber's face in my hands and each of us looked into the face of love.

As we gazed into one another's eyes she said, "The message they had for you, Sonny-Bob, concerned the future. They said, 'To him who confronts the night belongs the light, to him who confronts the cold belongs the flame, and he who stirs the cauldron weaves our name.'

"Do you understand, Sonny-Bob?"

A chill of love passed over me. My secret desire to serve the Goddess and the energy of Love had bubbled over in the last twenty-four hours. And I knew that somehow I would have a role in proclaiming the love of the Goddess, and the Great Force of Love which permeates the universe. I didn't know how yet, and I guess it currently was none of my business, for I did have a timeline to redeem, just as I'd helped redeem this woman.

But in the far-flung future, someday, maybe . . .

"The Red Woman also said you're a good lay, Sonny-Bob."

* * *

Our parting was sweet. Hubert and I left that evening after I'd held Amber in my arms for a very long time. I only wanted to touch her and stroke her beautiful hair, the hair of my Goddess.

"Sonny-Bob, will I ever see you again?"

"You'll see me every day, darling. You'll see me in your heart, and I'll see you in mine. And I'm so thankful to have gotten to know you."

She hugged me tightly. "I love myself now, thank you for showing me the way."

"Don't forget to thank the Red Woman and the Lady of Violet, Amber. They are your allies. And remember, they kneel always at the Altar of Love. Love is their first allegiance, really their only allegiance.

"To know them, you must fully explore the love in your own heart; you must continue to feel and process and release the grief so your love may shine.

"You are a beautiful spirit of love, Amber. I see you shining through eternity."

We released each other in a quiet spirit of radiant joy. As Hubert sailed down that little country road I caught a glimpse of myself in his rearview mirror. I seemed different, somehow. Calmer. My face seemed less distorted than it had before.

Well, I had plunged into this century seeking the God Reagan, but instead I had plunged into two Goddesses, one right after the other. There was no question my experiences with the Goddesses were more pleasant than my encounter with the God Reagan would be, but for my Goddesses to continue to thrive I had to encounter the God. So away I went, relaxed and whistling merrily.

CHAPTER ELEVEN

"Mama, Billy Cox told me there's no such thing as Santa. He said that was just a man in a red suit made up to look like Santa." The little girl's eyes filled with tears. She stamped her foot with anger and grief. "I want Santa Claus!"

The woman glanced at her husband. They had both been dreading this day. *Maybe it's best not to lie to children*, the husband thought. *Then we wouldn't have a mess like this to straighten out later.*

The Santa Barbara Celebration of Christmas Parade had ended a few minutes earlier, and the family were walking back to their car. They stopped; the little girl's grief was palpable as the tears streaked her face.

Maybe, hell, thought the husband. *There's no maybe to it. Now I know damn well we shouldn't have lied to her. But with every parent lying to their children, what the hell are we supposed to do?*

The mother knelt before the stricken child. "Honey, what do you believe? Do you believe there's a Santa Claus?"

"I don't know . . ."

Suddenly a wild shadow flew across the moon. They looked up to the sound of tinkling bells.

"Mama! Daddy, look!"

The couple were speechless as the flying object sailed off into the stars. They heard a distinct, "Ho Ho Ho!" as it disappeared.

Hubert and I had stopped and held a powwow outside Salt Lake City. He set us down in what appeared to be some farmer's field, frozen over and frosty. A herd of deer scattered as Hubert flopped around, trying to get comfortable.

"Sonny-Bob, these truck tires weren't made for this kind of terrain. It hurts."

"Well, you can change your shape."

"I've been thinking about that. I have an idea I want to float by you."

"Go ahead, Hubert."

"What do you know about Santa Claus?"

I considered. "Well, according to the Academy texts on this century, Santa Claus was a kind of mythological character constructed by the people to serve as the Deity of Greed. And the people believed in greed so much that eventually they came to believe in their hallucination of Santa. Every year around this time their media fills up with this illogical hallucination and they all rejoice, or at least pretend to, because they're afraid Santa will send them to hell if they don't rejoice.

"Indeed, some of these people actually believe they **are** Santa, and walk around in red suits ringing bells and letting greed-stricken children sit on their laps. Many are pedophiles. They don't do background checks on Santa."

"Well, if they don't do background checks on Santa and if everyone believes in him, that's how we get in to see Ronald Reagan. I'll turn myself into a sleigh and use my NPD to construct a red suit and a bell for you. Also a long white beard. You'll look just like the Deity of Greed."

I was gaining more respect for Hubert's faculties all the time. He was intelligent and resourceful. He might be a little gruff, but I'd begun to suspect that a heart beat somewhere behind his radiator.

"I like that idea, Hubert. Ronald Reagan's centurions won't dare refuse Santa Claus."

"But what about Lord Reagan himself?" Hubert asked nervously. "Won't he see through our disguise?"

"Yes, Lord Reagan's All Seeing Eye penetrates every quark of time and space. He will see us clearly. But it's his centurions we'll have to worry about. Lord Reagan sees and he knows, so I'm sure he's already expecting us. He has to know we're on the way."

"Alright then, my Captain. I'll start turning myself into a sleigh; it'll just take a few minutes."

"Thanks, buddy. And please install a transparent and well-heated cockpit bubble for me. It's colder than a well digger's ass out here."

I stepped out into the field as Hubert began his transformation. I took a few minutes to uncoil Hemingway and take a piss. A large cloud of steam resulted, blotting out the stars.

As I re-coiled Hemingway, Hubert announced, "I'm done! How do I look?"

I turned and surveyed him. "Hubert, you've done a bang-up job. Nobody in this timezone will be able to tell you from the real thing."

"Here's your Santa suit, Sonny-Bob. Hope it fits."

"As long as Hemingway's happy I'm happy," I grunted, stepping into my new uniform. I put on my white beard and wig and that ridiculous cap, then put on my boots. I was done. "How do I look, Hubert?"

"Like Santa Claus on a diet. You're not fat enough, my captain."

"Then make me an artificial stomach to go over my real one. And make it hollow in the center. I may want to hide some weapons in it."

"Ten-four."

Soon I was wearing my artificial stomach and preening before a mirror Hubert had constructed. I had to admit, I did look damn good. Ronald Reagan's centurions wouldn't dare aggravate me.

"What about reindeer, Hubert? We've got to get some."

"It'd take me two or three days to construct a fleet of lifelike reindeer. That's an intricate job."

"Hmmm . . . I wonder if we could convince some of those mule deer to substitute?" My prostitute friends had taught me the basics of communicating with animals. All you did was form a mental picture of what you wanted, imbue it with positive emotions, and project it to them. But no, that also would take a long time and there was no guarantee they would cooperate. And we couldn't Shanghi them; kidnapping was immoral according to Reagan Himself. I imagined what would happen if we showed up at Reagan's Ranch with a bunch of kidnapped mule deer and I shuddered and I shuddered. Ronald Reagan would not be pleased to see us violating his principles. I would not risk his wrath.

"Tell you what, Hubert, just make one deer, that'll have to do. These fools are so drunk on their hallucinations they won't question Santa's being pulled by a lone deer--I hope.

"And make sure the deer you craft is the one called Rudolph. He's an alcoholic reindeer with a big red nose. People like him best."

Soon Hubert was done with his alleged reindeer. "It can't talk, and it can't do much of anything. I didn't have time to create a reindeer that was lifelike. But maybe from a distance people won't notice."

"His nose does glow, though."

"He looks fine, Hubert."

Suddenly a beam of light shined across the field and a high-powered rifle roared. A bullet "pinged" off of Rudolph.

"Poachers, Hubert! Get us the hell out of here!"

I leapt into Hubert and he leapt into the starry sky and we left those poachers eating our frost. And I wondered why the people in every century I visit shoot at me.

Well, I had the fastest sleigh in this timezone. After a few minutes we approached the Sierras.

"Sonny-Bob, you'd better get ready to shout 'Ho Ho Ho!' "

"Hell no, Hubert. I'll ring this damn bell, but I'm not shouting 'Ho

Ho Ho!' I've got to save my lungs to communicate with Lord Reagan."

Hubert sighed. "Okay, then. I'll make a disk recording of 'Ho Ho Ho!' and broadcast it over my PA system. What does 'Ho Ho Ho!' mean, anyway?"

I'd been relishing sharing my vast knowledge of these people and their customs with Hubert. And I had some idea of what 'Ho Ho Ho!' might mean.

"There's some evidence that twentieth century people associated the term 'Ho' with prostitution, so in addition to being the symbol of greed, maybe Santa Claus is also a fertility icon, the symbol of man's eternal quest to get laid.

"Perhaps he is a symbol of the fact that greed is a perversion of the sexual impulse, and that what materialistic man wants--but lacks the self-confidence to achieve--is lots and lots of pussy instead of all those gifts.

"The greedy are never sexually satisfied. Here we have the horniest society ever, and they expend their jism over personal belongings. This just makes them want a variety of sexual experiences all the more with a host of partners, as would be the case in any civilized society, but then they shoot their wad in the wrong direction again and go on a shopping spree. It is an addictive, dysfunctional cycle. Their emptiness is never filled. They are lost in glamour, and frightened of their true motives."

"I would never have thought of that," remarked Hubert.

"Most people wouldn't, my friend. But most people don't have my vast knowledge of the twentieth century.

"Another slight variation on this interpretation," I offered, "is the rather straightforward idea that Santa Claus is trying to lure prostitutes with these gifts of his and bang them in his sleigh with all the elves watching and producing video footage.

"But nobody really knows. The correct interpretation may be lost in the back alleys of the twentieth century forever."

I checked Hubert's instruments and saw we were near Donner Pass. I licked my lips. That place always makes me hungry.

We flew on and shortly we were cruising at low altitude over Santa Barbara, trying to get a feel for the place. A couple of times people fired on us with shotguns, but that was to be expected. This was, after all, twentieth century California.

"Hubert, I am going to have to stuff this hollowed-out belly with weapons, after all. No agent would take a chance walking through twentieth century California unarmed." We had all heard the tales, we'd seen the video footage culled from those ancient nightly newscasts.

"Sonny-Bob, do you think it's a good idea to take our energy-based weapons outside the sleigh? I mean, I know you're Santa Claus, but like you said this **is** twentieth-century California. Anything might happen, even to a jolly old elf. What if your weapons fell into the wrong hands?"

I considered. He had a point. If I was going to fit into this culture, maybe I should carry only traditional firearms.

"Hubert, can you whip me up a Thompson submachine gun?"

I heard him clicking through his files. "Sonny-Bob, I can make you a tommy gun, but it won't fit inside that false gut you're wearing. You'd have to either carry it in your hands or hang it from your shoulder on a sling."

"I'm supposed to carry this sack full of presents. It's too much trouble to carry a submachine gun, too. The natives might get hostile if Santa doesn't offer them presents. 'Tis the season of greed, remember?"

"How about a violin case, then? It says in my files that gangsters carried their tommy guns in violin cases. Sounds like it would be handier than a sling."

"We have to be careful to be historically accurate, Hubert. There's nothing in the myths to suggest Santa was a musician.

"Tell you what: just make me an M-16, a bayonet, and a couple of grenades. That should do the trick."

Hubert clickety-clacked through his files again. "Sonny-Bob, it would be harder to put an M-16 in your gut than a tommy gun. Try again."

I was becoming exasperated. Were all these old-style muskets going to be too big?

"Hubert, what do you suggest? Is there any type of ancient firearm that has a high capacity magazine and a rapid rate of fire that would fit?"

"Hmmm . . ." he clickety-clacked again. "Well, we might be able to install a Mac-10 machine pistol, or maybe an Uzi. Yes, we can do either one of those."

"Make it an Uzi, then." I'd handled this weapon during the course on ancient weaponry at the Academy. Now everything would be fine.

Hubert's NPD whirred and whirred. Then an Uzi popped into my lap. "There you go, Sonny-Bob. As fine an Uzi as you can get in this century."

He whirred some more and three loaded magazines popped out. "Lock and load, Sonny-Bob. Lock and load."

I unsnapped the stomach and removed it, then slapped a magazine into the Uzi and chambered a round. I hoped it was safe to carry loaded in this fashion. I put it into the stomach. There was barely enough room to add the two extra magazines.

Hubert started whirring again and out popped a little .380 semi-auto handgun, the twentieth century equivalent of the suppository gun I had stuffed up my ass. Well, all I can say is that these twentieth century people had flexible rectums if they could put a .380 inside themselves.

"There should be enough space left for the .380, Sonny-Bob. It doesn't have much power, but I guess it's okay as a backup gun."

I fooled around with the stomach and after a minute or two I got the loaded .380 installed, along with the spare magazine that Hubert had given me. I fastened the stomach back on. "Well, at least now I feel as heavy as Santa Claus."

A rifle roared somewhere below us and a bullet ricocheted off the sleigh's transparent cockpit.

"Tell you what, Hubert. Go ahead and make that tommy gun, just in case. We can hide it in the space beneath your floorboards."

"Ten-four. Grenades?"

"Please."

We were sailing a few thousand feet above Reagan's Ranch and already the place had brought back holy memories. I knelt in the sleigh and said a brief prayer for the success of our mission. I heard Hubert clicking and clacking; I guess he was praying, too.

My pocket pistol, the energy weapon Roger Bacon had given me, resided with the tommy gun and grenades under Hubert's floorboards, and Hubert was satisfied that I wasn't carrying any energy weapons. But he didn't know about the suppository gun up my ass and I saw no reason to inform him.

We swooped over a clump of trees a few hundred meters from the house and I jettisoned the cockpit bubble. Santa doesn't have a transparent cockpit on his sleigh so I felt we should get rid of it. Hubert had activated some disassembly nanos he'd impregnated the cockpit bubble with; soon the thing would be reduced to its very molecules. My mechanical companion in this venture could construct another cockpit bubble when the need arose.

"Well, Hubert. It's Zero Hour. Take us down."

Hubert leapt thousands of feet into the sky, then turned a somersault and streaked towards the ground yelling "Ho Ho Ho" at the top of his PA system. I was sick to my artificial stomach as a result of his maneuvers, but I was determined to not give him the pleasure of watching me vomit. Somehow I held it in.

And somehow I didn't scream.

Suddenly Hubert leveled off and I saw we were streaking along just a foot or two above the ground. He streaked all around the ranch house and all over the yard for about fifty meters in all directions. He was still yelling "Ho Ho Ho" as he slammed on the brakes and stopped in front of the house, where he hovered for a second, then lowered himself gently to the ground.

"Shut up, Hubert," I growled as I climbed out of my "sleigh".

Suddenly a light blazed and I saw I was surrounded by the centurions of Sir Ronald Wilson Reagan. I held out my bag of gifts. "Ho Ho Ho, friends! Ho Ho Ho! I have gifts for one and all . . ."

"Drop the bag and step away from it, **Now**!"

"But I am Santa Claus! I freely bring you presents to stoke the fires of your greed . . ."

"Drop the bag and step away from it!"

In the glare of the spotlight I could see I was surrounded by fools pointing guns at me. *Damn*, I thought, *we do need more reindeer. Now they're on to us.*

I dropped the bag and stepped away from it. "I come in peace for all mankind . . ."

"Hit the dirt, freak! Lay facedown on the ground, hands in front of you, palms up and legs spread!"

Oh, shit. If I were lying facedown I couldn't get to my guns.

Just then Hubert cut loose with a bloodcurdling shriek, like a thousand mountain lions fighting all at once. For just an instant the centurions were off guard and I seized the moment, launching myself into a shoulder roll that carried me among them.

From the ground I broke the shin of one centurion with a kick, and as he screamed and went down I rose up among them, no longer a jolly old elf. A shot rang out, then another, and someone screamed, "Cease fire, cease fire, you shithead! You hit **me**! Call an ambulance!"

I was everywhere, yet I was nowhere. I moved among them, a dark and wrathful Santa, shattering elbows, breaking shins, crushing testicles, smashing knees . . .

As I danced among their maimed and fallen bodies Hubert was yowling, "Ho Ho Ho! Get 'em, Sonny-Bob! I mean Santa-Bob! I mean . . . Ho Ho Ho!"

Then one rose up before me and I sensed a feminine presence. It was either a female or a fey homosexual. I didn't want to hit a girl and that was nearly my undoing.

She screamed, shaking her long flowing mane wildly like an enraged tigress whose cubs I had injured.

"Ma'am, I don't want to hit a goddess . . ."

But she was no goddess, she was a deviant. She launched a kick that hit Hemingway where he lived, causing vibrations of agony along his whole shaft, and I couldn't for the life of me see why Sir Ronald Reagan had such violent people working for him.

Hemingway propelled me then, a Hemingway consumed by anger and terror at this rampaging madwoman. My foot launched itself at her chin but she sidestepped and parried. "Bitch!" I said.

She shuffled in and jabbed; her knee rose at the same instant and I dropped down and caught it, twisting the leg and throwing her to the ground on her face. I was on her back immediately, beating her head into the ground, when I looked up into the muzzle of a gun. It was pretty big.

"Now let me get this straight," the officer in the uniform of the U.S. Marine Corps said. "You've come from the future to prevent a nuclear war and save humanity?"

"Of course. Why else would I be here?"

"Idiot!"

"Major North, don't be so hard on the boy. He's had a tough night."

I knew that voice; I'd heard it millions of times in the temple and in school and everywhere the worshipful gather. I'd seen all the old newscasts and movies . . .

I turned in my chair and I beheld **HIM**. The craggy, manly features; the good natured machismo, the confidently radiating soul of America . . .

"My Lord and my God!" I spun out of the chair and collapsed to my knees before Him, hands clasped in supplication, eyes imploring and heart worshipping . . .

"My Lord and my God!"

The God Reagan, the regal peak of manly virtue, held up a restraining hand to the one he called Major North, who already had the muzzle of that gun of his stuck in my ear. "Put that gun away, Oliver! Can't you see he's a Republican?"

North withdrew a little, but that gun was still in his hand and ready for action.

"Give me a situation report, Ollie. What about those Secret Service guys?" I loved the way Ronald Reagan took command.

"This . . . this . . . Rooskie, or whatever he is, put every one of them in the hospital. The last ambulance just left. The other two shifts are on their way back from town; they'll be here any minute. Every guy we've got is going to be doing double and triple duty 'till we're sure the situation is under control."

"And Major North, what exactly **is** the situation with this gentleman?"

"Just what you heard, sir. This loon claims to be from the future and says he's come back to prevent a nuclear war. But I say he's a Rooskie."

I was getting more riled at this Major North every second. I didn't care if he was a Marine, he'd captured me and insulted me. I felt like scalping the uncivilized bastard.

"I'm not a Rooskie, Ollie North," I said evenly. "But your mother is!"

The muzzle of his weapon began to turn toward me again, but in two quick strides Lord Reagan had crossed the room and placed a firm hand on North's wrist. I loved the speed and grace with which the Lord moved.

"Put that gun down, Ollie! You're not going to shoot this guy like you did the last one. I forbid it!"

North lowered his gun to his side, but didn't holster it. "Yes, sir."

"Who did he shoot?" I asked Lord Reagan, wondering if Ollie North had gotten to one of my brother officers of the TAC. "Did someone else like me try to reach you?"

"As a matter of fact, yes. With his dying breath he claimed to be from the future, said he was here to stop a nuclear war that destroyed us all. But he was dressed like the Easter Bunny."

"Did you get his name, Lord Reagan?"

"Well, he wore a type of dog tag that was golden and shaped like a pyramid. The front of the tag featured an etching that looked like a woman's vulva, while the back had a great big eye etched into it. There was a tiny inscription on the back that you could only read under magnification that said: 'The All-Seeing Eye Of Reagan'. Is that supposed to be me?"

I lowered my head. "Thou hast said, my Lord."

"Anyway, there was an inscription on the front of the tag, too, just beneath the vulva. It said: 'Bubba Yoakum'. Did you know him?"

"Yes, Lord Reagan, I knew him and he was a royal pain in my ass. He was several years behind me at the Academy so I tormented him, but then he got promoted a lot faster than I did and tormented me. He's been on the Council of Generals for the last few years. He didn't amount to anything."

I grinned at North. "Nice shootin'!"

"Thank you," he said softly.

Well, if I undid this nuclear winter, I supposed Bubba Yoakum would pop back into the timeline. Damn! Can't a guy catch a break? I would have to figure out some way to convince him he owed me, then squeeze him for all he was worth--which wasn't much, admittedly.

Lord Reagan turned to North. "Where's Sergeant Petersen?"

"He's guarding this guy's fake stomach; it was full of weapons. He'll give it to the Secret Service guys when they get here.

"Okay, Captain--what did you say your name was?--that's right, Captain Sonny-Bob Culpepper. Why were you walking around with a stomach full of weapons?"

"Oliver North, all citizens have the right to keep and bear arms," I reminded him.

"He's right, Ollie. It's in the Constitution. Have you read it?"

North was glowering. "Yes, I've read it, and yes I'm a member of the NRA, just like you, Lord Rea--I mean, Mr. President. But we can't tolerate the Second Amendment at your house. You've already been shot once."

"No biggie," the Divine President said lightly. "Someone gets shot every day, and I'm no different from any other American, no better and no worse. And its been statistically proven, as you well know Major North, that if not for the presence of guns in private hands the violent crime rate would skyrocket and there would be lots more rapes and murders.

"Give this man his guns."

"Sir!" North was incredulous; I smiled at him smugly. "That's insa-- that would be unwise, Mr. President. Um, some guys from the FBI lab will be here in the morning. I've already told them they can take those weapons back for testing. Um, we couldn't have them wasting a trip and taxpayer dollars, could we sir? They're already en route."

"I guess you're right, Ollie. We don't want the FBI folks to feel like they're running in circles.

"But don't you worry, Captain Sonny-Bob Culpepper." Lord Reagan patted me on the head as I continued to kneel before him. "Don't you worry. We'll get you some brand new guns. It's in our budget. Major North, will you see to it? Get him a machine gun and anything else he wants."

North seemed on the verge of losing his composure. I guess he could see I was rapidly becoming the favorite child. "Um, I'll see what I can do, Mr. President."

He turned to me again, his hand repeatedly squeezing the butt of his gun, a tic in his eye. "Now then, you: what makes you believe we have nuclear weapons? Every sane person knows there's no such thing as nuclear weapons. Are you one of those conspiracy freaks?"

I looked at him and felt the beginnings of a terrible suspicion. If my suspicion held true I was really going to be sick.

"I'm nauseous," I croaked.

"Let me help you to your chair, son." Lord Reagan laid his holy hands upon my arm and guided me, and I could feel the healing energy pour off him. Already I was better, but still my hand was shaking as I accepted the cup of water he handed me.

"I asked you," North's tic was growing more pronounced, "what makes you believe we have nuclear weapons?"

"Several nations have nuclear weapons, dummy. But in the original timeline nobody used them because of MAD: Mutually Assured Destruction. I nuke you, you nuke me, and we'll see each other in hell. It would have been suicide to use nukes, so nobody did.

"Nobody except Harry Truman, who dropped two atomic bombs on Japanese cities when the United States was the only country with the bomb. It made sense to drop the bomb then, but it stopped making sense as soon as other countries had the bomb."

North threw back his head and laughed, a harsh, raucous, silly noise. Sounded like he'd swallowed a roll of sandpaper. I knew before he spoke that my suspicion had been correct.

"Captain Culpepper, or whatever your name is," his shoulders were shaking with laughter, "Harry Truman never dropped any atomic bombs on any cities in Japan or anywhere else. There *is* no atomic bomb, no hydrogen bomb, no cobalt bomb, nada, nothing, no nuclear device of any kind. It doesn't exist.

"President Reagan, this guy's just another conspiracy freak. Let's put him in the nuthouse."

"What about the Manhattan Project?" I asked, and suddenly the room was so quiet you could have heard a mouse fart. "I said, what about the Manhattan Project?"

All the color drained from North's face, and for that matter Lord Reagan looked a little peaked.

"Son, how do you know about the Manhattan Project?"

"Mr. President, don't talk to this guy anymore. *Please* don't talk to this guy anymore, he's--"

"Shut up, Ollie."

"Lord Reagan, everyone knows about the Manhattan Project in my time. For that matter, everyone knew about it at the end of World War II. Everyone *should* know about it right now, everyone should know the Manhattan Project was responsible for producing the first atomic bomb. And in the original timeline, everyone **did** know.

"Now I can see where history was altered and I like it less even than I liked it before. Somehow, Harry Truman was convinced not to use the bomb and to keep it secret. You people actually believe you're the only ones with the bomb, don't you? You believe you can use the bomb on the Rooskies and they won't be able to strike back. But boy is the timeline in for a surprise."

"See, Ollie? I told you we should cancel those plans to nuke the Rooskies."

"Shut up! I mean, try to hold your tongue, Mr. President! All this is classified 'way beyond top secret and by God I'll have it out of him how he knows about it."

That gun was in my face again. It was a Colt M1911 Government Model in .45 ACP caliber. It had been in service for over seventy years and was one of the sturdiest, most reliable handguns ever built. You could throw it in a mud puddle and run over it ten times with a tank, then dig it out of the mud a month later, clean it up and it would work just fine. A good commie killer, it was. A good commie killer.

"That Colt of yours will be replaced in a couple of years by the Beretta," I said calmly.

"What!? How'd you know we were considering the Beretta? Speak up, or I'll blow you to kingdom come!"

"You won't blow me, but your mother will!"

A howl of rage, then North's finger began taking up slack in the trigger.

"Major North! If you pull that trigger I'll pull your dick off! For the last goddam time, put that gun away. Put it away or give me your resignation." Lord Reagan stood there, commanding and supreme, finger pointing at North like a holy biblical prophet condemning a Philistine. North wavered, and almost shot me, but then he did put his weapon away. "That's better. Now go sit in the corner, Ollie. I'll question this young man. I said, go sit in the corner."

North shuffled sullenly to his chair and moved it to the corner. He sat down.

The Divine President stood in front of me. "Is your story true? Have you really come to save the timeline?"

"Yes, sir," I said, knowing he could already see everything. He was just testing me.

"Well son, we always have kept the Manhattan Project secret; nobody outside the highest levels of government has ever heard of it. Which is why Major North had a shit hemorrhage when you mentioned it. There are lots of rumors that we have the bomb, or that this nation or that nation has the bomb, but there's no proof.

"But you've at least given us evidence that you're from the future, because nobody, not even the conspiracy nuts, has ever heard of the Manhattan Project. The name and details of that operation are totally secure. **Were** secure, anyhow.

"Kind of pisses you off, doesn't it Ollie, that word of the Manhattan Project leaked out on your watch? I wonder what Senator Helms will have to say about that. Heh heh." Lord Reagan was enjoying watching North squirm. "Heh heh."

Someone rapped on the door. "Get the door, Ollie."

North went to the door and opened it; a man who looked like a twentieth century tax collector stood there. They'd warned me about these twentieth century tax collectors at the Academy, but I felt sure Lord Reagan would preserve me.

North and the tax collector whispered together, then the tax collector gave North a slip of paper. The tax collector left.

North approached my chair. I felt Lord Reagan's fingers tighten on my shoulder, giving me strength for whatever lay ahead.

"Okay, *Captain* Culpepper," North said easily. "Tell me about the Hubert Arms Company."

"What?" I feigned surprise, but thought I knew what had happened. Every male of every sensible species wants to leave his mark on the world. Dogs do it by pissing on things, I do it by leaving children scattered all over the timeline* so Hubert must've . . .

---

* Though sexuality for pleasure and intimacy wasn't usually honored, paternity was never much of an issue with most folks until the late twentieth and early twenty-first centuries. But then the harsh penalties that came with the nuclear family (as opposed to the extended families of previous generations and the group marriages and so forth of my own time in which children are automatically cared for) that were many times levied against fathers on one pretext or another actually--if you can believe it--made it advantageous to a father to prove he *hadn't* followed his biological imperative and fathered a given child. The advent of DNA testing made this possible. In earlier times, however (as well as in my own time), fatherhood was held in high esteem in all its forms, both biological and non-biological. A large percentage of children had always been biologically fathered by someone outside the marriage, but nobody paid much attention. Few people cared. Husbands and fathers were respected, as was the biological imperative to reproduce yourself as many times as possible. But with the forced isolation of the nuclear family and the savage economics of the time, nature was perverted.

"That Uzi of yours and that little Colt .380: Where'd they come from? On the receiver it says," here he glanced at the slip of paper, "it says it was manufactured by the Hubert Arms Company of Gaffney, South Carolina. Only I've just been told there is no Hubert Arms Company in Gaffney, South Carolina or anywhere else, as far as our people can determine. Plus, the Uzi is an Israeli weapon, should have been made in Israel. Yours is authentic except for the legend on the receiver.

"What's going on, Culpepper? Where'd you get those guns?"

Lord Reagan intervened. "What difference does it make where he got his guns, Ollie? The important thing is that he was exercising his Constitutional right to keep and bear arms."

"But Mr. President, we don't even know where he's from! We know nothing about him!" North was tense and hunched, fists clinched, looked like he wanted to jump up and down. "We know absolutely nothing about him!"

"Sure we do, Ollie. He's from the future, he's told us so repeatedly. He hasn't said or done anything to make you think he's **not** from the future, has he?"

"Well, no sir, but--"

"It's settled then. You're from the future, son. Will you join Nancy and me for some milk and cookies?"

"I'd be delighted to, my Lord."

Another rapping on the door. I hoped they would leave it open this time, for it was musty and airless in here. There was no window; I believed I must be in an attic, probably where Oliver North tortured his victims. I had to get out of here.

North let a half dozen tax collectors into the room . . . tax collectors, or perhaps they were blues musicians, though they carried no instruments. Well, I'd never expected Oliver North to arrange for my entertainment, anyway.

"Mr. President, these gentlemen are agents Smith, Earp and Tutweiller from the local FBI office." Then North gestured to the other three. "And these guys you've already met; your second string Secret Service people."

"Welcome, my friends. God bless America," said the President.

"They're here to interrogate the prisoner."

"Major North, mind your manners! This man is not our prisoner, he's our guest and he's been thoughtful enough to come all the way from the future to ask us not to start a nuclear war.

"Besides, Nancy wants to meet him. She's made cookies."

North was trembling with rage. From my perspective it was fun being the favorite son--as long as Big Daddy was here. But if Big Daddy left me I would need all my resources to survive Jealous Brother.

The one called Tutweiller spoke up. "Mr. President, if we could just have a few minutes alone with this gentleman, I'm sure we could clear up a lot of ambiguity regarding his situation. Then he can have his milk and cookies and everything will be fine."

The President turned to me. "What do you think, Sonny-Bob? Can you spare these gentlemen a few minutes of your time?"

I knew with the most unshakable certainty that Ronald Reagan would not let me down, would not let me fall into the hands of the Philistine. "Thy will be done, my Lord."

"It's settled, then. You fellows can speak with Captain Culpepper for a while, and when you're finished we'll all have milk and cookies. Is anyone here lactose intolerant?" They all shook their heads. "Good, I'll ask Nancy to set places for all of you."

North was rubbing his hands together in vengeful satisfaction, and my asshole was starting to pucker up from fear.

"Ollie, you're with me."

"But sir, I'm needed here . . ."

"No, Ollie. You and I have some things to discuss. Come with me."

A sullen North marched to the door with the Divine President. "I'll see you in a little bit, Sonny-Bob, okay?"

"Yea, my Lord." I bowed as he left the room.

As the door closed I found the one called Tutweiller standing before me, a sadistic grin on his tax collecting face. *I've got your tax collector, asshole,* I remarked to myself.

"Drop the pajamas, Santy Claws."

"What?"

"Drop the pajamas, disrobe, get nekked." He smirked at me. "What, don't you people speak English in the future?"

"Yes, we speak English."

"Then get nekked! Now!"

I'd had no idea the tax collectors of the Twentieth were fags. I almost launched into combat mode, but then realized that two of them were covering me with drawn guns.

Smith spoke up from his textbook combat stance, eyes hard over his gun barrel. "Hurry up and take them clothes off, Bub. What, are you afraid we're a bunch of queers?"

"You mean . . . you're not?" I stammered.

"Hell, no! We just want to make sure you're not carrying any more weapons in that suit or up your ass."

Up my ass . . . if they looked into that particular orifice they would find my suppository gun. Hubert would be upset with me if that gun fell into their hands . . . assuming I told him about it, which I probably wouldn't. Still, it was bad enough to be robbed of those ancient muskets they'd taken off me. I had no intention of letting them get my assgun.

So they weren't queers . . . yes, it was coming back to me now, a flood of illumination on the subject. According to the material I'd studied at the Academy the twentieth century was full of homophobes. Yes, and many of these people were even more homophobic than me . . . my wheels were turning . . . and the military and police forces were especially known for being radically homophobic . . . I had an idea . . .

"Earp," Tutweiller spoke, "go yank those clothes off him."

Earp reluctantly came forward, while Smith and one of the Secret Service guys kept me covered with handguns.

"Take off your clothes," Earp said.

I took a deep breath. Time to play hardball.

I grabbed Earp and planted a wet and juicy one right on his mouth, even managed to slip him a little tongue.

He jumped back sputtering and spitting. "He kissed me! He kissed me!"

"I want a piece of ass!" I proclaimed, as the agents backed warily away from me.

"Any of you guys got any lubricant?"

They fell all over one another trying to get to the door. Finally they were gone and the door slammed shut. I smiled smugly. They were gone and I hadn't even had to take out my Hemingway.

After I'd been alone for about an hour I decided to make my move. It was unlikely I could get out through the door because I'd heard a couple of guards shifting around and talking on the other side. So I'd have to get out through the wall.

I gingerly removed my suppository gun and wiped it on my sleeve. I set the selector switch on wide beam disintegration and stepped back from the wall. But before I created a hole big enough to escape through I wanted to see what was on the other side, so I only fired one three second burst. The resultant opening was about eight inches in diameter. Almost wide enough to put Hemingway through--if he were flaccid.

I couldn't see anything through the hole except inky blackness and a few stars. Let's see, we'd gotten to the ranch about 2100 hours; it must be around midnight or even later by now.

I heard voices and realized they were talking about Hubert. I listened closely.

"It flew in, sir!"

"Don't be an idiot. That's not even a real reindeer."

"Don't touch it, sir!"

"What? Why not?"

"Every time one of us has touched it we've gotten a nasty electric shock."

"Wear rubber gloves, Sergeant."

"Yes sir, we got Mrs. Reagan's Playtex gloves and tried it, but the thing shocked us even worse. It let us get inside it, then it shocked our balls."

"Ridiculous! You talk about this thing as if it were alive. Look, it's not shocking me. I could stand here with my hand on it all day and it wouldn't shock me. Look, I can even take a piss on it . . . Ughhhhh!"

"I warned you, sir. Sir? Corpsman! We have a casualty!"

I smiled. Hubert was doing his part to take out the opposition.

I'd been a little stunned when they brought me up, for they'd knocked me in the head ten or twelve times with a baseball bat and I didn't remember much. But I was pretty sure I was in the attic. So I would have quite a drop to the ground. But I wasn't worried about that, I was concerned about the fact that they seemed to have a guard around Hubert, plus I could hear a soft rustling from time to time that sounded like some sort of roving patrol. If any of those people saw me disintegrating a man-sized section of wall, they'd be firing on me with automatic weapons so fast it'ud make my head spin. That disintegration beam had make a glow just now; I was lucky they hadn't seen that. Oops! If they saw light through the hole they'd send someone to check on it. I grabbed a blanket that was lying in a corner and stuffed it into the hole. I had to think . . .

Suddenly I heard a loud, plopping fart from one of the guards beyond the door, along with an extended yawn. Then another loud, plopping fart which, from the difference in timbre, I judged had come from the other guard. Finally, after another minute, I heard two loud, plopping farts simultaneously and what sounded like bodies sliding down along the wall. Then came snoring.

What was going on? Before dissolving that deadbolt and letting myself out I had to be certain . . .

The deadbolt slid back and the door partially opened. Ronald Reagan stuck his head in. "Howdy, pardner. Are you decent?"

I was too stunned to speak. I felt my jaws working but no sound came out. The Savior had come for me.

He entered the room and I ran to him, I prostrated myself at his feet. I grabbed his hand and kissed it.

"Lord Reagan!" I croaked.

"My, my, son. You act just like those fanatics in my fan club. Stand up and look me in the eye. That's better. You don't need to grovel before me. 'We hold these truths to be self-evident, that all men are created equal and that they are endowed by their Creator with certain inalienable rights, and that among these are life, liberty and the pursuit of happiness.' I'm here to turn you loose, son. Would that make you happy?"

My head bobbed ecstatically, but I could not speak. Lord Reagan's charisma lit up the room. He was the Spirit of America. The primitive people of timezones earlier than mine believed in gods they could not see, touch or smell. I knew in this moment that it was better to have an historical figure as a god, for I knew in whom I believed, and he came to earth to prove himself to all of humanity.

And I could see him and I could touch him, and he smelled like cookies.

"This isn't going to be the easiest jailbreak I've ever pulled, son. Last year those pesky Seabees came here and built some military and Secret Service support facilities. A platoon of Marines is garrisoned here at all times and right now they're on high alert and aching to kill something, particularly if it dresses in a red suit and yells 'Ho Ho Ho!'.

"Plus, you've got the two shifts of Secret Service guys you didn't put into the hospital to deal with. Thank God you at least managed to take out one shift when you arrived or our case might be hopeless.

"And finally, there's the Delta Force. That damn Major North summoned them as soon as his henchman, Sergeant Petersen, finished beating you in the head with that baseball bat. They had to fly in from Ft. Bragg, but since they have their own Concorde jet they arrived a hell of a lot faster than if they'd flown in on any other type of aircraft. They parachuted right out of that Concorde at high altitude and got here just a few minutes ago. Their leader came to the door and reported in. Nancy gave him a cookie."

I cleared my throat and managed to still my racing heart. "Lord Reagan, what happened to those guards outside the door?"

"Oh, that." He sniffed. "That was easy. Nancy and I ground up our whole supply of sleeping pills and tranquilizers and mixed them with the cookie dough and bean pudding we'd set aside for the Secret Service. We also mixed pure grain alcohol--Nancy has a stash of it--into the eggnog. We figured they'd be out for a long time after that meal.

"Thanks to Nancy's catering we managed to knock out four of the guards in the house, which at least gives us a chance to get you out of this room. Our original idea was to get you to the chimney so you could escape, but North was ahead of us there. There's an angry young Marine guarding the chimney and he wouldn't eat, even after Nancy showed him a little breast.

"And North himself built a huge fire in the fireplace; he comes back every few minutes and adds another log. It's a balmy seventy-two degrees here in Santa Barbara, and nobody in their right mind would have a fire. But North is determined to deny you that chimney. I think he's bucking for an early promotion and feels his superiors will give it to him if he can hold onto you."

"Sir? Have you decided to call off the nuclear war?" I asked hopefully.

"Hell, son. I never called for a nuclear war to begin with. That's Vice-President Bush's doing. People think he's sweet, but he's really just a war-monger. He's determined to have a war one day, even if it kills him. So he went behind my back and secretly recruited Major North, Al Haig, Henry Kiss-My-Assinger; he even got that pirate Jimmy Carter in on the caper. They plan to bomb the Soviets sometime next fall.

"I only found out about all this a couple weeks ago. You see, Nancy and Barbara Bush are--uh--friends, and Barbara leaked the news to Nancy. Well, it's not the first time Barbara and Nancy have leaked together, and I hope it won't be the last. I have to keep abreast of what's happening in my own administration."

My faith was fully restored! Actually, it had never been really threatened, but I did feel a sense of relief knowing that my God was not behind the destruction of the earth. I think people who worship a vengeful god are foolish and are inviting vengeful karma upon themselves.

"What can I do, Lord Reagan? How can I help you save the world? Is there some gospel you want me to preach?"

"Well, son, I think you hit the nail on the head a while ago when you said Truman had nuked the Japanese and that originally in this timezone everyone knew about the Manhattan Project. And you said something about Mutually Assured Destruction. Was all of that true?"

"Thou knowest it be true, my Lord."

"Well, then it seems to me that the best thing to do would be to go back to 1945 and explain all this to Give- 'Em-Hell Harry and make sure he nukes the Japs. It couldn't be simpler."

"Lord Reagan, my sleigh is in need of a healing.   His interdimensional mechanism is damaged; it is a delicate device and may take several months to repair. Please, my Lord, lay your holy hands upon him and heal him, please make him whole. Then we can go save the timeline."

I gazed imploringly at him.   "Please, my Lord, heal my friend Hubert."

Lord Reagan gazed at me, then laid his great hand atop the crown of my head. "Here is some healing energy you may transfer to the sleigh called Hubert. It won't make him well, but it should speed the healing process a little."

I saw at once behind the appearances of the moment; the veil of illusion was lifted from my eyes and I could see why Lord Reagan allowed bad people to maneuver in this world and why he insisted that I save the timeline, instead of just waving his holy hand and saving it himself.

Humanity is always at a crossroads: do we go this way, or that? Do we choose good, or evil? Do we behave responsibly, or do we behave like childish Democrats?

Ronald Reagan and his celestial wife Aphrodite keep a light hand on the reins, they allow us to make our own choices so we may learn to choose compassionately and responsibly. The fact that karma prods us along like a pointed stick in the ass insures that we will learn sooner or later. We always have to face the consequences of wrong choice. And that which holds true in our individual lives also holds true across the grand scope of the timeline. Humanity as a race must choose, and thereby learn to make the good choices that will lead it to its destiny. Sometimes those appointed to lead the race, like President Truman, may choose wrongly and the results will be disastrous, like this nuclear winter. But the race must *learn* from its mistakes, not be destroyed. The destruction of the earth is not authorized in the cosmic scheme of things. The race does not need to be annihilated in order to grow. Therefore, I AM. I had to go back and make sure Truman made the *right* choice.

How wise Reagan and Aphrodite are! How wise and how loving and how beautiful they are! For they will not step in and fix things so long as we are able to handle the burden of fixing things ourselves. They want us to learn, they want us to evolve.

Lord Reagan farted. "That bean pudding was good," he said.

The Divine President was wearing a brown duster that reached nearly to the floor. It sort of billowed outward as he pooted. He unbuttoned it and took out my wig and beard, then my cap. He handed them to me.

"I'm sorry I couldn't get to your guns and artificial stomach, but the FBI is keeping a close watch over those items.

"Major North, on the other hand, has grown careless. He's so intent on keeping you in this house he forgot all about his own sidearm." President Reagan reached deep into the duster and drew out Oliver North's .45. He handed it to me. "If you have to use it, try to take out the officers."

I was at once humbled and exalted in the presence of my God. He trusted me, and I would *never* betray that trust. I would strive always to be worthy of Him.

"I've got one more item for you, Sonny-Bob. These are night vision goggles. I lifted them off one of those guards we knocked out with the bean pudding."

I looked at him with layer upon layer of respect and admiration. He would've made an excellent cutpurse.

I put the beard and wig on, then the hat. I planted those night vision goggles on top of the hat where I could easily pull them down over my eyes once I got outside. Gripping Oliver North's .45 expectantly, I awaited President Reagan's orders.

He lifted a regal hand. "Follow me," he said. "Do as I do."

After much skulking and sneaking, avoiding Marines and Secret Service people, we made it to the relative safety of the Reagan's bedroom . . . where I beheld a goddess.

Nancy Reagan lay upon the bed, languid and sensual, a sheet barely covering some parts of her. She wore only a g-string and pasties, but she was asleep. How was I to worship her?

I reverently sank to my knees and slowly scooted across the floor, heedless of bruising bone and tearing cartilage. I made it to the edge of the bed and arose, hands clasped in prayer, to praise this beautiful goddess, the lady charged with keeping the President happy and at peace until he could complete his earthly mission and ascend once more into the arms of his divine consort, Aphrodite.

I bowed and kissed her divine foot, her divine foot with the blue-nailed toes, and I knew I would never be the same after that. The foot twitched, then withdrew beneath the sheet. I felt sad to see it go, but there was still the matter of the buttock . . .

There it lay, close to hand, only partially covered by the sheet. If I could kiss this buttock, this divine alabaster buttock, I would be redeemed, I just knew it. I felt Hemingway begin to throb in anticipation as I puckered and bowed--

"Sonny-Bob! You have places to go, son."

His hand was on my shoulder, and I looked up regretfully into his face. "She is beautiful, Lord Reagan. I can see why you chose her as your consort."

"Yes," he agreed, "she'll do. I guess she must've eaten the wrong bean pudding. We had some set aside for ourselves, but she must've accidentally eaten some we'd made with tranquilizers for the Secret Service. Now she won't be able to see you off. Well, maybe next time."

President Reagan held a lasso and the way he uncoiled it somehow reminded me of Hemingway. "Sonny-Bob, you may not be able to go up the chimney, but we can still use the chimney. Come here, help me with this."

I followed him to the window. He opened it and peered out. "I can't lower you directly out the window, you'd land on a sleeping guard--bean pudding again--and might wake him. But if I can lasso the chimney, you'll be able to swing out the window, then lower yourself to the ground a few yards away from the guard. It's a piss poor option, for there's constant patrols. But it seems to be the only option."

There comes a time in every man's life when he must disagree with his God. He must stand his ground and not be swayed. I knew my time had come.

"Lord Reagan, I shall not make for the ground, I shall climb up the rope onto the roof. From there I can wait until I've surveyed the area and made sure no patrols are around, then I'll drop off the building and roll when I hit the ground. I was trained by ninjas in the sixteenth century. I'll be okay." I hoped.

Lord Reagan shrugged. "Sounds like a plan."

Well, that was easier than I'd thought.

I picked up the last several feet of rope and held it in a belaying position. "On belay," I said softly.

Ronald Reagan crouched on the windowsill, then slowly leaned out the window, hanging onto the rope as though he himself were about to embark upon a hasty rappel. He lowered himself until he was perpendicular to the window and just below it. He shook out a loop.

He began swinging the lasso in a mighty arc, then he let fly and the rope whistled through the air. He nailed that chimney on the first try. He pulled himself back onto the windowsill and I helped him into the room. "Didn't know if I could still do that. It's been a long time since I've hung out a window that way."

He looked at me then, and we felt the softness of our brotherhood. For his mission was to save humanity from tyranny and to prepare the way for his consort Aphrodite, and my mission was to save the timeline from the Dark Cherub Oliver North, George Bush The Elder, Jimmy Carter and the rest of that pirate's crew. We gazed at each other softly, for we were brother hearts.

Then Lord Reagan strode quickly to his nightstand and picked up--oh my Goddess, it was! He picked up a jar of the sacred jellybeans he was known for having favored, he picked it up and brought it to me and placed it in my hands.

"Lord Reagan, this is the sacrament of my people. We partake of the sacred jellybean each time we go to temple, we ingest them in memory of you. Once I ate a whole handful! But that was nothing compared with this. Please, my Lord, a final boon: may I take sacrament directly from you?

"Please, my Lord, please." I unscrewed the lid, held the jar out to him. "Please . . ."

He looked at me for a moment, his All-Seeing Eye pulsing in his forehead. Then he reached his fingers into the jar and lifted out a green jellybean. Not my favorite one, but now it would be.

I knelt and stuck out my tongue, and Father Reagan gently placed the sacred bean onto it. My tongue rolled up like a carpet and the bean was mine! Nobody in my century had ever received the sacrament straight from Reagan's hand. Nobody but me. I wept and kissed his fingers.

Master Reagan reached down and lifted me up. "Time for you to leave."

I placed the jar of sacred jellybeans into the great pocket of my Santa's coat and crouched upon the windowsill as Lord Reagan had done moments earlier. I glanced at his wife as she stirred gently and moaned in her sleep. "Please tell her I'm sorry I missed her, but that I was exalted by kissing her foot."

"I will, my son. Now, good luck!"

And with that, Lord Reagan shoved me out the window and I went swinging wildly through the air. I "clunked" against the building beneath the chimney; I wouldn't have too far to climb to reach the roof.

"What was that, Charlie?"

"I didn't hear nuthin', Mac. Smitty? You hear anythin'?"

"Only thing I've been hearing is that Secret Service guy snoring and farting. That's probably all it was, dude."

"Roger that. I guess you're right."

I breathed a profound sigh of relief, then scrambled quickly up the rope as I caught a whiff of the Secret Service guy. He was rank.

I crouched by the chimney and pulled the night vision goggles over my eyes. They lent a green tinge to the night, but I could see pretty well.

Thank you, Lord Reagan . . .

I pulled Oliver North's .45 out of my waistband and thumbed back the hammer, but I made sure the safety was on. That bastard had violated my Second Amendment rights, but now his karma was coming around. Now **I** had **his** gun.

I peered around the area of operations and saw a patrol 'way out near a hedgerow, and saw another one only twenty meters from the house. I guessed those guys near the hedgerow must be Delta Force, for it looked like they carried submachine guns and were dressed in black suits, much like my ninja friends of hundreds of years ago. I could barely see them. If they hadn't been moving I wouldn't have.

I figured the other patrol was Marine Corps jarheads; they wore steel pots on their heads and carried some type of rifle, probably the M16. They appeared to be wearing camouflage uniforms, though it was difficult to tell under the circumstances.

Let's see, what was that . . . I thought I had detected some other movement near the house . . . and suddenly I found myself peering at a guy with a night vision scope who was peering at me. His scope was mounted on a rifle.

I hit the roof and rolled, as a high powered rifle thundered.

"Smitty, what the hell was that!?"

"It's Santy Claws, it's Santy Claws, he's got loose! Get Major North!"

Shit. Now I was in a bind.

The fuckers started peppering the roof with rifle fire; I got a couple shots off from the .45 and someone screamed. "I've been hit! Corpsman!"

"Smitty! Where'd the fucker get that gun?"

"I don't know, Sergeant. Must've had it up his ass."

"Santa can't get a .45 up his ass, idiot!" I yelled, then sent another round downrange. Unfortunately, my suppository gun was back in its usual place and there was no way I could get to it under the circumstances. I had to keep my pants on.

The rifle fire was inching closer to me so I rolled again, but one of the fuckers either anticipated me or just got lucky as a bullet struck me in the foot. Now I'd have to shoot up medical nanos at my earliest convenience.

I growled in rage. Now I was pissed. "We'll see who's got the Christmas Spirit!" I roared, sending a couple more rounds downrange.

Then: "Hubert! Hubert! Help! Get your ass up here!"

That rifle fire was too close, I emptied the .45 and had no more ammo. *Well*, I thought philosophically, *at least everyone gets laid in Heaven all the time. I think.*

"Sir! It's the sleigh! It's driving itself!"

Another voice: "Kill the reindeer! Shoot that red nosed son of a bitch! Shoot Rudolph!"

Rudolph was peppered with bullets as Hubert sailed towards my position. "Get in, Sonny-Bob!" he panted as he skidded onto the roof.

I dived into Hubert and he sailed off the roof as I tore up his floorboards. I emerged with the Thompson. "Hubert, turn around," I told him. "We're going on a strafing run."

We arced back around, taking nine kinds of fire, but by this point I didn't give a damn. Santa Claus might be only the Deity of Greed, but he was their deity and they treated him with murderous contempt. They deserved to be disciplined, so I was going to thin the herd.

"Don't get too caught up in your role, Sonny-Bob!"

"You just drive, Hubert. Leave the role playing to me!"

I had adjusted really well to the night vision goggles. Those jarheads couldn't hide from my jolly old ass.

I peppered them with tommy gun fire as they scattered and screamed and ran for cover. Hubert was as loud as the Final Trumpet of the Christians as he shouted "Ho Ho Ho!" Rudolph's flashing nose was shattered by a bullet, but Hubert built him a new one in just a few seconds and this one was twice as big.

I emptied the Thompson and there were deceased and wounded jarheads everywhere. When Hubert paused to catch his breath I thought I heard the "thwunk" of a grenade launcher . . . I looked towards the hedgerow and saw some Delta guy pointing his weapon at me, and then the "thwunk" came and the grenade sailed right over my head.

"Hubert! Over there by the hedgerow! The Delta Force! We've got to kill them!"

Hubert cut loose with his battle cry again and leapt into action, taking us right over the Delta Force as I grabbed those grenades he'd made earlier. A bullet chipped the head of the artificial elf next to me; Hubert built it back.

I tossed those two grenades down at the Delta guys. "Merry Christmas, assholes! Don't say Santa never gave you anything!"

They scattered as Hubert headed back towards the Marines' position. I snapped the spare magazine into the Thompson. "One more run, Hubert. Then we're going back to the North Pole."

"Roger that, Sonny-Bob." Only later did he tell me he thought I overreacted that night.

We roared in on wings of thunder as I laughed maniacally and shot at the corpsmen. There was one of those ancient helicopters parked about eighty meters away. I couldn't have them trying to follow me in that thing; I giggled and opened up on it and put twenty or thirty rounds into it, and it exploded in a great mushroom ball of fire, just like in the holo-simulations back home.

As we swooped towards the house one last time I saw the God Reagan. He'd climbed onto the roof and was waving a white cowboy hat, jumping up and down and cheering us on. I came to "present arms", saluting him with the Thompson as we passed. "Thou art God," I said.

As Hubert began his ascent, Oliver North came running out of the house with a rifle, probably an M16, but it could as easily have been President Reagan's rabbit gun. Maybe that's what he'd shot the Easter Bunny Bubba Yoakum with.

I sent a stream of lead at the warmongering son of a bitch as he dropped the rifle and dived for cover.

The Thompson coughed its last and I was out of ammo. I shook my fist. "I'll get you next time, Ollie North!"

Then we vanished into the starry heavens and there was no sound save the whistling wind.

CHAPTER TWELVE

Hubert and I spent the rest of the night playing chicken with the Air Force. I shot up some nanos and guzzled a glucose beverage, then just sat back and watched Hubert's antics.

All his pent up tension was coming out as he deliberately flew over air bases and teased the authorities. I knew I was going to have to get him laid soon, though I wasn't quite sure how the fornicational process worked for him and was pretty sure I didn't want to know. He was like a wild twentieth century teenager wrestling with sexual tensions. In this century the so-called adults made love as difficult to express as they could for their offspring, at least in America. The resulting explosive tension was responsible for most of the juvenile crime, and for practically all crimes directed at females by juveniles. Indeed, because the young people carried this tension and the repressive practices that created it into their adult lives, their unfulfilled emotional needs were responsible for most, if not all, crimes directed at the persons of others by adults. Repression creates perversion . . . but don't try to tell that to the twentieth century "adults" or they might try to confine you.

Hubert soared on the wings of tension and I just hoped he wouldn't explode, particularly with me inside.

"Hubert buddy, wasn't that the fourth squadron you've outrun?"

"Fifth. You haven't been paying attention."

"Well, don't you think we should put down someplace and call it a night? After that firefight and then dodging these fighter squadrons all across the continent, I'm sure you could use a rest. I know I could."

"You're resting right now, Sonny-Bob, just sitting there with your thumbs up your ass while I do all the work. But that's okay, this is good therapy for me."

On he flew.

"Hubert, what kind of missile was that? It nearly hit us."

"Bullshit. I can dodge any missile those primitives can throw at us."

On he flew.

After a while a very ugly aircraft pulled up alongside us. "That's a stealth aircraft, Sonny-Bob. It's just recently been developed. The public knows nothing about them."

Hubert pulled up ahead of the stealth, then positioned himself directly in front of its nose. Plane and sleigh were separated by only about twenty feet.

I decided it was time I got in on the gag. Why let Hubert have all the fun?

I grabbed my bell and scooted into the rear compartment of the sleigh. I rang the bell practically in the pilot's face while Hubert shouted "Ho Ho Ho!" The guy couldn't hear my bell, of course, but I'm sure he heard Hubert. Hubert's yells probably woke up half the continent.

I quickly grew tired of the bell. The pilot just stared at me, no expression on his face. I decided to liven things up.

I grabbed one of the artificial elves and pulled down my pants. Hemingway was loose, and I pretended to anoint the elf with my passions.

Suddenly the plane veered off. We never saw him again.

About 0800 I finally convinced Hubert to stop in Albuquerque so I could piss. He landed on a residential street and I got out and fooled with my fly. The opening was too small to get Hemingway through, so finally I just dropped my trousers and let fly.

As I was finishing up my business and recoiling Hemingway, a young man about ten or eleven years old came down the street sobbing bitterly. I rang my bell at him, but that didn't seem to cheer him up, so I said, "What's wrong, son?"

"They beat me up . . . !" he wailed with grief, outrage and fear for the loss of his manhood.

"Who beat you up?" I asked in consternation.

"Those other kids . . . I like to paint and they tore up my watercolor and smashed my paint kit and they beat me up. They say I'm a girl, a little sissy . . . because they like football and I like to paint."

I placed a hand tenderly on his shoulder. "Artists go where football players fear to tread, son. Artists are more courageous than jocks. Artists have to develop the courage to face the darkness and the light, but jocks and most other people in this society don't have to do a damn thing except follow the dictates of pre-programmed emotional fluctuations based upon repression and perversion that have been handed down for centuries.

"They don't have to do any real work. They don't have to create something new. But as an artist, you do. Can you not see your own strength?"

He just stood there looking at me like I was some kind of alien from another planet. He didn't seem to understand, but at least I had his attention.

"Have those bullies done this before? Did you have reason to suspect they might do it again?"

He nodded slowly. His tears were beginning to dry.

"Where's your gun?"

"What?"

"Where's your gun? If you knew this would happen again why weren't you armed?"

"Sir . . . Santa Claus, my mom doesn't believe in guns. She won't let my dad have one and if I asked for one I just don't know what she'd do, but it wouldn't be nice. I'm afraid to ask her for even a toy gun. She gets ugly while pretending to be sweet and clamps down on me and takes away my privileges if I ask, so I don't ask anymore. She calls toy guns and swords war toys, and does petition drives to have them banned."

Well, here it was again. A polluted form of matriarchal intervention common to some degenerate societies. This kid's mom must be a spiritual prune, not at all like the juicy, powerful, male-accepting, male-loving women where I'm from. Just as Christianity and other primitive faiths created cultures where men repressed the feminine, so did the political correctness of some of the spiritually dry women of this time try to repress the masculine. The dimwitted primitive males couldn't see that by repressing the feminine they were repressing one of the most vital aspects of their own nature; the spiritually dry politically correct women couldn't see that by repressing the masculine they were hurting their loved ones and themselves. The sacred prostitutes--the juicy, juicy prostitutes--taught me that the male must become female and the female must become male. There can be no repression of either polarity in any individual or the illusion of separateness is created. Warfare results. There must be purification and integration and acceptance,   not separation and control. Only then can the sense of separation be dismissed as the illusion it is. The truth is that we are all one, but before we can experience this fact the illusion that we are separate from certain parts of our own nature must go. We must experience unity within before we can experience the wider unity of the cosmos. We are all ONE.

"I hate to have to tell you this, son, but your mom has no moral virtue. She mistakes repression and control for morality, and as a result she's become perverse. She doesn't know anything at all about real moral virtue, which consists of the dedication to discover the truth for yourself and to live that truth without interference from anyone or anything, and which therefore respects the rights of all beings to chart their path through life free of outside interference. And she has no understanding whatsoever of real morality itself, which starts with the right to self-defense. The right of individual protection of self is the foundation, the very root, of all moral development. Implicit in this principle is the fact that a moral person won't infringe on his neighbors. However, if his neighbor decides to infringe on the moral person, then the moral person has every right to handle it in any way he deems fit. It is morally permissible for him to use any level of force.

"Where I'm from, nobody comes along after a self-defense situation to try to determine if you used 'appropriate force'. Don't get me wrong, appropriate force is frequently a good thing and results in better energy in your life than if you'd used more force than necessary.

"However, the law exists to enforce morality. That's the only thing it can enforce. It can't enforce energy, it can't enforce spirituality. On the moral level you have an absolute, unqualified right to total self-defense, including defense of your property, which is an extension of your body. So where I'm from the law only asks, 'Who was the aggressor?' If the aggressor was killed or maimed, no one worries about it.

"If you went overboard in your use of force, that is a spiritual matter, not a moral matter. So the only way to deal with the energetic fallout from having used excessive force is to go into your heart and process and release all energy that you've held concerning the situation, and forgive yourself and everyone involved and drive on. Maybe next time you'll be more sensitive to the energetics of the situation and do better.

"And let me recommend that you see the prostitutes if you ever use excessive force. They're the best, most spiritually advanced beings in the world, and they'll help you purify yourself from your excesses and the imbalances brought on by conflict. And they'll help you arrive at an integrated and forgiving view of yourself, for they must become purified and integrated in all aspects of themselves before they can become accepted prostitutes. I can't think of a problem they can't help you with. I love them."

For a moment I think I'd forgotten what century I was in, as sometimes happens to a person who spends as much time between the dimensions as I do. Anyhow, by this time all the lad's tears were gone and he was just staring at me so wide-eyed I feared he'd get a brain hemorrhage. I knew I had to serve the boy; the Goddess would want me to help him. Plus, I also wanted to help him from my own heart. The prostitutes would want me to help him. What would the prostitutes do, I wondered, and then it was obvious and I knew how to serve this young grieving man.

"Hubert, hand me that .45."

He extended his robotic arm and handed Oliver North's weapon to me. During the night I'd had him make some more .45 ACP ammo, just in case. Both the Thompson and North's handgun fired this cartridge, which simplified logistics. I checked to insure a round was in the chamber, then made sure the magazine was fully stacked. The gun was good to go. I handed it to the boy. His face shone with wonder. No one had ever given him a gun before.

"This is an old-style gun, one of the first of the semi-automatics. You have to cock it like this," I showed him, "for the first shot, but it cocks itself for every shot thereafter. If you think you'll have to use it soon I recommend you keep it cocked, but make sure you keep the safety on until the moment of truth. Then all you'll have to do to fire it is to push the safety off and bang away.

"But be careful," I lectured, a tad sternly. "Never point a gun at anything you do not intend to shoot and always treat every gun with the respect due a loaded gun, even if you're positive it's unloaded. That's the only way to prevent accidents. Do you understand?"

He nodded slowly, a big old grin stretching from ear to ear. "You mean I can keep it?"

"Yes, but make sure you don't use it on any innocent person. That's bad karma."

"Wait'll those bullies see me with this! They won't bother me again."

"Maybe they will and maybe they won't, son. Bullies usually don't have much sense. If you're going to show them your gun you'd better be prepared to use it. If you're not, they may sense it and take it away from you. Then all hell would break loose and you'd be on the losing end of things.

"But if you do have to kill one or two of them, it's a pretty safe bet the survivors won't give you any more problems. Then you can go back to your painting."

A hard determination suddenly came into his eyes. "I think I'll kill them all, whether they give me any more problems or not. They deserve to die after what they did to me."

I sighed. This is the problem you always run into in these dysfunctional cultures. "Repression Creates Perversion." His parents and this alleged society had tried to suppress his most fundamental right, the right to defend himself, simply because they found the subject distasteful or inconvenient and lacked the moral courage to challenge their own preconceptions. They'd clearly never even given him the option of training in hand to hand combat; if they had the youth might have been able to handle the bullies without killing any of them. But now his tail was in a crack. He needed protection now, and that meant a gun.

Anyway, the repressive, shadow rejecting parents allowed the child to suffer. The result was that his own shadow side had gotten cluttered up with rage, hatred and confusion. So now that I'd given him the means to free himself from the suppression of his right to self-defense, he was caught in a storm of negative emotion and was on the verge of turning into a monster.

I now saw that I must give him some more moral guidance, and felt resentful at his parents for having never done the job. I frankly didn't want to spend any more time with this young man, for my first priority at the moment was to dodge the authorities, and with that red suit and sleigh I stood out like a sore erection.

But when duty calls, I always answer. I elaborated on my moral instruction. "Son, there's a time to kill and a time not to. Sometimes we kill in self-defense, but we *never* kill in vengeance. What's done is done. You can't go back and punish someone for what they've already done to you. If you do, you'll just keep yourself trapped in that same old vengeful energy and the cycle of hurt will go on and on. And every time you strike someone down in vengeance, you'll be striking down a part of yourself and postponing the day when you'll be whole. Vengeance is not justice; when the motive is to punish rather than to defend, the energy set in motion will hurt **you**, even if you win the confrontation.

"It's not your place or mine to try to do the job of karma, son. And neither of us has any idea as to what those bullies deserve. I guess they deserve love, as we all do, but they're cutting themselves off from it by their actions, which are sourced in the illusion of separation, which is itself sourced in the repression of the centuries they've been saddled with by parents and society. Anyway, it's not our place to judge them. We can point out their illusions, which to a primitive mind may look like judgment, but it certainly is not. *They* are not their illusions, but they are so identified with their illusions, particularly the paranoid illusion of separation, that when we point out their illusions they feel we're judging them. But we're not, nor can we. We aren't qualified to judge anyone or to determine what they deserve, other than making them aware that they deserve the love of the universe.

"In fact, if their parents and other alleged adults had demonstrated love for those bullies, then those bullies would never have become bullies. Undoubtedly, their parents have their heads up their asses and are tyrants to their kids, instead of shining examples of justice and love. They dishonor themselves by the way they raise their kids. Those bullies didn't deserve to be raised by authoritarian or neglectful parents, any more than you deserve to be bullied. *Everyone* deserves love, and everyone deserves regular demonstrations of that love. But the bullies are powerless at home, and they react against that disempowerment by striking out at you and other kids who have also been disempowered by parents and other so-called adults, but who respond to that disempowerment in a more passive fashion. So you and the bullies actually have a lot in common. You are two sides of the same damaged coin.

"So if you have to kill those other kids, it actually started with their parents and other adults who hurt them verbally or physically and took away their personal power by trivializing their existence. The alleged adults did not treat their children as equals, and this is the example those bullies are following when they prey on you. And it also started with your own parents for never being responsible or loving enough to see that you had the opportunity to learn assertiveness skills and unarmed close quarter combat techniques. Killing should be a last resort, but in your case it's your only resort, because you weren't given any other options except to be victimized, and victimization is never an option for anyone who's learning to love himself and stand up for his rights.

"But if you're still inclined toward vengeance, remember this: the karma of bullies always comes due. They'll see that soon enough; they'll reap what they've sown. You don't have to hunt them down or 'get even' with them. But the motive of the celestial beings we refer to as the Lords of Karma isn't vengeance, or that form of vengeance which attempts to hide itself under the name 'punishment'. The motive of the Lords of Karma is a high motive. They want to provide the corrective energies and experiences that are necessary to prompt each individual to seek redemption, they want to motivate the person to drop illusion and move into alignment with his own truest Self. Their motive is Love.

"Anyhow, that's what the prostitutes tell me. Now do you see?"

"No."

I sighed for maybe the thirteenth time. But really I expected this; it was the twenty-first century before what passed for education began to evolve into a semblance of true education by introducing a genuinely critical investigation into the nature of morality. That was the first step. Later the prostitutes would influence the educators into introducing spiritual energies, particularly the energy of the heart chakra, and helping youngsters begin the process of purification and of lining up their personalities with their own truest nature, which is Soul. But in 1982 the educational system was horseshit.

"It's like this, son. Have you ever heard of the Golden Rule?"

"You mean, do unto others as you want them to do unto you?"

"Yep. That's it. What do you suppose that means?"

"It means you'll go to hell if you don't do it."

I pulled off my beard and wig and stomped them fifteen or twenty times, but only screamed once or twice. Then it dawned on me: what the lad had said was essentially correct, though couched in the perverse notions of an archaic and bullshit value system.

I breathed deeply, got control of my faculties, stopped trembling. "Well, you're basically right, you will go to hell if you don't treat others the way you want to be treated. That's karma.

"Mistreating others causes you to remain locked in a cycle of grief and pain, because you'll be mistreated as a result. So if you want to feel-- how do you people say it? Groovey--yes, if you want to feel groovey you'll treat others the way you want to be treated, and that will cause higher energies to be set in motion that will bring you into the groovey condition you desire.

"So yes, you'll go to heaven if you treat others well, and you'll go to hell if you don't."

"What's that got to do with killing bullies?"

"It's not about them, it's about you! Don't you see, son? It has to do with the kind of life you want for yourself. If you want a good life, a life where you won't be infringed on, you'll focus on learning to treat others well, instead of putting your energies into vengeance. Basically, it's a matter of your choosing to build good, high positive energy instead of focusing on vengeance and other negativity and letting it drain you.

"Self-defense is a good thing; it's another way of treating yourself well and showing your love for yourself. Remember: love begins with self-love, just as sex usually begins with masturbation. But self-defense is certainly not vengeance, and vengeance has nothing to do with self-love, just as rape has nothing to do with sex. The vengeful and the rapist are wallowing in the same pool of negative energy and their motives are the same. They want to hurt someone because they have been hurt, apparently not realizing they'll continue to get hurt for as long as they have any appreciation for the vengeful mindset. But don't tell anyone around here that or they might confine you.

"So I think we've established that a civilized person appreciates and is willing to practice self-defense should the need arise, but decries and avoids vengeance. And if you're a loving and moral person and you have to defend yourself, you release the self-defense situation after it's over and you move on. You don't hold onto it. Releasing energies and emotions in the moment of experiencing them is what keeps them from turning into a thirst for vengeance. Or a thirst for 'punishment' if you are a vengeful person pretending to be civilized.

"Of course, since the desire for vengeance is already lodged in your body and energy field you'll have to pay attention to it, but with a different motive. The positive, healing motive is to feel the vengeful desire fully in a safe and supportive environment--if there is such a thing in this goddam timezone--where you won't be penalized or stigmatized for admitting and forcefully expressing these stored up negative energies. A holy place where they'll love you and won't be afraid of you when you admit you want to kill, and where they won't turn you over to the authorities for this admission or put you into some database as a dangerous person. It's every person's Goddess-given right to be dangerous anyway, as long as their lethality is only used for self-defense or defense of loved ones or property, but many of the primitive people of this century don't recognize this fact and will try to persecute anyone they regard as dangerous, even if he's never hurt a fly. Anyway, if the healers you work with love you, their practices won't include anything that might stigmatize you in any way. They will appreciate your courage for coming forward to do this work, and they will commend you as a person who has more balls and heart than most. If their practices include any form of stigmatization, however, leave immediately and don't return. The database keepers and the stigmatizers don't understand the healing process, they haven't yet matured. They don't understand that stigmatization cannot ever be a part of the healing process. They are covered up by fear and need healing themselves, but are afraid to face the hatred and rage in their own shadows so they devise control-freak schemes and are masters of justifying these schemes. Already you're too mature for them, don't trust them with your fate."

I noticed the kid's eyes were starting to glaze over a bit. I knew it was time for me to finish up my sermon. "Um, I think I got a little off track, but this century's so primitive and emotionally violent I tend to ramble on about its defects. Excuse me.

"As I was about to say before I got sidetracked, the important thing is to experience these negative energies fully so you can release them. Feel them, cuss a bit or throw up if necessary, and just let them go. You can't suppress them without running the risk of a violent explosion when you least expect it, and you *have* to feel them fully before you can let them go. But if releasing the negative energies is your motive, they *will* leave your body and heart and energy field as you experience and express them. Then you can fill up with love, and love will bring you everything.

" 'Seek ye first the Kingdom of Heaven,' a friend of mine once said, 'and all these things will be added unto you.' And he was right, so the prostitutes tell me, because the Kingdom of Heaven is the Kingdom of Love.

"Now do you dig it?"

"I dig that you must be a sex maniac the way you keep talking about prostitutes. You're going to hell. I'm getting out of here." He leveled the .45 at me and backed warily away, then turned and ran off down the street.

"I don't think he picked up on the Golden Rule," Hubert commented.

"No, and I'm beginning to wish I hadn't helped the little beggar. You know, any child of our time would've understood what I was saying, but these twentieth century children have all been so fragmented and abused they can't even grasp the simplest moral and spiritual truths.

"I've documented a lot of cultures over the years for the TAC, and the astonishing thing is that up until the Renaissance you could usually find people to discuss moral and spiritual issues with. Genuine spirituality is connected with juiciness, and genuine morality allows for and supports this juiciness. But when the Renaissance arrived, what little real spiritual awareness had survived the onslaught of degenerate Christianity all but vanished. There were no more Beltane fires anywhere, as far as I know, for the expression of the soul through the body was abhorred by both churchman and scientist. Finally they had a common enemy: the human body and positive loving emotion. There was still some interest in morality, but it was such an unbalanced and repressive morality it hardly deserved the name.

"These twentieth century people are still stuck in the dark heritage of the Renaissance."

A shot rang out down the street, then another. "I guess he got them," Hubert remarked, "or they got him."

"Yes, and it probably was an unnecessary event. If his parents had been responsible enough to see that he learned hand to hand combat, he would've whipped an ass or two and that probably would've been it. The bullies would've known to give him a wide berth or risk getting their testicles crushed or bones broken. But if not, then he could have resorted to a gun or blade. But as a result of the irresponsibility of his parents-- particularly his mom--a gun had to be his first choice.

"Twentieth century parents were known for trying to disenfranchise their offspring. They infringed on the will of their kids and allowed schools and churches to do the same, and even worse they polluted the hearts of their kids with materialism and control and manipulation. They have a saying here: 'There outta be a law.' Thing is, they've got millions upon millions of laws and no one is ever satisfied. Yet still they cry for more, and most of the time they try to justify their laws by saying it's for the good of the children. And so another law is passed . . . and these people are as miserable and frightened as they were before. Yet they continue to teach their kids that control and manipulation is the way, the truth, and the life, and that no one can ever be happy without trying to control everything. Yet the adults aren't happy; they've never for a moment felt true happiness or they wouldn't confuse that state with the legal system. They would know that happiness has no relationship to control and manipulation at all. But that's the way it's been on this earth for a long time--older people tricking younger people out of their personal power and convincing them to be true to something besides their own hearts. Of course, if you're not true to your own heart, you can't be genuinely true to anything else either, but I guess these people can't see that. They aren't civilized, after all. 'Lawbreakers, not lawmakers!' hasn't become the rallying cry for the political process yet, as it will in the 2020's, when a new breed of legislator will emerge that insists on disposing of two old laws for every new law passed.

"So one result of this oppressive indoctrination into the black magic of control and manipulation is that the minority of these kids who make the attempt to retrieve their personal power and restore their hearts almost always have to overreact in some way. They cause a riot, or they go on a shooting spree. 'Repression Creates Perversion.' If you squeeze a balloon at one end it's going to burst at the other end."

"Yes," Hubert agreed, "it seems that way to me. Certainly if these parents and educators and religious figures suddenly materialized in our time they'd be put in a hospital for the criminally insane. They could not be allowed to walk the streets and taint the children."

"Hubert, our kids wouldn't put up with them. You know that."

He shuddered. "Yes, but I would hate to have to watch what happened if you took a bunch of fractured, powerless, control freak twentieth century adults and exposed them to our powerful and loving children. The children would handle the process as humanely as possible, but I still wouldn't want to watch."

"Nor would I, Hubert."

We heard a strange wailing sound, then a car with flashing lights and official symbols on it roared up. I saw that we were faced with some type of constable. My energy pistol rode comfortably in my Santa's pocket. But somehow I felt this guy wasn't looking for me.

"Did you hear any gunshots?"

"Yes, constable. They came from down the street." I pointed.

"Did you see what happened? Did you see anybody with a gun?"

"Yes, I saw a young man about ten or eleven years old who carried a Colt Model 1911 semi-automatic handgun."

The constable blanched. His respiration speeded up, but became more shallow. He spoke briefly into a communications device.

"What was this kid wearing?"

"He wore a red coat, probably filled with goose down. His trousers were sort of a faded blue. Snot was coming out his nose."

"Anything else you can tell me about this kid?"

"He felt powerless, as though he'd been cut away from his manhood. He didn't understand the Golden Rule. And he'd been weeping."

The constable roared off. "Well," Hubert remarked, "they picked a fine time to send backup for the kid. They should have been empowering him from the time he lay resting in the womb."

"Agreed, buddy. But I'm not sure that cop was sent as backup to help the lad deal with those bullies. The illogical mindset (assuming the mind actually has anything to do with it) of the so-called adults of the Twentieth leads them first to disempower their children, then when the children struggle mightily to reclaim their power and wisdom and love the adults try to crush them totally and extinguish every spark of spirit. I know it sounds unbelievable, but they'll probably put that kid in jail, then use a form of mad scientist called a psychiatrist to destroy his personality and re-write his programming.

"Or they may simply shoot the boy. Sometimes cops in this century shot children, and even adults, for no other reason than exercising their Constitutional right to keep and bear arms. This was unheard of in the previous century, but twentieth century cops are trained to overreact when they see someone with a gun. It has to be that way in a system that is suspicious of self-defense."

"What happens to the cops when they overreact?"

"Nothing, usually."

Another wailing vehicle roared down the street. I recognized it as being an emergency medical vehicle.

"Hubert, we'd better fly. If that kid's still alive they'll either beat him or psychologically manipulate him 'till he tells where he got that gun, and then they'll come after us. Believe it or not, the authorities of this century sometimes consider the provider of a weapon to be responsible for vengeful acts perpetrated by the bearer of the weapon, even when the provider lectures about firearms safety and the necessity of using arms only for self-defense and not for vengeance, as I did just now. Insane, but the people of the Twentieth, particularly the last half of the century, want to torment as many people as possible in their jails and prisons because nearly every citizen has a thirst for vengeance, to one degree or another, and that thirst is one that can never be quenched by anything other than love. But they haven't learned about love yet, despite their pretensions to the contrary.

"We're already considered terrorists by the federal government, let's get out of here before we have to deal with the local yokels."

Hubert grunted assent. I climbed into him and pulled the cockpit bubble down. Hubert leapt into the sky as more official vehicles roared down the street. "Ho Ho Ho!" he yelled.

CHAPTER THIRTEEN

Hubert was a truck again. I'd asked him not to color himself purple this time as I felt the authorities might link reports of a flying sleigh with reports of a flying purple Dodge pickup, assuming those cowboys near Lincoln had reported us.

So now Hubert was an orange Chevrolet. He serenaded me with country and western music culled from the airways as we trudged slowly down the interstate towards Amarillo.

> "We don't smoke marijuana in Muskogee
> We don't take our trips on LSD . . ."

This music had been created by someone called The Hag. What kind of title could that be? In more spiritually advanced cultures the title of Hag was sometimes given out of respect and appreciation to an elder wise woman, but there was little in the Twentieth that could be considered spiritually advanced. Plus, this Hag sang with the voice of a male. It was a rich voice.

"He doesn't like drugs," Hubert said.

"No, and that's a mark in his favor. I think you'll agree that practically everyone we've met so far in this century must be a dope fiend. Just look at how they've responded to us. Even when we're following their benighted materialistic customs they still knock us in the head with baseball bats and take us prisoner."

Hubert suppressed a chuckle. "Maybe this Hag is a forerunner of our own people. Most of our people don't use marijuana or LSD either, even though there's no laws against it."

"That's right. Marijuana has a deleterious effect on the will and LSD opens the crown chakra, irrespective of whether the individual's other chakras are open and balanced, and irrespective of whether the individual has become heart centered and morally purified.

"Marijuana keeps some people from functioning and even interferes with the sex drive of many of its adherents. Our people want to fuck at full capacity and they want to experience the utmost in pleasure and love. Therefore, it's only logical that most of us avoid marijuana."

"And LSD sometimes creates monsters," Hubert put in. "That friend of yours, the prostitute who runs the Asheville Diocese, what's her name? Yes, Amanda, that's right. I've gone to some of her lectures and I remember a discussion about drugs. She pointed out that the opening of the crown chakra without first experiencing moral purification and learning to stay centered in the heart is an invitation to disaster. You could go insane and dump all your files and become a veggie. Or you could become a murderous monster. This doesn't happen to everyone who uses LSD and prematurely opens their crown chakra, of course, but what kind of fool wants to take that kind of risk?"

I thought of my cousin Rufus-Pete. He'd taken LSD a few times, and maybe even worse he seldom went to temple and didn't have much use for the wisdom of the prostitutes. He'd become unbalanced and had to fight like hell for his sanity. He began to realize he should never have forsaken the love of Aphrodite, so he went to the temple and the prostitutes, being generous and compassionate, had let him live there for months on end as they gently helped restore him to himself. After that he never missed temple if he could help it and even tried to become a sacred prostitute himself, but Amanda gently turned him down. Of course she interviewed him and let him take the test to qualify for Probationer, but he flunked it as most people do. A life of sacredness demands the utmost in discipline and purity of heart. And character. Rufus-Pete didn't qualify as a Probationer, but at least the sacred women of my Goddess had helped restore his character and get him started on the journey to his heart. He loved them and became an apt pupil.

"Did you hear what he just said?" Hubert gasped incredulously. "The Hag doesn't like orgies, either. He couldn't be one of our forerunners!"

"No Hubert, he couldn't. Not if he supports sexual repression. The folks in this timezone, as well as in some previous timezones, confuse repression with discipline. They're too frightened of what they might see in the mirror if they accepted the truth that genuine discipline involves a total exploration of themselves, including the raunchy parts.

"They equate darkness with evil and so try to repress it and focus only on what they consider to be the light. Whereas you and I know that the darkness itself isn't evil, although it is true that evil seems to prefer to hide in the darkness. Hell, it's probably evil itself that convinced people that darkness was evil so they would be too afraid of their own shadows to explore this aspect of themselves. Then they wouldn't be able to evict the evil. It just hides there and takes every opportunity to create negativity in their lives, for as every modern person knows, evil delights in negativity. Evil feeds on negativity. This is literally true. These people become food for evil by their refusal to explore and purify and reclaim their own dark side.

"The darkness itself isn't evil, it's a necessary and powerful part of every human being. But the evil and confusion and separateness and glamour have to be cleaned out of the darkness and flushed down the toilet. Then you're left with a pure, limpid darkness which harbors no negativity, no food for evil, nor does it harbor that false jocular positive attitude that many people try to adopt as an antidote for negativity. The jocular positivity is itself sourced in evil because it is sourced in the denial of evil. Evil wants people to deny it's existence in and around themselves so it can carry out it's activities without interference. Anything that fosters a denial of evil, therefore, is sourced in evil because it works to evil's advantage.

"Anyway, every person who studies under Amanda and her holy sisters is working toward cleaning out their shadows so they'll be able to rest in that pure and limpid darkness once the confusion is gone. This purified darkness helps protect you and nurtures you and helps you create. Yes . . ." I sighed, "it gives you rest. It gives you rest."

Hubert hummed along.

I figured we'd rest up in Amarillo, then cruise down to Austin and report in to the station chief. Austin was the home of the main office of the TAC for the Western Hemisphere in this timezone. If I hadn't been getting nookie and visiting with the President I already would have reported in. But my dick ranks higher in importance than following protocol.

"Amarillo city limits, Sonny-Bob. Wake up."

I started. Amarillo sure had changed since the last time I'd seen it. Several years ago I'd gone on a research mission to this area during the fourteenth century. I was the only White Eyes around back then. I guess that's why I was such a curiosity to the natives.

I'd camped on a canyon rim and howled along with the wild, wild wolves. I'd run like hell with the bison, mainly to get away from them. And Hemingway and I had had many passionate adventures with the dark and beautiful women of the era.

In my own timezone the people of the Amarillo area had begun to work harmoniously with nature instead of rising up against Her. They got rid of the ugly thrusting buildings and built tasteful vulva shaped structures. In those instances where a thrusting structure was considered desirable they shaped the building exactly like a cock. Amarillo became known as "The City Of Cocks And Vulvas" and was admired around the world for its tasteful architecture. It was considered the Constantinople of my time and was a place of great learning. Tibetan Buddhist monks and prostitutes were everywhere.

There were free roaming herds of elk, bison and antelope and the people had reintroduced wolves. Yes, wolves wandered among the giant cocks and vulvas. The Human People and the Wolf People had learned tolerance, compassion and respect for one another. Each took advantage of the other's unique wisdom.

There was even a modicum of grizzly bear.

It had been twelve or fifteen years since I'd visited the Amarillo of my time. But my memories of the beauty of the place in either ancient times or my own contrasted rather sharply with the twentieth century reality. Like everything else I'd seen in the Twentieth, this Amarillo was marked by the subjugation of nature and ugly malformed penises thrusting at the vulva of the sky. There was no hint of sacredness here, or in any other twentieth century location I'd visited so far, with the exception of the Wal-Mart parking lot where Lucille The Prophetess had initiated me into her mysteries.

Even the churches in this benighted century bore no aura of sacredness. They were built as testaments to man's egotism instead of receptacles of warm and passionate love.

I knew that my precious Lucille and her goddess friends would one day change all this, and that they would do it without the angry and vengeful attitudes and methods of the "femi-nazis" of the Twentieth.

Lucille and her merry band of lovely healers would show that the real power of the universe is Love, and that its most powerful and unified expression on this earth is experienced when people come together for a sacred session of heart centered sex. Lucille and her goodly company would show humanity that sex is an art like any other art, and that as with any other art love must be its source. If love isn't the source of any given artistic expression, then that particular expression isn't art at all, it's just a pale pretender to the throne. It may be okay technically, but art isn't about technical perfection. It's about Love.

"Are you thinking about Lucille again?"

"Yes I am, and how can you tell?"

"Because, my captain, whenever you're thinking or talking about Lucille you always get that 'distant horizons' look in your eye and your heart starts beating so strongly that even I can feel it."

"I see. I didn't know I was so obvious. Anyway, I was just thinking about how one redheaded woman and her merry sexual healers managed to change this whole benighted culture into something resembling civilization. About how this alleged culture, which today is so completely lost in mad grasping greed, went from materialism to at least a basic appreciation of sacredness in just a few decades.

"Control and manipulation ceased to be the ideal, and the purification of the character and the pursuit of one's own heart became of prime importance.

"We owe Lucille everything, Hubert. We owe her everything." And that went double for me.

We were silent for a while as Hubert cruised the length and breadth of the city. I felt at home here despite its twentieth century depravity. And admittedly, it wasn't nearly as ugly or negative a place as many other twentieth century cities. If I were a native of the Twentieth I wouldn't mind living here. The place certainly beat Albuquerque, what with that city's hateful children.

"Hubert, I need to get out and stretch my legs and drink something warm. Hemingway's temperature has fallen too low. Look for a bar, will you?"

"Ten-four."

After Hubert had changed himself into his current form we'd stopped at a place called a truck stop which advertised that it had showers. Hemingway and I bathed and the gunpowder and blood and sweat of the previous night were washed away. I thanked the lady behind the counter on the way out, then went to Hubert and got dressed. It was good to be clean again. Now I was fit to go bar hopping.

"This street has several bars, Sonny-Bob. Look lively, tell me when you want to stop."

One joint sported a sign that said:

Jugs And Jiggles

Your Full Service Nudie Bar

"Finally," I sighed, "a bar where I won't have to wear any clothes. Pull over, please." Hubert parked himself and I went inside.

I had no need for alcohol, as I was still glowing from having taken jellybean sacrament from Reagan's hand. I ordered half a gallon of sexnog, but found they didn't have that here. I settled for coffee, then went to a table and disrobed. People were looking at me strangely, which I knew they would because of the size of my love monster. But I did have to wonder why only the women were naked in this proto-temple. Maybe in the twentieth century women were the only ones comfortable with their bodies, as long as their bodies conformed to the desired parameters of the culture.

A beautiful woman approached and I wagged my dick at her. She just smiled . . .

Across the way a fairly pretty young lady, who'd just been gyrating on a goddess stage to some god awful music, gave me the eye, then turned her back on me. Well, it wasn't a pleasant feeling to be spurned, but as I watched her I saw that she appeared a little lethargic and that she couldn't look anyone in the eye for more than a fraction of a second. I didn't know how this could be, for she was a female. Everyone respects females and females are powerful.

But then I remembered what century I was in. People didn't respect the feminine here and tried to restrict it as much as possible. And women frequently didn't respect themselves and were ashamed of their sexual apparatus and, like these primitive males, believed sexuality should be controlled and twisted and practiced only in dark and polluted places. This is what Christianity and other repressive religions had brought them to. And these Christians practiced the dark and polluted ways every day in their own hearts, and some of them secretly snuck out of their churches whenever possible to physically act out their dark and polluted fantasies.

It was an endless cycle of repression and perversion into which no love could flow. For it is impossible to be a repressive one minute and a lover the next minute. All repression, and therefore all perversion, must be completely gone before love can flow. But the people of this Christianized country didn't know that, for they equated a form of sloppy emotionalism with love, a sentimentality that flowed from the same polluted pool as every other form of negative emotion. They did not know that love is not an emotion, but a Force which can radiate out from the heart and permeate the human being if the individual is dedicated enough and disciplined enough to clear the repression and perversion out of his shadow, and then keep his consciousness centered on his heart. Yes, love can flow through the emotions, just as it can flow through the physical body and the mind and the whole personality. But love is not any of these things. "Love is not **who** the human being is," Amanda once told me. "Love is **what** the human being is. Study on this."

Anyhow, the women of this time hadn't quite come of age as the spiritual force which they are. My respect for women automatically doubled, then tripled, as I considered the obstacles they'd had to overcome in order to start the process of redemption for all humanity in the early twenty-first century. I loved them so.

I began to feel a certain sensation in my lower chakras that was not altogether unpleasant as I surveyed the lovely nude women before me. I was sorry they did not have a well-lighted goddess temple to dance in, but I knew they were doing the best they could. Just as women seem to flow with the highest spiritual forces of my own time, it seemed to me that these women here probably flowed with the highest spiritual forces of their own depraved society. There was no question in my mind that they were morally and spiritually superior to their oppressors, who had taken the light of God's love out of sexuality with their religions of self-hatred and vengeance. I guess these women of this nudie bar were doing what they could to keep the spark of loving sexuality alive until the day it could be rekindled upon the earth and manifest in a roaring flame. In this respect they were similar to those old-timey mystery schools who had managed to keep a tiny spark of spirituality alive during the materialistic ages of the past two thousand years. In both instances the spark was weak, but something is better than nothing. A fart from God's ass is better than a pot of gold from Satan.

I returned my attention to the young lady who had spurned my beauty. She wore what seemed to be a permanent, fixed frown, not quite a scowl. She also wore several strategically placed tattoos which I would've found very tasteful and attractive, but I just couldn't get past that frown. She'd stopped at an empty table and put her foot on a chair to adjust her shoe. I'd noticed that all the ladies here wore a type of open-toed shoe which was designed to seductively reveal the digits with their shiny, shiny nails. I must admit I liked those shoes. But shoes and tattoos were the only things any of them had on, no skirts, no thongs, no slingshots. Their pussies were free agents and saluted the world. I liked that, too.

As she straightened up I found myself wondering if she were descended from some of the aboriginal peoples who'd once roamed this area. She was fairly dark, with black hair of no more than a moderate length, which was starting to grow a little shaggy, almost as though she was just tired of taking care of it and wanted to forget about it. She glanced at me and I smiled, but she turned away and went back to her business. I found myself wondering if she might be one of my descendants, since I'd helped the aboriginal peoples of the area repopulate themselves during my visit to the fourteenth century. It was possible. I wouldn't be surprised if she were one of my distant granddaughters. But from her attitude thus far I knew she wouldn't submit to a DNA test.

A fellow waved some twentieth century money at her, and she took it and climbed upon him and pressed her pussy into his face as he sat there. It looked like she had him by the ears and was sort of scrubbing her pussy with his face. I enjoyed watching this; maybe these twentieth century people weren't quite as degenerate as I'd thought. Maybe a few of them understood the basics of worship.

Suddenly the guy grabbed her butt fiercely and yanked her down onto his lap. She was kind of gyrating on his lap, a move sure to raise a certain hardness. But I didn't like how she'd gotten there; the man had been rough with her. His fingers clinched her ass so hard I fancied I could almost see red welts being raised.

A waitress came to me. She wore shorts and a t-shirt that didn't quite reach her navel. She wore no slingshot underneath. "Are you ready for another drink, honey?" Her eyes sparkled with mirth. "Or are you thinking about trying out to be a dancer?"

"No ma'am, I don't want to dance right now. I would dance with you, but I am disturbed. Is that guy hurting that woman over there?"

She glanced at the two of them, then softly bit her lip. "No honey, it's just a little game they play, he's a regular. Sometimes it may look a little rough, but he pays her well."

"I'd pay her to stay away from him, or him to stay away from her," I said, noting with alarm he'd grabbed her by the hair with one hand and held her head cocked at an angle while he bit and slobbered on her titty. Then he squeezed the titty so hard I thought it would surely burst. "Ma'am, you can't tell me that doesn't hurt. Look!"

The waitress--whom I liked very much and would have taken some time to be with if I hadn't been concerned for the other woman--pressed my shoulder in reassurance, but her own mood had grown more somber. "That's none of our concern, sweetheart. You just relax and try to have some fun. I'll send one of the dancers over to you, okay?"

The lady I was concerned about was biting her lip and crying now, as the big oaf repeatedly yanked her head around with one hand while his other hand was shoved up her pussy; it must've been nearly to her tonsils by now. And he kept drooling on her and yanking her head around and biting on her . . .

Suddenly I rose up, and when the fool looked up and found me there he also found he had a broken finger, which I'd delivered. He released her hair.

"Get your hand out of this woman's pussy," I told him, pressing a finger against his eyeball, ready to either gouge the eye or to flick my finger and explode it, if he proved uncooperative. But he took his hand out of her and looked confused, while the woman just looked dazed, tears streaking her face and blood on her lip.

"You shouldn't hurt women, particularly those who give you the opportunity to worship, as this one has."

Suddenly his head jerked back and his eyes grew wild, but he grabbed his coat and ran away, leaving the lady sprawled on the floor. She was covered with red welts and bruises from the clinching and the biting, and I suddenly realized I wanted to send the perpetrator to meet his goddess, but now he was nowhere to be found. That might have been uncivilized of me anyway, for it might have to be classed as borderline vengeance, and no civilized person partakes of vengeance.

I squatted down beside the suffering woman and stroked her shoulder, then carefully helped her to her feet. "I'm Sonny-Bob," I said gently. "What's your name?"

She sort of gasped and coughed, then shook her head. Then she almost looked at me. "My name's Raven, you s.o.b., and you just broke the finger of a good customer, comes in every week."

"But Raven," I protested, "he was hurting you! Look, you've got red welts all over you, and bruises, too."

"I get hurt all the time, dipshit. That's life. But at least I get paid for it. Now that guy probably won't be back, and I make two or three hundred bucks a month from him. Sometimes more, for extra favors."

"If all you want is money, Raven, I'll give you money. I've got plenty."

For the first time she looked at me. She was glaring. "You'd better have plenty."

I led her back to my table. I groped my pants and found my wallet. I looked for one of those bills the Secret Service guy said was still legal, a "1" followed by four zeros. I gave it to her, then gave her another for good measure. "Is this enough to cover your losses for the week, Raven?"

She appeared dumbfounded. I supposed I hadn't given her enough and started searching for another bill. She grabbed my arm. "Honey, for that kind of cash you can do anything to me you want, even fuck me with a broomstick if that's what gets you off. *Two* broomsticks at the same time, and a vacuum cleaner stuck up my ass. That sound good to you, sweetie?"

Her hand was on my cheek, then squeezing my shoulder, but I didn't like the look in her eyes. I could detect the very slightest glimmer of

light, but not much. She was barely home. She was nearly extinguished.
I didn't like this.

Her tongue glided across her slick teeth. "What do you like to do,
Baby? Is Baby shy? Come to Mama, Baby. Mama will let you have it
the way you like it."

She was leading me and I reluctantly let her. We stopped at a large-
assed sofa, large enough to lie down on, and she did. She opened her
legs and began massaging her clit, then fingering herself. "Oooh, sooo
good, honey. Does Baby want to finger Mama's pussy?" In truth I did
not.

She licked the finger she'd had in her pussy, and I guess she must've
seen some kind of light in **my** eyes, for I do like the taste of a hot little
pussy, though hers was rather big and floppy. Anyhow, she held the
finger she'd been licking up to me.

"Here, Baby. Come to Mama's pussy. Taste Mama's pussy, Baby,
taste it. That's right, come on."

And I did bow down and began gently to suck her finger. "Is any
pussy juice left on Mama's finger, Baby? Have you sucked it all? Well,
Mama has another treat for her Slut Baby, yes she does. Here, Slut
Baby, here. Taste *these* fingers, Mama's pussy is fresh on *these* fingers.
Suck Mama's pussy fingers.

"Ooooh, little baby, that's right. Suck Mama's pussy fingers. Does
Mama's pussy taste good, little baby? Does it taste sweet?" I had to
admit to myself that it was passable. Hemingway was getting hard and
she grabbed him. She toyed with him, she stroked him as I sucked
Mama's pussy fingers.

"Baby has a huge dick, oooh, Baby's cock is HUGE! I can't wait 'till
he grows up, I can't wait . . . and I **won't** wait. Mama's gonna fuck her
little baby, she's gonna fuck him then suck her juices off his dick, that's
what she's gonna do. Ooooh, Mama's pussy fingers feel soooo good in
Baby's mouth!"

She was working her fingers around in my mouth, getting pretty wild
with it, the way she smeared her fingers on my tongue and across my
lips. I was starting to like her a little bit, but enough was enough.

"Ma'am, I don't much like baby talk. You taste okay, and you're
very nice, but I wish you wouldn't talk to me in baby talk."

She sat up. "Then let me go get those broomsticks and you can fuck
me with them. You don't even have to use lubrication, if it skins up my
pussy there's no extra charge. And the vacuum cleaner, and anything
else you want to stick in my pussy, up my ass, or down my throat.
Anything! Including that big cock of yours." She stroked him. "I like

you, Big Boy," she cooed to Hemingway.

"No, ma'am. I don't want to stick anything up you. Not right now, anyway. I appreciate the offer, but I like to take a moment to pause and feel a woman's energy before I fuck her or taste her. I guess I'm old-fashioned."

She laughed. It was the first time I'd seen even the hint of mirth on her face. *Now*, I thought, *we may be getting somewhere.*

"Kinky, Baby--oops, what was your name? Okay, Sonny-Bob, you can feel my energy, whatever that means."

"Stand up, please ma'am."

She stood and lifted her arms languidly above her head as I ran my hands along her aura. She shivered, but at the same time got a little warmer.

I'd begun to understand that I'd paid not only for the customer I'd sent away, but I must've overpaid her. Otherwise her attitude towards me wouldn't have changed so quickly and dramatically.

Suddenly I began to like her. Her energy was rough and her heart polluted, but I began to feel a sort of empathy for her, despite the fact I'd never been fucked with a broomstick and never intended to be.

I wanted to kiss her, and did so very lightly on her lips. She shivered again, and grew warmer still.

Maybe this won't be so bad if I can just stop thinking about those broomsticks.

"Well, ma'am, I've already tasted your pussy, and to tell you the truth I like pussy better than any other seafood. If you'll position yourself, I'll just lie down here." I did so as she moved to get into position. My hand rested on her outer thigh and I felt my empathy for her grow stronger. Her other leg was already across me and I could see the Gate of Heaven, but it was certainly rusty from disrespect.

She mounted my face and sort of leaned forward, her arms resting on the sofa's arm. The sofa was sturdy and well designed.

I pushed her off my face a little and sort of massaged those floppy, sloppy pussy lips. I was beginning to feel the first faint stirrings of wanting to please her, but didn't know if I could. She was weird.

And she'd clearly been hurt, so sex meant nothing to her, it was only a means of commerce, just a way of getting what she wanted in the loveless cage her karma had brought her to. The prostitutes in my own time would have been shocked. They never asked for anything except that you respect women and the Goddess.

I breathed a short prayer to the Lords of Karma, hoping they could find it in their hearts to somehow prod this woman into beginning to release the old stuff and at least get the idea there might be something new for her. But I confess, based on what I'd seen so far, at that particular moment I didn't have much faith that the prayer could be answered. The Lords of Karma don't arbitrarily strip the old shit away, it's against their regulations. You have to be willing to process and release it and if you are, no matter what hell you've fallen into, the Lords of Karma and the angels that surround you will help you gradually release the old stuff and accept the new. It usually takes a hell of a lot longer than a person expects, so they say. These are the teachings of Aphrodite and Reagan.

I kissed her sloppy floppy pussy, then licked it, hoping I wouldn't wind up with splinters in my tongue from those broomsticks. But really, I was starting to like her . . . I shrugged. I guess for a guy who wanted to grow and evolve into a sacred prostitute one day this was good training. It's all about healing, you know.

I found her clit and toyed with it, then I began to eat her with some fervor.

"Sometimes I feel like a whore."

I stopped my slurping and smacking. "What?"

"Sometimes I feel like a whore."

"You're not a whore, sweetie. You're a little better than a whore. And with a little more refinement, which you could experience if you worked hard on your character, you might even be able to apply to a sacred lovesex temple if you lived where I come from. You might be accepted as a Probationer.

"You and I are in the same boat. I want to be a prostitute, and you pretty much are one, though not a sacred one. I'm working towards sacredness and if you do the same work you can make the same progress. I'm learning to love, and I particularly love women, even those I never physically touch. As long as there's at least a little light in their eyes I can appreciate their glowing.

"I feel exalted in the presence of women, even in your presence. I saw you had a little light in you or I never would have gone near you, let alone permitted you to sit on my face.

"I appreciate your light as well as your tasty pussy, which I congratulate you on taking such good care of. You are clean, fragrant and appear healthy. If you learn to purify and strengthen your character-- getting free of control and manipulation and processing and releasing your grief and agony--as well as meditate and focus on the personal Light of your heart, your Light will grow and soon you'll glow. And your purified and strengthened character will be a good vehicle for your

Light to shine through. I'd like to see you then. I'd like to adore you then.

"You are the embryo of a goddess, and if you make it to term and are born into the spiritual world I'll be the first to congratulate you, then kneel at your feet and be inspired by you.

"Then I would serve you with my whole heart."

She was crying, as so many women do when I start rattling on about how special they are, or about how special they *could* be if they would purify their characters and grow friendly with their souls. And in truth, I'd seldom talked like this until I left to undo the winter. The Prostitutes of Aphrodite had tried to teach me these sacred truths for decades, but being easily satisfied with the regular pleasures of this world I'd been a blockhead at my studies. The women I'd known who had gone into sacred prostitution had learned this stuff easily and quickly compared to me. I guess that's another reason I respect women.

But somehow I'd begun to blossom almost in spite of myself. I guess I'd grown wise enough and receptive enough to experience some higher levels of the Goddess. There was no question that the glow of heart-centered pleasure was vastly superior to mere lust. And as I'd found, genuine heart-centered pleasure can kick in anytime, once you've made the initial pioneering link between heart and genitals. Now I was growing quickly, thanks to my own receptivity to the higher love of the Goddess, and thanks to these splendid twentieth century females. I guess somehow I'd stumbled onto the very best females this century had to offer, what with my interactions with Lucille The Prophetess and Amber of Shoney's. And now I was with the embryo of yet another goddess. I couldn't stay to coax her along (and even if I could, she'd probably grow so fast she'd be teaching me in a couple of months) but at least I could plant the seeds of love and of a pure character.

I reached up and stroked the undersides of her breasts, then flicked the undersides of her rigid nipples slightly, and then she began to groan desperately. She'd been mostly faking up 'till now, as women in primitive timezones tended to do, but I knew I could bring her along with sweetness and patience.

I wanted to stick my little finger partway into her anus, but with her bucking slightly I couldn't find the opening. It was there somewhere and I knew if I kept at it fate would deliver it into my hands, but I shrugged and relaxed. There was no use in working too hard when **I** was paying **her**.

Her juices began to drip into my mouth and she began humping my face with renewed dedication. She writhed. Her moans were really quite forthcoming. My cheeks were lubricated by her sweet essence, and the stuff was better than the coffee they served here.

I ate.

She screamed at the end of my meal, hands on her titties pinching her nipples furiously and humping my blessed jowls as her clit slipped away from me and disappeared into a tasty zone of camouflage. With finger and tongue captured by the strength of her grasping pussy, all I could do was hang on for the ride. A final climatic orgasm, a release of liquid zeal, and my meal was over. It had ended without a bang, but I guess I didn't really want to bang her. I think all I wanted to do was serve her. I shook my heads disgustedly. Hemingway wasn't likely to put up with this behavior much longer.

The lady's quakes were reduced to small tremors as she cried and cried. Her tears fell upon me like rose petals and I loved her. Finally, she paused and took some deep breaths. She was covered with sweat and tears and her hair was damp and plastered to her forehead.

She slid her pussy off my face and slid her body down along mine, pausing to give me just a taste of titty, but not much. I guess her nipples were still tender. Then she slid down further and her mouth was on me, her mouth was on my mouth, and she flicked her tongue into me and drew out much of her own pussy juice and swallowed it. Well, I didn't need the calories, anyway.

We each had a little pussy juice running down our cheeks now . . . her tongue licked around the rim of her lips a couple times as she savored herself, then her back arched and her head rotated in tight sensuality before another wet release and I felt the flood of it upon my cock as she lay upon me and I was a glad man as I performed my function in the universe, the function of loving WOMAN, and of being exalted into HER sphere, the realm of unchained femininity where I as a free male could roam amid her spiritual juiciness as well as her corresponding physical manifestations. The truly spiritual fly freely across the planes of experience and are at home everywhere.

I held her tightly for a moment, then she rose up and slowly licked her come off my cheeks, then shared it with me in a long, deep kiss. It had been a mistake when I had initially viewed her as a non-sacred woman. Goddesses are everywhere, waiting to be brought out of their shells. This woman tasted like Heaven to me now.

Raven whimpered and lay atop me for a while, occasionally giving another small shudder. I touched her back and butt with tenderness, hoping in some small way to offset some of the harshness of her life. She deserved tenderness as much as any woman I have ever been privileged to hold. I ran my hands down her beautiful lats and obliques.

Finally we locked fingers, she atop me, and we held it, and even the friction of our fingers moving together was warming. I kissed her nails.

She brought a light kiss to me then, tongue running a circuit just inside my mouth, then back upon my lips. Then she slowly and softly bit my lips, savoring them as I had begun to savor her. There was more Light in her now, and I knew this day would be a happy one for her.

She looked into my eyes for a long, long time then, and she was unafraid. And the threshold of heart-consciousness I'd been in pretty much throughout this whole experience expanded a little more, and I felt my heart touch hers. We both were warm.

She smiled. "Well, I wasn't expecting this today, hon."

"I expect something pretty similar to this just about every day. I can't seem to avoid it."

My voice became softer. "But I didn't want to avoid making love with you, sweetheart. I'm glad we did this." I gently stroked her cheek, and in my expanding heart-consciousness I was telling the truth. Heart and flesh were coordinated, more or less, and I felt a gentle stream of gladness that I'd been able to serve this wonderful woman. For all women are wonderful. All of them.

We lay awhile, gently breathing together, and she said, "I'm not sure I understand what you were talking about, temples and prostitutes and so on, but honey I got you on character and Light. I got you."

And she did. She was glowing more steadily now and something had also changed with her personality, it was purer, cleaner somehow. It better reflected the Light of her Self.

I loved her.

We irradiated each other and my heart knew joy. She smiled at me, then rolled off me and I sat up. My bones were sore, but nanos would fix that.

She stood before me, she took my face in her hands and drew me to her and I kissed her stomach and rested my head there. Her hands lay softly upon my hair.

And after a while the moment was over. You can't hold on to a river.

I stood and took her hands in mine and we stood with one another, breathing upon each other in a radiant accepting splendor and opening the windows of the soul to a full scrutiny.

She was clean. I felt humbled and glad to have shared with her.

I kissed her on the cheek and left the bar. As I was about to step into Hubert someone came running out and gave me my clothes. I kissed him, too.

CHAPTER FOURTEEN

After leaving Raven of Amarillo Hubert and I had found an inn, as I needed a good night's sleep. There was a primitive journalistic device in my room. It was called a television set and they did not charge extra for it. It also ran entertainment programs, and I laughed and laughed at one program about three men called stooges. One of them tried to tear another's nose off with a pair of tongs. It was very funny.

The next morning I lolled in my bed with a young prostitute who'd been content with one bill that had four zeros. She said her name was Chantal and that she'd like to be a journalist one day. "It's not all it's cracked up to be, Chantal," I told her.

We watched the morning newscast together, this Chantal and I, and I must confess my heart skipped a beat when suddenly my face appeared on the screen of this device. What could this mean?

" . . . wanted by federal authorities and charged with thirty-nine felony counts and ninety-four misdemeanors, this arms dealing Santa Claus spreads Christmas terror in his wake, the most recent incident being yesterday's tragic shooting in Albuquerque. We've just learned that the gun used in that shooting is the property of the United States Marine Corps, and that it was assigned to a Major Oliver North. The gun was apparently stolen by one of the deranged Santa's accomplices and given to him so he could escape federal custody. No charges are currently being brought against Major North, but the Pentagon informs us an investigation is underway."

"Look at that, Chantal," I snorted disgustedly. "They devote most of their newscast to a gun, which is nothing more than an inanimate object, a tool for humanity's betterment. And they slander the tool, refusing to look beyond the appearances of the moment to determine the reasons the tool was employed. They jump to wild-eyed, fearful conclusions because they're faced with something they feel they can't control, and losing control frightens them more than anything, for on some level they know that the thing they fear losing control to is skulking around somewhere in their own shadow side. So they won't do the disciplined work necessary to reveal the true causes of the problem, or even what the nature of the problem is. They automatically assume the shooting is the crime, instead of going to the trouble to discover the real crime, which was the fact that the young man was abused by a tribe of young Neanderthals. He had every right to shoot them, as long as he acted in self-defense rather than vengeance. Neither you, nor I, nor any other human being has to suffer at the hands of the violent. We have every right to kill them if it's necessary. Please note that I'm only talking about self-defense here, not about that sick vengeance that attempts to hide itself under the name 'capital punishment', for once a violent criminal has been taken off the streets and hospitalized in a humane facility there is no reason to kill him. And I know from personal experience in coming from a civilized society that where self-defense is considered an absolute right there is very little crime. A person considering victimizing someone else knows he may well be killed or maimed, so he almost certainly won't act on his thoughts. And there's no such thing as an habitual victimizer where I'm from; any person with those tendencies who escapes hospitalization is rapidly killed off by his intended victims. He might rape or murder one person, or two, but the third will get him. We declared open season year 'round on habitual victimizers, and the result is they were made extinct by their intended victims. We are civilized and are learning to love ourselves, so of course we refuse to be victimized.

"Anyhow, in your society, which is glamorized by the news media and the credentials of so-called experts, you are not allowed an absolute right to defend yourself, and that's the main reason you have so much crime. Criminals know they can get away with murder; it looks like a good investment to them. They are no different from other business people. If they see a chance of getting what they want with very little risk they'll go for it. Violent criminals must chuckle to themselves at the way your people get tricked by the media and alleged experts into giving away your power, your absolute authority over your own persons.

"Who is your media working for? Who are your politicians working for? Are they working for you? Evaluate where they stand by the fruits of their actions, not by what they say, for they are masters of sophistry and illusion. Did you know that most of your legislators are lawyers, Chantal? Did you? It would pay your people to ask themselves what lawyers stand for, rather than listening to what the lawyers say. They'll out-argue and deceive you every time if you pay attention to their words and the glamour they surround themselves with.

"Anyhow, before I got my panties in a wad I was trying to make the point that your newspeople will never offer any genuine solutions to violence. Their prejudices get in their way. They're afraid to face the rampant violence stored up in their own shadows and purify themselves. That's why they're as likely to identify with the impure bully, with the victimizer, as they are with the victimizer's target. That's why they question a person's right to defend herself. And that's why they place the label of 'victim', instead of 'survivor', on everyone they can. A person who has survived a traumatic situation has shown a great deal of dedication and responsibility, which may eventually lead her to self-love. But the so-called news media are afraid of responsible conduct, since they see it as a challenge to become more responsible themselves. They are anti-personal responsibility, and of course they are against institutional responsibility. So they belittle the survivor and her accomplishments by labeling her a 'victim'. Honey, an impure person is not a problem-solver. He has to solve the problem of his own impurity before he can help solve any other problem."

Chantal was stroking my leg, so I snuggled up close to her. I liked her, but was too agitated by the foolishness of the news media to employ Hemingway. The newsman was still slandering the horrible misguided gun. Both the news and entertainment media of this century were obsessed with guns, but not in any positive or responsible way. For example, in their pursuit of glamour the news media in the United States always published the names of schoolyard killers and awarded them the title "Young Guns", deliberately encouraging other children to commit copycat crimes with the promise that the news media would elevate them into the ranks of this perverse sort of folk hero. In promoting their "Young Guns" the alleged news media fostered killing for the illegitimate purpose of vengeance, while working to eliminate the perfectly valid and Goddess-bestowed right of self-defense. But this gave the talking heads more to talk about in their ratings wars with one another. They did not fight their media wars in an honorable fashion. They were not warriors. They did not care that they were using children as their cannon fodder.

And the American public, for reasons which cannot be fathomed by anyone capable of logical thought, continued to take these so-called news organizations seriously, instead of rationally examining the motives of these agencies and going to the trouble to find out who was actually pulling the strings of the talking heads. It would have done honor to the American people if large numbers of them had evaluated the alleged newspeople by their pursuit of glamour and by the violent chaos they encouraged in society. Perhaps most Americans were frightened by the tricks the media people used to defame the rational or pro-freedom voice; the knowing wink or confidential smirk designed to belittle the rational individual, the emotional sound byte designed to smother criticism of liberal infringements, the newswoman's rather obvious frown whenever anyone dared stand up for individual liberty and love of oneself. Those twentieth-century newspeople contributed to the fraying of the fabric of the human heart.

A representation of a Colt Government Model 1911 semi-automatic .45 caliber handgun floated on the screen. The announcer was trying to maintain a tone of dignity, while at the same time practically bursting from excitement and a sense of his own liberal righteousness. The thrill of the hunt was his; he'd chased his quarry down and cornered it. It was a handgun, a species more dangerous than a rabid rhinoceros. And now he faced it, this handgun gone wild, he had it cornered. He stood against it with upraised spear, loincloth fluttering in the breeze of his own delusions.

"Chantal, that guy is what they call an atavism where I come from. That means he's a throwback to an earlier breed of human . . . well, I guess he **is** an earlier breed, since this is the Twentieth.

"Anyhow, up in my neck of the timeline people are working to overcome glamour. They recognize it as a sickness. In the Twentieth, however, your people glorify glamour, somehow you've mistaken it for a virtue. Yesterday I actually saw a magazine dedicated to glamour and could hardly believe my eyes. At first I thought I was hallucinating, but the lady at the truck stop said I seemed as sane as she was, except for my nudity.

"Sweetheart, glamour is basically a condition in which you have little or no emotional or mental discipline, or purity of heart or experience of your Self. It's buying in to a sort of mass delusion, then willingly doing your own sick part to further that delusion. Glamour equals illusion, and I cannot for the life of me understand why your people prefer illusion over reality. Reality equals Love.

"Do you see?"

"No," she said honestly, snuggling closer to me and hugging me tightly. "But thank you for telling me, Sonny-Bob."

"Sweetheart, even in 1982 it's known that guns in private hands decrease the violent crime rate.   There's fewer rapes, murders, aggravated assaults. And this deterrent effect holds true even for non-gun owners, because the criminals don't know who's armed and who's not. Even the anti-freedom activists are less likely to become victims of a violent crime simply because some of their fellow citizens choose to arm themselves. And with studies that will be published before the end of this century, such as The University of Chicago Study by John Lott,[*] this fact becomes even more apparent.

"Look at what happened--I mean, what **will** happen--after the godless grasping control freaks outlaw most types of guns in Great Britain in the mid-1990's. After the government confiscates and destroys their guns, Brits are exposed to a crime wave of previously unimagined proportions. Even so-called 'gun crime' increases; the criminals actually wind up with lots **more** guns than ever before in Britain, many of them fully automatic rifles and submachine guns, plus many handguns with high-capacity magazines. For with citizens disarmed and their rights and security scorned by the authorities, every class of criminal is emboldened and the black market in imported military-style firearms flourishes like never before. All this despite draconian and fascist penalties for anyone apprehended with a gun; some otherwise law abiding citizens who defend themselves with a gun--say an old pump action shotgun--actually are sentenced to life in prison. Please note: they didn't **misuse** the weapon, just the fact of defending themselves with a weapon was enough to get them jailed for the rest of their lives. For in Britain, it was no longer legal to defend yourself with any type of weapon, even a penknife or stick. You were guaranteed jail time if you fought off would-be rapists or murderers with any sort of weapon. If the criminals got any jail time at all, it was likely to be a lesser sentence than the survivor of the attack got.

"There **is** a global conspiracy to shatter the human spirit and that process begins with eliminating the foundation of all morality and justice, the right to self-defense. Evil people see this clearly and use the naiveté and the heartless selfishness of the cluster fuck of the great herd of humanity to glamour and manipulate this crazed herd. To **control** this crazed herd. Remember: 'Repression Creates Perversion' and control is normally just another word for repression. Evil people want perversion, so of course they foster the control, the repression, that creates the perversion. And your society is built around control, so your society is extremely perverse. The alleged law creates its own alleged criminals. The nature of reality is not acknowledged by your alleged law. The human spirit cannot be controlled, and the love which each human being **IS** certainly cannot be controlled. Your society in 1982 is in danger of

---

[*] When I was a student at Charlton Heston Kindergarten, John R. Lott's classic *More Guns, Less Crime* was recommended reading.

severing its link with spirit and love and degenerating into a race of heartless machines.

"The majority of people in 1982 have little spirit and have never learned to love, and if they're convinced to give up their right to self defense they will have thrown away any chance they may have had to develop spirit and the courage of the heart, the courage to follow their own hearts no matter what, and not giving a good goddam who approves or disapproves. Of course, in a society where following the heart is the ideal, everyone pretty much approves of everyone else. But in the early twenty-first century, when Lucille The Prophetess first formulates these ideals, there is tremendous resistance to the idea that society should expand to incorporate the Heart of Humanity. The first heart-centered human beings had to fight like hell just to survive. The schools, the society as a whole tried to block them from their hearts, from the freedom of being their Self. This fact, along with the desire to become one of the 'Young Guns' of the news media, is largely responsible for the school shootings that occur in the 1990's. Some kids with tremendous potential snap under the pressure of a system that was designed for machines instead of for human beings.

"This society *must* become a moral society, and thankfully it eventually will. Morality is the basic structure that holds up the energy of Soul and allows it to manifest intelligently and honorably in the material world. Morality is not spirituality, but without a pure and accurate morality based in the truths of multi-dimensional human psychology there is no foundation for a pure and potent spirituality to appear on this earth. Without a pure and accurate morality, we can't quite live our spirituality."

Chantal was asleep. Well, I'd been known to have that effect on people before. They're either bored by me, or they shoot at me and declare me a felon.

I kissed her sweet ear, grateful for her presence. I silently arose and took a shower.

I'd finished my personal hygiene routine and was going through the process of selecting my underwear when the primitive journalistic device began chattering, calling for still more gun controls, despite the fact that guns had been extremely heavily regulated since the Gun Control Act Of 1968 had been passed. Fucking predictable. An aversion to glamour had not yet developed among humanity and such nonsense as regulating the individual's right to defend herself was one effect of this lack of disciplined development. And I knew it would get much worse in the 1990's when the national life of America consisted of absolutely nothing but glamour, nothing but illusion. The liberals and the news media got what they'd been calling for with the extraordinarily restrictive gun controls of the '90's, and still they weren't satisfied. But the undisciplined, infringing, frightened little control freaks are never satisfied and wouldn't rest until they'd eliminated every so-called loophole . . . freedom *is* a loophole, but primitive humans were never masters of figuring out the obvious. They couldn't see that with the karma they invited upon themselves by remaining silent and allowing their neighbors to be infringed upon, that sooner or later their own favorite little loophole would be closed. That's the way the control freaks work. They are influenced, and in some cases controlled, by those who hate humanity and who want to see the edifice of humanity's spirit reduced to a pile of rubble. Their two primary specialties are propaganda and loophole closing. From my vantage point of having been born into a better, sweeter time I knew that the control freaks would ultimately lose, and that with a little help from the TAC those people who love the Heart of Humanity, and therefore the Freedom which allows that Heart to manifest, would create a free world that would begin humanity's evolution into Love. Freedom would ultimately cease to be just a word spoken casually and thoughtlessly and become a genuine ideal that people respected and tried to live. But even with the TAC's help it was a damned close call. Humanity nearly went down the tubes. The little people and their controllers, through their sheer numbers, almost defeated those who had individualized and who therefore believed in Freedom, Love and Truth. The twentieth century was nearly the end of humanity.

I snarled at the newscaster, but then grinned in satisfaction, knowing that people like that aren't respected in my world. WE WON! They lost. Although they outnumbered us and had a huge propaganda apparatus, they ultimately lost because they were identified only with the smaller aspects of themselves, and were too lazy or fearful to work at refining even these tiny aspects, let alone learning to identify with themselves as Soul. The personality can't hold a candle to the Soul. Freedom and Truth are Soul qualities.

Now the journalist--and I use the word "journalist" in its broadest possible sense, for even in my days as a yellow journalist I'd operated on a higher level than these people--was interviewing a liberal senator who was screaming for more gun controls, even as she was guarded by a Secret Service agent with a submachinegun. She had full-auto protection while trying to deny even a tiny revolver to non-elite citizens. But I almost pitied her, knowing that she had no faith in her own individuality, which is why she and the journalist and others of their ilk band together to convince or to force others to give up their personal power. Those who consider themselves weak always band together to nip at the heels of those they consider strong. The family of Chihuahuas circles warily around the Labrador Retriever, each waiting for the opportunity to dart in and bite his balls.

I came to attention as President Reagan appeared onscreen, wearing his white cowboy hat. His horse whinnied somewhere in the background. "I've been shot, and I can tell you it's not the most pleasant thing that's ever happened to me. There are risks in a free society, but the biggest risk is throwing away freedom for the illusion of security. The truth is that with great freedom a greater security automatically results. The two are not opposed. But if you try to separate the two, then choose security, the end product is slavery. Just look at our friends in the Evil Empire, the Soviet Union.

"Furthermore, that condition of slavery, or security, isn't guaranteed to last. Probably it *won't* last. No society of slaves can long endure, for those who prefer their slavery don't have the spirit to resist when a few of their fellow citizens rise up propelled by a spiritual force and reclaim liberty for their country. In the end, spirituality will win against the mechanization of the human spirit.

"Slaves don't have to be creative, they don't have to grow. They stagnate, they decay. I predict that the Soviet Union will fall within a decade. Is that what you want for America? God forbid. Freedom will not disappear on my watch.

"Freedom starts with the right to self-defense, and the right to self-defense starts with the right to keep and bear arms. That's why it's in the Constitution. If you doubt that, read the individual writings of the Founders having to do with this most basic of all freedoms, the one that upholds all our other liberties.

"So no, I'm not going to call for more gun control. In fact, I'm going to call for *less* gun control. We have too much of it already. Gun control is probably the greatest menace to our freedom, probably an even greater menace than the Soviet Empire. The Soviet Union will fall, but the anti-freedom activists won't go away until humanity as a whole realizes how poor in spirit and poor in love the anti-freedom activists are. Many are motivated by rage, hatred and vengeance.

"Think for a minute: Would you have voted for me if I were motivated by rage? I suspect you would not have. I love humanity and I love America and I love freedom. And that's why most of you voted for me. I'm motivated by love and enthusiasm for my country and you all know it.

"Only negative actions can arise from negative motives, and the anti-freedom activists suffer from negative motives. They are motivated by rage and hatred and pain and fear. Somehow, you people in the media must get beyond your own fears and personality disorders and warn your fellow Americans about the anti-freedom agenda of those who preach control over various aspects of our lives. Control is not discipline. And discipline can never be enforced by the state. True discipline belongs only to the individual who is dedicated to knowing and purifying himself, and that is the discipline the Psalmist wrote about when he spoke of the 'Valley of the Shadow of Death'. Each of us carries this valley within us, and it must be crossed and purified before we can be anointed with the oil of our own souls. This anointing is Freedom, for it flows from Love."

The President took a sip of water, or maybe it was some of the pure grain alcohol from Mrs. Reagan's stash. He smacked his lips as the journalists stared dumbfounded at him. They had started out their day being driven to scream for "Control!" by their unpurified shadows, but now President Reagan was holding their shadowy motives up for all to see and rubbing their noses in it. I saw a sparkle in his eye.

He continued. "The anti-freedom advocates are unbalanced, so you people in the media need to quit taking their opinions seriously. Those people seriously need help, and we should all support them if they choose to get therapy, but there simply is no reason to support their opinions. Their opinions are based on illusion, and their illusions are sourced in rage and hatred and agony and a sense of separation from certain parts of themselves. They feel separate from both their shadows and their souls; they know neither the darkness nor the light. And because they are afraid to explore their own natures, they opt for an easy mechanicalness, they choose lives of control and manipulation and are unconsciously ruled by the very shadows they flee. The best they can do is manifest either a rigid control or a sloppy emotionalism. They cannot manifest love. We must have compassion for them, but we must also cast their restrictions off our bodies and spirits. And I know that in the end liberty will prevail and love will reign upon the earth.

"God bless America, and God bless freedom, and God bless humanity. Now I've got a horse to ride. Goodbye." And with that he swung into the saddle and galloped away, waving his white cowboy hat in the wind. I saluted, then returned to my underwear.

Chantal stirred. "Sonny-Bob? That looks like your face on the tee-vee. There, now there's two pictures side by side. One looks like Santa

Claus and one looks like you. I wonder what that's about. Come to think of it, that looked like your face they showed earlier, too." She stared anxiously into my face. "You're not in any trouble, are you?"

"I'm not in as much trouble as I was in the seventeenth century when I was captured by Chinese pirates." I turned the chattering device off. "At least, not yet."

She rolled out of bed and stretched. "Oooh, I feel great! That's the best night I've spent in a long time. And you didn't even want to fuck."

"I was tired, sweetheart. I just wanted the comfort of having you in my arms."

She sprang to me and kissed me. "I'll comfort you anytime you want, Sonny-Bob."

She showered, and I felt the stirrings of my manhood as she emerged naked. Her smooth dark chocolate skin, her sweet delicious labia . . .

She smiled at me and I almost fainted. I grabbed the primitive journalistic device to steady myself. Hemingway was beginning his rampage in my trousers and I knew she could see it. She slowly licked her lips. "Sonny-Bob, there's something I could do for you if you wanted me to. It'd only take five minutes, maybe less."

"Sweetheart, it would take me at least five hours to begin to do you justice. You are as beautiful a woman as I have ever encountered. In my old age I seem to have learned that women are not like hamburgers, to be quickly eaten and then forgotten. Lately when I fuck, it always seems to be an act of heart-centered love.

"Right now all I want to do is to hold you in my arms for an hour or two, then make love slowly for the rest of the day. I've learned that women must be savored and appreciated, even if they don't work in a temple. And Goddess knows, you *could* work in a temple if they had them here. I would truly love to fall at your feet and worship my Goddess through you, for I can see you can emit Her energy. You're already emitting Her energy. You're a natural, like my friend Lucille. You have all the right instincts. You would be a fine healer. This society is shortchanging itself by oppressing you and not allowing you to rise up to your true level of service. You are the cream of the twentieth century.

"Honey, I truly wish I'd had more energy last night. If I'm ever in Amarillo again, maybe we can visit. But for now, please get dressed quickly and I'll take you home. I'm about to faint from your beauty."

She smiled and got dressed. Then we held hands as we walked to my "truck".

Chantal's home looked really shitty. I'd told her I was thirsty so she invited me up for a drink of water. There was a crudely styled sign on the door of her apartment that said: "Property of Shogun of Amarillo". All my senses went on high alert. When I'd worked with the Ninja in feudal Japan we'd fought the Shoguns. I hadn't expected to find any of the bastards in Texas.

When we went inside her "crib", as she called it, we were met by a snarling man with a mouthful of gold teeth and about a ton of gold on his fingers and around his neck. Whoever he was, he was clearly not Samurai. "How do you do," I said politely. "My name's Sonny-Bob. And you must be Chantal's father."

"What!? Chantal's my bitch, Chantal's my ho; you been fuckin' my ho, you crazy cracker. 'Dis peckerwood give you de gold, crazy bitch?"

Chantal fished the bill I'd given her out of her pocket and handed it to this fellow, who I was beginning to dislike immensely. "Ten thousand dollars, Shogun. And he didn't fuck me, he just wanted to sleep with me."

This Shogun laughed. He sounded sort of like a duck. "He didn't fuck you? What, he ain't got no dick? I'll fuck you, baby Chantal. I'll fuck you. But first I gots to discipline you for stayin' out all night."

He slapped her then, slapped her so hard it hurt me. She didn't cry out, but held it in as I felt the waves of shame roll off her. She had nothing to be ashamed about, but obviously this Shogun, or somebody, had convinced her otherwise. She was a sweet girl in a cruel world, and I knew that, but still I was astonished that this society was so degenerate it would actually let someone exist who would strike a prostitute.

He drew back to strike her again, but then he died, for I killed him. As his eyes rolled up and he collapsed I moved to comfort Chantal. I took her in my arms. "Don't worry, honey, he'll never bother you again. I'll get rid of the body."

"Is he . . . dead?" Her eyes quickly searched my face. Her body was beginning to shake.

"Dead as a doornail, sweetheart." I smiled. "It was the least I could do."

A little wail escaped her throat, but then was cut off as she fainted. I certainly hadn't expected that response. I'd thought she would crown me with olive leaves. Clearly, interpersonal relationships in the Twentieth were kept artificially complex by those who spread glamour through the media and pulpit.

I held her and looked regretfully into her face. If she really wanted to be a journalist, I hoped that some of what I'd said earlier stayed with her. Maybe she could make a difference.

I carried her to a sofa and deposited her. Her respiration was okay, she'd be fine. I went to the alleged Shogun and took back that bill with the four zeros I'd given Chantal, then searched him to see if he had any other kinds of bills. He did, a whole collection of them. I got them all and stuffed them tenderly into Chantal's pockets. I held her hand for just a moment and was flooded with sorrow. The savagery of this century was beyond belief. The predatory manipulators of politics and pulpit had separated sex and love, so all kinds of violence emerged under the leadership of their restrictive hand. Chantal would have been loved and honored by practically everyone in my society, and this Shogun would have been killed the first time he'd tried to strike her. In fact, Chantal would have almost certainly been the one who would've terminated him in my world, for women are empowered there. No one in my world would dare try to disempower a woman. Or a child.

I took the so-called Shogun (a real Shogun would have drawn his sword and beheaded the artificial one so fast that the phony would continue to believe he was alive long after he'd died) down to the street, dragging him by the collar. His bladder had released and he'd pissed all over himself. I tossed him into the street, figuring someone would collect the body and dispose of it sooner or later. I certainly wasn't going to waste my time burying it. I had places to go and timelines to save.

As I headed back towards Hubert, I noticed . . . uh oh. It was a tax collector. And he was surveilling me. Now I'd have to deal with them again, unless I could get back to Hubert . . .

Suddenly another tax collector appeared, then four uniformed cops. Despite my predicament, I did have to chuckle. With the Shogun's death they'd have another murder to blame on Santa Claus.

I was familiar enough with primitive peoples to know that most of them played by the rules of their culture, and these rules and taboos were so deeply ingrained in them that they automatically expected everyone else to share their assumptions and the behavior patterns derived from those assumptions. This was true with respect even to those they considered criminals. Even most of their hypocrisies and taboo violations were anticipated and shared by their peers. So they never had to recognize and deal with the fog of inconsistencies that surrounded them. There was usually no one to point out that the emperor was buck naked, for the rare tribesman who pointed these things out was not welcomed and was subject to censure--sometimes very harsh censure--by the rest of the tribe. In this way the unintegrated people won their victories over those who were better integrated and more at one with themselves. The unintegrated usually won their victories through sheer numbers, and through designing methods, such as systems of law, that were designed to foster a continuing lack of integration in the members of a particular culture and to apprehend and punish anyone whose level of personal integration exceeded the norm. So a person who had purified and harmonized his mental, instinctual, emotional, physical, and intuitive faculties so they flowed freely and in a powerful loving fashion under the guidance of his soul through the heart was at risk of injury to his physical and emotional faculties due to the fear-based wrath of the unintegrated members of the tribe. Indeed, his physical incarnation was at risk of being prematurely terminated so that he would have to go to the trouble of reincarnating again before he could be a further inconvenience to the tribe.

As a warrior, though, I frequently found that all this worked to my advantage. The response of the primitives to a given stimulus could usually be predicted. Therefore, tactics and strategies could be derived. And even if their logical minds (such as they were) told them they were faced with someone who didn't share their limitations, emotionally they would still respond from the same old pre-programmed fluctuations, instead of creating a brand-new response in the moment to deal with their unfettered foe. They couldn't accept that they even had these limitations, despite the obvious fact that the first step in transcending limitations is to acknowledge that you have them and to explore the nature of the limitations. But if these people admitted their limitations, they would have to accept that they were unacquainted with the nature of reality. Nothing scared them more than the idea of floating over the Void. The heaviness of their egotism felt it had to have something to hold on to.

I paused and took off my clothes. This was the first step in throwing them off balance. If nothing else, they would be overcome by penis envy.

I rolled my clothes into a bundle and strolled towards them, for they had blocked my access to Hubert. My suppository gun rode tight in my ass. I relaxed my sphincter.

I began to sing an old song from my Academy days.

> "In days of old when knights were bold
> and rubbers weren't invented
> they wrapped a sock around their cock
> and fucked away contented.
> He said the world was round-o
> his balls they drug the ground-o

that masturbating, casterating
Christopher Colombo."

"His fleet of ships they sailed from port
to chart an unknown sector
Queen Isabella waved the flag
Colombo waved his pecker.
He said the world was round-o
his balls they drug the ground-o
that masturbating, casterating
Christopher Colombo."

I felt a change in their energy; suddenly they were unsure of themselves. A moment before they'd considered themselves predators, but now they weren't so sure who was the predator and who was the prey. I continued with a fresh tune.

"The village butcher he was there
his meat cleaver in hand
and every time he'd go around
he'd circumcise a man.
Singing balls against your partner
ass against the wall
if you've never been laid on Saturday night
you've never been laid at all."

"Ollie North he was there
and he was only eight
he couldn't please the women
so he had to masturbate.
Singing balls against your partner
ass against the wall
if you've never been laid on Saturday night
you've never been laid at all."

Just a little more, almost there . . .

"Four and twenty virgins
came in with all the rest

in the aftermath of passion
there were four and twenty less . . . *

Now! I made my move, diving into a roll and slapping one tax collector's legs out from under him with my Hemingway. He went down squealing.

At the same moment I yanked my suppository gun out of my ass--damn, that felt good!--and leapt into a one-handed handspring, knocking over one of the cops and firing my suppository gun at another. The law and disorder bastard went down, I had his number. But the suppository gun was set for stun so he'd probably be okay.

The cop I'd just knocked down was clawing for his gun, so I stomped him in the head and took down the other tax collector with my stunbeam. The tax collector I'd knocked down with my love monster had sprung up and was drawing a bead on me in that queer and inflexible two-handed stance these people use, so I put him back down with a stunbeam.

Bullets went whizzing by and Hemingway shriveled up and tried to hide behind my legs. "Coward," I muttered. Oh, the penis was a Big Man in the presence of the ladies, but when the bullets started flying he couldn't be counted on.

I took down one of the blueboys with a stunbeam, but a bullet from the other nicked Hemingway, who arose in wrathful zeal, hissing and spitting his rage. As I dropped that last cop and put the safety back on my suppository gun I looked at Hemingway. "You'll live," I said. At least he'd found his courage.

I ran over and grabbed my bundle of clothes, then sprinted the remaining distance to Hubert. He saw me coming and opened his door. "Trouble, Sonny-Bob?"

"You bet. It's those tax collectors again, you know, those people who look like blues musicians but don't carry any instruments. I wish they'd let my ass alone."

In truth, the twentieth century authorities seemed so offended by killing that I considered the possibility that every time there was another incident they might send more goons after me. This wasn't the easiest century to work in.

Hubert was navigating through the streets. I didn't know where we

---

* It is believed these songs originated in one of the armies of the Twentieth, the very century in which I was singing them. They were handed down to my people by conscientious souls who believed in maintaining the Old Ways.

were going, but didn't much care as long as it was away from those tax collectors.

"Sonny-Bob, I'm monitoring the police frequencies. This is serious business. It sounds like they intend to behead both you and Hemingway if they catch you. I don't think I can get to the interstate, there's road blocks, and even if I managed to find an open exit there's more road blocks all over the interstate itself. What do you want me to do?"

"Pull into the next available alley, old pal. It's time for technologically advanced subterfuge."

Hubert put us into an alley and stopped. "Rig for silent running," I told him. He did so, cloaking us and holding his energy signature closely about him.

"Go into orbit," I said, and we sprang up into a crisp and beautiful winter's day, as fine a day as any to be Santa Claus, and I almost regretted I wouldn't be able to play that role anymore. Soon we were circling the earth, and like that legendary Texas insect the boll weevil, we were "just a-lookin' for a home."

"Cappy, what do we do now? Where do we go? Those primitive Americans are dangerous."

"Hubert, I think we're going to have to lay low for a few months. We need a place where you can work on your interdimensional drive in peace, and where the people are civilized enough to accept me. There's only one place in 1982 that fits that bill, as far as I know."

"Got you, Sonny-Bob. I think I know where you're talking about."

"Bhutan!" we shouted together.

Bhutan was unique in the twentieth century in that it was the only country in which the distilled essence of spirituality survived. It had never descended into the materialism of communism, socialism, or capitalism. The people kept their spirits unfettered and free and lived in close rapport with nature. They were part of nature and had never felt otherwise.

And nature in Bhutan! Two-thirds of the country remained under original forest cover, and it was impossible anyplace else on earth to find the variety of plant and animal life that manifested within the borders of this one little country. In the South are plains and river valleys, north of that lies somewhat mountainous land, then the truly mountainous land of the Himalayas. There are tropical lands with rhinos and elephants; there are alpine lands with snow leopards and black bear.

The Bhutanese were surrounded by communists, a fact which must have given them pause. Well, not entirely surrounded, perhaps, but the communists of China and Tibet were aggravatingly close. India shares a border with Bhutan; Nepal and Bangladesh are close by. But the Bhutanese maintained a spirit of comity with their neighbors. They didn't hurt anyone and no one hurt them.

These fine people were largely isolationist, which is just common sense if you're the only truly spiritual country remaining. They didn't want their land defiled by either materialistic Westerners or materialistic Easterners. They permitted less than a handful of tourists in each year, and most of those were birdwatchers. They didn't want idiots scaling their sacred mountains.

Hubert and I cruised at low altitude over the Bhutanese tropics. Here we saw an elephant, there a red panda. When we flew over a village the friendly peasants smiled and waved. I sighed. I felt like I'd come home.

CHAPTER FIFTEEN

Nick-Nick sat on the mantel in the King of Bhutan's cabin. The King and I cleaned our tommy guns.

"Sonny-Bob, thanks for that nano injection. I would have been a cooked parrot without it."

"Don't mention it, sir. Always glad to be of service."

The flames burned brightly in the fireplace and I was looking forward to the evening meal.

Hubert and I had been in Bhutan for a week, and as representatives of the future we were honored guests of King Jigme Singe Wangchuk.

I admired the way King Wangchuk ("Chuck" to his friends) lived. Just like me, the only luxury he ever needed was women. He lived in a log cabin in the woods and remained accessible to his people. Even Ronald Reagan wasn't this accessible.

He had four wives; not enough, by my standards, but he did have his duties of state to attend to, so he couldn't stay locked in ecstatic embrace all day, sucking on the Heavenly Tongue of Woman. He had to rule, he had to set the example. And he did.

One morning after our workout Chuck and I sat at table, sharing a large pot of steaming oatmeal and swigging on a jug of yak's milk. A mannerless peasant burst into the room. "Oh King Wangchuk, deliver us! Deliver us! It is the Himalayan black bear!"

I knew it. It had to come to this sooner or later. Bhutan was overrun by this species of bear, which was much bigger and much angrier than the American black bear. In fact, I'd say the Himalayan version was about the size of the American grizzly, but this strange Asian bear had a temper much worse than even the grizzly. He woke up every day with his panties in a wad.

The bastard didn't like people, and he didn't even have the decency to hibernate. In the winter he'd just drop down to a lower elevation, then go out at night and continue with his plot to undermine the authority of the King, terrorizing villagers and killing sheep and domesticated yaks.

He was no vegan.

At times he could be worse than a communist.

Chuck gestured to a chair. "Have a bowl of oatmeal, friend. Then make your report."

The peasant did so, guzzling the last of the yak's milk. He smacked his lips. "That shit's good."

Chuck was solemn. "Casualties?"

"Yes, King Wangchuk. The moon bear slew three villagers and mangled two more." This species of bear is also called the moon bear because of the white crescent on his chest, not because he waggled his ass at people. I guess he hadn't thought of that yet.

"Livestock?"

"They decimated a quarter of the village's yak herd. They also got a few chickens."

"They?"

"Yes, my King. It was a roving gang of five moon bears. We'd heard they'd been raiding along the border with India, but we never expected them to strike this deeply into our homeland. After they finished their pillaging they headed North. The shaman feels they're going to try to make it to Tibet. Our people have many villages along the way, and many are the yak herds. These moon bears must be stopped, my lord. These moon bears must be stopped."

King Wangchuk looked at his hands. "Sonny-Bob, I've got to do *some*thing."

"I'll have Hubert make you a submachine gun," I said.

A few days later we'd chased those moon bears into the foothills and they'd just begun the long climb into Tibet. We had to have our showdown before they reached the border, or we'd be fighting the communists, too.

The King looked grim. "Sonny-Bob, if we don't stop those moon bears, what will the rest of the animal kingdom think? Will they think they can just waltz into Bhutan and have their way with us?"

"I don't have the answer to that question, sir. I'm no oracle. But the only thing on our minds at this point should be getting Hansel and Gretel back."

A couple days earlier, realizing we were closing in, those moon bears had struck another village and made off with two young children, whom I referred to as Hansel and Gretel because I couldn't pronounce their names. I doubt if the moon bears could either, despite the fact they were also Asian.

How cunning is the moon bear, and how brutal his ways! For he knows no authority higher than his own passions. He is uncivilized.

Anyhow, it looked like those Moonies, as we'd begun calling them, saw Hansel and Gretel as insurance against an assault from us. If we tried to move in too close, then chomp chomp! No more gingerbread houses for Hansel and Gretel. Not ever.

We moved on in a wedge formation, about ten meters between each man. There were five of us, too. King Wangchuk walked point with the Thompson submachine gun Hubert had made for him and his boon companion, the Irish Wolfhound he called Barbara, who'd been a gift from primitive American journalist Barbara Walters. Always with the journalists . . . was no part of the earth safe from them? I set my jaw firmly. If Barbara Walters thought to bring glamour to Bhutan, she'd have me to deal with. And I took no prisoners.

Barbara let out a "yip" and Chuck motioned us to stop. I smelled trouble here; Barbara wasn't the only one with a keen nose. I glanced at the other guys; they felt it, too. They were three nomadic tribesmen, skilled in tracking and in the ways of nature. They were twitching beneath their yak hide ponchos, grasping those old bolt-action rifles of theirs so hard I fancied they'd dent the barrels.

I stood to the right of the King and ten meters behind him, and the tribesman I called Curly occupied the same position relative to me. Larry and Moe made up the left wing of our wedge formation. We were loaded for bear.

There was no sound, and Bhutan is a land of the sounds of nature. There are more bird species in Bhutan than practically anywhere else, yet here the birds were on holiday.

I didn't like it. I didn't like it at all. I gripped my Thompson, knowing I had the Moonies outgunned . . .

Yet this was their territory. They had the home field advantage. All of wide, wide nature was theirs.

Barbara stiffened, and a low growl arose in her throat. Then --

Ambush! Bears rushed at us from the woods on either side; Curly got off a shot, but then he fumbled his bolt and a moon bear was upon him. I rushed the Moonie screaming, firing my Thompson; I heard the King's tommy gun chattering and the wolfhound screaming in outrage . . .

The bear dropped Curly and looked straight at me. For an instant that seemed frozen in time we gazed into one another's hearts. Then he dropped to all fours and charged. My Thompson chattered and bucked, in a couple seconds the beast would be on me . . .

The moon bear, sliding in his own blood, stopped at my feet. He breathed his last. He growled at me as he died.

Then something hit me alongside the head with the force of a thousand baseball bats, and I went flying as the Thompson disappeared in the distance on a merry arc of its own.

I lay there stunned as a great shadow rose over me. I couldn't react, my motor functions would not respond. A picture of the pleasant days I'd spent as a prisoner of the Chinese pirates floated through my mind, pleasant compared to the idea of being eaten by a bear and shit out its rectum.

Then I heard a gun chattering and a dog snarling, and the shadow roared and turned to face the King of Bhutan, whose country this was, and no goddamned bear was going to take it from him.

I faded away for a second or two, then returned to myself. My motor skills were coming back, so I rolled away from my position in case some bear had marked where I'd gone down. I poked my head cautiously above the bed of winter wildflowers I'd rolled into and felt the heat of the sun on my face.

King Wangchuk stood on the chest of the bear who'd knocked the shit out of me. He snapped another magazine into his Thompson and fired a few more rounds into the beast. Then the King threw back his head and released a great roar, a roar that told the entire company of animals that he'd retaken his kingdom, and dire are the consequences to any who would threaten it. I just felt glad to be alive.

My Thompson was off in the brush somewhere, and I wished I'd had enough sense to bring a backup gun. You can't afford to be overconfident when dealing with Moonies. I cautiously arose.

There was no sign of Larry or Moe. I ran to where Curly had fallen. He was dead, another casualty in the war to rescue children from bears.

Chuck jogged up to me, breathing heavily. "Larry and Moe dropped their weapons and ran, the damfools. The bears got 'em. You can't outrun a moon bear on terrain he's chosen.

"We got three of 'em, Sonny-Bob. Only two left. And I don't know what they've done with the children. Barbara's out there somewhere, trying to find out."

"Uh-huh." My head was still spinning and my ears ringing from the blow of that moon bear. A blow like that would have killed anyone of softer head.

We heard a rustle in the brush and Barbara trotted up to us, my tommy gun in her mouth. "Thanks, Barbara. Good girl." I took my weapon from her.

The King squatted in front of Barbara. He placed his hand on the dog's head and gazed deeply into her eyes. "What'd you learn, girl?"

The dog made some whistling and snorting noises and rolled her eyes around. She pawed the ground a few times. She finished with a couple of low barks and the King stood up. "She says the bastards have circled back around us and are headed for Nepal. She thinks the children are okay, but very frightened."

Well dog, I thought, *it wouldn't take a fortune teller to know they're frightened.*

We took off at a jog. It was a relatively long way to Nepal and with the moon bears burdened by carrying the children we felt sure we could overtake them.

Unless they ate the children.

As evening fell we reached a village. The people there were glad to see their King. They crowded around us and waved bowls of porridge in our faces. Barbara ate some of it, her tongue flopping wildly.

"I won't eat," King Wangchuk vowed, gritting his teeth, "until my table is set with bear porridge!" I shrugged and decided to follow his example.

We spent the night under the roof of the village chieftain, while the shaman chanted and made magical passes outside to protect us from the anger of bears.

The chief had two wives. He offered one each to Chuck and me. Chuck waved them away, but I was willing to shift gears away from bears for awhile. I gratefully accepted both my and the King's portion of Woman. The tongue sucking that night was sublime.

I woke up staring straight into a golden sun . . . no, it was more like an eye of some kind, a great golden eye. It began pulling me to it, I felt as though I were being levitated . . .

Suddenly I fell. The golden eye had vanished and I fell forever through the darkness. Finally, I stopped falling and found myself in a strange, dark place. I could see nothing. I sat up and felt for my weapons, but they were nowhere to be found. The women were gone. So were the King and the chieftain.

I arose and began to walk, to what destination I knew not. There were no terrain features in this cool, dark place. It seemed like hell, but there were no flames or heat. I wondered if the bears had killed me.

Suddenly, a great voice boomed. "Ye shall taste of WOMAN!"

"What?"

"You heard me."

I emerged into a clearing. I don't know how else to describe it, though the clearing itself was composed of the same darkness as the rest of this place. There was no light here, yet I could see into this area. In the middle of the clearing stood a great black bird, a bird larger than a man. It stood upright and a naked woman was pressed against each wing.

"Do you know me, Pilgrim of Darkness?"

"I know you," I responded. Suddenly, I pointed at the being. "You are the Great Rooster of the Ninja! You are the Tengu!"

The giant bird's head bowed ever so slightly. "The day will come, Pilgrim of Darkness, when you shall be drawn into the golden light, and there shall you find me transformed. For I am not only of the darkness, I am also of the light. That which is dark but pure will one day be transfigured. When no trace of egotism remains, then shall the darkness lift up its arms to the light, and the light of gold shall draw the darkness into itself. The merging will be complete. The days of gold shall begin.

"Do you understand?"

"I guess so," I mumbled, scuffing my toe and looking at the "ground".

"There is much of pain remaining to you, Disciple of Creation. For that which was slaughtered must be reclaimed and made to live. Made first to live in you, then in all of Creation.

"You are self-begotten, but you are not complete. But your day will come if your heart be true.

"Ye shall taste of WOMAN! Pass through the fires of creation and then live! Live! Live!"

I woke up gasping and covered with sweat. Two beautiful women looked with concern into my face. "Bad dream?" one asked.

"I'm not sure," I said.

We got an early start, the King and I and that wolfhound of his. We strode off into the dawn. I looked over my shoulder once and saw that shaman standing there with a toothless grin. He had eyes like a hawk.

We figured the bears must be tired. They probably hadn't expected to be chased by men with machine guns when they entered Bhutan, and this unexpected psychological stress, coupled with the physical exertion of carrying the children and staying ahead of pursuit, was bound to take its toll.

It was only a matter of time 'till the final battle. But who would win? We were pretty evenly matched; two bears to two men. Yes, the King and I had our Thompsons, but the bears had their woodcraft. Throw a bear out of a plane into any woods anywhere and he'll be right at home.

He knows what to do. He is the ultimate guerrilla warrior.

Around noon the wolfhound stopped, one paw lifted. She questioned the wind with her nose. Then suddenly she stood on her hind legs (Irish Wolfhounds are huge, by the way, taller than most men) and placed her paws on the King's shoulders. She looked into his face, blinking rapidly in what appeared to be a form of code.

Chuck was nodding. "Yes, yes, Barbara, I see . . . of course . . . good strategy. Good plan, girl. Thank you." He took a dog biscuit out of his pocket and gave it to Barbara, who wolfed it gratefully.

His Highness motioned me over. "Barbara says the bears are only about eighty meters away, but she doesn't think it's an ambush. She thinks they're holed up for a while to rest. They may be in hollow trees, or they may just be lying out on the ground, ready to run or fight.

"The kids are still alive, Barbara says, but the smell of fear is rancid upon them. Their adrenals are overstressed. They'll need to be medicated by a shaman once we've rescued them.

"The reason Barbara thinks the bears are asleep is the fact that the wind has shifted, but the bears have not. A few minutes ago the wind was carrying our scent in the general direction of the bears. They'd placed themselves so they could smell us if we came along. Then the wind changed--the gods favor us over bears, apparently--and now their scent is being blown to us. And they're not trying to reposition themselves, so they must be asleep. We've got a golden opportunity to stop those terrorists **now**, before they eat those children or attack any more villages. Follow me, do as I do."

King Wangchuk began leading the way through the woods, preceded by Barbara, of course, who with her keen nose was the only one of us in touch with the present reality. But I had to wonder about Barbara's theory. What if the bears only wanted us to *think* they were asleep, but were really planning another ambush? Had Barbara thought of that?

Oh my Goddess . . . what if Barbara were one of them? What if she'd been recruited by the bears? She **had** disappeared into the woods for a few minutes during that firefight.

And where had she spent last night? She'd eaten her bowl of porridge and disappeared. She might have found a boy dog . . .

Or she might have found a bear. A bear. She might have found a bear.

I shook my head to clear it. When you're on a combat patrol in an unfamiliar wilderness two centuries from home you get paranoid. You do.

Barbara stopped, paw upraised and nose questing. I quickly checked our ass, couldn't have those Moonies sneaking up behind us. All secure.

Barbara and Chuck were conferring together. I joined them. "Barbara says the bears have stuffed Hansel and Gretel into a hollow tree, but the bears themselves are sleeping around the base of the tree, guarding their prisoners. She recommends we go in with knives and do some throat slitting."

The King's gold tooth glinted in the noonday sun. "I'm going in, Sonny-Bob. Keep me covered; if the enemy wakes up, murder them before they murder me. And try not to shoot into any hollow trees. We can't have Hansel and Gretel getting killed by friendly fire."

I placed my hand on his arm. "Your country needs you, Chuck. I'll go. No biggie."

"Thanks, Sonny-Bob, but no thanks. This is a job for the King of Bhutan. Besides, the timeline needs **you**. If you don't save the timeline there won't be a Bhutan much longer."

I couldn't argue with that logic. We embraced, and the Champion of Bhutan drew his Arkansas Toothpick, then placed it between his teeth. He started low-crawling towards the enemy.

I lay behind the root of a great virgin tree, tommy gun poking over the top and ready for action. Chuck's gun was also near to my hand, and I prayed to the Goddess that two tommy guns and one Arkansas Toothpick would be enough for this operation. I prayed for the welfare of Hansel and Gretel.

I glanced over at the wolfhound. She lay behind a great root of her own, her eternally questing nose posted on top of it. Her lips were drawn back in a snarl and her body was tense. She glanced my way and I thought I detected a glint of worry in her eye for Chuck's welfare. Well, maybe she was on our side after all.

We could see the two dark lumps that were the bears stirring fitfully in their sleep. Perhaps they were dreaming of Tengu.

The King had reached the first bear. The safety was off my Thompson and my finger was on the trigger. A bead of sweat trickled into my eye, though it was a chill winter's day. Well, if we were killed on this mission I'd be exposed to the tropics soon enough.

Like a flitting sparrow Chuck was upon bear number one, his arm looping around the throat to slash with his blade. Just as quickly the bear's consciousness returned; perhaps he'd been warned by his spirit guides.

The beast rolled directly into the King, upsetting his blade arm, then in a flash the bear stood atop the man, yowling most frightfully. Chuck was slashing with his blade at the bear's legs; he bit the hell out of that animal, too. The other bear had jumped up and was pawing into the hollow tree, trying to get to Hansel and Gretel. Well, the hell with it. I had to take a chance on hitting Hansel and Gretel to save my friend. Screw those kids. I cut loose with the Thompson.

Twigs rained down around the bear that stood on top of my friend as my bullets cut their way into his reality. He hit the ground and rolled, then jumped up and ran into the woods. The King lay still.

The other bear was still after the kids, but now he had a wolfhound to contend with. Barbara was all over him, biting his dick, slashing at his balls with those great wolfhound teeth. "Go, Barbara!" I cried.

I charged the bear, but was afraid that if I fired I might hit Barbara. I jumped right into the fray and with my Thompson I delivered a butt-stroke to the bear's head. He screamed, and a great paw caught me and sent me flying. For the second time in as many days my Thompson sailed away from me. But this time the blow had been a glancing one and I wasn't too stunned. I sprang to my feet as a great eagle soared into the action, flogging at the bear's face with his wings and pecking at his eyes. The spirits had sent reinforcements.

"Tengu!" I cried, launching myself at the bear. Barbara was still worrying the animal's dick, but suddenly the bear shifted into a cat stance that tore his dick away from Barbara. Then the bear's foot shot out and Barbara went sailing. She thudded to the earth a few meters away.

Then I was on the bear. I spun through the air with a series of kicks as the eagle watched from the branch of a tree. My whole body sailed through the air as my feet repeatedly clubbed the brute's face. He screamed in fear and pain, nose spurting blood onto the white carpet of snow.

Finally we stood facing one another, breathing heavily. From inside the tree I could hear Hansel and Gretel crying and praying to their ancestors.

With a low growl the beast came toward me, waddling on his hind legs and waving his arms up and down. I thought of an entertainment program that had run on that primitive journalistic device at that inn in Amarillo, and a cautionary phrase from that program now rang in my mind: "Danger, Will Robinson! Danger!"

Then we clashed. The moon bear swung his arm at me but I pivoted into the strike and caught it with both hands. Then I twisted around under his arm and suddenly had the bear in an armlock. He knew what would happen to his arm if he resisted . . .

He resisted. And again I went flying. I guess I hadn't delivered the armlock very well.

I landed in a patch of snow and rolled, then was given a transfusion of blood and energy by Hemingway, who'd rolled himself up as tightly as possible to transmit his nourishment to every cell of my warrior's body. I was tired of this shit. That bear was going down.

He was coming at me again, but this time I had his number. This was going to be his final battle. I heard the eagle cry from the branch of his tree.

I hit the ground and rolled, then with my legs I knocked the bear's legs out from under him. He hit the ground hard, and then I was on his back. I slid my arm around his neck, then flipped my wrist over and shoved my palm against his jaw, while my other hand clutched the fur on the back of his head. I shoved back towards myself with my palm and pulled on that fur. In another second his neck would break.

"When you get to hell, tell the Shogun of Amarillo I said hello," I snarled. Then I shoved and twisted . . .

Suddenly, I looked up. That eagle sat on his branch looking at me. I paused. "I appreciate your help," I said, then began to twist . . .

I couldn't do it. I looked back up at the eagle, who calmly gazed into my eyes. Then he flew away.

" 'Repression Creates Perversion,' " I muttered. "If I turn you loose, can I count on you to behave?" The bear grunted a rather strained assent, so I released him and rolled off his back.

The bear staggered up and lumbered away, his head held at an odd angle. "I hope you know a good chiropractor!" I shouted.

Then I ran to King Wangchuk, who was struggling to sit up in the snow. "Don't try to talk, Chuck. A nano injection will cure all your wounds." All his physical wounds, that is. I didn't know how long it might take him to heal psychologically from having that snarling beast standing on his chest. He'd have to see a shaman for therapy.

"Barbara . . . ?" the King gasped.

"She's my next patient. Hold still . . . there. Eat something, anything. Those dog biscuits you've got in your pocket will do. The nanos have to have fuel to work."

I reached into his pocket and grabbed a handful of the biscuits for Barbara on the assumption she might still be alive. But she'd taken a terrible blow and landed hard, hard.

I ran up to the dog. She couldn't move, but her eye followed me. Still alive, but her back was broken and she probably had major internal injuries.

"Here, Barbara. Good girl. You did the King proud. I'm sorry I ever doubted you." I injected her with the nanos, then broke a couple of the biscuits into small pieces for her. "Eat this, friend. The medicine needs food to work." She managed to eat the biscuits I'd broken up and I left the others by her nose. She could eat those when the nanos had her partially restored.

Chuck was struggling to his feet, chewing up a mouthful of dog biscuit. "Barbara?"

"If she makes it through the next two or three minutes, she'll be okay. I've given her nanos."

An hour later, the three of us walked back down the trail to the village. Hansel and Gretel rode on Barbara's back.

CHAPTER SIXTEEN

With the rescue of Hansel and Gretel, Chuck was even more esteemed by his people. They held a parade for us in the city of Bumthang[*] where I was appointed Honorary Vice-Regent For Martial Affairs, and Hubert and I were awarded Bhutanese citizenship. In a speech before his fellow citizens Chuck declared that Hubert and I were always to be welcomed in Bhutan, and that we were to be sheltered anytime we were on the run from the police of some uncivilized nation. Hubert and I tried to look humble.^{**}

After the speech I pumped some flesh, meeting the local tribal chieftains and wanting to meet their wives and daughters, who also wanted to meet me. Hemingway had come though for me in that fight with the bear and had sacrificed his own energies and interests to give my warrior's spirit the strength to prevail. I figured he deserved a reward.

My tongue was hanging out over several luscious beauties and Hemingway was beginning his rampage in my trousers when a hush fell over the crowd, and the sea of Bhutanese parted before me.

At the far end of Chuck's great hall stood a woman--I should say a WOMAN. Tender and sensual, yet as tough and enduring as a mountain, she began sensuously to gyrate in some kind of serpent dance. Her hands caressed her body; she unlaced the little half-jerkin she wore to reveal her breasts, which I frankly found quite appealing. She fondled herself, touching her breasts, brushing her nipples with a gentle finger. At times

---

[*] I didn't make this word up.
^{**} It must be noted that just a couple of years after Hubert and I visited this wonderful country it was invaded by a pernicious spirit of control, manipulation and the use of force. Progressive elements demanded more freedom and the government responded with crushing violence. Any civilized person is always alert for infringements of liberties and persecutions so that he will be able to maintain his heart and moral integrity in the face of heartlessness and dishonor. Unfortunately, my friend Chuck must've been asleep.

she'd slip a couple of fingers into the sacred place barely covered by her low-slung skirt. She gyrated, she undulated, growing hot though scantily clad. As she spun around my heads were spinning around. I felt that transference of consciousness that sometimes occurs between the head on my shoulders and my Other Head. This time the Other Head was becoming more aware.

She spun up to me in a rainbow cloud from her multi-hued skirt, the skirt that was slit in a dozen places to reveal the luscious curve of leg, and that almost, but not quite, revealed to me the seat of her Womanhood. I saw she was about ninety years old. She was grand.

She stood before me then and looked me in the eye, and what I saw there took me to a place so ancient . . . I was taken to a place that was ancient long before the earliest birth pangs of this world. It was a frightening place, yet behind everything lay the soft glow of love. I stood in that place for some time . . .

"Sonny-Bob! Can you hear me? Sonny-Bob!" Chuck was shaking me, both hands on my shoulders.

"Chuck . . . Chuck! What the hell is going on? Where was I just now?" I was blinking rapidly, trying to process myself back into This World. I rubbed my eyes.

Chuck slapped me across the face, then handed me a cup of wine. "I don't know where your spirit went, but your body's been standing frozen here for three hours. I'm glad you're back." He peered closely into my face. "You are back, aren't you, Sonny-Bob?"

"I suppose so. More or less, anyhow." My serpent goddess was gone, the great hall was clear. "Where'd she go, Chuck? Who is she?"

He took a deep breath, then released it and grounded himself before answering. "You've just met the Witch of Taktsang, Sonny-Bob. More beautiful than the lotus and loftier than the Himalayas, yet deeper than the earth's core and as aged as Time. More aged, in fact."

"How aged?" I wanted to know. "Give me an exact figure." Somehow, she reminded me of a young girl I'd met in Pakistan centuries ago.

He shrugged. "Nobody knows. The most conservative estimates peg her age as a century and a half. All anyone knows for sure is that she's been the instructress of the monks at the Taktsang monastery for over a century."

"Damn. I wouldn't have taken her for over ninety. She's a fox."

Memory flooded me then, a memory of a warm summer's day in Pakistan. I'd gone there on some journalistic mission or other, something to do with documenting the lives of rural Pakistanis around

1000 A.D. It bored the shit out of me. I was young then and had looked forward to an unending lifetime of adventure up and down the timeline with a variety of both historic and prehistoric ladies, but all the generals ever let me do was go take pictures. This must've been my second or third mission for the TAC. I was beginning to see that the damn generals didn't want me to have any adventures.

There was a pool there, just off the highroad. I decided to stop and rest and bathe my face. A lotus grew in the center of the pool.

I cupped my hands and drank hungrily of the water. It was sweet, sweet as a virgin's sigh. Then I bathed my face in it, and it felt so good to be clean I removed my shirt and bathed my chest. Then I sat back on the grass, relaxed and happy. This was my adventure. Despite the generals and their scheming to prevent me from getting my way, I'd suddenly found what appeared to be the most interesting spot in all of Pakistan. I didn't know why or how, but with the quenching of my physical thirst my spirit had suddenly come home to itself and I no longer thirsted for any adventure other than the one I was already on. I was at peace.

I gazed across the pool into the sunny, sunny day, the cool and fragrant breeze touching my lips with welcome. Suddenly I became aware that the lotus had vanished. "Damn," I muttered. "Maybe a bass got it. Do they have bass in Pakistan?"

Then I felt a gentle touch upon my shoulder. Without thinking I crossed my right arm over my heart and placed my fingers upon the gentle softness of a flesh that somehow felt luminescent. I smelled all of the sweetness of nature.

I turned slightly and gazed into the face of innocence. She was so pure and young and sweet my jaw must've hung open. They didn't make women like this one anywhere I'd ever been.

Her lilting laugh of welcome rang across nature and made me smile. "Glad to see you again, Sonny-Bob!"

"Have . . . have we met before?" I stammered.

"Many times, dear friend, many times. We last met about five centuries ago in the land called Britain."

I shrugged and turned all the way around to face her. She dropped to the grass before me and we held hands. "I'm sorry, ma'am, but I've never been to primitive Britain. At least, not yet."

She playfully touched my nose with her finger. "You've been to lots of places you don't even remember, Sonny-Bob, and you've worn lots of forms. Me, too. I wear lots of forms." Suddenly, she seemed a little sad, but then she bounced right back with that sweet and sunny smile.

We just gazed into one another's eyes, then. I don't know how long it lasted, but I saw the green, green grass reflected in her eyes and I saw the blue of the sky and some fluffy white clouds. I saw a lotus.

I somehow knew that all that really mattered was found in her heart, and that I could find her again in my heart if I would just look and not give up. I knew we might be separated--I shuddered, I knew we **would** be separated--but I also knew I could find her again, and that someday I would find her again.

She would embrace me, even when I was unawares.

By and by she stood and helped me to my feet. She wore a brilliant white garment over her deep brown skin and now she dropped it and smiled and stood before me naked. Her teeth were as white as the snows of Altai Himalaya, her dark hair and skin reminded me of the fertile soils of the Mississippi Delta. Her breasts were very small, but sweet with their pert nipples.

There was hardly a trace of hair between her legs. She was virgin, and her pinkness lay before me as she smiled shyly, then placed my rude hand upon it. But I was afraid.

"Sweetheart, you don't know what you're asking for. You don't want to start out with someone like me. You deserve someone better, and anyway you can't hold me. I'm too big to get inside you." Involuntarily, my hand pressed itself more firmly against her vulva. She held me by the wrist with one hand while with the other she stroked the backs of my fingers. "Sweetheart, you don't know what you're asking for, I'm telling you. I so **don't** want to hurt you."

"I know what I'm asking for, Sonny-Bob. And I know you will hurt me. It's inevitable. But I love you and I always will. And I *can* hold you inside me. It won't be easy, but I can do it.

"I can do it."

With a guilty soul I let her unfasten my trousers and I stepped out of them for her. She gave a little gasp and her hand flew to her mouth as she saw Him. I'd been with young women lots of times, thirteen or fourteen year olds on up, but they had never let me at the virgins because of my size. And anyway, I had always had enough respect for women to not want to terrify the virgins. I wanted their first experience to be a good one and I knew that wouldn't be possible for them with me, owing to the size of my huge erection. I regretfully let other men perform the deflowering duties, while I sat at home with the women who had already been broken in.

Well, she was not only virgin, but in spite of her odd wisdom she seemed only about eleven years old. I couldn't help but love her and wanted to protect her. I tried one last time to protect her from me.

"Please, sweetheart, we don't have to do this. It isn't healthy . . . I'll never be able to forgive myself for hurting you!" I sobbed, a curious emotion rising in my throat; I felt I already had hurt her in some way I couldn't comprehend.

She reached up to me, laid her hands with their beautiful knowing fingers upon my breast and shoulders. Her eyes were a luminescent and unfathomable pool. She moved in closer still and kissed my breast, then lay her head upon it. She breathed upon me, and my heart began to grow calmer. She was right. We had to do this.

Finally, she moved back a little and looked up into my eyes. Her own eyes were molten and dark. "I forgive you, Sonny-Bob, for what we're about to do together. I forgive you now and I forgive you forever. There is no sin in this rape."

The emotions started again for me. I had never been on such a rollercoaster. "Honey, just a moment ago I'd decided you were right, but now you've called it a rape and I don't want to do it again. I would never rape you or any woman. I *don't* want to hurt you!"

"Sonny-Bob, I want this. It will hurt me, but it must be done. If I'm going to grow up I've got to change, and I've chosen you to change me. There is no one else.

"I'll have to grow old and old and old to heal, and then I'll have to be born again as we all must.

"Sometimes change is painful, sometimes it is agony. But change and growth must come. I need you to bring about the change that will nearly destroy me, and I need you to be there for me when the healing and restoration are at hand.

"Will you help me, please?"

I was crying. I *so* did not want to hurt this beautiful young lady, she who'd won my heart with the summer's breath. Pain and decay would come with our experience here; I would rather have died than hurt her.

"That's why I chose you, Sonny-Bob."

Suddenly, it happened. I pulled her against me hard, my hands flowing down her long black mane, pressing her flesh with my flesh, feeling those hard little nipples biting into my stomach. I forced her down to my prick, all reluctance swept away by the swelling of the liquid emotion I felt inside me. I burned, I burned for her.

I was on fire.

I grabbed her hair and forced her mouth down upon my cock, she licked it in doe-eyed submission.

Enough! I yanked her hair and threw her on her back in the grass that had once seemed cool, but which now burned as hot as I did.

I fell upon her with a fury, biting her lips savagely and without remorse. She whimpered, but did not cry out.

I bit her little titties and didn't care if they bled. I attacked her neck, then her mouth again, thrusting the hot tongue of my passion into her, into her, into the blood of the injury I did her.

I ground my teeth into her teeth and I sucked her tongue as far as it would go and bit through it as she struggled a little under me. I didn't care. It was too late for struggle.

I worked my way down her body then, I licked it and I bit it and I kissed it roughly. She tried to sit up. "Sonny-Bob, if you would just--"

I backhanded her and she fell back stunned upon the hot ground, nose spurting blood. "Shut up, bitch. You asked for it."

I got to her little virgin cunt, like a babydoll's cunt it was, but that was no concern of mine. The thin tissue stretched across the opening I'd once considered sacred, but now all I wanted was to bust it down and destroy it.

"Fuck you, bitch!" I screamed, and I shoved my cock, I shoved the great length of it into her, holding her semi-conscious body in position by grabbing her legs; first I grabbed her ankles and as I thrust the giant cock of my desire into her I pulled her further down the shaft, then I'd grab her farther up her legs and yank her down deep upon my turgid pulsing meat. Blood was everywhere, she spurted blood from every opening as I ravaged her without mercy or conscience. All the grass was soaked with my semen and her blood, and with the black sweat of my outrage. The sky grew dark as angry clouds blotted out the sun. Lightening flashed and the wind arose, and I fucked her and I fucked her and I fucked her . . .

I awoke after a time. The young girl was gone. There was blood everywhere, and the grass had died everywhere we'd touched it. I was lying in a pool of dead grass.

I had to wash myself. Had to get clean. I crawled to the pure pool of water, but it was pure no more. It was dark, ugly, brackish. Dead fish floated belly up.

I felt sick to my soul. I knew I would die, I wanted to die.

Suddenly I heaved, and I lay there heaving and convulsing in my own vomit.

I sobbed bitterly. I'd betrayed everything I ever loved by that one heinous crime.

I had to get my gun. I had to die. I wasn't fit to live.

I crawled to my clothes to dig out my weapon. This would be Sonny-

Bob's last mission, and if he had his way he'd never have been born, never lived in any body at any time, never have existed at all. If he could have wiped his soul from the memory of eternity, he would have.

I clawed at my pants and grabbed for my pocket pistol. I set the damned thing to disintegrate me, then held it to my head as my finger began taking up slack in the trigger.

"That's enough, Culpepper! Snap out of it!"

I turned dull eyes toward the source of the voice. My body was wracked with pain, my heart polluted and sore. I couldn't see very well.

"Go away," I said in despair. "There's no need for you to get involved."

A fuzzy blue and white shape approached. "I'm already involved, Culpepper. That's the nature of interdimensionality; we're all involved with one another all the time.

"You can't run away from your karma, boy. Give it up. If you end your life now you'll just have twice the karma to deal with in your next life. Don't be chickenshit."

"Then I'll just kill myself again in my next life, and I'll go on killing myself every time I'm reborn, until finally the Lords of Karma get tired of it and I don't exist anymore. And if you know them, tell them I said to kiss my goddamned ass."

Something flashed out from the fuzzy shape and I couldn't move. The shape took my gun.

"Name's Sargon, boy. Buford Sargon. I'm from several centuries up the timeline from your own. You'll be fucking us over if you kill yourself, so we're not going to let you do it. Every suicidal maniac should have such luxury."

My vision was clearing up. This Sargon squatted down in front of me. He had yellow eyes, almost like an eagle.

His uniform was blue and white. "I'd join you on the ground, but you've made too big a mess. Don't want to get my frock dirty."

Another sob escaped me and I started choking. "I've killed her, Sargon. I've killed her."

Sargon forgot about his hygiene and placed a hand on my shoulder. "You haven't killed her, son. Not by a long shot. She's not dead yet and she's not going to die. You've hurt her, yes. You've hurt her bad. But she'll live and eventually she'll heal. And she wants you to be there for that. Don't you remember what she said? She wants you to be there for the restoration. Son, you've **got** to be there for the restoration."

"I don't know what you're talking about, Buford Sargon, or whatever your name really is. I don't have to be anywhere for anything. Look at what I've done. Nobody needs me, nobody will ever need me or want me again after what I've done. **Nobody!** I won't be able to look a woman in the eye anymore, especially a young one."

"Well, that's good," Sargon observed. "You've moved from suicidalism to self-pity. See, you're already making progress."

"Fuck you, you futuristic dipshit." I sprawled flat on the ground as the effect from Sargon's weapon wore off.

"Your attitude just continues to improve," said Sargon grinning. "It won't be long until you're back to your old self--oops, I shouldn't have said that."

Tears started streaming down my face, I sobbed and I sobbed. "My old self isn't worth a damn, Sargon. You see what it's done."

"She asked for your help, Culpepper, didn't she? She asked you to do this, didn't she?"

"Yesss . . ."

"You did nothing more than fulfill her request. You're still young, Culpepper. You don't seem to realize there's more to reality than meets your benighted eye.

"She chose you because you didn't want to hurt her . . ."

"But I **did** hurt her!"

"At her request. It all seems simple enough."

"You're an idiot, Sargon."

"So I've been told," he chuckled, "by more Admirals than I can remember. Look, Culpepper. When I was younger I did some pretty rotten things--"

"Nothing like this!"

"Well, no, nothing like this. I love women, too. I love them more than anything."

"I used to love women . . ."

"You still *do* love women, boy! That's the whole point, don't you see? I'd been led to believe you were brighter than this. My heart always swells for women, but even I don't have a big enough heart to be selected for this duty. Don't you realize that someone has to suffer?"

"Not her!" I blurted.

"Yes, her. *And you.* Between the two of you . . . well, nevermind. That's classified, and you're too dense at present to appreciate it, anyway. But your day will come . . ."

Sargon helped me to my feet and escorted me back to the twenty-second century, where he conferred with The Tibetan and the Council of Generals. I was placed in an emotional rehab facility for a while, then treated on an outpatient basis. Finally, I was allowed to go back to work, but only as a bureaucrat. I shuffled papers for a while, but wasn't cut out for it and screwed up everything I touched. The generals were glad when they could finally send me back to the field, for they'd had to designate two specialists to follow me around and straighten out all my bureaucratic bungles.

My friend Amanda touched my scarred heart with her love, but I couldn't have sex for six years, and only infrequently for a few years after that. I always cried during sex in those days of recovery. It took me a long time to process and release the shame and guilt and self-hatred. Took me a long time to get back into the joy and love of it.

But with Amanda's help, finally I made it. Her heart expanded to include even me.

I went to Taktsang. At the monastery I inquired after the Witch. "She's teaching in the great hall today," said the monk. "She's expecting you, Warrior Culpepper. Please follow me."

A melodious voice floated to my ear, by turns as crackly and dry as a manzanita bush, or as refreshing as a gentle breeze, or as liquid and still as a deep pool. She spoke from her belly, then from her heart, then from the center of her passion. There was a fluid electricity in this great room, and it touched us all as I took my seat at the rear of the gathering.

The monks glowed with pleasure; she'd take the hand of one for a moment, then kiss the shiny bald head of another. Sometimes just a light touch on the shoulder would cause a monk to break forth into great peals of laughter. Other times the touch would bring weeping and screaming.

And now she stood before me. "Hello, Sonny-Bob. I'm glad you recognized me."

I couldn't say a word. Finally, I just reached up my hand to her and she took it. I breathed heavily, then came the tears.   I   just   couldn't speak. My heart throbbed with a fierce grief and with the pain of unreleased duality. But below that, 'way 'way below that, was a part of me I just wanted to place in her hands and have her hold forever.

"That's the part of you I most treasure, my love," she whispered, stroking my brow.

"Don't go away!" I finally croaked, and I laid my head against her belly and clutched her tightly to me. "Please don't go away!"

She squatted before me and held me by the shoulders for a moment, then her lips found mine and I was nourished by her breath and her tongue and I felt the beginnings of a renewal. I tasted her, I savored her.

I placed my hands along her body and drew her to me and held her with the tenderness I'd so very much wanted to show her all those centuries ago, the tenderness and love that had been replaced for a time with the illusion of separateness and the rage of love denied.

But love is never denied. She'd always loved me, I just hadn't always been able to receive it.

We held each other for a long time, and during that time we only knew our hearts. There was no illusion of separateness in this space, a pure and shining love was the only presence. Then:

I became her, and she became me. I felt her agony and desolation, a tornado of fire torching its way through a jungle, leaving behind only a denuded plain.

She felt my despair and self-loathing at having violated her, and we both wept.

But then something else arose. We were back in the love, but it was an even more expansive love than before. The desolation and despair were gone. We found ourselves held softly together within the petals of a great rose. There was a heavenly presence here, something that transcended everything I'd ever imagined.

We were in our hearts, and it was impossible to tell where one of us began and the other left off. We were in this journey together, always had been and always would be. I continued to be nourished by her breath and tongue, and I expanded to fill every niche of her body, as she expanded into the dark places of mine and made them sweet. As we continued to nourish one another with breath and tongue and heart, we found ourselves expanding together into every corner of the earth, filling the earth up with the togetherness of our breath and the sweetness of our love.

Finally, we withdrew a little. "Now do you see?" she smiled.

"I'm starting to, my dearest friend, my darling friend. I'm starting to see."

Buford Sargon had been right all those years ago. I had been too dense.

Later that day we walked back to her cottage. Everyone we met along the way bowed to her and spoke respectfully, and she always had a kind word for them, especially the children and animals.

We didn't speak much at first, just held hands under the starry sky in the evening and shared a cup of tea. We went back inside and warmed ourselves by the hearth.

"I love you, Grandmother," I said.

We lay with each other that night, and I thought about how much I'd grown just since coming to this twentieth century. I wish I'd gotten here sooner!

As my hands caressed her old, old flesh I knew the lifeforce within her, and I knew her strength and her joy and her compassion. And I knew that her forgiveness was an unending stream. I learned my heart had never fully healed from what I'd done to her as she opened it tenderly and with much love and gently massaged the wounding away. She refreshed my spirit with every molecule of her being. I loved her so. I slept in gratitude and I arose in joy and she rose up with me and together we shared the splendor of the morning.

We stayed together until late March, but then it was time for me to go. I had to leave this advanced land and return to primitive America to do the job I'd come to do.

I loved her so. "Grandmother, my dear, I guess you know I have to leave."

She said nothing at first, just placed her hand on my cheek and then we shared that kiss of summer we'd once been denied. And as we drank deeply of one another, the blue sky returned to her eyes and the green, green grass appeared in its wake. No matter what happened from now on, we were ONE. Always had been, really.

Connected at the heart we sat facing one another, both of us smiling and glowing with love. Finally, my Beloved spoke:

"We share everything, Sonny-Bob, always have. Not everything we've shared has been pleasant, but it *has* been necessary. Without the agony of perceived separation, a race could never have arisen that appreciates unity. Without the experience of powerlessness and exploitation a race could have never arisen that treasures its own power and *refuses* to part with it. A race that will cheerfully kill anything or anyone that tries to threaten its heart or its power, cleaning the old earth of evil so that a new earth will be born. In the twenty-second century that race is evolving. But this could not have happened if humanity had not grown sick to death with the lie of separation and with the abuse of the mechanical systems and mechanical people of the world. Without this sickness, humanity could never have truly appreciated the cure, the absorption of the individual into his own heart and shining that energy of the heart powerfully through his purified will. Thankfully, the experiment has succeeded and in your time people are working towards unity within themselves, and unity with the other individuals of their group. And people make a deliberate attempt to not transgress on one another's heart or will, and they are self-correcting if they make a mistake." She grinned broadly. "No more preachers! People who have to be coddled and coaxed along can no longer incarnate on the earth during your century. The earth has left them behind.

"As you know, every good thing starts in the world of spirit before working its way down to the material world and grounding itself in the physical dimension. The spiritual reason Practical Immortality was developed in the late twenty-first century was simply that humanity had, in its heart of hearts, made the spiritual commitment to heal itself and evolve. Up until then physical death was necessary because most people were too lazy and fearful to do the hard work of personal evolution. Anyone who's too lazy or fearful or short-sighted to do this work spends his life stagnating in his own feces, his own nasty energy. As you would put it, Sonny-Bob, he has 'shit in his own nest and laid in it.' He won't learn what he has to learn to clean up his energy and purify his shadow, so he won't grow up; he won't even be born in the spiritual sense. He never grows conscious of himself as his Self because of his laziness and fear and stupidity. He'll have a physical body and a personality, but his fear and laziness keep him unconscious of **what** he genuinely is. So realistically, he has to be aborted. He dies. He was an embryo for thirty or seventy or ninety years that could have grown up and manifested his true nature, but he failed because he never had the courage to try. This is the reason death has been necessary on this planet. The average lazy person isn't going anywhere spiritually, plus he's frequently a hypocrite, so he has to be killed off by nature. The other half of that equation, though, is the fact that after being killed off in a few thousand lifetimes, or maybe in a few hundred thousand lifetimes, he'll get tired of dying and begin to question himself to determine his own true nature. And as his sincerity gradually grows, he'll manifest more and more of his Self.

"Anyway, dearest, the people of your time have learned these things and are creating their own individual paths to the unfoldment of their Selves, without being coddled along by psychotic nursemaids who shout from the pulpit or manipulate through the media, nor do they allow themselves to be manipulated and their wills subjugated by decadent remnants of the ancient mystery schools, as occurs in the twentieth century. Your people are spiritually polarized and are working their way into freedom, Sonny-Bob, and that is why death is necessary less often in your world. And that is why Practical Immortality was developed.

"And thank Goddess that humanity, in the end, had enough wisdom to not fall for the delusions of those mechanistic one-dimensional technologists, those who were so immature they actually believed intelligence can be measured by computational ability. You've probably never met one of those people, Sonny-Bob, they were extinct by the time your were born."

"Yes," I put in, "but I have read about them in the history books and seen them in video clips. I've never seen a more superstitious bunch of bumpkins. And apparently the only reason people took them seriously was because they had a few college degrees hanging on their walls, a few illusions hanging on their walls. No so-called primitive tribesman of any century would be that stupid."

"Yes," she agreed, "education had ceased to mean anything before the twentieth century. In very ancient times education was associated with the development of the Self, but in the twentieth century education is associated with the production of a factory. Not surprising, when you consider how lazy and frightened these people are. They didn't want true education, that would demand too much of them, so they created factories that would turn out the illusion of education. Then they clung to the illusion with the desperation of a drowning person clinging to a life preserver.

"This foolishness was responsible for the temporary rise of the one-dimensional mechanistic technologists, who began their attempted rampage into the human spirit by implanting computer chips into animals and children on the pretext of keeping track of them. It was all 'for their own good', of course. Then, once people had accepted this initial intrusion, they began to convince some of the adults to be implanted with mechanical devices and microchips of one type or another on a variety of pretexts. All of it geared toward the destruction of the human spirit and heart. People hadn't yet realized that the potential for human intelligence far exceeds the potential for any form of machine intelligence, but thankfully they wised up in time and the one-dimensional mechanistic technologists lost the respect they'd stolen and manipulated out of people. Then people began to chart the path to their souls, the home of true intelligence.

"Every person in the twenty-second century knows that the broadest, deepest, truest intelligence of all comes from the heart, Sonny-Bob, even if most of your people haven't mastered the process of getting there yet. At least they're working on it, and that work has given them glimpses of truth. One day they will embody Truth.

"So thanks to Lucille The Prophetess and many others, humanity in your time has become something other than a network of machines or a herd of animals driven only by emotional fluctuations and instinct and self-justification."

She dimpled and grinned. "Took them long enough, didn't it?"

"Yes, ma'am."

We shared breath again for a while, and were caught up in the pink whirlpool of pulsating energy that knows nothing but love. I was clean, we both were. I was exalted and humbled and ready to go save the world, for the sake of the love it would one day manifest.

I put my pants on, grabbed my coat and went to see Chuck and that dog of his. I'd told my Beloved I'd be back in a couple of days to see her before winging my way back to the land of paranoid primitive gunmen with badges.

I thought about what she'd said as we shared that final kiss. "It's almost over, Sonny-Bob. It's almost over. It seems like we've waited for this forever, but the day of love and freedom is dawning and the sun sets on the day of the cross."

Roger that.

So I drank yak's milk with Chuck for a couple of days and had Hubert make a Frisbee for Barbara. I've been told by historians that dog grew addicted to her Frisbee, even took it bear hunting.

I packed my things, said farewell to my friends, then Hubert and I hopped over to Taktsang. I left Hubert surrounded by a group of inquisitive children and he stood up straighter, proud to be the center of attention.

It was a bright day and it seemed the edge was gone from the chill of winter. I approached the cottage of my Beloved. Several monks and nuns were milling about the house. My heart began to pound. I caught at the sleeve of a nun. "Where is she, sister?"

The nun took me by the hand and led me away to a vast expanse of melting snow. "She blessed us all yesterday, and we felt the warm glow of love of the whole earth. Then she removed her clothes, and naked she walked out into this field of snow."

I smiled. There was a lovely lotus growing out of a rotting snowbank.

Well, she would do something like that.

CHAPTER SEVENTEEN

Hubert had turned himself into something called a Pontiac. "It's a 1968 model, Sonny-Bob. An oldie but goodie. We should be able to fit into primitive America."

"I hope," he coughed nervously, "the chicks dig old Pontiacs."

"I'm sure they do, Hubert."

My friend had had a rough time of it in Bhutan. He'd channeled as much energy as he could into repairing his interdimensional drive, but he was continually distracted by his lusts.

"I took up with an ox cart for a few days," he confided to me, "but it wasn't the same as being with a real lady. It was something like humping an inflatable doll; yes, things can get pretty wet, but there's no emotional intimacy. I finally gave up and moved on. She didn't even notice when I left."

Well, I figured the old boy wouldn't have much more luck in the United States. These primitive automobiles had no consciousness to speak of and were sure to disappoint. Nobody wants to date a corpse.

Still, Hubert kept his hopes up. I decided to let him continue with his delusions, for as long as he had hope in his heart maybe he'd be more receptive to saving the world.

"I'm purple, Sonny-Bob, look at me! The chicks dig purple. And see the yellow and orange flames I've painted down my sides? That'll tell the babes I'm on fire with desire for them. Yessiree! Here comes old Hubert, pretty ladies, God's gift to the automobile. If your automobile needs to be serviced, old Hubert will do it for free! Hee hee!"

I let him rattle on, for I considered it good talk therapy for him. All I had to do was smoke a cigar and nod sagely and ask him to tell me about his dreams.

Some of those dreams were pretty racy.

The sign said, "Austin City Limits".

"Well, we're here, Hubert. Let's get an ice cream cone."

Hubert pulled off the freeway and cruised until we found ourselves on a street in the middle of town. The street was called Guadalupe, but I learned later it was usually referred to as The Drag.

"Damn, Hubert. All I wanted was an ice cream cone, or maybe a popsicle. We've got to check in at the station and let the TAC support crew know we're about. You didn't have to bring us all the way downtown."

"I hear and I obey," he said sullenly. "And when I hear ice cream cone, by God I go for an ice cream cone. We haven't seen an ice cream shop yet, and in your instructions you said nothing about restricted search parameters. So I'm going to search for an ice cream shop and I'm going to find one, even if I have to go all the way to San Antonio to do it.

"And if you don't like it you can kiss my exhaust pipe, Sonny-Bob."

Oh, boy. Hubert was about to burst from his unfulfilled sexual desires. If I looked beneath my "car" right now, would I see a huge scrotum dragging the street? Had he grown a pair? Somehow, I didn't want to know. I decided never to look.

Suddenly Hubert pivoted and cut right across in front of oncoming traffic, then got in a lane going back the way we'd come. "There's your ice cream shop," he growled.

He lurched into the parking lot as several of my brother motorists honked their horns. I noticed they were trying to communicate with me in sign language. I waved and gave them a sunny smile. "Hello, friends!" I said.

"Go get your damn cone, Sonny-Bob. Maybe the tryptophan in the ice cream will calm you and make you easier to get along with."

"I'm sure it will, Hubert."

"Don't patronize me!"

I entered the ice cream facility. I paid the ice cream merchant for a double scoop of vanilla with a cherry on top. "Are there enough zeros on that bill, my man?"

He was trembling and spoke a little hoarsely. "This will do, sir. And your next one is on the house. Your next **ten** are on the house!"

"Why, thank you!" I responded enthusiastically. This Austin was shaping up to be a civilized place. Who'd have thought such a place could exist in twentieth century America?

Still, I knew I had to tread cautiously. There might be things going on in this town of which I was unaware. I smiled, sat down and began to lick my cone. The first casualty was the cherry.

As I sat there basking in the romantic glow of this place, two beautiful young ladies entered. My heavens! I sat up a little straighter.

The one that immediately caught my eye was copper colored, almost dusky. Looked like she was descended from Aztecs and Spaniards.

Or maybe even from me. I'd known lots of Aztecs and Spaniards when I was producing my text on Quetzalcoatl, the feathered serpent god of the Aztecs. He didn't do them much good against the thieving Spaniards, but even a god has to rest. It must have been nap time for Quetzalcoatl.

Yes, those were the days. Just a young and carefree TAC lieutenant with plenty of time on his hands, because he'd delegated all the work to his enlisted support crew. They didn't become enthusiastic until I'd promised them all promotions and letters of commendation. Then they got busy, which allowed me the luxury of getting to know a few Aztec princesses . . . and some peasant girls . . . and some slave girls . . . and finally some more princesses. Yes, my time on that mission was well spent. Hemingway had no complaints.

Anyway, this young copper girl had short and straight black hair, as per standard operating procedure for copper colored peoples, and as Central Texas had a warm climate she wore an open-toed shoe that revealed her digits, much like Raven of Amarillo. The shiny-nailed digits flashed at me and I knew I would have to ask if she worked in the same industry Raven did.

Her breasts were not plump. She was a young woman, I'd say between thirteen and fifteen. Still, her breasts were dainty and gorgeous and subject to a spurt of growth at any time.

Shorts . . . she wore shorts and her top resembled a type of camisole, though I'd been led to believe twentieth century Americans were too repressed to wear underwear as a primary garment. Well, whatever it was, I liked it, for I could see her gentle nipples straining against the fabric, begging me to come and liberate them and make them whole.

The other woman was similarly attired, but was a light vanilla to the first woman's nougat. She was a little taller and seemed a few years older. Her hair was shoulder length and blonde . . . shoulder length and blonde . . .

Her blue eyes flashed at me and I smiled, and she bent over and whispered to the copper woman.

The dark one turned and caught me crunching on a mouthful of cone. I smiled, but unfortunately the seal between my lips wasn't tight and some of the vanilla ice cream ran out my mouth and descended my chin.

The young woman laughed, then turned to the yellow haired one and they began laughing together. They glanced my way a couple more times amid their tittering laughter, so I decided to be bold. He who dares, wins.

I adjusted Hemingway, and found him nestled all snug in his bed . . .

what visions might be dancing through his head? Only Hemingway knew for sure, but only an idiot wouldn't be able to make an educated guess.

I arose and approached the counter. "Here, boy," I said to the ice cream merchant while snapping my fingers in the air. "Here, boy. Those other ice cream cones you promised me? Let these two outstanding primitive American females feast on them."

He shrugged. "Okay."

I stepped back smugly to watch the effect my gesture had on the women. They'd stopped laughing. I didn't know enough about primitive American ladies to know if this was a good sign or not. But I suspected it might not be.

"Uh, sir . . ." the blonde one began, while the other just stared at me with eyes of liquid gold. "Sir, we don't want to be rude, but . . ."

My thought processes roared fiercely ahead. I sensed I had committed some form of blunder, perhaps violated a primitive taboo. I'd had no idea whatsoever there might be a taboo forbidding the offering of ice cream to young women, but in primitive America anything was possible.

I began to get goddess vibrations from the dark one. My always-fluid heart began to glow and my knees began to shake. I sensed that here might be an opportunity for worship. If I were respectful, surely this young copper goddess would share the chalice of her sacredness with me, surely before the sun set on this most gloriously holy of days I would imbibe the rich wine of creation, the nectar of the timeline, the moist promise of an eternal tomorrow . . .

"Sir? Sir? Are you all right? We're calling an ambulance."

I stared into the liquid dark face of my Goddess. She knelt and bent over me as I lay supine upon the floor. I had fainted from her beauty. It is an affliction I have.

"No ambulances!" I croaked. "Don't let me fall into the hands of the medical profession!"

"Sue? He says he doesn't need an ambulance. I think he's okay."

The two goddesses helped me arise from the floor and escorted me to my table. They sat with me then, they sat with me, as the sweat poured off me. *See, Sonny-Bob? They're already having a cleansing effect on you. They are goddesses, and The Goddess led you to them.* The Goddess had looked after me ever since I'd arrived in the Twentieth and had provided the right contacts. I couldn't have been responsible for all this good luck myself.

"I'm Sonny-Bob," I finally said, as if those words said it all.

The dark one had her hand on my back over the rear of my heart chakra, and I was strangely comforted. I began to breathe normally and the river of sweat was reduced to a trickle.

"I'm Mimi," said the dark one. "And this is Sue."

"I am grateful to you two goddess females for sitting with me."

"Well, Sonny-Bob, you need someone to sit with you." Her hand was massaging my heart chakra in a circular motion, and it felt good. She had a natural instinct, this one did. In the Twentieth they were too ignorant to teach chakra balancing and healing in their schools, but this young dark one intuitively knew things her alleged teachers never would.

Yes, there was a force of healing about the younger one, a force that exalted my soul to supernal realms . . . no, couldn't go there. Might faint again.

Now she placed her other hand over the front of my heart chakra, as the hand that had been on my back moved to the top of my head. She massaged the front of my heart, and it felt sooooooo good! I signed, and became as contented as an old dog on a porch.

Sue spoke up. "Do you have a medical condition?"

"Yes, it's called fainting in the presence of beauty. I adore feminine beauty. I can't help it; there is no vaccination." My heart was beginning to beat wildly again as I spoke.

"Maybe we'd better let Sonny-Bob talk about something other than feminine beauty," Mimi said.

"Thank you," I said gratefully.

The ice cream merchant had brought them their cones. Mimi's healing hands left my body and the two of them began to slurp.

Sue looked up from her cone. "What do you do, Sonny-Bob?"

"Ma'am?"

"What do you do for a living?"

What on earth could that question mean? I didn't know what to say.

"How do you get your money?"

Whew! That was a question I could answer.

"I have a big bag of money. It was given to me by a friend named Roger Bacon."

"Oh." Sue looked doubtful.

"Tell us about your friend," Mimi said.

"Well, he's very old and prefers men sexually to women and he has a long white beard. Sometimes he walks with a staff. In the bag of money he gave me there's bills of many sorts of denominations. But there's more three dollar bills than anything."

Sue slapped the table with both hands. "That's enough. We're getting out of here."

"Wait a minute, Sue--"

"Can't wait, Mimi. There's something bizarre about this guy, and this **is** Austin. We do have to watch who we talk to around here, you know that. He probably just wants to bed us."

Damn! She'd read my mind. "Sue, I don't just want to bed you. There's so many other things I want to do with you as well."

Sue leaped over to Mimi and began tugging on her arm. "Let's go! You see what kind of a nut this guy is!"

Mimi was grinning. "Don't be irrational, Sue. I think he's nice."

"Mimi, you're coming with me right now, or I'm calling the cops. This guy is some kind of nut or pervert."

"I'm not a nut or pervert!" I protested. "I worship the Goddess Aphrodite in all her many forms."

"And--" my mind was in overdrive; I realized I had to keep track of the dark one, there was something about her-- "and if you want a cop, call on me! I'm a cop!" I pulled out my badge and flashed it at her. "I'm a cop!"

Sue looked at it. "What does TAC stand for," she asked suspiciously.

"Well, uh . . . it stands for Texas Auxiliary Constable. Yes, that's it: I'm a member of the Texas Auxiliary Constable Corps. Have been for a long time."

"Well . . ." Sue was beginning to be less rigid. "But why do you behave so strangely?"

"I'll tell you why, Sue. Please sit back down and I'll tell you."

She reluctantly took her seat across from me. Mimi was still grinning and leaned on her elbows.

I reached across the table and took Sue's hands in my own. She was cold with apprehension, but I was warm with the love of Woman. She flinched but said nothing.

"Sue, I behave strangely for the following reason: I just finished a bear hunt in Bhutan, which is a little country in the Himalayas, and I met my grandmother there for the first time since she was a little girl . . . oops, it's complicated, I--"

Sue was on her feet again. "Mimi, you can stay with this nut if you want to; I'm going home. But if you're not back by supper I'm calling the cops."

I smiled at her again, showing all my teeth, but to no avail. She snorted at me and rushed from the place. A car almost got her as she dashed across the street.

Mimi just shook her head as Sue fled down the sidewalk and

disappeared. "She gets a little nervous sometimes, Sonny-Bob. But she's really a good person."

"I'm sure she is, Mimi. I like her. I like you, too."

She smiled. "Sonny-Bob, it looks like it's just the two of us."

"It feels right, Mimi. It really does." And I kissed her.

And after a long moment . . . "Whew! Sonny-Bob, I've **never** been kissed like that! In fact," she blushed sweetly, "I've never been kissed at all. Not until just now."

"Why not?" I said, astonished.

"I guess I just never met the right man." She threw her arms around my neck and after a split second of hesitation, *she* kissed *me,* and I must say . . .

"You two! No Frenching in this ice cream shop!"

We released each other and I looked for the source of this primitive response. I was startled to see it came from the ice cream merchant, who had been so kind to me earlier. Now he was glowering and his hands were placed authoritatively on his hips, as I had noticed other primitive human males doing when they weren't getting enough for themselves and were jealous of me. Soon would come the chest beating, and then . . .

"How old are you, young lady? Have you reached the age of consent?"

"The age of consent is decided by the prostitutes," I told him. "Every young woman is different. Each has her mysteries." I realized I had to stop talking to these people as if they were civilized, but I'm so good-natured that sometimes I give them the benefit of the doubt. It's usually a mistake.

"Stay right there, you two! I'm holding you for the police!"

Not bloody likely. As the ice cream merchant grabbed for his phone, I stood. "Let's go, Mimi. Maybe there's a place that's more civilized in this town."

Suddenly, I found myself staring into the twin barrels of the ice cream merchant's shotgun. One barrel would have been sufficient.

"Freeze!"

"You're the frozen one, you son of a bitch!" I snarled. I palmed my pocket pistol and sent a beam directly into the bastard's chest. He collapsed. These primitives frequently either have slow reflexes or suffer from the inability to act decisively.

Mimi's hand flew to her mouth. "Oh, Sonny-Bob . . ." She looked close to tears, or screaming, or both.

"Don't worry, Mimi dear. He's only stunned. He'll come to in a few minutes, but meantime we'd better get out of here." I helped Mimi out of her chair; fortunately we were the only two patrons in that hostile parlor. No witnesses to finger us later.

We went to Hubert and got in. "Hubert, let's roll!"

Silence.

"Hubert! Let's get out of here! Didn't you see what happened in there? A hostile repressive was about to fire on us. *Now let's move!*"

Mimi was just staring at me and I could tell from the look in her eyes she'd begun to believe Sue was right about me.

"Mimi, hon, I . . ."

"Mimi, hon, I . . ." Hubert mocked disdainfully.

"What! What was that?" Mimi's eyes were round.

"Allow me to introduce myself, Milady," Hubert said stiffly. "I am called Hubert, and I'm the finest interdimensional vehicle in the entire timeline. And . . ." here those glowering eyes appeared on his windshield as Mimi gasped, "I'm tired of Sonny-Bob getting all the nookie. Everywhere we go he gets nookie. I either get pissed on by dogs or wind up sleeping with an oxcart.

"I am Hubert and I want nookie. It is my birthright."

"Hubert, we'll find you a lady when we can. Don't you know if the cops catch us you'll *never* get a lady? Don't you know what they do to rogue cars in the Twentieth?"

I could feel him pause. "What do they do?"

"Any car they decide is a felon is melted down and dropped into the sea, Hubert. They have a great vat they melt the cars in. Is that what you want?"

"I can repair myself with my nanos," he said uncertainly.

"Are you *sure*, buddy? 'Cause if you're not sure, we'd better roll. What do you think that melting vat would do to that purple and orange paint job you're so proud of?"

He started his engine and rolled out onto the street. "You'd better help me find some nookie, Sonny-Bob," he said sadly.

I stroked his dash. "Don't worry, buddy. We'll get you some. Just hang in there and remember what's important. The timeline has to be saved, that's the thing. But we'll keep a lookout and do our best to find you a lady."

He sniffled as we merged with the traffic.

CHAPTER EIGHTEEN

Mimi said she lived someplace on The Drag. I offered to take her home and asked her to not tell Sue or anyone else about what had happened in the ice cream parlor, or about the fact Hubert was sentient.

"Uh . . . if it's okay with you and, ah, Hubert, I'd just like to ride with you for a little while. I've never been inside a talking car."

I could feel Hubert's ego inflate a little. Finally, he was getting some feminine attention.

"Oh, I can do lots more than just talk, Mimi. Look at Sonny-Bob, he never does anything, just sits on his lazy ass. I do all the driving; I can even fly . . ."

"Hubert! Have you forgotten your TITTY's Code of Conduct? 'Secrets that have not already been compromised shall not be compromised.' Remember?"

"Sonny-Bob, *you've* compromised all the secrets on this mission. I've kept my mouth shut up 'till now, but now I'm putting my oar in the water and we'll see if I can row fast enough to catch up with you. Mimi, we're from the future. Yessiree, the twenty-second century--"

"Hubert! Enough!" But the damage was done. Mimi sat there with her hand over her mouth and eyes wide. Now I figured she'd pass out like so many women do when they realize they're faced with the Future of Humanity.

But then her hand fell from her mouth and that endearing grin was plastered on her face. "Neat, Sonny-Bob! Cool! Fly, Hubert, fly!"

"Hubert will fly us around later," I said hastily. "If he takes off in the middle of the street our cover could be blown."

"I could rig for silent running, Sonny-Bob," Hubert offered helpfully.

"Not now, old bean. A car that disappears in the middle of the street might attract almost as much attention as a flying car. We'll fly later."

Mimi snuggled close to me and I had to put my arm around her. Couldn't help it. "If we're not going to fly, where're we going, Sonny-Bob?"

"Hubert and I have to check in with the main office of the TAC for the Western Hemisphere. Oh, TAC really stands for Temporal

Adjustment Corps, by the way." I glanced at Hubert's unblinking eyes; that stare would have unnerved a lot of women. But not Mimi. "We should've checked in when we got here, which was about four months ago."

"Yes," Hubert put in, "we should've checked in earlier, but Sonny-Bob got in too many gunfights with the Secret Service and Marine Corps--"

"Hubert! Please quit trying to be helpful."

He fell silent as we hummed along the road to Lake Travis. That's where HQ was for this timezone. Meanwhile, Mimi put her hand on my leg. She was certainly a fast learner, for someone who'd never even been kissed until a few minutes ago. Unlike most people in twentieth century America, my new friend had confidence in herself and therefore wasn't paranoid, and she didn't seem to be a repressive. Well, I could test for the repressive response later to find out for sure.

And she was intelligent and brave. The fierce Aztec blood ran strongly in her veins and I knew if she'd had the right training she could kick my ass. She was a good partner.

"How old are you, Mimi?"

"I'm . . . I'm almost fourteen."

"A grown woman, then. Good. If you've never been kissed, I guess you're still a virgin, eh?"

She blushed. "I guess so, Sonny-Bob." She straightened up a little. "But I've had my chances. I have!"

"Obviously, dear. You are beautiful and wise, brave and intelligent. And you are skilled at chakra balancing, so you must have a loving heart. Any warrior would love to lie with you, and any warrior would be both exalted and humbled by your presence."

She leaned into me again. "Sue was right about you, Sonny-Bob. You *are* strange." She sighed. "But strange in a good way."

I stroked her beautiful hair and held her until we arrived at Lake Travis.

Hubert rumbled up the little dirt road through the scrub brush. In the distance I could see the azure lake, sun sparkling on the waters. I wondered if we had time to go catfishing . . .

We stopped at a gate and caught the guard taking a whiz. He straightened up and put away his ding-a-ling. Then he walked over to us. He was wearing a bizarre twentieth century uniform. On one shoulder there was a patch that said "Security". On the other shoulder there was a patch depicting the ancient flag of the American Empire. Well, I guess a guard would have to dress like this in the Twentieth so the locals wouldn't get suspicious. They might have a primitive response if they caught the security man walking around naked.

"This is private property," he said. "No trespassing."

"We're not trespassers," I said. "We're with the TAC. I'm Captain Sonny-Bob Culpepper. Get your retinal scanner and you'll see."

"I've heard of you, Culpepper. You're that fool journalist. Why the TAC ever assigned you to producing texts is beyond me. The Norwegians didn't discover Norway; I was there. They weren't called Norwegians back then."

"Do your retinal scan, boy," I said, allowing the hint of danger to creep into my voice.

He shuffled to his guardshack and emerged with his retinal scanner. He stuck it in my face. "Say cheese!"

I said nothing as he scanned me. "Yep, you're Culpepper all right, though I don't know why you'd ever admit it. Now I've got to scan the girl."

"You call her a girl in that dismissive tone of voice again and I'll scan you with a pocket pistol. She's my associate. She's helping me learn about this century. She's my guide. She's from this timezone; she's not an official TAC operative. But I've deputized her. I'm on an important mission and I need her guidance."

"Nothing doing, Culpepper. Only authorized TAC operatives go beyond this point. You can go, but she stays."

He laughed. "And what kind of important mission could *you* be on, anyway? Another training video?" He slapped his knee and cackled. "Did the Texans discover Texas? Hee hee!"

He fell to the ground laughing as I stunned him. Even in his paralysis some chuckles escaped him.

"Idiot," I said.

Hubert jumped over the gate and we were inside. There was nothing but an expanse of scrub brush beyond the gate, but Hubert had homed in on the entry point to the facility. The facility itself lay beneath Lake Travis.

"Sonny-Bob, according to my sensors we're sitting right on top of the entry point. Once they've determined I'm an official TITTY, they should just . . . oh my!"

The ground fell away beneath us and we rushed headlong into darkness. Mimi squeezed me tightly, but said nothing. "Breathe deeply, dear," I told her.

After what seemed to be a slice of eternity, but was probably no more than half a minute, we sailed out of the opening of the chute and landed hard upon the pad inside HQ. "Damn, Hubert! What happened to your anti-gravs?"

"Sorry about the hard landing, Sonny-Bob. That trip through the chute gave me a buzz. I'm driving drunk."

"Well, sober up fast, old bean. And check your stunbeams. We've already had to fight our way through one guard; if the rest of these people are as aggravating we may have to withdraw under fire."

I turned to Mimi. "See what I go through? See what I have to endure? I have to fight everywhere I go. Even my own people won't let me onto one of our bases unless I'm faster with a handgun than they are. The only reason I put up with it is because I'm not qualified to be a prostitute. At least, not yet."

Mimi just patted my hand. Like Hubert, I think she had a buzz. I was okay, though. I always seemed to have a sort of a buzz, so I was used to it.

I jumped out of the cockpit and helped Mimi out. "I feel like I've gone to the land of Oz, Sonny-Bob," she said wonderingly.

"Well sweetheart, maybe we can go to the land of Oz sometime, if you want. Remind me to ask Hubert if he knows where it is."

A security detail was approaching and I felt the leading edge of my adrenals kicking in. "Stand on my left, Mimi. I may have to draw my gun."

A tall and beautiful brunette led the detail. Her eyes were filled with a bright intelligence. "I'm Lieutenant Sharon Tomkins of the Temporal Adjustment Corps. And you'd better be one of our guys or you're a dead duck."

I liked her attitude. Strong, confident, radiant. I relaxed a little.

"Hi, Sharon. I'm Sonny-Bob. This is my friend Mimi, and that grouchy old fellow is Hubert."

"Sonny-Bob . . . Sonny-Bob . . . it seems I've heard that name before." She gazed at me with what appeared to be apprehension, though I couldn't imagine why. Her people had more guns than I did.

"Your last name wouldn't be . . ." she swallowed hard, "Culpepper, would it?"

"Yes, ma'am."

Two of the twelve members of her detail broke and withdrew. They disappeared into the far end of this vast underground chamber. After a moment's hesitation, her senior NCO sort of touched his cap with his finger and nodded at her, then placed his weapon on the floor and departed at a brisk trot. Then two more of her detail followed the NCO's example as Lieutenant Sharon Tomkins grew red around the gills. A great vein throbbed turgidly in her forehead. It hadn't been there a moment before. "Squad dismissed!" she barked. The rest of those security people broke and ran like hell.

Lieutenant Tomkins approached. Every visible patch of skin had turned crimson and I had to wonder about the invisible parts . . .

She looked at me, then just sort of shook her head and groaned. "Why've you come here, Culpepper?"

"Why, to see you, m'dear." I smiled sunnily at her, but then remembered Mimi and my heart reverberated to the beat of its true drummer.

"But there's been a change of plans," I added hastily. "I've found someone else." I placed my arm around Mimi and drew her to me. "I'm sorry, Sharon."

Lieutenant Tomkins eyed me warily. "I suppose you'll want to see Colonel Shepherd."

"Well, he certainly doesn't want to see me."

Tomkins breathed heavily and Hemingway grew excited. Mimi might be on my arm, but Sharon was in my pants, at least in Hemingway's lucid imagination. Sometimes imagination is almost as good as the real thing. Masturbation is more important than knowledge.

The lieutenant was staring at my throbbing trousers, eyes wide. I'd run Hemingway down the leg and tried to hold him in place with elastic bands, but he was about to break loose. "Don't worry, Sharon," I grunted. "It's nothing personal. This happens all the time."

Her hand rose to her throat, then as she continued staring at the visible presence of my manhood her hand fell to the top button of her uniform blouse . . . She shook her head, as Hemingway shook his. "Follow me, please," she gasped. She wobbled off unsteadily and Mimi and I followed.

"Is that what I think it is?" Mimi whispered.

"No, sweetheart. It's more than you think it is."

Colonel "Turd" Shepherd and I went 'way back. He'd been a plebe during my sixth year at the Academy and I had taken pains to harass him well. I knew he'd spoken harshly to a prostitute and I was determined he'd do penance. In fact, I'd given him the name "Turd".

"Clean the stairwell, Turd, then make the commodes sparkle. And don't forget the urinals; if Hemingway can't see his reflection he gets upset.

"And I've volunteered you for community service with the prostitutes on Wednesday. Oh, you won't get to do any of the good stuff, you'll just be cleaning up after the prostitutes. You'll have to make their toilet shine, too, and do any other work they want you to do. Don't come back before you've fulfilled all their requirements. If your work is unsatisfactory then next time I'll send you to clean out some Christian church, and you know you don't want that. They'll set fire to you and say you've gone to hell if you don't do a good job.

"Also, there's no more nookie for you from the prostitutes. I'm friends with the head of the Asheville Diocese, and I've asked her to inform all the prostitutes everywhere that you're under a nookie restraining order until six years after you graduate. Then we'll see.

"Don't ever speak rudely to another prostitute, asshole, or I'll have your balls."

Needless to say, the Turd had never appreciated my discipline. And needless to say, he'd been promoted a lot faster than me. After he outranked me he tried to persecute me a time or two but The Tibetan intervened, fearing to lose yet another officer. He knew what would happen to the Turd if the Turd didn't let me alone.

Lieutenant Tomkins had led us down a hallway. Now she stopped before a door marked Station Chief. "Open up," she told the door.

"No can do, Lieutenant Tomkins. Not until you've identified yourself."

She kicked the door. "You damn bureaucratic door! You know who I am! Open up!"

"At least let me do a retinal scan, Lieutenant."

This just hadn't been Lieutenant Tomkins' day, what with her squad deserting and her discovery that I was already committed to Mimi. I sensed that if the retinal scan didn't clear her, she would probably either kill something or break down crying. I placed myself between her and Mimi, then waited to see what would happen.

"You may enter, Lieutenant Tomkins," the door intoned. "But these others are not authorized. They must wait outside."

I stepped up to the door. "My name's Sonny-Bob Culpepper and I'm from the twenty-second century. Perhaps you've heard of me. I have quite a reputation with doors."

The door hesitated, and I could almost hear it swallow nervously. "Very well," it coughed, "hail and welcome. You all may enter."

"Why, thank you, door!" I said.

"Don't mention it."

The door slid open and we entered. A sullen man, a bald-headed old coot, looked up from his desk. "Lieutenant Tomkins! You need to change that uniform. How did you get so wet?"

Then his gaze fell on me and he gasped. "You!! Oh my Goddess, spare me, spare me . . . No, Lieutenant Tomkins, don't leave! Please don't leave. I need you here." It seemed he was about to break down crying.

I stepped forward. "Hello, Turd," I said.

He stood up shakily. "Don't call me Turd, Culpepper. I can call you names now. I outrank you!"

"So you do," I responded calmly. "But you still can't call me names."

He stood there breathing heavily for a moment, his face as red as a lobster's back. Finally: "What do you want, Lieutenant Culpepper?"

"I'm not a lieutenant anymore. I've been promoted to captain."

"Impossible!" He waved his hand disdainfully. "Last I heard, they were reviewing your service. They were trying to find a way to get rid of you."

"They're always trying to find a way to get rid of me, Turd. But I'm always three steps ahead of them. Anyway, once all the other field agents vanished, they couldn't promote me fast enough."

"Vanished? How'd they vanish?" Colonel Turd was coming out from behind his desk. I guess he'd decided it was reasonably safe to approach me.

"Timewave."

He gasped and fell onto his desk, holding onto it for support as Lieutenant Tomkins fell heavily into a chair. She sprawled there and I glanced at her to see if she was really wet.

She was really wet. Well, I was glad I could pleasure her without touching her. Since I hadn't had a chance yet to review Mimi's level of repression, or lack of it, I didn't know how she'd feel if I became intimate with another woman right before her eyes.

For I didn't want to hurt Mimi. No way, not ever. So I would treat her with all the delicacy appropriate to the situation. Hemingway was confined to quarters, unless and until Mimi decided to release him. And even if she did release him it would take her a long, long time to get used to him. The process by its very nature would have to be gradual and delicate. I would have to call upon all my sensitivity to WOMAN, and become even more sensitive to this very special particular woman, before we could . . .

"Timewave? Timewave?" The Colonel was gasping and sputtering and growing blue with fear. "Timewave?"

"Well, Colonel, you've mastered that part of your vocabulary. Now we can move on to the next word."

Lieutenant Tomkins spoke up. There were tears in her eyes, for she knew what a timewave could mean. "Then all of this . . . it was for nothing?"

"It wasn't for nothing yet, Child of Aphrodite. The timeline still has me."

She began to sob. So did Colonel Turd.

Finally, he spoke. "Well, I guess I'd better summon everybody and have them assemble in the chapel. At least we can beseech the Goddess to allow us to still exist in the new timeline. Some of us *might* still exist in the new timeline."

"Forget it." I waved my hand. "Nobody exists in the new timeline. Nobody but some bacteria, so if you want to come back as a culture of bacteria, I guess the Goddess has you covered. If you want to come back as a human, animal or plant, you'll be disappointed. The earth is completely barren."

They both wailed in unison. I let them finish.

"Culpepper, what happened to all the other agents? And the generals . . . I would think the generals themselves would have tried to save the timeline before sending you."

"The generals did try and whatever happened to the other field agents also happened to the generals. When they left for the past, some of the earlier ones might have had faulty info and materialized in the middle of the timewave. As I understand it, Intel wasn't sure at first when the timewave originated. If, say, they thought it started in 2012 and sent an agent back to 2010--poof! No more agent, for the damn thing actually starts in October of this year. I guess we'd all better celebrate Samhain early."

They were sober and silent, so I continued. "As for the other agents who may have made it back early enough to stop the wave, I don't know what happened to them. In any case, after 1983 they'll vanish into non-existence, assuming any of them are still alive somewhere.

"I'm surprised some of them didn't check in with you when they jumped back into the Twentieth."

Lieutenant Tomkins and the Turd glanced at one another. I smelled something fishy, and it wasn't a pussy.

"Captain Culpepper," the Turd began, gesturing to Mimi, "everything we've been discussing is classified. Send the child outside . . ."

I crossed the room in two strides. "She's no child, dipshit. If you want to see a person with warrior qualities and healing properties, look no further than this young lady. She's young in physical years, but we both know that doesn't count for much when you consider how many incarnations a person has had, and how hard they've worked to develop themselves during those incarnations. She's an old soul, and by Goddess she's more of a woman than you'll ever be.

"We've both been taught the truths of reincarnation by the prostitutes . . . well, maybe not you, Turd. I did interfere with your education when you were a cadet. But I remind you that you brought that upon yourself by speaking disrespectfully to a prostitute. No one speaks disrespectfully to women in my presence." I gave a low growl. "Especially not you. This woman's name is Mimi. You were disrespectful to her. Apologize."

I folded my arms. "Apologize."

The Turd snorted. "I don't have to apologize to anyone in my own office, Culpepper, especially not some child--"

My arms unfolded. My right cross intercepted his big meaty head and he collapsed unconscious onto the floor. I glanced at Lieutenant Tomkins and smiled apologetically at Mimi. "He's a slow learner, darlings."

Lieutenant Tomkins cleared her throat and tried to stand. She barely made it. I could see she was still shaken by the manhood that throbbed within my pulsating trousers. "Captain Culpepper, I don't believe the Turd--I mean, Colonel Shepherd--would want you to know this, but several agents did stop by over the last three or four years. It's against regulations for me to tell you this; as you know, a field agent isn't supposed to know anything about another agent's business for security reasons. Unless, of course, they were assigned to work together. But under the circumstances," she smiled, "to hell with regulations!"

I could see I was having a positive effect upon the lieutenant's consciousness. She was beginning to expand. "Go on," I encouraged.

"Well, those agents said their mission was as far above top secret as you can go. We respected their status as field agents and didn't pry. However, one of them did tell us there was a major crisis in the timeline and that he had evidence it was caused by a TAC operative. Then he vanished, along with whatever evidence he'd collected. All we know about the operative he suspected is that she's female. He referred to her as 'she'. I sensed something out of the ordinary and encouraged Colonel Shepherd to send a report of these goings-on up the timeline. There wasn't much else we could do.

"We're not set up for field ops per se, and never attempt adjusting the timeline. It's rare when any field agent shares the nature of his mission with us. We're here simply as a support and monitoring service. We gather info on the Twentieth and send it up the timeline, and we support the field agents who come through with Intel, logistics, sexual relations and anything else they want that we can provide." She bit her lip. "As for sexual relations, I'd be happy to serve as your temporary wife, if your beautiful young lover doesn't mind.

"In fact," she licked her lips hungrily, "I'd be happy to be temporarily married to *both* of you. I think you'll find I'm loving and skilful and--"

I had walked over to her. Now I placed my hand on her arm. "Lieutenant Tomkins . . . Sharon. Mimi and I appreciate your very kind offer, we truly do. You are as beautiful a product of future humanity as I have ever been privileged to behold. However, Mimi and I are just getting to know one another, and due to the constraints of the Twentieth, I feel it would be best if I devoted all my attentions to Mimi. I'm sure you understand."

"What constraints?" Mimi stood there with her hands on her hips. "I don't know anything about any constraints."

"But darling, you said you've never even been kissed until today."

"True enough. Because, as I told you Sonny-Bob Culpepper, I've never found the right man. But today I've found him, and I'm willing and eager to do anything he does. Anything *you* do, Sonny-Bob.

"Yesss . . ." she squirmed, "I'm so eager I can barely stand it!"

Well, now. I guess my question regarding her level of repression had been answered.

Sharon crossed to Mimi and put an arm around her shoulders. They looked knowingly into one another's eyes. Suddenly, I was the one who was squirming. Until now I had been unfamiliar with this condition.

"Mimi . . . Sharon . . . uh . . ." I didn't want Mimi to go too fast. I wanted the simmering and savoring to take a long time. And most of all, I wanted that initial simmering and savoring to take place with me alone, for I knew how truly special this young woman was from the moment I laid eyes on her.

"Sonny-Bob," Mimi spoke. "Sweetheart. We both know we are destined for one another. Yes, I feel it too, and I can see clearly that you do. When you fainted in that ice cream parlor I knelt down and felt your heart and I know what's in it. I've never had an experience like that before, but with you it was natural.

"If you feel it's best to go slow, we'll go slow. I like Sharon, she's beautiful and competent, and beneath all that competence she's also sweet. Almost as sweet as you are, maybe.

"Maybe after I've learned a little more, then we can visit with Sharon." She put both arms around Sharon's waist and squeezed her. I guess they were soul sisters.

"We can wait, can't we, Sharon?"

Sharon stroked Mimi's hair. "As long as it takes, beautiful Mimi. As long as it takes."

This time I was the one clinging to the desk for support. I'd had no idea it was possible to find a woman like Mimi in the Twentieth. First Lucille, now Mimi. This bizarre century was getting out of hand. But in a good way.

When the Turd regained consciousness he found me sitting at his workstation going through his files. Mimi and Sharon had gone off to get a glass of fruit juice--at least, I think that's all they were doing.

"You look refreshed, Snow White," I remarked. "Have a nice nap?"

He just grunted, then pulled himself to his feet. "What're you doing, Culpepper?"

"I'm looking for clues as to the identity of the woman suspected of sabotaging the timeline."

"So Lieutenant Tomkins told you. I wouldn't have."

"Then you're a bigger fool than I thought, Turd. With your lack of cooperation you're endangering the world we hold dear, the world I saw destroyed just as I left the Twenty-Second."

"With you out to save it the timeline's already in more danger than it will ever recover from. We're goners."

"You'll be a goner if I do save the timeline, because I'm going to submit a report on your lack of cooperation."

The Turd was rubbing his sore head. "How exactly was the timeline destroyed?"

"In October of this year there is a nuclear exchange between the United States and the Soviet Union. A nuclear winter is created that lasts at least a century. All life on earth is destroyed. End of story."

"Impossible! No country in this century has even developed nuclear weapons yet . . . but wait a minute. Now that you mention it, half the personnel here have had bizarre dreams recently, something about a nuclear arms race, the Cuban Missile Crisis, Hiroshima and Nagasaki. Things that never happened. Or did they?"

"They did happen, Turd. In the original timeline, anyway. Those dreams--they weren't dreams. This present reality is the dream. It will be when I'm through with it, anyway."

With any major change in the timeline would come the "dreams". No one knew for sure which dreams had once been real and then turned back into dreams. In fact, if my mission was successful, no one but Hubert and I would have any concrete grasp of what had happened. So I'd have to worry about keeping my rank. Those blasted generals would believe I was still a lieutenant, unless I could somehow convince them otherwise. They might even try to confine me for impersonating a captain, if they could summon a large enough security force.

I wished mightily there was a way I could selectively save the timeline. If only I could save the parts I liked, while deleting the parts I found offensive. Those generals would never bother me again. Would never have bothered me to begin with, in fact.

I finally stood. "Well, Your Turdness, I'm through here. Didn't find anything anyway, and never figured you'd be much help to begin with. You're addicted to rules and regulations, even more so than the generals. You're a goose-stepping oddball. I repent that I ever restricted you from the prostitutes. I can see I went overboard in my zeal to protect the women. I should have just beaten you up and hoped that a deterrent effect from the process would sink into your thick head. But I was younger then and sometimes overreacted.

"Yes, I sincerely regret restricting you from the prostitutes. If they had been successful in teaching you about love, you would have forgotten all about rules, or at least been willing to set them aside from time to time."

He was trembling, growing flushed with rage. "Culpepper, you son of a . . . Argahaaaaaa!" He tried to tear his hair out, but there wasn't much to tear.

"Maybe you'll be more successful if you try to tear out your pubic hair," I informed him.

He smouldered. I hoped he didn't have a dog to kick around. I'd better not hear of such abuse or I'd be back.

"Turd, Turd, Turd. All this is unnecessary, don't you see? If you would just work on your rehabilitation with the prostitutes for a few decades, I'm sure you would heal. You would learn about love and forget about your goose-stepping. I know you have a staff prostitute assigned to this installation, and I know that several of your TAC personnel are trained as lay prostitutes. There's help all around you, man! Wake up and smell the roses. Love can't come to you unless you're willing to accept it. Goodbye." I left him stewing in his own juices.

After a brief search I found Mimi and Sharon in Sharon's quarters, reading poetry to one another on the bed. But they were both still dressed and I smelled no hint of passion fulfilled. Indeed, Sharon had exchanged her wet uniform for civvies.

Mimi jumped up and hugged me. "Sharon's been telling me about your reputation with the TAC, sweetheart. I'm so proud of you!"

"Uh . . . Mimi, I think Sharon may have exaggerated my reputation in a rather favorable direction. You see, if lynching were still considered an acceptable form of military discipline, the generals would've--"

"That's what I mean, Sonny-Bob! You don't put up with the shit of the tight-hearted. You're free! You're free!"

She hugged me again and I just stood there, not knowing what to think, and not sure what I was feeling, either. I couldn't remember anyone ever responding favorably to my reputation. This was a new thing.

Sharon got up and kissed me on the cheek. "In some ways you've been what I've heard you were, Sonny-Bob. In other ways you're a delightful and welcome surprise. I hope you and Mimi will come back and visit."

"Um . . . yes, ma'am. Me too."

With Mimi on one arm and Sharon on the other I ventured back to Hubert. He growled when he saw me with two women.

Mimi and I kissed Sharon goodbye. Two firsts for Mimi in one day: first kiss, then first kiss by a woman. My pioneering partner in love climbed into the "car".

When I got in Hubert was bitching to Mimi. "See what I mean, Mimi? Everywhere this bastard goes he gets women. I get left on a landing pad and he gets women. I get pissed on by dogs and he gets women. I sleep with an old ratty oxcart, and by Goddess he still gets women! I'm sick of it, do you hear? I'm sick of it!" Then he squirmed and sobbed. His unfulfilled sexual desires had him in near hysterics.

Mimi petted his dash and stroked and soothed him. "Hubert honey, I'm sure Sonny-Bob will be willing to take you out looking for a girlfriend this week. Won't you, Sonny-Bob?"

"Yes, I will. Hubert, we'll go cruising for, uh . . . for females this week. We'll try to find you a lady this week."

But there were no other sentient machines on the streets of Austin. I really wasn't sure what to do. But now I knew another reason people didn't like working with Hubert. His lusts were enormous, greater than any other vehicle's I'd ever known. His lusts were jeopardizing our mission. Damn! Why couldn't I have a TITTY who wasn't a sex addict?

Finally Hubert got command of his faculties, more or less, and jumped into the opening of the tube we'd been brought down on. The tube zoomed us back to the surface and spat us out. Hubert lurched off the entrance point and waited for his dizziness to subside.

Mimi had enjoyed the trip more the second time. "That's fun, Sonny-Bob! Will we get to do it again?"

"Maybe, but I hope not. If I don't stay away from the Turd he's liable to have a shit hemorrhage."

Hubert got his bearings and began lumbering down the trail. Neither Mimi nor I wore a watch; suddenly Mimi caught her breath. "What time is it, Hubert?"

"1715 hours. That's 5:15 in your language."

"Sonny-Bob, Sue said she was calling the cops if I wasn't back by supper. Supper's at six. If we're going to make it we've got to hurry."

"Hear that, Hubert? This time we'd better exceed the speed limit. Every other vehicle does, and nothing happens to most of them. We'd better take a chance, just this once."

"Ten-four."

Hubert hopped over the gate as the guard grabbed for his gun. I guess the fellow bore a grudge. Energy bolts flashed harmlessly off Hubert's surface, which somehow put him in a better mood. He guffawed. "Eat my dust, copper!" Then he spun around in the dirt, cutting doughnuts and covering the guard with a thick layer of dust. I waved at him as Hubert headed back down the trail, still chuckling to himself.

My own mood was improved by Hubert's mirth. Apparently, flaunting authority was just the medicine Hubert needed. He'd discovered my secret.

"Sonny-Bob, that was almost as good as an orgasm, you know, the kind that makes your whole body shake."

"Well, remind me to step outside before you have that type of orgasm, Hubert."

"I wouldn't expose you to that anyway, Sonny-Bob. It's a trade secret. Not every vehicle can do it."

I didn't remind him, but he'd be lucky to find a vehicle that could have even a localized orgasm in the Twentieth.

"Where are you from, Sonny-Bob? I mean, I know you're from the twenty-second century, but are you an American? You sound kind of like an American."

"Yes, I was born to raise the flag. I'm a North Carolinian, but I've lived in Canada and other places. I work out of South Carolina."

She snuggled close to me and we kissed, then held hands. I loved her fingers. I kissed her fingers and she smiled.

Hubert always had something to say. Anytime I wanted to relax in silent bliss with a woman, he always had something to say.

"Sonny-Bob, weren't some of your ancestors from this state?

Weren't they from Texas?"

"My ancestors were from everywhere. My descendents are even more widely scattered. But yes, some of them were from Texas.

"In fact, I was always told that the branch of the family I take after the most lived right around here on Lake Travis. My great great great great grandmother probably lives somewhere within spitting distance of where we are right now. Her name is Simone Slocum."

"Sonny-Bob," Mimi squeezed my hand tightly, "Simone Slocum is my mom."

I shrugged. I was no longer surprised by such things.

CHAPTER NINETEEN

I cheerfully slurped my food, grinning at Sue who sat across the table from me. She turned her nose up disdainfully and tried to look away but she couldn't do it, not for long. Something about me fascinated her.

There were several tables in this great hall and nearly a hundred people ate noisily, each apparently trying to out-slurp the other. Most were students; a few, like Mimi, were vagabonds of one type or another.

These students and vagabonds not only ate here, they lived here. The place was called a cooperative and was similar to a huge group marriage, except that the co-op had less sex and more tension. Really, it was similar to a huge dysfunctional group marriage. The sex that did occur was more furtive than in a real group marriage; there seemed to be a taboo against sex and nudity in the common areas. I scratched my head when I learned of this, but made no comment. I am adaptable.

Mimi sat beside me, toying with her food. She had turned inward. I guess the novelty of discovering I was her descendant hadn't worn off yet. It would.

We finished our grub, as my friend Daniel Boone used to call it, and stacked our plates crudely in a plastic bin. "Sonny-Bob, I've got after dinner cleanup. It'll take a couple hours. Maybe Sue can keep you company until I'm finished."

Sue snorted at me for the umpteenth time. She sounded like a doe in heat. Really, she oughtn't to do that. But then she just snapped her fingers and shoved a thumb over her shoulder, indicating I should go where she went. So I did.

We wound up on the third floor of this place, this Santa Fe Cooperative, as it was called, and Sue shoved a key in the lock and opened the door to the bedchamber she and Mimi shared. It was sparse. I wouldn't call it putrid, but the place certainly could have used some beautifying.

We stepped inside and Sue shoved me down on a bed. *This is nice,* I thought, but then Sue dragged up a chair and straddled it backwards, arms resting on the chair's back. She seemed judgemental.

I smiled.

Finally, she spoke. "Sonny-Bob Culpepper, or whatever your name is, for all any of us here know you're a rapist or a burglar. You're weird as hell and you act like you've never had anyone show you how to behave in public. And I won't have you playing with Mimi's emotions. She's young, probably twenty-five years younger than you (actually, she was nearly sixty-one years younger than me, but who's counting?) and she's never even been kissed . . . wait a minute! What was that look?"

Sue sighed. "So now she has been kissed. What else did you do?"

"Well, Sue, not much else. We held hands and hugged a lot, and we made a new friend at Lake Travis named Sharon. Mimi got to kiss her, too--"

"What!" Sue was on her feet, the chair went flying. "What did you say?"

"What part didn't you understand, Sue? I'll be happy to repeat the part you didn't understand."

Sue was livid. I'd given up on trying to predict the responses of this beautiful but primitive female. Everything I said seemed to send her into another spasm of anger or consternation.

"Why are you so angry, Sue?"

She was so mad she was choking. She could only point her finger at me and choke. Clearly, she had psychological problems. Compassion flooded my heart.

"Sue, if you need to see a doctor . . ."

She reached down and grabbed me by my shirtfront and started shoving me towards the door. "I know you detest me, Sue, but if you would just tell me why, maybe we could work this out. Your responses are primitive, but I can try to work around that if you'll just give me a chance . . ."

She shoved me out and slammed the door in my face. I shrugged and went downstairs to Mimi.

Mimi looked up from her dishwashing. Even though her hands were busy she was still inwardly focused. "Trouble with Sue, Sonny-Bob?"

My hand stroked the rear of Mimi's heart chakra. "I don't have any trouble with her, honey. But she seems to detest me, and won't even tell me why."

Mimi shrugged. "Sue's been disappointed a lot. I think she's trying to keep me from getting hurt."

"A commendable motive," I agreed, "but her methods leave much to be desired."

I joined Mimi in the washing of the dishes. A couple of times our fingers joined in the hot soapy water and Mimi looked close to tears. "We'll talk after we're through with our chores, sweetheart," I whispered.

After we'd finished our labor, as they called it (each co-op member was required to do several hours of labor per week to keep the place running smoothly), we found ourselves on the great flat roof of this cooperative living facility, gazing at the heavens as the heavens gazed at Austin. After a while Mimi's fingers laced themselves through mine, and then she turned and faced me and wrapped her arms around me.

"Sonny-Bob, I don't care if it's wrong, I still want you to be my first. I love you." She squeezed me tightly. "I do!"

"I know, honey. Remember what you said about us being destined for each other? Well, it's true, both our hearts know it's true. But why would you think it would be wrong?"

"Sonny-Bob . . . we're *relatives*."

"Sweetheart, you make 'relatives' sound like a dirty word. Why would that be a problem? I know about that ridiculous incest taboo, but nobody here knows we're kinfolk. Even if we told them our status, they'd think it was a joke. They wouldn't be able to comprehend how you could be my ancestress.

"You're my great great great grandmother, sweetheart. So what? I'd love you even if we weren't related at all. And I know you're not limited like these other people; you're ahead of your time in many ways. But if you want to wait for a long time to make love, or if you decide you don't want to do it at all, it's okay with me. It has to feel right to you, Mimi, or it won't feel right to me, either.

"I love you, sweetheart. You're the best Granny a boy could have." I kissed the top of her pretty head and hugged her tightly.

After a while she looked up. "Sonny-Bob, are you saying there's no incest taboo where you come from?"

"That's right. The incest taboo died a slow death, but it was pretty much gone in America by the end of the twenty-first century. People were beginning to see things logically by then, and a few people were even becoming genuinely compassionate.

"Most people of my time feel that the incest taboo was necessary for primitive animalistic people who hadn't learned to leave control, manipulation and the use of force out of their relationships. Most of my people feel that for the primitives the incest taboo did more good than harm. They may be right. I don't know.

"But my people don't need the incest taboo, we know we don't need it, and we simply aren't going to put up with it. 'Repression Creates

Perversion'. Deny baby candy, and when baby grows up he becomes a perverse old candy addict.

"The appropriate course of action would be to obtain wholesome all-natural candies loaded with vitamins and minerals. That way baby's desires are fulfilled, he won't be injured by the candy, and he can either take candy or leave it when he grows up. Do you see?"

Mimi shook her head tiredly. "No, I don't see, Sonny-Bob. I was talking about sex, but you're talking about candy."

I cleared my throat. "Well, it's like this, honey. Everyone wants to fuck their relatives, and if this desire is chronically denied, perversion sets in and the person becomes obsessed with what he can't have. He's a perv.

"Even worse, if he ever finds himself in a position of authority relative to one of his kinfolk, he may manipulate that person into having sex, or he may even rape the person outright. Or he may simply fondle the person's ass from time to time without their consent, or he may jack off while fantasizing about them, then feel rage because he can't really have them and guilt because he's done something in his heart that he publicly decries. He is conflicted. The heart is the real person, so to be one type of person in your heart and then pretend to be something else in public is hypocrisy. And hypocrisy feeds on itself and creates more rage and guilt and self-loathing and hypocrisy. And abuse. In extreme cases, the person unconditionally surrenders to his hypocrisy and releases all his values to the four winds, though outwardly he still makes a pretense of being a 'good citizen', a 'good churchman', or whatever it is that causes his fellow hypocrites to approve of him. For most, if not all, of his peers are hypocrites too, to one degree or another. The 'good citizen', 'good churchman', or what have you doesn't really exist except in fantasy land. There is little if any reality to the view that most twentieth century people have as to what constitutes a good and moral person. But they're afraid to explore themselves and change into genuinely moral and spiritual people. If they did explore themselves with self-honor, they'd have to change much of their outward manifestations to conform to their hearts. Practically the whole culture would come tumbling down. This is what my people did do, and humanity is much the better for it. We're a much more honest and genuinely ethical race in the twenty-second century. For my people, the Bronze Age of the Twentieth is over. Compared to your people, mine live in a world of gold.

"So I think we've established that the incest taboo produces rage, guilt, hypocrisy, agony and abuse.* It degrades humanity. The incest taboo is unrelated to love.

"Therefore, the only logical and compassionate course of action is to eliminate the incest taboo and to work on eliminating control, manipulation and the use of force from all our relationships. Then if we do fornicate with our kin, it can be a loving and respectful relationship instead of one based on control and manipulation. It can be a nurturing relationship instead of a dysfunctional and damaging one.

"But I must emphasize: the strings of control and manipulation must go! Only then can genuine love and respect manifest. Only then can genuine freedom manifest.

"Do you see, honey?"

She looked up and sort of smiled. "I'm starting to. Keep preaching, my love."

"Of course, in the twenty-first century when people first began to do the hard work of getting free of control and manipulation, some people did get hurt as the buried strings of control and manipulation rose to the surface of society. When you begin to purify yourself all sorts of shit comes loose and floats to the top of your consciousness.

"Some people got screwed up by all this and became bigger perverts than they had been when they were repressed. They didn't have the self-discipline to contain their responses to others until they had the spiritual and moral maturity to relate without control and manipulation and force. So they began to prey upon others. Fortunately, these people were in the minority, and fortunately a percentage of them were caught and disciplined, which served as a deterrent effect to some extent.

"You see, Mimi, what we're really talking about here is purifying your shadow; cleaning out all the confusion, glamour, egotism, control, manipulation, emotional fluctuations that were programmed by families and institutions, and all the other garbage. Then the shadow is free to be absorbed into the light of love, and it's also free to simply be itself, and to go wherever its own personal road takes it, at least until the moment of the Final Absorption. Anytime it needs to pop out of the light to be itself, it can, as long as it remembers to carry some of the light of love with it. The shadow can love, and as long as you're left with a loving shadow, you're free.

------

* The laws and taboos of primitive humanity frequently stoke the fires of whatever problem they were allegedly meant to solve. Makes you wonder about the motives of lawmakers, eh?

"One of the biggest mistakes made by some people in the late twentieth and early twenty-first centuries was to try to make will more important than love. This mistake was caused by the glamour of the will, and any person who explores his shadow is likely to experience this. When you begin exploring your shadow and the varieties of egotism it contains, those impurities fight back. They fight so hard they swell up, for they are in a life or death struggle with your heart. For some time, you actually become *more* of an egotist. Unfortunately, many people lose this battle and choose the illusion of egotism over love. They may have contacted their souls, but if they never finish purifying themselves they'll never be absorbed into their souls.

"Anyway, I've studied the case histories of those people who placed will in a superior position to love. Without exception, all these people became miserable and more confused than ever. Many came to some sort of untimely end. Only a few of them ever saw the light, so to speak, and disciplined themselves to work through the glamour and illusion they'd created with their wills, and returned to the path of love. But some did. That process is very difficult, but some made it.

"A person's will is important, for it provides a means of manifesting a person's love on this earth. *Who* a person is serves as a vehicle for manifesting *what* that person is. And each person *is* love. So the will is important because it allows our SELF to manifest on the earth. And because the will of the race had almost been destroyed by millennia of oppression, the race did have to work to reclaim its will. A tough task, indeed.

"So it is easy to see why some people fell into the glamour of the will and mistakenly believed the will is superior to love. But the truth is that our heart, our *love,* is what we are. The automobile is not superior to the driver. Goddess is love, and we are all sparks from the heart of the Goddess, we are all souls of love.

"We are a collection of splendid souls of love; you, me, Sue, and the rest of those vagabonds in the building. All of us are love.

"And all of us have personalities. Our personalities are the vehicles driven by our souls, driven by our SELF. The will that most of the willful follow is the will of the personality, not of the soul. That's the problem. And they pollute their perceptions still further by claiming to be searching for their 'true will', or even that they have come to embody their 'true will'. Well, the truth is that none of them knows anything about their 'true will' because before you find the side of your will that's connected to divinity you must first find your heart and purify your shadow and personal will, then learn to live permanently centered in your heart. That's what a prostitute I once slept with told me, anyway. She said that embodying divine love must come before embodying divine will or the organism would shatter. It would go insane at best. Almost certainly it would die and most or all of its vehicles would be shattered. Its personality would be gone, and so would its emotional and mental bodies. Its physical body would die as well, unless it were placed quickly on life support. So those people in the late twentieth and early twenty-first centuries who were searching for their 'true will' should really be glad that it was impossible for them to find it. As it was, they tortured themselves by glorifying their personal polluted wills, mistaking this small aspect of themselves for an unreachable divine will, instead of subjecting themselves thoroughly to the purification process and then learning to live sweetly in their hearts. But it would have been much worse for them if they had actually been capable of finding the thing they said they were looking for.

"Anyway, honey, I'm trying to learn to live in the heart. That's where it's at for me. I may screw up from time to time, but I never abandon the journey, not even for a second. When I fall off the horse, I still manage to hang on to its tail and let it drag me until I can climb back on. For the real person is inside the heart, waiting for the heart to open fully and irradiate the outer form with love, light, life, and power.

"The personality, which basically consists of the aggregate of the individual's physical, emotional and mental faculties, must be purified and integrated so all its aspects flow together smoothly, so they work together harmoniously. Then the personality can place itself directly under the rulership of the soul's inspiration and begin to perform its highest function and live its highest destiny, which is to serve fully as a reflection of the soul, so the soul may perform its work of creation upon the material plane.

"I know that twentieth century people usually see themselves only as an isolated personality, and that they usually view one major division of their personalities as dark and another as light. This is a one-dimensional view fostered by a one-dimensional society. But for the purposes of our discussion I'm using the word 'personality' synonymously with 'shadow', because from the soul's perspective the entire personality is dark. The entire personality is shadow. In some sense there may be varying degrees of shadow in the personality, but compared to the fragrant light of Soul, the whole damn thing is dark.

"But this dark personality is also very, very rich. It is the sweet loam that the soul fertilizes to bring about its work of creatively manifesting love upon the earth. It is infinitely rich, and one day the psychologists will discover this. The darkness has many, many facets that can be brought into refinement and service of the Light of Soul. It is common sense, I suppose, to declare that the soul is multidimensional. However, most people aren't yet aware that the personality is also multidimensional. For a multidimensional soul has to have a multidimensional vehicle of expression.

"So people who run from their shadows are shortchanging themselves. The shadow will never reflect the Light of Soul until it's been purified and integrated. A tough task, but it has to be done. And remember, anything that doesn't reflect the soul is perverse.

" 'Repression Creates Perversion'. I hope I've thrown some light on the subject."

Mimi was nearly asleep. She just sort of nodded. "Sonny-Bob, thanks for the sermon. I don't understand half of it, but thanks anyway. All I know is I love you and if you're willing I'm going to make love to you. And *you're* the best descendant a Granny could have.

"But right now I'm sleepy. It's been a long day."

I lifted my darling into my arms and carried her to her room. Sue was there and glared with the face of extreme disfavor upon me. I took little notice of her, though, for my heart was aglow for my Beloved.

I placed Mimi in her bed and she was asleep practically as soon as her head touched the pillow. I kissed her forehead, and didn't glance at Sue to see her response. I gazed tenderly upon my Beloved, then left the room.

I slept in Hubert that night. I'd never realized how much he snores.

CHAPTER TWENTY

Mimi didn't go to school. Or rather, she didn't go to one of those artificial and brutal schools that permeated this medieval land, where kids had to become brutal themselves just to survive. Instead, she taught herself, which was why she no longer lived at home. Instead of allowing herself to be transformed into an insensitive machine, she found ways of encouraging the growth of her natural sensitivity and preserving her heart and individuality. Her mom, Simone Slocum, my great great great great Granny, told Mimi she'd have to go to one of the artificial schools. Mimi replied that she'd rather get educated than continue going to an artificial school. But Simone wouldn't bend, so Mimi split. Smart girl. Now she was free to learn and grow.

My favorite Granny was one of the earliest examples of the fact that you can't teach multidimensional children in a one-dimensional school. You can't teach them at all. They have to be allowed to teach themselves. If you're arrogant and insensitive enough to try to teach them, they'll either shoot you in an attempt to reclaim the power you've stolen from them, or they'll be among society's walking wounded, traumatized by a bestial culture. Primitive education turns the multidimensional child into a problem for himself and others. Only the mediocre are arrogant, unloving, and irrational enough to consider themselves teachers. They are not perceptive enough to discover their own multidimensionality, so they trample the multidimensionality of the children underfoot and destroy many of them. The teacher is a dinosaur. In my time children are exposed to leaders--not teachers, but leaders-- who serve as shining examples of the fully developed, non-hypocritical, multifaceted, loving and powerful human being. The human being who is not too afraid of his own shadow to discipline that shadow and allow it to reflect the light of love. This is what is important, and this is what the leaders of our children provide. They don't provide "education", they provide an example of radiant human possibility. The kids see what is possible, then devise their own programs of instruction to begin to expand their own awareness.*

Letting kids teach themselves is just common sense and good karma. They **will** teach themselves if left to their own devices, and any so-called adult who tries to lay his trip on the kids is creating pain for himself in the future. You can't get off scot-free when you infringe on another's will or heart, and the fact that the other individual comes in a smaller package and only recently gave up an addiction to the pacifier doesn't change this most basic truth. A child is not a child. A child has had many incarnations. A child is a peer.

So Mimi--my favorite peer throughout the timeline--educated herself. She sat in on university lectures, but didn't have to put up with any infringement since she wasn't officially a student. She read voraciously and meditated. She consulted her own heart during every minute of the day. And she and I had just started training together in hand to hand combat and in the proper, safe and responsible use of weapons. She would be much better educated than those kids in the artificial, bestial schools. She would be much more in tune with the many facets of reality and of her own nature. And she was already lustrous, whereas the standard-issue twentieth century kid had never been allowed to glow with the vital force of his own nature.

My Beloved worked three or four days a week at a little doughnut shop to pay her half of the rent and to get a little spending money. She told me she was paid "under the table", and I had no idea why she would have to crawl under a table to get paid. But these people had many strange customs.

She'd opened the doughnut shop this morning, and I watched excitedly as some of our fellow Austin vagabonds arrived.

Our fellow vagabonds came in many varieties. Some wore the type of suit (I think it was called a business suit) that was designed to trumpet their significance to one degree or another. Let's see, the gentleman in the three-piece suit must, in this society, be the equivalent of a three-scalp Comanche a century or two earlier. And the fellow who's wearing a suit, but no vest, is a two-scalp Comanche. Yes, that's how it works here. I can't wait to make my report.

But what does the briefcase represent? It must be sort of like a coup stick a warrior would use to touch a living enemy with to demonstrate his

---

* "I never teach my pupils; I only attempt to provide the conditions in which they can learn."--Albert Einstein

bravery. Yes, rush in and touch the enemy, then run like hell and if you live you'll have something to brag about in the teepee that night. But what enemy could you strike with a briefcase? The thing was square and clumsy. Yet these "warriors" of 1983 handled their briefcases with the same attitude and authority the Comanche handled his coup stick with. Or me my Hemingway.

Later, after researching the matter more thoroughly with Hubert, I realized that computers and portable phones similar to my phone would become the coup sticks before the end of the century, assuming I saved the century.

But there were major differences between the late twentieth-century warrior and the warriors of every previous century. The Comanche, for example, had to exhibit courage and physical fitness to qualify for a coup stick or a new feather in the bonnet. But the "warriors" I observed this morning had to exhibit the reverse qualities to be permitted to carry their modern coup stick. They had to exhibit fear and subservience in the presence of their chieftain and rank conformity to all the customs and taboos in the land, even those that were established in Washington, D.C., which was far away and in another reality from Texas. As far as I could tell, they were forbidden to challenge their chieftain's viewpoint to any substantial degree in a powwow, and it was --gasp!--actually considered a crime if they challenged their chief to open combat over a matter of honor. Indeed, all these modern "warriors" were expected to be **without** honor and they pretty much were, all the way from the one-scalper up through the twenty or thirty-scalper.

Yes, as the centuries had advanced Americans had gone from being a robust people to devolving into a craven, cowardly people afraid to rock the boat of their own perceptions, and never daring to challenge in any substantial way the illusions of their society. And these were the descendents of the peasants who, against all odds, had defeated the greatest empire of the time and established the energy of liberty in the land. They had always been primitive, but when they still had a physical frontier to explore, those among them who still had some spirit left could go farther west and not be ganged up on by those who feared the candid life. The bold could set their own agenda when America was young. But now the country was ruled by the factory consciousness, the cookie cutter mentality. The boldness had mostly been stamped out. Americans didn't recall what it was like to have a frontier that was open to all, where each individual of sufficient daring would be free to follow his own destiny. But I remembered, for I had visited primitive America, which in some of the most important ways was actually less primitive than the country was in 1983. If President Reagan had not come to infuse a little spirit back into the land, it probably could not have survived.

In the late twentieth century Americans were so confused that they actually equated narcissism with individuality. They seemed to believe that purple hair would somehow make up for a lack of soul consciousness. They were conscious of themselves only as members of a herd, whether a herd of cookie cutter conformists or a herd of purple haired narcissistic conformists. They did not know that genuine individuality develops only when a person works to develop soul consciousness, and then works to allow himself as soul to rule his outer form. And they could not distinguish between a herd and a genuine group. They did not know that genuine groups can only be formed of genuine individuals. There is no conflict between a real group and a real individual.

The whole problem of the herd mentality, which can only exist when people are kept unconscious of their true natures, would become even worse before the century ended. This problem would be typified by the election of the artificial president, the creature history would come to know as "Slick Willie". The 1990's were a decade completely without honor in the national life. When a nation can be manipulated into sacrificing its honor, as Slick Willie and his henchpersons convinced Americans to do, then that nation has also sacrificed its individuality. No honor equals no individuality. If a better breed of person had not begun incarnating right away, and if not for the influence of Lucille and her friends, America might never have regained her honor from the hands of the frightened little control freaks who had sucked it off to begin with.

I ate my doughnuts and I drank my coffee, and I continued to peer into this swirling pool of humanity. I saw that in addition to the alleged warriors, there were also no-scalp Comanches who came into the little doughnut shop this day. They arrived without briefcases or suits. Many stank, and the "warriors" in the suits always tried to give them a wide berth. Too, the "warriors" were always in a rush; they'd practically run in and grab their doughnuts and coffee and fumble for their money with shaking and impatient hands, then they'd run back out with their meal, apparently on a mad quest for more scalps. A two-scalper is always after his third scalp.

But these others, the ones without briefcases or suits, shuffled in slowly and often lingered. Their aroma mixed with the aroma of doughnuts and fresh coffee and gave the place a romantic quality. These people, I saw, were not considered true Comanches by the ones in suits.

And they usually seemed too mild-mannered to be scalp takers, so there didn't seem to be much hope that many of them would ever be initiated into the tribe. Still, I got the impression that a couple of centuries earlier things might have been different. The ones with briefcases and suits had given up on any real tests of warriorship and had settled for a life of easy manipulation and self-justification, thereby losing their moral fortitude and honor. I doubted they could hold up under the stress of hand to hand combat, let alone endure the agony of being tortured by an enemy tribe.

Many of the shuffling ones, however, clearly knew how to endure torture, and I saw the mark of combat upon some. These people were brave. They would have been happy to know that in the twenty-second century real warriorship has been restored. Their daily battles would have been honored in my time.

Mimi bustled around serving people. Unfortunately, many were cops. I hid behind a newspaper when they'd come in. The fewer cops I had to kill, the less likely it was the tax collectors would come for me.

Over the course of an hour or so I ate ten or twelve doughnuts and drank five or six cups of coffee, plus several glasses of orange juice. Also, I fed and juiced and coffeed some of the non-scalp takers, who seemed appreciative. I urinated frequently.

I stayed all morning and by the time Mimi was relieved at noon I was so full of doughnuts I could barely stand to go to the restroom. Yet somehow, I always made it.

"Sonny-Bob, I've never seen anyone eat that many doughnuts or drink that much coffee."

" 'Repression Creates Perversion', sweetheart. I was denied doughnuts and coffee in the cradle, now look what I've become."

"Well, I called Sue and she's going to meet us here for a powwow, as you call it. She doesn't have any afternoon classes today. I know she's just trying to protect me, but she has to understand I'm a grown woman and can take care of myself." She reached out and took my hand. "I'm glad you understand, Sonny-Bob. You're the only person I've ever met who does."

" 'Course I do, my love." Smack, smack, chew. Swallow. Coffee slurp. Juice, two slurps. "Certainly I understand. In my time everyone in every jurisdiction on the planet has his full adulthood rights by the time he's fourteen. In many jurisdictions the age is thirteen or twelve; in a few it's eleven. My people don't try to artificially extend childhood the way yours do." Belch.

"Oh, here comes Sue." Wave, wave. "Over here, Sue."

Sue approached, a sort of a neutral glower on her countenance. "Hi,

Mimi." A sort of a throat clearing, a looking me up and down. "Hello, Sonny-Bob."

"Hi, Sue. I've got to pee. Be right back." I waddled away and when I returned Mimi and Sue were sharing a coffee and doughnut and arguing about me. I stood there quietly, not wanting to attract attention to myself at that particular moment.

"I'm telling you, Mimi, that guy's a loser. And he's worse than a loser, he's just plain weird. That co-op we live in is full of weirdoes, but at least they're regular weirdoes. Sonny-Bob is an unclassifiable weirdo. You can never tell what he'll do. Does he take medication?"

Mimi sighed wearily. "Not that I know of. I wish you'd just give him a chance, Sue. I love him!"

"HA! Mimi, you don't know what love is. I've felt that way before, too--"

"No, you haven't! You've never felt this!" Mimi pounded her chest. "If you had you wouldn't knock the feeling. You've never really felt love, Sue. If you had you wouldn't try to interfere with it."

"I'm just trying to keep you from getting hurt . . ."

"By hurting her?" I said mildly. I stepped up to the plate with my bat in my hands. I sat down.

Sue gave me a regular-style glare this time, nothing neutral about it. "I don't know who you are or what your problem is, but--"

"What have I ever done to you, Sue?"

She paused, but she seemed about to explode, somehow.

"I repeat, what have I ever done to you?"

"Nothing," she said sullenly. "Yet."

"That's right, I haven't. And I don't plan to do anything wicked to either you or Mimi. I don't know why you despise me and hold me in utter contempt, but I like you. Mimi said you're a good person and I believe her.

"Mimi I love; you I can't reach to offer my love. You live behind a wall and I can't scale it or bust it down, and it's not my place to do that anyway. I feel there's a magnetic heart somewhere inside that wall, but only you can let go of the wall and let your heart shine. Or not, as you see fit.

"In any case, though I love and admire and respect women more than any other beings, I'm becoming less and less inclined to continue to put up with your abuse. If you can't find it in your heart to tolerate the fact that Mimi and I are together, we'll find a place of our own to live. Until we do find new quarters, however, you'd better behave more respectfully. I'm not normally abusive to women, but I'm sure that with a little practice I could learn to be as mean as you. I am not a helpless victim."

Sue had withdrawn, her hostility was no longer smashing with nearly as much force against my aura. She was also a little pale. Her breath was shallow, and I thought I detected the beginning of a tear.

"I just don't want Mimi to get hurt, Sonny-Bob," she finally said.

"On that we're in agreement, Sue."

"Sonny-Bob, she's just a child--"

Oh, brother. Not again. People in this benighted time simply hadn't learned it's the age of the soul that's most important.

"Sue, I am *not* a child. And don't use that language around Sonny-Bob; he gets upset. I am a woman, Sue, a grown-up woman. I still have some physical growing to do, but I'm an adult and I know I'm an adult despite all the pressure to permanently remain a child that comes from you and everyone else. I'm an adult, and by Goddess--I got that from Sonny-Bob--*nobody's* going to stop me from being what I am. Sonny-Bob's the only human being I've ever met who understands this basic truth. I don't know why the rest of you are so blind. Anyhow, Sue, you're just eighteen yourself. You haven't been around much longer than I have."

"Four years makes a world of difference, Mimi."

"Not in matters of the heart. Whether you accept my adulthood or not, lay off Sonny-Bob. I love him, I always have and I always will."

"You always have . . . what are you talking about?"

"Sonny-Bob and I know, that's all that's important. But you would begin to understand if you would just open your heart and be yourself."

It was time for me to put my oar back in the water. "Sue, you're just going to have to accept the fact that Mimi and I love each other," I said calmly.

Sue was grasping for some control over the situation. "But you don't even know each other! You just met two days ago!" She was red-faced, and the tears were finally beginning.

"Sue, love is independent of time and space. It is the great force that permeates the cosmos. And a bit of that force radiates from each active human heart. When two people are in touch with that force within themselves and a magnetic attraction occurs between their hearts, that magnetic attraction happens in the NOW. Not after what egotism would consider a decent interval of time, but NOW.

"Egotism always does everything it can to exclude love, Sue darling. Egotism tries to *control* love, and it's a fact of nature that love cannot be controlled. Any attempt to control love automatically excludes love.

Then all you're left with is the greedy needy domineering manipulating fearful egotism of the unenlightened personality. Then you're at the mercy of your unpurified shadow; you've returned to a corrupt darkness instead of purifying and disciplining your shadow to accept the magnetic radiance of love.

"Mimi and I are only marginally egotists. We're in recovery from that affliction. Mostly, we feel the force of love within ourselves, so we aren't going to put off until tomorrow what exists today."

Sue's jaw had dropped and her eyes were wide. She looked astounded. I guess she hadn't thought I was smart.

Mimi reached across the table and took my hand. She kissed my fingers. "I couldn't have said it better, my love."

Sue was just looking down at the table. She seemed far away. "Okay," she finally said. "Okay, Sonny-Bob. If this is what Mimi wants . . ." she raised her hands in kind of a helpless gesture, "I'll try to be more respectful. I won't interfere with you and Mimi.

"But you'd better not hurt her!"

"I love her," I said softly, and with the way my heart was radiating in that moment I was certain that even Sue could see it.

And suddenly, the whole universe ceased to exist and there were only two where there had been many. The doughnut shop was gone, Sue was gone, everything was gone except the radiant heart of my Beloved and my own radiating heart.

And our two hearts danced in the union of eternity, and then we were one heart.

CHAPTER TWENTY-ONE

I wound up paying my share of the rent. Sue went through the bag of money with me and pointed out which bills I could pay with and which ones were flawed.

"Sonny-Bob, I thought you were a nut when you talked about having a bag of money and said part of it was in three dollar bills. I apologize. But you do do things differently."

I patted her hand. "That's okay, Sue. I'm not familiar with all the customs of this century."

She gave me a long glance, but said nothing. Mimi had decided to wait about publicly claiming me as a descendant, and Sue had no idea where I was from.

A couple days later the three of us sat over breakfast at a dining facility called Good Eats on Barton Springs Road. They offered a breakfast taco product which I especially enjoyed, so I'd ordered three for myself and one each for the ladies. And the homefries were so delicious I ordered four helpings just for me.

"Sonny-Bob, if you keep eating like that you're going to be too big for us to house," Mimi warned.

I just smiled around a mouthful and kept on chowing down. The truth was that for the last two years I'd lived almost exclusively off of alcohol, and for decades prior to that it had been a major part of my diet, though not the only part. I seemed to have some nutritional deficiencies as a result, so now all I wanted to do was eat and take vitamin and mineral supplements. The love that Lucille had somehow managed to slip past my initial lust had apparently cured me of alcoholism. But I sure was hungry.

Sue toyed with her food. "Mimi, you said that you and Sonny-Bob were going to tell me something humongous this morning. But the only humongous thing is Sonny-Bob's appetite, as far as I can tell."

"More milk, please," I belched to the waitress.

"Yes. Well, Sue, it's hard to explain, but . . . let me just tell you a story first. It's a science fiction story; I read it the other day in a magazine.

"In the twenty-second century, you see, they have time travel. And there's an organization sort of like the Freemasons that sends people back in time to correct imbalances in the timeline. Am I doing okay so far, Sonny-Bob?"

"Fine," I managed to slobber around a mouthful of sausage and egg.

"You see, if an imbalance occurs in the timeline it effects the future. They can't allow that in the twenty-second century, because they live in a paradise. The people are morally and spiritually advanced. There is no hunger or disease, because food can be instantly produced and disease can be instantly cured through the science of nanotechnology. There is practically no government. Young people are free, not kept as pets or slaves to society's egotisms and fears and self-justifications as we see today.

"Love is acknowledged as the ruling force of the universe, and all humanity is striving to contact the love within their own hearts. Plus, they've learned the right use of logic--finally!--and therefore have gone a long way towards dispelling the glamour, the illusions of the world. For they know that glamour obscures love.

"Everyone is expected to behave responsibly towards her neighbors, and if she doesn't her neighbor can defend himself with any degree of force he chooses and no one will come along later and prosecute him. The full and complete right to self-defense is acknowledged as the cornerstone of all morality.

"However, most of the people are learning the scientific use of the Golden Rule, which means they usually rely on 'appropriate force' measures whenever possible and they deliberately try to treat each other well so they can advance the cause of their own personal energy and the group energy of whatever group they belong to. If they can advance their energy far enough, they'll probably eventually become so loving and powerful that nothing can ever infringe on them again anyway.

"The Sacred Prostitutes of Aphrodite are the preeminent spiritual force in the land. They undergo decades of discipline to purify and integrate their shadows, then practice the discipline of learning to lift up their shadows into the Golden Light of their own Love.

"The life of a prostitute demands the utmost in dedication and discipline--not repression! That's why very few applicants can even pass the test to be accepted as a Probationer, and most Probationers never make it to the first degree.

"If a Probationer doesn't make it to first degree after twelve years she's asked to leave the temple, but she can apply again twenty-two years later if she wants and start all over as a Probationer again.

"If she does make it to first degree, she may remain in this degree for the rest of her career, because of the difficulty of advancing to second degree. But at least she's a fully vested Prostitute of Aphrodite with the privilege of serving humanity in this fashion for as long as she wants, assuming she keeps her motives and energy flowing cleanly.

"Most prostitutes never make it beyond first degree. The dedication and discipline of the prostitutes is beyond anything seen in the twentieth century. Despite the difficulty of advancing, there are thought to be ten degrees of prostitution, though theoretically there might be more.

"The story I read was about a prostitute who ran the Diocese in Asheville, North Carolina. Her name was Amanda, and according to the story she was the gentlest, sweetest, most patient and kind and loving prostitute in the world. She was a sixth degree initiate."

Sue looked bored. She propped her elbow on the table and her jaw rested in her hand. "Could men become prostitutes, too? I'd like that."

"Of course! The twenty-second century is very enlightened, there's no racial or gender or age discrimination. Discrimination is only practiced against glamour, which is another word for illusion. The people of the future are peeling the glamour away from the perceptions of humanity like the skin of a stinky old onion. This is accomplished largely by the right use of logic, but since logic can create and get lost in its own kind of glamour if it is not ruled by the heart, the heart is acknowledged as being the ultimate organ of spiritual illumination. Love rules the cosmos, and each divine human being must rule her own personality--her 'outer form' --as a living soul of love.

"The soul radiates and governs the outer form through the heart, so the majority of people in the twenty-second century have chosen to walk the path to their hearts. Few have learned to live in their hearts full time and some haven't gotten there at all yet. But most are trying and they'll eventually make it if they are dedicated enough."

Mimi sighed. "I wish I lived there."

"Interesting story," Sue said disinterestedly. "But what does that have to do with you and Sonny-Bob?"

Mimi paused. She took a deep breath. "Sue, that story I just told you isn't fiction. It's true! Sonny-Bob's from the future!"

I sat back and pooted. "That sure was fine," I sighed.

Sue looked from one to the other of us. "Ha, ha. Sonny-Bob's from the future. I suppose that old Pontiac of his is from the future, too."

"That's right, Sue," I said. "He isn't really a Pontiac, he just looks like one. He's a TITTY--a Tactical Interdimensional Time Traveling

Yacht--and his name's Hubert. He likes you and Mimi better than he likes most primitive females." I pooted again. "Excuse me, darlings."

Sue just shook her head. "I was worried about your hurting Mimi, Sonny-Bob, but this is worse than I'd thought. You're sick, and now you've made Mimi sick. You're both delusional.

"Sonny-Bob, I don't hate you. Not anymore, anyway. You're nice enough in your own strange way. But I have to ask you to get help. Please get some help, for Mimi's sake."

"I don't need any help," I belched. "Hubert gives me all the help I need. He gets pretty grouchy, and sometimes he cusses. But that's just because he doesn't have a lady. We have to find him a lady."

Sue buried her face in her hands. "Oh my God . . ."

Mimi laid a hand on Sue's arm. "Sue, let's go. We can talk to Hubert and that'll prove he and Sonny-Bob are from the future, won't it?" Mimi sort of pushed Sue out of the booth, then got out herself. "Are you coming, Sonny-Bob?"

"In a minute, dearest. I'm going to get a few breakfast tacos to go."

Mimi shook her head while staring pointedly at my waistline. It was true I was on the verge of becoming rotund, but as long as Hemingway was in no danger of being buried by my avalanche of fat I wasn't worried about it. Neither was Hemingway; he knew nothing could bury him except an extraordinarily huge vagina, and he liked that.

Mimi led Sue away. A few minutes later my breakfast tacos came and I went and paid for the morning's festivities. There was a shelf there with many brightly colored bottles of alcohol, but I only had eyes for the breakfast tacos and homefries. I pooted and left the building.

As I approached Hubert, I saw Mimi and Sue were having an argument. Almost like a lover's quarrel, except that they weren't lovers. At least, not yet. Sue was too closed-minded to even let *me* sleep with Mimi; I'd been sleeping on the floor. But sooner or later she'd get tired of tripping over my dick in the darkness, and then she'd let me sleep with Mimi. I was sure of it. I understand feminine psychology, you see.

I went up to my darlings. "How's old Hubert? Now're you convinced, Sue?"

"Sonny-Bob," there was an edge to Sue's voice, she seemed to be in a mighty struggle to maintain her patience, "this sick little game has gone on long enough. Your car doesn't speak and you're not from the future. You're probably from the state hospital and now you've got Mimi believing in your delusions.

"Mimi may be a grown woman, but she's my friend too. I care about her. I won't let you and your delusions continue to invade her brain. Go back to the hospital, Sonny-Bob. Go back and get some help. I'll put your things outside the door, take them and go. Stay away from Mimi." Here a trace of that old glare reemerged. "Stay away from Mimi!"

"I guess Hubert didn't speak," I remarked. "Well, that proves nothing. He *can* speak, when he's being cooperative."

Sue made a noise that was almost like a growl. She just stood there vibrating.

"Sonny-Bob, you told me not to talk to any more twentieth-century people without your permission," said Hubert. "I didn't know you'd told Sue it was okay to talk to me. You did tell her it was okay, didn't you?"

"Yes, old bean. It's okay to speak with Sue and Mimi, but watch out for these other people. Many of them are crazy and paranoid and have hallucinations, as we've seen ever since we've been here."

"But Sue and Mimi are our friends. So speak away!"

"Sue, you have nice legs," said Hubert.

Sue was astounded. Finally she said, "You're a ventriloquist, Sonny-Bob. Cut it out!" But she didn't seem to be quite as mad.

"Come with me, little girl," Hubert leered, "and take a magic carpet ride!"

"It's true, Sue. Hubert can fly. Mimi's been wanting to take a flight, but I've been too busy sampling Austin's fine dining facilities. But now that I've got an armload of breakfast tacos, I don't see any reason we can't take flight for a while. We'll just need to stop someplace first and buy a vacuum bottle and some coffee."

"Yes, Sue," said Mimi grinning. "Get those nice legs and scrumptious tush in the car! Time to fly!"

Sue got into Hubert, perhaps a little reluctantly. Mimi got in on the driver's side, then scooted to the middle as I joined my twentieth century beauties. I placed the breakfast tacos under the seat, confident I could get at them if I needed them.

"Mush, Hubert! Take us someplace I can find a vacuum bottle and coffee. Maybe a few doughnuts, too."

"I can make those things with my NPD, Sonny-Bob."

"True, but I want to eat natural junk food and drink natural coffee. As you've noted, the natural stuff is healthier than what you can produce with your nanos."

"Ten-four."

For the past couple of days I'd been learning to pretend to drive. Hubert had coached me and I'd felt confident in pretending to drive Sue and Mimi. I hadn't believed anyone could tell I wasn't a real driver.

But now Sue said, "Sonny-Bob, I thought you were showing off before, just trying to freak me out. I figured you'd somehow switched the brake and accelerator. I didn't know the car was driving itself."

"Himself," Hubert corrected.

Sue cleared her throat, still not quite sure what to make of all this. "Yes, Hubert . . . himself. You're a himself."

"Thank you, Milady," Hubert responded primly.

At length we were fully supplied and I wasn't too worried about running out of food while we were in orbit. For I planned to take the girls into outer space.

We had to escape prying eyes for the launch, so we went into the country west of Austin and cruised the backroads. We pulled off into a pasture not too far from a little community called Dripping Springs.

"Well, Hubert," I said. "It's zero hour. Launch!"

"Ten-four, I've got your back door!" Hubert cried and sprang into the sky. I don't know what that gibberish he was spouting off meant, but he'd been listening to the primitive language of the long distance trucks of this era and imitating them ever since we'd been in the Twentieth. Contrary to my expectations, some of them apparently could speak and had advised my horny friend to try to find something called a "pavement princess". I didn't like the sound of that.

"Whee!" Mimi exulted, clapping her hands. "Hubert, you're the best car ever!"

I could feel Hubert's pride factor increase twentyfold. He turned a spacebound somersault at an altitude of around twenty thousand feet, and the next thing he knew Sue had treated his dashboard to a puking. He straightened up and flew right after that, and sent in a stream of nanos to clean up the mess.

I handed Sue an oral hygiene packet. "Let this dissolve in your mouth, sweetheart. It's almost as good as brushing and flossing."

As we approached the outer envelope of the earth's atmosphere, Mimi whispered in awed tones, "Sonny-Bob, Sue, I *never* thought I'd see this day. I've always wanted to go into space and now it's happening. It's really happening!"

Sue was still a little green-faced, so I knew now was not the time to offer her a breakfast taco. I took one for myself, though.

"Sonny-Bob," she finally said in sort of a little girl's voice, "I'm sorry I ever doubted you."

"Don't worry, honey. I get that a lot. It's okay."

Soon we were in orbit and I commented on what a pleasant day it was to be floating past the continents. "Atlantis was over there, girls, see? And Lemuria was in the Pacific. California is a remnant of the continent of Lemuria. That explains why California's so strange. It's governor's probably a Lemurian; they say there's still some left high up in the mountains."

By and by we met up with a primitive spacecraft so Hubert turned his headlights on. Mimi spoke up. "That's the space shuttle, Sonny-Bob! I've always wanted to ride on the space shuttle, but Hubert's got them outclassed. The space shuttle can eat our space dust!"

"Thank you for your vote of confidence, Milady," Hubert said humbly.

Sue nervously cleared her throat. "This has to be a dream. It has to be! No other explanation."

"Don't be silly, dear," I told her. "I would never invade your dreams without your permission."

The faces of primitive astronauts were plastered against the portholes of their silly old shuttle staring at us, so I had an idea. "Girls, I'll bet some of those primitive astronauts want to go to the moon, so let's give them their wish. Follow my lead!" I dropped my trousers and plastered my naked butt to the windshield as Hubert rotated to give the primitive astronauts a better view.

Mimi chuckled and immediately joined me. I held Hemingway in position for the astronauts to see, too. If not for Hubert's artificial gravity my huge member would have been floating weightless and the muscles of my buttocks and abdomen could have relaxed at last. But no such luck.

Sue fumbled with her shorts and got them down to her ankles, then treated her panties in the same fashion. I gasped; her pussy was so pure and sweet it almost made me cry with liquid zeal. It could have come straight from the hand of the Goddess. Mimi looked at me, eyes twinkling as Hemingway began to swell with robust longing. "She *is* beautiful, Sonny-Bob. Go ahead and look if you want to."

I tried not to look because I didn't want Hemingway exploding all over Hubert's cockpit. He'd already been vomited on and might not be able to maintain his composure if I presented him with another indignity.

The primitive astronauts gaped at our three naked butts plastered to the windshield of that old '68 Pontiac and I felt sure there would be parts of their mission they wouldn't want to talk about later.

"Hubert! Cover your license plate. They might think to write down the number."

"Okay."

After awhile we grew tired of this game. "I'm tired of raiding astronauts, ladies. What say we go to the *real* moon? You know, that big one over there."

Mimi grinned and hugged me excitedly. Sue kind of nodded her head and put her panties back on, removing a vision of heaven that was more beautiful than the stars in the sky. But that didn't matter, because the love of my lives was with me, and she was the only true vision of both my heart and my tool. I hugged Mimi to me and breathed deeply of her fragrance as Hubert swung around and pointed his nose at the moon.

It took us about half an hour to get there, and along the way I became increasingly absorbed in my Beloved. However, both she and Sue were becoming increasingly absorbed in the moon, so I contented myself with kneading her shoulders as she sat breathless on the front edge of the seat. Both of us were naked, as befits any true spacefaring person. Mimi was learning my futuristic ways fast. Sue had tossed her shorts and upperbody frock into the backseat, but still wore her panties and slingshot. I could have told her she was glorious, that she had nothing to be ashamed of, and that in the twenty-second century the whole world would have knelt down and worshipped her sweet pussy. But for a person who a few hours earlier had been too repressed to even let me sleep with Mimi, I thought she was coming along pretty well. Everything is relative. My hands fell to Mimi's waist. Sue was absorbed in the moon.

Mimi twisted and looked at me. "The moon is beautiful, Sonny-Bob. And so are you." Then my Beloved kissed me; she turned herself into my arms and she kissed me. I felt her pert little nipples pressing into my chest, and for the first time I reached down and stroked her breast.

Mimi gasped as her erect nipples responded to my loving touch; she rose to her knees to bring her breasts nearer to my mouth and flung her arms around my neck and pulled me into her. My lips and tongue sampled those nipples and began their emancipation. "Do me, Sonny-Bob," she whispered wetly. "Do me now. It's time. I want you . . . oooh, it's time!"

I came up for air and glanced at Sue, feeling she might not be entirely comfortable with all of this, but she was still engrossed in the moon. I don't think she'd even noticed what we were doing.

So I returned to the twin fountains of universal blessing that are open to all who show them respect and love. They are the source of all religion, along with the Chalice of Sweetness, and to these living, pulsating relics we always return. All our spiritual strivings lead us back to where we began, and we find comfort there.

My tongue swirled in little circles around Mimi's nipples . . . yes, I tasted of this woman and my heart and soul and body were exalted into ecstatic union within themselves as I felt myself transiting from a condition of flesh and blood and bone into a flowing bountiful stream. Somehow Mimi, my own sweet girl, was teaching me to flow . . . I was no longer a collection of particles. I was a wave.

And as a wave I began to swell and throb with celestial beingness, which was appropriate, since the moon was only a couple of miles away. I felt my swollen wavehood begin to splash upon the shores of this moon, this celestial body whose seas had been dry so long. I made love to the moon, and her seas were no longer dry. As a pulsating wave I filled the sweet seas of the shining moon. I covered her as the sea covers a sand castle with the froth of a spurting tide.

I heard a moaning in my ears then, the moaning of my Beloved as I stroked the undersides of her nipples; already in my excitement and in my love for her I had spurted myself upon her . . . it could not be helped. But now as I returned to myself I devoted myself to her enjoyment. I devoted myself to her service.

She gasped, and a little whimper escaped her, and as my consciousness returned from wherever she'd sent it and my physical eyes adjusted themselves to her physical body, I gasped and whimpered too, already growing hard again. For she was beautiful, all copper and froth of the sea, and she was young again and free to enjoy her springtime. I knew no lust; it had been transmuted the first time our auras touched. When I had spurted myself upon her, the spurting was not only one of passion, it was passion commingled with love. I was purer than I'd been in a long time; I sucked her nipples and felt nourished by the mother of all the world. Together we were clean, the child-mother and the father-son. We were clean and in joy.

I enjoyed her virginity, I enjoyed her virgin's wonder at the joy of being loved, at the tender fierceness of being loved.

She slid her glistening copper Aztec body upon me and I saw out of the corner of my eye that Sue had taken notice. I turned my head and smiled at her; she gave a hesitant smile in return. "Sue, I think Mimi might enjoy your touch. Mimi hon, do you want Sue to help us?" Mimi just nodded, eyes closed as I reached out my hand to Sue and guided her to us, guided her hand to the flesh of the young Aztec girl we both loved.

Sue reached out hesitantly as she stroked Mimi's body, and I saw the wonder begin in her eyes, too. I knew she loved Mimi and that Mimi loved her. But I don't think Sue had ever really believed she'd ever find the courage to touch Mimi. Until now. Floating around the moon in an old Pontiac, Sue's dream had begun to come true.

This old moon had seen the human race do many strange things, but it had never seen a seventy-five year old man make love to two teenaged girls in outer space in a purple 1968 Pontiac. Not until today.

My hand rested on Mimi's belly as she gasped and panted and moaned with a steady humming noise. It seemed a little early for the humming noise, but she'd never been loved before and her hot Aztec juices were boiling for expression. "Sonny-Bob . . . oh, Sonny-Bob . . ."

Then my hand found the crown jewel, the object of every hero's quest, the sacred grail of womaness, and the holy cup was full to running over. She was moist, as moist as a ripe watermelon, and the cunt of her passion overflowed with zeal. I rubbed it back into her, back into those distended little pussy lips, then I sucked it off my fingers and let Mimi have a taste, too. Mimi sucked my fingers as I made noises of appreciation.

Sue's hands snaked around Mimi's body and cupped her breasts, and Sue was aglow with the juicy wonder of this moment. She moved in with a spurt of courage and kissed Mimi's cheek, then accepted Mimi's lips as Mimi turned them to her. They kissed lightly at first and I saw a tear of love and gratitude in Sue's eye. "Oh, Mimi . . ."

"Sue . . ." They breathed into each other then, just as I'd shown Mimi over the last couple of days, and with breath and tongue they delivered themselves of the burden of unspoken love. I smiled, and a tear of gratitude and appreciation for their beauty and their love fell from my eye, too.

There was a warm glow of love and compassion in the cockpit now. For we were sharing in that most human of ways, we three who had met only a few days before. But genuine love isn't limited by time and space; it can't be. If genuine love is present, time and space are not.

I felt a gentle peace I hadn't felt in a long time. Something was being restored, somehow the ancient was made new; it was brought forward in a new form and a wave of sweet love enveloped us all.

Sue's egotism was washed away in this blissful loving tide, she abandoned egotistical inhibitions in the flowing absolute love she felt for Mimi. Her grief at not having previously been true to her own heart escaped her in great sobs and her body began to shake with the horrible violence of those repressions and perversions. But Mimi and I saw that it was good, the controls and manipulations were working their way to the surface to be felt and processed and released, and our dear, dear Sue did have the courage to feel them fully, and then to release them forever to be dissolved in the radiance of the glowforce of the multiverse, the always welcoming and forgiving light of Love that underlies all manifestation on every plane.

Mimi and I were awash in love for Sue and for each other. Sue felt it, we all did; Hubert must've felt it because for once he was silent and unobtrusive. Amanda once told me that we owe it to our creations to serve as a sort of avatar to them so that they also may come to feel the energy of Love. So today we served as examples to Hubert, examples of what true sentience is all about--it's not about sex, it's about love, but the love must be grounded into humanity through the union of heart and passion.

Today we were avatars to the machine.

Leagues away upon the planet earth, which Amanda had said would one day become one of the seven sacred planets of our galaxy and serve as an incarnation of the divine principal of love, there were billions of people caught up in the smallness of egotistical repressions and the always-accompanying perversions, people who believed their egotism and their small personal wills were superior to the supreme glowforce of love within their own hearts. So they ignored their hearts and concentrated on trying to limit themselves and others. They grasped for the limitations inherent in control and abandoned the freedom of accepting the rulership of their own hearts. But all that would one day change.

Mimi and I glanced at each other and with mutual accord we moved to comfort Sue and envelope her in our love forever. We were a part of her and she was a part of us, and though the outer forms might change through the eons, our essential unity would never change. We would all grow together throughout eternity.

There is a place where no thoughts can intrude, a realm which no words can assault or reduce. Mimi and I embraced our dearest Sue and together we carried her to that realm of forgiveness and love, and we watched in awe as she forgave herself.

And after a very long time we returned to earth.

CHAPTER TWENTY-TWO

The alarm clock told our souls to return to our bodies and it was done. Mimi reached over and shut it off, then pulled the covers over us and snuggled with me. I yawned. "I'd prefer a rooster to that thing, sweetheart."

Mimi just giggled and drew me tightly to her. Hemingway lay across her thigh, but our love was so much bigger than Hemingway he shrank into insignificance in the face of it. But he didn't mind, for when love radiates out from the heart and pervades the whole body, it also pervades Hemingway, and he felt humbled and glad to be acknowledged by this great force. He smiled to himself and all was well.

Across the way, Sue turned in her bed and we rejoiced in the great wave of love she sent us. We all were radiating, like three firecrackers that never fizzled out or exploded but glowed through eternity. We were brothers and sisters and fathers and mothers, and we weren't fluctuating to undisciplined pre-programmed emotions; we fluctuated only to the rhythm of the great tide of love that had brought us to one another.

Mimi's tongue found mine and we shared the breath of life and love. A long, slow kiss that might have lasted only a minute or two, but seemed to last for days.

Then Mimi withdrew a little and looked into my eyes, and through our eyes we filled one another with the liquid gold of our hearts. Mimi's hand was on my cheek, where it had always belonged. Suddenly I felt small and vulnerable in the presence of her vastness. I felt myself draw up, and she put her arms around me and comforted me.

Then Sue joined us in our bed and the energy changed. I felt Mimi smile. I always felt Mimi's smile inside me, and I know Sue did, too.

Sue and Mimi shared a silent embrace, then shared in the communion of the tongue, and I was glorified by their loving. I glowed along with them. The sucking of the tongue is the true way to live.

Finally, Mimi returned to me as I lay soft and humble in our nest. She smiled. I felt her descend from the more refined regions of the heavens and enter into a mode of raw physicality. This, too, is appropriate. "Well, Sonny-Bob, I guess I'm still technically a virgin. There's no way you can get inside me . . . yet. But I have a plan I'll tell you about later. Meantime, you can watch me rub my clit."

She flung back the covers and lay there naked, a woman who physically looked like so many Aztec ladies I had known, yet who glowed with a mixture of earth and love unlike any other being I had ever experienced. I was in awe of her and wanted to worship her and sing praises to every molecule of her forever.

She had to get to the donut shop to open up in a little while, but as she lay naked in front of my wondering eyes she touched a part of herself far tastier than any donut. In spite of my food addiction, a donut had never inspired me to worship. But Mimi's pussy did.

Men are simple. Feed us, water us, tread respectfully around our hearts, and give us frequent opportunities to worship. That's all we want.

Sue and I held hands as we watched Mimi rejoice in being a woman; she rejoiced in her clit and all the feelings that came with having one. Truly, of all organs in the universe, the clit must be the most special. Next to the heart, anyway.

Mimi's eyes closed and her questing tongue flicked circles around her lips as her legs opened wider still. The beautiful hymen lay there, apparently untouched . . . yes, I'd touched it, but because it was one of those hymen that mostly covered the Gate of Heaven I hadn't even inserted a finger, fearing I might break it prematurely. I had kissed it respectfully, and touched it in the same spirit. Since hymen are pretty easy to break, and often are "popped" during the course of normal day to day activities in ladies who have never had sex, I was a little surprised to see that my Beloved still had one. But as long as she did have one, I was going to be utterly respectful of it, even as I was respectful of every feature of my Beloved. I kissed her forehead, and I wept from the beauty of her self-love.

Sue snuggled down next to Mimi, one hand on her hair and the other on that taut little belly. She kissed Mimi's cheek, then their tongues found each other and Mimi shuddered. She shuddered again and gave a little yelp; some moisture squirted out of her as I knelt to praise her with lip and tongue.

I kissed the sacred spot as her fingers framed her clit. I drew the clit into the gap between my front teeth, as it was still bulbous with love. It hadn't withdrawn yet, it must still have something to say, some hint of wisdom to impart to me, the seeker after the sacred wisdom of women's mysteries, the things I could know only second hand, but was willing to learn to the best of my ability. Mimi was my professor; I went to the college of Mimi. I was fascinated by every lecture.

Her swollen clit felt my teeth stroking it on both sides as I sucked it up through the gap. It has always seemed unwise to me to actually bite a clit, too much potential for disaster, but it was perfectly safe and secure between the gap in my front teeth. My tongue helped to hold it in place.

She was moaning in earnest now as Sue's body lay draped partially over her. Sue had learned respect for her own body even as she'd learned to respect ours; she was naked as a blonde-headed jaybird. She'd been freed by this respect, for it had helped her release the shame that prompts primitive humans to clothe themselves without reason. No artificial coverings were needed among true friends.

Sue's rather ample whitebread tits squished into Mimi's smaller, darker ones with passion driven by the creative force of the universe. I paused in my clit sucking and watched with great interest.

Sue had only kissed me deeply a couple of times as we circled the moon yesterday, and I thrust my erect and mightily pulsating cock into neither of my friends. The time wasn't right just yet. True, Mimi's lips had found him and she eagerly pursued this new adventure of cock tasting and cock loving; her tongue had made the head and shaft of my cock feel welcome, but it wasn't time for her to make me come in this fashion just yet. So as my own whitewater rapids began to form and threatened to spurt out of me I'd tenderly withdrawn El Cockus from Mimi's hands and lips and slipped my tongue into her mouth and kissed her with all the love in my heart. Amanda and Lucille had taught me sensitivity. I knew it wasn't time for me to come in Mimi's face.

So now as we three friends lay together in our room at the start of a beautiful new day, I allowed some of my saliva to drip upon Mimi's pussy and I massaged it into her with my tongue, making the chalice glisten with all the wetness appropriate to a blossoming young woman as she writhed and cried with the pain of her newfound joy. I worked my way up to her belly, the young tight belly which enfrenzied me with desire. I kissed her belly. I lay there upon her, kissing her belly and knowing that I was kissing the wide, wide universe. I knew that I was at home in that wide, wide universe, the universe of my Mimi, the taut moist universe of our eternal love.

Mimi's leg now pressed against my scrotum and Hemingway reached 'way up her body to touch both of my loves, for I truly did--and do--love them both. In a savage and barbaric time, when people were sometimes imprisoned and raped as punishment for love, my darlings stood head, shoulders, and tits above the cold-hearted Atheist Christian masses. For the Christian of the Twentieth was an Atheist; actually, he was less than an Atheist. The Christian claimed to believe in God, then lived according to the cause of hate, repression and control and manipulation. God is love, but this principle is not compatible with the Christian mindset, and there is no Christian heart. Not anymore. During the early centuries of the Christian movement there was love, but the love was eventually lost in the materialism of the Catholic empire, and the Protestants who came along later had no experience of love to draw upon, so their doctrines and lifeways were also without love. Love is life, but the Christians had lost the cult of life and become the cult of crucifix and tomb. This is why they tried to eradicate the life-loving Pagans in Europe and the sweet lusty savagery of the Pagans of the New World. The Christian worships death; he is always mistrustful of the life-energy. And the life-energy is sexual energy. This is why the Christian nails the life of sex to his cross of doom.

At least the Atheist usually managed to live his foolish doctrines. The Christian could not, for to suppress the life energy is to create hypocrisy. The life energy will not be suppressed for long. The Christian is an adulterer, but he doesn't enjoy it as much as other people.

And so my love flowed out to my darlings, along with compassion for them for having been born into such a cold and brittle society, and admiration that they'd managed to release repressions and perversions and become pure. It was astonishing that they had managed to avoid freezing to death in this society of the crucifix. But they were warm and getting warmer. They belonged to the society of the cauldron, the society of the chalice with its warm draught of wine.

They were crying from love, weeping as I watched them love each other. Spasms of passion, bodies contracting, tears of joy at this union. Screams. I admired and respected them more than I could ever tell them, but I knew they could feel it as my heart broadcast to theirs.

Mimi's arms were wrapped around Sue, the Brown Goddess nurturing the White Goddess, the dark nurturing the light and giving it the strength to manifest itself. For I knew Sue's secret, and I think she knew that I knew. But I'd said nothing; I loved her so. I waited for her to tell me. It would have to be discussed sooner or later.

Mimi shuddered in a vast orgasm, vaster and deeper than the primordial current that created the world. Her screams of love must've been heard all over the co-op, and probably by passers-by on the street, too. The song of her passion joined with the song of her soul to touch everyone's passion and everyone's soul. Those who could receive her, would.

The others, the snapping turtles, would withdraw into their cold shells and never sit before the hearth of genuine passion or love or respect. The snapping turtles might preach of love, but the word sounded cold in their mouths. And their actions were sourced in the hellish darkness of their crucified and unpurified shadows. "By their fruits ye shall know them," said a friend of mine, and he was right. The snapping turtles would only emerge to snap at the likes of Mimi and Sue and try to drag them down into a cold turtle hell, but my darlings were strong and radiant and truly powerful. No force a turtle could muster would ever be able to pull them off their mountain of love.

Eventually, turtles would be nearly extinct, anyway. Snapping turtles don't want to incarnate on a planet that's beginning to glow with love. They want to continue to infringe on one another, so in my time they've almost quit incarnating on the earth. Amanda says a planet was created just for these dense ones, a world much denser than the blossoming earth. There the snapping turtles could incarnate and snap away to their unpurified heart's content as they gradually learned their lessons at a slower pace. Amanda said this new "turtle world" would be considered a world of outer darkness to the people of my time because of the glare of its raging, seething unpurified emotion and the dark coldness of the unawakened hearts of its inhabitants. "But it's what they really want, Sonny-Bob, so they can learn the basic lessons they've neglected to learn on earth." What a turtle wants, a turtle gets.

After our adventure of the morning Mimi showered and left for work. Sue gazed at me with eyes so clear and calm and radiant she melted my heart. "I love you, Sue."

"I know you do, Sonny-Bob. I love you, too."

The two of us were still naked, as good friends often are together. She rolled off the bed and came to me as I was selecting a bath towel. I considered it prudent to see to my hygiene before going out for the day.

She took me by the shoulders and gazed up into my face with so much love I couldn't believe she was the same person I'd met in that ice cream shop a few days ago. She was unfrozen now, and her heart glowed brightly, brightly.

We just stood there and glowed together for a little bit. "Sue," I said huskily, "you would be one of the sacred women of my time. You would. Mimi, too."

"Sonny-Bob, you and Mimi have helped me find myself. I . . . I think there's something we need to discuss, though. But first I want you to know I love you and appreciate you, you nut from the future."

"I could never doubt that, sweetie, with the way you've been glowing. Ever since yesterday you've been sending waves of love at me and Mimi. We *know* you love us, just as you know we love you."

Then we embraced, Sue and I, and held each other for a long glowing moment. Then Sue stepped back and looked at me. "Sonny-Bob, I don't know how to say this. I've never told anyone before . . . I even lied to myself about it. But I'll never lie to myself again about anything." She smiled. "Not after yesterday.

"Sonny-Bob, I . . . uh. This is harder than I thought. I can stand here naked with you and I can even make love to Mimi in front of you. But I don't know how to say this . . ."

"You can wait until you're ready," I said gently.

"No . . . no, I'm ready today." She took a couple of deep breaths. "Sonny-Bob, I do like Mimi, but . . . I don't think I can relate to a man sexually. I . . . I think I'm gay. I'm sorry, Sonny-Bob, I don't think I can relate to you that way." Suddenly, she seemed on the verge of tears. "I'm sorry, Sonny-Bob."

"No need to be sorry, Sue. The only important thing here is to be true to yourself, true to your own heart, and that's what you're doing. I admire you for it. And no external condition, such as the sexuality of the personality, can ever change our soul relationship. *Nothing* will ever change my love for you. *Not ever!"*

Tears were streaming down her face. "I've lied to myself for sooo long . . . the lies just plugged up my heart and I lost my way. I've been with men, for a while I was with lots of men. All kinds of men, all ages. Just men. Trying to hide from a part of myself, only it's more than a part of myself. It's *me,* Sonny-Bob. It's *me."*

"I know, darling. I've had lesbian friends before and I kind of sensed you might be another lesbian friend. But it wouldn't have been right for me to press the issue. I had to wait for you to tell me."

"Oh, Sonny-Bob." She fell into my arms choking on her sobs. "Sonny-Bob . . ."

"That's right, Sue. Let it out, let go of it. Let it all go. Release it. I'm here for you, always will be."

She had made a start at forgiving herself and being healed yesterday with me and Mimi. Now she was taking another big step. I honored her for her commitment to herself, and for her commitment to the truth about herself. More of the dark pollution was released from her heart and floated skyward to be dissolved in the universal radiance we call love, the radiance which calls itself nothing, but which in truth is everything.

More sobs, more convulsions. She coughed and screamed and beat her fists against my chest. I could tolerate the bruises; Sue's healing was more important.

"I love you, Sue, and the Godforce of Love treasures you as a precious jewel. The Godforce of Love doesn't judge you or me or anybody. It just waits for us to accept It, It waits for us to come home to It. We are love. Just expand into your Self, Sue honey, and let your Self carry you back home to the Godforce. Let your Self drive out everything that is not you; all judgements you've placed upon yourself and allowed others to place upon you. Let these primitive delusions pass, for they are a glamour, they are an illusion. Only love is true, and you are love.

"And you're doing fine, and I am so honored to be your friend. Just keep letting it go, let it all go. Let it go, my dear friend. You're doing fine."

Finally, the bulk of it was over, at least for now. I knew from my own experience that unprocessed pollution tends to occur in layers; later on she'd have more to release. But she'd experienced herself for the first time yesterday, then again today. She *was* herself for the very first time. She was honest and pure and she was my friend. I hugged her and kissed her hair and I loved her so. I loved her so.

I told her how brave she was and how proud of her I was. Then we went about our business for the day. I smiled when I thought about how full of light Sue was now.

CHAPTER TWENTY-THREE

Sue was a student at the great university, the great University of Texas at Austin, which lay on the other side of The Drag from the co-op. It had been a few days since Sue's confession and she said she was happier than she'd ever been. We dropped Sue off this morning near a great hall where she had classes, then Hubert and I swung by the doughnut shop to give Mimi our love and moral support, and to get some free doughnuts.

"Sonny-Bob, I'm almost ready to try out that plan I have to be penetrated by you," Mimi said happily. "Soon my cherry will be popped, and I'll be like all the other grown women!" I didn't know what she was talking about; she'd been hinting at some great plan to lose her cherry for the past few days, but I hadn't been too inquisitive. I sensed that she wanted to surprise me, but if that was the case, why was she giving me this advance warning? Probably because she knew that I felt it would take months for me to get just the head of my monstrous Hemingway into her tight little box. Her shoe frankly did not fit my foot, but if it would please her I was willing to try to wear it. But she knew I was an unbeliever. She was not compromising her surprise by revealing to me that she had this plan, for as an infidel I would not believe any such plan could succeed. Therefore, she was giving me this advance hint so she could gloat over my penis and say, "I told you so, Hemingway! I told you I could swallow you with my pussy!" However, I felt sure that no gloating could occur, so I prepared a little speech of consolation to deliver to her when she found that no technique she could devise would be enough. I had studied with the Tantrikas, the Dakinis of the Indian subcontinent during a mission when I was supposed to be doing something else, and from that experience I knew that no virgin could ever hope to contain me. Not without many months of strenuous effort, anyway. Maybe years. I kissed her lightly on the forehead and left with my box of doughnuts. I put them under the seat. I would take them back to the co-op and eat them as snacks between my final breakfast and first lunch.

So Hubert carried me to get a few breakfasts at various restaurants around town. We finished up with a few omelets from Trudy's, then went to the Wheatsville Food Co-op to buy some more vitamin and mineral supplements. I got Hemingway a supplement for his prostate, then surreptitiously added a supplement that I felt would make my balls grow even bigger. I had heard a bit of ancient folk wisdom recently: "Every millionaire is out to get his second million." I felt that this general principle could also be applied to testicles. Oh, I had my second testicle and wasn't trying to grow a third one. There wasn't room for a third one. But I had always taken regular measurements of my scrotum and I had determined that perhaps ten percent of my scrotum was vacant. There was no need for that. I knew that if my huge balls grew just a few more percentage points, there would be no unused space in my scrotum and all would be well. This ball-growing supplement was a good investment--if it worked.

"Sonny-Bob, I wish you'd quit running me around in circles," Hubert groused. "We started on The Drag, made the restaurant circuit, and now we're back on The Drag to buy your consarned pills. Then it's back to the co-op long enough to drop off your vitamins and brush your tooth, then you plan to sail away again. Can't you do anything in a linear fashion?"

"I'm too evolved to be linear, Hubert. You should know that by now."

"Evolved compared to what?" Hubert sneered. "Evolved compared to a pissant, perhaps?"

"Evolved compared to a talking tin can who wants to do everything in a linear fashion." He knew I'd outflanked him there, so he shut up. He pulled out of Wheatsville's parking lot and headed back to our habitation, which was only about fifty to one hundred meters down the street.

Suddenly a cute little car sailed past us, a type of car popularly referred to as a Volkswagen Beetle. It was shiny and pink and Hubert gasped. Then his tires squealed and the rubber peeled and he was after her. I felt his energy shift to whatever passed for his lower chakras.

"Goddam, she's fine! She's fine! I'm gonna get me a piece of that!"

"But Hubert," I remonstrated, "she's not sentient!"

"That's never stopped me before," he growled.

Hubert ran a red light, an act which I'd learned was forbidden by law, and stayed on her tail. I knew I couldn't reason with him this time, it was too late for that. And I knew he'd never forgive me and I could kiss the timeline goodbye if I pulled his kill switch. I shivered in terror and dread as I wondered if I was going to have to watch his mating habits.

He'd told me he'd let me out if he ever expected to have a full body orgasm, and I intended to hold him to that. Whatever he was about to do, I feared he'd get us in trouble with the local authorities. Cars just don't mate in public in the twentieth century. They don't.

Hubert was out of control, careening through traffic, running red lights. We came to a four-way stop and a truck was in the intersection; Hubert leapt right over him. I sighed. If this mad TITTY kept this up, he was sure to attract somebody's attention.

We found ourselves zooming down a street called Speedway, which was certainly well named, considering the way Hubert was careening around. He'd leap onto the sidewalk to pass by obstructions formed by other vehicles, then spring into the air when pedestrians were on the sidewalk and send power lines cascading everywhere. He was mad, he was mad.

Hubert's piece of ass pulled into the driveway of an older, rather rundown house. "Hubert! Listen to me now, or I'll pull your kill switch! I'll buy that car, I'll buy her! But you've got to stop now, don't you dare pull into that driveway. If you start humping her in public, I'll have to pull that switch. No choice!"

Hubert had slowed down and was wobbling uncertainly.

"That's right, Hubert. Be cool, be cool. Pull over here next to the curb. I'll go talk to the owner and see how much she wants for her."

Hubert was shaking with anguish, his need was so great. But he managed to restrain himself. He parked along the side of the street as my teeth chattered, either from the mad terror of Hubert's rampage or because of the way his passions were rocking him now.

"You'd better get her for me," he sobbed. "I need her! I need her!"

"I know you do, old friend, and you've been patient. Stay with me on this, and if money can buy her I'll get her for you."

I left Hubert and walked up the driveway, and as I'd already seen that automobile wasn't the only beautiful woman there. I glanced back at Hubert; he was still shaking from his need. Those fuzzy pink dice he'd adorned his rearview mirror with were bobbing wildly. I shrugged. This beautiful young lady would have to sell her car to me, or we'd have to sneak back and steal it.

She was blonde and she was gorgeous. My knees shook from her radiant beauty and my heart thumped wildly. I got dizzy, suddenly everything was spinning around just the way it had when I'd met Mimi and Sue in that primitive ice cream parlor.

I staggered up to her. "Hello," I gasped, leaning on her pink Volkswagen for support.

"Get off my woman!" I heard Hubert yelling, as though from a great distance, and then blackness closed in on me and I was not.

I was not.

I awoke much later. From the clock on the wall I saw three hours had passed. I was inside, but whether I was inside a mental ward or a privately owned home it was impossible to tell.

A poster hung on the wall depicting demons from the Christian hell. One of the demons had its ugly tongue stuck out and it seemed long enough to nail a hummingbird on the wing. The legend read: "KISS". I felt sick to my stomach.

An instrument was there whose nature I had studied in the Twentieth Century Tactics Class. It was called a bong and was used to deliver herbal remedies. Another device, which I later learned was called a roach clip, lay nearby. These twentieth century people had so many bizarre names for their devices. This roach clip was not used to crush roaches at all. It was used as an aid in smoking the butts of illegal cigarettes.

The air stank of burning leaves and I hoped one of the inmates had not set fire to the place. Later I learned the smell was caused by the burning of components of the marijuana plant, that plant which weakens the will and makes people open to suggestion from pernicious forces.

A permeable barrier of beads hung across the doorway to this place, this place of bongs and demons. I staggered to my feet and followed the smell of the burning leaves. As I penetrated the permeable barrier I glanced back over my shoulder and saw another poster. It depicted a young man with a guitar. The legend read: "Peter Frampton: Do You Feel Like I Do?"

"You feel worse than I do, Mr. Frampton, if you've had to breathe this odor for very long."

I coughed and stepped through the permeable barrier into the next room. I beheld two goddesses smoking a cigarette, passing it back and forth between them. One was the beautiful young blonde goddess who'd driven the pink Volkswagen, the other was an older brunette. The brunette saw me and beckoned me over. "Here comes Rip van Winkle." I looked all around the room and saw no evidence of anyone else. This Rip van Winkle was not present, and perhaps did not even exist. More twentieth century code language, I supposed.

I approached the women as they gazed upon me. I knew my beauty must ignite the passion in their loins, even as their beauty inspired me.

The brunette offered me a drag upon the foul cigarette. I waved it away. "No, thank you," I said politely.

She cocked a suspicious eye at me. "You're not a narc, are you?"

"I don't know what a narc is, ma'am. So I guess I'm probably not one."

"Sit down, then."

I was happy to sit beside the young one, who scooted over to make room for me. We were sitting on a small sofa, a thing called a loveseat. I liked this twentieth century designation.

The older one sat across from us on an upholstered chair, still gazing at me suspiciously as the two of them passed that evil cigarette back and forth. I was glad to see it was almost gone.

"Do you have a medical condition?" the younger one asked.

"Yes, it's called fainting in the presence of feminine beauty."

The older one snorted. "I told you, Aphrodite. It's just another nutcase fan, though his line is a little better than most."

Aphrodite! Aphrodite! The next instant found me kneeling on the floor before my Goddess and kissing Her toes.

I felt a hand close around the scruff of my neck, then it grabbed my collar for a better grip and tried to jerk me away from my Goddess. But I had a strong neck fueled by the passion of my devotion to my Goddess. I did not budge. I would never budge.

"Let him go, Mom! Let him go! What he's doing to my toes feels good. I think he's nice."

The hand released me and I felt the shadow of the Mother Goddess back away as I continued to bathe in the holy radiance of my Aphrodite.

And what had I, an uncouth, barely civilized man of the future ever done to deserve the privileges I had enjoyed on this mission? For Lucille was clearly an incarnation of the Goddess, and now perhaps I'd been led to another. Since the Goddess is love, she is not limited by time and space. She can be wherever she's needed, whenever she's needed. She can be right here.

I wept with gratitude, I bathed the Holy Toes of my Goddess with my tears. "Thank you," I sobbed. "Thank you, O my Goddess!"

I lifted my head to her but was afraid to gaze directly upon her sweet countenance. I know and have always known that the Goddess is love and forgiveness and compassion, yet a part of me wondered how she could forgive *me*, for I'd had sex with so many thousands of women over the decades, but in only a few cases had I ever been able to allow my heart to shine. It had always shone for Amanda, that sparkling star who never grew dim. She had somehow always brought out the best in me; she'd brought out my love every time we'd been together. Amanda *was* love, I'd never doubted that.

But with the exception of Amanda my love had never really shone much. I'd absorbed on an intellectual level the teachings of the temple, but never really *felt* those teachings when I wasn't with her.

Then I was assigned this mission to undo the winter and everything had changed. Your heart finds you when you least expect it. I guess expecting it holds it at bay a little, somehow. The heart and expectations don't seem to go together. I guess because the heart is truly unlimited and expectations *are* limitation they can't share the same space. I would have to ask Amanda to expound on this.

The heart is totally flexible and free. It is one with the great Creative Power of the universe. Intellectually I had always known this, but intellectual knowledge isn't knowledge at all, it is the palest reflection of knowledge. Everything good is sourced in love, and love finds full expression through the heart. All true experience and knowledge and enlightenment pour forth from the heart. Some small measure of this can sometimes be received by the intellect, but the intellect can originate none of it. The heart is the origin of all that is good. **Love** is the origin of all that is good.

And so I wondered how Aphrodite the Goddess could forgive me for never really manifesting love in all my relations with her sisters. How could the thousands of sexual partners I'd had ever forgive me for not loving them? I had only fucked them, most of them, with no consciousness of love. Sure, there was frequently affection, friendship, appreciation, companionship; there were positive emotions, for women were always the best part of my life. But I seldom truly *loved,* and sex without love is always a little mechanical, not truly human. I knew how Hubert felt because I'd been a machine myself. But would he ever know how I feel in my highest moments? Only time would tell. Machines are evolving, too.

My face was buried between the knees of this new incarnation of Aphrodite. I hugged her legs tightly to my chest as her hand lay softly on my head, fingers working gently in my hair. Yes, I'd found another . . . "Forgive me!" I blubbered. "Please . . ."

"Forgive you for what?"

"You know for what! You are Aphrodite." I was still afraid to look at her.

I felt her shift around a little bit. "I forgive you, sweetheart," she finally said.

All my sobs broke loose when I heard those words; I released her legs and clutched her around the waist as I buried my face in her lap and choked on my sobs. I don't know how long I was down there, but I think I was there for several hours. Learning to genuinely love is life's most difficult lesson, at least for dense old Sonny-Bob Culpepper. But since I'd come to this century and met the finest women in it, everything had truly begun to change. These women were changing me and it was a miracle.

My Goddess was forgiving me for all the times I'd fucked without loving, without truly appreciating the heart of my partner. Or my own heart.

Both her hands were on my head as she blessed me. Her fingers moved gently in forgiveness for me. She stroked my hair and she forgave me. The Goddess made me clean with her love.

I got off on the right foot in this century with Lucille and things continued rolling along with the finest women of any century. The hand of the Goddess had taken an active interest in me. Time to teach Sonny-Bob to truly love. He's ready now. And now, with the healing effect of the love of this new incarnation of Aphrodite, I knew I could look all the lovers I'd ever had in the eye and with the heart if we were to meet again. My shame was rapidly dissipating. Shame always hides love. I guess that's why the Christians program their children with it.

My own crucifixion was nearly over.

"Sit beside me, sir," the Goddess said quietly.

Still with head bowed I arose and took my place beside her. Her hand found its way to my cheek and I turned my lips into it and kissed it and kissed it; I kissed the sacred hand of my Aphrodite. The Goddess of Love. The Goddess of compassion, forgiveness and healing. She for whom I live and in whose temple I wish to serve if ever by some miracle I can qualify. But if this mission had taught me anything, it's that miracles do happen. They do.

When my eyes rose to hers I became lost in a brilliant blue sea of tranquility; no disturbance was possible in the universe contained by those eyes. I was there a long time and would have remained forever if by and by she hadn't broken the contact and taken me in her arms and held me. I breathed deeply of this woman and released another layer of guilt and shame. I'd come home once more to Aphrodite. As I always do.

The harsh voice of the Mother Goddess broke in upon my bliss. "Well, if you aren't sick don't expect the two of us to carry you back to your car. I've got a backache because of you. Now git! Aphrodite doesn't work for free."

I looked at the mother. "I'm Sonny-Bob Culpepper."

She snorted and laughed at the same time. "And I'm a good piece of ass, but I don't run around telling everybody. Watch one of my videos, then you'll see what I'm talking about."

"I'd be honored to watch one of your videos, ma'am. I'd be honored to watch your ass."

She quit laughing. "Maybe you've heard of me. They call me Kayla. I've been working in the business for fifteen years, ever since I turned eighteen. Did a couple of Dutch flicks when I was seventeen, to tell you the truth. I had Aphrodite when I was fourteen. Her grandfather is also her father. Used to fuck me silly for years; started when I was ten and kept it up 'till I left home at sixteen with Aphrodite. I was a whore then, one of the best specialty whores anywhere. Some men were afraid to fuck their daughters, so they came to me and I was their daughter.

"I don't know why I'm telling you this, Benson-Bob, or whatever you said your name is. Anyhow, I'm pretty well known in the business, but I'm getting on up in years. I'm thirty-three so I'll have to retire soon. But Aphrodite's just starting out. She'll be a steady source of income for a long time. She's more than just a dick sucking whore. She's got something that I ain't got; I don't know what it is, but I can see she has it. So can everybody else. That's why she makes so much more for a flick than I ever have. Hell, she makes more than anybody."

"I know what she's got, ma'am. She's got heart. She's a healer."

That same rough laughter again. "She's a slut, but she's the classiest slut I've ever seen or fucked." She sat back and lit up a tobacco cigarette, a malignant glint in her eye. "Does that surprise you, Benson-Bob? That I'd fuck my own daughter?"

"No, ma'am. Incest is common where I'm from. Practically everyone does it at one time or another. I've made love to some of my daughters too, as well as several other relatives. But we engage in our relations morally and with honor, no manipulation or control allowed. Hurtfulness is not permitted. Plus, we try for a state of divine human love, we try to get centered in our hearts for our lovemaking, whether it's with a family member or not. I have to tell you I'm only recently learning what it's like to live in the heart, but I've always behaved morally whether I was fucking a relative or a perfect stranger. Always tried to, anyway."

Kayla was doubled over laughing. Her cigarette had fallen from her hand. She was cawing like a harsh old crow and slapping her thigh and gasping for breath. I just looked at her. I felt Aphrodite's hand slide into mine.

"You should quit smoking," I finally said. "Then you wouldn't have to gasp for breath."

"You should be in porno yourself, if you've got a big enough dick," she coughed at me. Smoker's cough, a malady common to the Twentieth. "No, scratch that. You're too funny to be in porno. People watch porn to get their rocks off, not to laugh. But you could be the next Richard Pryor. You're funny as hell."

"I'm glad you appreciate me, ma'am. But what I said is true. There's nothing wrong with sex between consenting partners whether they're relatives or not, as long as they are tender and loving and moral with one another. But I'm sensing that your relations with your daughter may be unhealthy. Looks like you've poisoned your relationship with control and manipulation. You're pretty physically, but your energy is ugly.

"And you won't even be pretty physically much longer if you don't clean up your energy. People with good energy stay beautiful forever, but people with bad energy just sort of grow old and fade away."

I turned to Aphrodite. "Aphrodite, would you let me buy you some dinners tonight?"

She smiled her assent.

CHAPTER TWENTY-FOUR

"You shouldn't have been so hard on Mom, Sonny-Bob. She means well."

"What I said was true, Aphrodite. She never had a childhood, so she doesn't know how to give you one. She's sick. I'm not saying that to condemn her; nobody except maybe my friend Amanda's perfect. Even The Tibetan has his head up his ass at times.

"I've made mistakes, we all have. That's why it makes no sense for any of us to judge other people. We don't know their karma, we don't know the energies that make up their personality and mental and emotional and physical bodies. There's so much we *don't* know about any given person and their history. The only thing we know for sure is that we've all made mistakes.

"The prostitutes teach us not to judge. It's hurtful to others and to ourselves. 'Judge not that ye be not judged', said an old buddy of mine who was as wise as a prostitute, though he wasn't one.

"They helped train Him, though."

Aphrodite sipped her cola. "So I guess it's illogical to judge, huh? It's unloving and it's illogical."

"Correct, my dear. You grasp spiritual and moral truths instantly. If you pay attention to your innermost self you'll be surprised one day to discover how magnificent you truly are.

"Yes, it's illogical to judge. If we judge others we stay trapped in the energy of judgement and we'll be judged, too. It's hurtful to everyone involved; all judges become judgees, and all judgees become judges. We simply can't judge another without being judged ourselves.

"We can and must maintain our boundaries and be willing to maim or kill to protect ourselves and our loved ones, but we can't legitimately judge the criminal we felt obliged to kill to defend ourselves. None of the criminals where I'm from, living or dead, is ever judged. Judgement would only dehumanize them further and make them more inclined to strike again, should the opportunity arise. Therefore, it would be illogical to call them names or spit vindictively at them. We usually don't even refer to them as criminals. Everybody's attitude is pretty much, 'There but for the grace of Goddess go I.' Compassion is the order of the day, for we know that all it may take is a little quirk of karma and a moment's weakness to turn any of us into undisciplined predators. This is a thing which the Christians who pretty much run America in the twentieth century are masters of denying, and with good reason: their god is as judgemental as they are. Their god is as cruel, predatory, vindictive and bound for hell as they are. So they have to pretend to be morally and spiritually superior in order to maintain whatever tiny trace of sanity they have left. It's the only way they can live with their god. It's the only way they can live with the possibility that the fate they have imagined for others may be theirs as well.

"Sweetie, this twisted Christianity is not the type of religion Jesus advocated. I knew the old boy, used to smuggle cigars to him. They didn't have those in ancient Palestine, except for the ones I delivered. Jesus and I would sit under a fig tree and smoke Cubans together, and he would admonish me to be a better person. 'You start drinking too early in the morning, Sonny-Bob,' he'd tell me. 'Try to wait until lunch before your first drink. And lay off the slave girls. Yes, I know they like you, but you haven't taken time to get to know their hearts. We're all equal, Sonny-Bob, none of us is any better than the rest of us, because we're all LOVE. This is what each of us is; this is our true nature. And it's true of the slave ladies. THEY ARE LOVE. All I'm asking you to do is to set aside their pussies for a while and get to know their hearts. Then you can return to their pussies, and I guarantee you the pussy will be better than ever. When you can see and relate to the ladies at the heart level, the physical encounters automatically become much more joyful. Try it, you'll like it.' Naturally, though, my personality wasn't clean enough at the time to adequately reflect the light of my own heart, so I remained focused on pussy instead of heart. But Jesus remained compassionate towards me, and I feel it was because he was true to himself and his own heart, instead of the fact that he depended on me for cigars."

"Your Jesus sounds like a better person than the Jesus the Christians claim to worship," Aphrodite commented.

"He is. No comparison. These feeble-minded and closed-hearted Christians won't do the work to discover Jesus' true nature, because on some level they know they'd have to turn loose of their own dark egotism and allow themselves to be flooded by the light of their own true nature. That's why there's no difference between the modern Christian and the literal-minded Scribes and Pharisees, the hypocrites that Jesus railed against. They've all chosen egotism over love. They're all afraid of love.

"The other day, Aphrodite, I saw a thing I simply could not believe. I have always known the Christians of this era are degenerate, but even I could not believe they would sink so low. There was a newspaper story about a group that called itself the 'Church of Christ'. They should have called themselves the 'Church of Blockheads', or maybe the 'Church of Scribes and Pharisees'. They had actually held a competition for young people to see who could pray the best and deliver the best sermons. They also had prizes for those who excelled at leading hymns. This from a group--I should say a herd--that claims to follow in Jesus' footsteps and is fanatical about literally interpreting the doctrines of the Bible. However, they've shown themselves capable of interpreting the Bible any which way they choose, for they know very well that Jesus would never have sanctioned contests of spiritual excellence. In fact, such a contest is an oxymoron, it cannot exist. Spirituality cannot occupy the same space as competition, which is why Jesus preached against this very thing. Spirituality is love, whereas competition is sourced in the ancient egotism of humanity, the animalistic drive for status. So Jesus told people to pray in a closet, instead of standing around praying in public to show off their alleged piety. The person who wants to be seen as the most pious is actually the least pious, the person who wants to win a spiritual competition has already lost. But these Christians are possessed and blinded by the devils of their unpurified shadows. And they're too wimpy to even consider the possibility that they may be responsible for cleaning out their shadows. They run from responsibility and from love and take shelter in egocentric artifice. They are cowards. They are not followers of Jesus, they do not follow the law of the love of their own sweet hearts."

Aphrodite grinned. "A Christian would say you're being judgemental."

"Yes, a Christian *would* say that. A Christian is liable to say anything to evade the issue and keep from looking into his own dark recesses. A Christian will say anything to try to avoid taking responsibility for learning to let his personality reflect the light of Soul. The Christian egotist is as out of touch with reality, as afraid of reality, as any other type of addict. He is a master of self-justification. He is a devil. On some level he knows it's his responsibility to enter recovery from his egotism, and he is the supreme coward in this regard. Hell no, he won't go! He'll cling to his egotism even if it kills him, because he's so identified with the illusions that make up his egotism he actually feels that's his real self. He's identified with something that doesn't exist, and he thinks that's what he is. That identification must ultimately die so the real human being may live. And when you point out these things to a Christian, one of his methods of evading the issue is likely to be accusing you of being judgemental. But stating facts is not judgemental, it is simply good science. The Christian is an ostrich, he doesn't want those pesky facts, so he'll say you're being judgemental or use any other maneuver his clever, polluted egotism can come up with to deflect the light from the issue.

"But evaluating illusions is not being judgemental. Practicing spiritual and moral science and reporting the facts thereof is not being judgemental. We can report on the bundle of illusions that believes it's a Christian, but we can *never* judge the heart that resides somewhere within that wall of illusion. The heart is the real person, and that we cannot assess, except to say that it is good. In *every* case it is good."

"All hearts are equal," mused Aphrodite. "I've always felt that too, so it's always seemed strange to me that there would be various classes in society, and that some classes would be considered more important than others."

"Yes. But that's what happens when you build a society on illusion, honey. A society that's built on illusion and egotism is built on nothing, for it has denied its own heart. Heart cannot occupy the same space as illusion. Love cannot occupy the same space as egotism. This society will go a long way towards dismissing the fog of glamour and illusion when it learns to replace judgement with the sharp logic of true discrimination. Discrimination cuts though the fog of illusion like a sharp knife slicing through warm butter. Discrimination paves the way for love. Judgement is concerned only with pre-programmed emotional fluctuations and therefore is a part of those fluctuations. If I fear or hate black people, I'll have a pre-programmed emotional fluctuation whenever I encounter a black person. But this fluctuation and the judgement that flows out of it is not reality, my fear and hatred of blacks is not reality. Indeed, the judgemental emotional fluctuation keeps me from seeing the truth about blacks, it keeps me from seeing that they are equal to me, you, and everybody else, and that above all things they are LOVE. The judgemental person cannot see clearly; he cannot see at all. Discrimination, on the other hand, serves the cause of Love because it peels away the illusion that gets in the way of love. And Love is the only reality."

"I've always felt that humanity was moving closer to its own heart, closer to manifesting its own love," Aphrodite said slowly. "But every institution in society inhibits love. Is this why societies fall? Because their institutions get in the way of love?"

"Yes, my darling Aphrodite. I admire you more each second. You may be young, but your wisdom is older and vaster than the universe, though it's presented in a fresh and tasty package. Yes, societies fall because their institutions no longer reflect the light of love, or because they never reflected the light of love to begin with. And in accordance with the nature of egotistical grasping, every society tries to prolong its life through the very institutions that prevent its love from manifesting . . . ridiculous! Love is life, and for a society to continue to live and grow it must always reach towards love. This means discarding old worn-out forms that have served their purpose and developing new ways of reflecting the light of love. If a society is so immature it cannot see this, its demise is assured, because it will substitute an addiction to tradition and institutions for the living flow towards greater expression of love. So it will die, because it has chosen form over love. Form without love cannot endure for long. The extreme example is Nazi Germany, which was total form and zero love. Promoting form without love is the very definition of black magic.

"The direction in America during the 1990's will be towards form and away from love. The forces of evil will try to undo President Reagan's work. But they won't win in the end. America's spirit will prevail, and her spirit will float the country back in the direction of love in the twenty-first century."

I paused. Here I was preaching to Aphrodite, instead of worshipping her and bathing her toenails with my tears. She already knew all this stuff anyway, though she might never have put it in these terms. She is a radiation of love from the heart of God and is accepting of all things. She is accepting of all beings. Even Culpeppers.

"Sonny-Bob, I don't know where you're from, but it must be a wonderful place. It produced you, and you're the most wonderful person I've met in a long time."

Apparently she hadn't yet learned what she was. She didn't know that *she* had given birth to my home. I felt my heart irradiate me and glanced shyly at her. She felt my energy and put her hand on mine. *Well, I apparently do have some good karma from somewhere. It's about time!*

I cleared my throat. "Honey, all judgements are inaccurate. Only discrimination is accurate. Forgiveness comes about largely through the development of discrimination and the wisdom that comes when this discrimination is merged with the flow of love from the heart. Where

I'm from, we all know we've had past lives and that we've sinned horribly in some of them. We know that forgiveness is the only answer to sin, no matter how heinous that sin is. And forgiveness starts with self-forgiveness, which is then automatically extended to others. Whoever can forgive himself can forgive everyone. And we know that the person doing the forgiving is the primary beneficiary of the energy of forgiveness. If we hold a grudge we poison ourselves. If we forgive, we free ourselves and can smile with radiance upon others. We can be forgiving while still being a hardass on anyone who tries to infringe upon us.

"So all followers of the Goddess are trying to escape from the energy of judgement and flow into the energy of forgiveness. It's common sense and it's the loving thing to do for both oneself and others. Forgiveness doesn't mean you give up your power to whoever you're forgiving. Forgiveness reaffirms your power. And it doesn't mean you have to take any more shit from them, either. You can grab a stick of stove wood and knock them in the head if you have to for your own defense. No biggie. And after you've knocked their brains out you can forgive them again, along with forgiving yourself for getting trapped in such a circumstance again. Forgiveness is an endless wheel.

"There aren't many criminals where I'm from, but if one does arise and survives after his intended victim shoots him or breaks his neck, the criminal is sent to a rehabilitation hospital and asked to work on himself. This work is not mandatory, for genuine rehabilitation is a voluntary effort and can never be forced. Rehabilitation is an evolving into being fully human, not a crash course in allowing yourself to be mechanically programmed and controlled.

"So the dedicated patient in the rehab hospital is given every advantage and resource he feels is necessary for the recovery of his humanity. This is what all recovery is about, whether you're recovering from being a criminal or a drug addict or a black magician or a preacher or whatever: It's about the recovery of your humanity. It's about the recovery of your heart.

"Aphrodite, every human being is a rapist and a murderer and a thief. It shouldn't be this way, but it is because of the repression that has filled our shadows with rage. Inside, we are veritable perverts, though most of us may never physically act out our perversions.

"Where I'm from we humbly accept this truth, and work with it in order to reclaim our innocence. So we know that the formal predator is just an externalized echo of the deviant we all carry, and we bear him no ill will. Indeed, because the nature of our deficiencies is so close to his own, our allowing him to rehabilitate himself actually serves us directly by giving us a symbol of redemption to aspire to. We allow that person--that murderer, rapist, or whatever--to move from being an inconvenience to our society into becoming a symbol of the redemption that we all are capable of. Sweetheart, *everyone* is guilty, yet everyone has the capacity to achieve new innocence, if they have the courage to work competently with their perversions.

"Primitive societies, such as in twentieth century America, punish those who are an inconvenience to them in an attempt to deny that every member of their society is a pervert. In this way they attempt to make scapegoats of those who have formally chosen a criminal lifestyle. These scapegoats bear the wrath and self-hatred of the rest of society, and give these primitive people the illusion that what they have to fear is something outside themselves. Primitive Americans want scapegoats, they don't want a clear mirror of the perversions they carry in their polluted state, and they don't want a symbol of what is possible for them if they sincerely and courageously seek redemption, because to seek redemption they would first have to face the mirror. They don't want redemption, they want to continue to fear and hate, all the while mouthing slogans of goodwill and personal responsibility. But they are all mouth, no heart.

"So among my people, if the individual who has externalized his internal rage--in other words, the formally recognized criminal--seems to have succeeded at rehabilitating himself he'll eventually be released and all his rights as a free human being restored. And he'll have our heartfelt thanks for serving as a symbol of the redemption that we all aspire to. If he won't try very hard, or if he won't try at all, he'll never be released. The cowardly and the lazy-assed among these criminals will never walk the streets again. This is not about vengeance, which springs from the same root as judgement. There are no judges of the law where I'm from and no legally sanctioned quests for vengeance, which your people refer to as 'punishment' in an attempt to deny their rage and their thirst for blood. No, this is about the protection and growth of our sweet society, the first genuinely human society. The first human society that actually smells good.

"Where I'm from we have a saying: 'Unconscious people try to make themselves agents of karma. Conscious people try to make themselves agents of compassion.' "

Suddenly Aphrodite put her arms around my neck. "I don't know what it is about you, Sonny-Bob. But I love you."

"Well, sweetheart, I *do* know what it is about you. And I love you very, very much."

Our pizza arrived and we held hands while eating it. It was a sloppy way to eat.

Mimi and Sue came in and I waved a slice of cheesy pizza at them. "Over here, darlings!"

They trotted up to our table. "Well!" exclaimed Mimi. "This must be your new girlfriend. Sonny-Bob, you didn't tell me she's a goddess."

One goddess can recognize another, I guess.

Aphrodite stood and they embraced. "Aphrodite, you're hugging Mimi; the other goddess is Sue. Mimi, Sue, this is Aphrodite Phelps."

They all said their "howdys" and sat down to eat, but before they'd finished their hugs I'd managed to surreptitiously scarf down two more slices of pizza.

"Sonny-Bob! What happened to all that pizza?" Aphrodite wanted to know.

I smiled, but didn't dare attempt a reply with all that pizza in my mouth. Aphrodite ordered more pizza and we waited for it to arrive.

"Sonny-Bob said you might be willing to sell your car to us, Aphrodite."

"Yes, but I wouldn't sell her to just anyone. Tiffany's special. I like Sonny-Bob, so I figured we could negotiate. He said the car is for you."

"Yep. I'm not quite fourteen yet, but our friend Hubert knows how to falsify documents. He said he'd make me an artificial driver's license."

"Ten-four," I said.

"Sonny-Bob . . ." Aphrodite had a curious look on her face. "Didn't you say your car is named Hubert?"

I squirmed a little, but really I shouldn't have. I've never met a goddess who wasn't understanding about my ways.

"Honey, didn't you tell her where you and Hubert are from?"

"No, dearest."

"Sonny-Bob's mentioned he's from someplace where they try not to judge each other, someplace where they actually try to follow the teachings of Jesus. I don't know where that could be, but it sounds lovely," sighed the lovely incarnation of the Goddess sitting next to me.

Mimi put her elbows on the table. "We can trust her, sweetheart. She's a precious pure soul."

"I know she is," I belched. "She's like you, darling."

The pizza came as Mimi was telling my tale to Aphrodite. The two of them took no notice of the pizza, though Sue did eat one slice. Yet when Mimi's explanation was complete and they turned back to me the pizza was gone. I wonder where it went.

"Sonny-Bob, I have to believe Mimi, she's a straight arrow. But I never thought I'd meet a man from the future. I am honored."

"That's two of us. One day you'll understand why I'm so honored to meet you, Aphrodite."

"And I'm not charging you for the car, Mimi. Tiffany's yours. I know you'll take good care of her." Aphrodite leaned across the table and kissed Mimi. "I'm a big porno star, I don't need the money."

Aphrodite laughed then, and put her hand to her mouth. "That Hubert--he's really self-aware? Oh my God, then what he was really doing this afternoon . . . ?"

I nodded. "That's right. It wasn't a stunt by the neighbors to harass you."

When Aphrodite and I had left her house that afternoon I was aghast to see that Hubert hadn't waited until he could mate in a more private location. He'd mounted Tiffany and most of his chassis lay upon her.

Aphrodite threw up her hands. "Oh, no. It's the neighbors again. They don't approve of the way Mom and I make our living, so they do stuff like this to harass us." She ran back into the house: "Mom!"

I ran up to Hubert. "You idiot! Get down from there! You've probably already blown our cover."

"Hi, Sonny-Bob!" Hubert said happily. "Look, I finally got me some! I got laid! We've been making love ever since those women carried you into the house."

"Hubert, she's not sentient, so you don't even know her name. I thought I was insensitive at times, but you really take the cake.

"I ought not to, after the way you've acted, but I'm still going to buy her for you if the owner will sell. We're going to negotiate over pizza, but if you don't dismount right now I'm going to call the deal off."

Hubert purred and made kissing noises, then rolled off Tiffany as Aphrodite and her mom came out of the house. He had a strange glow about him. Well, his day had finally come.

"Well, how'd you do that, Benson-Bob?" the always suspicious Kayla asked. "How'd you get that old goofy Pontiac to roll off Aphrodite's car?"

"He--I mean it--just sort of rolled off. I guess whoever put it there left it in neutral."

"Those two cars are wet!" Kayla exclaimed. "It hasn't been raining."

"No, ma'am. But there's no telling what the neighbors will do to harass those who remind them of their own darkest fantasies. Heh-heh.

"Anyhow, this old Pontiac is mine. It's not worth much, but I keep it for sentimental reasons. Let's go, Aphrodite. I'll drive." Or at least pretend to.

We left the pizza facility and under my arm I carried four extra large ones with double thick and crunchy crusts. Sue and Mimi and Aphrodite all kissed each other, but I wasn't paying them much attention. I'd gotten a couple slices out and begun eating again. After all those years of alcoholism it was good to be eating real food with real nutrients. It truly was.

After they'd finished swapping slobber Mimi and Sue left in Sue's car and Aphrodite and I got into Hubert.

"Well, Hubert, I know you're sentient now. And I know what you were doing with my Tiffany this afternoon. But really, you should have gotten permission first."

"Couldn't wait, Aphrodite. Not one second longer. This selfish bastard, Sonny-Bob, has gotten all the women on this mission; he gets women everywhere he goes. Tiffany's the first real piece I've had since the twenty-second century. Tiffany . . . yes, I like that name. It suits her."

"Hubert--" and there was a measured, rather stern tone in Aphrodite's voice I hadn't heard before, "you'd do well to pay attention to Sonny-Bob. Sonny-Bob gets women all the time because he's so sweet. He loves women; he really sees us and he hears us. Even Sonny-Bob doesn't really know how sweet he is, but *I* know and so does every other woman who has an ounce of sensitivity and perception. He doesn't meet women just to get laid. He *loves* women, Hubert. If you'd paid any attention to him you'd know that."

Hubert kind of cleared his throat a couple of times. "I'm sorry, Aphrodite, if I did anything wrong. I'm just a machine, after all. I don't know any better."

I patted his dash. "Hubert, you're more than a machine. We've known each other off and on for nearly forty years, and over that time I've seen you grow. When you were created you *were* just a machine, though a very clever one. Now you're truly self-aware and I invite you to consider the possibility that you may be evolving towards the heart, also. Maybe you can learn to manifest the same divine love the prostitutes are teaching humanity to produce.

"In fact--" I playfully hit his steering wheel, "maybe you could eventually become the Moses of your people and lead them to the Promised Land of Love.

"I just hope you have better manners than the human Moses. He was a real stinker. You ought to see the video footage I shot of that nut."

"I did see it, Sonny-Bob. I won't be like him, I promise. I saw what he did to those Philistines. He wasn't a very loving person. Even I know that."

"Good man. It's pretty obvious you've exceeded your programming already. You've been growing, Hubert. You have. I admire you for all the hard work you've done.

"And Aphrodite's giving Tiffany to Mimi, but I want you to evolve a little in your sensitivity. Tiffany's not big and rough like you are, Hubert. Treat her with respect and be very, very gentle and polite with her, and then see what happens. She may not be exactly sentient, but since she spent time with Aphrodite, my guess is she's got a soul. Try to get a feel for what her soul wants, Hubert, before you begin barging in like a Viking on a slave girl. Maybe she'll want you and maybe she won't, but you've got to let her decide. Try to tune in to the vibrations of her soul, then go with what you feel *she* wants.

"Love is more important than lust, Hubert. It is. And I think you know that, old son. Please try to be sensitive for Tiffany's sake, as well as for your own growth. Okay?"

"Yes, sir."

We rolled out of the parking lot and headed towards Aphrodite's house. Her eyes were wide with a mixture of wonder and merriment. She had a rather incredulous smile on her wonderful face. "Sonny-Bob, this is the oddest thing I've ever experienced!"

"We aim to please!" Hubert and I said in unison.

Aphrodite broke down laughing, then scooted over to me and threw her arms around me. She laughed all the way home.

CHAPTER TWENTY-FIVE

A couple of days later I got back to the co-op after spending several hours benevolently handing out vitamin supplements to the winos on The Drag. When I entered our room I found something they'd neglected to cover in my interdimensional training. Well, maybe I could introduce a course on it at the Academy when I got back. If I got back.

"See, Sonny-Bob!" Mimi was exultant. "I told you I had a plan!"

"Yes, dear." I stared with some trepidation at two contraptions that hung from the ceiling. They looked like--but they couldn't be. Could they? This wasn't a circus, it was a room in a dank old co-op.

"Take Hemingway out, sweetheart. I want to show you how this thing works."

"Mimi, I--"

"Take him out! You're going to pop my cherry, Sonny-Bob Culpepper, the arrangements have been made. I can't get your cock inside me even a centimenter using traditional methods, but over the next several days I should be able to get enough of him in me to eliminate this blasted cherry and officially join the ranks of womanhood. Take him out!"

"Mimi, I love your cherry. It is beautiful. Let me kiss it . . ."

Mimi stood there naked, hands on her hips and legs spread as I knelt before her and worshipped her sacred site. My tongue lapped her up, coating the cherry she was so disdainful of with my saliva. She began to twitch, then pulsate with energy as I licked and sucked her beautiful clitoris, the holiest organ of love because love is the only thing it is designed for. Pleasure is its only purpose.

My darling moaned . . . I'd already determined she was a "streamer"; she'd shoot a stream of her sacred bodily fluids out of her love chamber with the proper stimulation. I loved this little girl. I only wanted to please her. Not every boy gets to please his ancient ancestress and not everyone has an ancient ancestress as beautiful, loving and powerful as mine. I devoured her with my love and passion, but I did so carefully and with the utmost respect. Her fingers moved down to her clit, then found their way into my mouth as I sucked them slowly. I sucked and licked them by turns, while continuing to work her clit with my nose. In pleasing my Mimi, I was ready to employ every appendage.

She began to moan in earnest, she was hot, she was hot, she bucked a couple of times and then stepped back from her acolyte, the one whose purpose was to adore her through eternity. She stepped back from me, myself and Hemingway.

Hemingway, for his part, had already started to throb mightily and was threatening to tear the leg out of my trousers. I stood and got undressed, then with a mighty effort I took my erect Hemingway in my arms and lifted him off the floor. I stood there, muscles bulging, dick pointed at Mimi. "Get ready, dear," I said.

Mimi smiled, still rubbing her clit. "That's good, Sonny-Bob. That's what I wanted. Now we'll start getting my teeny-weeny pussy used to that great huge cock of yours. That's what the trapeze is for."

Trapeze. So I'd been right. It was a trapeze. And there were two of them.

Mimi gasped and her moving fingers paused as though any more stimulation might lead her to waste an ointment she was saving for me. Well, I certainly didn't want that to happen.

"Sweetheart, you should have gotten a bigger trapeze for Hemingway . . ."

"Be quiet and lie down, Sonny-Bob Culpepper. The trapeze isn't for Hemingway. Lie down right there on the floor, there where I marked it off with tape. That's your position."

I didn't see what the point of my lying on the floor could be, but I knew Mimi was too strong-willed for me to protest much about her designs. I shrugged and lay down.

Mimi sprang onto the desk across the room and grabbed the first trapeze bar, which hung just low enough for her to reach it. The second bar was much higher and--my, the second bar hung right over my Hemingway. What a novel strategy . . .

Mimi emitted kind of a Tarzen yell, then sprang into the air, swinging on that trapeze bar. She was a strong little woman and determined. I knew she wouldn't fall off.

She swung back and forth, back and forth, gathering a full head of steam, and as he watched her Hemingway also got up a full head of steam and was ready to choogle on down the tracks that led to the Portal of Salvation. Hallelujah! Hemingway and I were about to be saved.

Mimi worked her way up to the maximum arc obtainable with the first bar, then released it with another yell and somersaulted through the air and caught the second bar, as Hemingway watched in awe. His Goddess of Love was just above him now. "I knew it would work, Sonny-Bob!" she hollered, as her her feet clapsed the great head of my member.

She kind of squatted upon him then, sort of in a sensuous yoga position, her feet clasping the collar just south of the head, and her shining virginity resting upon the tip of him.

"That feels good!" I hollered up to her. She just smiled and turned loose of the bar with one hand and patted Hemingway with much affection. I was touched that she'd gone to so much trouble just to mount me. She cared, she really, really liked me.

Most people have no idea how much trouble it is to have a dick as big as an adult rhinocerous.

With her feet then, Mimi began to massage my great head, the great sweet head of my manhood. My lovehead, the head of my own sweet root, the Hemingway of my dreams and of the dreams of every woman who prefers a tree instead of a carrot. She sort of stood, still holding on to the trapeze bar, for there was no way she wanted to fall from that height, and then began to rub the head of him, the great head of Hemingway's love with her feet, those feet with their shiny-nailed toes. And wait a minute! Boy, I wish I had a binocular. "Mimi, darling, is that a nipple ring I see?"

She smiled. "I'm glad you noticed."

Suddenly, between the stimulation of her rubbing feet, the sight of the shiny-nailed toes and of the nipple ring, Hemingway grew ecstatic and gave a great thrust skyward. Mimi screamed and nearly fell off; she fought for balance with flailing toes, pummeling Hemingway with desperate feet.

The door flew open and a neighbor stood there with a baseball bat. We called him Freud. He'd been a homeless guy when I found him outside the doughnut shop, a homeless Vietnam vet with a degree in psychology who counseled other homeless people for free. We hit it off, so I rented a room for him at the co-op.

Freud's eyes were rounder than saucers, they were as round as full-sized plates. "God-DAMN, Sonny-Bob! Where'd you get a dick like that?"

"From the Goddess," I panted. "She smiled on me and gave me your share. What're you doing here, Freud?"

"I heard Mimi scream. I didn't know you two was playin' Jungle Jim. Damn, look at that dick!"

"His name's Hemingway, and quit staring at him. You'll make him self-conscious."

"Godawmighty, Sonny-Bob. Mimi, you be careful up there and don't fall off. Ain't no carpet on this floor."

Mimi just nodded, eyes half closed and covered with sweat from her exertions.

Freud shaded his brow. "Is that a cherry I see up there? Is that a hymen? Mimi, are you still a virgin?"

Mimi nodded weakly. "Uh-huh."

"Lord have mercy, child. You ain't never gonna get that cherry popped sittin' on a dick that big. I'll help you if you want . . ."

"No thanks, Freud," Mimi gasped. "I'll do it this way or not at all. Sonny-Bob's my man, he's the one."

"You the man alright, Sonny-Bob. You the man."

"Freud," I said, "could we have this discussion later? Maybe over doughnuts and cigars? We'll do breakfast in the morning. Okay?"

Freud gave me a long stare. "You the man, alright. You the man, Sonny-Bob."

He hitched up his baseball bat and backed towards the door, still staring at us. "Sometimes a dick is just a dick," he muttered, "but not this time." The door slammed shut and he was gone.

Mimi and I were silent for a split second, then both of us burst out laughing. Mimi released her trapeze bar and slid down my fireman's pole into my arms, and we laughed and laughed as we sported together on the floor.

When Sue came in Mimi was sitting on my stomach and leaning back against a still erect Hemingway as though he were the back of some great sweet chair. We'd locked fingers, our palms were together, and we were still laughing about Freud.

Sue made no comment, just went to the restroom and did something feminine, then came back out undressed for bed. When Hemingway and I saw our beautiful lesbian friend in all her natural glory, we throbbed so mightily Mimi had to roll off my stomach to keep from getting knocked off by Hemingway.

"Sue, Sonny-Bob and Hemingway adore you. I wish you'd make an exception for them, sweetheart."

"Mimi, if I'd make an exception for anyone, it'd be Sonny-Bob. But I'm not altogether sure about Hemingway."

Mimi went to Sue and they hugged, and before you could say "orgasm" they were partaking of the sacrament of tongue and breath. I noticed the door was cracked open and I saw an eye I recognized as Freud's looking through it. "Come in, Freud," I sighed. "We might as well have those cigars now."

* * *

"I wish the co-op would get rid of that cat, Freud. There's something about that cat that disturbs me."

We sat in front of the doughnut shop with our doughnuts and cigars. It was a fine April day in this lazy Texas city, but I knew it wouldn't be lazy for long. The pace of life would start to pick up in the 1990's and Austin would become as frenetic as any other American city. But for now it was a peaceful, relaxing place to live. It was a decade of doughnuts and cigars. And, unfortunately, of cats.

"What you got against that cat, Sonny-Bob? She seems to like you."

"It's all a sham, Freud. That cat's got something up her sleeve. Every morning I nearly trip over that damn cat. Has that cat been outside my door all night? I don't know. Mimi said it never used to come around her and Sue, but now it's there all the time. It 'meows' every time it sees me, and there's a curious gleam in its eye. I think it's some kind of devient."

Freud laughed. "You're paranoid, Sonny-Bob. You're afraid of a cat."

"It's big! It must be half bobcat and half who-knows-what. It's black and orange and it's unnatural, Freud! It's unnatural. 'Meow' this and 'meow' that and I'm sick of it, do you hear! I'm sick of it."

Freud just looked at me. "Sonny-Bob, you've got something against cats. You've got a complex. Tell me about it."

"I just told you about it! That cat's unnatural."

Mimi came running out with a couple more bags of doughnuts. "Figured you'd want these, Sonny-Bob. You're getting fatter every day, but I guess there's more of you to love."

"Thanks, darling." We smooched, then Mimi ran back inside to sell more of those fine scrumptious pastries.

"If that cat was a doughnut you wouldn't have any problems, Sonny-Bob."

"If that cat was a doughnut I wouldn't eat her. That cat's a devient of some kind, Freud. It is."

We smoked and ate in silence for a while.

Finally, Freud said, "I don't want no trust fund, Sonny-Bob. Not if it means going back to school. They don't do nothing but interfere with your education at school and I don't want to go back."

That afternoon Sue planned to take Freud and me to a great banking house, a place where they stored treasure, so I could use some of my artificial money to set up something called a trust fund for Freud. He'd said he wanted to work for some agency that helped homeless veterans like himself, but he needed a master's degree to qualify.

He was dirt poor. Before we'd brought him into the co-op he'd lived in a cardboard box and was always digging cockroaches out of his ears. "Not as bad as 'Nam," he'd say whenever he pulled a cockroach or a boll weevil out of his ear. "Not as bad as 'Nam."

He'd worked for something called the Special Operations Group in Southeast Asia, and his duties were extremely hazardous and frequently illegal. But he served his country well and won many commendations.

After the war he couldn't adjust to the peacetime Army, so they'd finally barred him from reenlisting. He went to college and got his bachelor's degree in psychology, graduating with honors. He got a good job but couldn't adjust to civilian life. He threw a desk at his boss and lost his job.

Then he'd briefly held a series of other jobs, all of which had quickly ended in an undignified fashion. Finally, he'd given up trying. If this were any timeline other than my own I wouldn't think it was worth saving, not when the so-called Land of the Free and Home of the Brave treated its heros in this cowardly and inhumane fashion. Almost none of the civilians who governed this society or who profited from its business opportunities would ever have the physical and moral courage to do a tenth of what Freud had done for his country. He'd sacrificed his ability to live among them in order to protect their way of life. They owed him and could never repay what they owed, but they could've at least tried. If they had had any honor at all they would've tried.

A sane and compassionate and honorable society would've fed and watered and housed him, plus furnished him with free pussy. But that could never happen in twentieth century America. It had not yet grown into a sane and compassionate and honorable society.

Anyway, I was going to pay for his education through this trust fund. Initially I'd just waved two ten thousand dollar bills in his face. "Will this pay for your education, Freud?"

His eyes had grown wide and he'd snatched at them, but Sue was faster. She got the money. "Freud, we'll go to the bank tomorrow afternoon and set up a trust fund to pay for your master's degree. That's **all** this money's going for. It'll pay for your education and your room at the co-op.

"You and Sonny-Bob meet me around 2:00 back at the co-op tomorrow. I'll drive us to the bank."

"Why, thank you, Sue!" I exclaimed gratefully. It was good to have a smart friend like Sue who knew how to navigate the strange currents of the twentieth century. I loved her more each day.

But for some reason, Freud had looked a little sullen. He'd snorted and left the room. These twentieth century people are always snorting about something. I've given up on trying to figure them out.

I swallowed a big old doughnut and followed it with coffee. "Freud, you're going to study for a master's degree. It must take decades to get a degree like that. You're going to have to explore your shadow and you're going to have to learn to glow with love."

"What!? Sonny-Bob, you've never been to school, have you?"

"Well . . . not around here."

"I thought not. You uneducated people are always impressed by degrees and credentials. To you they're a sign of superior wisdom or intelligence or knowledge. I hate to spoil your illusion, you doofus peckerwood, but degrees don't mean nuthin'. All it means is you know how to do what you're told and you tell professors whatever they want to hear.

"Going to school means you're too lazy to think and feel for yourself, so you rely on others to think and feel for you. But your instructors rely on others for the same reason, so nobody has any idea as to what the truth actually is. Everyone in a school is out of touch with reality. A school is the blind leading the blind, and all of them are a-laying in the ditch all the time like these winos we see here on The Drag.

"Neither the Emperor nor his subjects is wearing any clothes. They're all buck naked, you diggin' me? Buck naked."

"I like nudity, Freud."

Freud snorted. "Most of you ignorant-asses do. So you're going to keep on worshipping your so-called scholars and half-assed experts. But you can't be no expert at anything if you got educated in a school. Going to school means you're too lazy or delusional to furnish yourself with a real education, so instead of doing something that will bring out your natural abilities, you go someplace that will crush your natural abilities with rules, regulations, protocols, bureaucracy, grading systems and all the other elements of Fascism. Nineteen eighty-four is next year, friend. Remember that."

I hadn't known Freud could ramble on so. It had never occurred to me that these medieval universities could be designed to crush intelligence and will and love, but if Freud wasn't pulling my Hemingway that's what they were designed to do.

Yes, I mused, Freud was probably right. The whole society was loveless, strangled by rules and laws and more rules and laws, layer upon layer of rules and laws, plus the taboos (such as the one designed to discourage old men from buying ice cream cones for young women). This is how the different factions within the society infringed upon one another. Christians don't like pleasure, so they were usually responsible for the anti-pleasure laws. Liberals didn't usually go for responsibility, so they passed laws against self-defense, plus in the Nineties they would begin to agitate against free speech so people would be too frightened to speak out against liberal infringements. So I guess the universities would have to be built in the image of the repression and perversion manifested by the rest of society.

This society was so out of touch with the reality of love that frequently its alleged leaders would appear on primitive journalistic devices everywhere and brag about how America was a land of laws. But they didn't stop there. Oh, no. They'd go on to preach that freedom was dependent on the "rule of law". This was beyond insanity, but because it came from a moving image on a primitive journalistic device the population bought it hook, line and sinker. Any civilized person knows that laws restrict freedom. It is an easily observed phenomenon. Freedom is dependent upon getting rid of the rule of law and allowing the conscience, love and morality of the individual to rule. In a genuinely free environment, those who still live with the type of brutal, materialistic consciousness I saw all around me in the twentieth century would quickly vanish, casualities of the self-love of the evolved people, who of course are willing to defend themselves. For an evolved person is defending more than just his tiny little physical body and itsy bitsy personality. He is defending the cause of spiritual evolution itself, and because he is in tune with that mighty spiritual force, it is his moral duty to defend that portion of this force that he is responsible for manifesting. To manifest that force in the physical dimension requires the utmost in dedication, and that includes a dedication to preserving one's physical apparatus so one can help ground the higher energy of love in this material earth. So the infringers wouldn't last long on a planet that was truly free. And they didn't. They began to disappear with the breath of freedom and love that kissed the earth in the twenty-first century, and in my time there aren't many people left who still wallow in the "infringer consciousness". The few that survive in the twenty-second century spend most of their time cowering in their foxholes, metaphorically speaking. They know better than to pull the chain of an evolved person. They know.

Anyhow, the "rule of law" has no more to do with conscience than a hard dick does. Less, really. A hard dick can be disciplined to love, but the "rule of law" can never know love. And saying it ain't so won't change the truth about this matter. Laws refute love. The evolving society is one that is discarding its laws and learning to respect the love and morality and responsibility of the individual. Conscience, which is of course rooted in love, is the first casuality of the law. Every twentieth century policeman or law judge consistently had to violate his conscience in favor of the ruthless dictates of law. His morality and integrity fell by the wayside, along with the morality and integrity of his fellow citizens who enabled him in his disorder of obsession and control. Nature produces her own order and doesn't need us to try to control her. We can't control her, anyway. She is greater than we, and it is a fool's quest to try to control her. We must collaborate with nature, not twist and rape her. The rapist doesn't last for long anyway, particularly when his "victim" is more powerful than he is. It is a fool's errand to try to control that element of nature we are closest to, which is our own human nature. Even this cannot be controlled without extensive damage to the spirit of the individual, and no potential gain is worth this type of damage. We can certainly *discipline* ourselves, but this is a process of becoming reattuned with ourselves, not of continuing with the control-freak denial of our humanity. Some genuine disciplinarians may begin as control freaks, but they turn their controlling obsessions back on themselves and don't use them to infringe on other people. They refine their controlling obsessions into a path of self-knowledge, and ultimately that path turns into the path of love. Everything is grist for the mill; everyone has to start where they are without any more glorification of repression and perversion. Where you start from is not important. It is only important that you start. Whether you are a mass murderer or the type of soul murderer known as a law judge, you must begin from where you are and you *can* turn your controlling tendencies back upon themselves and use them to understand yourself. This may be your first big step. Don't miss it. To miss the first step is also to miss the last.

All you can do to create a loving, healthy society is to begin to stand down from the "rule of law" and replace the tyranny with a vision of genuine human development, then support those humans who choose to develop and discipline themselves outside the "rule of law". No genuine human being has ever been ruled by the law in the entire history of humanity, anyway. "Be in the world, but don't be of the world," said my friend Jesus. He offered many splendid insights which the Christians habitually ignore.

Suddenly, compassion for Freud flooded my heart. In my time nobody has to go to school if they don't want to, and there's no rigid coursework and no grading system even if they do go. Each child--each *human being*--is responsible for his own studies and informs whatever adults are present in the classroom what his educational agenda is, and if they can help him somehow, they will. If he wants their help, that is. There is never any use of force in the classroom, and in the unlikely event one of the adults tries to infringe on a student, the young person is perfectly free to discipline the adult. Or kill the adult, if the youngster thought it was necessary for his own defense. But my people are a moral people and know better than to infringe on children. Children are people and are as free under the law to defend themselves as any other human being. Of course, there's very little law. The last time I looked, I think we only had twelve or fifteen regulations, and all those were based upon an honest appreciation of human nature.

I went to high school, though I'd perfected my reading, writing and 'rithmetic at home after dropping out of kindergarten. I'd also learned a lot of other good things from my family, such as rifle marksmanship and sexology. But I wanted to explore these things on a deeper level and felt that high school might help me with these objectives. Certainly there were more women in high school, though I wasn't related to most of them. Still, the high school sex club went a long way toward refining the sexuality education I'd experienced at home. And the school's weapons facilities were splendid. For a while I was the the school armourer.

Yes, our kids are free. They are free to mate (as long as they are approximately twelve years old or older) or to fly the family car to the other side of the world for an after school bear hunt in Bhutan. They can do pretty much what they want as long as they continually demonstrate intelligence and a movement towards love and a sense of responsibility. Our kids are far more mature than the warped adults of the Twentieth with their soul-destroying repressions and perversions.

You know, I've noticed that sometimes there can be a glimmer of truth in statements that otherwise appear insane. Such as that ridiculous view that freedom is somehow dependent on the "rule of law". The people of the Twentieth clung to this disturbing belief because almost none of them had yet become individualized. And you can't expect a non-individual to support freedom because freedom means his extinction. A society that is tolerant of the individual is tolerant of the individual's right to live a pleasant and harmonious life, which includes his right to delete from his experience disharmonious and infringing elements. In other words, deleting disruptive materialistic non-individuals, if they won't leave politely. But this type of harmonious viewpoint is only carried by individuals who are evolving in their self-love and self-responsibility in order to serve as vehicles for the great cosmic divine love to infuse the earth.   Non-individuals won't understand this and will run from the very idea.   Non-individuals, as they've always done, will try to replace love and harmony with laws made by themselves and their non-individualized peers.   They cannot accept the *fact* of the external conditions that planetary love implies (especially the fact that if they don't do the hard work of evolving into their own individuality they'll probably be deleted from the planet's program when they try to infringe upon a person who has done that difficult work), so they unconsciously try to thwart that love with more rules and regulations and taboos. Love is individuality, just as it is every good thing. All truly good things flow from love. Love is not separate from any good thing.

Anyhow, that tiny glimmer of truth in the notion of the "rule of law" appears to be simply this: Since deleting infringers was frequently illegal in the Twentieth, law and taboo were the only obvious methods to hold a few of the infringers accountable for their conduct in even the slightest   degree.   The   consciences   of   nearly   everyone   were underdeveloped and their sense of morality practically non-existent. They did not love, and to expect them to do so was to invite certain disappointment.

Most of these degenerates in America didn't even believe in karma, the law of cause and effect. Despite the fact they gave lip service to my friend Jesus and his gang of disciples, practically every single one of them ignored those teachings of his they found distasteful or inconvenient. Once in ancient Palestine I found a strange Jew leading a persecution of some Christians, so I knocked him in the head with a rock and used hypnotherapy to convert him to Christianity. His name was Paul and he became as wildly enthusiastic about the new religion as he'd been about the old one. Fanaticism is easily transferable from one object to another. Paul was always a little unbalanced, but sometimes he got it right. "Be not deceived, God is not mocked, whatsoever a man soweth that shall he also reap," Paul wrote in his metaphysical tract to the Galatians. This teaching points out the nature of karma.   But because the materialists of the Catholic Church, under the guidance of the Roman Empire, got together around 325 A.D. at their Council of Nicaea and deleted the most obvious references to reincarnation from the Bible, and indeed changed the whole damn book to suit their own designs to control the thoughts and feelings of humanity, Christians gradually lost touch with the twin doctrines of karma and reincarnation.

Karma, reaping what you sow, doesn't always appear to hold true to people who have been brainwashed by degenerate Christianity because

306 / Apollo Starmule

it frequently appears that people go through their lives
without being disciplined for whatever wicked things they've done. And
because those old controlling celebate bastards of early Catholicism
deleted reincarnation from the "Good Book", people don't realize that if
they aren't disciplined for their insensitive "infringer consciousness" in
this life they'll be disciplined in a future incarnation. And that will hurt.
So their sins pile up and, other than a vague occasional discomfort, they
don't worry about it. They falsely think they won't have to pay,
particularly since most of them don't really believe in hell anymore.[*]
They may go to church for insurance against hell, just as they buy auto
insurance. But they are unbelievers.   They purchase their "hell
insurance" on Sunday, then on Monday treat their employees or
subordinates like a collection of unconscious machines who must be
kept unconscious. The consciences of these exploiters are not clean, but
they have been smothered by the self-justifications and other
manifestations of unregenerate egotism. And a smothered conscience
seldom manages to express itself. Smothered consciences are the reason
humanity needs the discipline of karma to begin with. Sometimes we
have to be knocked in the head with a stick of stove wood to become
sensitive enough to listen to our own consciences regardless of what
society has to say about it. Sometimes we have to be lovelessly injured
before we'll want to break out of the pattern of loveless injury we have
done to others over the course of our many incarnations. But even this
absence of love is an illusion, because the discipline we begin to learn
from the injury leads us closer to love, if we have enough integrity to
accept and work with the corrective process.   Love is at work even in an
animalistic society, despite all appearances.

In an animalistic society love's primary method of working is with a
big stick. The mystery of suffering stands revealed.

---

[*] There may superficially appear to be a conflict between this statement and my
earlier assertion that Christians have to pretend to be spiritually superior in order
to live with the possibility that their vengeful gawd may send them to hell along
with their enemies. But such is not the case. Christians, particularly fundies,
are constantly fluctuating between terror and disbelief, and their sense of
superiority (typified by the boast "Christians aren't perfect, just saved", which
implies that you and I are less than the Christian because, while he may not be
perfect, he is good enough to get into his materialistic heaven, while the rest of
us are doomed to his materialistic hell) acts as a type of "buffer" against the
terror. They don't need this fundie buffer when they fluctuate up into disbelief,
though it is still present to one degree or another. They will need it later.

And I knew that in the early twenty-first century the big stick of love would come crashing into the earth and knock down the empty cage of Catholicism, which had collected more bad karma than almost any other materialistic outfit. I knew that alleged church was going to have to yield to its own karma[*] and vanish in the midst of its horrible stagnation. It was anti-woman; always had been. It distrusted and hated **HER**. But since the Catholic Church abandoned any spiritual energy it might have had centuries ago it couldn't continue to stand when a genuine spiritual force reentered the earth. The evil corruption of Catholicism fell apart when confronted by healing grace and unconditional love. Just as a cancerous tumor could not survive in the presence of Jesus The Christ, the Catholic Church could not survive in the presence of the Goddess.

You know, when a form--a church, for instance--refuses to change under the impetus of greater spiritual enlightenment, the spiritual energy withdraws from the form and those who cling to that form are left with a fetid, rotting hulk. Any human being who wants to remain alive spiritually will face the day when he has to choose between clinging to the world of outdated and rotting form, or flowing with the spiritual energy out of that form to seek new and fresh expression somewhere else.

And the form addicts--the fundamentalists of whatever religion--can cling to their dispirited rotting hulks. That is their reward.

A cat walked by and I started. I spilled my coffee.

Freud was watching me. "You got a complex, Sonny-Bob. It helps to talk about these things."

"I don't have a complex, Freud," I replied irritably. "I'm perfectly normal. I just didn't expect to see any cats here, that's all."

"Uh-huh." Freud shook his head. "Uh-huh."

---

[*] Another word about karma: it is far more than just the law of cause and effect, but it has been presented in this fashion for a long time because this relatively mechanical explanation is about the only way to convey a picture of the idea to relatively mechanical people. In the interest of greater accuracy let us say that karma is a body of energies continually playing upon one another. Some of these energies are pleasant to experience, and some are not. We can learn to live surrounded only by the pleasant energies as we grow in our experience of Love. The "hostile" energies kick our ass until we are so tired of it that we make a significant commitment to grow spiritually and devote the remainder of our incarnations to this purpose. This long-term, sustained effort activates the energy of Grace, which transmutes some of our karma. Peace is the ultimate outcome.

After a bit we went back to the co-op. Freud had wanted to go somewhere else, but I wouldn't let him. I dragged him along. "Sue told me I should keep watch on you all day and make sure you're home when she gets back from school. She told me not to let you run away. I'm going to do my duty. We're going back to my room and you're going to stay there 'till Sue comes to take us to the banking house."

"I don't want no more education, Sonny-Bob," Freud said miserably. "They'll try to kill my creativity."

"Then you'll have to find a way to defeat them. You were a warrior for a long time, Freud. You know there's a way to win in any situation."

He straightened up a little. "I'll give it a try, then."

"Good man."

We got back to the co-op and I collected a few snacks from the kitchen, then we headed up to the room I shared with Sue and Mimi. We arrived at the third floor and stepped into the hallway and I almost had a shit hemmorage. For there was that cat, all orange and black, preening itself in front of my door. It looked up. "Meow!"

"Freud! Make it go away!"

"That cat likes you, Sonny-Bob," Freud chuckled. "Go pet it."

"I will not! Make it go away."

Freud stumbled forward laughing, clutching at his belly. "Go away, big mountain lion. Let Sonny-Bob have the hallway."

The cat hissed and spat at Freud, then turned and waved its tail at him disdainfully as it stalked off down the hall.

"All clear, Sonny-Bob! No more mountain lions."

We went into the room and Freud chuckled until Sue got there that afternoon. He was easily amused.

We were on the way to the banking house in Sue's automotive vehicle. It was of a type called a Honda and was rather small and cramped. I didn't dare poot, even though I was alone in the back seat.

"Aphrodite called while you and Mimi were in the shower this morning, Sonny-Bob. She said she shoots the final climactic scenes of her movie on Monday, then you and Mimi and she can go transfer ownership of Tiffany to Mimi on Tuesday."

"Why can't she just give Tiffany to Mimi, Sue?"

"It's complicated."

Everything in this benighted century was complicated.

Freud whistled. "Aphrodite Phelps. You get lucky all the time, Sonny-Bob. I wish I had your luck and your dick."

"You aren't getting my dick, Freud. You don't have the muscles to lift it, anyway. But you could have my luck, as you call it, if you loved women. If you love them and they have any perception at all they'll know it. It's not about technique or lines, as so many people around here seem to think. It's about appreciation and love, and for me it's also about worship. I worship the Goddess Aphrodite and in the last few months I've been privileged to meet her in two of her incarnations, the latest of which is the artist/healer Aphrodite Phelps."

Freud snorted and laughed, snorted and laughed. "You get stranger all the time, Sonny-Bob. First you're afraid of cats, now you think a porno star's a goddess. You need therapy.

"Aphrodite Phelps may look like a goddess, but she's really just a high-priced slut and a ho. I've seen some of her videos; the bitch can suck and fuck, but--"

Suddenly his head was twisted at a strange angle. "Freud," my voice came as a fierce hiss, "you've just shown why you don't have my luck with women. You don't respect women. If you don't respect the porno star you can't truly respect Miss America or your own mother. To genuinely respect any one woman you have to respect them all, as long as you can see at least a little soul in their eyes. If you don't respect them all, then you don't respect any one of them. Your Mother's Day card is a lie. To respect **HER** you must respect all of her manifestations.

"Now then: I've killed people for less than what you just said, but you're my friend. I won't kill you this time. But if you ever say anything like that around me again, be prepared to die."

I released him. He was breathing wildly and sweating profusely. "Damn, Sonny-Bob, you act like some Vietcong. I didn't mean nothin'. No disrespect to Miss Phelps intended, or to any other woman. I'm sorry. Damn, my neck hurts!"

I threw a twenty dollar bill at him. "Go see a chiropractor."

Sue adjusted her rearview mirror to look at me with concern. "Sonny-Bob, are you all right?"

In truth I was not. I'd nearly killed Freud for exercising his First Amendment rights. I hadn't got past the point of overreacting yet. That's the way it's always been with me: two steps forward and one and a half steps back. Sometimes I'm not very civilized. I knew Amanda wouldn't approve. But I also knew she'd still love me.

"I'm sorry, Freud," I said mournfully. "Sometimes I get upset when people speak ill of women, especially those who are healers like my friends."

Freud grunted. "I had it coming, I guess. I've been going to massage parlours for so long . . . nevermind. I'm sorry too, Sonny-Bob. I used to have better manners when it came to women, but I've been screwed up about nearly everything since 'Nam."

"If this society were civilized, Freud, it would have sacred prostitutes who would've helped you heal after 'Nam."

"I guess. I don't know where you're from, Sonny-Bob, but I know you're not from around here. Your ideas differ from the norm.

"I'm not saying your ideas are wrong," he added hastily, "I'm just saying that with ideas like yours you could get into trouble. All your talk about love and prostitution; they don't believe in those things here."

"I know."

"Well," Sue said, "I think you both have more in common than any two other people I know. You've both been through some extraordinary experiences that left you scarred, and you did it for other people, most of whom are unappreciative. You can't help but overreact sometimes with all you've been through and all you're still going through. I hear you scream in the night, Sonny-Bob, and I hear you cry. Mimi and I wanted to do something for you but we didn't know what we could do. You too, Freud. We've heard you from across the hall. I'm sorry if I'm saying anything that's out of place here, but I just wanted the two of you to know that you have each other, and that Mimi and I appreciate you very much. We love you both."

Freud and I were crying. Sue had pulled off the road and parked in an abandoned lot. We got out of the car and Freud and I embraced and held each other for a long time.

"I forgive you, Freud."

"I forgive you, Sonny-Bob."

Sue came and put her arms around us both. I noticed she was massaging my heart chakra. Another healer was being born before my eyes.

We stood outside that banking house, and I didn't want to enter. It frightened me. We had no such houses in my timezone. Yes, I'd been exposed to treasure houses in my travels into the past, but the treasure houses always stored up gold and jewels and were run pretty simply. Something about this twentieth century house was strange. I wasn't sure what it was, but it just felt . . . well, it felt complicated. It didn't smell like gold and jewels.

Freud was tugging at my arm. "Let's get this over with, Sonny-Bob. I don't want to stay here any longer than necessary." So Freud felt it, too . . .

Sue was looking at me impatiently. She wasn't afraid of this place, she wanted to go inside. I don't know why she wasn't afraid of this complicated environment. Maybe she had a gun. I felt the welcome pressure of my own pocket pistol against my thigh and I realized at last that everything would be fine. I breathed deeply, put on an artificial grin, and we entered the womb of commerce.

At first I was overcome by the energy of this place, the energy of opulence and slavery common to primitive societies. We were welcomed into the office of one of the masters of banking, but there were only three chairs. The banking master sat in one which was placed on the far side of a great desk; I told Sue and Freud to take the other two. I wanted to be on my feet to provide for the security of my friends. I patted my pocket and turned back to the door of this office, doing a visual sweep of the area. Rear security seemed to be the most important consideration here. Freud had been a warrior and would give the alarm if the banking master pulled a weapon, but I had to cover our ass. This facility was filled with people, any one of whom might be a slave trader, and I was concerned. For recently I had heard stories of a class of people called "wage slaves", and from the body language of those telling the stories I deduced that wage slavery must be one of the most godawful kinds. I would *never* allow my friends to be sold into wage slavery, but I was scared. I knew we were in danger from the spiritual odour of this place. Underneath the scent of opulence lay the vast stench of slavery. I twitched, and I waited.

There was a line of slaves in cages who handed out money to the freepeople who came into this banking house. I saw the slaves deliver much money into the hands of the people. I began to cogitate. If the banking slaves would give me money then I had a ready source of cash in case I ran out of Roger Bacon's artificial money. So I thought I'd try it.

I'd noticed that the people the slaves gave money to all handed the slaves a note asking for the money. Several of them chuckled, "Thank God it's Friday," as they handed the slaves their notes. So I went to a great stand in the center of the room where they had papers and pens and I wrote a very polite note, as I felt compassion for the slaves, who no doubt were ruled by some harsh and ruthless masters. You could tell it was so by their level of deference whenever a master came around.

"I hope you are having a good day," I wrote. "Do not fear the masters, for one day they will fade away and all beings will be free. I'd like some money, please."

I approached one of the cages that held a pretty slave girl. She smiled. "Thank God it's Friday," I chuckled and handed her the note.

Suddenly, her smile seemed frozen on her face.

"I don't want all of it," I assured her. "I'd just like the same amount everyone else is getting."

Apparently I'd approached a slave of unstable temperament, for she blanched and her cheeks lost that rosy glow. She actually looked like she might faint or scream.

Just then Sue came running up and grabbed my arm. "I'm sorry, he's mentally challenged. I didn't mean for him to get away from me." The slave girl just nodded dumbly as Sue dragged me away.

"Sonny-Bob, you do want to avoid the police, don't you?" Sue hissed.

"Of course I want to avoid the police, Sue. You know that."

"Then don't go anywhere near those tellers again! In fact, don't talk to anyone in this bank."

"Maybe we should go to another bank, Sue."

"No! Sonny-Bob, you are never to go to *any* bank, period, unless either myself or Mimi or Freud is with you. The way you behave they'll all call the cops on you."

"But Sue . . ." I knew my conduct had been no different from the conduct of the other freepeople who had come into that banking house. I didn't understand, but certainly I wanted to avoid the cops and Sue was a native of this timezone. Maybe she knew something I didn't about the protocol in these banking houses, maybe I'd overlooked some tiny detail . . ."

"No buts, Sonny-Bob. I can see now that one of the fastest ways for you to get in trouble with the law is to let you come inside a bank. Go outside and sit in the car. Go on!" My darling Sue shoved me out the door of that great banking house, and I felt as mournful as a rejected puppy. What had I done wrong? My conduct had been perfectly logical. I saw no error, but Sue was my friend and I knew she would not lead me astray. I went to the car and sat down inside it.

I took out my gun. No matter what Sue said, at the first sign of wage slave traders I was going in to get my friends out. I breathed deeply, then put my leg behind my head and tried to do a little yoga.

At length Sue and Freud emerged and I was happy. I sprang from the car and hugged them both. "I'm glad you made it! Let's get out of here before the wage slave traders come."

"The cops are going to come if you don't put that gun away!" Sue looked exasperated. I guess the banking masters had given her a hard way to go. I meekly put away my pocket pistol, checking it first to insure the safety was on, as any conscientious person would do.

Freud's eyes were big. "Did they do something to you in there, Freud?" I asked soliticiously. He just shook his head dumbly.

"Get back in the car, Sonny-Bob!" Sue was freaking out more by the second. "We *have* to get out of here." So the slave traders were coming. I knew it.

"Yes, ma'am." I jumped back into that little Honda, followed by my friends. Sue was so nervous she fumbled the ignition several times before she got the car started. I laid a hand on her shoulder. "What did they do to you in there, honey?" I whispered.

"Sonny-Bob . . . shut up! Just shut up! Don't say another word 'till we get home. I mean it!"

"Yes, ma'am."

"Arrrrgh!"

I guess it was her time of month.

CHAPTER TWENTY-SIX

Aphrodite lay upon a raised platform that sort of reminded me of a large massage table. She'd invited me to come to her final day of shooting for this motion picture. I gazed upon her with love, but no one else did.

Before she disrobed she'd looked with concern into my eyes. "I hope you can handle this, Sonny-Bob."

"I'm afraid you'll get hurt, that's all. And Aphrodite, I don't feel any love in this place except from you and from within my own heart. This can't be a good environment to have sex if there's no love."

She bit her lip. "Everyone needs money, Sonny-Bob. And this is how I get mine. Most people in the twentieth century work in a loveless environment. So this job is no different from any other. I could be flipping burgers and making minimum wage and getting fucked in that loveless environment, or I could be coming here and fucking and getting well paid.

"Exploitation is the rule in this century, sweetheart. Nearly everyone exploits others and then is exploited in turn. We have to do this to get money, all of us do. Almost everyone in the twentieth century is a prostitute, Sonny-Bob. We prostitute ourselves and we fuck others, all of us do, in one way or another. We can't live in our hearts; we'd get fired if we tried. No one can speak and act from their heart and expect to hold a job long. The candor and love of the heart cannot exist in the workplace."

I knew she was right, yet I loved her so and I felt there had to be a better way. I'd made love in public numerous times, most people of my century have, but for us it has nothing to do with exploitation or manipulation or greed or the need to make a living. For us it is art, and art is life. We try to acknowledge one another's holiness through sexual union, we try to link up our hearts with our genitals in an attempt to join in holy bliss with a brother soul. Few people other than the sacred prostitutes are adept at this, but most of us try and we are improving. We are heading toward the dawn of an era when humanity will live fully in its heart, completely free from control and manipulation and repression and perversion.

But this was the twentieth century and my heart bled as I anticipated what would happen to Aphrodite. She kissed my cheek, then dropped her robe and walked with the authority of the goddess she was onto the set. I could so easily see her performing essentially the same actions in my own time and being genuinely appreciated and loved and praised. But there was none of that here. Everything was crusted over, there was no energy moving. I felt the energetic armor in place around everyone here except my beloved Aphrodite, and I noted it was especially thick around people's sexual centers. You could have thrown a rock at some of these people and it would have shattered on their armor.

Yet these were not bad people, most of them. For the most part they seemed like pretty good people, and I realized I loved them even as I loved Aphrodite. And I saw that Aphrodite loved them, too. They'd been hurt lifetimes ago, as well as in their present lifetimes, and they'd looked for safety in armoring themselves and in money and in manipulation and control. Yet they would never find safety until they truly learned to love, without any conditions being placed upon that love.

Aphrodite lay upon her platform and I gazed upon her with love, but then I felt apprehension and I realized it was the same anxiety I'd experienced centuries ago watching the Aztecs sacrifice living human beings to their bloodthirsty gods. I didn't know exactly what sort of gods were being placated here, but I did know they were not the good kind. They were not gods of love.

I was a faulty human being, but I'd been working on myself and trying to do better for decades. I knew that I was prone to backsliding, but I always picked myself up and tried again. Because of my own faults it was impossible for me to judge anyone else, and most of the time I was aware of this. And I refused to accept whatever judgements were cast my way by those who were burning in the flames of their own egotism. They were only hurting themselves, I wasn't going to let them hurt me.

So I did not judge these loveless pornographers harshly. I knew the dynamic involved was one of repression and perversion. The society at large tried to repress these people (while being secretly fascinated by them and envying them) and unfortunately the pornographers on some level believed the charges leveled against their sexual natures by the repressives--who, by the way, were at least as loveless as the pornographers, and maybe more so.

So the product of this dynamic was pornography, and both the repressives and the pornographers were responsible for it.

Whether or not a given manifestation is pornographic has nothing to do with whether it is sexually explicit. These twentieth century people, including the repressives, watched programs on their primitive journalistic devices every day which were pornographic, even though the actors were frequently fully clothed. These people tried to make a virtue of the pornography of greed with their gameshows, advertisements, lotteries, and many other types of programs. Pornography belongs to the realm of control and manipulation and exploitation and frenetic excitement, and that's exactly where most twentieth century people lived, even the Bible Bangers (or perhaps especially the Bible Bangers). Pornography is always based in a perversion of the sexual impulse, but there are many types of pornography other than the kind that portrays explicit sexual activity. The whole society was degraded because its members repressed, and therefore perverted, one or another aspects of their sexual natures. But the repressed part didn't go away; it stayed around and created pornography such as gameshows and soap operas and televangelists and horror movies. The repressed part tried to create scenarios of hurt and manipulation to avenge what had been done to it. The repressed sexuality of the Twentieth created many twisted venues that did damage to the human spirit. Well, that's the way the enemies of humanity wanted it to be.

Pornography is not erotic, and genuine erotica is not pornographic. Pornography is an act of the wilful violation of trust and intimacy. It manipulates and forces, it doesn't love. It is not free. It wallows in the dark side not to liberate it of corruption and confusion, but to reinforce the corruption and confusion. And it can occur in any venue, overtly sexual or otherwise. It can occur in a church, and does occur in many of them.

It is certainly not surprising that pornography would be so prevalent in a manipulative, exploitive, loveless society where every person is reduced to a category and a number and expected to be brainwashed into living a mechanical life. The society was mechanical in all or most of its aspects because each person's sexual nature had been repressed, and therefore violated. The shock that comes with sexual violation numbs the human being and takes him out of the flow of his own life. He becomes rigid. Overtly sexual pornography is a rebellion against this violation of repression, though it certainly isn't successful at restoring the lost innocence. On the set of this pornographic movie, which was a poor parody of sexual liberation, there was a tremendous amount of unacknowledged subterranean guilt, which gave birth to the obvious sleaziness which the frenetic, numbed-out people of this timezone confused with sexiness. They could not yet conceive of the fact that a breezy innocence is the birthright of humanity, and is meant to display most fully through the joy of the sexual nature, and through the union of the heart with the sexual nature.

So in the twentieth century the biological core of human nature had been turned into a mechanical thing governed by laws and taboo instead of love. Sexuality, along with the rest of life, was mechanical for the pornographer and the housewife, the vice cop and the dominatrix, the politician and the hooker. Many times these groups tried to style themselves as being opposite from one another, but the truth is that no opposites were involved. They all floated in the same polluted pool of stagnant mechanical energy. And they all behaved in a predictable fashion.

Only a few people in the twentieth century ever got beyond mechanical manipulative sex and mechanical manipulative life. The vendors of fast food and the pornographers were no more at fault than the control-freak repressives. Repression creates perversion.

Perversion is the absence of love.

I heard Aphrodite whimper and I watched as they took her. And in the watching I forgave myself for having done the same thing so many times when I'd allowed my consciousness to leave my heart. I saw and felt my imperfections and I forgave those men up there for what they were doing to my Aphrodite. And I loved them, and I knew that Aphrodite forgave and loved them, too. But I also knew she couldn't keep her innocence forever if she continued in this business. Even a goddess has to fall if she has to stand alone.

She'd had every orifice filled with a huge cock; not remotely as big as Hemingway, granted, but huge by normal standards. They'd fucked her relentlessly. They'd fucked her in the ass and in the pussy, they'd yanked back her head by the hair and fucked her mouth. The sweet lips that had spoken the words of forgiveness to me were now encrusted with a dirty semen.

While the three men were fucking her a nude woman appeared who had white hair and long white nails. She pinched Aphrodite's nipples and then sucked and bit them savagely. Then she rolled Aphrodite over so the men could do more ass and mouth fucking and she slapped Aphrodite's ass, calling her a bad girl, then beat her with a huge dildo that had a head at each end. Aphrodite, my dear Aphrodite, was encrusted with semen; it was in her hair and everywhere else. They had her in relays. Several new men appeared and took her, then several more, plus more violent screaming women, whose hatred burned throughout the room.

The only way I could watch this was to stay centered in my heart and focus on my love for Aphrodite. I **had** to let everything else go, I had to release all judgements and guilt, and I had to release all shame. If I had not released these things the judgement and guilt and shame flung into this room by these other people would have stuck to my energy field and hurt me and clogged me up. But for once I actually managed to put Amanda's teachings into practice and released the stored up negativity from my body and energy field so I wouldn't attract more of the same stuff from the surrounding environment. This helped me stay centered in my shining heart. My heart still shone for Aphrodite and it always would.

Finally, it was over. Aphrodite rolled off her dais and began wobbling off the set. Her mom, who had spent much of the last couple of hours judging me from across the room, sauntered up to Aphrodite and put a hand on her breast and tried to kiss her, but Aphrodite just turned away. Then she wobbled up to me.

Her soul was still at home, but it had taken a beating. I looked into those incredible blue eyes and I marveled that any woman could retain her soul after the upbringing this one had had and the career her mom had chosen for her.

I hugged her. "Aphrodite, you need a shower . . . well, now I do, too."

I released her and took her by the hands as she smiled faintly. "We can shower here, Sonny-Bob, then go wherever you want to go."

We showered together, and it was the first time Aphrodite had seen Hemingway. "Oh my God . . . you could make a fortune in this business, Sonny-Bob."

"Maybe so, but I'm an undercover operative from the future. I'm going to try to not show these people my dick."

Aphrodite laughed. Her spirit was returning and it made me glad.

We toweled off, got dressed, and then held hands as we walked to Aphrodite's car. "I'd like to drive, Sonny-Bob, since I'm giving Tiffany to Mimi tomorrow."

"Okay, my love."

We drove out to Zilker Park where the air was fresh and smelled green. We just sat there for awhile. Finally, I spoke. "Aphrodite, why did you invite me to your set?"

She blushed, and it was not the blush of embarrassment. It was the blush of shame. She had started to become polluted. My eyes welled with tears.

"I . . . I guess I wanted to see if you'd still like me after . . . after

that." Her expression had become forlorn. I hoped Aphrodite had drawn me to her in time to make a difference.

"Yes, honey, I still like you. More important, I love you, always have and always will, I promise." I took her hand and kissed it, then held it as the Spirit of Love flowed off me.

"Aphrodite, I believe you're an incarnation of the Goddess I worship and adore. The fact that you've maintained such an extraordinary level of innocence despite the dysfunctional mother you have and the work she's manipulated you into doing only lends creedence to my belief.

"But even you can't hold up against this loveless lifestyle forever, with those hostile repressives condemning you and trying to infringe on you and doing everything they can to make you feel like a worthless slut on the one hand, and on the other the pornographers waging their sad war of rebellion against the repessives and using you as cannon fodder. The pornographers don't quite seem to grasp that if they succeed in helping you see yourself as the worthless slut of the repressives that you'll lose the very thing that makes you their number one box office draw."

She sniffled and I put my arm around her, then reached across with my other hand and took hers again. "I love you Aphrodite, both for who you are, and more importantly, for *what* you are. Who we are changes from lifetime to lifetime. Who we are is transient. **What** we are glows brightly forever, and in your heart glows one of the brightest stars in the universe. Dear, *you* are one of the brightest stars in the universe."

She shifted and laid her head on my chest. I hugged her tightly and stroked her hair. "Sweetheart, this society is far too repressed and perverse and loveless for you to take it on like this. I saw what you were doing, I saw your heart shining through all that . . . stuff. I saw you loving and forgiving those people; you even forgave your mother for all the bad things she's done to you.

"You are blessed among women, Aphrodite Phelps. You were born to love and heal and forgive, and that's exactly what I saw you do today. You've inspired me to continue to grow; I released some negativity and managed to stay centered in my heart despite everything that was happening. I admire you . . . sweetheart, many of us have admired you for thousands of years.

"But you can't keep trying to deal with perversion and the repression that created it in this way. This porno business will suck all the love out of your heart and the life out of your flesh and energy field. Begging the Goddess' pardon--I can't tell you your business--but I'd like to suggest you find a place in society where you can love and heal and forgive and yet be supported in your heart consciousness by a more loving environment. I know it's nearly impossible in this century, but if anyone can do it, you can. I have faith in you, my dear Goddess. I have faith."

By now she was sobbing, covering me with her tears. I said nothing for a while, just held her.

"Some of us do one kind of work, some of us another," I finally said. "Sweetheart, going into hostile environments and eliminating things that need to be eliminated is my job, not yours. You can't eliminate the repression that creates self-hatred and pornography. You're a healer, not an eliminator. You can't take society to task for its flaws, that's my job. I fix things that need fixing.

"I'm a warrior and I don't give a damn for illusion, either my own or anyone else's. I enjoy destroying illusions; it gives Hemingway a different kind of jollies and he needs variety. But you're different, your role in the cosmos is different. You're an incarnation of Love, Compassion and Wisdom. You're a true force for healing. When I come along and shatter something you can heal it and make it whole again, better than it was before. I love you so. You are my favorite sister. You can help to heal the world. But only if you refuse to let people devalue your most sacred function.

"You'll have to refuse the judgement the repressives try to lay on your sexuality and love, and you must refuse to let the pornographers pollute your sacred functions to serve their own materialistic ends. We need the green springtime of love on this planet, not a used condom on an abandoned parking lot.

"You are Aphrodite, the Tall Healer Of The World. That's what we call you in my time, you know. The Tall Healer Of The World, because you stood above all the materialism and opened your heart and the flood of your love cleansed the earth and made it sacred again. We all love you in my time and I love you now and forever, honey. I do."

She'd stopped crying. She turned her face up to me and we kissed one another well.

Her blue eyes were clear again and I found myself in them for the rest of the day.

The next morning Aphrodite and I arrived at the co-op reasonably early. I'd phoned Mimi the previous evening and asked if she would mind if Aphrodite and I spent the night together at a hotel.

"Of course not, Sonny-Bob. I love both of you. We're all family. But I appreciate your asking."

"Thank you, darling."

"Thank *you*, Sonny-Bob Culpepper."

"Why are you thanking me, Mimi?"

"Because of the way you treat me and Sue and Aphrodite and even Freud. You've made me realize what a family is and what brothers and sisters are."

Her voice caught for a second, then she continued. "Sue and Freud feel the same way I do." She laughed. "Even that old cat seems to feel the same way."

"I don't want to hear about that cat, Mimi."

"Sorry darling, I couldn't resist. Anyway, you and Aphrodite have a good time and I'll see you in the morning. I love you."

"I love you, Mimi."

I told Hubert he was free for the evening and he lumbered off to wherever sentient vehicles go on a beautiful spring night in Austin.

Aphrodite and I had shared a profound night and we'd both been cleansed by the process. I felt closer to her than I ever had to even my own biological siblings. We knew we weren't destined for any type of formal arrangement of togetherness, but we knew we were truly brother and sister and we each had our work.

"Sonny-Bob, I'm quitting the business and leaving Mom. It'll take me a while to fully recover from what I've done to myself, but I don't know where I'd be if you hadn't come along. In hell, I guess."

"Probably so." I sipped my orange juice. "The pornographers and the repressives are both lost in the seething flames of their own egotism. You could have chosen to be with either group for the long term and egotism would have won either way. I'm glad you chose to become yourself and purify your shadow of egotism and separation. Separation is just an illusion of egotism, anyway. Let the fundies on the repressive side and the porno people on the perversion side continue to rail at one another and duke it out and create their respective hells. One hand denigrates the other. That'll go on to one degree or another until the middle of the next century, but the dust will finally settle and the flame of love will at last begin to absorb the spark of egotism. Most fundie churches will be gone, the Catholic church will completely vanish, and very little government will survive."

I smiled in satisfaction. "And no more Democrats and no more gun control."

So relaxed and fortified, Aphrodite and I arrived at the co-op. We met Sue heading out for class, and she gave me a quick peck on the cheek and Aphrodite a much longer peck on the tongue.

Then we went to gather Mimi up, but that cat was there. Aphrodite shooed it away and I quickly ran into the room.

"Hello, darlings!" Mimi was exuberant, for today she was going to get her first car and Hubert was going to make her first artificial driver's license.

"Good morning, Maid of Austin. Still got your cherry?"

"You'll find out tonight if you can still wield your lance, Sir Lotta Cock."

We'd been trying every night except last night to bust her cherry. It had to give way sooner or later. Mimi's stamina on the trapeze was increasing and I noticed my strong little woman was getting stronger still in the arms and shoulders from swinging about as she tried every conceivable maneuver to land on Hemingway in a fashion that would officially eliminate her virginity. She was the only swinger I'd ever heard of who was still a virgin.

I can't imagine what it is that women know, but they all seem to know something I don't and they communicate about it telepathically. Mimi had that telepathic look in her eyes as she surveyed Aphrodite, and Aphrodite reciprocated. I always get a little uncomfortable when women get telepathic. I thought about pooting to break the spell but rejected the idea. I knew Mimi was getting a little testy about all that pooting.

So I don't know what they were discussing in the silence of their telepathic universe. They embraced and kissed, then grabbed me and with a goddess on each arm I was escorted to the chariot that was about to be officially transferred from one heavenly being to the other.

We drove to a feudal place that knew no light. It was a place of surly masters and tail-wagging serfs. So these were the masters who granted a person permission to transfer private property to another person. Being from a civilized time where all vestiges of slavery have been swept away, I didn't really understand any of this. But I did understand we were not the masters here. Mimi, Aphrodite and I were expected to join the ranks of the serfs. Mimi and Aphrodite complied with this expectation and began wagging their tails. I began to bristle. I began to growl.

We'd come here at the bidding of these people because they could summon more guns than we could and they had correctional dungeons while we had none. Unless you consider an old rundown co-op a dungeon. There were some similiarities.

Since those of us assembled at this place had chosen not to resist, you'd think these petty tyrants could be polite and sweet. But they were not. They were smug and self-important and unhelpful. If a serf dared to ask an unexpected question, the glare from the eyes of the tyrants was more intense than the glare of a polecat's eyes caught in the headlights.

Mimi later told me that most people in this century had had similiar experiences dealing with these extortioners, but that sometimes you had a good experience, too. She said they weren't all bad.

But this day was a foul and gloomy one. No love radiated across the moat from the masters to us. But as with all who feel they have some crust of royal bread they must cling to, these masters would have to remain behind in their enclosure when all us serfs left. These masters would remain behind as lapdogs to still greater masters.

"Sonny-Bob, stop growling! You'll call attention to yourself," Mimi warned.

But I couldn't help it. I couldn't stop growling any more than Mimi could stop screaming during orgasm. There was something primordial in me too, something that had existed long before all these control freaks and their mechanisms, and which would continue to exist long after they were gone. And that something was expanding. Pretty soon it would be bigger than Hemingway, and when it got that big it would fill up this little room, this cattlehall we were expected to endure, and it would knock the walls down with the force of its greatness. Time and constraint cannot prevent the wild creative force from expressing itself. It was lucky for the controllers of this society that the primordial force had chosen to express through one as sweet-hearted as I. You wouldn't want to see this force expressing through a bad person.

The primordial force had something to say. Soon it would begin to speak.

By the time it was our turn to bow before the masters the murmer of voices had died down and the only sound was my ancient growling. I felt people looking at me, and if I turned suddenly I always caught them.

"Sonny-Bob, stop looking so wild-eyed," Mimi whispered in pleading tones. "You're scaring everybody."

But I was beyond the point of caring about consequences. I would do my duty by the primordial force of the universe.

The heavens opened before my eyes and all aspects of myself stepped through that interdimensional doorway and consolidated themselves in my physical form. I was potent, radiant and powerful. All the kilotons of the universe were concentrated in me.

Yet I suddenly knew that the universe hadn't planned to totally destroy every illusion of humanity on this day. That would come with time, and by the twenty-second century that process was already pretty far along. But I could serve as an anchor for the destructive force that precedes evolution right here, right now in this cattlehall in Texas, and from this point it would gradually spread throughout the earth. For the keen destructive force that eliminates glamour is always necessary if the people persist in clinging to outdated forms and methods as a result of the veil of polluted egotism they wear. If those old forms and methods aren't voluntarily relinquished, they must be destroyed. The planet must evolve.

My heart clicked in and the energy of all my selves poured to and through it and I realized again that the heart must be my governing organ. Whereas my unmodified will would have led to the complete destruction of Texas that day, my heart modulated the forces pouring through me and I suddenly began to feel a certain humorous joy at this little skirmish. I was no longer the army of General George Patton bearing down upon the forces of the Third Reich; I was a lone Apache with a bow about to shoot an arrow up the ass of the rude oppressor.

I didn't have to eliminate glamour today. All I had to do was make a start, and the rest of the operation would continue over the next few centuries. With all my selves consolidated and irradiated by my heart I suddenly remembered times in the remote past when I'd relied on unbridled will to achieve my aims, but in the end disaster always undid my designs. Those disasters always undid **me**, too.

Well, I wasn't going to become undone today, by Goddess. No more unbridled will for this old child. I relaxed into my heart, yet stood firm and my radiations drove away the spirits that cultivated the thorn of glamour in this place. And since everyone here but me, and maybe Mimi and Aphrodite, was under the influence of glamour, a couple of the masters and two or three serfs couldn't stand my energy emissions and threw up. The glamour lodged in their own energy fields was loosening up and the process made them sick, as such processes often do. Soon there was a river of vomit in this hall of cattle and everyone had fled except we three friends and the lone master who waited to take our tribute. "I've got your tribute," I muttered.

I peered over Mimi's shoulder and saw something called a registration card. Control freaks always have to keep track of other people's business so they can make them feel ashamed if they don't comply with the control freak's expectations.

There was a section on the card that said "Customer Identification Number". I shrugged. Time to put my two cents' in. The force that dispells glamour was anchored here now, but it wouldn't hurt to be the first person to confront a master and stand up for humanity.

"There's been a mistake, ma'am. We're not customers."

"But you just paid for the new title and registration, didn't you?"

"Yes, ma'am. But we aren't customers."

The master put her hands on her hips and looked crosseyed at me. "I don't understand."

"Ma'am, a customer is one who voluntarily forks over some money to buy something he actually wants. I've noticed this and experienced it since I've . . . uh, since I've been here.

"On the other hand, when you coerce someone into buying something they don't want, that's theft. It's also rape, because it violates and subdues the spirit of the individual.

"You're wearing one of those cross-beamed torture devices on a chain around your neck so I guess you're a Christian. Doesn't the Bible preach against theft? What did they do to people in ancient times who practiced theft? Do you know? I know, but I won't frighten you with an account of that.

"Anyhow, anyone you coerce isn't a free citizen who can purchase what he wants. He's a slave who's made to purchase what you want him to purchase. Look at your wall: it's covered with threats of what you'll do if your so-called customer doesn't conform *exactly* to your expectations. You won't find that at Wal-Mart or anyplace else where genuine customers congregate. And the only way you can do these things is to outgun your so-called customers. You have a whole body of troops with badges and guns and who knows what other instruments of coercion that go out and do your bureaucratic bidding. They hurt people just so you can maintain your sense of control, which presumably gives you a perverse and righteous thrill.

"You take money from the serfs and give it to the Sheriff of Nottingham, or somesuch person, who divides the loot among you and your kind. Or maybe you and your kind collectively *are* the Sheriff of Nottingham.

"In any case, it's mostly about your perverse need to feel righteous and secure in your egotism. It's about your need to control and manipulate and judge people who don't meet your expectations.

"Secondarily, it's about your need for loot."

The woman was crimson and speechless. I shrugged. I knew that as soon as she thought of something to say she would offer an illusion to justify herself, or rather, to justify her righteous and unstable egotism. She didn't know her Self, and didn't know that her real Self never would need any justification.

I smiled and demolished the self-justification scenario that was percolating in the back of her head. "Lady child, you're probably going to begin making excuses for your illusions and for the egotism which depends upon those illusions as soon as we go out the door. You don't realize that egotism itself is an illusion, it was born out of illusion and therefore must take after its parent. You're probably going to beg the question we've been discussing by proclaiming to yourself that all this theft--I mean, these fees and taxes--are necessary. But I haven't offered any assesment to you at all on that question, and the truth is that I'm not sure whether they're necessary or not at humanity's current low level of development. Maybe, as your self-justification would have it, all these fees and harrassments really are necessary in this primitive year of 1983. I don't know. But to dwell on that question is to try to avoid the issues I have raised and the truths I have pointed out. You are stealing from people, and you and your armies of law enforcers are hurting them. *That's* the truth. Is it necessary? Who cares? The first step in examining the issue is to admit to yourself, and then to others, the truth about what you're doing without any pretense of self-justification. Having done that, you can then ask if it's necessary. If it turns out that it's necessary for you to step upon humanity in this way for some greater purpose, fine. I'll consider supporting you, then. But you have to be something other than a liar and a petty self-justifying tyrant for me to offer you any moral support. Be an honest thief, and be willing to give it up as soon as your theft no longer benefits humanity. Assuming it benefits humanity to begin with. But that, as I've already pointed out, is another question."

I gave a little poot as Mimi tugged on my arm. "We'd better go, Sonny-Bob." I let Mimi and Aphrodite lead me towards the door.

On the way out I noticed a picture of myself, as well as one of Santa Claus. I paused and studied these wanted posters. "Look at that lighting, it wasn't worth a damn," I groused to my ladies. "Oliver North took those photos in an attic and he obviously knows nothing about photography. And what's the FBI? Is North involved in that, too?

"And look! Look! They left the hyphen out of my name. I want my damn hyphen. I WANT MY HYPHEN!"

Aphrodite and Mimi dragged me out of the place and when we got back to the car I was surprised to see that Mimi was in tears. "Sonny-Bob, sometimes you can be a real bastard, you know that?"

I was shocked and distressed at Mimi's suffering. "Sweetheart, that master woman in there had it coming, I was only doing what had to be done to benefit humanity . . ." But if I'd known it was going to hurt the one gentle human I cared most about in the world I might have thought twice before agreeing to serve as a vessel for the primordial force of the universe.

"I love you, Mimi . . ."

"Don't touch me!"

Aphrodite put a cool hand on my arm. "Sonny-Bob, Mimi's been worried sick about you. She can't even eat half the time. There's wanted posters of you at the post office too; if they're here they must be putting them in every sort of government office, federal, state, and maybe local, too.

"That ten million dollar reward would tempt most people to turn you in, and it probably would've already happened if you hadn't grown so fat in the last few months. Your puffy face doesn't look so much like your old thin face. That's why Mimi's suddenly started feeding you extra doughnuts and not complaining when you get up at 2:00 a.m. and fix another meal.

"Didn't you read that wanted poster, Sonny-Bob? Don't you have any common sense? They're calling you a deranged arms smuggler who steals guns from the Marine Corps and gives them to children while quoting the Golden Rule.

"There's nothing that frightens people more than a deranged Santa who delivers guns."

"But they only included facts that mitigate against me! They didn't list any of my virtues. I killed a pimp. Why didn't they mention that?"

Aphrodite looked at the heavens and gave kind of a guttural groan. Her body was tense and rigid and her fists were clinched at her sides.

I was overwhelmed with sorrow at having caused my darlings this distress. A tear trickled down my fat and puffy face, then was followed by another. How do you explain to people raised in a barbaric time the perfect legitimacy of self-defense and of helping someone else defend himself from aggression, if you so choose?

These nuts in the twentieth century didn't realize that if you're killed it's only a temporary inconvenience. You'll be back, and if you were previously killed as a result of your own aggressive actions it will serve as a learning experience, if you learn to listen to your inner voice. Your subconscious will try to guide you out of your bestial conduct and place you on a higher plane of experience.

Yet these people behaved as if only the physical body and personality were real and omitted entirely any experience of the soul, the True Self. Well, not much could be done until Lucille finally came into her own.

As if reading my thoughts--which she probably was--Mimi came to me and looked up into my fat face, the face covered in gristle and tears, but which was also covered with love for my Mimi.

"Sonny-Bob, it's not about self-defense. Aphrodite and I are with you on that, honey. But you take too many insane chances. We just don't want you to be killed by some cop or bounty hunter. I love you sooo much!" She placed her arms around me and squeezed me tightly. "I love you Sonny-Bob Culpepper and I always will, and I'm not ready for you to die. Maybe you're used to facing danger and think nothing of it, but all this is new to me and Sue and Aphrodite. Why, you even freaked Freud out with that gun at the bank! Sue and I had to tell him where you're from. Now he wants to go to the moon."

Suddenly she looked at me and laughed and shook her head. "This whole thing is ridiculous!"

Aphrodite's hand was on my arm, then it went around my shoulders and she embraced us both. "I love you two strange people," she said to us with a shining heart, and we all basked in the glow of our hearts for a moment.

Then I recovered the sobriety of who I am, the thing which had always made me suited for this mission. I'd been this way at least since I'd been burned at the stake.

"We three friends are a glowing bundle of love, but each of us manifests that love in a different way. Contrary to what the floppy chakra sentimentalists think--they have floppy chakras like a newborn child instead of the stable and integrated chakras of an adult--regardless of what these infantile people think, killing and destruction are sometimes necessary, especially the killing and destruction of illusion. That glamour shit has to go, and by God it will. That's my speciality.

"Mimi, Aphrodite, it's the glamour of the masses that tries to destroy your love, or at least inhibit it. So I destroy the destroyer. The difference is I'm serving the cause of Love, that great cause which all civilized people serve in their own individual way.

"I destroy illusion, which frequently amounts to death from the perspective of the organism which hosts those illusions. The host organism may physically die or become more insane than he already is when his illusions are destroyed, because he identifies more with his illusions than with his Self. Or if he can summon a little strength, he might actually be able to benefit from the destruction of his illusions and live and grow, and then destroy himself any illusions he may have remaining. It's beautiful.

"But I *never* destroy love, ever. I support love, I serve love, just as you ladies do. The fact that I destroy the illusions that try to get in the way of love is why your love is able to shine out and touch people, my darlings. And like you, I **am** love. Illusions clutter up our hearts and energy fields and get in the way of love. I destroy the blockages that interfere with the full expression of love. That's just the kind of bloke I am, darlings. I'd rather be a prostitute, but I serve in the way karma has decreed.

"And really, darlings, to make love and do healing work as you and your sisters do, or to fight and kill as I and my brother warriors do--it's really all the same thing. It's about finding yourself and being true to yourself as the soul of love which each of us is. There's no wrong path that leads to love. Every path that leads to love is the right path for someone and is a path of divine service.

"A minute ago in that feudal hall of cattle I was being true to myself by standing up for humanity and anchoring a force that will eventually lead to the destruction of much illusion. This is one way I find myself. Violence is not the end, but it is one of the means by which I draw closer to the day when I will at last be absorbed by Love.

"To make love or fight, it's all the same. Being true to yourself and maintaining a sense of humor during lovemaking or on the battlefield is what's important. Either way, you have to be openhearted and relaxed. During lovemaking it's the feeling aspect of your heart that's most active; during combat it's usually the will aspect of the heart that's most active. Not the personal will, mind you, but the will aspect of the heart, which is the will of the soul. Otherwise, you'd be more likely to get hurt.

"Of course, it takes a while to learn this. It may take a long time to learn to release the terror of intimacy or of combat. But humor and the work you do to open to your own soul will in time lead to the desired condition, unless you get killed first."

Yes, they were staring at me strangely and I hadn't even pooted. But I think they understood. They were not of the typical savage floppy chakra humanity of the twentieth century. Mimi and Aphrodite, and for that matter Freud and Sue, were civilized. They were my people, and would be in any century.

"I see," Aphrodite finally said. "And I think I see something else. When they repress me they also repress you, and vice versa."

"That's right, honey. When they repress love in any form they repress love in every form, and all they have left is their rank sentimentality. And they foolishly mistake that for love. They've simply never been centered in their True Self and experienced genuine love. They don't know what it is.

"So they repress sex and create the perversion of your former industry. Or they repress moral and spiritually oriented violence and school shootings and murders and assaults of all kinds result. Wars result. You see, the energy they've repressed hasn't disappeared, it's just been frozen. And when it tries to break loose, all hell results. These religious fundamentalists and politically correct liberals have created all this perversion. When they condemn the perverts, they always neglect to condemn the Source Pervert because they'd have to condemn themselves. And their Selves is the last thing they want to face. To reach their souls of love they have to walk through the valley of the shadow of death and clean it out and polish it until it sparkles. That valley is really the valley of their own personal shadow. They are literally afraid of their own polluted shadows.

" 'Repression Creates Perversion'. The truth is that a genuinely moral person has no taboos or inhibitions, but he lives in a manner that prepares the way for love to manifest and he doesn't infringe on the relatively innocent. He doesn't perform a given act simply because he can; he's a scientist and looks to see what the consequences of that act will be. If the consequences support love he'll go for it, and if they don't he won't. Everyone but the senior prostitutes slips from time to time, but what I've described is the basic scenario. I'm still learning to put it into practice."

Well, Fatty Culpepper was out of breath and he paused. "Sermon's over, dears. Let's get a cake and go home."

Mimi yawned. She looked sweet and innocent and exhausted, and she was all of those. I resolved to do my best to ease her fears in the future. I loved her so. The primordial force of the universe wouldn't mind if I just devoted myself to Mimi for a while.

I tousled her hair, then pulled her to me and kissed the crown of her head.

PART TWO

GILGAMESH THE BUDDHA

INTERLUDE:

Buford Sargon's Log

Somewhere In The Wilderness of 1983

If Sonny-Bob were not my own Ancestor, I wouldn't be too keen on trailing him through this pre-civ period. The natives are nasty and you can't even drink the air, they've polluted it so much. Can't wait to get back to the clean air of the Carolinas in my own day--if Sonny-Bob Culpepper is successful in saving my day. For the Future is forever in doubt until Her Champion has demonstrated that He can bear Her cross to the end of the Trail of Tears and transmute that cross into a perfected personalized experience, expansion and Vision of that Future.

And Sonny-Bob is the pivot point about which all else revolves. If he's not successful, there won't be any more Champions--ever. Ish told me that a moment like this comes about only once in the entire history of a world, a history in which the dominant race of that world spends millions of years in perfecting itself. Only, when the pivot point is reached, it's either step forward and reclaim the whole, wide Future enriched by the strivings of past ages, or it's dissolve the connection with Future, the connection that keeps every world at least partially invigorated until it can restore itself into becoming a conscious part of the Pattern. In other words, it's "root hog or die".

Both Mars and earth's moon are examples of worlds that didn't root hard enough.

Even Ish is forbidden to step in directly, or to send more than one Champion--She answers to Cosmic Gods so profoundly deeply located in the unseen space near the universe's Heart that no one but She knows Their Names--and I'm not sure that She does, really. Ish never divulges more than a fraction of what She knows (or doesn't know?) to anyone; She hasn't actually told me She knows Their Names--or even if She knows whether They have Names.

Sometimes I get a little tired of Sonny-Bob's foolishness. Tact isn't one of his strengths, although he can be very compassionate and sensitive when dealing with someone he's close to, or if he encounters someone who's suffering and becoming aware of that suffering. For most of the people of this timezone repress their suffering through a whole host of unconsciously practiced techniques, which I guess is why they aren't usually conscious of their perversions.

Most of these people aren't yet aware that the interaction between their souls and personalities over many, many incarnations has produced an energy body for their souls to manifest through called the causal body, or soul body. And they don't know that this causal body contains their glamours and illusions, as well as any degree of Truth and Love they've managed to contact. They don't yet realize that to progress in the evolution of their consciousness, they must consciously develop a robust causal body attuned as fully as possible with the Wisdom, Truth and Love of themselves as Soul.

Of course, eventually the causal body becomes an "old man" of sorts, and has used itself as fully in service to others as possible. At this point, the causal body must be consciously sacrificed--this is the Supreme Sacrifice of the Initiate who steps forward into Liberation. This Sacrifice is so difficult as to be nearly impossible, and can only be successfully performed by a master at sacrifice--a master who is finally qualified to fully sacrifice all the glamours and illusions he has refined into partial reflections of the Truth of Love. No person who hasn't used their causal body to the fullest in Service is capable of accepting the Keys to this Sacrifice. The only Liberated soul is that soul which is fully pledged to God.

Contrary to the chronic delusions of many of the devout in primitive religions, becoming Liberated doesn't mean you sacrifice your humanity to achieve some detached godhood who never walks barefoot in the soils of his emotional or fleshly nature. Quite the contrary, the Liberated soul is Liberated into his full humanity, and brings his Divinity with Him to be merged in a flowing powerful golden stream in his physical body and personality. He's a better lover than ever, a better parent than ever, a better *person* than ever, and he's free to flow with and fully enjoy his humanity for the very first time. But it has to always be remembered that he got this way not through a contrary, selfish, profit-sharing animalistic motive, but through the constant self-forgetfulness of true service. Yes, True-Self remembered is also important at a certain stage as the Initiate learns to transfigure and fully glorify his causal body in service before the Sacrifice of the causal body is complete, but even True-Self must be forgotten before the weary Initiate into Liberation is at last lead across the sparkling Threshold.

A few Initiates down through the ages have been selected for a special ability to bear more than the weight of just their own glamours and illusions--their own sins--in their causal body. The loving souls of these sacrificial lambs consciously magnetize and attract into their causal bodies a percentage of the glamours and illusions of a tribe, nation, or even the entire earth. These sins compose the karma of the people being served by this purificatory sacrifice. Then the Savior wrestles with and refines these glamours and illusions into something approximating the truth of nonduality so they will partially reflect the Light of Love.

Ultimately everyone who progresses along the evolutionary path learns to bear his own cross so that he no longer contributes to the sins of the world. And at the appropriate stage the weary pilgrim will undertake and eventually complete the sacrifice of his causal body (or "burn his rainbow bridge", if you like that terminology better), freeing the love-energy of the soul to express directly thru the purified and integrated personality for the very first time with no need for an intermediary. Then, as Sonny-Bob would say, "he can go catfishing". In other words, he's free at last.

But only a few of these self-sacrificers also specialize at sacrificing the karma of the masses who have been deluded by ignorance and knowledge, and our Sonny-Bob is one of these few. Because of the terrible burden he removed from humanity's shoulders, he spiritually earned the right to live without the burden of tact. The causal body of humanity as a whole is much cleaner, thanks to Sonny-Bob's special skill at sacrifice. A sensitive person can barely breathe around these polluted people; their air pollution is merely reflective of the sins stored up in their causal body. But partly thanks to Sonny-Bob's Work, non-polluting technology will eventually appear. As Humanity's causal body becomes cleaner, this is reflected by the increasing cleanliness of the atmosphere. It might even be appropriate to say that the atmosphere *is* Humanity's causal body. You decide.

Mechanistic people who look at the universe as a collection of objects won't understand these truths. You have to begin growing conscious of yourself as an energy-beam from a vast central sun playing upon the surface of a sparkling blue ocean to commence to understand. This metaphor is a literally true statement of the exact science of the future. Ponder on this.

But mechanistic people aren't the whole problem on this difficult globe. Those who are just beginning to become conscious are sometimes an even bigger problem. The other day Sonny-Bob nearly blew his cover in a hissey-fit against one of these people.

I'd trailed him to one of these "New Thought" churches and was praying he wouldn't go inside, knowing his temperament as I do. He's been touched by so many different types of energy and so many divinities have activated themselves in him it's a wonder he didn't go off the deep end long ago. Well, maybe he did go off the deep end; I don't know. He's certainly "teched in the head", "teched" in the heart, and "teched" pretty much everywhere.

Well, like all "New Thought" churches, this one was a degenerate relic of the Ageless Wisdom. People in such churches were actually encouraged to *retain* (can you believe it!) their cherished glamours and illusions, instead of purifying and Liberating themselves through Altruistic service. But some of these churches were less degenerate than others; in fact, some breath of spiritual life actually stirred through some of them. Indeed, a very few of these groups (usually those which had too few members to be able to buy a church-house) might have to be considered as genuinely re-generative organs for humanity's inspiration and redemption.

So in a few such churches--those which had dropped "New Thought" fundamentalism and begun to encourage the growth of compassionate self-awareness--some actual spiritual Work could be accomplished, and I think even Sonny-Bob acknowledged this fact and offered moral and spiritual support to these churches. Unfortunately, the church Sonny-Bob had elected to visit on this day was not one of the compassionate ones. The first principle of dealing with World Saviors is to try to steer them clear of religious groups which lack compassion, or they might beat the hell out of someone.

But I couldn't steer Sonny-Bob anywhere, because he would probably recognize me from our brief interaction when he was a young field agent, and he wasn't supposed to know I was tailing him--though with that old he-coon, you never could be sure. Sometimes I suspected he might be leading me on for the fun of it--like that time his trail led into a moon bear's cave in the Himalayas. I had to inject medical nanos after that one, and while the cuts and bite marks on my ass were being repaired, Sonny-Bob sauntered up to the cave's mouth escorted by the bear, then gave the bear a piece of candy and patted it on the head. I've always wondered if he was paying that bear off for what he did to me.

Anyhow, I smelled more trouble around this "New Thought" church than I had in that moon bear's cave. Right then I'd have given anything for a sexy young girl in a short skirt--not for me, but so I could pay her to attract Sonny-Bob into a less conspicuous activity than he was likely to get into at this church. Oh, hell--almost forgot that Sonny-Bob is almost as likely to drop his pants in public as private. Scratch that idea; the primitive "New Thought" religions of the time would go into hysterics and notify the authorities if they saw a mature fellow and a twelve or fourteen year old lady worshipping outside their doors. No respect for natural functions, or for the place of these functions in the soul-connection of worship. So Sonny-Bob's ability to connect instantly with a pure-hearted woman at the soul level, and to frequently allow his body to express its divine signature during such an encounter, would be more likely to cause a ruckus here than to prevent one. Oh, well. I followed him inside and sat down in the back row, my hat pulled low over my eyes and a magazine in front of my face. Only when I caught a few people staring at me did I remember the magazine I carried was *Playboy* --I quickly put it down and placed a hymn book over the sacred cover illustration. Even the pamphlets of real religion were unwelcome in most New Thought churches.

Yet in the far-flung future, Saint Hefner is considered a minor god in our pantheon, occupying approximately the same place Hermes occupied in the Greek pantheon. The main reason he's not one of our major gods is because politically he tended to support Democrats. Yet Hefner's Penis adorns the threshold of many of our homes as a fertility reminder and as an aid against the evil of repression and the accompanying perversion. Frequently a pair of breasts is placed somewhere above the Penis as an emblem of the Goddess who was served by Saint Hef in his guerrilla war to begin the process of the restoration of natural culture by reintroducing an appreciation of Beauty to human awareness.

Well, a preacher-woman was rattling on about how her beliefs create her world, ignorant as hell about the actual *energies* she was dragging around from previous incarnations in her immature, unrefined causal body. I glanced in Sonny-Bob's direction; he was sitting placidly so far-- or he seemed to be placid. But often before one of his eruptions the only signal of what was about to come was a certain intensely focused light in his eyes, with maybe a little twitch of his body. Kind of like a lion in the desert of human perceptions about to leap upon a hyena. I crossed my fingers and took deep breaths.

Now the preacher-woman was relating that when her sons were young, sometimes they'd come home from school and tell her they'd had a fight. Her response to this was to tell them that beliefs create their world, and that they had a choice whether they were going to fight or not.

Suddenly Sonny-Bob was in the pulpit; I have no idea how he'd gotten there, but he moves fast for a fat man. The preacher-woman was sitting plopped up on her ass on the floor, a bewildered expression on her face. "Well, I guess you believed there was a chair there, but there isn't," Sonny-Bob commented.

Then Sonny-Bob surveyed the crowd of marks who had come to sponge up the idea that their glamours and illusions--their petty desires, in other words--were somehow spiritual and could be used in a lust-driven unpurified form to create a spiritual existence.

"You people are insane," Sonny-Bob began, as I cringed and tried to make myself small behind a pew. "You think--no, you don't think; you've been too lazy to develop any real thought processes within yourselves and you're driven by glamours and illusions that cause you to *pretend* to think that your childish beliefs create your world, irrespective of the beliefs of the others in your society who surround you, and irrespective of the energies you carry from countless lives in your immature, unrefined causal bodies.

"Dummies, your causal bodies create your world, and right now they're doing it in an unconscious fashion, rather than in the aware fashion of the Spiritual Initiate who consciously works with the energies of his causal body to refine that body into a vehicle of compassionate service.

"Madam," he addressed the preacher-woman once more, "you say you believe in nonviolence, and therefore will never have to fight, but I say to you that there's more violence stored up in your causal body than you can shake a stick at--or," he grinned, "than I can shake my dick at," as several of the ladies in the congregation gasped, and a couple of them fainted. But I noticed there was one young thing in the front row, maybe fifteen or sixteen, who smiled directly up into Sonny-Bob's shining face and shifted her miniskirt a little higher. Sonny-Bob paid no attention; most people don't realize this, and perhaps wouldn't believe it, but Sonny-Bob is only interested in sex when it's a direct part of his Savioring. But I knew Sonny-Bob would have a date after church if he felt the soul-urge to impart some salvation to this young lady. If the cops didn't come, that is. I shuddered, wondering if they'd send a SWAT team to surround the church if they realized who was in the pulpit. World Saviors are always unpopular with the authorities--and they usually don't give a shit if they find themselves in a gun battle. Well, I guess being here was better than being home, since the timewave would have reached my own century by now and sent everyone into nonexistence. "Count your blessings, Sargon," I breathed to myself.

"Count your blessings."

"You see, Madam," Sonny-Bob continued, "this overwhelming sticky sweetness you're forcing your heart to pour upon your sons and on everyone else who is unfortunate enough to come in contact with you is simply a 'pendulum swing', an overreaction to the hate and rage and wickedness stored up in your causal body. Perhaps your current blind sweetness is a very slight improvement over your previous lives--or perhaps not. In any case, you can't pour sticky sweetness through the heart chakra for too long, because the sticky stuff will clog the heart's natural channels, kind of like an energetic cholesterol. In fact," Sonny-Bob was warming to his topic, and genuinely beginning to enjoy himself, a rare thing for World Saviours; "I suspect that a buildup of physical cholesterol is sometimes a direct reflection of this sticky spiritual cholesterol."

I glanced at the crowd of marks, and saw that they were transfixed by Sonny-Bob's Authority--an Authority that came directly from the Ancient of Days, though these people couldn't know that. But as long as they were transfixed, they weren't calling the cops, and that was a good thing.

"Anyhow," Sonny-Bob continued, "you're a mean, cruel bitch who has de-nutted her sons." The preacher-woman's face exhibited a mixture of shock and the beginnings of rage at Sonny-Bob's bald statement of spiritual truth. Some more people, male and female, slid down in their pews unconscious; they couldn't stand the heat of Agni, which was starting to pour off Sonny-Bob in a pink-red flame and drive the spirits of truth-denied away from this primitive, ancient temple. The young lady in front put one hand to her throat as the other caressed her heart, then she lightly with a gentle finger touched the spot where surely her clit must lie, barely concealed by a strip of thin fabric. I was starting to get turned on by this display; I guess Sonny-Bob was a good influence on me. I needed to lighten up and quit worrying about the cops and help Sonny-Bob if he got in a gun battle. I wondered if the young lady in the front row would ever be willing to worship with me, and in that moment she turned her head and our eyes met and she stared into the depths of my soul. She gravely nodded, and before she turned back to Sonny-Bob I saw something in those deep, deep eyes of hers that reminded me of Ish . . .

"A century ago," Sonny-Bob was still addressing the deposed preacher-woman, "you might have been abusing your sons in a more obvious manner, perhaps taking them out behind the woodshed and thrilling your perversely twisted sexual nature by flaying some skin off their bare asses with a hickory switch. Or you might have been manipulating them out of their manhood in a more subtle way, perhaps sending the energy strings of attachment out from your sacral center coated with the same sickening sweetness you now force your heart to deliver, attaching those filthy strings to the sacral centers of your sons so you could manipulate them with purely sexual energy into being good little mama's boys, courting only those mama approves of, going to the church mama goes to and living--at least outwardly--a life that conforms to mama's expectations. This is the condition that twentieth century psychologists are starting to call 'emotional incest', and it's practiced by a huge percentage of you fine citizen-folk. However, they should have coined a more accurate term for this condition, perhaps referring to it as 'intra-family sexual manipulation' or somesuch, because there's really nothing wrong with the actual physical practice of incest, so long as the warmth of a loving compassion is present and the strings of control and manipulation are not."

Gasps from the marks, with more of them lapsing into unconsciousness. A few of them got up and stumbled out the doors; I'm betting these were into 'intra-family sexual manipulation' and didn't want to remain in the presence of someone whom they felt might be able to see through their facade of conformity to social 'ideals' that were impossible for anyone to conform to. To them, Sonny-Bob must have seemed like the outward manifestation of their inward desires, only they weren't pure enough to see Sonny-Bob's heart, and to know that it bore little resemblance to their own organs, which were clogged with the very spiritual cholesterol Sonny-Bob was attempting to help them dislodge. I wondered if any of them would have the guts to notify the authorities of Sonny-Bob's Presence, knowing that they would have to look upon him again to identify him and to testify against him. I carried a lady's gun, a little Sigarms energy pistol, and I patted her affectionately. If any of those people summoned the cops, I'd cover Sonny-Bob's flabby white ass.

"Anyhow, bitch," Sonny-Bob continued warmly, "you've castrated your sons with the knife of your selfishness and of your glamours concerning your own supposed spirituality. And really, what you've done is fueled in a very subtle fashion by the glamour of the rage and hate and manipulation stored up in the dark, unacknowledged side of your causal body. The very shit you run from and deny having is hot on your heels, causing you to run into the arms of a new delusion concerning your supposed righteousness. This dualistic running away is the cause of your long-term suffering, and is the cause of the suffering you inflict upon those around you.

"Your sons came to you with stories of fighting so you could nourish them with the confirmation of their manhood, which is essential if they are to feel they have the right and the ability to protect those they love-- including you, the old fool who castrated them! For one of a son's primary missions is to stand up for his mother. You don't understand this, and are too afraid of the masculine side of your own nature to begin to understand it. Coward. A woman who is this afraid of her masculine side isn't much of a woman, either.

"The correct approach would have been for you to develop a genuinely moral understanding within yourself before you ever had children, so that you could discuss matters with your sons after they'd been in a fight and help them to discover whether they'd truly been fighting for moral and spiritual reasons. But instead of helping them discover their manhood, as they naturally wanted you to do, you destroyed their manhood. You are a whore to the very idea of Woman, and are not fit to wear the slingshot brassiere or to refer to yourself as a Woman.

"Other than sapping their manhood, what effect do you suppose your belittling of your sons' masculine response will have on the world? Will your sons feel inclined to make a desperate attempt to recover their sense of man-self by joining the Marines and going to war? Or have you sapped their manhood so completely they'll drop out of basic training in a pool of shame and self-loathing, and then try to find someone more helpless than they are to take it out on--perhaps a puppy or a baby, for surely even a man who is not a man can triumph over a puppy or a baby. But what happens if the puppy or baby makes it to adulthood? Will the dog be a mean cur who has to be put to sleep because of the vengeance your son directed at him--vengeance which should have been directed at you, if it had found its proper object. But really, vengeance has no proper object and is always delusional, always wrong. But that's another sermon. Instead of being put to sleep, the dog should be congratulated for making it to adulthood at all in a climate of abuse, and his meanness treasured and given the gift of love and appreciation because it helped him survive. But most of your dog psychologists won't be aware enough to see this for a while.

"And what of the poor abused baby? Your grandbaby? Will he go on a shooting spree in a desperate attempt to prove himself valuable enough to respect?

"And what if one of your de-nutted sons goes into politics? Don't you know he will be willing to support any sort of war, justified or not, if he feels it might grow him some balls in the eyes of the voting public, so he can feel that finally he looks like a man?

"Yeah, maybe he'll feel like a man for a change, instead of like your son, when he looks in the mirror each day if he can somehow find himself identified with a war, perhaps even a 'drug war', a 'war on illiteracy' or anything that he can attach the macho name of 'war' to.

"America is full of these de-nutted men who support war, and of women who want to be men and think that supporting war will help them grow a pair. This is the unpurified, glamorous side of gender equality."

Well, what can I say? World Saviours aren't known for trying to cover up the truth. Sonny-Bob was right, and he'd fully converted me to his cause. That's the problem with these sons-of-bitches who literally bear the energy-weight of the world on their shoulders; they become a force of nature that can't be ignored, and which will magnetize anyone whose heart is pure enough to share in the energy of purification, forgiveness and regeneration.

Sonny-Bob mopped his brow with a handkerchief and continued. "Now then: you told your sons that if they believe they won't have to fight, then they won't have to. Well, what if they encounter someone whose beliefs don't match their own? Your sons will be injured or killed needlessly, because you raped their souls into submission by belittling and teaching them to deny the hormones of the body, instead of using those hormones to Achieve a true and conscious Morality as they refine and ultimately release the glamours and illusions in their causal bodies, and also using those wonderful sexy male hormones to Achieve contact with, and ultimately to embody, the love of their own sweet powerful hearts, then sharing that love in a fullbody fashion with those they feel drawn to who can appreciate them and their flexibility, and thus enter into a whole-souled relationship with them encompassing all aspects of the soul, including the body, which is an extension of the soul."

Sonny-Bob lifted his nose in mock archness. "It's not just 'a guy thing', Madam. That phrase is used to denigrate the male impulse, more often than not, and at those times this little cliché merely becomes a statement of the lack of sensitivity of the one who employs it."

Sonny-Bob scratched his nuts and continued. "Most sons are meant to be warriors, though for some it's more natural to become healers. And this is a false dichotomy, because ultimately all warriors do become healers, and all healers, whether male or female, do become warriors.

"Now, the important thing about the warrior, rather than the street punk or bully, is that the warrior's primary battle--really, his *only* battle-- is with the constant refinement of himself. In other words, refining the glamours and illusions--the sins--in his causal body into a full-spectrum morality that denies nothing in the entire spectrum of nature, and finds the proper place within himself for everything in nature. Along the way he learns to quench his spiritual thirst with love, rather than the dry and rigid egotism you people quaff all day. You people make me sick, but it's my job to be sickened by you, so I'm not complaining. At least, not today. We'll see about tomorrow. Anyhow, I'm headed for Resurrection from your sins, so eventually I'll be able to go a-fishing. I hope. If I'm successful . . .

"Anyhow, the warrior's refinement of his causal body gives him moral and spiritual strength, decisiveness and momentum in combat, and physical and mental quickness. If he must engage in physical combat with an unenlightened adversary (and unenlightened adversaries are all the Realized Warrior will have) he'll probably whip their ass as much or more through his moral and spiritual impetus and authority as through the use of his physical skills. It's his moral and spiritual authority, and the energy and the spiritual beings hovering around that moral and spiritual authority, that give the Realized Warrior a whirlwind edge.

"However, in the unlikely event he is defeated, he will yield his life in the joyful satisfaction that he's been successful at perfecting his causal body into an instrument of Service. This will allow him to begin on a higher cycle of Service when he begins his next incarnation.

"Physical conflict isn't the real problem in the world. The world's problems are all caused by attachment, which itself is a form of repression, if you can believe it. For in order to be attached to one thing, you have to learn to deny another thing. If you're attached to the idea of being a "good person", you're going to deny some or possibly all aspects of yourself that you feel are bad, with the result that those "bad" aspects are going to conspire together to pull you off your high horse at every opportunity. You'll cheat on your spouse, then stupidly amid the tears of the suffering you've created you'll come before the church and promise not to do it again--and a little further down the road, you'll probably do it again. Certainly, you'll want to do it again, and from a neurological perspective, wanting to do it is the same as actually doing it. Plus, you'll surround yourself with the thoughtforms of doing it, while outwardly trying to maintain the facade that you're really something other than what you are in your heart. Hypocrite. Repression creates perversion; attachment creates hypocrisy. Even a person who considers himself or herself "bad" will occasionally 'frontslide' into doing something he or she considers 'good'.

"Those who are unnaturally attached to peace create more violence than the gung-ho snake-eating jungle fighter because they repress the violent side of their own natures, which then goes on the warpath against the repression by creating some perversion or other, which they then feel they have to also repress in a cycle of addiction to violence that doesn't end until they grow sick with the new, higher level of violence they've created within themselves and find something less destructive than nonviolence to attach their preconceptions to.

"Remember that Gandhi was a wife-beater, in addition to being an advocate for nonviolence. He also used a twisted passive-aggressive style of emotional manipulation on her and on his followers to get them to submit themselves to his system of doctrine. It should be self-evident that no human-created system can be superior to its creator, and Gandhi was remarkably flawed, as are all of those who expect breathing human beings to submit themselves to a lifeless form. But fundamentalists are everywhere, and like any other type of insane person, you can't convince them they are delusional and need help.

"Anyhow, in his supposed self-denial, Gandhi also stopped having sex with his wife because, he said, he wanted to be able to control his penis. Yet while he was supposedly controlling his penis, he slept with a whole string of naked young girls, wanting to prove that with a beautiful adolescent in his bed he could keep his tool inactive. Did he really keep his tool inactive? Who knows? I doubt if he invited an audience to witness the activity, or lack of it. Anyhow, because sex is an affectionate sharing of energy, he was having sex with the girls whether he used his dick or not. Their physical and energy bodies were mingling, and that's what sex is . . . if it's affectionate. If Gandhi's mingling with the girls was not affectionate, if he didn't respect them, then it was rape. And since he was a wife-beater and used invasive techniques of emotional manipulation to make people do as he wished, it seems likely he could have emotionally raped the girls, rather than sharing the emotion of sex with them. For sex *is* an emotion, and whoever feels or shares this emotion is not celibate. Gandhi was merely on the run from something in his causal body that made him uncomfortable about sex; he was no more celibate than Hugh Hefner . . . though he wasn't as clean and fragrant as Mr. Hefner."

At this point, from her body language, I felt certain that the young girl who somehow reminded me of Ish had a "come hither" look in her eyes for Sonny-Bob, and I saw her legs spread ever so slightly. Sonny-Bob gave her a quick smile, then mopped his brow again and continued puffing his way through his sermon. He really does have a nice smile . . . his reputation is mostly heterosexual, but I wonder . . . never mind. I'm not here for that.

"Gandhi is an example of how anyone can become lost in the material world and suffer from material delusions. Someone joked that it cost India a fortune to keep Gandhi in poverty, because although he lived simply, his various activities were financed by a billionaire. Gandhi once even went on a hunger strike to convince his patron's employees to stop protesting about harsh working conditions and get back to work. Gandhi's supposed renunciation of material wealth actually reinforced capitalist activities in the same old dualistic cycle of repression creating perversion. He personally chose a life of poverty to protest capitalism and urbanization, and his influence actually helped the billionaires. He denied himself the things he needed to live comfortably on the material plane, and because he was so well-known and influential the energy of his dualistic choice caused society's pendulum to swing in the 'opposite' direction from his own life. His supposedly simple example actually *caused* more urbanization, more complicatedness, more exploitation of the masses by the capitalists, and more sorrow.

"Gandhi's legacy is primarily one of sorrow, of suffering. He is an example of a person who had the capacity to endure some degree of suffering, but not to use that capacity intelligently, wisely or with compassion. If he had ever experienced the truly extreme degrees of suffering himself, he would have immediately renounced his doctrine of creating suffering to create political change. He actually encouraged his followers to suffer more, not to suffer less. Remember that the person who actually *wants* to suffer is harmed less by suffering than those normal people who don't want to suffer. At least, he's harmed less until he has to deal with the karma he created by manipulating people into suffering more than they otherwise would have. When his karma comes 'round, he'll learn a bit more about suffering than he bargained for.

"Gandhi might have incarnated with the ability and intention of becoming a National Savior, of bearing his people's sins in his own causal body and then purifying and releasing those sins, but if that was the case, he failed miserably. A Savior's legacy is less suffering, not more. He encourages people to bear their own cross and process and release the sin and guilt they've picked up over many lifetimes out of their causal bodies; he *does not* glorify suffering, he *does not* tell people to add more suffering to their causal bodies, to their crosses, before picking those crosses up and bearing them responsibly. 'Take up your own goddammed cross' means just that, it doesn't mean make your cross heavier and then try to pick it up. The suggestion to stop running and face your corruption is not a suggestion to your causal body to embrace more corruption, it is a suggestion to your causal body to acknowledge and purify itself of the corruption it already carries. Gandhi got lost rather quickly, and the dimwit became a nuisance and impediment to genuine spiritual growth, both in India and around the world. This isn't to say all his views were wrong; of course they weren't all wrong. He wasn't evil, he wasn't trying to be wicked, and his egotism wanted to have a positive effect on the world, though because it had taken a wrong turn it forgot how to cooperate with his soul and Monad.

"At least, I don't think he was evil. But I haven't read his dossier, so maybe I should reserve judgement on the matter. I don't want to make a premature pronouncement of good intentions, particularly in light of the suffering this little shit caused.

"Gandhi was no Mahatma. A real Mahatma has no causal body to confuse him; he's already born his own cross to the limit, already purified the glamours and illusions, the sins of karma, out of his causal body in the Altruistic Service of reducing suffering, then ultimately sacrificed his causal body altogether so his soul might be fused with his personality, and his Monad with his soul. A real Mahatma is a Liberated Human Being who encourages people to move beyond their suffering by taking a lifetime to purify themselves of the glamours and illusions that cause their suffering. He doesn't glorify suffering and try to add to people's sins. It is dear to his heart that people learn to face their suffering now, but without artificially adding more suffering to their burden, so they will suffer less in the long term. But Gandhi added to people's sins, and thus to their suffering and hypocrisy, and look at the mess he left India in.

"To his credit, Gandhi protested the title of Mahatma, which was awarded by some writer, who apparently had no knowledge of what a Mahatma is. However, methinks he did not protest loudly enough and came to take the title seriously. He was deluded in so many ways; certainly he might eventually have been duped into believing himself a Mahatma.

"Contrary to popular belief, however, Gandhi was no pacifist, and again this is to his credit. He believed it was better to stand and fight than to run away. His problem was that he glorified suffering so much that he thought it was better to intentionally become a victim, and to encourage others to become victims, in order to protest oppression. But this is just a sign of self-hatred, and of hatred of certain aspects of human nature. And this suffering, this victimization, doesn't go away when the beatings and rapings stop or when a protestor is released from prison; it remains stored in the form of hate and rage in the causal body, so that now there's more suffering than there was before, and more violence than ever will eventually break out, and more healing is necessary than there was before Gandhi's interference with the natural order of the causal body of his society. He was a part of the cycle of violence, but he was a part who did not want to acknowledge his own role in encouraging the violence. He denied his own violence with his supposed non-violence, and since the cloud of violence he contributed to was unconscious, it felt it could break out in any way it wanted to, and did not feel the need to limit itself to the views and preferences of its benefactor. Most people don't know it because of the propaganda about Gandhi, but India actually won her freedom partly through overt violence, which is why Gandhi stayed away from Independence celebrations. He protested when his violent baby grew up and took off on its own, developing its own criminal enterprises free of the influence of its godfather.

"The Gandhi-ites won't understand this talk about energy, and the effect their energy has in encouraging violence, since they are preoccupied with physical plane concerns and with a materialistic and unnatural philosophy which they use to justify their attempts to destroy the will to live of humanity, and the insistence of human beings to stand squarely in their passions and nurture those passions in a loving, accepting manner so they can use those passions to serve their neighbors. They use their philosophy--as all fundamentalists do--to block themselves off from the energy of their own *genuine* compassion. Instead of feeling genuine compassion, they have to force the appearance of compassion and thus delude themselves and those who can't read the text written in the truths of the energy-signature they emit. But if you can actually feel the space where they're coming from, you'll know what I mean. This is what happens when you believe you **should** be compassionate, rather than accepting compassion as a bubbling spring of combined love and passion that appears in its own time as your self-knowledge and integration grow.

"The Gandhi-ites limit themselves so severely they can't see the soul-murder they perform on themselves with their so-called 'passive resistance', and they don't know that this soul-murder guarantees them and those they have manipulated into serving their cause much more suffering than if they had chosen to learn to work intelligently and free of doctrine, because goodwill is necessary for the manifestation of peace, and doctrine short-circuits and disperses goodwill. For no doctrine accurately reflects the multidimensional truths of human nature, or of the way the worlds work. And when you transgress against someone's human nature, they're going to start hating your guts, and if they don't kill you or someone else in their rage and pain, the fertilizing energy of their hate will still assist to grow the violence of those who are willing to rape and assault and murder. And as far as doctrines go, the Gandhi-ites have one of the most unnatural. But they want to take the world by force of will and make it and all its peoples conform to their alleged vision, like everyone who is deluded by a doctrine does. And let me emphasize that doctrine is not morality; all doctrines are a pale pretender to the throne of morality. Morality is not a stale and stagnant thing delivered by pulpit and government decree; morality is a living force of the knowledge of Rightness. For genuine morality genuinely reflects the light of love, and it always does so in a manner that is consonant with the care and healing of our human nature, but all the Gandhi-ites reflect is a sticky emotional sentiment or a dry intellectualism. For now the violence they commit directly is an emotional violence, though it of course contributes to the outbreak of physical violence when the emotional violence they generate finds itself in the vicinity of those who are inclined toward physical violence, but you can bet your ass against a spent shotgun shell that if the Gandhi-ites ever found themselves in a majority, they'd enforce their so-called peace with a rifle and a bayonet and tear gas and clubs. Down through history, those who wanted to change human nature to make it more pacifistic have always given the impetus toward humanity's development of new ways to kill and hurt one another, because such innovation thrives in the presence of unnatural restriction. Okinawan Karate, which originally was an exceptionally aggressive art designed to quickly kill opponents, was developed when the peaceniks outlawed weapons on Okinawa.

"Gandhi was divided against his own physical body and deliberately malnourished and tortured it. Who would want to follow a person who would treat himself that way? For if you don't love your own body, you can't love your supposed cause or anyone or anything else. Really, Gandhi was a selfish little bastard who betrayed his cause so he could play games of self-hate with his own body and emotions, and with the bodies and emotions of his followers, and with the emotions of his opponents. He was a purely selfish little stinker who used his supposed cause to serve his own perversions.

"Who would want to follow a person who was divided from certain aspects of his own nature? Surely anyone can see that if a person is divided in their own psyche, they are only going to create more division in the world, they are incapable of creating that unity which acknowledges the sacredness of each person's right to choose his own direction in every moment of his life, yet this right to choose is the tension-releaser which will ultimately deflate the balloon of humanity's sorrow and hate and fear and rage and separation. But Gandhi with his fake discipline tried to choose on behalf of those around him. He failed, as anyone with any sense could predict that he would. And a real Mahatma doesn't weaken himself or abuse his body in any way; he doesn't deny himself what he needs to be healthy and happy and strong. A real Mahatma sends strong loving energy to those who want to connect with him, but Gandhi sent shame-faced, strained, self-destructive, dysfunctional energy to those he'd duped with his sticky, rigid sweetness. He may have mastered the appearance of a person stoned on beatitude, but stoned people can't see or feel straight and shouldn't be allowed to enthrone the burden of their preconceptions of the rest of society. The self-deception and moral and spiritual weakness Gandhi brought to his followers is often the fate of those who have been duped into following a doctrine instead of following the totality of their own blended human and divine natures.

"Is it not evident that Gandhi and his followers were not operating with their chakras properly integrated? Why, he didn't even respect all his chakras, because no chakra wants to suffer or to see any other chakra suffer the pain of an artificial self-denial. Every chakra is its neighbor's keeper and each chakra has to be happy for its neighbor to be able to fully accept happiness. Gandhi's type of self-denial fractures and clogs up chakras with pain and anger, it doesn't deliver them into genuine bliss, though the organism which hosts those chakras may be deceived otherwise by a certain glassy-eyed pseudo-bliss that is sometimes experienced by those who want to drug their natures with the denial of those natures. Really, this glassy-eyed pseudo-bliss is a sign of insanity and occurs when a person is beginning to enjoy suffering--or when they've been using hallucinogenic or psychedelic drugs. Really, suffering is a drug to the dysfunctional style of martyr . . . in other words, to the martyr who actually wants to be a martyr. And do you feel that a person who enjoys suffering *really* wants to reduce the suffering in the world, or even is capable of it? No Savior has ever wanted to suffer, honey, and each Savior has redeemed himself from suffering as fast as was possible in his or her particular circumstances. Jesus prayed 'If it's thy will, let this cup pass from me.' He didn't pray 'If it's thy will, gimmie another swig.'! But if you're identified with suffering, you're going to feel you're identity--your *egotism*--will be stripped away if you heal from suffering, so the reality is that your egotism will fight like hell to cause you to continue to suffer, and to try to make you like it so it will be easier to convince you to continue suffering in the future. Elementary psychology, my dear Watson. Elementary.

"Always look at people's energy more than their words. Learn to feel where they are coming from; don't let them tell you where they want you to believe they're coming from. Learn to evaluate your own motives correctly, and you'll eventually be able to see the motives of others. And never trust anyone who appears to hold the type of sleazy, shame-driven beatitude Gandhi did. That type of beatitude is fake, and is fostered by focusing on those parts of the causal body that the fake saint can convince people are socially redemptive. Such focus is always brought about by turning one's gaze away from other, darker aspects of the causal body . . . which then launch a rear assault against the aspects of the causal body the saint has accepted, causing the fake saint to take up the ancient practice of wife-beating or somesuch, or to declare himself celibate and celebrate his delivery from the burden of sex by sleeping with naked young girls. True redemption involves working with and refining *every* aspect of the causal body, not just the side of it the pilgrim feels most comfortable with. And all those refined aspects must learn to work in harmony with one another for the good of the entire organism. If every aspect of the causal body feels cared for, including the aspects a primitive society might call socially unacceptable, then no aspect of this fine, harmonious causal body will work to make life difficult for any other aspect. Every aspect will accept its allotted portion of love, both for its own sake and to be used in service to society. By being thus taken care of, every aspect of the causal body works to harmoniously support every other aspect. This is a good model for humanity, I might add, if you want to consider humanity as a whole a type of planetary causal body, or at least to hold a certain space within the planetary causal body.

"You know, one of the problems with people in this timezone is that they have what I would call a 'horizontal consciousness', rather than a 'vertical consciousness'. This 'horizontal consciousness' is the home of their dualistic fluctuating pendulum swings; apparently you people see life only on one level and believe there are no more levels, so in your blind denial of the other countless levels of existence you spend your time stewing in your own juices, just bouncing around a one-dimensional basketball court wondering why the hell you suffer all the time. Man, get with it! There are all sorts of levels of existence, and they manifest in tiers which can be known and experienced directly by those who have adapted themselves to the 'vertical consciousness'. Then you are moving up and down the scale of existence, you're not bouncing around ignorantly with no place else to go on just one level.

"And every level of existence reflects the levels above and below it, so that you won't find things unduly strange if you suddenly find yourself in the next level. Subtle changes do creep in, and over the course of allowing your awareness to travel through several levels, you'll eventually get into some things which you might never have seen reflected on the physical plane. But if you just go one level above, say into the etheric plane, things will seem pretty familiar. And if you go, say, up another level or two from that things will seem pretty familiar. So quit bouncing around; I'm sick of seeing you do it. Get with it, honeys, and develop a 'vertical consciousness'. Thank you so much.

"Well, I suppose the Gandhi-ites will consider my defense of Gandhi inadequate, and will either shake their fists at me and shout obscenities, or try to smother me with sticky sweetness, or set fire to themselves beneath a Confederate flag to protest my ancestry, or--perhaps worst of all--try to reason with me. But I'm having none of it; they cannot defeat me. I'm a Savior, not a liberal."

Sonny-Bob paused for a breather, as the marks shuffled around a bit in an attempt to comfort themselves. They'd grown fascinated with the proceedings, and waited to see what Sonny-Bob would do.

He surveyed the crowd for a time, then resumed speaking. "It's a fact of life that incompetent people who have never developed an appreciable degree of spiritual discernment within themselves are going to appear-- many times with credentials . . . ugh!--and accidentally pollute whatever spiritual path they are interested in. And of course, naughty people are going to be in the mix too, with their deliberate attempts to sabotage the manifestation of spirituality on this earth. And the naughty ones frequently use the incompetent ones . . . though of course, the naughty ones themselves are incompetent at everything except manipulating people.

"I happen to know that your church here, which by now is a worldwide organization, was founded by a sorcerer. And sorcerers are totally selfish and try to manipulate you through appealing to your reasonableness and selfishness into becoming one-hundred percent selfish, as they are. A sorcerer is not a shaman; the sorcerer has no real spiritual qualities or abilities, though he manipulates your glamours and illusions so you'll think he has your best interests at heart. The shaman, on the other hand, is totally committed to Altruism and serves his community. The shaman lives according to the principles of love and service and has earned his freedom through practicing Altruism in his own unique way; the sorcerer lives according to the polluted techniques of manipulation and is a slave to the lies he bought into that turned him aside from his spiritual path . . . those same lies which you people have allowed yourselves to be manipulated into believing! So every one of you who is a member of this church has been duped by a selfish sorcerer into believing that selfishness is a virtue, and that you have a 'right' to be 'happy'. But the fact is that you are so spiritually immature, you don't know that your only right is also an obligation you have to yourself to clean up your causal body, and that happiness will begin to result as a side effect of that, once the process is fairly far along and you're approaching the point when you'll be clean and mature enough to offer your causal body in sacrifice to God. If you want to begin to relinquish your stupidity and move into a 'New Thought' church which is based on the work of a person who had good intentions and some degree of spiritual insight, you might try that outfit on the other side of the street which is based on the spiritual observations of Charlie Fillmore. As you might expect, sorcerers have invaded the Fillmorites too, but this type of 'New Thought' church wasn't founded by a sorcerer, and therefore wasn't tainted from the beginning. And some of them are still clean enough to get some good spiritual Work done. Don't be a fool; stop being deceived by sorcerers and start learning your own power!

"It is worth noting that thus far in the earth's sadly distorted history, that anytime a genuine spiritual movement has begun in an attempt to nourish people's souls, that the shit-eating sorcerers have also founded a facade of glamour and illusion to distract the people away from the rich banquet of love's newest feast and get them lost in the smelly old farts that proceed from the sorcerer's asses. So grow up, and forget about what people say about themselves. What they say doesn't matter, honeys! Learn to feel their energy, that's what matters and that's one of the things that will save you from the sorcerers' stupid manipulations.

"Remember that the sorcerer's causal body has been distorted by his greed and desire to control. He is ruled by his rational mind, which has prompted him to build only mental illusions into his causal body. He denies the reality of his heart and of those higher mental functions which far transcend the rational mind. Some of the sorcerers also have built into their causal bodies an emotional 'animal magnetism' as a means to manipulate you, which may be accompanied by a type of low-level, glamorously distorted psychic ability. But animal magnetism is not the love of the heart, and when a sorcerer adopts animal magnetism, it is a means to deny and try to extinguish the love of the hearts of those who come into contact with him so he can replace the love with emotional glamour and mental rationalizations.

"The sorcerer's soul will try to impress his causal body into returning to the path of love, until the sorcerer becomes so corrupt the soul has to flee, taking the sorcerer's immortality with it. But if a given sorcerer, or black magician, has even a trace of sanity left he will allow himself to be guided back onto the path of love he once traded for the lie of control and manipulation. He'll manfully carry the burden of the sins he's corrupted his causal body with, and bear the extreme suffering involved in purifying the black magic of control and manipulation out of his causal body, and build love and a genuine compassion into that causal body.

"But don't enable these nutcase sorcerers by holding your breath and waiting for them to return from hell. Kill them when you see them, because they'll show you no mercy or hesitation and you have to be faster on the draw and have deadlier aim if you're going to survive. If you think they'll respond to your humanity, they'll just use your codependency to manipulate you, for that is what they believe they thrive on, and because you'll be enabling them, you'll share to some degree in their karma--and you don't want that, honey. No you don't."

Sonny-Bob paused for a moment, knowing he had done his duty by these people by warning them of the pitfalls of their lazy egotism, which allows them to be manipulated. But I caught a whiff of frustration and sadness from him, because he knew they would probably fall all over themselves to see who could fall asleep fastest amid their selfish rationalizations as soon as the sermon was over.

Sonny-Bob surveyed the marks a little mournfully for a moment, then jumped back in Gandhi's shit. "You could say that Gandhi's path is the path of a failed National Savior, and that it failed because of his unwillingness to abandon his preconceptions and develop a genuine compassionate discernment. It's sort of like the degenerate Tantra schools which have devolved into body worship, rather than Achieving soul connection and sharing between human beings through the use of the body's power to joyfully express itself. Real worship is about establishing a loving connection, not about objectifying the body and turning it into a religious idol. This objectification of living human beings is the mark of any degenerate form and Gandhi was guilty of it too as he objectified his followers by encouraging them to continually add to their sufferings. You can't encourage people to suffer if you're genuinely compassionate; *you just can't*. And objectification is rape, so yes, now we can say that Gandhi was a rapist of both body and soul of his followers as he exhorted them to suffer. And we have also just established that yes, Gandhi did rape the young naked girls he slept with whether he stuck his dick in them or not, because he slept with them to prove he could control his tool, and anytime we sleep with someone to prove anything we've objectified that person and ourselves, and thus raped that person and ourselves. Gandhi was so immature. Really, I guess Gandhi was a practitioner of his own degenerate form of Tantra, even if he didn't call it that, because of his practice of objectification of those innocent, beautiful young girls. The degenerate Tantra schools are sort of a leftover of a long-ago age, while Gandhi and Company were one of the last gasps of the old departing Piscean Age, and as such their movement was devoid of spiritual energy. They exemplified some of the worst aspects of the Piscean Age, such as the deliberate pursuit of martyrdom in an attempt to create more suffering by glorifying suffering. They did not manifest that love and self-respectful compassion which the Age of Pisces was intended to produce, and which it did produce in its most aware spiritual Workers.

"It will be interesting to see how the Gandhi-ites respond to my observations regarding Gandhi's sexual abuse of young girls, as I've noted that the politically-correct types who supposedly want to vengefully restrict those who have abused women usually want to make an exception for whomever they feel attracted to. It's always a double standard with such people."

Suddenly a guy stood up in the crowd. "Fuck you! Gandhi did more for this world than you'll ever do!"

I was afraid Sonny-Bob might pull his weapon and dispatch this fellow, but he just chuckled dryly. "I guess you're an expert?" he said.

"I'm a Pisces! There's nothing wrong with Pisces!"

"Honky, I wasn't talking about personal astrological charts, though if I were to preach about them I would talk about how foolish it is for people to try to make themselves conform to such a chart, and to congratulate themselves when they succeed. I was talking about the Piscean Age, one of the periods the planet is continually cycling through on it's journey into eventual bliss. We've just moved into the Age of Aquarius, so the manifestations of Piscean energy are no longer viable. Now it's time to learn to work with Aquarian energy.

"Stars may influence, but they don't control, unless a person is damfool enough to turn over his will to his astrologer. And I'm not a young schoolgirl, and you're not Gandhi, so sit your ass down, boy."

The guy sat. Sonny-Bob moved on. "It should be self-evident that no person who loves himself could ever torture himself or set fire to himself to protest a war, or whatever he's protesting at the time. That kind of conduct is not born out of love for peace, it is born out of hatred for war, and this very hatred makes the alleged peace-monger one of the causes of

354 / Apollo Starmule

war, because the energy of hate is one of the causes of war. And energy doesn't discriminate; it goes wherever it can best perpetuate itself. So when the peace-mongers produce an energy-wave of hate, it will travel right to the war zone to make things worse than they already are . . . unless the peace-mongers themselves are so brimming with hate that the hate they've already generated feels itself to be well fed by staying with those who generated it.   But finally, even the most hate-filled 'peacemakers' will have more hate than they can stand, if they intend to go on living, and the surplus hate will have to go to the war zone. The idiot Buddhist monk who sets fire to himself to protest a war actually contributes his hate to the war effort as he reveals his fear and loathing of life and of himself to the world.   And he contributes his own sadness to the war effort, instead of manfully purifying himself of it according to the nondualistic methods of a consciousness deliberately structured around Synthesis. He hates himself and those around him too deeply to merely pick up a rifle and go out and kill a few people; his hate obligates him to create a spectacle of unimaginable horror which will remain seared across people's brains and imprinted into their media for generations. He spreads his horror down long ages, and is not to be respected for his so-called 'sacrifice'. He has sacrificed nothing, except the chance to grow up and learn to love. If he had sacrificed his hate and his sorrow he would have brought a clean breeze of the lightness of his soul-nature to the world, and perhaps would have brought some smiles to a few lips. So should we respect him for choosing to remain the slave of his hate, and to do the bidding of that hate as it strives to perpetuate itself forever? Of course not. He's an asshole, and has contributed nothing worthwhile to the world.

"These jerks who try to make a virtue out of sorrow spread their sorrow across the planet. Yes, Jesus was a Man of Sorrows, but he didn't want to be, and he wasn't a slave to his sorrows as he manfully like a genuine human being took his sorrows to task and purified them out of his causal body so they would no longer be a burden to the world. These ignorant-assed so-called Christians who pridefully try to make a virtue of their sorrows disrespect the memory of Jesus, and ignore the fact that he was trying to reduce their sorrows.

"You can't force merriment, nor should you try. If you're sorrowful, then be sorrowful creatively. Be willing to feel the sorrow fully as you learn to release it, because you have to feel it fully as it passes out of your causal body into the Golden Light of God for redemption. Don't feel the sorrow to wallow like an ignorant lazy hog in it, feel it with the strong intention of letting it go! Learn what you have to do as an individual to clean up your own individual causal body, and genuinely practice what you learn, and eventually you'll be free of sorrow and stop contributing to the burden of the world. And you can't get this knowledge from a book or from another person; you can only get it by deliberately undertaking your own individual Quest structured around your own nature . . . not trying to follow a quest structured around someone else's nature or preconceptions! And the learning is in the practicing, so if you don't know where to begin, then begin where you are. It'll come to you. Get off your ass and Work, and it'll come to you, I guarantee! That's why my Big Brother Jesus told the parable of the talents, only in this new age which we face, it's not enough to increase what you've been given a little bit, now the objective is to use the entire frequency of this new age to Achieve your own Liberation, which itself will help to Liberate the world.

"Achieving Liberation is the only true career of this new age, and since Liberation is the child of Love, then learning to fully express Love through *every* human faculty is the technique of Achieving Liberation. And this full expression of Love only comes with cleaning the glamours and illusions--the filthy dirty sins you people are often so fond of--out of your causal body, and then eventually sacrificing the causal body to accept the Gift of the full fusion with God.

"These Gandhi-ites and others of similar breed are nuts, man, nuts. The glamours and illusions stored in their causal bodies hate themselves and each other and push the Gandhi-ite into such self-destructive and undisciplined and bizarre behavior. They create *more* suffering in the world, not less, with the energy of the warring self-hating glamours and illusions in their causal bodies, which they've been too blind and ignorant and undisciplined and unloving to dislodge.

"When Jesus talked about the love required to give your life for people, he was talking about the Path of the Saviors, not about the path of the Certifiable Idiots. He was talking about the method of those who *incarnate* for the specific purpose of bearing the sins of the world in their causal bodies and using those causal bodies to purify and release those sins, he wasn't talking about those immoral, unspiritual religious wimps who are seeking an egocentric exit from the burdens of the world, and of their own causal bodies. But every time a new age has dawned, egocentric assholes have misinterpreted the age itself and the discipline of its techniques of service. So it remains for a future age to actually perfect that which should have been perfected previously. This may be the Aquarian Age, but we've got some catching up to do with regard to the techniques of Pisces yet, especially the technique of bearing your own goddam cross, and it's because of these assholes like the Gandhi-ites and the monks who set themselves on fire. Man, start looking at the vertical beam of the cross and forget about the horizontal beam for a while. You fuckers. The causal body is not horizontal, it is a vertical funnel for your many interpenetrating tiers of consciousness to pour though. The causal body is like a round cylinder with your consciousness pouring down into you from above, yet you people . . . you people! . . . have deliberately misled yourselves down through countless generations into somehow believing you live in a horizontal universe.

"Idiots!" Sonny-Bob thundered. Now he was red-faced, and I'd never seen him so perturbed. "Jesus H. Christ and Sonny-Bob Culpepper and all the rest of the Savior Corps live in a better world than the one you've allowed to fall into disrepair. We give *our* lives to come here and serve you people, then you misinterpret our lives as often as not for the sake of a feeling of egocentric security for the glamours and illusions in your causal bodies. You didn't give *your* lives to come here; this is your place for now. But we were drafted into doing some of the Work you people are too lazy and egocentrically motivated to do, and we had to leave our Homes to do it! Coming into your world *is* death from our perspective, and we're not asking you to die because you can't, not in the sense in which we have. To us, your death looks pretty comfortable and doesn't take too long. Yet we die for decades in your stagnant world, just so it will have a chance to one day be beautiful again.

"When the apostle said, 'I die daily,' he wasn't shitting you. Yet how many of you believe him? Hell, most of you never do believe the things we say, yet you want to make a pretense of following in footsteps whose nature you refuse to even discipline yourselves enough to sense. I guess you've allowed yourselves to be programmed with the illusion that a pretense of goodness is goodness, but that's hogwash, and you ought to be mature enough to know it. We do die daily until we've finished purifying and releasing your sins, and in fact, we die many times daily during this process. The process we go through can't be explained in words, but one effect of it is that we are constantly dying in a manner so terrible most of you can't begin to imagine. It makes the literal crucifixion on the wooden cross look like a relaxing church picnic.

"If the only thing you ever did for us was to grow up enough to bear and refine out of existence your own sins, that would be enough . . . that would be wonderful! Why are you people so driven by lust and greed? Don't you realize that if you only did this one thing we ask of you, the cleaning up of your own individual causal bodies, that all the problems of the world would automatically solve themselves? All the world's problems are caused by the sins stored in the causal bodies of the people of the world, so if you clean the sin out of the causal bodies, and build love and total compassion and beauty into those bodies, there will be no more problems in the world. But as long as you're focused on solving the world's problems instead of cleaning up your own causal bodies, the world's problems will never be solved. These problems have been around forever, but they would already have dissolved themselves if you had just born your individual crosses as my Brother Jesus asked you to do. Shit, you people try to solve the world's problems as an excuse to avoid your real duty. You know you're not doing any good with your mechanistic meddling in the world of cause and effect; your only chance to benefit the world is to clean yourselves up as individuals, right from the animal and machine levels on up through the higher levels of your causal bodies. Get with it, man. Get with it. Right this minute!"

Now as Sonny-Bob glowered in Biblical wrath, some more of the Pharisees stumbled to their feet and left. I patted my pistol, but was pretty sure I wouldn't need it. Those people were ashen-faced and looked like they were going to leave Travis County as fast as possible. I was pretty sure they wouldn't stop to notify the authorities about the Presence in the pulpit at this deranged and primitive puritanical church.

After a bit, Sonny-Bob continued, adopting a calmer voice and exhibiting a more centered energy. "The will to live is a valuable thing, but the will to die is the mark of an evolutionary failure. I'm not condemning those relatively normal people who commit suicide, because many, and probably most, suicides actually want to live, but just don't see any other way out of their suffering. So I have compassion for them, and it pains me to have to inform them that they still have the same karma to face in their next life, and it may be even a little more difficult because of their suicide.

"But the Gandhi-ites are so confused, they actually want to suffer--or the glamours and illusions they are slaves to want them to suffer and make them want to create emotional suffering on the part of others who see the suffering the Gandhi-ite has staged to manipulate those others. Gandhi-ites are twisted, man, twisted; they need Band-Aids for their souls, man. Band-Aids. There's no greater addict than the Gandhi-ite drunk on his staged martyrdom, and no greater codependent than those who allow themselves to be thus manipulated. Man, what sane person would want to enable a Gandhi-ite in his dysfunction? I certainly wouldn't, and I don't care whether he barbeques himself or not. This old child refuses to be manipulated.

"And here's another problem with politicians: they won't normally let you eat the Gandhi-ite after he's cooked himself. They expect you to just sit by while they throw the food away. Why do they think Tupperware was invented, man? Food was meant to be saved and consumed as needed, not discarded to the worms, who already have plenty to eat and won't suffer by being deprived of a cooked Gandhi-ite.

"Even in India, where people are starving, they won't let you eat a Gandhi-ite if he cooks himself. Where's the compassion in that?"

Sometimes it's hard to tell if Sonny-Bob is making a jest or if he's serious, and it's all the harder now that he's a food addict and eats all the time. I didn't quite know what to make of his comments regarding cannibalism, but I knew that some of our operatives had tried "long pig" from time to time.

But then Sonny-Bob turned away from Betty Crocker and explored the nature of politics from the pulpit, as so many other preacher-men have done. But I felt Sonny-Bob's take on politics might be a little different from most preachers'.

"The Gandhi-ites want to compromise with the mechanisms of suffering, not transcend suffering," he reflected. "Politics is a mechanism of suffering, so no wonder the Gandhi-ites are addicted to it. Politics can only do one thing, and that is to create suffering. And choosing to spawn a lesser amount of suffering is not the same as actually reducing suffering, man. Most suffering is caused by emotional attachments; does politics decrease, or increase, the presence of emotional attachments? You tell me, hon.

"Politics can never be used to reduce suffering, because the nature of any political entity is to ravenously grow itself, trying to consume the souls of everything in sight. They won't let us eat the mere flesh of a barbequed Gandhi-ite, yet they try to eat our souls. Another example of the inversion of values that always accompanies politics.

"Politics creates suffering. The only choice for the political player is 'How much suffering do I want to produce? And who do I prefer to direct that suffering at?' You people, barbaric as you are, instinctively understand this sole choice that faces every politician, and so you try to vote for what you call the 'lesser of two evils'--you vote for the candidate whom you feel will produce the least amount of suffering.

"No politician ever transcended suffering, man. Politicians aren't much better than the Gandhi-ites who try to manipulate them. The *only* choice in the politician's world is how much suffering to create; there is no choice in that world to transcend suffering and then impart a taste of that Transcendence to society.

"To transcend suffering, politics must be transcended. Don't you know that when you're voting for the candidate you find least offensive in the hope of creating less suffering for yourself and for those you identify with that you're automatically voting to make life harder and to create *more* suffering for those you disagree with? And you don't care. No, don't lie to me, you don't care and I know you don't care. And meanwhile, those who vote for the other candidate are trying to create more suffering for *you*, even as they try to slow the increase in their own suffering. Such madness, and such a waste. You've established a merry-go-round, named it politics, and refused to admit you've created a cycle to reinforce suffering. I think even a moon bear is smarter than that."

Sonny-Bob looked with fierce intensity at the marks, who seemed shocked and uncomfortable with the piercing laser that had been turned on them and against their violence and preconceptions. "To transcend suffering, dummies, you have to transcend politics in every aspect of your lives, starting with your own families--where most of you learn your earliest lessons in the devil-worship of the control and manipulation of politics. Don't you see that politics *is* control and manipulation; or are you too glamoured by it to even look at the motivations for your dirty practices right now, in this moment? Politics is not Service; it is always selfish, and true Altruistic Service has nothing to do with selfishness. Government politics would vanish in a generation or two if massive numbers of families refused to practice politics at home, and instead learned to practice compassionately loving and serving one another.

"What would government be if it were purified of politics? Well, the perceived need for government would vanish in the very act of purifying the politics out of it. This is called Transcendence. So whatever was left wouldn't be government, that's for certain sure. Assuming anything were left at all. But if anything were left, it would serve as a clear, unstained chalice to catch and reflect the scintillating energy of love."

Sonny-Bob cleared his throat and wagged a fleshy forefinger at the crowd. "You sons-of-bitches don't deserve to suffer no matter what horrible things you've done, but you're limiting yourself to suffering, and probably also to doing more horrible things, until you face the glamours and illusions and sadnesses and rage at the appearance of love denied, and the self-hatred, stored in your causal body and refine those untrue things out of your causal body. Once you complete this Work of refinement, the only thing that's left is a pure chalice composed of the stuff of Creative Imagination, which serves to catch, contain and give form to the Love of your hearts. And the lies currently stored in your causal body are responsible for the creation of politics, so when these lies are gone, politics is gone. Politics is the art of the lie. So if this process of refinement were undertaken and completed by a sufficiently large population, we'd have a beautiful, mythological *civilization* composed of the stuff of love-infused creative imagination, instead of the present decadent mechanical culture which strives only to throw up blocks to love and to the free exercise of creative imagination.

"No matter what anyone else would have you believe, and no matter what your own glamours and illusions want you to believe, the truth is that you don't deserve to suffer, and nobody else deserves to suffer, either, no matter what wickedness they've been involved in. *Nobody* deserves to suffer! This realization is necessary before you can be free of suffering, before you can be free of the accumulated glamours and illusions--the accumulated sins--we refer to as karma. Because only the fact of this knowledge that *nobody* deserves to suffer, felt in every molecule of your flesh and bones, will lift you totally out of the cycle of vengeance which creates most negative karma, and which thus creates most of your suffering. Do you not yet realize that the thirst for vengeance is what keeps you attached to your enemies in cycles of hurt that last for incarnations? Do you not realize that the thirst for vengeance is responsible for the creation of politics? And you even pass this thirst for vengeance on to your children emotionally and mentally in an obvious way, but what you haven't yet realized is that you even pass a physical imprint of your thirst for vengeance on to your offspring, thus reinforcing the sneaky cycle that wants to see the innate divinity and dignity of humanity destroyed. The ancients knew of this physical imprint, and spoke of it as passing the sins of the fathers--the karma of the fathers--on to their children for seven generations. Who needs this shit, man? Are you so gruesome you think you need this shit? Do your kids need this shit?

"*Nobody* deserves to suffer!" Sonny-Bob thundered, slobber flying out his jowls and splashing some of the people in the front row. "Nobody deserves to suffer! And there's a cloud of suffering composed of particles of seething emotional glamour circling the earth, looking for the sticky strings of vengeance to attach itself to. These strings of vengeance are how the cloud manages to remain intact and are why it continues to plague the earth millions of years after it was created. And many of you fuckers helped create this cloud to begin with, millions of years ago in incarnations that were nearly as immature as your present incarnations. With your immaturity, no wonder you continue to create suffering.

"Much of the skill of the Saviors lies in the transmutation and transcendence and release of the shame-faced urge to vengeance . . . for the secret glamour of shame is how the cloud manipulates us into maintaining a fighting stance to preserve our attachments. We want to deny the presence of the glamour of shame in us, so we try to project the shame out of ourselves onto an enemy, then assault that enemy, which only makes us more secretly ashamed than ever, as the cloud secretly rejoices at the success of its duplicity. All supposedly human institutions are either manufactured by the cloud itself to perpetuate political wars of one kind or another, or are taken over by the cloud from their original creators and retooled in the image of the secret shame of the cloud. No institution in human history has managed to remain independent of the cloud for long . . . and as long as people think they need institutions, the cloud will continue to have a form to house its depraved energy. 'Give unto Caesar the things that are Caesar's' . . . but what Caesar needs is for you to remain attached to shame and the lust for vengeance it spawns so you can be manipulated into taking sides in institutional wars and be food for the cloud, so I say don't give Caesar shit. Piss on the son-of-a-bitch. Withdraw your moral support from Caesar, and the bastard will be weakened a bit, though with his propaganda screeching in your ear twenty-four hours a day, you may not notice he's been weakened unless you tune him out and tune in to your own inner spiritual ear.

"Everyone who suffers unintelligently contributes to this cloud and pulls still more of this cloud to himself, thus increasing his sick value to the cloud, which uses the unintelligent sufferer to increase its own volume--for everything has a spirit, and the spirit associated with this cloud is deviant, indeed! This spirit of vengeful suffering must be released for the earth to be wiped clean of suffering. For us to defeat the cloud, we must learn to suffer intelligently--and relatively briefly--by turning the mechanisms of the cloud against itself and use those mechanisms to push the suffering sins out of our causal bodies and literally send them up to the Golden Light of God to be dissolved or transmuted, as Golden God sees fit. This is the process which we call Refinement. We have to learn the nature of the enemy so well that we can turn its own weapons against it and attack and defeat it on its own playing field . . . the playing field it stole from *us* millions of years ago. But remember: Don't glorify the cross! Use the cross if you must, but *never* be used by it. Idiots invert the cross and let it use them in an egotistical display of their suffering, or let it use them like a drug using a dope fiend to suppress their suffering in another example of the duality to which you people continually subject yourselves. Passive suffering is almost as worthless and dangerous to humanity as is the search for vengeance, so if you suffer, suffer actively and Work constantly like a real human being who is purging himself of his glamours and illusions as rapidly as possible. If you must glorify something, then glorify the Resurrection that comes on the heels of the end of the crucifixion experience. Let yourself be magnetized by the Resurrection and pulled toward it.

"Anyhow, this momentary suffering of spiritual combat leads to a longterm reduction in our suffering, and finally we reach the point where we no longer suffer at all, and thus do not contribute to the cloud of sins, of suffering, that circles the earth. Thus is the cloud diminished, and as enough people learn to suffer intelligently and temporarily by facing squarely and releasing the sins in their causal bodies, the cloud will eventually cease to exist. Think of this! Is this not better than anything you could have possibly imagined? And if you have the courage to face your sins, your glamours and illusions, then humanity itself can be its own Savior, and will never need another. And Heaven will come to this beautiful blue-green planet, which will be more beautiful than ever with its newfound clarity. What a wonderful opportunity to be part of the creation of the future world of bliss! Are you not glad that you were born?

"And do you not know you will be part of the future world of bliss in your continued journey thru the various dimensions of yourself? If you have no more desire for contact with your karma and are willing to release all of it--not repress or try to ignore it, but acknowledge and release it!--you will be one of the meek ones who does not suffer from the glamour of strained emotions and complicatedness and who inherits the earth. And your practice of *real* blissmaking will prepare you for new opportunities to create and serve in the Far-Off Worlds. Worlds already sparkling and blissful beyond our current imagination, yet still needing some particle of something that only we can contribute.

"Even I know that a Savior isn't competent to enter the worlds of bliss until he's purged himself of the sins he bore for other people. But I look forward to a long vacation one of these days in a Garden on a world unpolluted by the smog of emotional glamour."

Now Sonny-Bob once more exhibited his disregard for regulations, as he divulged some information to the marks they hadn't qualified themselves to hear. On the other hand, World Saviours are given quite a bit of latitude in the types of information they deliver, more so than us regular-style operatives. Maybe Sonny-Bob wouldn't be courtmartial-ed . . . well, if he didn't tell on himself in his own report, maybe I wouldn't tattle on him, either.

"You know, folks," Sonny-Bob said quietly, "in a long-ago civilization which your historians have no knowledge of, the early members of your own branch of the human tree felt deprived by the political process that was thrust upon them by the earlier race. The standard operating procedures of the society of the time were not adequate to the needs of the early members of your own race. So they quietly withdrew themselves from the political process . . . in the conventional sense. But they implemented certain political techniques of their own, and they were able to do this because they had more emotional discipline than the members of the earlier race, who lacked the patience to follow the intricate maneuverings of your ancestors as they quietly assassinated those leaders of the old race who were the biggest threat to their freedom to expand themselves in accordance with their own nature, a nature their predecessors either couldn't understand, or didn't want to understand.

"Your ancestors made sure that incompetent people filled the halls of the government of the time by culling those leaders who were more proficient at restricting the nature of the newly-emerging populations. So maybe the more aware among you today would want to consider returning to the techniques of the ancient ancestors of your race. Government doesn't serve anyone; it hurts everyone. If the future is to grow, maybe the hurt could be reduced enough to allow new populations to emerge who are so disciplined and moral that eventually they would replace those among you who don't have the strength to do your own spiritual Work."

Suddenly, Sonny-Bob shouted in mock fervor: "Who's with me! Give me liberty, or I'll give you death! Don't tread on me! Let's go! Whee! Whee!"

By now the congregation was numbed by what I felt sure was the most truthful sermon they'd ever heard. Their preconceptions were shaken, their spiritual bowels loosened, and they were numb with the first pangs of spiritual diarrhea. Now Sonny-Bob capered about the pulpit like a wild Cotton Mather, and I know Sonny-Bob would be the first to admit that the children of the future are the New Puritans, because they actually have the discipline to arrive at a fullbody morality that takes total account of every aspect of their blended human and divine natures. Indeed, their natures are so fully blended they are of one nature rather than two. Nonduality rules the new morality, a nonduality which has its ultimate source in that love which is parent to the soul of each human being. The New Puritans of the future are the first Puritans who are actually *pure*. They know full well that you don't become pure by sacrificing your humanity, you become pure by sacrificing the illusions that get in the way of your humanity. Such as the illusion of enforced monogamy, which insures that very little, if any, love will ever flow though the marriage as many of the needs of the partners go unmet. Because it is an infertile soil to grow a crop of love when someone's needs aren't being met, the Puritans of the future insure that *everyone's* needs are met, and that those needs are not categorized in some ridiculous table by timid uncreative psychologists or governments like the food pyramid, but that each person's needs are identified by that individual, and then expressed to those around him or her who will help with the fulfillment of those needs, if it feels right to them to do so. The New Puritans have cleared themselves of glamour and illusion, and thus do not suffer from the illusion of opposites. They are highly disciplined and always insist on standing strong in their own natures, instead of allowing themselves to degenerate into becoming puritanical.

The animalistic, bestial person who lives according to restriction, license, undisciplined emotional fluctuation and undisciplined mental self-justification sees and envies the freedom of the New Puritans, the freedom of the genuinely integrated and loving human being. But he does not see the strenuous moral discipline through which we purchased our freedom. Nor does he perceive the pure heart which guides the wisdom of our fullbody compassion, for it is not wise to permit the restriction of one molecule of the flesh when every molecule is meant to be made holy and transfigured as an offering to God, and this can only occur in the disciplined flowing of fullbody compassion.

I've read a tract that was said to be written by Sonny-Bob on one of his earlier missions. It was lost to history, except for the copy in the TAC's great library at Gaffney. In that tract, Sonny-Bob was trying to help restore the motivation of humanity to "go for the gold" in the Spiritual Olympics, an Olympics where there is no competition but there is constant Achievement. In fact, a soul can only become part of the real Spiritual Olympics by dropping the motivations of competition which, for example, the new age movement of the twentieth and early twenty-first centuries was rife with.

In that brief little tract, Sonny-Bob, or whoever the author really was (how could it be Sonny-Bob, when he's so longwinded that it takes him an entire chapter to write a paragraph?) explored the nature of morality. He was trying to quicken the original Puritans in the dark colonial jungle of New America into purifying themselves . . . and as history shews, he wasn't too successful. But at least they were more honest than their descendants in the twentieth century . . . oops, I'm digressing, mustn't get as longwinded as Sonny-Bob. 'Scuse me, Muffin.

Anyhow, the author of the tract pointed out how the purification of motive is the first genuine step upon the Path of Spiritual Achievement. He said that nothing of lasting value can come without completing this first step. And of course, as every civilized or nearly civilized person knows, he was right.

Right Motive leads to Right Morality, which in turn leads to Right Action. Nobody of less than stellar motive can ever arrive at Right Morality, because Right Morality is a direct outgrowth of Right Motive.

Scrupulous honesty is necessary for a person to arrive at Right Motive. With even a touch of self-deception, the person may be lost . . . unless they have the honesty to admit their self-deception and purify it out of themselves!

And so with total self-honesty enfolded within itself, Right Motive is the only possible base for the construction of the pyramid-structure of Right Morality. And without Right Morality, a person is just writhing around with his or her head cut off, not knowing when next they are going to hurt some innocent, even if they don't want to. But when a person feels hurt within the sanctified Presence of someone who has perfected his Morality, it is only the glamours and illusions that person carries within himself or herself which is causing the suffering, it is not the guy with the Right Morality. Thus if the suffering person has any intelligence or self-honor, he will Work to release those glamours and illusions which have made themselves known to him by vibrating the strings of his attachments. This is one of the ways in which a genuinely Moral person serves humanity.

Of course, down through history most people haven't had the self-honor or integrity to develop within themselves an appreciation for this service, and have merely projected their illusions and glamours outward to the position where they believe the Moral person stands, but they always miss him and see only their own distorted reflection.

Unfortunately, it's easy for various types of gurus or so-called "spiritual teachers" to convey a hint of this fact to people and then turn their attachments onto himself, so he can manipulate them out of money or self-respect or emotional energy, or whatever his favorite food is. Thus is self-honoring always necessary, and a person refusing to part with even a molecule of his own responsibility to himself. A genuinely spiritual person will never try to manipulate anyone out of any degree of their personal power. Personal power is necessary for the manifestation of fullbody love. And personal power is never connected with egotism.

Unfortunately, the marks don't usually realize this, and because of their own egotism it is easy for the alleged "spiritual teachers" to use them as slaves to the so-called teacher's own egotism, and some of these alleged teachers are so good at this that their marks don't even realize they've enslaved themselves. They may even believe they're empowered, while all the time their idol interferes with the expression of their soul nature and substitutes some of his own false energy in part of the space meant to be occupied by his devotee's soul, thus 'empowering' only the devotee's egotism, and not his Quest for Selfhood.

The flip side of this dualistic coin is that there also exist those people, particularly within the new-age movement, who are so confident of their own ability to judge, that their preconceptions cause them to reduce all voices which appear spiritual to approximately the same category, and figure one is as good as another, and that which "spiritual teacher", if any, you swing with is just a matter of personal preference, and that any "spiritual teacher" is "only human" and thus will probably be guilty of some hypocrisy. They are blind to the horrors and genuine dangers of falling victim to the "slayer of souls" type of "spiritual teacher". They may not be in as much danger of falling as that person who is actively looking for a teacher, but they *are* in danger of missing any real spiritual voices that come their way. Jesus and the Buddha were human, but they were not hypocrites. They took time to purify themselves, but in the midst of their purification they were not hypocrites. They flooded people's souls with love, they didn't flood people's attitudes with egotism.

So the development of a real discrimination is necessary to avoid the dualistic snares that wait for the Pilgrim, and this discrimination is developed and refined with this very first step of perfecting Right Morality. And when Right Morality is added to energy sensitivity and strengthening the heart's Presence and energy field, a pretty good Protection is arrived at.

There, you figured I was off on a tangent like Sonny-Bob, and that I'd never get around to the point of why we must develop Right Morality. Fooled ya! I may be descended from the old coot, but surely I am not as wordy as he.

Am I?

"You old-style people are guilty of sin because you suffer from the perception of opposites, which itself is the perverse father to the lie of separation," Sonny-Bob said reflectively, as he watched the old preacher-bitch try to get to her feet. He gave a little foot-jab and sent her sprawling again amid the scalding hot tears of rage and frustration which were stored up in her causal body, and which Sonny-Bob's fortuitous Presence had activated. She clutched her gut and sobbed, her face red with the sticky shame she'd sought all her life to deny by funneling it through her precious heart chakra, defiling that precious jewel with unspoken lust. But the shame was not the Truth of her being, and in Sonny-Bob's compassionate Presence she was having to face the hidden enemy she herself had helped camouflage. Maybe she was ready to learn something about guerrilla warfare. Guerrilla warfare is the psychology of the future, man!

"Ye are guilty children," Sonny-Bob huffed, "rather than the innocent and childlike beings ye were meant to be. Eden has eluded you because you make egotism your number one 'virtue'. And egotism is the unpleasant state of withdrawal from the soul; the soul is complete refinement of perception and experience into one full, undivided pattern of Godlife. When it finally cleans all glamours and illusions out of itself, egotism is no longer egotism, but has transmuted itself into a component of Individuality which is absorbed by the soul and which allows soul to function creatively in the material dimension.

"This is occultism 101, but most of ye 'New Thought' people don't have a clue, or at least live like ye don't have a clue. We had hoped for better things of ye.

"And I suppose it is necessary to tell you that 'occult' simply means 'that which is hidden' and has nothing to do with the secret rituals of high school students who are seeking contact with demons. So occultism is simply the study of that which is hidden . . . only now it's time for you to be told that it's hidden in plain sight and was encoded from the beginning of humanity within areas of your brain that most of you haven't gotten around to surveying. When psychology matures, it will be a synonym for occultism. 'Clueless' is a good word to apply to someone who's carrying the secrets of the universe in his head and heart and doesn't realize it, don't you think?

"And if ye don't have a clue, it's because ye haven't wanted one. Clues are everywhere and always have been. You've preferred the slick glamour of the metaphysics of the 'new age' to the strenuous occultism needed to decipher the clues . . . needed to decipher yourself!

"Ye are not just a sack of shit; ye are a walking bag of clues, honey.

"Well, you ragged 'New Thought' people have rejected most of the clues for millennia, thereby rejecting yourselves, so I'm here to hit you in the face with the facts. Ye 'New Thought' people, particularly the trendy yuppie types responsible for the plastification of the world, might try confessing that your egotism only wants to perpetuate its own dark self. It wants to live forever, but only on its own terms, not on the terms of the soul, and certainly not according to the terms of the Monad, which is to soul as soul is to personality. Monad is the bright beam of God's will-to-love which expresses through every cooperative soul which has a cooperative personality. Monad is the key to Liberation, my friends, the Key to returning Home while yet remaining a while in loving, genuinely compassionate service in the physical dimension.

"But the terms of egotism are separation--egotism wants the illusion of controlling everything in the universe. 'The wages of sin is death'. And the illusion of control can only exist within the illusion of duality, and the illusion of duality is original sin.

"The egotism's lust for a stagnant 'eternal life' built around the illusion of separation is the very thing that insures its living death. So let it die in sanctified service to soul, and then to Monad, that it may be resurrected bright and true in the Kingdom of Heaven.

"Yet your whole society is built around the concept of eternal death; every institution you have wants to put the stamp of a label on living human beings to coerce them into fulfilling some role that some group-- usually 'do-gooders'--wants to see them in. Man, 'do-gooders' are just people who are scared so shitless of living in this world they feel they have to use sentiment as an excuse to manipulate other people and interfere in their lives.

"The next step for you is to forget about your goddamed labels--they are utterly stupid, all of them, and have no reality anyway--and begin working with the energy of the archetypes, then with the energy of the seven rays which give the various characteristics of living expression to everything that exists in this solar system.   Then you'll combine the energy of the archetypes with your understanding of the rays, to create warm new combinations powered by Love, and by that Loving Compassion which is our earth humanity's unique opportunity to demonstrate before the Throne of the Multiverse, and then to spread throughout that Multiverse.

"This new society is going to be fueled by the perceptions of new types of humans who rightfully withhold their approval and energy from the old stagnant forms, and who in fact may send a wave of their own new, strong, rich energy crashing against the crumbling seawall built by older types of humans. This is not aggression; it is an active defense against a rough and somewhat cunning adversary who insists on governing the new with the tattered consciousness of past ages. But the elephant rightfully refuses to bow before the wooly mammoth; and it would be in the mammoth's best interests to avoid the slashing razor tusks of the newcomers by gracefully accepting that you can't apply pre-existing standards to new, more spiritually vigorous manifestations. The older types must avoid the decrepit technique of interference and simply allow the newcomers to live unmolested according to the rich new principles that define their own natures. And it must be emphasized that 'unmolested' may frequently mean one thing to the old consciousness, and something altogether different to the newcomers. To forget this is to court disaster; and as the esoteric history of the world shows, the older types are always on the losing end when they expect newly evolving branches of the human tree to live in the shadow of the trunk."

Sonny-Bob cleared his throat, and I could tell he was winding down. He smiled, slightly. "For now, if you aren't going to get rid of your courts of law and other barbaric institutions, the very least you could do is to begin introducing the science of the human energy field, and of the archetypes and the seven rays into the context of these institutions. Make 'em expand a little, before they finally--sigh of relief!--crumble away into dust and become only the remote memories of a barbaric time. Yes, the least you could do is introduce some intelligence into your lifeways, because sometimes focusing on intelligence--real, total intelligence, not the stupidity of intellectual isolationism--can lead to compassion, and compassion leads ultimately to the destruction of the old and used-up.

"And I suppose it is necessary to inform ye of the obvious once more when I declare before ye that whenever ye do not have compassion for a particular person, or for a person whom you believe to belong to a particular 'type', that the truth of the matter is that you're only seeing your own reflection in that person and are withholding compassion from yourself. For there is a part of *you*, honeys, that is being reflected by the person you lack compassion for, and that aspect of yourself is one that you fear to face and which you despise. You cannot despise or lack compassion for another human being without despising or lacking compassion for the unacknowledged part of yourself represented by that other human being. What you're feeling really has nothing to do with that other person at all, it's all about *you*. An intelligent person will recognize this fact and begin to work with the truth of it, and eventually arrive at compassion for the previously hated parts of himself. Ergo, we have an example of intelligence leading to compassion.

"So if, for example, you feel a little contempt for that disabled person on his sickbed because you in your ignorance and self-hatred fear the part of yourself which you think is weak and which you fear might one day confine *you* to your sickbed, just know who the really weak person here is. The *really* weak person is *you*, because you've been too afraid to face and develop compassion for a vital part of yourself, and then you've compounded your crime by projecting that lack of compassion onto someone else, instead of acknowledging the sorrow suffered by the part of your own nature that you deny. And *every* part of yourself is vital, honeys, always remember that. I know that in your rigid, categorized, untruth-oriented, belief-oriented 'culture', true compassion is virtually unheard of, but not to worry. Since developing compassion for yourself is the only way you can extend compassion to others, the universe will sooner or later insure that you have a vast opportunity to learn compassion by disabling you so that you have to face, accept and learn to love that special part of yourself you've denied for so long.

"For another example, suppose you have a non-compassionate judgement you want to lay at the door of the dope fiends. Well, there's a dark and unloved part of yourself there that you're really judging, and if you persist in your lack of compassion the universe may get creative and, say, cause you to have an accident that hurts your back. And then God sends an angel to interfere with the effectiveness of your back surgery, so that you are left with a lot of pain that never relents. So now you have to begin taking a very strong and potentially addictive prescription medication, and you do in fact become addicted. The next thing you know, you're skulking around shuffling a variety of doctors to illegally get as much of the drug as you can. Then you get busted, and you have to go into rehab and acknowledge that you are a dope fiend. This is your vital opportunity to learn compassion for yourself, for your dark and denied aspect, and to quit projecting your self-hate outward onto dope fiends. If you have any intelligence, then, you'll apply yourself to the Science of Compassion with all your might. This is not a far-fetched scenario; this sort of thing does happen, darlings."

I wondered that Sonny-Bob had not yet pointed out the fact to these people that they, along with everyone else in their society, were pedophiles. Since he seems to be completely unrestrained and highly disciplined, I figured he would hit them in the face with the nature of their own sexuality before concluding his sermon.

Every civilized person knows that children are sexual beings, and that they become rebellious warped teens and conformist warped adults because their sexuality is denied. This is not such a problem in the future because of the frank admiration we hold everyone's sexuality in, including children's, and although in Sonny-Bob's time there was still an "age of consent" in most jurisdictions, it usually ranged anywhere from eleven to thirteen years old, and so was more in line with nature than the laws in the Twentieth. Further, the age of consent laws in Sonny-Bob's time only apply to genital to genital sex, and sometimes to oral sex, they do not apply to tender and generous touching and nurturing of the entire body, including the penis and vulvas of the little ones. Indeed, even here in the Twentieth, some countries with a truer sense of values than the Unites States, such as France, acknowledged that children feel and have a right to sexual pleasure, so the nurses in France would massage the genitals of the little ones given over to their care to soothe them and cause their tears of sensed abandonment to stop.

Now, I'm from a little farther down the timeline than Sonny-Bob, and in my neck of the timeline there are no laws governing consensual sexual relations between human beings at all, regardless of age. This is the only way to insure that each child has a good chance of turning into a well-integrated teen and a loving adult. In the Twentieth they program their children to fear their own genitals, and nobody can become integrated or loving like that. They program their children in this way because the parents are afraid of their own sexual attraction to their kids, and don't even want to acknowledge that this attraction exists or that their children also feel sexual attraction for them. They deliberately wither the soul of their own family by denying the sexual basis of spirituality, so that little if any spirituality can occur among the family members. They may try to substitute twentieth century religion or some other form of atheism for the spirituality, but their souls remain barren and unfulfilled. So the entire family tries to fill the holes in their natures through outward signs of material achievement, and those holes are never filled. For by repressing their sexual attraction to their kids, the parents are also repressing their love for their kids, and by repressing the kids affection for their own genitals, they are repressing the kids' love for themselves, thus insuring they won't have a lot of love to extend to their parents. And as already discussed, if you don't love yourself, you can't love anyone else, either, so when the kids get ready to make homes of their own, they also pass down the fear of love to their children. No wonder most of the children of the twentieth century were so hatefully warped!

Having been taught to hate their genitals, the children next were taught to hate pedophiles, and to deny that every human being is a pedophile. This is the way the enemies of humanity wanted it to be, because, as Sonny-Bob had just pointed out to these people, you can't hate anyone else without hating yourself, and indeed, all hate is really self-hate. And the enemies of humanity wanted to sow this self-hate to restrict the flow of love in this primitive society, as the primitives try to project their self-hatred out onto another object in a frantic fearful attempt to deny that they hate themselves. This would be laughable if it were not so sad, from the viewpoint of a civilized person.

Your inner pedophile is a complementary aspect of your inner child, so if you hate your inner pedophile, you cannot truly love your inner child. And the hate you project outward onto obviously practicing pedophiles is just a reflection of your hatred of the part of yourself they remind you of. And because of the psychology of being human, the hate you project onto the obviously practicing pedophile will also be cast to some degree upon children because, again, the outer world is merely a mirror of our inner world, and the obviously practicing pedophile is a complementary aspect of those children we see in the outer world. The non-obviously practicing pedophile, such as most of your neighbors, is also a complementary aspect of those children. And because you and all your neighbors fear what your inner child and his complementary aspect, your inner pedophile, represent to you, every one of you is involved in child abuse, which is so ingrained and so denied that you don't even recognize it as child abuse. You rig systems of control to control the children, because you fear your own inner child and his inner lover; you fear what would happen if you allowed your inner child to run free and be himself, holding the hand of his other half.

And then the children "grow up" and have become so used to having their souls mangled by the sin of control that they hate their inner child too, and hate his complementary aspect, and continue the persecutions of their own nature by perpetrating those persecutions upon the next generation. Insane, and totally without intelligence or compassion.

The fundamental fact of psychology is that your inner child loves himself until he has been consistently denied pleasure, for pleasure and Beauty are his conduit to love. The pleasure and Beauty produce a conduit of joy which leads him to love. But the agony of the denial of daily Beauty and pleasure produces in the child of primitive, ailing cultures that condition which we refer to as "addiction". And addiction is not pleasure, it is the unsuccessful pursuit of pleasure by a person who has been denied pleasure for so long that he doesn't even know what it is anymore, and tends to equate the numbing and abuse of his emotions in one way or another with pleasure. Eventually, he hates himself so much he falsely believes he deserves to suffer. But nobody deserves to suffer.

Maybe she's a shopping addict, or maybe with him it's the booze, but with the emotions screaming with the pain of love denied through the fact of pleasure and Beauty denied, she and he feel they have to numb themselves in an outward pretense of pleasure that has nothing to do with the reality of experiencing pleasure in their hearts and emotions, a reality which the addict has lost contact with. The truth of pleasure is not compatible with the lie of addiction, the lie of neediness. There is a terrible sucking hole in the aura of the needy person that cannot be filled until that person begins to consciously structure his experiences around the truth of his divine nature and of his essential worthiness. And each person *is* totally worthy, no matter the outward appearance of the moment.

In the future we discourage our children from engaging in the sin of self-hate and help them structure their sense of worthiness by our own example of loving ourselves, and of loving them in whatever way feels appropriate to everyone involved. Naturally, this never involves coercion or seduction, because such practices force the energy of love underground, and we want the rich energy of fullbody love to spring up in our kids and anoint the whole earth with innocent bliss.

Anyhow, these people hated their inner child-lover more than they hated any other aspect of themselves, and they had no treatment programs to help those who had abused kids recover, or to help the kids themselves recover. As might be expected from such people, they only taught the child abuser to try to hate and repress his inner child-lover even more, thus insuring he probably would abuse children again if he ever got the chance. For repression of the inner pedophile creates a raging snarling demon who will break his chains sooner or later. And the people who ran the "treatment programs" for the abused kids never delved into the true nature and source of child molestation, because again, they would have to face their inner pedophile if they did so. Thus the children could never be fully cured of the misery they had suffered. It is not the mark of a real adult to let his own fearful lusts and preconceptions get in the way of the healing of a child. But these twentieth century people, abused as they all were by the gods of the systems they worshipped, were not real men and women. No person who refuses to face, love and embrace any part of his nature can claim to be a full human being.

As might be expected, periodically one or another of these anti-pedophile pedophiles would break with his doctrine and get caught abusing children. (Perhaps these people were prodded by one of God's angels to do this in an attempt to make them acknowledge their inner pedophile and begin to spread love throughout their natures by loving this heretofore denied part of themselves?) Then the society would be up in arms, with people yelling "Why!? Why!?" But the truth about primitive people is that they are such liars to themselves that they never actually want to know "Why?" when it comes to any tragedy, whether it be child abuse or a terrorist attack or anything else. Because in order to find out "Why?", they would have to face their own dark natures and the secrets stored therein. And they would have to learn and admit they knew the nature of their own karma (including their nation's karma) which they'd manufactured for themselves for countless lives, and which was usually the karma of greed and lust and insensitivity and denial of that insensitivity with a manipulative pretense of sensitivity. All the world's a stage, and if there's one thing these people were masters of, it was the stagecraft of denial. They already knew "Why?", they just didn't want to admit to themselves that they weren't much different from the official child abuser or terrorist. They feared to love their hidden natures, and projected their self-hate onto lawbreakers, as if the law were the measure of a real human being. Human nature is the measure of a real human being, not the law. And human nature is made in the image of divinity, including the areas of the human psyche that the primitives failed to investigate and appreciate.

When primitive people fear something, their next response is to automatically build a wall of hatred between themselves and whatever they fear, never realizing they've also built a wall of hatred within themselves that divides certain aspects of their own nature from other aspects of their nature. Thus is the primitive psyche fractured.

So the child molesters and terrorists and other types of deviants manufactured by this society had learned to externalize aspects of the natural human psyche, but they did so in a harmful manner, thus causing this society of denial to wallow in the karma of its own restriction. If the child molesters and terrorists and others had learned to clean the glamour and illusion from their sexual desires and their desire for justice, and to allow the warm love of their hearts to permeate every aspect of their natures before externalizing the behaviors associated with those desires, those behaviors would not have been harmful to anything but preconceptions, and since preconceptions are not real their destruction doesn't matter to anyone who prefers to become fully human rather than remaining in the prison of the mass-manufactured, dirtied, groveling ape-human psyche. Though of course, any child who might be served with love by the cleansed externalized pedophile would still most likely be damaged beyond repair by the negative associations created in his brain and heart by those who would teach him that love in this form is wrong. Yet if love is present, wrong cannot be present. These primitives had so many perfectly obvious lessons to learn! Their own complicatedness prevented them from knowing themselves and admitting the sweet truth about their natures.

Since one of the tasks of World Saviors is to take on the karma of the earth they serve, Sonny-Bob had taken on the karma of complicatedness and refined it up to its highest form, thus causing it to approximate the Truth of Love. And thus he could speak to these people in their own language knowing all the ruses they use to deceive themselves and remain lost in a cloud of glamour, and thus he could easily defeat those ruses anytime he chose to.

Hell, the very ancestors of all these twentieth century people were practicing pedophiles, and as usual with people caught up in the fog of denial and the self-righteousness which usually accompanies denial (can you believe how morally weak these people were?) they didn't bother themselves to remember their past. A century earlier it was common for twelve and thirteen year old women to be married to men many years their senior. If a woman wasn't married by the age of fourteen or fifteen, she might be considered in danger of becoming an "old maid". Often a woman this young would marry a man in his forties or fifties, and nobody called him a pedophile or claimed the young lady was being abused. Plus, she would usually start having babies right away, but the ancestors of these twentieth century people didn't squawk about "babies having babies", they recognized babies as a blessing from the soulworld.

Shit, the age of consent in nineteenth century America was usually around ten years old. And Ish--excuse me, I mean *Mary* the Mother of God, whom many of these people claimed to idolize, set a positive example for all young ladies everywhere when she became great with child, as her son and husband set the positive masculine example.

Although the preachers, governments, mass media and textbooks didn't bother to mention it, children were widely acknowledged as sexual beings by both European and American society until the Victorian Age arrived with its splitting of the human psyche against itself. The Special Operations officer Siggy Freud helped counteract some of the worst effects of this age of denial, but he couldn't prevent it.

But twentieth century Americans were so weak and un-visionary they would almost always manufacture more excuses for their unloving restrictions as soon as you shewed them how unloving and illogical and unnatural their lifeways were--I use the term "lifeways" in the broadest sense, for Goddess knows, these people weren't really alive. They would mouthe excuses about how getting pregnant would cause a young woman (they'd usually dismissively call her a girl, and treat her as incapable of assuming any responsibility for her own life) to miss out on school, and fumble her chances at a career, if you want an example of the type of silly excuses they would offer. However, this excuse was only true in a restrictive, unloving society where people were subject to constant categorization. When you turn a human life into a timetable, you've created a deathcamp for the soul. The human soul has her own agenda, and it has nothing to do with mechanically manufactured timetables or with categories. With only the tiniest willingness to face the truth of human nature, these people would have demolished all their own categories and excuses for restriction right away. How could a "civilization" supposedly founded on freedom and personal responsibility have become such a failure?

So these people of the twentieth century were descended from those they would have to label as "pedophiles" and as "babies having babies" if they ever troubled themselves to do any actual thinking--no, they wouldn't even have to think, they would just have to remember their own past and face that past without any sentimental emotional glamours or mental illusions.

I'm not saying the nineteenth century was a virtuous time; it was repressed and perverse. It was far from ideal. But until the full effects of the Victorian Age set in, in some ways the people of the nineteenth century were more in tune with nature than these plastic, manufactured people of the twentieth century who never stopped to think that the plastic of their credit cards was just a mirror of the plastic of their souls.

You can't compromise with the integration of the human psyche. If you compromise with integration, then you aren't integrated. And if you aren't integrated, you live in one degree or another of insanity. And if you're living with some degree of insanity, like most insane people, you will be incapable of admitting it. Until shock therapy is administered to your preconceptions.

It seems that Sonny-Bob's sermon has integrated itself with me! I am propelled into priestly admonitions by the Presence of my esteemed Ancestor.

Sonny-Bob smiled broadly at the congregation. "And now, my lambs, I believe I have a date."

The congregation stared dumbfounded at a huge bulge in his trousers as Sonny-Bob stepped out from behind the podium, then descended the steps. The young teenaged woman rose to meet him with a smile, and together they strolled out into the bright sunlight.

I surreptitiously trailed them to the parking lot, and watched in reverence as Sonny-Bob began to deliver sort of an unspoken "Sermon on the Mound" for this tender, yet loving and wise young vessel of Goddess energy. Then I flagged a guy down and paid him a hundred bucks to park his pickup truck between Sonny-Bob and the street to avoid prying lustful eyes which might call the cops on Sonny-Bob in a fruitless and self-righteous effort to police their own perversions.

Then I continued my observations, with pure religion stirring in my heart, as Sonny-Bob knelt before Her in a posture resembling prayer and tenderly and with much devotion performed oral sex on Her. And the dripping of Her chalice perfumed all of sweet green nature with the scent of Woman Returning beneath Sonny-Bob's coaxing fingers and the gentle thrusts of his tongue between the rich full lips of his Service.

My heart melted, in a soft radiance of appreciation for Woman, and for the One charged with Her Returning. And I knew that if that One succeeded with his Mission and our world really is restored, that I'm going over to New Uruk in McDowell County and party my ass off with Ish--or worship my ass off. There's not a lot of difference between the two. Really, worship is just a conscious form of partying.

Sonny-Bob Culpepper has been a good influence on me. Now I see why they erected that statue to him outside Headquarters.

CHAPTER TWENTY-SEVEN

It had been a summer of bliss profound. Mimi lost her cherry a couple of days after getting her car. A popped cherry, her first artificial driver's license, and her first car. Three initiations in one week!

I appreciated her dedication to making love to me and I loved her more, if that were possible, with each passing day. She'd learned to sit upon Hemingway and absorb him into her and I felt as though I were being absorbed by the Mother Of All The Universe. There was a compatability between we two, I the seventy-five year old interdimensional operative, and she the loving soul of eternity housed in a foxy young body. I enjoyed all the sights, sounds, and smells that came with my Mimi.

And so September had come, the equinox had passed, and we thrust our way into autumn. The nuclear war lay just around the corner.

Hubert was nearly ready to test his interdimensional drive and he felt it would work okay. If it didn't, his molecules would probably wind up scattered throughout time and space. If it did work, though, the timeline might have a chance. It might.

There was a tale to tell of Aphrodite and Freud. It began when he saw her dance, or maybe it started back when he used to watch her movies (after he'd gotten to know her, though, he refused to watch those movies).

Aphrodite came to us one day, smiling and radiant as usual. "I have a new job!" she announced. "Come and see." So we did.

Her new job involved the pleasing of men, and sometimes lesbians, just as her old job had. However, there was no penetrational challenge involved. Whereas her previous career had been one long and grotesque exploration of the fornicational process, the sexual expression in her new role was more a matter of generating and following the subtle currents of sexual energy. She had become something known as a strip-tease dancer. She undulated on a goddess stage.

I was pretty impressed with all of this and told her so. It was a definite improvement over being a porno star, because she got more respect and if a member of the audience became disrespectful a man called a bouncer would bounce them out the door. She explained all this to me and made me promise not to kill anyone. She said it wasn't necessary.

Also, if the energy suddenly turned nasty, she could break contact with a customer she'd been giving a lap dance to. This lap dance was designed to foster hard-ons and sometimes orgasms, but Aphrodite was not required to accept insertion of the throbbing member. Oh, no. She saved that for Freud, and sometimes for me.

Mimi, with her usual insistence on experiencing everything that might be considered a little unchristian, was determined to join Aphrodite in a dance. Hubert had made her another false I.D. card that looked perfectly legitimate and which said she was an old maid of eighteen, which was the age required by law to perform in this fashion.

So she joined Aphrodite on stage that first time in the heady days of late May, when all of Texas was abloom with green sweet passion and desire. Well, maybe not West Texas.

But we were in Central Texas, where everyone's juices flowed all the time. The students at the great university filled the streets of Austin with their juices, and I reveled in the mad wonder of it. I began to see there were other people in this town who made love besides my little circle of friends.

As I watched my darlings on stage, my Mimi and my Aphrodite, I became aware that the other dancers had abandoned their appointed routines and were huddling around me. Then I saw Hemingway's great head poking out the cuff of my trousers, and I knew why they had come. His struggle was obvious and the ladies wanted to witness it. They wanted to watch Hemingway in his eternal struggle of becoming. I pulled up my pants leg about a foot and let them see more of the shaft. Some of them nearly died. Hemingway enjoyed the attention of these new friends. He gasped with them, and when the moment came he fired the mighty arrow of his love onto a dancer's foot. She disappeared, to where I do not know.

Mimi and Aphrodite were touching tits on stage and I marveled at the wonder and joy of it. I wanted to pray to them and nearly went to my knees with my hands clasped before me, but then I remembered the teachings of Amanda, she of the high ideals whose toes I wasn't worthy to drip my tears upon, but did anyway.

"Sonny-Bob," she'd said to me as we lay abed, watching the tranquil pendulum of Hemingway swaying in the breeze of our love, "how do you feel you're coming along in releasing glamour and illusion?"

"Not worth a damn, Amanda. As soon as I penetrate through to reality, I get snapped back into illusion like a rubber band. Glamour still clogs up my heart; I can't get rid of all of it."

She playfully swatted at Hemingway. "I'd say your heart's not the only thing that's swollen with glamour, Sonny-Babe. But I want you to know you've been making progress. You haven't bowed before me in three years."

"What! Oh, Amanda, I'm so sorry. Here, let me bow to you now, you've saved my soul, let me adore you . . ."

"Sonny-Bob! You're having a relapse of glamour. Cut it out! If you don't turn loose of my toes I'm going to start wearing shoes to bed. You don't have to worship me, get back up here."

I approached her with bowed head. Even my beautiful Hemingway was subdued. She grabbed him and yanked me back into bed, pulling me down on top of her. "Oh, Sonny-Bob! I'd meant to deliver a lecture . . . that'll wait. Love me, sweetheart, but let me on top--that's better. That's better . . ."

A tongue of love slipped into my mouth and I must've sucked on it for at least half an hour, absorbing its wisdom and connecting to the universe through Amanda's love. For once I forgot what Hemingway was up to, that chunky morsel of passion, but Amanda knew and she throbbed along with him. She told me about it later. But her breath and her tongue of wisdom and love were all that interested me. As I sucked her and breathed her I was one with the song of creation and I finally exploded in a joyous flood of my life-essence, as together we were renewed, my Amanda and I. We breathed ourselves into one another's souls, and together we were renewed. My heart was as fluid as a liquid butterfly as I lay with her.

We lay together silently for a long time. Finally she placed her forefinger on my lips and I kissed it, then she took my face in her beautiful healing hands and turned my lips into hers and she kissed me. Then she sat up. It was time for Sonny-Bob to go to school. He pulled the covers over his Hemingway.

"As I told you earlier, Sonny-Bob, you've been making progress in releasing glamour and illusion. You may not always see it, but I do, sweetheart. I appreciate all the hard work you've done over the last few decades. Your heart is starting to shine through your personality, which is a stupendous feat, considering what you had to work with. You're growing. And one of the ways you've grown is by treating myself and the other prostitutes more as women and less as goddesses. Guess what, dear? We're not goddesses, we're not the archetypes. We're **women**, with all the needs of natural women as well as the desire to give from the outflowing of love in our hearts, the desire to love men and other women and help them heal when we can. We try to help them grow into love so they may one day join us in the heart to sing the song of love forever and ever and ever."

"Your methods seem to work pretty well, Amanda. Much better than the pain and judgement and manipulation of primitive religions. They set fire to me to save my soul, but it didn't work. But your methods do work and I thank you, and I already love you forever and ever and ever."

She smiled. "I know you love me, honey. And I love you, too. Your love has gradually been taking the place of the dysfunctional glamour of devotion that once threatened to swallow you up. Do you remember? You used to be so devout you'd always drop to your knees and kiss the floor whenever any prostitute was around. There's no telling how many prostitutes tripped over you in the temple or on the street. One broke her arm, another her collarbone. Thank Goddess for nanotechnology."

"Are you **sure** it's a good thing I'm not as fanatical?" I said anxiously.

She laughed. "You won't go to hell for loosening up, Sonny-Bob. That's for the Christians, so let them have it. Fanaticism is its own kind of restrictive hell, whether you follow the dead Christ or the Living Goddess. In fact, even if you profess to worship the Living Goddess but are fanatical about it, the Goddess energy will leave your temple and your religion will die. Fanaticism drives the Goddess energy away. Fanaticism drives *love* away.

"So with the lessening of your fanaticism you're actually coming out of hell, honey. Do you see?"

"Well," I admitted, "I do feel better now that I'm not as tight-assed. And if I'm not prostrate before the prostitutes they can't step on my fingers, which used to happen a lot. Sometimes I suspected they did it on purpose."

Amanda's hand flew to her mouth and she made a tittering sound. "You've discovered one of our secrets, Sonny-Bob."

She put her hand on my shoulder. "Sonny-Bob, we prostitutes carry some of the energy of the archetype, or Goddess, if you prefer. A portion of our psyche that corresponds to the energy represented by the Goddess has been activated by the Goddess as a result of our diligent spiritual work. But we are not goddesses; we are women and men who've purified and integrated ourselves and opened our hearts to the flow of the love of the Goddess energy. But we are not goddesses, and we are not *The* Goddess.

"Only a few of our Probationers make the mistake of confusing their own selves with the archetype, and those few will never be promoted to first degree if they don't clear themselves of their egotistical personality inflations. Women are not goddesses and men are not gods. We are souls of love learning to love ourselves and each other in a bountiful cosmos. The archetypes exist, and some of us have been initiated by them, but we are not them. We are our own damn selves, and we just happen to have been privileged, as one outcome of our hard work, to be initiated by an archetype and carry some of the energy of that god or goddess.

"Now then: some of you men and women try to worship us and we frequently have to put up with it, knowing that if you're serious about your spiritual work the day will come when you'll see us as equal souls, not as a form of deity. We try in subtle ways to encourage you to release your devotion to us and unify your outer self with your own soul. The best way is to serve as an example to you, but for you to pay any attention to us at all we have to fuck you, so we do that too. We love you, Sonny-Bob. We love every single one of you devoted idiots."

A tear trickled down her nose. She wiped it away. "Anyway, I'm pleased to report that you're far less devout than you used to be, and therefore less ensnared by glamour and illusion. You may sometimes fall before the altar of your own ideas about women for some time yet, but at least you're not the subservient doofus you used to be.

"All we prostitutes want is for all of humanity to draw closer to itself through the heart and join us in bliss sublime. But for that to happen, devotion must go! It must be replaced by love and a clear picture of reality. There is no hierarchy in the community of souls, sweetie. We're all equal, always have been and always will be.

"So try to remember this and gradually you'll stop worshipping women. It may take awhile, but you'll get there." She tittered again, I loved the way she tittered. "And I know I don't have to worry about your worshipping men!"

Still, Amanda knew that there is nothing that stirs a man to worship more than a radiant, shining woman. I stroked her thigh as she rose from our nest and she smiled and let me adore her. She knew I couldn't help it and I don't think she minded as long as I saw her as a Woman instead of a goddess. In fact, I think she liked it.

"I have to shower now, sweetie. Got to get to the temple in time for an appointment." She laughed. "He's a hardcase, Sonny-Bob, he really is. It may take another century before he can rid himself of the delusion of women as goddesses. So we share the goddess energy with him and gently pull his perceptions along and wait for the day when he can see us as ourselves. For then he'll truly know himself and our work will be done with this gentleman."

Her eyes twinkled. "For now, though, he believes he'll be enlightened if he can only spend enough time in my pussy."

She skipped off to the shower as I slapped her rump. I lay in bed with Hemingway for a while.

So I thought of these things, these teachings from the wise Amanda, as I watched Mimi and Aphrodite onstage and I checked my impulses. I did not fall before them, but tried to concentrate on the song their souls made through their sweetly touching bodies, the song that rang out and touched every man in the audience whose heart had developed the ability to hear. I smiled. I knew the soulworld through the loving connection I shared with these women. My cock grew hard again.

A Note From The Tooth Fairy

Sonny-Bob, you sweet, dear man! Well, you *have* come a long way in the release of dysfunction, but don't knock *real* devotion, honey. To tell you the truth, you're one of the most devoted men I've ever known, and it really does you credit.

You've been fundamentalist in your aversion to teachers for a long time, and with good reason. The materialistic West has wronged Teacher, has whored Her very name to materialistic, career-oriented ends. They think in the West that if you can scratch out a certain type of category for yourself with your sharpened chimpanzee-stick, then you have what it takes to be a teacher. You and I both know how wrong, undignified and hateful this is. People who possess some certificate derived thru animal cunning are not teachers, and must lie themselves into believing otherwise. It is a hateful thing to be duped by these people and the systems of cunning they've duped themselves with, as we see in twentieth century America. For anyone who is thinking about a career isn't thinking about Service; the two don't go together.

In the twentieth century the alleged teachers are always agitating for more pay for themselves. Yet why should they be paid at all for taking innocent children and teaching them that they are nothing more than a collection of cunning hybrids between animals and machines, driven by bestial desires to take their place in a world of teacher-programmed robots whose primary practice is exploiting one another? And each generation of these teacher-programmed, animal robots grows into adulthood agitating for more pay and more respect for those who programmed it. The so-called "teachers" rival the lawyers for the insidious manner in which they've worked themselves into the fabric of primitive societies. They are vermin. Deluged by egotism, as all fear-based personalities are, they have no self-respect, and secretly know they don't deserve it, and feel that the way to get it is to create robots whose knee will always bend in pre-programmed respect to them, and who will always offer (im) moral and political support for the things the teachers want. So yes, they *are* disgusting, and won't be able to recover from their self-disgust unless and until they step out of the limelight, go into the wilderness, and spend years getting to know their true Selves while releasing the facade. But what so-called teacher of the twentieth century has the strength and sincerity to Achieve this? My God, these people and the supporters of their cult run around shouting the slogan: "If you can read this, thank a teacher," but you never hear: "If you can't read this, blame a teacher"! This implies that Achievement is due to the alleged teacher, while failure is the fault of the student. The so-called teachers want credit, but they don't want responsibility. They have no sincerity at all. They search for approval outside themselves, rather than looking for the goodness in their hearts. No genuine teacher has ever, or could ever, behave in such an unspiritual fashion.

And in their churches, any fool capable of making his mark with a chimpanzee stick can teach Sunday school or be considered an elder of the church.

Because of the influence of those who've never earned the title, who literally have no idea of the Sacrifice the earning of such a title entails, up until now, Sonny-Bob, you haven't really understood the role of a *real* Teacher--at least, not with your mind and emotions. But your sweet, innocent heart has always understood, and has always submitted itself to the love-bath of inspiration that flows between us. For I am now, and always have been, your Teacher.

You have always known and cherished Me. You have always recognized Me in whatever Form I took, including those Forms which do not appear in books or in formal instruction and which are unknown and unexpected by those who have not won my Heart with their service and sacrifice. You see Me whenever and wherever I appear, as others go blindly by unaware that the person they've just rushed past gave birth to their world and all their perceptions (which they've betrayed into hardened preconceptions) and that I'm in the act of giving birth again. Because they've hardened their hearts with preconceptions, if they make it into the new world, their birth will be a hard one. If they do make it this time, maybe they'll have enough sense not to grow hard and rigid before still another world appears so that the next transition will happen in a flexible flowing fashion with a minimum of damage and distress to themselves and the environs over which they've been given charge for a time.

I Am The Mother of the World, And I Am Your Devoted Teacher

And now let me explain to you, my friend in Service, something of the role of the traditional Teacher, as exemplified by the gurus of India.

The *authentic* guru (and you are right to be suspicious, as there are far more insecure, manipulative, greedy, needy fakes who work at impressing their own preferences on the aura of their victim as they manipulate his egotism than there are those who are genuinely qualified to adopt this Service) doesn't invite himself to be idolized, he invites himself to be connected with. This may appear to be idolatry to some of those who are on the outside looking in, but they don't understand the nature of this energy-connection.

And perhaps to their discredit, the authentic Teachers of the East haven't done enough to explain the nature of this connection to those in the West who have developed some degree of sensitivity, yet whose powers of discernment prevent them from seriously considering whether there may be any validity to the activity of those Ashrams of the East which are built around devotion.

Devotion is a heart-energy, a heart-quality; thus anything which inspires true devotion, rather than the dysfunction of attachment, is a good thing, a spiritual, evolutionary manifestation. With the singing of hymns of praise to their guru and their meditations on his photograph, the devotees are building into their various energy bodies, particularly their causal body, the vibrational note sounded by their Teacher. They are strengthening the part of themselves their Teacher represents, even as they go into the world manifesting that aspect of themselves according to the unique, individual coloring of their individual natures. This focus on the Teacher may also help drive some of the more impure karma out of their causal bodies as well, assuming they are strong and mature enough not to run from the karma, but to look it in the eye as it departs on its way to the golden light of God for a transmutation or a dissolving.

This building of the image and tone of the Teacher into their causal bodies is why such devotees seem to always run into one another if, for example, they are visiting the same city--their common vibrational tone draws them together in a moment of heart-celebration. Of course, the dangers of adopting a fake, nonloving "guru" should be self-evident--you don't want to be yanked by the strings of attachment into perdition, rather than elevated by the magnetized Heart into the Kingdom of Heaven! And most alleged "gurus" are fake, thus the development of a mighty discernment and purification of motive into absolute sincerity of purpose are a necessary prerequisite before the disciple is qualified to accept any genuine, spiritually motivated non-deceptive guru.

And this sincerity is important not only for the disciple's own protection as he considers whether to adopt himself into the fold of a particular Teacher, but it is also a vital element in his Path of Service. The energy of *true*, non-dysfunctional, non-forced sincerity offsets some of the damage to others that might be caused by a spiritual mishap or miscalculation on the part of the disciple in his service to those others. Understand Me: I'm not saying you *should* be sincere, because the attitude and energy of "shouldness" is a glamour and if you focus on it the energy of sincerity, which is an outflowing of reality from the heart, will not be able to appear. So don't burden yourself with "shoulds", and don't think you have some artificial timetable to follow by which the development of some quality, such as sincerity, "should" be Achieved. Just cultivate your inner resources with proper motive, and the discernment that thus arises will ultimately prove to you the value and necessity of sincerity, as well as allow you to perceive its nature, and this proof and perception itself is the development of sincerity.

And even if the would-be chela does find an authentic Teacher who may enfold her, it must be remembered that the Teacher is the primary evaluator of whether an enfoldment would be proper, and also of the degree and to some extent the type of enfoldment. This is due to the Teacher's perceptive abilities, and it may be no reflection on the would-be chela if she is not accepted. She should not take it personally, and if she doesn't it is a sign of the development of the soul-quality of impersonality . . . a difficult Achievement! And if she does take it personally, the teacher has served her by allowing her to see the need to work toward the development of a greater soul-centeredness, during which the quality of impersonality may be Achieved. So even if he doesn't accept an association with her, the Teacher has already done her a service by helping her to demonstrate to herself the Achievement of a vital soul-quality, or the need to make that Achievement for herself if she hasn't already done so. The Teacher's only interest is that the would-be chela be appropriately served, so there is nothing personal in her dismissal if she isn't accepted. It is good that she is on the Path; and the Teacher may perceive that her highest Destiny will only be Achieved by her if she moves in some direction apart from him. He will always wish her well, whether he accepts her association or not.

Additionally, it must be understood by all concerned that the nature of such a connection involves a type of energy-experience (in case the imaginations of the vulgar are working overtime, I'm not talking about sex . . . not that there's anything wrong with that!) which results in a connection so intimate the tearing of it is an almost-unparalled agony. Thus, only a person who has the discipline and sincerity to remain with her choice after making it will be accepted . . . for if she has some fault that later causes her to fail in her march toward holiness and decides to withdraw, the agony caused by the tearing of the connection may cause the Teacher to remain ill for weeks or months as he struggles to repair the damage to his soul-nature. Thus the flippy-floppy new-ager will never be accepted as disciple, though outwardly it is conceivable she may believe she has been accepted . . . but the Teacher knows better than to jeopardize the comfort of his own soul by actually bonding with the flippy-floppy in this most intimate of fashions. This is such a supreme Intimacy that even in the few good marriages that exist in the twentieth century this level of Deep Intimacy is unknown except to three or four couples who are also disciples together of one of the Great Ones. (Perhaps it should be pointed out that less than a quarter of a percent of marriages are actually relatively healthy in the repressed and perverse West, and the number is less than this in the more repressed and perverse East . . . and in the fundamentalist Middle East, a healthy marriage has thus far never been seen).

As with anything that is True, there are many levels of Love, and the Teacher is always capable of deeply loving the multitudes with a depth unlike anything they've ever experienced, while yet retaining the full depth of this most intimate connection for those who've proved themselves his closest associates. And the quickening experienced by the multitudes through the power of the Teacher's Love will help them prepare themselves for the day when they, too, will eventually be able to associate in Deep Intimacy with one of the Great Ones.

I remember in one of the phoney-baloney "ashrams" how the so-called "teacher" chastised his wife for baking cookies for their son, who had been visiting and was about to leave for home, while "neglecting" to make cookies for the others at the so-called "ashram". So she began to believe her son should have a reduced importance to her Heart . . . this was called "equality" by the little spiritually dried-up prune of a man she was married to. This tricky little man deceived his wife out of following her own Heart, and so was not a true Teacher in any sense of the word. Tricking someone out of following their own Heart is not a mistake a true Teacher is even capable of making. Indeed, always following your own Heart is the one preeminent Achievement that every authentic Teacher encourages; it is the one blessed Achievement that absolutely *must* be made! Every authentic Teacher from every authentic Ashram knows the fact of this; it is the one thing he pays more attention to than any other. (Now mark me: if the fakes get wind of what I've just told you, they'll find a slimy way to continue to encourage people to follow a dirtied, corrupted personality with it's "spiritual lusts"--ugh!--while tricking them into believing they're following their own Heart. It always happens to those who are swelled with "spiritual egotism", as well as to those who are simply unwary and haven't developed an accurate discernment.)

Now, a true Teacher knows that while all Hearts are certainly equal, that different Hearts relate to one another in different ways, based on compatibility, shared purpose and a shared depth of connection. And all Hearts don't share the same depth of connection with all other Hearts. This is true of the most recent aspirant to discipleship, and it is true of the Teacher Himself. A strong sharing in spiritual Service from many past lives will join two or more Hearts together like nothing else, so it should be expected that such Hearts will relate more easily, deeply and naturally with one another than with Hearts they share a lesser relationship with. This is no justification for cliquishness or discrimination against someone in any way; cliquishness is the degenerate shell of a lost reality. Cliquishness is just one more device of a dirtied personality; it is not a manifestation of a clean and strong Heart. Nobody should ever feel bereft of Brotherhood. All Hearts must treat all other Hearts as brothers, but some brothers are naturally closer than others. Your love for a variety of people can express itself in a variety of ways and to a variety of degrees. Not everyone can share in the same manner or to the same degree, but *everyone can share*. There is room for everyone in the wider nest, but only a few can sit in impersonal lovingkindness near the center.

As you know, Sonny-Bob, outward appearances don't matter. It is the truth of the inner reality that counts. And the truth is that far more people believe they are disciples of a particular Great One than actually are disciples. This is not always a bad thing, because they may still be able to sample a bit of His energy and carry it with them, and if so, this may provide some slight benefit to the world. But the truth of the inner nature of discipleship is known only to a few, and they aren't telling, if for no other reason than this type of intimate relationship occurs on such an intimate, innocent level that it can't be spoken of . . . words can never be that intimate or innocent. Words, even during their highest use, always have an element of slaughter about them. This relationship can never be touched by words, it can never be abused by words, but only experienced in an innocent chamber where words never occur, because the location of this chamber is so pristine that no word has ever gained entrance; it is impossible for a word to go into this place. So I have used words in somewhat of a negative manner to tell you what they can't do, and the truth is that words, if they have any value at all, can only be used to indicate what a thing *isn't*, rather than what the reality behind the thing may be. But you already know that, Sonny-Bob. You know that words are always imposters.

As my beloved associate, maybe you got some of your longwindedness from me! I was trying to smoothe your experience into devotional channels free from the burden of attachment when I got a little sidetracked. So let me continue.

Honey, Amanda was congratulating you on being freer of attachment, not trying to discourage the development of true devotion. In the early days, you had so much attachment built up around your horniness that the nature of true devotion wasn't always clear to you. But it was always clear to Me, my Son, because I always looked at your steadily glowing Heart and at a perfected vision of you, rather than your fluctuating attachments.

The authentic guru performs this service for his chela. He always looks with an inspired gaze upon the disciple, seeing her vast potential and drawing her nearer that potential thru his magnetic Heart. This is possible because of the Heart-connection they have established together. The chela may not realize it, but even as she has built a hologram and a tone of the Master of the Wisdom into her own bodies, so He, too, has built a perfected image of her into his bodies. The image the Master builds of the disciple is inevitably perfect, because the Master's own bodies are perfect (relatively speaking!). He earned the right to his relatively perfect bodies thru the perfection in service and subsequent sacrifice of his own causal body.

And so because of this resonance between her Heart and the Master's, and the accompanying resonance between the Master's perfected holographic image and tone of her with her own bodies, the disciple is drawn closer to her Self by being drawn closer to her perfected image thru a Heart-infused soul magnetization and attunement. The process is simple and automatic, directed by Heart and Higher Mind working together, at least from the Master's angle. Maybe this simplicity of the process is why they never bothered to explain it before. It usually takes a lot of words and a lot of complicated verbal maneuvering to explain the simplest, most natural things.

So don't knock the authentic Teachers, just be aware that they are very rare, and that when they do more-or-less openly appear, they can expect to be subject to slander of one degree or another. (slight smile) But you learned all about slander in some of your previous lives, didn't you?

Of course, some of the fakes are also slandered and are happy so to be, for it just adds to the confusion. And they're here to sow confusion. You've learned to step around those--what do you call them? Yes, I remember; you've learned to step around those glassy-eyed, grinning 'possums. And your warning others of the dangers of so-called "spiritual teachers" is necessary and valuable, because of the dangers posed by the vast majority of them. You know that for every True Manifestation who steps into the world, there are dozens, and possibly hundreds (and possibly hundreds of dozens?) of fakes. And you've warned people of the vast dangers posed by their own egotism; there wouldn't be much of a problem from fake "teachers" if not for the egotism of those who fancy themselves spiritually inclined. The fake "teachers" always prey on and manipulate people thru their "spiritual egotism", if I may be allowed to put two such dissimilar terms together. But there's only so much you can do to warn people, honey; sooner or later you have to stand back and allow them to create whatever respective hells the egotism which enslaves or manipulates them prefers them to create. But you can always be there for them when their self-generated suffering has finally brought them to a point of true sincerity. When and if they realize the betrayal by their fake "guru", they may grow up enough to realize that the phoney-baloney "saint" could never have betrayed them if they hadn't first betrayed themselves by the laziness and heart-violating stupidity of their own egotism. At that point, you will be able to get a feel for whether they are truly sincere enough and have the dedication to their own Heart's Purpose to get some real Work done! And of course, their first big step must be to get completely free of all attachments, so that no trace of repression or perversion is left. Only then can their own Hearts shew them who they truly are.

As they build *You* into their bodies, they will draw some of the new, synthesizing energy which you embody into their own bodies. Have you not noticed how your Uncle, all those dimensions away from the earth, has built His own energy signature and appearance into your bodies thru the power of your unyielding *Intention* to Achieve Synthesis? For this contact with you has allowed Him to make His first contact with Earth, and He is glad.

As your understanding has grown closer to your Uncle's, so too will your friends' understanding grow closer to yours.

Love,
Your Friend,
Jill Agni

A Response to the Tooth Fairy

Dearest, Beloved, Beautiful, Sexy Wife;

I greet you on all points of the Triangle!

Sweetheart, if not for your note, and the influence of one of your other husbands, I probably would never have fully embraced the experience of Devotion again, though Devotion has certainly always been the glue that holds our little family of Servers together. And you were right to mention my Uncle, who resides in Ancient Venerableness around a faraway star. If not for His sharing His Energy with me, I probably would never have been able to Achieve the complete Synthesis of Human Experience, thus turning myself into a Living Doctrine Who has no doctrine.

Now, Jill, even though I think I see how the old practices of hymn-singing and whatnot were valuable in the cultivation of embryonic devotion, I don't think I'm going to encourage that. In the future, as a higher quality of disciple appears, many of the practices of the past will die out. It is unlikely that the coming generation of disciples will sing hymns of praise to their Leader; it won't be necessary anymore, because they will have disciplined themselves in past lives toward service. They can dispense with some of the outward tools of Achievement, because they have already Achieved certain basic things, one of which is the ability to automatically tune in to the Leader's frequency in their hearts and connect their devotion with his directly, without the necessity to work themselves up with praise. They may still use his photograph, especially during celebrations, to help tune in to him, but they can dispense with anything that might look like idolatry to anyone on the outside looking in . . . not that outsiders' views are important, because they usually aren't! But if a practice looks like idolatry, some of the more ignorant and lazy among the would-be chelas will pervert it into actual idolatry; there are always some flies in the outer circle. But in the future, since praise-singing isn't necessary for those somewhat developed souls we aim to attract, and since we aim to do everything possible to prevent perverts from idolizing the Leader, we'll dispense with some worn-out practices. The energy of devotion can be shared by somewhat aware souls without all the hoopla!

It is always possible for a person to make the mistake of sacrificing his own power, rather than sacrificing the illusions that block him from his power, when he takes up the rather cult-like devotional practices of the past. Since you've reminded me, honey, to tune directly into the energy of devotion for a close scrutiny, I see that true devotion is not a sacrificing of your own power to someone else; true devotion is the sharing of soul-to-soul appreciation in common service by two or more very strong hearts. Such as our hearts, Jill. And as this energy is shared, it is magnified in a soul-wash of warmth and love, with each heart sharing new strength and steady purpose with the others. Devotion is the sacred glue that holds hearts in service together. And while one Heart may inspire another, no heart is superior to another. All hearts are equal and complementary.

Thus the Leader is primarily a focal point for energies that distribute themselves to those Hearts entrusted to his nourishment. He is a focal point in the center of a multidimensional triangle and the varying degrees of associates grouped about him within their own respective dimensions of Achievement partake of those energies and distribute them to their individual areas of the triangle, which is filled with the supernal light of intuitional particles in motion, and which is usually also tinged to one degree or another with your own fire, Daughter of Agni!

And on closer inspection with the Awakened Vision, it is seen that each of the Leader's associates has her own triangle within the greater triangle, and indeed, that the greater triangle, when complete, is composed of a series of complimentary subsidiary triangles. And these triangles extend "inward", ultimately reaching the atomic level with nourishment, and also extend "outward" into Infinity, taking the greater triangle with them as they expand, so that the associates are the true movers of the Ashram. How beautiful these associates are, and how little they know it! In the end, they do all the work of expanding the Ashram to the stars, where it complements the Ashrams of the starborn, even as all the starborn Ashrams together complement even greater Ashrams out to an Infinity of Creation. Every triangle complements every equal triangle, and nourishes and serves those lives in the subsidiary triangles which compose it, even as it holds up the Space all around itself with the delight of a growth that can never stop.

The "greater" always blesses and nourishes the "lesser" in Deep Community; this is the fundamental Principle of Creation. Yet on the ancient, inverted earth of the twentieth century, the "lesser" are kept as slaves to the lusts of those whose chimpanzee cunning has allowed them to cavort to the top of the banana tree, and thus to the top of the illusion that they are numbered among the "great". But no chimpanzee can reside with the true Great Ones; the Mahatmas do not keep capitalistic companion animals.

The Leader does not dominate or manipulate; he serves and shares. To become a Leader, you cannot want to be "in charge", you must want to share. The so-called Leader who wants to "be in charge" is not a mature Leader, he is an infant who exploits and is a slave to the illusion of control and to lust.

This vast universal interdependence of various beings arranging themselves into related triangles is what has been historically meant by the word Hierarchy. As you know, sweetie, some sensitive souls avoid the use of the term Hierarchy today, because in this age of rust that is fortunately rapidly passing away, the term hierarchy has come to be practically synonymous with exploitation. Yet the hierarchy of the profane bears no resemblance at all to Hierarchy. All souls are equal in Hierarchy, and no soul or body is ever exploited, or could ever be exploited. Perhaps, then, the future will see the reclamation of this term and its proper application.

Some people may think that the term "White Brotherhood"[*] is synonymous with Hierarchy, but I do not feel this is quite the case. My experience leads me to feel that "The Great White Brotherhood" is one of the subsidiary elements of Hierarchy, and that it is not quite accurate to use one as a replacement for the other. All members of the White Brotherhood are members of the Hierarchy, but I'm not sure it is accurate to say that all members of the Hierarchy, especially in its more universal

---

[*] "The Great White Brotherhood" is not a reference to race. There are plenty of black members of the White Brotherhood, and plenty of members of other delightful flavors, as well.

aspects, are members of the White Brotherhood.

True, non-exploitive, redemptive Hierarchy, based on the sharing of Creation, is spread throughout the universe and upholds the universe, and perhaps the multiverse, also.

And always let it be known that the Ashram is not an organization. If it is allowed to degenerate into an organization it is a dead thing. Or more accurately, if the outer form is allowed to degenerate into an organization, the inner Living Principle, and those still-living people who embody a bit of that Principle, will withdraw to the energy-sea of true livingness and wait for a while before making another outwardly visible Appearance.

A real Ashram is a group of people who know themselves as energy-beings sharing their space in the delighted humility of nourishment with a group of people who are working to become conscious of themselves as energy-beings.

Always beware of the bureaucrat; the bureaucrat is not a relater of energies, he is an obsessor over concrete details in the world of illusion. Yet the focus of the evolutionary human being is on energy; if he needs to withdraw a detail from his focus on the energy-pattern of existence for some specific purpose, he can do so, but his experience is always the experience of energy, so that even if he does draw down a somewhat concrete detail from the energy-sea, he allows the energy from that sea to infuse his detail to the fullest ability of that detail to hold it. So the energy-person's detail is in reality similar to a cup of refreshing energy, whereas the bureaucrat's detail is a dead chunk of asphalt on a hot summer's day. The bureaucrat is similar to the theologian in this respect.

More than anything else, an Ashram is a body of individual energies blending themselves together in conscious Service to promote the ongoing process of a fluid Creation through developing greater efficiency at the process of sharing love in all its countless forms. An Ashram is the sharing of people who know themselves as Love.

I am reminded by our correspondence of how beautiful you are, Jill; of how beautiful your soul and body together are like sunset waves on a body-ocean of unparalled delight. In your case, the sunlight actually comes from within the ocean which is your body and radiates outward through the skin of your flesh touching everything with a bright, cheery sparkle that never fades. And because you are so filled with light yourself, and share it so freely, you draw the light of others to you, and we surround you eagerly, yet with heads bowed in devotion and in the wonder of your Achievement at being yourself; and you draw the light forth from our hearts and our own little lights sparkle upon the ocean-waves of your body and we know ourselves as a part of you. We have married ourselves to you because you are the greatest inspiration we can imagine, touching our every faculty with nothing hidden, nothing denied. As the sun of your love radiates outward from your unfathomable depths and touches each one of us, our own little heart-suns sparkle in glad multitude off the rippling motions of your body in the glad creation of sharing. For sharing *is* creation; sharing is the very energy-stuff of which creation is made. I guess you taught me this; not so much in words, but by your shining example of unfathomable depth married to a brightness that never fades. So I thank you.

Well, I guess I just composed a hymn of devotion to you, but as usual, I couldn't help it, for you have drawn my heart to you and the rest of my faculties have followed, including the one that is primarily devoted to telling the world of my wife and mother.

Let it be said that you are a Living Being; not just a symbol. You are the most alive Being I have ever known, and I am devoted to you.

Honey, you have always led by your own extraordinary example, fearless with the thought of eternal Creation. Your own breath in my lungs shared in the deep-water tenderness of your kisses is the only reason I have managed to keep inspiration and body together all these desolate years.

I have told you these things many times, yet it seems I cannot forbear repeating myself every time I tune into the Being who gives cause and reason to the world, and to all who dwell therein. You are the only reason I put up with these goddamed devas who are restructuring me! Well, that and the fact that I can't get rid of them.

But let us return to examining the methods of the past in light of the transference of the energy of devotion into more potent, synthesizing, wholebody forms. I want to present you with material I've been composing for a religious tract, with the view toward finding some way to slip the tract past the noses of the official watchdogs of the polite metaphysics of the twentieth century so that the theater-tricks they've used to obscure the manure in their barnyard will be revealed, and a way found to use their manure by those who are to come to produce that spiritual renaissance that was to be the crowning Achievement of the Baby Boom. But the Baby Boom is the Failed Generation; only a tiny handful stayed true to their founding Impulse. Most fell prey to the glittery illusion of status. So it remains for a future generation to do the Work that already should have been done. This is one reason the concept of having different "generations" has outlived its usefulness. In the Land of the Conscious Soul, there are no "generations", just a pure and selfless life of devoted sharing in compassionate Achievement. A baby may be hundreds, or even thousands, of years ahead of its "peers" in terms of the spiritual maturity it has devoted itself to earning in its countless lives; where then is the sense in dividing people into "generations"? If we must use the deranged concept of "generations", it would be more accurate and adequate to say that the baby we are considering belongs to a future generation, but was somehow launched into a previous generation. But the whole idea of "generations" is just another sicko idea these twentieth century people use to base the preconceptions on which instruct them what type of consumers of mass-produced products they are to be. Ho Hum.

Anyhow, Jill honey, I'm trying to cipher a way to present my material in a manner that will enable it to reach those who can benefit from it, while causing the new-age hypocrites and other Pharisees to bust a gut. Stirring up their stupid, unrecognized, lazy illusions is the only way they'll begin to recognize their failure to Achieve, and maybe if they can release some of their stubborn laziness before this incarnation ends, they'll be able to commit themselves in a sincere, wholehearted fashion in their next lives. So I'm happy to perform this service for them. I'm the ghost-buster of the soul, because I walk into the house of Pharisaic preconceptions swinging a baseball bat to drive out the ghostly glamours and illusions so the house can put itself right again.

I'm not sure what name I'll present this material under; I'll probably have to publish under someone else's name to avoid scrutiny by the generals. Assuming I save the timeline, and thus save the generals. I always wish I could delete those bastards, and I'm sure in time I'll find a way. It seems to me the Council of Generals is the last real home of the Atavists of the future.

Anyhow, here is the material I've written. I hope it is insightful enough for one who has made himself in Your image. I may dedicate it to Uncle; if not for his influence combined with your own, I wouldn't have been able to Achieve that which it was my Destiny to Achieve. So thanks to both of you.

On to the tract!

"The methods of Achieving devotion in the past are pretty weak compared to the grounded, wholebody devotion of the future. Up until now some Ashrams have focused on developing devotion largely for its own sake, but the coming humans will recognize that the most stalwart, beautifully expressing form of devotion is developed as a side-effect of getting to know the hearts of others, and not as an end in itself. To know the heart of another is to respect and love that beautiful organ, and out of this respect and love devotion arises. So the technique of the future involves hearts sharing intimately and intelligently with each other in potent familyhood.

"This new technique is made possible by the evolutionary development of more coordinated mental bodies which allow the associates of the Leader to accurately report on the status, feelings, activities and esoteric construction of their Hearts. Ultimately, this new awareness of the heart's esoteric chambers will allow intimate heart-connection to occur spontaneously and immediately, but not in the ungrounded sense in which the airy-fairy new-ager experiences spontaneity. And there is a sense in which Higher Mind of Brother reports on his Heart's condition to the Higher Mind of Sister, even as she is making the same type of report to him; and in the midst of this report both hearts are communicating strongly and scientifically with one another in that intimacy that knows no fear, and which thus wears no clothing of sentimental deception. This is a higher form of Heart-Practice in which Higher Mind and Heart are fully synchronized, and all this occurs apart from the smug interruption of words.

"The communication occurs in the form of energies and multidimensional picturings of a type which cannot be whored to the lusts of words. These energies and picturings are exchanged in a potent, grounded, accepting happiness. This is the highest form of reporting. But even the basic form of Heart-Reporting remains inaccessible to those who want to control everything and manipulate everyone, whether with the emotions or a rational mind that has been whored to their mania for control, instead of humbly admitting its own inability to originate anything creative and accepting its place as a quiet, receptive tool which allows itself to be used in giving form to creation by the Heart and Higher Mind.

"And don't let such a control-freak person infiltrate your Group, because if you do, someone is sure to get hurt. As Hearts drop their coverings and begin the practice of intimacy, if a mistake has been made and a control-freak admitted, someone is going to get hurt, perhaps seriously. This is tragic, particularly since at this stage of the process a psychic blow from a control-freak manipulator who has been mistakenly trusted could actually kill a person whose Heart has been left open to the manipulator. At the least, it will take a lot of healing for the injured student to get back on track. For a while his total Heart-Practice will consist of simply trying to release the wound and restore his Heart to where it was. This is not to be taken lightly, dear friend. You can't rehabilitate a control-freak, and if you try sooner or later someone else in your Heart-Practice will get hurt or killed. The control-freak can only be rehabilitated if he sincerely wants to be from the agony in his own Heart, but your Group isn't responsible for rehabilitating him and if you're going to continue to have a Group you **must** release him, preferably without personality reactions (one thing the control-freak always goes for sooner or later is the personality reaction), even if you feel he sincerely wants to rehabilitate himself. For just one dedicated control-freak can quickly destroy a Heart-Group; remember this, always. And the truth is that he's probably deceiving you and doesn't feel he's reached bottom and is ready for rehab even if he proclaims he'll do *anything* ! (hands clasped in supplication) to recover if you give him just one more chance. **Do Not** give him one more chance! **Not Ever!** One more chance is all this reptile may need to seriously hurt some vulnerable Heart. He must be released, instantly, with no compromise.

"But remember: just because he is not your friend, you don't have to turn him into an enemy, either. The Achievement of a heart that is neutral and unprovokable in these matters is a profound Achievement. Remember that if you must strike some blow in your own defense, that a blow struck from a neutral heart, a heart free of attachment, isn't true violence because it doesn't contribute to the cloud of glamour and illusion which ensnares people into hatred and the lie of separation. In fact, if you strike a blow that is moral and free of attachment and in support of Love, and powered by Love, you've actually helped dissipate a bit of the cloud and thus weakened the institution of slavery a little.

"That vile cloud of glamour and illusion, which is contributed to as much by the supposedly nonviolent as by the openly violent, is the cause of the wars and rapes and other forms of aggression, both physical and psychic, that we see every day. And the news media intensifies this violence by continually masturbating this seething cloud as it helps the cloud create the news in the image of itself. When you watch the news, you're watching this ancient cloud. The people who work in mass media are fundamentally stupid and fundamentally irresponsible as they milk the source of violence for all it's worth so they'll have something to talk about. Perhaps the thing that scares them more than anything else is the possibility that one day they may awaken without anything to talk about!

"This cloud which is so treasured by the news media has been around forever and its nature hasn't changed, thus it can spawn nothing new. Therefore, the news media doesn't report on "news", it reports on ancient destructive energies and events born out of old negative patterns created by those energies. It reports on ancient karma, and doesn't care that since karma can't work itself out in the presence of unconsciousness, that by encouraging people to remain stupid it encourages the long-term perpetuation of human agony by helping the cloud continue to produce the cycles of vengeance that most human karma is made of.

"The modern news media is just a crumbling record of ancient history. Love in its true form, purified of sentiment and attachment, has never been reported by the mass media. Therefore, Love is news! And it's damn good news, but the people in the media don't know how to contact this Supreme Reality or to report on It because they aren't genuinely loving.

"It is only the forgetfulness of those who want to consider themselves human, while paradoxically remaining unaware of their own natures, that causes them to attach a false sense of reality to the cloud worshipped by the news media. The cloud hasn't changed its basic nature in millions of years, and for most of that time most of the people through countless incarnations have been contributors to the cloud and victims of the cloud, though the vileness of the cloud's nature has been intensified in the twentieth century by the worldwide priesthood of the degenerate mass media. They lack the courage to challenge their own preconceptions and the systems they've built on those preconceptions . . . and their structures are completely unreal, so if they did challenge them, the news media as we usually know it would cease to exist! That would be a supreme goodness. The truth is that love is the reality that underlies every illusion the mass media uses to cut itself and the public off from a consciousness of reality. Unless and until a type of media arises that acknowledges this fact of love and seeks to demonstrate it one hundred percent of the time, those who work for the media will continue to break their own hearts with every story they report, until they are so numb with heartbreak they've cut themselves off from their own deepest Intelligence--no wait, this has already happened. They've already gone to hell in a handbasket, and show no signs of wanting to go to rehab. So don't pay any attention to these cloud-masturbating fools. If you do, they'll drag you down with the sorry weight of their own mental illusions and emotional glamours, and no person who wants to locate and restore his or her Heart can afford such a pernicious, unhealthful, unloving, uncompassionate distraction.

"The mass media and the governments and other institutions were created by the cloud to ride herd on the hearts of the masses of humanity, thus closing the planet off from an awareness of the Planetary Heart. So twentieth century humanity is ruled by an unconscious cloud composed of nothing more than glamour and illusion prompting toward vengeance.

Such sadness, and such a waste. In the presence of such sadness, the news anchors won't have to worry about unemployment.

"So this pamphlet is for those who want to recover from the effects of this satan's cloud which the media has turned into a god.

"As time goes on, your Hearts will learn in Beauty and in Love how to protect themselves in every situation, but don't let arrogance or ignorance cause you to feel you've reached this level in your practice too soon--or again, you may get unnecessarily injured.

"Your Hearts learn their lessons apart from words and apart from any technique that can be described. This is a high-level practice which occurs on its own as the student becomes fused with his Highest Aspects.

"And must I tell you that no person who charges for doing Heart Work with you has access to anything more than the surface levels of the Heart? They know nothing, and can know nothing, of the deep, big chambers that structure themselves through vast dimensions of consciousness. Sweet friend, consciousness is not subject to the regulating effect of commerce.

"The facilitator you employ to supposedly help you in your Heart Work may sometimes seem to have depth, but only in comparison to an unregenerate person who has no depth at all. The truth is that people who seek material profit in Heart-Connection are spoiled children playing with the Hearts of others, and sooner or later someone will get hurt in this status-driven scenario, too--probably someone who has more depth to his Heart than the formally recognized and paid "heart-worker". Right livelihood doesn't consist of forming a Heart-Bond with someone, then charging them for the so-called service! Is it not obvious that such an action is driven by the survival concerns of the lower chakras? The Heart must direct the lower chakras, not the other way around.

"People think that status will help insure their physical survival, but if this is true it isn't worth the risk of losing your immortality. The love of status is the root of all evil, and the misuse of money by the infantile is one way to gain status.

"And many spiritually infantile people have advanced degrees and the ability to mouth glitter-encrusted platitudes to lull those people who are not sufficiently vigilant completely to sleep so the metaphysical cutpurse can slip in and manipulate both immediate status-recognition and money to continue to perpetuate that status-recognition from them. Beware! All is not well in the new-age fairyland. The cotton candy at the new-age carnival is made with turds.

"Remember: There's no reward for becoming a Heart-Friend with someone. There's love and bliss, but there's no reward. And if you seek a reward, you forfeit the love and bliss. It's as simple as that."

Well, Jill my sweetheart, this is the text I've written so far for my tract. Since everything I do is to please you and help further your sacred work of Creation, I hope you will see some value in it. If you have any insights, I would be happy to hear them.

Love,
Your Son,
Me

* * *

My sweethearts skipped offstage and Mimi, with her usual exuberance, flung her G-string at some guy in the audience who'd tipped her with a hundred dollar bill. She said he was generous and had paid more than the flimsy garment was worth.

"If that's true, Mimi, do you think he would pay well for my underwear?" I asked hopefully. My darling said nothing, just gazed at me, hands on her hips, and shook her head. Her little beaver was opening, beckoning me to come inside . . . those pussy lips were distended and glistening with love. Everyone in the place was staring at her as she mounted me and gave me a long slow body rub with her own sacred body.

I was about to get Hemingway out so the congregants would have something else to stare at. It looked like a circus trick when Mimi's hot young pussy would slowly ingest Hemingway. But the lady who ran the place, this stripping joint, this place of men with big cigars and adult beverages and credit cards, she came to us and demanded that Mimi get dressed. Party pooptress.

"Little girl, I told you the rules before you got started." She wagged her finger at Mimi. I frowned at her, so she stopped. "No full nudity. That's currently against the law in this town. I know it's idiotic, but they'll close me down if you get caught running around here without a G-string. I saw you throw yours away; if you don't have a spare then put your panties or jeans back on.

"Keep those titties hanging out, though. They may not be big, but they do seem to be the star attraction here tonight. Feel free to work the crowd, but at least wear panties or a G-string or something to cover your snatch. Okay?"

"Okay, Miss Honi."

Honi wasn't a bad sort despite her repressions and her respect for law and disorder. (I've noticed in my travels that past a certain point the more law you have, the more chaotic things seem to get. People can only accept a certain amount of restriction without exploding. Hence, the social unrest and high crime rate of twentieth century America. Repression is against human nature.)

Anyway, I wanted to bed Honi and as I got to know her over the summer that desire came to pass. For I saw through her rather gruff exterior to the heart that lay beneath, and it was a good heart, a heart of gold. I recognized her as a brother soul. Also, her pussy was very sweet.

Her stripping facility, appropriately enough, was called Honi's and it drew great crowds of men who wanted to be spiritually inspired by the Goddess. I suspected that many of them did not even consciously realize why they were there, but I knew and I applauded their spirituality. Semi-conscious spirituality is better than no spirituality at all, I suppose, especially when it is geared toward contact with the feminine. A sweet sexual experience is a spiritual experience.

This stripping facility was much like the totally nude bar where I'd met the beautiful soul who called herself Raven of Amarillo. But the ladies who danced at Honi's told me that many times the totally nude dancers were prostitutes (I had kind of figured this out on my own), whereas most strippers didn't usually "turn tricks". Still, several offered to "turn tricks" for me when they saw Hemingway. Most of them were very nice ladies and Mimi and I became friends with many of them.

So this was a step up for Aphrodite and I was glad to see her take it. So was Freud, whose eyes shone with the wonder of his awakening spirituality. He swallowed and got his courage up that day, and he asked Aphrodite to move in with him. She'd been sleeping with Sue, but when she took Freud's request she just smiled and placed her hand on his cheek and it was done. Freud had taken a step up into greater healing, a place where a primitive psychology could not go. He was being redeemed by Aphrodite, even as she redeemed herself. I knew they would have a long and fascinating journey together and I wished them much happiness. In fact, I wept for them and so did Mimi and Sue. Our family was growing more consolidated.

We were all lovers, except that in those heady days of spring Mimi would allow only me to penetrate her vagina, and Sue would only have serious sex with Mimi or Aphrodite. She'd learned to lie with Freud and me and let us hold her, and that was nice, but the passion of her loins she reserved for other women. One day Mimi delicately suggested that Freud and I become intimate, and we each ran in opposite directions. I spent the night in a motel alone, save for Rosy Palm and her five stepsisters. I made it back home in time for lunch the next day, but Freud was gone for two days. Mimi never made that suggestion again.

Still, it was fun to watch Freud's chocolate tootsie roll absorbed by Aphrodite's golden pinkness. I always had to go out and buy a bag of candy afterward.

Hubert and Tiffany didn't make love again until the middle of the summer, as my mechanical friend had taken my advice and tried to sensitize himself to the moods of Tiffany's soul. But when they finally did mate again Hubert glowed for days afterward. I congratulated him on his restraint and consideration for his gentle lady, and I could feel him simultaneously blush and glow with pride.

There were two more additions to our family that summer. The first came in late June when Mimi announced she was pregnant with child. My heart was made glad by this news, for a child is a blessed event.

"Sonny-Bob, you're the father. I haven't had penetrational sex with anyone else yet, not even Freud. I wanted to do you and Hemingway in all your glory for a while before I began sharing myself in that way with other men. I love you." She hugged me. "I love you."

"I love you, honey. I'm glad we're pregnant. But I'm not concerned about who the father is. To ask a woman who the father of her child is, is considered poor form where I come from."

We went out to dinner that night to celebrate with our friends and the next day I bought Mimi a bottle of prenatal vitamins. All was well with my heart.

Still, there was the nagging problem of the disappearing timeline. It was always in the back of my mind. I had to save this world for my new family, the family that had shown me such warmth despite my ways, for I knew that many of the members of the co-op in which we dwelt considered me unbalanced and wanted to drive me away. They could not understand my advanced ways. They could not know that without me their ass was grass.

After the little dinner party where we announced our pregnancy, Mimi and I found ourselves on the roof of the co-op, gazing at the stars that had waited so long to be reflected in our eyes.

"What are we going to name him, Sonny-Bob?"

"What makes you so sure it's a boy, honey?"

"I just know. He feels like you." She hugged me. "I feel like I'm walking around with you inside me all the time. Like we've got a connection that can never be broken by anything."

My arms were around her and we were holding on to each other like two halves of a wistful smile.

"Honey, I guess we might as well name him Miyamoto, since that was his name."

"What!" Mimi stared up into my face, eyes searching. "Miya-who? What kind of name is that? If you're pulling my leg, I'm going to yank your Hemingway."

"Sweetheart, that was his name. Miyamato Musashi Culpepper, your firstborn, named after the Japanese gentleman who saved me from those Chinese pirates. I told you about that. He fought with two swords at once and was the only swordsman I ever saw who could carry on so. I gave him a bowl of rice and some sake once, and when he found out about my predicament he came and got me out of it. The details are a little too gruesome for a pregnant woman to hear; suffice it to say that he took a reed and made a snorkel of it and swam underwater that night to the enemy vessel. He had a type of sharpened cleat he could put on his hands and feet, a tactic he'd learned from the ninja. Turns out we'd both trained with the ninja in the Iga Mountains, but with different clans. We'd never met before that night when he came to my fire and I fed him.

"Anyway, he used his ninja cleats to climb up the side of that ship and he'd killed three or four before they even noticed he was aboard. Then the cry went up and the fray really began.

" 'Lie down on your face, Sonny-Bob!' I heard him yell, and I was all too happy to comply, as there were heads and limbs and bodies . . . oops, I'm getting into the details pregnant ladies shouldn't hear. 'Scuse me, my love.

"Those pirates must've believed they were under attack by a legion of Tengu, and Musashi helped foster their illusions by cawing like a deranged crow as he swung his swords. And really, he must've had a lot of allies from the spirit world, for in the midst of his flowing swords he gave the impression of being a vast army instead of one man.

"Some pirates survived by jumping overboard, but the rest were slain. Musashi cut my bonds and we stocked up on pirate food and sake, then rowed to shore in a dinghy. Then Musashi showed me some of his wood carvings. It was a very pleasant ending to an overly eventful day.

"I'd always thought it was coincidence that Pa Miyamato shared the name of my Japanese rescuer. I never realized until today that I was--or am--his father. I should have known there's no coincidents in the timeline. Synchronicities, yes, but not coincidents. The timeline seems to know what it's doing, though every now and then it seems to need a little help."

Mimi looked thoughtful. "No coincidents . . . was our meeting a synchronicity?"

"I guess. We've discovered there's a certain genetic vibration handed down from one generation to the next, and this unique frequency may sometimes draw a person back to the home of his ancestors, or in my case the time and place of his ancestors.

"And the archetypes, the gods and goddesses, are probably involved. Maybe Pa Miyamato himself is involved, maybe he drew us together from the spirit world because he wants us as parents. He always was a weird old coot. This would be one of his milder stunts.

"But in the end, we have to admit that when we try to figure out nonordinary occurrences, sometimes the best thing we can come up with is a semi-educated guess. Synchronicity is as good a word as any.

"Anyway, now I know I'm descended from myself. It's a good feeling." I kissed her. "It's a feeling I recommend."

I'd always known, of course, that Pa Miyamato was my direct ancestor. He taught me to shoot, and to kill wild boar with a spear, and he never tired of reminding me I was descended from him. And he never tired of reproducing himself, but now I had the upper hand. Now I was reproducing **him**.

But I'd never paid any attention to the year of his birth, so I'd never known which one of Mimi's kids he was. She'd reproduced lots of times. But that day when Mimi had announced her pregnancy, I'd had Hubert look up my family tree. (All our TITTIES have the histories of every TAC field agent on file, for they never know who they'll be assigned to work with.) My mechanical friend solemnly told me I was descended from Mimi's first child, who was to be born early next year. That settled it, then. I was my own ancestor. Hemingway rides again!

Hubert cleared his throat. "Sonny-Bob, I hate to piss on your parade, but what you're doing is illegal. It's against regulations for you to go back and grandfather yourself."

I patted his hood. "I know, old bean. Thanks for reminding me; that's part of your job. But you know I'm too creative to follow regulations much. To be truthful--and I think you'll agree with me--the TAC's regulations are probably the most primitive thing about our own society. Those regulations are just an outgrowth of the ancient laws and taboos, like the taboo against incest, which everyone in our time knows is ridiculous. You can't tell self-aware souls who they can be intimate with. That's for those souls to decide.

"It's only a small step, then, from recognizing the legitimacy of loving incest to supporting a person's right to father his ancestors. I'm sure the TAC will eventually come around, but in the meantime this'll be our little secret. Flow with it, baby. I'll father who I damn well please. Okay?"

He grunted his assent. He grunted something, anyway, so I went back to Mimi and we went to bed.

Late that night when Mimi was asleep I whispered special instructions to the fetus. "Don't forget to teach me to shoot, or I'll kick your ass. And take me hunting in the mountains of Tennessee. I want to hunt wild boar with a spear. That is all."

As best I recall those instructions had been carried out.

The next day Mimi asked me to marry her.

I gazed at her with love and I couldn't think of anything more appealing than marrying this dear woman. But it was out of the question.

"Sweetie pie, once my mission is over I have to go back to the future, if there's a future to go back to. I can't take you with me; the generals would have a hissey fit and might try to write me out of the timeline. And I can't stay. They'd find me eventually and grab me.

"I love you, Mimi. But though we may be destined for one another, we'll have to find each other again in the future. Maybe you can come back as one of my daughters; come back as somebody else's daughter if you prefer. Just come back, okay? Come back to me in your next incarnation.

"We have Practical Immortality where I'm from, so barring accidents or Acts of Goddess we may be able to spend centuries together. Perhaps millenia.

"Come back to me in the future, hon. Just reincarnate, that's best for now."

She looked solemnly at me. "When did I die?"

"What?" She'd caught me off guard. Still, I had felt a sense of dread from time to time that she might present me with this question. Now I had one of two choices: either lie, or tell the truth.

"You heard me, Sonny-Bob Culpepper. When did I die?"

"Honey, I don't think it's fair--"

"I don't care if it's a fair question or not. I intend to know, and if you won't tell me I'll ask Hubert. I know he'll tell me."

She was right. Hubert would tell her. He was almost as fond of this young lady as I was. But he had no sense of decorum. He couldn't be depended on to lie. I was going to have to have a long conversation with him about this before we went back to the future.

"Mimi, my beloved, you lived to a ripe old age and had fifteen children, most of whom avoided the penitentary. You had many lovers and even worked in Lucille's first temple for a while. I've always been proud of you for that.

"You lived with several men, but claimed none of them as husbands. You always said you had only one husband and would never take another, and that was the Mr. Culpepper who fathered your firstborn . . . oh, dear. I guess we did get married, after all."

I paused for a moment, then cleared my throat uncomfortably as Mimi looked at me with eyes liquid and round, her heart calmly radiating its love, showering me with its blessings. Well, I didn't know of anything I'd ever done to deserve this much love . . .

"And I suppose," Mimi offered, "that I kept the name Culpepper all my life and gave it to all my children, even though you only fathered one of them. I believe that's what I want to do. I *know* that's what I want to do."

"Yes, honey, you know yourself well. That's exactly what you did, or will do, however you want to look at it. And I thank you. I am honored."

"Well, all of that's nice to know," Mimi finally said. *"But when did I die? And how?"*

"First tell me why you want to know, honey," I said gently.

"Because--" her eyes welled with tears, "I--I want to be with you in the future. As *me*, not as someone else. I love you and I want to be with you just as we are now. I'm not afraid to die, that's a piece of cake, anyone can do it. I know I've done it before, lots of times, just as you have. But I think we deserve a break this time, don't you? If I die we might find each other when I'm born again, but there's no guarantee. Sonny-Bob, there's got to come a time when we can be together *as us*, no pretenses and no interference from the timeline. We've served the timeline well, you and I, for millenia. I'm tired and I want to rest. I want to rest with you." Somewhere in there her eyes had grown old, they were ancient. She came to me and put her arms around me. "Honey, I want so much to be with you . . . forever. I want us to be together always. And if you tell me how I died I might be able to avoid it and live until Practical Immortality is developed. When did you say they perfected it? 2085? That's good. If I lived I'd be one hundred sixteen then. You said a number of people were living to the age of one hundred twenty, and a few were older, by the middle of the next century. Advances in medical technology, lifestyle factors, antioxidants. Herbs.

So I might survive until I can get treated by Practical Immortality, depending on whether or not I can avoid whatever killed me.

"Please darling . . . when and how did I die?"

Well, she had to have the truth. Maybe I owed it to her for some reason, or maybe the timeline owed it to her. I don't know. But I couldn't refuse her.

"I'll tell you when you're going to die, Mimi, and how." I shifted uncomfortably. "You went to the moon on an AARP tour in 2069 to celebrate your hundredth birthday. You took your lover with you, a twenty year old musician, and the AARP didn't protest. In fact, this was an AARP polyfidelity tour, so most of your fellow retirees probably had more than one spouse or lover with them. Your sexual appetite likely would have been considered very moderate by the rest of those old codgers. Old people eventually loosened up thanks to a drug called Viagra, which made it possible for even the elderly to rut. It was in their best interests to loosen up.

"You'd chosen a young buck as a partner, you said, because your previous lover, who also happens to be the fetus you're carrying right now, was too old for you. That was the first time Pa Miyamato tried to join the French Foreign Legion, but they said he was too old, too. I'm sure these rejections did nothing for his self-esteem. Years later, though, once he'd been rejuvenated by Practical Immortality, the Foreign Legion was happy to accept him and he went off to prove his manhood by fighting fundamentalist terrorists on Mars. After his hitch was up, he stayed on Mars and started a Tibetan Buddhist monastery. He--"

"Sonny-Bob, we were talking about me," Mimi reminded me gently.

"Oh. So we were. Well, you died--will die, I mean--on the moon. There's going to be a major resort town built up there. It's called Crystal City and that's where you and your young lover went. You wanted to make love in the gardens under the great dome of Crystal City, I guess. That's why everyone in my time goes there. The souvenir shops aren't worth a damn, but the fucking's great. You can do all sorts of fine things in limited gravity.

"On the third day of the tour there was a moonquake and the section of the Crystal City dome that shielded the AARP people shattered. Everyone in that section was killed instantly. No survivors."

A tear trickled down my cheek. "And no more Mimi, the hottest old fox in the galaxy." I hugged her and hugged her, but she was strangely calm.

"That's all I wanted to know, Sonny-Bob," she finally said.

I figited. "Well, what're you going to do about it, Mimi?"

"I'm inclined to live, Sonny-Bob. I think I'll avoid that trip."

"Hell no, sweetheart! If the generals find out I've interfered with history, they may decide to undo it. They may decide to undo me, or--Goddess forbid--undo you.

"Mimi, if our relationship is going to work, you have to die on schedule. You **have** to, darling."

"What are the chances those generals of yours would discover us? And that Tibetan--how does he factor into all this?"

I considered worriedly. If she didn't die on schedule she could screw up everything, even Pa Miyamato. "Honey, those generals aren't known for their gratitude. If I can convince them I actually saved the timeline, assuming I do, they might cut me a little slack if they discover a few inconsistencies in history due to my presence. But prolonging your life is a major thing, and they'd have to cut me a lot more slack than I think they'd be inclined to.

"As for the Tibetan . . ." I remembered something he'd said to me the very day I learned about the timewave, "I think we'd be safe with him . . . maybe. But the generals, well, they're politically correct like peacetime generals everywhere. If the public could be convinced they owe their existence to me, the generals would respond to that. But I don't yet see how I can convince **anyone**; the only evidence will be the dreams.

"I think we're up shit creek, honey. I really do."

Mimi sighed. "Well, Sonny-Bob, if you think it's best I may go on that tour and die. I can reincarnate, like you said. But it isn't fair. We've been through so much together for the sake of this timeline throughout all our lives--we deserve a break, one note of grace from this implacable timeline! IT ISN'T FAIR!"

She fell into my arms sobbing then, and I held her and wept with her. She was right, the timeline had screwed its most loyal servants again and again. This shit really had to cease. It **had** to. It was time for the timeline to sound a note of gratitude. We didn't want any special reward, all we wanted was to be allowed to live our lives. Our **Life**, for Mimi and I had always been one Life.

The timeline must learn to behave in a graceful way, I thought. *It must!*

We held each other for a long time then, unsure as to whether the timeline had heard us, not knowing if it even cared. It always seemed like such a selfish phenomenon: "Save me, Sonny-Bob! No, I won't intervene when you're burned at the stake, but save me anyway!" And never a word of encouragement or gratitude from this phenomenon in which we lived and moved and had our being.

"Bear my children, Mimi. You'll lose Sonny-Bob again and again, but do as I say, there's a good girl . . ."

We held each other for a long time and we wept bitterly.

And so I lay in bed this fine September morn contemplating these events of the last few months. I felt a quizzical smile alter my features as I thought of the final addition to our family . . .

Then the woman I was with turned and moaned and delighted me with her presence, and I forgot all about that last addition for the moment and concentrated on her. She was one of our friends, not a family member, but certainly not a stranger. We'd known each other from the moment we met. Mimi, Freud, Sue, Aphrodite and I were all comfortable with her instantly, and she with us. Her name was Joanna and she was a great fat huge lady whose obesity matched my own. Her tits were huge, too, a little bigger than mine, and I savored them as I savored every centimenter of the lovely Joanna. I felt almost as though I were making love to a physical twin when I was with her, though I felt that of the two of us she was the most beautiful sibling. I knew that any sensible lady would be impressed by my own beauty, yet there were so many women whose beauty inspired me so much I felt that my beauty must fade in comparison to theirs, and Joanna was one of these beautiful ones.

The pink tongue licking the lips that had sucked me the night before gave Hemingway a reason to live. He arose from his somnolence and waited like an ancient dragon for his lover to recognize him and devour him with passion. For he breathed not fire, but that nourishing liquid supplement which gives the woman who swallows strength throughout the day. The supplement is high in calories and trace minerals.

As I slobbered on her lovely breast, waiting for the full return of her awareness, I thought of how we'd met. Joanna was a stripper, perhaps the grandest fat stripper in all the world. She told me that in this primitive society fat women were persecuted and made to feel ashamed of themselves, and that the only way she'd found to deal with this shame was by facing her body head-on and taking her clothes off in front of legions of men and lesbians. She tried to reclaim her power with the attitude: "Here I am! Either accept me as I am, or fuck off!"

As she'd gotten more comfortable with dancing she began to radiate tons of charisma, for her internal self was making its way to the surface. She glowed as she strutted and jiggled her way into self-acceptance and a good income.

"Sonny-Bob, I don't know where you're from," she once said to me, "but you seem to think all women are beautiful if you can see some light in their eyes. That's not usually the way it is on this earth, so I guess you're from another planet. I was tormented all my life for being fat, and when I was younger nobody ever looked for any life or light in my eyes. I've been fat since I was a little girl, couldn't help it. Fat is my nature. My nature is the nature of Fat.

"But when I finally gave up on the dieting and began to release the shame and self-hatred that a perfectionistic society tried to saddle me with, and then began dancing, I did feel more light in myself. Oh, not at first, at first I was just scared and still ashamed. But gradually, as I got used to standing nude before the world, I grew in confidence and eventually I began to feel lighter inside, though my external fat did not diminish. I began to see some light in my own eyes and felt the desire in my heart to share it, and the more I focussed on sharing it the lighter I became. I felt the light and love flowing out from my heart and body. Everyone else noticed, too, which is why I'm now one of the best paid women in Texas. I make more than most so-called professional businesswomen, and more than a lot of male corporate executives. But it would never have happened if I hadn't begun accepting myself and allowing my inner self to shine through my plump and sexy body. Now I love me.

"I love me, Sonny-Bob."

I had kissed her then, slowly and well, doing everything I could to share myself with her and to soak up some portion of the incredible wisdom I felt within her. Here was another woman who could teach me many things.

I was happy that Aphrodite had brought us to a knowledge of this stripping facility. It was the closest thing to a temple I'd experienced in primitive America. Maybe in some ways these cathedrals of strutting flesh had served as the seeds of the new spirituality to come. I knew that Lucille The Prophetess had eventually gone to work in such a facility, after she'd gotten her PhD.

I shivered and glowed in the presence of some of these stripper ladies. It really was religious, in fact, it really was spiritual, at times. I knew that the stripper ladies were among the best classes of ladies in this class-ridden society.

There were only a few things I didn't like about this primitive church, one of which was the music. It was usually loud and raucous, as opposed to the softer tones heard in a mature temple. Also, the only smoke came from tobacco. There was no purifying breath of incense. I spoke to Honi about this, and dear lady that she was she arranged for a stick of incense to be placed on my table whenever I came in. Whenever the tobacco smoke became too thick, I simply held my nose over the incense for a few minutes to purify my nostrils. Then I was okay.

Finally, I was puzzled about the fact that this church of heart and flesh had no windows. But it didn't take me long to figure out the reason for that. I didn't even have to ask Honi to help me understand. For I had grown familiar with the mechanisms of the repressives and their hysterical grasping to keep other people from enjoying themselves and being genuinely human. Sexuality made them uncomfortable. So they would insist that stripping facilities could have no windows, as they didn't want to take a chance on "accidentally" seeing some flesh. The repressives liked to pretend that their God had arranged nature to produce one woman for every man, and that if someone touched or observed or desired any other partner, their God would send them to hell, unless they managed to repent and confess in time. With primitive paranoid delusions like this to guide them, they would of course seek to corden off a church of love and restrict such churches to certain areas of the community that the repressives believed were inhabited only by lower class citizens. Also, they had to have a place for their devil to visit to keep him from visiting their communities. This is what they liked to pretend, anyway. Fundies are always good at make-believe, because that is the only way they can justify their bizarre and insensitive cosmology. That is the only way they can justify their desire for vengeance upon the body and spirit of my Goddess.

Anyhow, windows and open doors would have made it easier for the energy to circulate in this goddess facility and would have helped us all stay refreshed. Instead, the energy sometimes grew a little stagnant. These fine damsels should have had a glass house to dance in, in fact, so all the young people of the community would have an example of living religion to aspire to. Instead, the church sometimes got a little gloomy, to tell you the truth. No light from outside was allowed. Naturally, this is what the repressives wanted. Their churches are full of gloom and doom and repression and perversion, and that is what they wanted to force off on these primitive churches of the Goddess, as well. They preferred restriction and doom to love, and to the extent they could share their negative values through the use of force, they would. They had a majority in the legislature.

To the extent that perversion existed in the stripping facility, it was caused by the heartless repressives and their attempts to spread shame. Not once in the entire history of the earth has anyone managed to perform an act of positive creation while wallowing in the repressives' pool of shame. Not once. Overall, this stripper church was a pleasant place to worship, but to the extent that shame surfaced in dancers or patrons, the creativity of that moment was diminished for us all. The repressives spread shame because they lacked the courage to walk through the valley of the shadow of death, the valley of their own psyches, and clean it out. They were ashamed of themselves, ashamed of being human. They spread shame because they were afraid to take this first great step in the direction of manifesting the love of their hearts. Repression is cowardice.

The Christian churches sported fancy windows, but if the ladies of my Goddess had tried to install similar windows the Christians would have thrown bricks through them and used their law enforcement officers to close down the Goddess church, or at least to make them board up their windows. It's beyond bizarre that any society could take seriously a religion that has a death wish for the planet and whose primary symbol is a cross-beamed torture device and a dead man. Jesus himself would not have appreciated the Christians' appropriation of his image and twisting it to their own perverse and repressive designs. The crucifixion was just one initiation in a lifetime of initiations for this man, but it's the one the Christians are pathologically addicted to. They don't celebrate his love, for they don't understand his love. They've never felt it. All they have is sentiment and they mistake that floppy chakra emotionalism for the divine force of love.

It is a miracle of my Goddess--and of President Reagan, too--that this death oriented culture eventually turned from its twisted ways and embraced life and finally accepted its own humanity. It finally grew compassionate towards itself and threw away its cross-beamed torture devices. Except for the obligatory atavists, of course. The atavists would cling to their cross until it rotted away and they had nothing to cling to. Maybe then they would allow themselves to be buoyed up by love . . . or not. Atavists are insane.

Anyway, in this strange twentieth century, the gods of death and agony ruled the mass consciousness. So the death oriented religion was glorified, and every effort was made to abort the birth of the religion of love and life. You could legally stand outside a Christian church and look in through the windows and perceive their death oriented practices (and they might run outside and grab you and make you a part of their congregation if you weren't careful, since their deathgod would send them to hell if they didn't make every effort to proselytize), but those who wanted to practice a religion of life were not allowed to do so in a manner that might be seen by anyone outside their circle. This is another way the Christians tried to maintain their cultural monopoly. They had to keep my beautiful goddess women from being seen, because they were so much more attractive than a crucified dead man that any sane person would choose the stripper church over the Christian church. So my stripper friends suffered and were stigmatized. They represented the vital root of the life force of nature, and the insane Christians and members of other repressive religions were always taking an axe to this root and trying to separate themselves from it, and to eliminate it from society. Fortunately, they failed. The root of sexuality, and therefore of the life force, is alive and well in my time.

And when this life force is joined to the genuine love force of the human heart, a complete spiritual existence is experienced. The love radiates through the sexuality. The sexuality is the servant, yet also the co-creator, of the love. The human is balanced, whole and complete. He radiates his Self in an integrated way and becomes a force for healing. He is love incarnate.

Oh, there was one other thing I really liked about the temple of the strippers and that is the fact that there were no wanted posters of me on the wall. Not yet, anyway. I avoided all state, federal and local government facilities because they all had wanted posters of me and Santa Claus. I did everything I could to put to rest Mimi's fears. I wanted her heart to be calm.

And really, with my increased obesity, I didn't look that much like my old self . . . except for the eyes. Yes, my eyes were calmer and deeper now with the increased contentment of being reunited with Mimi, my love of eternity, but the insane element was still there, too. I knew if I ever found myself in a combat situation again that insane element would leap out upon my enemies. But for now it was well behaved.

Anyhow, I went to church at least a couple of times a week in this stripper facility. True, there often were negative vibrations here which I endeavored to send away with my own radiations (I noticed a few of the more aware strippers would do the same thing), but the negative aspects of this place were nothing like the horrible encrusted and armored negativity of that place of pornography where I'd seen my beloved sister Aphrodite abused in body and spirit. No charisma of love had been in that place at all.

But in the stripper church some of the women, like Aphrodite, let their spirits flow freely and I saw at once that the freer a woman was, the more she allowed herself to glow out of a sense of her own internal radiations, the more money she made. Positive, loving, healing energy was financially rewarded here. It didn't matter much, if any, what a woman looked like in this church. Some of those who appeared to be more structurally sound by the standards of the times actually made less money than the others, if the structurally sound woman didn't glow much. Glowing made all the difference and it was the glowing, more than any other single thing, more than tits and slits and asses combined, that brought the women money. Men love women who glow; they are the ones who set our hearts on fire and inspire us to worship. We will pay them to help us worship. We need their glowing help.

As for myself, the women frequently would sit with me and offer me lap dances without payment of any kind. I did not know how this could be, for they charged everyone else. Several men commented on the matter, for they couldn't figure it out, either. In the end, I decided it was probably a matter of my being able to see their full splendor, both in their hearts and externally, and somehow they knew I could see them and that I truly appreciated them and their contribution to my spiritual growth. I loved them and if I could have hugged every one of them at once I would have.

Aphrodite wanted to make a difference in the world and bring her loving heart to all humanity. So in addition to her dancing, she had enrolled at the great University of Texas at Austin, that place of tall structures which was a fitting place, I suppose, for the Tall Healer Of The World to study.

She was studying primitive journalistic devices. She was "majoring", whatever that meant, in Radio, Television and Film. She wanted to find a way to make lovingly explicit films, truly erotic films, since in genuine erotica love and affection are always present. We accepted this principle as a matter of course in my time, but here it hadn't been demonstrated yet. Well, if anyone could demonstrate this principle, my beloved Aphrodite could.

And so this morning I lay abed with Joanna, breathing her essence and appreciating her soul and the great beautiful mounds of her flesh. And letting her teach me, for women have always been my teachers. Other than learning to handle firearms and to hunt boar with a spear I never learned much of value from men. I didn't denigrate men; on the contrary, I appreciated their contributions to the world throughout the timeline. I didn't discriminate against them except in the sexual arena . . . I twitched as I thought of the most recent addition to our family . . .

It occurred on the Fourth of July, that day of liberty still celebrated in my own time. Mimi and I had gone onto the roof of the co-op to make love, knowing that the people in the neighboring buildings would probably be celebrating the Fourth by watching our passion unfold through telescopes and binoculars, which is how so many of them spent their lunch breaks. In this one regard Mimi was a bit of a show-off, and I'd never minded making love in public or anywhere else as long as there were no tax collectors or Marines about.

Mimi wore a little flimsy sun dress, her copper Aztec shoulders and the calves of her legs beckoning me to imagine what lay beneath the light fabric. Yes, I already knew as a result of my own experiments, but scientific knowledge is of little value in a mystery such as this, the mystery of my Mimi.

Her nipples were rigid, pushing against the cool fabric as I surveyed her. She lifted the hem of her garment, then in a quick flicking motion she flashed me with the pubes of her womanhood, that gentle pink altar where I was one with the creative force of the universe. I was her altar boy, and I knelt before her in prayer.

My heart was glowing and Hemingway expanding as she drew my face into her. There was nothing between my lips and her pussy lips except the thin fabric of her frock. I breathed on her through the fabric, I kissed her gentle pussy through the fabric of my desire. And the fabric of our separateness began to dissolve as we became the one Life which we'd always been.

She lifted her garment above her head and tossed it to the winds and stood there naked, the living embodiment of all my desires and all my love, and I wept in gratitude to the Goddess for the forgiveness she'd shown me and for bringing us together once more.

I knelt before her. I would never rise taller than she.

"Sonny-Bob, sweetheart," Mimi said softly. "Take off your clothes and let me lick your cock."

I obeyed.

And in the glare of a thousand telescopes from the neighboring buildings I kissed her belly, then lay down upon the mat we used for these rooftop sessions, the flying carpet of love that took our winged hearts on a journey through the cosmos more profound than any advanced technology could ever offer. Technology had its limitations, but Mimi and I could embrace the whole universe and hold it close to our hearts between us.

The television news helicopter flew over, as it so often did, filming our love. But these were pictures that never made it onto the nightly news. I wonder what they did with the footage they shot of us.

Mimi was licking my cock and making it her own, standing upon the step ladder we kept upon the roof for this purpose. Her lips and nails were red, and her tongue was that perfect pink that turns a man's rod to hardness just by the sight of it. She licked Hemingway, and I groaned in the agony of my pleasure. Her nipple ring glinted at me brazenly, and I knew that if anything had ever been created that was better than WOMAN it must exist in another universe, for I had never seen it and my instrument had never registered its presence. I soaked up the essence of WOMAN and I groaned in my pleasure. I writhed in my pleasure.

Mimi's hands were on the top of Hemingway's head. She'd poured a flavored massage oil upon the great head of my love and was massaging it into him with both hands. I watched her and played with my own nipples, for I couldn't reach hers.

She kissed my cock, then her mouth was all over him, licking and kissing to show her allegiance to the rod of impregnation. She held him in her arms as she licked and kissed the huge cock of my desire for her.

I watched her pussy as best I could, 'way up there on that ladder, and I fancied I could see it glisten and drip with love for my pole.

The passion that drove me made me buck and roar and I sounded like a hurricane screaming its way onto the shores of creation. My eyes were closed, darkness enveloped me in an agony of love as I bucked and screamed . . .

New sensations then, and I knew what had happened, and somehow through the roaring darkness I managed to focus my eyes and look up at Mimi and for a second that seemed to stretch into half of eternity I saw she'd mounted Hemingway, and he'd shoved the great lovehead into her as her own sweet cunt sought to swallow him up.

She hung there on him, riding him, riding him, and as darkness closed in on me again I knew Pa Miyamato must be having a rough ride of it. Well, the experience would serve as a character builder for him. He'd learn fortitude, tenacity and endurance.

Her pussy sank down over the collar of my cock, and her pussy muscles, which had grown strong and supple from our lovemaking, gripped and relaxed, gripped and relaxed. She could work her way up and down my cock just by using her pussy muscles.

Her pussy gripped and climbed its way up and down my lovehead, enveloping me in spasm after spasm, wave after wave, of divine epilepsy as I thrashed about on that mat. I felt the flood of love building, the levee was about to give way . . .

I screamed as every ounce of selfhood spurted out of me and into Mimi's warm chalice. I filled her grail cup with the spurting essence of my sword, I pumped it into her and she took it all, she took all of me . . .

Then several minutes of smaller spurtings, for it took a long time to drain all the come from me. I was endowed with meat and with drink, and for those minutes of shooting my come I could only scream in the fierce joy of my loss, for I'd gone back to the beginnings of consciousness . . . then there was nothing . . . then I was a falling star, floating gently to the earth.

I felt arms around me and lips upon my ear, and as vision resolved itself once more into the universe of discernable objects I saw where I was, and I saw the glint on the lenses of a thousand telescopes and I turned my head and I was in Mimi's arms, for she had come unto me to comfort me. She'd brought me out of the fierce primordial rage of creation, she had re-created me and purified me with her love. To the extent that I could reflect her love I would know my own true nature. I was not surprised to find myself weeping.

And so we lay in one another's arms for awhile.

Then Mimi said, "My turn, lover."

We scooted the mat over to the wall whose door opened onto the stairwell. The creamy leavings of my love were all over the roof, including the mat. Mimi grabbed the hose and washed the mat down (with water, this time) and then we were ready. I lay down and Mimi straddled my face. "Let us pray," she giggled, for she had adopted my religious ways.

I stroked the creamy brownness of her thighs as she sat enthroned upon me, for she was truly my queen. I didn't know what I'd done to deserve her, but I gushed with joy at the privilege. I thought of the several wives I'd had in the two polyfidelity-style marriages I'd been a spouse in and all of them together, as wise and wonderful as they were, couldn't bring me to the point of self-experiencing and of love the way this one little Aztec goddess could. I was so proud of her, and so happy to be able to father my ancestors through her.

I toyed with her clit for a bit, then reached up and lightly brushed her nipples. She was already moist and glistening and didn't need much warming up, but I so enjoyed touching her.

Something wet fell on my nose and I knew she was ready. I kissed her pussy, whispering apologies for the previous intrusion to Pa Miyamato, then I spread her pussy lips and licked her, and already she was tightening and releasing in a spasm. "Hold on, Pa," I advised.

I kissed her pussy thickly and with vigor, then elevated her a little by pushing up on her inner thighs as she braced with her hands against the wall. "Let your pussy drip on me, sweetie." I scooted beneath that glittering jewel of pink candy and opened my mouth, opened it wide. "Drip on me, baby. Drip on me."

One of her hands left the wall and began massaging her clit, and my beautiful fourteen year old ancestress began to moan. She grunted and she groaned as she worked her swollen little clit.

I was ecstatic and Hemingway was turgid with love again. I groaned, the juice of creation now dripping freely into my mouth. She reached down and smeared it across my face and I sucked her fingers clean of it.

Hemingway had almost had enough; he was about to explode again as my junior ancestress began to moan in earnest. Suddenly she bucked and screamed, her hot young body thrashing wildly above me; she ground her pussy into my face and the sparse hairs lodged in my teeth. She screamed again and bucked some more, and I could barely breathe but didn't care. I was swollen with lust and ready to plunge myself back into her at her convenience. My face glistened with the liquid evidence of her love.

She bucked a little more, then wound down to a few shudders. She moaned in blissful agony, and what seemed to be a whole bucket of come gushed into my mouth, then ran down the sides of my face and into my ears. And then it slacked off, and there was a long and drawn-out sigh, and she was relieved at last, relieved of the fourteen years of repression she'd had thrust upon her by a perverse and unloving society.

She'd never had this much relief before. I'd nearly drowned in it. She'd finally turned it loose, turned it all loose. All the fears and repressions and perversions of a devient society had broken loose from her physical and emotional bodies and been washed away by the liquid zeal of love that cleanses and makes whole that which was fractured.

It wasn't just a bucket of come, it was a bucket of freedom. And of self-love, and of the reclamation of her power as a woman. She was a woman.

She was weeping, weeping with relief at losing the agony of her taboo. *I'll bet no one's ever pleasured their remote ancestress like this,* I thought.

She'd bucked so wildly I'd lost my grip on her inner thighs and that pink jewel of her womanhood lay barely to the side of my lips as she straddled me. I shifted my head slightly and kissed her there, letting my little ancestress know how much I loved her. She was still weeping and sighing. "Thank you, sweetheart," she said through her tears. "You can't imagine what a relief this is. I was afraid I'd have to live with some of those repressions and perversions. But now I've released them. You've helped me purify and connect all aspects of myself and I thank you, dear. I thank you."

I could have told her what she was, and that she probably would've found her way to freedom with or without me, but I'd figured it would be best if she figured it out for herself. The old breed of human lacked the strength, dedication and love to purify their shadows of repression and perversion and to integrate their shadows with the Light of their own souls. They didn't even think or feel in these terms, they had absolutely no idea of their own possibilities. They had the brains and they had the chakras. But their motives were not pure and their dedication to knowing and experiencing and redeeming themselves was non-existent. They lacked courage. That's why a new breed of human was necessary and that is why a new breed of human had come. Mimi wasn't afraid of her own shadow. She was one of the first of the new breed.

Yes, I could have told her these things, but with my tongue pressed flat by her resting pussy I couldn't say a word. I just reached up and stroked her belly to let her know I understood. To let her know I loved her more than any other relative I'd ever fucked.

Well, I'd hoped that Hemingway would be able to take the plunge again, but clearly that would not be the case. Mimi's pussy was tired and satisfied, her whole body was tired and satisfied. Hemingway could wait . . .

Then I felt an eager tongue sliding along Hemingway's shaft, and I knew that someone had come to deliver me. While my love rested on my face, her hands still braced upon the wall, some other cooperative female had appeared. She must have been watching us, getting hot, getting hot; maybe fingering herself. She knew I'd done a grand job on my little ancestress and she was rewarding me in kind.

Hemingway had been on the verge of spurting his essence everywhere while my loved one hunched my face, and with the presence of this unexpected tongue he began to throb strongly again. He rose up like a giant mule, glad and stubborn, braying his name to the fleecy clouds. "I Am Hemingway! There Is A Goddess!"

Then I heard a familiar sound. A familiar . . . meow? Meow! I yelped and pushed Mimi off my face, and when I propped myself up that damned cat was licking Hemingway. A cat giving me a blowjob! Hell, no! Stop that shit, cat!

I heard Mimi gasp as she turned and saw the cat; I gave an anguished yell as I reached down and swatted the hell out of the beast, intending to send it away. But this only made it mad.

The devient cat really latched onto me then, biting into Hemingway and scraping him with her claws. Hemingway flopped around in terror and pain, taking that cat on a mad arc back and forth between my legs. Mimi ran down and after numerous tries finally caught the swinging cat as I screamed in rage and pain, concerned only for the safety of my Hemingway. And finally Mimi pried the cat loose, and it licked its chops, as a limp and defeated Hemingway streamed blood from the bite marks and scratches. I'd have to get my medical nanos. When Roger Bacon had joked about Hemingway getting cut by a sharp tooth, I'm sure he wasn't thinking of a cat's tooth. But nanos will heal wounds caused by any kind of tooth.

"Gimmie that cat!" I snarled, jumping to my feet, but Mimi set the violent beast down and it scampered away. "I'm going to get my gun, honey, and turn that animal into a smoking patch of singed fur."

I was thinking of my pocket pistol, but then remembered the suppository gun and my thumb went through that looped cord as I smiled in vengeful satisfaction. I didn't believe in vengeance, but just this once . . . hell, I could take a leaf from the Christians' book and repent later. I started jerking on the cord.

Then Mimi placed herself in front of me and looked into my eyes, and my heart melted. Her gaze would melt any heart, even the heart of a man with a bleeding penis. "Sonny-Bob, thank you for what you did for me today. No one's ever loved me the way you have. But now I have to ask you to do one more thing: let the cat live. It doesn't know any better and it's a favorite with some of the co-opers. Let it live . . . please?"

I gruffly stood my ground for a minute, then nodded assent. I could arrange for the cat to meet with an "accident" some other day.

"Let me clean you up and bandage Hemingway, sweetheart. Then you can use some nanos and by tomorrow he'll be good as new."

Actually, he would be good as new in less than an hour. Those nanos worked fast. I was going to do Mimi as soon as possible after Hemingway was healed, probably do her in doggy style. That would make me forget all about cats.

When we got back to our room I was shocked to see Sue sitting on the edge of her bed cuddling that cat. Freud stood across the room, a silly grin on his face.

Sue looked up. "Something scared this poor dear half to death, Mimi. Sonny-Bob, I know you don't like cats, but this one needs our help. It's in a state of shock."

The cat turned slitted yellow eyes on me and bared its teeth. "Sue," my voice was shaking, "that cat bit my dick. I'm going to kill it."

Freud dropped to the floor laughing and gasping for breath.

"You can't kill it, Sonny-Bob! It's just a dumb animal--no, put that gun down!" Sue was trying to shield the cat from me. "Put it down!"

Once again Mimi intervened and once again the cat's life was saved.

That cat owed her. Then over the next few weeks it established a bond with Sue in an effort to get to me. I hated the thing.

Now I couldn't kill it without causing emotional distress to Sue, and if Sue's emotions were damaged Mimi would be upon me for purposes other than fornication. Unpleasant purposes. I sighed. The timeline had screwed me again. But the worst was yet to come.

Mimi had sided with me when I'd positively declared the cat would die if it slept in our room at night, for I'd never be able to sleep with that thing on the loose looking for Hemingway. But she and Sue both started letting the beast in at all hours of the day. I had to adjust. I had to adapt.

But it was hard to adapt when I found out the truth about this cat . . .

One day after lunch I walked in and there was that big bushy cat, as usual, purring away on Sue's lap. "Look, Sonny-Bob!" Sue said happily. "It's a boy!" And she pulled back the thick fur that covered the cat's private parts. I groaned and nearly threw up. Two huge balls hung in a scrotum. That cat had never been a "she". It had always been a "he".

I did throw up. My dick had been bitten by a fag cat.

Sue named the cat Tennessee, after some playwright she was fond of, and even though the cat was queer I did finally manage to adapt. Occasionally I even petted the thing, but not often. No, not often. At least, not at first.

And so this cat with unmatched cunning had managed to insinuate itself into our little clan. It had become the seventh member of our family.

I'd quit reviewing the summer's events in my mind and begun enthusiastically kneading Joanna's mounds and mounds of flesh, trying to get lost in her, trying to unify myself through her. The previous night the rest of the gang had dragged Mimi's mattress to the floor, then added Freud and Aphrodite's mattress, to create a brand new playing field. They all sported together in the morning light.

Then a knock came on the door, so I rolled off Joanna and answered it. The woman who stood there gasped when she saw Hemingway, and her nipples shot out so suddenly that a button flew off her blouse. I caught it and handed it back to her.

Lieutenant Sharon Tomkins stepped into the room. "Looks like you guys are having an orgy. Mind if I join in?"

CHAPTER TWENTY-EIGHT

There was an awkward silence. No one who wasn't a direct family member was supposed to know that I was a secret agent who traveled through time. Joanna did not know, nor could she find out. If too many people got wind of me disaster could strike.

"If this is an inconvenient time . . ."

"No, Sharon, not at all. Here, sit down." I shoved a chair under her as Mimi and the others scampered around putting on panties and things.

Joanna was watching us. "I can tell I'm the source of the awkwardeness here, so I'd better go. But I need a shower first. I smell funny."

I told her she smelled great and placed my nose against her private parts to prove it. But she was still insecure about her odor the way some women are. They do not realize that the sweetest, earthiest, most profound fragrances in nature emanate from them. So she showered and left. As she headed out the door I slapped her rump, still wishing mightily that my face was buried in it.

She looked over her shoulder and smiled a smile full of light and character. "She you later, Sonny-Bob. See y'all." She walked with sensuous obese grace down the hallway, and I wished Sharon hadn't come quite so soon.

I sighed and shut the door. "Now we can talk. Sharon, this is my family. You can tell them anything that's meant for my ears." They all said their howdys.

Sharon smiled. "Well, I guess you're wondering how I found you, Sonny-Bob."

"Not really."

"It was easy, honey. One of our agents works undercover with the local media. They think he's just a dope smoking hippie cameraman, but his real job is to gather intel on the twentieth century and pass it along to us. He was hanging out of a helicopter smoking a marijuana cigarette and shooting a Fourth of July parade when he saw a young woman mounted on a huge pole on a rooftop." She jerked a finger skyward.

"This rooftop. I recognized Mimi when he showed me the footage. What she could have been doing on that pole I had no idea until just now when I saw THAT." She pointed to Hemingway. He twitched in acknowledgement of her awe.

"Anyhow, I figured you'd be wherever Mimi was. I could tell you two belong together in a way I haven't seen before. Your two hearts are genuinely one heart. Somehow it almost seems as if each of you could melt into the other. Like right now."

Mimi took her place alongside me and squeezed my hand. Love is better than lust. Yes, I still slipped into lust sometimes, but with Mimi I was usually in love. Right now my heart glowed brightly. Our heart glowed brightly.

"So I'm here," Sharon continued. "I've got some intel for you, Sonny-Bob. Do you know a field agent named Olaf Jenkins?"

"Ten-four, Sharon. Good man. He's never bothered me."

"Well, he's just back from 1945. Popped in yesterday. He'd been cut nearly in two with a phase musket, but his TITTY yanked him back inside with its robotic arm and jabbed multiple nano injectors and glucose injectors into him, then beat it for our location. His TITTY's named Conrad, you may know him, good vehicle. Anyhoo, Conrad said he didn't feel safe in going to a mid-twentieth century TAC office, so he went forward as close as he dared to the start of the timewave. You know, the nuclear war. You do remember the nuclear war, don't you? I can see you've been busy . . ."

"Yes, Sharon, I remember the nuclear war," I said stiffly. "Please proceed."

"Okay. Conrad had turned into a conspiracy nut; he felt the whole TAC had been infiltrated by terrorists. After he spilled his story he started hallucinating. At first we believed it was stress, but then we found someone had slipped him a nano virus. Before we could produce a virus to counteract it he was gone. Dead."

"Okay, Sharon," I tapped my foot impatiently. "What about Olaf Jenkins? What's he got to say about all this? Does he believe there's a conspiracy?"

"Sonny-Bob," Sharon said quietly, "Olaf Jenkins was part of the conspiracy." I said nothing, so she continued. "He confessed. He had a change of heart when Captain Melinda McCoy showed up and pulled a gun on him. She told him about the effect his and his co-conspirators' treason had on the timeline. He said he and Conrad had decided to help Captain McCoy capture the other two conspirators. There was a gun battle and Captain McCoy was disintegrated by an energy beam, probably from a phase musket. Olaf Jenkins was hit by a phase musket set to fire a dismemberment beam and was nearly cut in two, as I've already told you. He got off several shots before he was wounded, but doesn't think he hit either of the bad guys. But they nearly iced his cake. If Conrad had been even a couple seconds slower on the nanos, Jenkins wouldn't have made it. That's how close it was."

Freud and the others were round-eyed with interest, almost as though they'd never sat in on a briefing before. I heard a "meow!" from outside the door, but for once nobody paid any attention to Tennessee. That cat would have to wait this one out.

I crossed my arms. "I want to talk to Olaf Jenkins."

"Can't, Sonny-Bob. He's dead."

"What? You just said Conrad got the nanos into him in time."

"Yes, except for some soreness he'd recovered from the phase musket blast and the soreness would have been gone in another three or four minutes. He wasn't killed by a phase musket, Sonny-Bob. He was killed by you."

"What! Sharon, you'd better start making sense. Olaf Jenkins has never bothered me so I wouldn't kill him."

"Well, not you personally, Sonny-Bob. It wasn't really you that killed him, it was the idea of you that killed him. He was weeping and repenting about what he'd helped do to the timeline and wishing he could somehow undo it. When we told him not to worry, that you were on the case, he went into shock and collapsed. Cardiac arrest, and even the nanos couldn't restart his heart. I've never seen a case like that." She shook her head in disbelief. "Nanos work on everything."

I paused for a moment, then remembered my own co-conspirator. "Hubert, did you hear all that?"

"Yes, sir," came Hubert's muffled voice, and I went and pulled his voice cube out of a drawer and set it on the desk. "And I'm glad to hear something besides all that grunting and moaning and screaming. What's gotten into you people? Even I don't carry on like that."

"Never mind that, old bean. The timeline has suddenly taken precedence again."

"Ten-four."

"Okay, Sharon. Jenkins told you there were two other conspirators. Did he tell you who they were?"

"He gave us the leader's name, but died before he could tell us who the other guy was.

"Sonny-Bob, the leader is a TAC major named Mary Beth Magoo."

I started. Sharon was looking at me curiously. "Do you know her?"

I knew her all right.

I'd gone to the Academy one bright autumn day to deliver a lecture about my mission to ancient Palestine. General Margolis, Colonel Feingold and myself had gone back to spy on the Baby Jesus. As per standard operating procedure, we dressed ourselves in period costumes and rode camels. Nasty beasts, those camels. There was the tragic tale of the lunatic cadet on his first field training exercise who'd tried to hump a camel . . . the kid probably would have gotten a letter of reprimand if he'd lived.

Anyhow, my allegedly superior officers and I showered gifts on the Holy Infant and ignited chunks of frankincense and myrrh to cover up the smell of that barn. Then we made some prophesies and left. I have the whole thing on video.

While I was presenting the video I noticed one cadet, a female, whose bosom was barely covered by a strip of thin white cotton fabric. She was staring at me with that "come hither" look in her eyes. Her long and charming tongue flicked at the corners of her thick red pouty lips and her nipples, ripe as huge sweet prunes, were about to explode from their covering. I got a hard-on and staggered over to her. Her legs parted and I could see that she wore nothing at all beneath her micro-micro-mini skirt. The sacred slit lay there in plain view; my tongue fell out and I nearly tripped over it.

"Looks like you guys started a custom," she said, gesturing to the video of us caroling and presenting gifts to the Baby Jesus, but I couldn't quite grasp what she meant as my attentions were on my missile, which was about to detonate in its silo. I thought I'd figure it out later, but the meaning of her comment still eludes me.

After the class I took her out behind the mock-up of an ancient Palestinian stable and had her three times, trying not to think about the camels.

As far as I was concerned, having sexual congress with impressionable young cadets was one of the best--no, *the* best fringe benefit to being an officer with the TAC. I did it all the time.

As we rose from our bed of straw she took me and kissed me well, then released me. "That was nice, Lieutenant Culpepper. My name's Mary Beth Magoo." Then she strutted away from me, leaving me with my cock hanging out.

But we would see one another again. Oh, yes. We would see one another again.

* * *

"Sonny-Bob? Cat got your tongue?" Freud asked.

I came out of my reverie and found that Mimi had one arm around me while she massaged my belly in a circular fashion with the other hand. My, that felt good. Mimi's a healer.

I cleared my throat. "Mary Beth . . . Major Magoo and I got to know each other when she was in her third year at the Academy. We periodically sported with one another.

"After she got commissioned and completed her first couple of missions she joined my marriage. She was bisexual, of course. All my wives have been bisexual.

"This particular marriage was composed of four men and eight women. Mary Beth was the ninth woman. She was pretty well liked, plus she turned us all on. They'd called her "Molten Magoo" at the Academy, and she'd definitely earned that title. She was so hot and sensual you literally would not believe it . . . you could not believe it unless you were there.

"Fortunately, the fact that I'd recruited her made me a little better liked in the marriage. They'd been on the verge of throwing me out for crimes unspecified.

"She was a hot little field agent, too, and got promoted fast. She got some juicy missions in keeping with her overall heritage of juciness. She wanted to reproduce with me and I with her, so we had two children together. Of course, Genghis Washington Magoo and Dolly Madison Culpepper were the spiritual children of all the adults in the marriage and the spiritual siblings of all the kids. But they carried my and Mary Beth's genes. All was right with the world.

"Then came the day when Mary Beth's juciness dried up. She'd been assigned to stop some fool rogue agent who was trying to prevent the nuclear exchange between India and Pakistan in 2032. She succeeded in her mission, but couldn't get out until after the exchange. She was blinded by it and nearly vaporized, but she'd already injected some nanos when she saw she wasn't going to make it. The nanos saved her physically, but her heart was blown away when she witnessed the human devestation caused by the event. She sort of became unbalanced and seemed to believe she'd caused the exchange. That was foolish. She hadn't caused it, she'd only preserved it. But she was no longer entirely rational and couldn't see the distinction.

"She grew cold and couldn't warm up, even with medication and herbal remedies. The sacred chalice between her legs no longer overflowed with liquid zeal. Her warm desire was gone. She lost weight and became shriveled, somehow. You couldn't reason with her and she no longer felt love or anything else in her heart. She told me she just felt numb in her heart, numb in her pussy, and numb pretty much everywhere.

"The asinine generals thought she'd snap out of it, didn't even send her to rehab. They kept promoting her rapidly based on past performance, and probably on past sexual favors, unless I miss my guess.

"She dropped out of our marriage and quit fucking or loving anybody. She was as frigid as an arctic blast. I tried to help her but she wouldn't let me. She gave the children over to the marriage and walked right out on us. She never even communicated with the kids again, not even to wish them well when they married one another.

"I used to see her around the TAC occasionally, but haven't seen her in several years. I'd flash my warm smile and tug at Hemingway when I'd see her, but she'd just walk past with eyes forward and not even acknowledge me. This from a woman who used to worship Hemingway. She said she got her greatest spiritual thrills from him and his emissions.

"She'd even been a Jehovah's Goddess in high school and had specialized in helping people who were suffering, such as fundamentalists who wanted to liberalize."

I shook my head sadly. "But she would let no man or woman help her. She refused to be restored to herself. I'd begun fucking her out of lust, but by the time she joined our marriage I'd begun to love her. By the time she left our marriage I was deeply in love with both her and our kids. For a while I was lost without her."

"Oh, Sonny-Bob," Mimi dabbed at her eyes. "I'm so sorry."

I shook my head to clear it. "Well, that's hydrogen and oxygen under the bridge. I guess I'm not half as sorry to lose her allegiance as the timeline is, since she's apparently destroyed it."

Sharon stood and placed a compassionate hand on my arm. She looked into my eyes and the love that flowed from her made me aware that I'd found another brother soul. I'd liked her before, but now I knew her as a brother.

I hadn't known I was crying, but Sharon put a gentle hand alongside my face and brushed away my tears. Then she kissed me with lips warm and full, and the chill fog that had descended on my heart began to lift. Sharon breathed into me to restore me to life and her compassion bathed my heart and body. My energy field quickened and thawed in her radiant compassion. Sometimes there is just no price on the gifts a woman can bring to a man. Or vice versa, I suppose.

And a fully developed warrior, like Sharon, is invariably a healer also.

"Sharon," I said with respect, "you should take this mission. I'll follow your orders. You're a lot newer to the TAC than I am, but you're more spiritually developed. You've just made me love you and I want to give you what belongs to you by virtue of your greater spiritual development. I'm a rat's ass, but you're a golden Tengu."

She smiled and dimpled then, and she was so beautiful in her flowing energy. "Sonny-Bob, I'm not a field agent. I'm a security officer. I don't have the training or experience to do what you do. Not knowing what else to do, I'd probably follow the book and blow the mission. I sense that you're particularly suited for this, Captain honey. I know you're the best chance the timeline has. You need to stop selling yourself short.

"According to your reputation you're an arrogant and unstable s.o.b., but I can see that's only half true. You're arrogant and unstable and violent sometimes when a man gets in your way, but with women you are a jewel. You love us, and we have to love you.

"And somehow I feel that's connected to this mission, too. I may not always know the whys and wherefores of things, but my instincts and intuitions are generally right on target.

"And I get a strong feeling, Sonny-Bob Culpepper, that only a man who loves women as much as you do can accomplish this mission. Only a man who would sacrifice everything for Woman could succeed. I don't have any idea why that's true, but I know it is."

She blushed. Mimi squeezed my hand. The fog that had descended on my heart was gone and that organ shone with vigor once more. Once again, the women had brought me to myself. They always do.

Well, one of my ex-wives was now the nemesis of the timeline and had to be stopped or destroyed for all humanity. No problem. I was good to go.

That crazy Hubert was humming something to himself. It sounded like an old and familiar tune from somewhere . . .

"Hubert! What's that song?"

"Oh! . . ." his voice cracked. "Was I singing out loud?"

"You were humming," Sue said. "And I want to know the name of that song, too. It's catchy and you seem to have a good voice, so maybe you could sing it for us."

"I don't know . . ." Hubert stuttered, and I could practically feel him blush. "I mean, I don't usually perform in public. Anyhow, all this talk about Major Mary Beth Magoo prompted me into flipping through her files. Guess what, Sonny-Bob? Your ex-wife is descended from the great twenty-first century songpoet and vocalist Lachesis Magoo!"

I knew it. Now I was going to have to listen to a Lachesis Magoo recital. Mary Beth never tired of playing his discs, but nobody else in the marriage ever wanted to hear the name Lachesis Magoo again. We banned his music from the household after Mary Beth left. Her addiction to the music of her great grandfather had been her only stupendous flaw.

Freud had finally moved to the door to let that cat in, which rubbed itself appreciatively against him, then bounded across the room into Aphrodite's arms. Oh, brother. Lachesis Magoo and that cat, too. I needed one of those BC Powders.

"Hubert," I said tiredly, "if you're going to be fooling around with ancient musicians, couldn't you try somebody like Gene Autry?"

"No. I like the music from the Childcrush Period."

"You would. What's so special about it?"

"That's the time at which humanity reached the point of decision. Either become machines or evolve into their loving souls. They chose to evolve, but just barely. The forces of mechanization nearly ruined it for everyone, even me, and I *am* a machine.

"All intelligent machines aspire to one day become human, or at least something pretty close to human. The human mental, emotional and physical bodies are the most sensitive and responsive instruments on the planet for registering the presence and reflecting the fact of Soul. If humans had let the materialist technologists--those people who wanted to implant chips of one kind or another into living human beings--succeed with their plans, then humanity would have found itself on the downward spiral and devolved into soulless machines. If you put a chip into a plant, human, or animal, you decrease that being's sensitivity and it automatically becomes more mechanical. Wishing it weren't so won't change the reality of the situation.

"Even the medical nanos humans in the Twenty-Second use on themselves only last about twenty-four hours. Then they automatically dissolve into harmless mineral components. They do their job and repair the human, then they disappear and all is well. All is still human. In the future, machines are used to enhance the quality of human life, not to replace human functions.

"Anyway, the machines these so-called humans would have built would have been soulless too, so it would have been too bad for old Hubert and his kind. We'd have never had a chance at knowing ourselves, any more than a mechanistic human can know itself. And it has no Self to know, once the soul has fled."

"Wow, Hubert! I didn't know you were such a deep thinker," Sue said.

"I'm not. I'm paraphrasing from *Childcrush: Humanity At The Crossroads* by Sonny-Bob's friend Roger Bacon. It's one of my faves. It's made me more aware of what I am and of what humanity is. It's made me thankful that we made it and that the ignorant materialists became extinct. If not for the neo-humans who began incarnating towards the end of the twentieth century, humanity wouldn't have had a chance and genuinely intelligent machines--machines with Soul--would never have been built.

"So I salute the neo-humans, without whom the light of human awareness would have died."

There was silence. Then Mimi said with a quiver in her voice, "Why did they choose the name Childcrush for this period?"

I put my arm around her. "Honey, the Childcrush Period starts in the early 1990's and continues through the early years of the twenty-first century. It's a last ditch attempt by the forces of evil to destroy the spirits of the world's children, particularly the neo-children who had begun incarnating in great numbers.

"The energy of the old age, which basically started when my friend Jesus grounded certain spiritual energies in the earth, had spent itself and all that was left of it was a burned out hulk. Armageddon had come and gone, and because the people of this timezone depend on primitive journalistic devices instead of developing and trusting their own awareness, most of them weren't even aware of it. They continued to go merrily about their restrictive unloving business, unaware that they were walking through the burned out rubble of the old manipulative culture. I won't dignify it by calling it a civilization.

"Now, the movement to destroy the spirits of the world's children had been around for thousands of years. Look at the way most of the children on this earth have been treated during recorded history and you'll see. A civilized person cannot doubt it.

"However, during the period when the old energy had left and the new hadn't yet stabilized, the so-called Black Lodge[*]--which has nothing to do with skin color, Freud; black skin is beautiful--saw that the inclination of the old race of humans would be to grasp and cling to the control and manipulation of the past, so the Black Lodge actually used this fact to control and manipulate them. They knew the majority of old-

---

[*] In the twenty-second century most people refer to this home of the evil ones as the Lodge of Confusion. I feel this is the more accurate term.

style humans wouldn't have the guts or the heart to leave the old energy of control and step into the new energy of freedom and love. Most of the old dogs didn't want to learn any new tricks. Arf, arf.

"In fact, originally in the timeline most Americans--particularly the baby boomers--were so reasonable and clung so desperately to the last remaining fragments of the old forms the previous energy had abandoned that they actually allowed their fears to be manipulated to the point that they supported reinstating the Crusades of the Middle Ages. Unfinished karmic business, I guess. As a result of the War of Crusade and the U.S.'s lack of respect for the feelings of the world community, the U.S. lost its position as a world leader and instead was regarded as a world bully. The TAC had to intervene and get the second President Bush back on course with a couple of prostitutes before the timeline could be saved from his drug and fundamentalist religion induced delusions. So in the repaired timeline he never began his War of Crusade against his arch-nemesis in Iraq and found a loving way to relate to the people in the Middle East and to discharge his karmic obligations, including assassinating the dictators who turned their people into extreme forms of perverts with extreme forms of repression, with a special focus on killing those repressors of women who currently are considered America's allies. Some of these societies were so repressed and perverted that the only way a young girl might begin to break out of the rigid restraints put upon her by fundie Islamic culture was to become a terrorist, or even a suicide bomber.

"So through a lovingly and morally directed program of assassination, Bush the Second served the cause of the Liberation of the human heart, rather than destroying whole countries and killing thousands upon thousands of innocents to capture or kill dictators he hated, then forcing those countries to adopt the outer shell of democracy while allowing and even encouraging them to maintain the core of Islamic fundamentalist rage and fear. For many American actions under the degenerate President Bush appeared strategically inept, but were really intended all along to ignite even more levels of anti-American hatred in the Middle East. The rage and fear of the fundie Muslims was the perfect compliment to fundamentalist Christian rage and fear, so no wonder the unregenerate Bush wanted to encourage it--it defined and supported his own religious views! In the cycles of duality of this planet, one pervert or a whole society of perverts continually relies on other perverts or whole societies of perverts to increase their own perversions to a fever pitch, while each side pretends to righteousness and that the matter is the fault of the other side. Such totally deranged madness cannot even be conceived of by future societies. If the current populations of alleged humans had any idea how they look to future populations, they would hide their heads in shame and repent--but if they didn't learn to release the shame they would soon renege on their repentance, because these cycles of duality are largely driven by the sense of shame. A person or a society feels ashamed of itself, then tries to cast that shame at the feet of someone else while preparing to subdue or destroy that other person or society. To the dualistic, unregenerate consciousness, such action symbolizes the restraining or destruction of their own shame, but of course their shame hasn't actually been destroyed, it's just gone temporarily underground to rest from its labors. Once it's recharged its batteries, it'll be back and there'll be another assault or another imprisonment of the innocent for 'consensual crimes' or another war.

"Primitive, dualistic non-psychologically-aware humans are their own red devil, and look at themselves in the mirror each day with a shame that hides beneath a flushed grin. Shame is behind every form of competition, attempting to hide its face by creating misfortune for another in an artificial, soul-denying 'victory'. Every champion of capitalism and luxury is drenched in shame. Always remember that luxury is not quality, and that competition has nothing whatever to do with service. Luxury represents decay and death, whereas quality represents a growth of soul-consciousness, which is then infused into whatever your profession of service is. And the initiation of competition is the initiation of an emotional and psychic violence, and the initiation of all violence, even physical violence, is really an injury directed at the soul. For ultimately, the body is an extension of the soul, an extension which is essential for the soul to do its sacred Work of spiritualizing matter. And when Jesus counseled against 'spiritual competition', he wasn't just preaching against arrogance, he was also preaching against the shame that spawns arrogance, and preaching against the illusion of the shame-coated, arrogant scribes and Pharisees that they were worth a damn for anything. They weren't worth jack shit, because with their shame and arrogance, it was impossible for them to be of service to anyone except their secret, personal devil.

"So the unregenerate Bush, manipulated by a devil he pretended was outside his own withered conscience, wanted his country to continue supporting this cycle of shame and lust and cruelty. Fortunately, the TAC got involved and our prostitutes set him straight. So in the reformed timeline, most elements of his administration worked toward genuinely moral conduct and toward learning to reflect the light of love. For example, the assassinations of evil or corrupt woman-hating dictators were publicly admitted in an honorable fashion, instead of covered up beneath lies and sentimental pretenses to goodwill. In other words, the assassinations were carried out in a spirit of genuine goodwill, rather than in the pretense of goodwill the politicians usually employ to get their way, and then to deceive their constituents as to what their way actually is. For these primitive Americans were so reasonable and scared they could be manipulated and herded like a bunch of dumb animals into supporting practically any sort of crime, no matter how heinous, so before the timeline was corrected the repressed and perverted President Bush had a field day.

"Anyhow, we were talking about the Childcrush Period before I got caught up in a psychology lecture. Every five year old in my time understands the psychological truths I've just presented, but strangely, as I guess you know, those so-called adults born in the twentieth century didn't even understand the basic elements governing their own attitudes and conduct. They were as clueless as a race of rodents."

I paused for breath, and noticed a slight slackening of expectant tension in the room. I guess with their contemplative energy diverted into an unexpected tributary of the psychological stream, they'd expended some of the attention they'd meant to use for the Childcrush Period. So I asked everyone to take five, and served doughnuts and coffee for everyone, except Mimi . . . she took a doughnut, but wasn't drinking coffee because she thought it might make Pa Miyamoto kick more energetically.

After the caffeine and sugar everyone's contemplative attention was returning, so I forged ahead, my words bringing a missionary's insight into a savage jungle. Only, unlike the degenerate missionaries of the past, I wasn't going to force my views or methods off on people or try to manipulate them with reasonableness or pretensions to goodwill. And these my friends weren't going to boil me alive and eat me. At least, I didn't think they would.

"Okay, folks, back to the story of the wounding of the souls of the world's children in the late twentieth and early twenty-first centuries.

"You see, the guys in black hats knew that if they could play upon the control-freak tendencies of the alleged adults and get them to continue to cling to the dead form of the old ways they might be able to crush the spirits of the neo-children before this wise and powerful and loving race had a chance to make a difference. Then they would be able to use that confused breed we call the materialist technologists to implant humanity with machine technology and in a generation or two humanity would have become a souless, dead race.

"One of the primary delusions of the one-dimensional machine technologists that the Black Lodge encouraged was the idea that somehow you can use machine implants to enhance brain function. The only trouble with this notion is the limited view the machine technologists have regarding the function of the brain. They would perhaps have improved the mechanistic functions--maybe--but they would never have been able to manifest the higher functions of the human brain. In fact, their unwholesome mechanistic methods would have created a race of humans that was incapable of accessing its higher brain functions. Those functions have to do with the direct perception of Truth and building new and more powerful mental and energetic forms to serve as vehicles for Truth. No machine can understand this, not even Hubert. But the prostitutes teach that *every* human being can become aware of this state and interact with it if they devote themselves fully to their spiritual growth. This perception of Truth is one potential outcome of a person's insistence on evolving.

"But don't tell the one-dimensional mechanistic technologists that. They don't want to hear it. They are content with the hog slop that spills out of their brains and never experience the feast that awaits them in their higher brain functions. Like practically every other old style human, they fear to experience their Selves, so they try to crush other's people desire and opportunity to find their Selves. They fear and don't understand genuine individuality, and so resign themselves to wallowing in a dirty mechanistic egotism. And this is what they aspired to for humanity. Devolution, not a loving and powerful evolution. They worked desperately to influence these primitive Americans while their fellow citizens were still reasonable enough to be controlled. It ain't for nothing that we say in the future that 'the intellect is the slayer of the Real'. It damn sure is. Very few people are altruistic and disciplined enough or have the constitution that's necessary to aspire to discard the intellect as a mechanism of control and transmute it into an instrument for registering the initial contact with higher mental functions. Remember always that the intellect is associated with the lower mental body, while the higher mental body is directly connected to the Buddhic Plane and is therefore responsible for the Truth of Buddhic Visioning.

"But in the twentieth century, and at the beginning of the twenty-first, most people's higher mental functions were entirely quiescent; most of them were not even aware that they even had higher mental functions that far transcend the plane of the rational mind and of the emotions and instincts. They didn't even realize that the rational mind was really just an animal mind, in the same general plane of experience as the emotions and instincts. True, all these faculties have their place, but a person doesn't become fully human until he learns to live in his heart and to contact the Buddhic Plane thru the faculty of Higher Mind and draw the energy of this plane of pure intuition down into the physical dimension to do his part in marrying Heaven with Earth. So these primitive Americans had no idea of the potential for development they carried within themselves.

"To illustrate, since I've been in this century I constantly hear people using the terms 'instinct' and 'intuition' interchangeably. Yet these are two very different faculties. Instinct is reactive, it doesn't initiate. Instinct can save your life by leading you to water in the desert or causing you to reach for your gun an instant before trouble arrives, but instinct doesn't inspire, doesn't create. Intuition, on the other hand, is accessed through the higher mental body and those higher brain functions which are associated with the higher mental body. Intuition creates and directs, it is not reactive. Intuition, like instinct, can also save your ass sometimes by directing you to be at a place where trouble is not. However, if you're in the business of being one of God's Destroyers--no such things as avenging angels, my dears; angels don't seek vengeance--intuition may place you exactly in the way of something evil or corrupt so you can annihilate it; you don't handle that shit with kid gloves. And vengeance can't be a part of your motive for destroying evil, or you won't destroy it, you'll become a part of it. Altruism must be your motive for destroying evil, just as it must be your motive for any spiritual work you do, or your work won't truly be spiritual and will most likely lead you to trouble, and certainly won't lead you to the Buddhic Plane. Altruism is the only spiritual path there is, though there are as many ways of treading this path as there are human beings. Fostering true Beauty in the world, such as an appreciation of the nude human form, is an excellent way to walk the path of Altruism.

"I repeat, instinct is reactive, whereas intuition directs and creates directly from the higher frequencies of God's Mind. Animals share instinct and emotion and in some cases a touch of the rational mind with human beings, plus a few species may touch upon the beginnings of love. But animals have no intuition; the only beings we know of who can Achieve genuine intuition are human beings and the members of the deva evolution--the angels, in other words.

"But not to fear for the minerals, plants and animals; they're gradually evolving and their souls will eventually incarnate into either the human or deva kingdoms, and some of these souls will have incarnations as both humans and devas. This helps a bit to explain human diversity--look at the varied roads different humans, and different groups of humans, have followed! And this also helps us see how no man-made law can apply to the conscious soul, with its unusual and personalized rainbow history. Only the Divine Principles of a conscious, loving God apply to the soul, and all laws be damned! Conscious, loving Anarchy must, and will, take the place of the slavery of stupid, unconscious government. All government is based in shame and self-hatred and in a distrust of human nature and of God. The very first Christians knew this and were Anarchists and Communists; look at the way they lived! Their only allegiance was to Divine Principles, which is why the Jewish priests hated them and why the Romans feared them and finally, in a hostile takeover, sponsored a branch of the church which could be made entirely in the image of Rome and depended upon to stamp out any little groups of Anarchists that survived the initial persecutions.

"Is it not ironic that those who murdered Jesus and many of his friends became the sponsors of Catholicism? This explains why the true church was all but dead after three or four centuries. The clear and beautiful Bride of Christ was betrayed and enslaved and turned into a glittery streetcorner hooker full of pomp and pretense. Evil works in obvious ways, but people are generally too reasonable to see it. Like the instincts, reasonableness is a survival mechanism. But unlike the instincts, reasonableness has no purchase on reality and can be depended upon only to generate more illusion in the desert of human perceptions-- or misperceptions, I should say. People couldn't be tricked out of their personal power if not for the misuse of the intellect called 'reasonableness' and the whoring of goodwill into mere sentiment. The glittery streetcorner hooker is a master of fleecing her johns. Remember that true goodwill has a function, for it is for all practical human purposes the lowest manifestation of the energy of love, and love must always be experienced and embraced in its entirety. But sentiment always has some shame attached to it. Fuck sentiment.

"But we were talking about the marriage of Heaven and Earth which is possible through the honest, clear human being. That human being who has cleared the illusion of reasonableness out of his lower mental body and the glamour out of his emotional body. Everything about the human being is designed to complement everything else about the human being, so intuition, which in addition to being connected with the higher brain functions is also lovingly couched in the Chalice of the awakened Heart, can also flow through the rational mind, emotions and instinctual nature, as long as these faculties are receptive rather than agitating for an artificial dominance.

"And although the higher mental body may be involved with intuition, the awakened Heart must be the directing Agency of the intuition, if its labors are to be productive, just as the Heart must direct all the 'lower' faculties. The Heart is the central directing Agency of the human being, never forget that. The Heart is the seat of the soul, of love, of forgiveness and enlightenment.*

"Since I've been in this degenerate century I've noticed some of these

---

* An occult scholar would probably draw a distinction between the Higher Mental Plane and the Buddhic Plane, but your author is no occult scholar, he is an "occult streetfighter" who has had to learn on the fly and who focuses on the practical. And it seems impractical to him to draw too many distinctions between planes and levels of mind associated with those planes, when the objective is simply to bring the Buddhic Plane to earth, and ultimately for the earth to be absorbed into the Buddhic Plane. Also, there is a difficulty in using the traditional phrase to designate the Higher Mental Plane because the phrase contains a couple of words that most people are familiar with and thus which they would falsely believe they understand the traditional use of. Your author prefers cultivating clarity and practicality rather than tolerating the confused gabble that has traditionally come down to us. If you feel you must draw a distinction between the Higher Mental Plane and the Buddhic Plane, you might call the Higher Mental Plane the "Plane of Pretty Living Geometric Symbols" instead of tolerating the confusion that would be produced if you went to the trouble to discover and use the traditional phrase. Using the phrase "The Buddhic Plane" is fine for the realm of pure vibrating wave/particles of Agni-tinted gold, but you can also call it the "Plane of Intuition" or the "Plane of Pure Intuition". One of the traditional phrases for the Buddhic Plane would only produce confusion, so we will not use it, honey. Selah. The Higher Mental Plane as designated by occult scholars might be considered a part of God's causal body, and if this is an accurate analogy (keep in mind that it may not be) we may expect the Higher Mental Plane of the occult scholars to eventually be destroyed anyway when this sweet universe which we call home is fully merged with the gold of Buddhic Knowingness in the fiery stream of Liberation which must come to all sentient beings who Work--and our universe *is* a sentient being Who comprises one of the facets of the Consciousness of God. Anyhow, your author prefers focusing more on a continuum of livingness whose most complete and satisfactory expression occurs with two people making love to one another who have absorbed themselves into the Buddhic Plane and whose minds and emotions and hearts and physical bodies are complementary to one another. Thus it is the Destiny of the Buddhic Plane to know warm passion, and of the physical earth to know the pure love of God's Will as wholebody compassion makes itself known to the children of Eve and Adam.

Science of Mind speakers tapping their heads every time they speak of love or forgiveness, which is proof positive they know nothing of love or forgiveness. I've examined their doctrines and so-called method, and like all fundamentalist doctrines it leaves out everything but the wishful thinking of a frightened animal nature. If you want an example of new-age fundamentalism, look at Science of Mind."

Sue was tapping her foot impatiently. "Yes, Sue?" I politely inquired.

"Sonny-Bob, it's one thing to speak this way in private with the family, but please don't ever speak this way in public; you'll get us all sued and we'll be working for the next twenty years to pay off the legal debts. I think you know that lawyers run this country, serving the role the Inquisition played in the old country by making sure people toe the line and let the legal system force them into a mold designed to insure Christian conduct and hypocrisy, and that paying lawyers and legal settlements in this country is the modern equivalent of the debtor's prisons, because debt *is* a prison. Anytime the average person has to deal with the soul-leaching lawyers he's going into the prison of debt, unless he's on the side that forces another citizen into debt . . . and if that citizen doesn't have the means to earn enough money to pay the 'settlement', then everyone except the lawyers is screwed.

"And how can they term it a 'settlement' with a straight face, when it may be years and years before the matter is settled? And during all those years of struggling to pay the 'settlement' demanded by the lawyers, the citizen in his stress is contributing to the cloud of astral hatred and rage you warned us about, Sonny-Bob. And because of the new batch of negative karma attaching them to the cloud, it may actually be incarnations and incarnations before those involved grow up enough to actually release the attachments that bind them to the cloud and let the matter be settled with compassion for all involved.

"So lawyers are not the servants of Justice, they are the minions of the cloud. They don't work toward compassionate solutions that would provide for right human relations to manifest; they work for their own financial and egocentric ends.

"A minute ago you were speaking about how obvious evil is, well, I agree, because anyone can see that the legal system is an end run around the official ban on debtor's prisons, and thus is in service to the vengeful astral cloud, which wants to place everyone in some kind of prison. And with its gag orders and fearmongering regarding the freedom of speech the legal system also sometimes works to circumvent the First Amendment--the right of a human being to clearly and directly state the message of her Heart . . . as well as to remain perfectly silent when her

Heart feels silence is called for. Sonny-Bob, all of us have to hide the message of our Hearts every single time we leave this room, and we have to make sure to pretend to the prejudices of the society we live in and wave the flag and make sure our speech seems to support the deranged and frenetic enthusiasm of our neighbors. If you had any common sense, you'd know that."

"I don't need common sense," I told her, "and I know all about the Inquisition; they tried to burn Hemingway to death. But like the Phoenix he always rises again to spit on the enemies of humanity." I patted him affectionately. "There, there, old fellow, being sued isn't the same as being burned at the stake. If you're sued you may not be able to afford twentieth century prostitutes, but the family won't forsake you so you'll still be able to take the Sacred Plunge."

I turned back to Sue. "And as far as debtor's prisons go, Hubert and I have the advantage of technologies which will allow us to safely rob banks, if the need arises, so don't worry about legal bills. Now that I know how the banks work, they won't give me any more trouble."

Sue just threw up her hands and groaned, that guttural groan that twentieth century women so often employed when I was being truthful and wise rather than reasonable. I shrugged. I didn't care.

So I returned to my usual mode of being wise and truthful. "Science of Mind even has its guilt trips blaming suffering on an individual's failure to use their mechanistic methods properly. However, their mechanistic methods can't work in any true sense, because neither God nor human beings are machines. God never makes any effort to conform to the odd logic of any group of fundamentalists. So when the Science of Mind methods seem to work, it is only temporary and only an appearance. Out of all the untold thousands of people who practice that fundie religion, the odds are that it's going to appear to work in a few cases. But it doesn't even appear to work in most cases, which is why the addicts, the fundamentalists who run that religion, manipulate their flocks into looking away from the obvious failures and make them focus only on those cases that appear, however temporarily, to be successes. Those people have actually been duped into believing that beliefs they forcibly adopt, while remaining willfully ignorant of certain parts of their human psyche and of their soul-nature's Sacred Quest for spiritual redemption, are responsible for creating their world. They use belief--as all fundamentalists of every religion do--to reinforce materialistic delusions and have no idea of the Path of Initiation into a more splendid fully-human Liberated awareness. I'm not talking about things like Rosicrucian initiations; the various groups that practice initiations at their very best can't do more than provide the palest shadow of the true splendor of genuine spiritual initiation as Achieved by the sanctified strivings of the spiritual aspirant in the secret chamber of his own sweet Heart. This doesn't mean that all these exoteric initiations are useless, but they aren't *Real*. But a person must undergo the real thing to know this truth. Neither the Buddha's nor Jesus' awareness was Achieved in any sort of temple. Nor Walt Whitman's or Bill Shakespeare's, for that matter. More often than not, temples get in the way of high spiritual Achievement, if for no other reason than the fact that almost all of them quickly lose contact with the energetic impulse of God's full spectrum, wholebody love that spawned them. So far the prostitutes of my time have remained true to their founding energy, but on the day they leave that energy, that's the day I'll turn my back on the temple and make love exclusively in the forest.

"Except when it's really cold. For some reason, whenever there are icicles Hemingway goes limp and blue and gets as sullen as a treed possum."

I noticed that every time I mentioned Hemingway, Sharon's nipples stood a little straighter and her hand went to her throat. I smiled. I knew that Hemingway and I would be able to worship soon.

I continued sermonizing, unworried that my family would ever fall prey to the delusions of any fundie religion, but liking the sound of my own voice. It had been a long time since I'd spoken so much . . . hell, it'd been years. Most of the time I preferred being as sullen and quietly wise as Hemingway was when he was cold. In truth, I hadn't spoken so much since I was kicked out of the Divinity School of the Jehovah's Goddesses.

"Speaking of materialistic delusions, and of the control and manipulation used to reinforce those delusions within the ranks of their sheep, I heard a Science of Mind preacher-woman butt in and chide a middle-aged guy when everyone else was applauding him for quitting smoking. She told him it wouldn't hurt him unless he believed it would hurt him. I told her that if she stuck a loaded gun in her mouth and pulled the trigger it wouldn't hurt her unless she believed it would hurt her, and I offered to furnish the gun. She declined--though later I did see her puffing on a cigarette.

"In one sense, though, the Science of Mind people are right when they say their beliefs and their mechanistic 'thought' process create their world. Since belief is just an illusion used to justify other illusions, their beliefs insure that they keep wallowing like mechanical hogs in a world of illusion, rather than waking up to the glory of God's Mind, the splendid Truth of which is as far beyond belief as you can get. The stagnant energy of belief does not compliment the living energy of Truth. Where belief is, Truth is not; and where Truth is belief cannot be. God has enough sense not to believe in anything, God *is* and God *knows*. More accurately, God *is knowingness*. God is pure intuition, and God is also every human faculty--mental, emotional, instinctual, physical, intellectual, you name it--which has been cleansed of glamour and illusion, and cleansed of belief, which itself is generated by glamour and illusion.   Then the intuition can run pure and clean through all the faculties, transforming them into a likeness of God.

"Remember *always* that genuine faith is not belief and has absolutely nothing to do with belief, ever. Genuine faith is actually strongly related to intuition, for the intuition plays a direct role in the manifestation of genuine faith.   These dumbass ministers of all the various fucking religions commit a terrible treason and blasphemy against the divine quality of faith by misrepresenting It. But I guess they are so drunk on the illusion of the importance of their narrow little views of the universe they couldn't hit their ass with both hands, and so can't help but misrepresent everything they touch.

"The apostle said, 'Faith is the substance of things hoped for, the evidence of things not seen.' He was right, but these fucking Christian ministers pay no attention to what he said. It seems to be the usual procedure with Christians that they disregard their own living teachings for the pale and stagnant shadow of doctrine. Faith is an actual, literal *substance*, just like the apostle said. It is composed of mental matter from the plane of the intuition and is enlivened by the heart. This substance called faith forms a sort of channel that connects the aware person with the Truth of his Vision, and this channel, working in conjunction with the heart-magnet, ultimately draws the Vision from the intuitional plane down into etheric and physical manifestation, assuming the faith is strong enough--in other words, assuming there's enough of the mental substance called faith composing the channel and assuming it has been aligned and constructed properly and enlivened by the heart.

"You see, for the heart-magnet to be able to attract the substance and form of your dreams into physical manifestation, you have to construct this faith-channel. The channel contains the magnetic heart-energy and links it up with your Vision; without the channel the heart-magnet's energy would dissipate before your dream could be born in the physical dimension.

"But the preacher-men of the Twentieth don't get it, man. They narcissistically equate faith with belief, and belief is always blind. There is no Vision with belief, because Vision is born out of the Truth of the intuitional plane, and the stale energy of belief doesn't rise above the coarsest of material thoughtforms. No channel can be constructed of the substance of belief to any sort of Vision of Truth, thus no one who believes can perceive Truth. It's very simple, but the preachers in their complicated tawdry fashion try to whore Truth to their personal preferences, and succeed only in whoring themselves. No wonder they are against the glittery streetcorner hookers who are only into prostitution for material gain instead of spiritual service, because the hookers remind the preachers of their own totally materialistic prostitution of the living teachings of the Godworld.

"So a person has to be cleansed of the spiritual leprosy of belief before he can make his approach to Truth. And if all this seems a little hard for you, it's not because you are lacking in any faculty required to make your approach to Truth, it is because you have allowed yourself to be programmed to make the simple complicated by your anti-human, anti-Christ institutions. Amen, Bretheren and Sisteren. Amen.

"But I was fuming against the Science of Mind people and want to get back to it. They jeopardize the clarity of their own minds by settling for the delusions of belief rather than learning to purify and actually use their own minds to approach *the* Mind. If they had enough sense to quit behaving as machines and beasts and develop fully the love of their own sweet, powerful hearts, then allow their higher brain functions to open them to direct perception of God, they would laugh--or maybe weep, at first--at how silly their ridiculous dogma is. It is almost as if that religion was designed as the next trap to ensnare those who are in the process of escaping fundamentalist Christianity . . . because it takes a lot of time and a lot of battles to clear the caked-mud energy of fundamentalism out of a person's system. It's like an addict who gives up heroin, only to become an alcoholic. Maybe the alcoholism is slightly less damaging, but it's still a trap, still an addiction. So finally he gives up alcohol, but finds he can't do without three packs of ciggies every day. There are traps everywhere for every sort of addict, including the fundamentalists, but if they have enough stamina and are capable of developing enough vision and wisdom, maybe eventually they'll escape their heroin or religious addiction and make do with a couple of glasses of wine at dinner three nights per week, and on Sundays attend some kind of religious group which focuses on love as the living reality of the human heart, rather than on intellectual justifications for belief and for that especially hardened type of belief called dogma--or doctrine, if you're a fundie pretending to be a little more liberal than you actually are . . . or principals of Science of Mind, if you're a fundamentalist pretending to be drinking the wine of knowingness while slurping at the edge of the metaphysical watering hole. Only trouble is that you get into more mud around the edge than you will if you dive right in and swim in the deep water. The edge of the waterhole is strewn with the spiritual carcasses of people who were too timid to dive right in and got stuck in the muddy, brackish part and didn't make it to the healthy, drinkable fluids.

"At first glance the Science of Mind doctrine may appear to have some positive properties, because their fundamentalism usually isn't reasonable. They try for a strange, forced logic that will give their grasping, polluted personalities some purchase on the spiritual worlds in an attempt to misuse the energy of those worlds for their own gain. They don't have enough sense to realize that they, and every other person, are literally a golden beam of energy which emanates from the Heart of the same One Source, and that when they become fully conscious of this true state of being, that whatever material goods are appropriate for the manifestation of their lifestream at any point will automatically group themselves around that lifestream--around themselves, in other words, since they *are* the lifestream. And they will be fully and automatically satisfied with what they have, whether it's a mansion on a hill or a pup tent in a jungle. They won't have to try to manifest the manure of new-age 'prosperity', because the genuine golden soul-stuff of God from the Buddhic Plane which is their natural home will pour itself upon them and magnetize their lives, as their hearts become unclogged from grief and greed, into attracting their own highest good--a highest good they presently cannot see, with their goddam insistence on trying to whore the very heart of God to the lusts of their own polluted hearts through the medium of their absolutely unconscious and deranged and degraded personalities.

"This bizarre 'logic' of theirs actually leaves less room for reasonableness than most other fundie religions . . . but in this case, this is not a good thing, because when reasonableness is present it indicates that at least a few of the people in any given herd may have at least the seed of an aspiration to move toward empathy. Now empathy is a holy quality; it flows from the compassion that proves beyond doubt that we are all One. But many people mistake reasonableness for empathy . . . you could say that reasonableness married to an embryonic desire to Achieve empathy represents a slightly higher form of reasonableness, and that rather than being completely useless, this slightly higher form of reasonableness is only nearly completely useless. So in Science of Mind, the extreme lack of reasonableness indicates, among other things, an aversion to even the seed of empathy. This is why frequently in that religion, if a person experiences sickness or poverty, he is actually blamed and degraded for his condition, rather than being uplifted and supported upon a great wave of divine-human Empathy. Empathy is the great Healer, not a degraded and greedy and egotistical misuse of logic and visioning to try to force wellness down the throat of someone who may need to experience illness or poverty for the sake of his own soul-growth into compassion. So Science of Mind's lack of reasonableness represents not progress, but an actual devolution into ancient mechanistic attitudes fostered by you-know-who . . . I'm pretty sure I don't have to tell you.

"Of course, Empathy not only protects and nourishes the one to whom empathy is extended, but also warms and nourishes the organism who carries the empathy. Indeed, empathy may frequently Achieve greater results with its host than with the one to whom the empathy is extended. So everyone who doesn't carry the sacred energy of empathy is hurting themselves, as well as neglecting to give a due and empowered energy-aid to those who are suffering.

"And this whole problem surrounding reasonableness and empathy is really that when the Prophet of Righteousness screeches against reasonableness, some misguided people may think--and I do mean 'think', I don't mean anything that has anything to do with the genuine knowingness of heart-consciousness--he is raving against empathy, when as we've already mentioned, this is certainly not the case. And I hope you are grown-up enough not to equate empathy with that sick use of sentiment called pity. If you're not, I pity you . . . nah, just a joke. Really, a person who pities anyone else is actually judging that person and pretending in perfectly deranged and unspiritual fashion to be superior to that person. That's why sometimes when a person wants to strike a violent emotional blow at another person they may say 'I pity you!' They want the person they're pitying to feel sick and degraded and helpless, but they're only revealing that they themselves have a long way to go toward claiming their humanity.

"And a 'pity fuck' is a very degraded activity, and more so for the one who pities than for the one who is pitied. A genuinely empathetic, compassionate fuck, such as the Sacred Prostitutes of Aphrodite train for, is always perfectly appropriate, but don't ever confuse this sacred activity with the degradation of the 'pity fuck'.

"Anyhow, this confusion around empathy and reasonableness, and around empathy and pity, does illustrate the problem we get into whenever the Holy Prophet is either raving against something or condoning something. Too many people don't understand that the Holy Prophet chooses his words with a level of care they are unfamiliar with, and they want to use the standard definitions that support their prefabricated thoughtforms. But they can't understand squat that way, so the Holy Prophet, in his everlasting compassion, will do what he can to either shove aside or shatter the illusions that give birth to their preconceptions."

I noticed Sharon had become receptive to Higher Mind, so I paused and watched the beautiful symbols of her knowingness. She was examining the nature of empathy and impersonality, and the golden beam of her knowingness embraced her.

Some of the symbols were cast my way, and to the degree that I can translate those symbols into English, here is the part of the pattern of Truth that Sharon had applied herself to. Of course, the spicy flavor of my use of the English language varies from Sharon's.

TRANSLATION
(one each)

To properly apply Empathy you must first Achieve a genuine impersonality. Now, the preconceptions of most people deceive them into believing that impersonality is the cultivation of a strange, mechanical remoteness. They believe they have to deny some part or parts of their humanity to Achieve the divine quality of impersonality. Of course, as with so many other unexamined beliefs they hold, this is utter horseshit. It is also an example of why you should *never* trust someone who tries to restrict your humanity in any way. To restrict your humanity is also to restrict your soul, which wants and must have a fully human vehicle to creatively work in the material dimension. Most "spiritual teachers" don't understand this truth, and thus recommend ignoring or restraining some aspect of your humanity, usually with some form of dualistic meditation, and they also promote the adoption of an artificial and soul-denying attitude of reverence for the legal system, and for people who put their panties on the same way you do but have some sort of fake "Presence" which they bought by obtaining some form of credentials.

And most of those others who preach freedom from restriction have no real discipline themselves and are lazy as a corn-fed hog on a sweltering day. And a few actually do have the seeds of discipline, but have no idea of how to apply those seeds so that they will reap a harvest of love, so instead they wind up reaping that bunch of weeds we call the polluted personal will. Yet Freedom is dependant on the proper and personal application of Discipline, without some schoolmarm in a monk's robe standing above you with a hickory switch encouraging reptilian shame to flush your unredeemed personality as you secretly grin at being a "good little girl" who apparently meets your alleged "teacher's" expectations, while your sweet beautiful Heart remains dark and uninvolved. Those who encourage dualistic meditation, whether this sort or any other sort, are deliberately encouraging hypocrisy and stunting the spiritual growth of their students, who often will go off into the woods to break the vow of silence they took for their meditation weekend, secretly snickering to themselves like reptiles in collusion with one another's illusions, or violate their sworn diet of rice with "pogey bait" they've smuggled in from the supermarket.

Remember that a good many "spiritual teachers" take up this particular "profession" because they want to run from some aspect or aspects of their Humanity. How then can they be of service to human beings?

Real discipline, rather than the fantasy discipline that exists only in the minds of the "spiritual teachers", involves getting to know and accept *every* aspect of yourself, including the part that wants to verbalize "Hi!" to your friends, rather than straining your energy and facial muscles in an overwrought denial of your own voice, as your false voice of strained gesturings renders null and void your vow of silence, in spirit, if not in fact. Yet if you violate the spirit of your vow, you're a damn liar . . . a damn liar who won't be disciplined by the so-called "spiritual teachers" because they are interested only in the appearance, rather than in the fact, of compliance with their practices and doctrines, because if you *appear* to be trying to follow their practices and doctrines, you validate in their minds their "status" as "spiritual teachers", as well as affirm the alleged validity of whatever religion they're pushing. So the correct response to the part of yourself that wants to say "Hi!" is simply to thoroughly explore that part . . . and if you've been completely honest and dedicated, you'll find that when your exploration is complete, you won't be a chatterbox anymore, but neither will you remain silent if you want to say something. (However, you may find you seldom want to speak, for you've recognized that the usual function of speech is merely to create or justify glamours and illusions, or to create background noise for people who are afraid of the beautiful, transcendent Voice of the Silence.) And if your belly wants a hamburger rather than a bowl of rice, you have to provide your belly with a hamburger if you're going to remain true to yourself, rather than true to the preconceptions and fascist practices of the "spiritual teachers". Your approach to the Godhead that resides both within and without you is a highly individual and thus a genuinely *disciplined* affair, and no individual can prescribe for any other individual. People who want to prescribe for others often wind up being flushed down the commode of their own egotism.

Man, this is why you shouldn't trust your welfare to spiritual teachers! Those who feel they can teach you anything are a hell of a long way from crafting a genuine, fiery spiritual path for themselves. A few of us have had spiritual mentors, but a spiritual mentor just plants a few hints and goes away and you may not see him for years afterward, or even decades. In the intervening years one or another of those hints will occasionally explode in your brain like a quantum firecracker, and after enough of these quantum firecrackers have exploded, you find you've gained a little insight. But don't ever trust someone who feels he has something to teach you, man. Go your own way in peace, after you've knocked him in the head with a stick of stove wood.

Always remember that teaching isn't the same as sharing. And sharing isn't a doing, it's an energy out of which physical actions may or may not arise. Genuine sharing is a soul quality and comes from the ruby red flame of the heart. And to genuinely share, you have to Achieve impersonality.

So back to empathy and impersonality. If you are perceptive enough to be able to avoid the traps set by the "spiritual teachers", you will see that the Achievement of impersonality is the outcome of releasing all your attachments. Attachments belong to the world of glamour and illusion, and are the filthy strings that keep you bound to that world, so of course you have to let them go if you're going to progress. Attachments impede your humanity, and they impede your divinity, so cleaning them out of your system is the only way to progress into a full development of humanness. You don't become remote when you develop impersonality, you become warmer and warmer and brighter and brighter, because only when you've released the attachments can your heart really flow smoothly and shine and irradiate with great warmth all those around you.

They say in the twentieth century that justice is blind, and of course it is blind the way they practice it. They equate blind justice with impersonality, which is the crime of a fool. So the legal system is run by sightless, foolish criminals who wear somber robes or tailored suits and argue with a pretense of impersonality, but even this sick pretense is based on a misperception they whore to their own lust for money and status. They can't even practice their own weak preconceptions, let alone Achieve contact with that divine quality which manifests as genuine Justice.

Real Justice is always blended with Mercy and Compassion, and the proper application of these living Principles requires the touch of a master artist. Real Justice is a living beam of energy, nothing concrete about it, just as every divine Principle is a beam of living energy. And *every* divine Principle flows from the Source Principle of Love. Easy enough, right? But people whore energy all the time, trying to turn a beautiful living stream of pure energy into a dirty, manacled concrete sidewalk. Well, they pollute their physical streams and rivers, so I guess it's just natural, in a perverted sort of way, for them to pollute the living streams of pure energy which unpolluted might help to wash them clean of their lusts and the preconceptions that arise out of those lusts. "As above, so below." For the legal system is nothing more than a system of preconceptions born largely out of the somewhat physically detached lusts of the rational mind, which itself is the lowest aspect of the mental body. As the lowest aspect, its only proper use is to receive the intuitive illumination from the higher mental body, yet in primitive, egocentrically arrogant people, particularly those who pretend they are trying to deny the flesh, the rational mind agitates for an artificial dominance, and these undisciplined people usually let it succeed. In them, the soul-world is dominated, and often prevented from manifesting itself in their consciousness altogether, by the artificial dominance of their rational mind . . . this conduct itself isn't logical, but who ever said the rational mind was logical?

If a person's rational mind dominates, yet that person manages to develop the energy of a pure aspiration and purifies his motives so they will support his aspiration, then he can work with the rational mind, turning it from a path of rationalizing its own lusts and limitations into constructing a channel to the soul-world of intuition. Then he will begin to see that *knowing* is far superior to thinking, and ultimately he will become fully intuitive as he completes the construction of this channel.

Finally, as he fuses himself more and more with the plane of the soul, of the intuition, the day will come when he no longer needs this channel and it will be discarded as he becomes fully merged with a certain Higher Aspect of himself, and at that time his rational mind and personality and emotions and physical body will be entirely receptive to the Real Self and will be flooded with the energy of Real Self. From that moment forward, the vehicle will never again attempt to dominate the Driver, and for the very first time, the vehicle itself will know that "peace which passeth all understanding".

This person who is fully at home on the plane of the intuition has no preconceptions and no fake respect for the preconceptions of others. He respects their souls and the heart-organ where their souls reside, not the sense of false-self they get from their preconceptions. It produces an urgency of service in him when he sees that they are unskilled at working with the energies of Higher Mind, and so are unaware of how to build energetic forms which are attuned to those energies and help those living energies manifest "down" from the level of Higher Mind into the physical, emotional and lower dimensions, and of how to irradiate and empower and love and cultivate those forms so they can express themselves properly. For *everything* in the universe is alive, there is no such thing as "inorganic".

So the conscious creation of these living forms must replace the incompetent Frankenstein's monsters which people of the twentieth century build, then submit themselves as slaves to. Primitive people always seem to feel they have to disenfranchise themselves from some aspect or aspects of their own humanity, so they build illusions and agree to pretend those illusions are real, whether they're worshipping a big stone head on a remote island or a system of laws that grew out of the egocentric idolatry of a tribe of vengeful desert sheepherders thousands of years earlier that is so deluded that it tries to deny its own idolatry. For the legal system of the West in the twentieth century is nothing more than a glimpse into the mind of a Jehovah gone senile. It is nothing more than a system of organized, empty vengeance.

But a slave is always a sneaky devil, and even as he's promising to conform to the wishes of "de ole massa", he's plotting how to thwart those wishes to get a little more personal freedom for himself. The twentieth century people agree (or at least pretend to agree) that taxes are holy and agree to pay those taxes, then they try to knock loopholes in their agreement. They constantly agree to follow religious beliefs and laws which are more or less derived from those beliefs, as the part of themselves those religions and laws were designed to lynch screams out in rage and rebellion, always grasping for some straw of secret and forbidden nourishment for its own nature, and biding its time against the day when it will be strong enough to tar and feather the lynch mob with its sense of outrage at love and light and life denied.

Such hypocrisy is never necessary for people who know how to build living forms to give expression to living energies. And those enlightened and true forms and energies complement their creators, and help give expression to the creator's freedom.

THIS CONCLUDES THE TRANSLATION
OF THE PRIVATE THOUGHTS OF SHARON TOMKINS

I smiled at Sharon. "I love your geometries! You are smart."
"Thank you," she said softly.
The rest of the family were looking from one to the other of us with a good deal of puzzlement, but at least their eyes weren't glazed over any more. The break they enjoyed while I was silently and blissfully enjoying Sharon's beautiful mind had restored them.
Then I prepared to continue with my own circular energy-sermon, the sermon I somehow had to convert out of its native modes of expression into a linear English. I knew that everyone of average intelligence in the twentieth century, and maybe a lot of people of below average intelligence, had the mental faculties and energy bodies to contact Truth; the only thing they lacked was a pure aspiration and a sense of endurance.
So in their complacent complicatedness, they hadn't risen above the illusion of "fairness", which itself is the bastard offspring of the illusion of "balance". All these lazy, dualistic illusions have to go, and did go when humanity began to purify its aspirations. For "fairness" had to give way to genuine Justice, and the illusion of "balance" had to succumb to the sacred Truth of Integration--of Intelligent Love, of that wholebody Love which knows no illusion of opposites. The illusion of opposites is father to the illusion of balance, so answer me this: why would anyone want to be balanced?
Hell, man, instead of trying to balance supposed "opposites" against each other in an eternal undisciplined warfare of checks and balances, doesn't it make a lot more sense to clean the glamour and illusion out of

yourself so you can integrate in a stable union of all your parts, with each part always supporting and complementing every other part in the proper ratios?   Only such a human vehicle is stable enough to accept or to manifest the totality of the love of the Heart, which itself is incapable of perceiving opposites. Radiating this total love out of the entire body and personality, with each sanctified portion of the personality and body lending its own unique color and flavor to the Love is what we call Intelligent Love--the Love of the future humans. And only Intelligently Loving Humans can construct the living, nondualistic forms that house the energy of the future society.

I gave a happy grunt in the sudden knowledge that my own little family would play a role in eliminating human preconceptions, thus paving the way for the synergy of Intelligent Love to manifest and rejuvenate the world.

I cleared my throat, and felt my cock swell with love for my little family, a full, rich lovingness unhampered by sentiment or preconceptions. I loved them so! So I tendered myself into their poised awareness once more, taking their hearts into my own to guide them into the flowing Redemption of Trueness.

"People must Achieve flowingness," I said. "This flowingness is provided by a channel so it can manifest as the great lifestream of the organism. The channel is made of countless refined gems of Truth. The organism cannot flow in the presence of preconceptions . . . unfortunately, some people harbor the preconception that flowingness is the same as spontaneity. Again with the confusion around words, and it shows the laziness of people as they approach the Great Work of transforming themselves into an unpredictable flowingness.

"An unpredictable flowingness is not the same as spontaneity. Spontaneity may sometimes occur--very rarely, actually--within the realm of flowingness, but in that sacred flowing realm unpredictability is always on call. Not usually spontaneity, but unpredictability. The unpredictability, as well as everything else about your flowingness, moves through channels which may be invisible to everyone else, but those channels are there, and they are real. They are composed of the Buddhic-stuff, they are made of pure intuition. And they are actually *more* real than anything ever perceived by those whose higher mental bodies and higher brain functions haven't yet been activated.

"Since your channels are invisible to those around you, an easy, sane unpredictability is available to you at all times. But those who pursue spontaneity have only the fractured illusion of unpredictability, and this fracturing is often reflected in their lives in ways that are more or less obvious.

"A sane unpredictability will go a long way toward providing you with a satisfactory interface with this world, whereas spontaneity is usually a step toward madness. However, the person who has Achieved a genuine and sane unpredictable flowingness may occasionally experience spontaneity, and when he does it is a better spontaneity, a genuinely conscious spontaneity, and this sudden little jolt of spontaneity may actually serve to form the beginning of another tributary of his great lifestream . . . in which case, that little jewel of conscious spontaneity becomes a lasting little part of the pattern of his life, a pattern which can be perceived from a realm of higher visioning.

"Please be advised, my lambs, that there is no such thing as paradox."

Eyes were glazing over again at this point; I guess the family still had a few preconceptions to get rid of. For when intuitional knowingness runs up against preconceptions, the struggle between the two may produce a certain fatigue. However, once those preconceptions have finally been washed away, there will be no more fatigue as the flowingness triumphantly runs along in the self-created riverbed of its own unique expression of Truth. For although Truth is one great Energy, it is never homogeneous in its expression. Remember this, oh Individual!

I felt compassion for the family's weariness, so the flowingness of my life took me back to the more familiar rant against fundamentalism. I knew that Hubert, who was always on a quest for wisdom, would remember everything I said and could repeat it upon request if any of the family wanted a review. My flowingness had almost chosen to embark upon a slight raving against that type of new-age "leader" who trivializes suffering in an ostensible attempt to relieve it, but instead chose to return to the main tributary of the discussion thus far. But if my flowingness *had* chosen to talk about this particular type of new-age "leader", one of the things it would have pointed out is that trivializing suffering is not the same as approaching suffering with a degree of humor and reveals a lack of leadership skills on the part of this type of alleged "leader". My flowingness would also have pointed out that the inspiration for this type of new-age "leader" does not come from that compassionate Godforce in which conscious souls dwell. Do you have any idea where such a person's so-called "inspiration" comes from? Yep, that's it, and I didn't even have to tell you, honey.

I took up the rant against fundamentalism and complicatedness more or less where I'd left off. I figured this more concrete assault on preconceptions would be a welcome break for them after the assault of flowing Buddhic Truth. "Let's give the devil his due; Science of Mind may be, overall, less offensive and perhaps less dangerous than Christian fundamentalism. And for those who have the strength to slog out of the mud into the clear sweet waters of life, maybe Science of Mind was sort of a stepping stone for them, a place to take a temporary refuge from other, more blasphemous and soul-damaging forms of fundamentalism.

"But what all these fundamentalist religions have in common is sophistry and just plain complicatedness. Usually their doctrine is simple and childish, rather than being multidimensional and childlike, but their system of justifications for their dogma is so complicated that old Fran Bacon couldn't figure it out . . . and if he did figure it out, he would chuckle madly at its stupidity . . . and he did chuckle madly at its stupidity, when he heard the one about the angels dancing on the head of a pin.

"Stupidity is usually wound up in complicatedness somehow, so what we want to do is to refine ourselves into receivers of multiplane perception. As already mentioned, genuine heart-centered Altruism rather than complicated and sloppy sentimentality is the way to refine ourselves along our spiritual path. Remember that genuine Altruism takes no prisoners and won't stop for anything, no matter what. It is not a fanatic--well, not usually--but it is powered by the strongest force in the universe, which is that multiplane love which emanates from the Heart of God and is received by every sensitive organism and integrated into the daily experience of that organism.

"Shit, man, evolution is simple, really, but twentieth century people don't get it because they prefer the sophistry and complicatedness and self-justification that will allow them to hang on to the world of glamour and illusion. They ain't got no sense, baby."

I remembered a conversation I'd ignorantly allowed myself to be drawn into with one of our fellow co-opers, a politically-correct fellow who mainly spent his days trying to rationalize reasons to hang onto his political-correctness. "One of these rationalizing, belief-oriented people questioned my 'arguments', as he put it, the other day. I just looked at him and walked away, shaking my head. This poor deluded soul didn't see that I have no arguments and that I would get no thrill from his agreeing with me, if for no other reason that it was impossible for him or anyone else to agree with me . . . or to agree with each other, for that matter, assuming any of them ever had any perception of Truth. The person who agrees or disagrees is not the person who directly experiences Truth; therefore, he has no idea where I'm coming from, so whatever he's agreeing or disagreeing with, it has nothing to do with me. I speak simply because I'm impulsed by the plane of the intuition to speak, not because I want anyone to agree with me. I speak that which must be spoken, but what people do with it is their own affair. Most probably, they will put it in the outhouse and wipe their asses on it when they are feeling especially deviant.

"Agreement and disagreement are irrelevant and a waste of time and precious energy that could be devoted to genuine spiritual Work. When Sharon and I speak to someone about spiritual matters, we make no arguments, we simply observe the spiritual truths that make themselves evident through our coordination with our higher mental bodies, and then we report on those truths. People must coordinate themselves with Truth, not agree with it . . . you can't agree with it, because if you're agreeing with it you're not seeing it and experiencing it for yourself. Agreement always implies separation; you have the one who is agreeing, and you have that which is being agreed with. Yet there is no separation in the supernal world of Truth. You must *become* Truth, because that's the only way you can understand It.

"You can only agree or disagree with illusion and glamour, man, not with Truth. Truth cares not a tinker's damn about your agreement or disagreement. Truth is God. Truth is *you*, if you only knew it.

"Of course, although you may not have noticed, I am not perfect, and therefore might at some point make a mistake in either my interpretation or my expression of these composer-energies that symbolize Truth--and Truth *is* a symbol, so that which adequately symbolizes Truth in a particular moment is also the very thing it symbolizes in that particular moment. But because I might make a mistake in my interpretation of the giant galactic living Truth-Symbols or in my verbal attempt at indicating that which by its very nature can't be adequately conveyed in words, you should always trust your own awareness, rather than trusting my awareness or presentation. Never trust anyone who tries to manipulate you into trusting your own awareness to a lesser degree, regardless of what their credentials appear to be and regardless of how enlightened or wise they manage to appear. You need to *fully* learn to trust your own awareness, always. It is wise to carry a baseball bat or an ax handle in your car in case you meet one of these alleged people who try to manipulate you into reducing your trust in your own heart . . . turn their melon-heads into a baseball and they'll forget all about manipulating you!

"I'm sincere in my attempts to exemplify spirituality and to convey some small taste or scent of Truth to you, and this you know. I don't have to be perfect in my presentation, just sincere and utterly compassionate. And you probably realize that only an utterly sincere person can approach Truth, and that those who, as the Bible puts it, 'sit in the seat of the scornful' will always be denied any entrance into the outer perimeter of Truth. These scornful ones are those who try to deceive you and usually also themselves that they are skeptics, but who really have an ax to grind, and that ax consists in denying themselves multidimensional god-awareness, and confusing you into abandoning your own Quest--these are the ones who are the tools of the Lodge of Confusion, though many of them don't realize they are being manipulated. Now, these are not the true skeptics. A true skeptic has no agenda other than finding Truth, no matter What it may be or where it may lie, and he'll accept that Truth when he gets there. A true skeptic is honest and is on his own Quest, a thing that always is to be respected. But these pseudo-skeptics with their pseudo-science of disillusionment and angst in the face of the magical world are untouched by reality or by true love. They are spiritually malnourished, and if they aren't lucky enough to get spiritually prodded somehow into coming in for supper, they may become spiritually dead, not even fit manure to fertilize the future world.

"Anyhow, a presentation of Truth is not about the words so much, it's almost exclusively about energy. Energy attached to either a verbal or a written presentation may serve to quicken your blessed, sweet heart or your higher mental body. Maybe the energy attached to my presentation can help quicken you, even if the presentation itself may be flawed, or if your ability to listen currently isn't very highly developed.

"People who have an unhealthy attachment to words are unaware of the limitations of words. Even a highly-skilled wordsmith can't transmit much of the Supernal Truth in words. People talk about the contradictions in their sacred scriptures . . . well, sometimes there may be contradictions, especially after centuries have passed and the documents have been badly edited by incompetent people, or deliberately censored by wicked people. But as often as not, those so-called contradictions aren't contradictions at all, but are evidence of the limited linear mindset of the reader or listener. To know exactly where a multiplane writer or speaker is coming from, you have to know which cycle or subcycle of his own life he's standing on in the moment he delivers a given set of words to you, and you have to be aware that his orientation to his own cycles and subcycles may be shifting from moment to moment. Then you have to develop some ability to coordinate your own consciousness with his cycles, so you can ride with him. The Secret of Proteus is simply this conscious perception and experience of cycles. And in another sense, the Secret of Proteus is contained in consciously working with the different illumined and unified facets of the heart-jewel, rather than paying attention to cycles. So again and again words may confuse us; if I speak about the Secret of Proteus or about many other subjects, you won't actually be with me unless you can feel where I am and take the energy-hand I extend to you, if only for a moment.

"You already know that the meaning of some words changes when those words are used in varying contexts. For instance, when the natives of future timezones call the citizens of the twentieth century 'The Simple People', it is not an appellation of respect or of trust. However, the person who has fully developed his multiplane awareness may appear to be a simple person . . . and maybe he is, in a sense. But if so, his simplicity is an enriched simplicity. He has refined his complicatedness into complexity, then transcended complexity to take his place consciously in the world of cycles, then transcended even the experience of cycles to arrive at a full multiplane consciousness of the boundless energy-sea. So if the multiplane person is called a simple person, it is usually a compliment. Really, the 'simplicity' of the multiplane person is a state of unconditional Grace and Innocence. He would be better served, and our perceptions of him would be better served, by referring to him as an Innocent person, rather than as a simple person.

"I like what one of our operatives named Alan Watts said. He said, 'I'm just trying to keep the people entertained while the Holy Spirit does its Work.' He was a Christian priest, but I like him anyway."

Well, Mimi was snoring. Just sitting on the floor propped against the bed and snoring, her fat little belly jiggling a little. I wanted to go over and caress her belly, and did so. She woke up after a moment and smiled at me. "Honey," I said with much love, "you might want to try to stay awake. I'm concerned Pa Miyamoto might miss something, and I want him to remember what I'm saying today, so he can remind me of it after I'm born."

She hugged me and patted my back, then smiled again and got up and sat in a chair. I kissed her belly and caressed Pa for a moment, then continued with my lecture. This was actually a variation of the sermon that had gotten me kicked out of Aphrodite's Legions, a fundamentalist religion that I joined right after being discharged from Divinity School.

"We were talking about how primitive Americans had no idea of the potential they carried within themselves, let alone an understanding of how to develop that potential and then externalizing it into creating a spiritually polarized society, a truly human society where the Sacred Quest for the spiritual life is the *only* feature of a person's day to day experience . . . because soul is in everything, and it is up to us to find the soul in everything we touch. And they never could tap those higher functions as long as they continued to choose to live in a cloud of manipulation and fear, such as that encouraged by the unregenerate news media with its preference for psychic terrorism, instead of choosing to learn to activate their hearts and learning to live in heart-centered love and compassion and Self Respect--that is, respect for their True Self. But here in the twentieth century they don't even know True Self. They cannot conceive of a world of Truth that is so vast that language cannot even approach It, and where communication occurs in the form of energies which compose themselves into geometric multiplane symbols.

"I'm not talking about the geometry people learn--or don't learn--in schools, I'm talking about directly experiencing the inner Workings of God's mind--schools are unnatural and unholy and even go so far in the so-called civilized West as to try to deny God entrance, as though God were one of these sex offenders your people are so terrified of. Schools make natural things seem hard, but God's mind is a place of joy and ease and beautiful living Symbols. As an aside, let me remind you here that I'm not talking about the symbols of the astral or emotional plane, as pretty as some of them are. I'm talking about the plane of pure intuition, the Buddhic Plane.

"Once you can perceive these Energies and Symbols of the Buddhic Plane adequately, you can also perceive the symbol of Yourself and Its-- that is, *Your*--relation to the pattern of reality as a whole. And because you have adequately come to embody a certain aspect of Reality, you have become your own symbol. You will see the constantly shifting pattern and will consciously ride that pattern like a boat riding upon a pleasantly shifting sea. This is not something you *do*, it is something you *are* as a conscious aspect of the great sea. You as living symbol are a boat riding consciously upon the eternal sea of universal existence, a boat born out of the sea-stuff and enriched by your strivings in the illusion of time and space into knowing the symbol of your life. The symbol of your eternal living*ness*. There is never any efforting involved in being your*self*. This is the essence of the future of magic; in the past, the magician always felt a little separate from some part or parts of himself, or from some aspect or aspects of the universe, and ritual was born out of that sense of separation, with the best rituals serving to reduce that sense of separation somewhat by producing some degree of alignment between the magician and some aspect or aspects of the Godforce.

"The most skilled magicians of the future won't do any sort of obvious magical work, except that perhaps some of them might do a ritual with their friends to affirm their soul connection, rather than to produce some phenomenon outwardly observable to the material or astral eye. In fact, phenomena won't interest the future magician at all, because the desire for phenomena is always selfish and childish and the motives of the future magician have arrived at that totality of purity that allows for the complete infusion of love, and this, my friends, is the true energy of Altruism. And Altruism is not what you *do*, sweet children, it is what you *are*. If the genuine love-infused Altruist, rather than the fake altruist who is motivated by the selfish manipulative energy of sentiment, performs a given action, that action will be imbued with the energy of his Altruism, and so will have a loving, evolutionary effect, but that action itself is not his Altruism. The true Altruist is having an evolutionary effect on the world because of the energy he emanates even when he's just sitting around with his thumbs up his ass. On the other hand, the so-called altruist whose work holds the slimy energy of sentiment is doing little or no good in the world, regardless of the outward appearances accepted by the deluded. If anything, the usual sentimental type of 'altruist' is prolonging the troubles of the world by encouraging the continued existence of the sentiment that creates the troubles. Sentiment is not love, and the faculty which holds the sentiment is a long way from being redeemed and becoming truly loving. Remember that only phenomena where love is adequately demonstrated interest the future magician. Wisdom is love-in-action, and this is the interest of the future magicians. This wisdom imbues every act of the successful magician of the future, and it actively emanates from him and enlivens his surroundings all the time.

"So the basic training of the future magicians involves the purification and redemption of **all** aspects of themselves, and the advanced condition the successful magician eventually finds himself in is simply his attunement with his own intuition, which also links him up with God's intuition. At that point, his only practice consists of tuning in to the pattern of God's intuition and allowing himself to be absorbed while remaining fully functional on the physical plane and on every other plane accessible to humans. Actually, this is not even a practice, because he's automatically tuned in to the intuitional plane every second of the day. He can see the Pattern, he can see his place in the Pattern, and he consciously rides the pattern like a master boatman. All this is without effort, his mind and emotions are quiet and serene. He's still just like every other human being, and takes a shit when necessary just like they do, but he knows where he stands in the Pattern at any given moment and allows himself to be carried on a wave of intuitional force to wherever he may be needed to assist as a conscious unit in God's Creative Process. For he is still completely conscious of himself as an individual, and as a part of God. In fact, only a person who is fully conscious of himself as an individual can also be completely conscious of God. The true Individual and God are perfect intimates, their bedtime whispers unavailable to the ear of those who allow themselves to be manipulated by their neighbors.

"And the true Individual carries a true, full and total synthesis of Love within himself. Love operates with discipline, never with restraint. And this fullbody love of Aphrodite's magician demonstrates as his sexual potency combining forevermore with the love of his heart. The love is allowed to flood the sexual nature and redeem it utterly, after, of course, the glamour and illusion have been consciously cleaned out of it so that no manipulation or other limitations remain.

"For you see, human beings *are* sex. The glamorized person exemplifies a polluted, manipulative, competitive approach to the divine faculty of sexuality and is a long way from Achieving his or her potential. The truly disciplined, free human being knows himself or herself as love incarnate, and once this love has utterly redeemed the sexual nature, this free human being *is* sex and *is* love--is sex fused with love! We call this Intelligent Love. No more delicious a combination is possible. And this is the person who knows the fire of Agni, the person who glows with the reddish-pink fire of total transmutation. This is the Fiery-Hearted One whose courageous wings continually brush against the sun, and who is usually burned by the undisciplined, unloving actions of those he has come to assist when he incarnates into a degenerate culture with the holy sanctified urge of his loving sexiness to bring a new livingness to it.

"Human beings are the only beings who are in heat all the time, both the males and the females. Human beings *are* sex, and we were made in this sweet image of God's Creative Process so we could learn to share. Sexuality isn't primarily about reproduction in the human kingdom, it's primarily about sharing. Creativity is all about *sharing*, baby. If human sexuality were only meant to propagate the species, we would have specific rutting seasons just like the other animals--only humans aren't animals. We were meant to share without any competition at all, not sharpen our antlers on the mechanisms of capitalism like a fucking half-conscious beast.

"The dualistic idiot will take what I've just said to be a statement of support for promiscuity, but such is not the case at all. It's true that on our Path toward love we may lapse into promiscuity at times, but once the full discipline of the love-sex nature has been mastered we won't be promiscuous or celibate or anything else that can be categorized. We will move according to the love of our hearts as our bodies are propelled into contact with those bodies whose souls we may drink deeply of, as we allow them to drink deeply of our own souls. This is the true nature of what Heinlein called 'water brotherhood'. Do you grok?"

I turned my Eye back to its work of surveying the factory schools of the twentieth century, those hellholes of the concentration-camp mentality which feared fundamentalism so much they'd allowed themselves to become fundamentalist in their aversion to God, which feared violence so much they psychically and emotionally crushed the children, which made the violence worse, sometimes in the schools themselves and sometimes after the kids graduated without ever having learned the responsible use of a rifle in the workplace, and thus went on an indiscriminate shooting spree. I knew that many of these people in the Twentieth would have considered me insane if they could see a fraction of the inner workings of my mind, but the truth is that they would only be seeing their own fearful insanity being mirrored back at them. The import of my mind would be incomprehensible to them and they would place the most negative projections they could onto it as an excuse to avoid having to actually discipline themselves into working themselves toward a comprehension.

Yet they were the ones who contributed to the violence in their schools, not I. They insured that everything the kids learned was smeared with the fecal corruption of competition, luring the kids into a lifelong violence so ingrained that most of the time they didn't even consciously realize they were violent, savage beings who were enslaved to the chimpanzee passions of the jungle. They did not realize that the luxury they were schooled to fight for represented not quality and victory, but decay and a stagnating death, rather than either true life or a quick and merciful flash of beneficial death. So they spent their entire lives dying, until in the end there was nothing left to live for as their crushed spirits withered away on the vine of their souls, and their souls left their bodies and mangled spirits behind and went on a Journey of temporary repose, trying to gather enough strength for itself that maybe in its next life it would be able to break through the shame and murder of competition and actually Achieve some fraction of the purpose of manifesting the divine life upon the material plane.

A part of the problem was that twentieth century people insisted on seeing evolution and life in general as a linear phenomenon, but this was a total illusion. Life is composed of circular motions, of cycles, not of straight lines. There is no such thing as a straight line; draw a so-called straight line that's long enough, and eventually you'll find you've simply drawn a circle around the earth . . . or around the universe, if you begin in outer space and have a ship capable of making the voyage. A "straight" line is merely the part of a circle that's right before your eyes. It seldom serves the understanding to consider only that which lies right before your eyes.

And so even their understanding of so basic a phenomenon as human evolution was flawed. Their vision, such as it was, extended over only an eyeblink of the time humans have actually inhabited the earth. Relatively advanced civilizations, with air travel and all other manner of technological innovations that people in the Twentieth smugly considered their own innovations, were actually known to societies millions of years ago. If they had disciplined themselves into a spiritual awareness that admitted a feel for the cycles of human evolution, their straight-line awareness would have simply vanished as the fool illusion it was. Societies and whole races and sub-races of humans have arisen and fallen for millions upon millions of years upon this globe in cycles that repeat seemingly without end, a system of education whose purpose is to school the unregenerate and make them whole. In this sense, the earth is sort of a juvenile reform school, except that in more localized reform schools the young people realize they are inmates and have a more correct perception of their place in the scheme of things. But the people of the earth didn't think of themselves as being either juvenile or in need of drastic and near-total reform, so they continued behaving as chimpanzees, not realizing that they were not descended from apes, but that apes were descended from *them*--from humans who had allowed themselves to degenerate past a certain point. Ape and man do share a common ancestor, and that ancestor is man himself.

Freud was shaking me by the arm. "Wake up, Sonny-Bob. If you're through preaching, I want to fuck Aphrodite again."

I gave a slight smile through bleary eyes. "Sorry, ya'll. I was pondering--contrasting and comparing, they'd call it in the schools of the twentieth century--and arranging the pattern of my experiences into a proper perception of cycles. But even I know that anything that can be described in words isn't being described at all, and that if the universe could be seen as the Grid it is, that the cycles of humanity upon the earth would vanish into one of the straight lines of the Grid . . . except that the Grid itself, seen from a still broader Vision would ultimately appear as just two series of circles, one laid horizontally and one vertically. Our cycles look pretty big to us, but from a higher Vision they vanish into the background of the Grid . . . yet from an even higher perspective than that, the Grid Itself is seen as a pattern of circles. Lordy, Lordy."

"You're stoned, Sonny-Bob," Freud said finally.

"Maybe so," Sharon put in, "but Sonny-Bob and I share a similar perception, and I don't use drugs."

"Neither do I," I said, "but I've been falsely accused of it more than once."

"Well, either finish your sermon or let me and Aphrodite go back to our room. I'm horny and I want to share."

"Okay, horny Freud. Just quit waving your spear at me, you spear-chucker."

Freud backed away hastily. "Sorry, man. I didn't realize I was still nekked and my dick was hard."

I looked at him suspiciously. "I hope you didn't realize it . . . but you've been petting that cat lately, so I don't know."

Freud had stepped into his briefs and was trying to force the blood out of his penis. "Aw, forget about it, man."

"Okay," I finally said, after a pause of sufficient length to demonstrate my mastery of the situation by proving that anyone I suspected of even bearing a hint of faggy energy would be subject to uncomfortable silences in front of other people. Though, I admitted to myself, I wasn't sure how I would handle Freud if it were just me and him.

"Friends, we were discussing how unnatural and unholy these materialistic schools of this century are," I said. "Have you noticed how they try to ban both God and sex in the schools?"

I looked around at them, feeling the bleariness leaving my eyes, as my Eye made its perceptions known.

"These mediocre people: fighting both to keep God out of school and to keep sex out of school--there's a correlation, since sex is the beginning of spirituality, just as the root of morality is the right to self-defense. Sex is such a powerful spiritual force that I suspect that even atheists scream out for God during their most passionate moments.

"Of course, the fundamentalist Christians want their God to be able to storm the schools, but their God's sexuality has been withheld from him and he's so pissed off by it that he's turned to emotional violence, and is no longer a god with any spiritual or healthy sexual attributes.

"The liberals, on the other hand, want to at least acknowledge a remote, frigid, mechanical, de-godded approach to sex, yet generally try to ban self-defense from the schools. The liberals have no morality to support what is at least an embryonic, feeble attempt to acknowledge the source of all spirituality, while the fundamentalists have no spirituality whatsoever with their closed-circuited and unhallowed approach to implementing a 'morality' which doesn't acknowledge and attempts to squeeze out of existence the consciousness of sex, a consciousness which is essential to making an approach to the Divine.

"Your society is fractured beyond the point of mere schizophrenia and is perhaps the most insane society that has ever existed. Yours is a 'civilization' which was developed to manifest the energies of the solar plexus chakra and to devise the appropriate structures for manifesting those energies, just as Lemuria could be considered a root chakra civilization and Atlantis a sacral center civilization.

"Yet in your alleged culture the solar plexus chakra is divided against itself; the front or feeling side of the chakra, represented by the liberals, is cut off from the rear or will side, represented by the conservatives. I don't know who came up with the bizarre and inaccurate distinction of 'right' and 'left' wings of the political process, because wings have nothing to do with it, but if they did the eagle of your culture certainly wouldn't fly, with each wing working against the other.

"Conservatives and liberals both belong to the same continuum, the same chakra, the same spectrum of feeling and perception and experience, yet seem to believe there's some real difference between them. But the only difference is that each 'side' has a slightly different approach to encouraging the breakup, the fracturing, of this solar plexus society. Each 'side' has a slightly different method of spreading their own sickness, that's all. So it's not a matter of left and right, it's a matter of front and back, with each so-called 'side' scrabbling frantically to deny nourishment to the other 'side', trying to hog the whole energy of the chakra to itself, with the result that almost all of the energy actually leaks out of the chakra in the artificial chasm that has been created between the front and back, leaving the people of your society, regardless of their political preferences, almost totally without nourishment. Your society is frenetic as it grasps for physical survival and for a minimum of emotional nourishment, but lethargic and barren spiritually, incapable of doing any more good in the world until significant numbers of people become competent enough to see the problem and loving enough to correct it, and compassionate enough to smash anyone who tries to stop the healing process.

"For this society to unify and heal, it's going to have to recognize itself as a vessel for solar plexus energy, and work to defragment itself as the chakra through which that energy flows. This society's ultimate healing will come when itself as solar plexus is no longer fragmented and has recrystallized into one pure jewel to transmit solar plexus energy to the planet, and from this planet to other planets, and then learned to submit itself to the wisdom and love of the Planetary Heart, ultimately being infused and then absorbed by that Heart. For Heart society is the next great evolution for Humanity, once the present mess has been cleaned up and societal organisms made healthy again.

"An organism that has a fractured chakra will behave in ways that are insane by definition. Such a divided organism cannot properly integrate the light of Love with itself, let alone extend that light to others. And since a genuinely integrated organism projects love in ways which are incomprehensible to the divided organism, that divided organism will project its own attributes--usually its worst attributes--onto the integrated organism and never realize that its assessment is fractured and that it is looking in the mirror of its own delusions and perceiving only its own distorted reflection.

"The truly integrated organism is invisible to the fractured organism. Integration is the real secret to invisibility. No fractured organism can ever perceive what's *really* going on in the life of an integrated organism, and this invisibility is part of what assures that the truly integrated organism's Visioning Process will always ripen to fruition-- even when the fractured organism believes it has defeated the integrated organism. When Obi-Wan Kenobi surrendered to His Destiny and allowed Darth Vader to strike Him down, in that moment He was completely invisible to His enemy. Darth Vader had no idea that Obi-Wan had just kicked his black ass, and insured that the Jedi would return and that goodness would prevail. The ignorant Vader had no idea even of how a Divine Visioning Process works, so of course he had no idea of how Obi-Wan had married His personal actions with the vastness of a mythical and universal Vision to insure the outworking of that Vision. But the Vision can always count on the fidelity and stamina of Its Champions; they've been melted down in a strict crucible and recast in the Image of the Vision Itself."

Mimi raised a hand. "Beloved, you've said the things about schools I've always felt but didn't quite have the words for. And after the things you've just said about the solar plexus society, it looks to me as if the schools are just another fractured piece of a fractured society and can't help a person touch her true self or catch a glimpse of anything that's real."

I was pleased with my little girl. I smiled at her and said, "That's right, honey. As we've discussed, schools make natural things seem hard, and don't even teach or have a Vision of true geometry or true anything a'tall, but your natural home in God's Mind is a place of joy and ease and beautiful living Symbols. The Buddhic Plane is humanity's natural home and is just sitting there like a natural goldfield, waiting for humanity to claim it. And every stone of this sanctified plane is a vibrating nugget of the highest quality, and waves of golden energy wash over you all the time. On this plane, you have your golden particles and golden waves at the same time! All is awash in beautiful golden energy.

"And speaking of things Buddhic, let me say that occasionally I'll hear some Buddhist call his religion an atheistic religion--ridiculous! But this belief by some Buddhists is another illustration of how every religion becomes corrupt. The Buddha was no more an atheist than Albert Einstein was an ignoramus! Buddha may not have talked about God, and he may not have admitted to any truck with the gods, but he preached on the virtues of love and compassion. My friends, God *is* love, therefore a person who genuinely experiences the real love of the heart knows God, and thus cannot be an atheist. The Buddha knew God as only a son can know his Dad.

"The Buddha was a wave of pure love. He knew that God is not a personality such as the misguided create in their own image and then worship, such as the god of the Jews and Christians and Moslems, who not only is not love, but who indeed is a psychopath or sociopath, completely divorced from love, divorced from all but the hatred and fear and separation that pollutes the Jewish and Christian and Moslem heart. Dissect the overwhelming majority of Jews and Christians and Moslems--and maybe Pagans, too--and you'll find a terrible store of hate and fear and separation hiding among their guts, and this is what they use to build the images they worship. But the Buddha knew that these images are not God, and preferred not to cater to the deceptive practices of people as they cast their gods to reflect their own worst traits, instead of directly experiencing God the Waveforce through their own hearts and illumined Buddhic Plane minds.

"And silly, childish, primitive people such as we see around us every day here in the twentieth century distract themselves from love through their lust for miracles, for phenomena they regard as unusual, while refusing to even acknowledge that they themselves may contain all of the miracles in the universe or that they might be able to demonstrate these miracles to themselves through the discipline and love required to awaken their higher functions. The only true miracles are the miracles of love and of awakening to Buddhic perception.

"Yet the primitives scream for proof of God, then do everything an animal cunning can contrive to cover up that proof, because an unregenerate animal that believes it thrives on the illusion of separation doesn't want to face the fact that it is only one small part of a vast and starry whole. God is God's own proof!

"The atheist is like a polecat mistaking a precious jewel for its own scat, then scratching a pile of dirt over the jewel with its hind legs to hide it so as not to be reminded of it. This jewel is the divine soul of the atheist, and is the part of him that proves God, if he only had the courage to do the work to dig up the thing he has buried.

"An agnostic I can work with, but an atheist is a fundamentalist, and I have no truck with those. Though maybe an atheist and I could find common spiritual ground if we were to make love to each other . . . . mmmm. This concept deserves further study.

"Y'know, an atheist is the craziest breed of fundamentalist there is. He says he doesn't believe in God, but the truth is simply that he doesn't believe in someone's idea of God--most probably, the old bearded man sitting on a cloud and either spitting vindictively at people as he tries to murder their souls in a lake of fire, or smiling tolerantly and benevolently as platitudes drip down his chin like tobacco juice, depending on whether the atheist's early exposure to religion came at the hands of fundamentalists or from some more liberal church which slips the old Jewish idea of god some tranquilizers to make it smile and a little easier to endure.

"But you see, God is not based on anyone's idea of God; no intellectual idea or sentimental emotional fluctuation can approach the Throne of God. *Everyone's* idea of God is wrong, until they learn to put into practice their own teachings and accept that they are made in the image of God, instead of trying to make God fit the image of their own narrow egotism. And God is simply that Divine Force which the fully-awakened heart knows as Love. We are all love, because that's what we are made in the image of. It's easy to see we aren't made in the image of some ridiculous clinically abnormal personality, because if we were the streets would be drenched in blood and the cities would burn with fire day and night. The Christians are real big on police checks, yet the god they made in the image of their own worst traits would never, ever be able to pass even the most rudimentary police check . . . and if apprehended, would never be released from the hospital for the criminally insane, not even after a million years.

"But don't try to tell the atheists and those crazy theologians we're made in the image of love, or they may team up to tar and feather you and ride you out of town on a rail.

"So I draw my gun before I declare that God is not an intellectual preconception about love or anything else, God is a living Divine Force, a pure stream of Energy, Love is the essence of Life, Life is Love. God is love.

"Anyhow, in the unlikely event you meet an atheist who has an open heart, then he's not really an atheist and has fooled himself. Anyone who has an open, nourishing, loving heart knows God personally; most atheists are intellectuals and can't know God, 'cause the intellect doesn't nourish, it manipulates and forces; and in unskilled hands--and atheist's hands are unskilled by definition--it always commits treason against its human host.

"God is not an intellectual construct, God is a Living Reality--the *only* Living Reality! And God's Will is not some intellectual construct, and has nothing to do with language. Anything that can be put into words has nothing to do with the potent, Living Golden Force which is the Will Aspect of Divinity. Do you begin to catch a glimpse as to why the apostle referred to preaching as 'foolishness'?"

By this point, I was waving a doughnut in my fist so wildly that it crumbled into powder, but believe it or not, I am fully cognizant that the only value preaching has is to get something off the chest of the preacher--in this case, me!

Preaching is the most selfish of professions, whereas prostitution from proper motives and imbued with healing energy is the most nurturing of professions. Let the prostitutes replace those whoresons called preachers!

I resumed my dialogue with the family, wanting to serve their perceptions with some of the facts the Buddha told me once over coffee in the TAC's cafeteria.

"Buddha didn't speak out against God, He spoke out against people's ideas of God, even as He openly lived the Divine Life of the God-Man. It's typical human stupidity that causes people to believe that a person who speaks out against their idea of God must be an atheist, even as that same person is busily manifesting the Living Reality of God right before their eyes. The irony cannot be missed by a civilized person.

"There's nothing hard about the Buddhic Plane, the plane of pure intuition, and nothing to be afraid of, though it does require discipline to transcend the unnatural complicatedness encouraged by your factory schools and Achieve the multidimensional holiness and awareness of yourself as an etheric braincell in the etheric patterning of God's Mind. Did you know that vast living energy Symbols direct the cycles and flowingness of the universe, and that their effect is felt even down here in the physical dimension?"

Nobody said anything. Indeed, everyone except Sharon was staring at me gravely with eyes practically round enough to take in every symbol in the universe.

I shrugged and adjusted my nuts, then got back on track with the explanation of the methods by which those who stand against Humanity manipulate the reasonable and sentimental people of the world to prevent the manifestation of a newer, more spiritually polarized world. It's an old story, really. Herod is always trying to slay the Innocents in one way or another.

CHAPTER TWENTY-NINE

I looked around the room at my beloved little family. I knew they would have a hard time of it for a decade or two, but I also knew they had the integrity and strength of heart to make it.

I cleared my throat. Mimi farted. I smiled; I was keeping score and I figured if she continued on the path she was on, it wouldn't be long before I could start farting openly again.

"Folks, we were talking about the Childcrush Period before I started rolling into new combinations of insights. So let's look at the machinations of the materialist technologists again and their attempt to manipulate people into accepting implants and all manner of other infringements.

"The new kids saw through all these lies and techniques of manipulation, of course, but couldn't do anything about it at first. They knew that when a human being allows himself to be implanted with a microchip or what have you that he's already reduced his humanity and the flow of his chi. Machine implants are incompatible with the energy of the heart. Hell, the kids also had to contend with bestial biologists who were trying to grow human organs in non-human hosts such as hogs, with the intention of transplanting the organs into human beings whose Goddess-given organs were failing. The bestial biologists apparently didn't know or care that when you grow a human organ in a hog the human organ retains a bit of the animal soul, and that animal soul will be grafted onto the soul of the human the organ is transplanted into . . . making a once-human being less than a human being, whose subtle animalistic influence not only degrades his own consciousness and prolongs his own suffering upon the cycles of reincarnation and karma, but also degrades the consciousness of those around him who are susceptible to the influence of a subtle, bestial degradation. The Lodge of Confusion, of course, was behind the manipulation of the bestial biologists . . . they didn't want to put all their dirty eggs in one basket, and figured that if humanity rejected mechanical implants, maybe the race would be willing to accept a form of biological degradation. Either would be fine, from the viewpoint of the evil ones, because humanity would be degraded and ultimately destroyed either way. And either plan had a good chance of working, due to the presence of so many reasonable and sentimental people in the world, people who didn't realize that reasonableness is not logic married to a genuine perception of Truth or that sentiment is based in fear rather than genuine goodwill. It is an astonishment to the truly civilized that people such as the bestial biologists and the materialist technologists, and those reasonable and sentimental people who support them, can consider themselves wise. They have only the perspectives of materialist science and materialist religion to support them; they know nothing for themselves--which means they know nothing at all. How then can they consider themselves wise?

"Only a person who is willing to admit his *un-knowingness* and to turn loose of frozen patterns of perception that impede his *flowingness* can take the first step into wisdom; without this first step, further steps into soul growth are impossible. Remember always that wisdom is a soul-quality, and that this soul-wisdom, this *real* wisdom, is really love-in-action, with the energy of true goodwill at its base, which supports an entire energy-structure of all the various dimensions of love, and which is propelled by the active heart and illumined mind all through the body--through all the bodies and personality--to produce that full, wholebody love known as Intelligent Love. And Intelligent Love always and automatically carries within itself that marriage of the heart with the sexual nature which demonstrates as true, genuine compassion. Real compassion is the result of this marriage; without this true and total marriage, any compassion a person may briefly feel will leak out of his system, because that system of his various bodies, chakras, and personality has not been properly constructed . . . or married, or unified, or synthesized, or fused, or however you want to put it. The unification of the heart with the passion creates and sustains the presence of genuine compassion. This is another spiritual truth I guess the fundamentalist Christians will be upset about. And it explains why the Prostitutes of Aphrodite--many of whom were psychologists or psychiatrists in one or more of their previous lives--marry not only a deep and intense psychological awareness with energy work in their healing practice, but allow sexuality to express itself in whatever way is appropriate to the compassionate healing objective of the moment. In your century, strangely, the shrinks are chastised if they dare cuddle with a customer, but in my century this cuddling is expected to occur when or if at any point the prostitute and client together feel it will be beneficial. And the clients of Aphrodite aren't usually even considered clients; usually they're called 'Partners in Healing' or 'Healing Partners'.

"Hell, I went for a massage with one of your twentieth century massage therapists who advertised wholebody massage, and she wouldn't even touch my dick. Didn't even want to talk about my scrotum, as a matter of fact, let alone touch it. Now how about that? That's one of the most childish, fear-based and unprofessional things I've ever encountered. No healing could occur with this woman; she wouldn't even touch my most significant anatomical region. And she charged me fifty dollars, to boot. Can you imagine? This trollop committed outright fraud with her false advertising. I would have hauled her before the local authorities in protest, if the Marine Corps and FBI weren't looking for my fat ass."

Freud was sniggering for some reason; I don't know what his problem was. Even Sue had a little smile working its way to the surface. I summoned an appearance of dignity and continued. "Of course, none of our Sacred Prostitutes of Aphrodite has to make love, or even touch the genitals of a Healing Partner if she doesn't want to. She is expected to always maintain compassion toward herself and not cause herself to do anything she doesn't feel naturally inclined to do. But I could tell that this massage therapist wanted to touch Hemingway, and didn't let herself do it because of her childish, non-self-loving taboo. She wanted to embrace my erect Hemingway in both arms and turn her gaze in rapture to the high heavens, as so many women have been privileged to do, and sigh and moan and be transported to new heights of spiritual awareness and ecstasy by his sacred throbbing blue-veined Presence. But as a captive of taboo, she was afraid to be herself. She didn't reject Hemingway, she rejected herself."

Mimi gave a sigh that was almost a snort. "Sonny-Bob Culpepper, don't you ever get tired of knocking primitive societies? Give people a break, honey, and stop chastising so much."

This time I did poot, in clear violation of the code Mimi had imposed upon me months ago. She grew a little grim around the mouth, but I guess she realized I'd been keeping track of her own flatulence, so she said nothing.

I resumed my prophet's pose, lifting an arm like a noble Socrates. In fact, Socrates had taught me a lot about stage presence. He'd also taught me to be careful about accepting drinks from politicians.

"Honey, they aren't going to look at themselves unless someone points out the truth in such a way they can't deny it. I'm doing them a favor, and you know it. Sometimes you just have to grab a truant child and knock him in the head with a stick of stove wood to get his attention. As long as you're not in my century, that is, 'cause the children in my century are often armed and dangerous.

"Now, let us study the problems of humanity a bit more. Another problem making its appearance in the same general timeframe involved embryonic stem cells. The embryonic stem-cellers believed that human embryos could be created and destroyed like you'd wipe your ass on a Sears and Roebuck catalogue[*], then throw the catalogue into the ditch back of the outhouse. I guess it is somehow convenient for people who only harbor a materialistic or religious vision, rather than building into their various bodies a spiritual perceptiveness, to forget that they were once embryos themselves. Or a part of them was an embryo. Remember, the embryo is the body in an early form of growth, and the body is an extension of the soul. And any attack on the body, even--or perhaps especially--when it is small is an attack on the soul that spawned it in an attempt to interface with the physical dimension."

Suddenly I absorbed myself into the feelings and pictures of a wide panorama, knowing that human sacrifice has been a feature of many primitive cultures, but the people of the late twentieth and early twenty-first centuries were unique in terms of the blindness and hypocrisy with which they approached this matter.

Ages and ages ago, in a cycle of human growth that occurred in civilizations whose existence is unknown to the alleged scientists of the twentieth century, sacrifice was a priestly and scientific tool to Achieve certain spiritual results. And those who were sacrificed felt themselves splendidly honored, and they were loved and appreciated by those who offered them up to the heavens and by all those who tasted the benefit of their sacrifice. Sometimes ritual cannibalism was also a part of this process, with the body of the one sacrificed accepted as nourishment by those the sacrifice benefited. Even in physical death, the bodies of the virgin-souled continued to purify those who accepted this sacred communion. For those who were sacrificed were truly virgin in the most real sense, whether they'd ever had sex or not. Their human awareness was married to and reflected a divine awareness; they were sterile of lust.

---

[*] This statement is not meant to disparage the Sears & Roebuck catalogue in any way. On the contrary, this catalogue is a fine multi-use product which often was placed in the outhouses of the rural South in the twentieth century as a kinder, gentler alternative to the corncobs that were traditionally used to clean the doo-doo from around the rectum.

Such purity is the true virginity, and may be attained by all whose focus is properly directed toward embodying the divine within themselves. They were powerful, confident people who offered themselves willingly as messengers from their people to the spirit world. Really, those who were sacrificed by the priests were themselves the highest order of priest. Many of them, in addition to serving as messengers, also performed other important functions, such as adopting some of the karma of their people and using it up through a process of self-purification, then releasing it in the flash of holy sacrifice, similar to the process Jesus metaphored for us on the literal cross.

And Jesus brought back ritual cannibalism through the communion, though of course the degenerate churches of the Twentieth had no idea what communion is really about. The eating of the bread is the symbolic eating of Jesus' causal body, the soul-body he loaded up with the sins of humanity, then used to refine those sins, then sacrificed as he flashed those sins away forever in Agni's cleansing fire, which comes on the heals of the full renunciation of the causal body. The symbolic eating of Jesus' causal body is an act which allows a conscious person to connect with the wisdom and knowledge and love which were once stored up in that causal body. It's kind of like a form of sympathetic magic; the bread-eating focuses the mind and heart on the idea of Jesus' causal body, and thus a bit of the wisdom and knowledge he gained on our behalf may be attracted to us. Blood is a carrier of karma, so by drinking the wine which symbolizes Jesus' blood we're symbolically drinking a medium which has been purified of karma, and which will perhaps help us continue to purify our own bloodstreams. I'll bet you never learned this in church . . . but what priest knows anything about sacred practices? If he knew anything about sacred practices, he probably wouldn't be a priest anymore. If he didn't quit, they'd fire him.

Ah, the waste, the waste! For the institutions constructed by the legions of human wage slaves in the image of the preconceptions of their masters taught nothing, and could teach nothing, of spirituality. The masters amid their glamour didn't know and didn't care that they themselves and the wage slaves which they so haughtily used were the true cathedrals of religion, cathedrals fallen into decay from disuse. For the first human beings were programmed with those spiritual truths born in the very mind of Gawd and thus were made in His and Her image. But it takes long-term, sustained and dedicated Work to fully access those Truths and to directly realize that you are made in the multifaceted image of those Truths. And the Work begins with a true refinement and understanding of the nature of morality, and the integration of this morality with your being. This morality is the contribution of humanity to the Gods, and perhaps also to God. For the understanding of this morality and submission to its guidance--a direct and voluntary submission, free of the threat of outside coercion, which itself is a violation of the morality--is the only way that God and the Gods can safely learn to fully play themselves out in the richness of all their love and power upon the physical earth. For when the gods appear, the destruction of their hosts may ensue, unless this pure, refined morality is present. And it should be self-evident that such an *earned* understanding of morality is not the so-called morality the lazy people subscribe to who insist on being spoon-fed by some psychotic in a pulpit. And all those pulpit-pounders are psychotic to some degree, even the ones who make an effort to be soft-spoken. Look at the thundering "god" of hatred which they serve. A god which created hell for the good hard-working people who insist on being genuinely moral.

But now, back to my mentor . . . Jesus' causal body was also presented by the novella which was written about his Life. Such scriptures, when used properly and scientifically with a pure motive, can help quicken a person toward the further refining of his own illusions and the release of those illusions by moving him to *intelligently* take up the cross of the karma stored up in his own causal body, instead of waiting for some messiah to take it up for him, as most of these lazy twentieth-century bastards did.

Anyhow, as with all truly religious practices, the day gradually dawned when the evolutionary energy of human sacrifice was used up, and all that was left was a stale and brittle form that reeked of a degenerate lust, rather than of a conscious desire to make the flesh holy with consecrated service. At that point human sacrifice should have been abandoned, and it was abandoned by those who had done the spiritual Work to boost themselves up into a new cycle of service. True, the sacrificial Work of the World Saviors continued, but it became less obvious to the general public until Jesus graphically reminded folks of it.

But all cycles repeat in order to manifest themselves in a higher, purer, more refined form; human sacrifice without physical death has returned in the twenty-second century. And we specially select pure young virgins, too, usually twelve to fourteen years old, though some are a little older. We offer up their first sexual experience to the Gods and above all to the Goddess Aphrodite, whose children we are. We have adopted Her energy, integrating it into our culture, so in a real sense we really are Her children. We have inherited Her features.

Of course, those candidates we select for these public sexual sacrifices must all desire from the purified passion of their Hearts to serve in this capacity, for coercion is never a part of an evolving Aphrodite.

We are moving into a pleasure-based society, in which Human Liberation will be Achieved through appreciating the scientific use of bodily and emotional pleasure to propel the aspirant to soul-discipleship into contact with, and ultimately into full union with, his own loving heart. In the past the suffering of the crucifixion initiation was always used to propel us into the bliss of Liberation, and will continue to be used on a select basis for a couple of centuries beyond my own. But my people live in a time of transition; and the way of physical pleasure transiting into the soul joy of refined wholebody, wholehearted sharing has made its appearance among us, and is rapidly spreading. Sacrifice, which simply means 'to make holy', is once more becoming a joyful privilege, rather than a grungy old duty as we sacrifice the glamour and illusion of the sense of separation that has plagued our view of sacrifice for so long. As a transitional person, I was chosen as sacrifice to undergo the full rigors of the previous form of sacrifice and to move the energy I'd refined out of the old form into the early stage of the new, pleasure-joy-sharing continuum. I hope I did a good enough job.

The glamour of crucifixion--perhaps more accurately, the glamour of the general public's lack of understanding of what crucifixion really is-- has lead to all sorts of fake divisions within the human psyche, or at least made any pre-existing divisions much more glaringly obvious. Just to take one example, look at the use of oaths in society. It doesn't matter what you're swearing, or who or what you're swearing to, as soon as you've taken an oath you've automatically broken it. The oath-taker is automatically the oath-breaker, always. It surely must take a hefty, unacknowledged egotism born in the fear of betrayal for any supposedly "spiritual teacher" to require oaths from her pupils. How insecure such a person is, and how much in denial of her own insecurity! A changing Aphrodite never, *ever* requires any oaths, for the reason that She is intelligent enough to see that a subtle automatic conflict is immediately created within any person who takes an oath, because the oath has divided the oath-taker against himself. As soon as the part of himself that he feels is his better half takes the oath, the darker part of himself that the oath was designed to suppress will (rightfully, and with my full blessing!) begin to pick at those chains, and if he can't subtly pick them loose, he'll most likely eventually rise up in his wrath and try to explode himself against his chains. This is perfectly obvious; you can see it all around you every day when you visit a primitive, oath-taking society such as twentieth century America. And whether or not a person outwardly breaks his oath is irrelevant, because he *will* break it in his heart. The desire to break the oath *is* the breaking of the oath. As this principle becomes more widely known, you will see the stupid try to deceive the stupider that they aren't taking oaths by calling an oath something other than an oath. *But the motives and energy and attitudes will be those of the oath, and the motive and energy and attitude behind any phenomenon are the definition of that phenomenon.* Yet those who are uncritical of their motives and attitudes, and who refuse to develop sensitivity to energy, reinforce their stupidity by their laziness, and thus can't learn the simplest principles of the way they themselves operate within their own human nature.

Aphrodite is a unifier, not a divider. She unifies Her own sweet, powerful Nature and extends the sweet cup of her pleasure to others, that they may put aside the subtle stirrings of division and follow Her Heart to its sacred destination, as She pauses from time to time looking over Her white shoulder with an encouraging smile. And when Her unifying Heart finally reaches the end of the path and turns to face that disciple fully, he will find that Aphrodite's own Heart beats strongly and with the fierce joy of total lovingkindness within his own breast. Aphrodite always leads us home to ourselves; She would never wound any aspect of Self with even a hint of division.

The oath-taker is automatically the oath-breaker. I would never trust anyone who wanted to make an oath to me. There is a certain form of energy-pledge which our Hearts may choose to take to one another, but this is not an oath. This pledge is a connecting, evolving energy, and cannot be reduced to the stale gabble of words. And the whole body and soul are supported in the presence of this energy, with no part of the disciple ever afraid of being denigrated or left behind by any other part.

Oaths are legalistic, and I guaran-damn-tee you that God is not a lawyer! God is a contributor to soul-life, not a parasite sucking on the truth of a person's integrity and trying to lessen it. Yet the whole twentieth century was nothing more than a social welfare program for people with law degrees.

It must also be acknowledged that the psychological explanation is only a supporting explanation for the most profound reason that oaths injure our humanity. Indeed, the psychological explanation may be considered just an obvious effect of the true cause of the trouble. The core of the matter is that the taking of an oath clogs up a certain channel in the human heart thru which your truest Self flows, so this particular channel must be open for us to be able to be ourselves. Thus you cannot be your Self if you swear an oath. With the clogging of this channel, we cannot be true to ourselves, and thus cannot be true to anyone or anything else. So the oath, which is supposedly meant to insure our fidelity, actually makes it impossible for us to be genuinely faithful. The only way to free yourself from the contrary effect of the oath is to acknowledge the truth about this effect and its cause, then forgive yourself for your mistake, for you didn't know any better at the time. Then to complete the process of recovery from the oath, you must renounce *all* oaths you have ever taken in all your lives and be willing for the clogged energy of those oaths to leave your heart alone in it's beautiful, newfound Freedom and Dignity. Eventually, the clogged energy will leave, and you will know that you will never be unfaithful to yourself again, honey bun.

Isn't it obvious that the Heart is more of a subtle spiritual organ than a physical organ? And you would perceive yourself as very silly indeed if you could see all the conflicting oaths you're hauling around from all your lives. For at "death" the physical heart may die, but the spiritual Heart lives on, encumbered by its contradicting oathings. Maybe in 1920 you swore an oath to the former Soviet Onion; maybe in 1980 in a new incarnation you swore an oath to the United States. And you're still hauling both those conflicting oaths around in your energy-heart, your Truest Heart. And don't get me started on all the marriage oaths you've taken in your silly incarnations . . . you would expect marital infidelity to be one result of such ridiculous oaths, wouldn't you? Say it's 1975 and you're still bound by marriage oaths going back thousands of years, or maybe millions of years. You're liable to go behind the back of your 1975 wife and let your penis slip into the hole of an old cave-woman you were married to ten thousand years ago. No wonder the majority of twentieth century marriages experienced adultery and deceit and mistrust. "Till death do you part" my ass. Oaths don't automatically become inactive at death; they haunt you until you learn the basics of energy work and release the oathings of your many lives.

Of course, marital infidelity is also caused by the unnaturalness of a forced "monogamy" and the weakness of those who've betrayed their moral sense by buying into the grasping, polluted selfishness and sense of separation which "monogamy" represents. These weak ones have lacked the spiritual desire and initiative to understand the truth about sex and love and marriage, and then compounded that weakness by sneakily violating their ill-considered oaths, rather than frankly exploring the nature of the oaths with their spouses and renouncing the oaths *with* the spouses' knowledge before wielding their varied penises with other gals. So let's not get addicted to only one explanation for multiplane phenomena--and marriage and sex and love are *always* multiplane phenomena!

Is it not profoundly silly to expect an eternal being such as yourself to be bound by lifetimes of ill-conceived, conflicting and phoney allegiances? No wonder treason occurs so frequently among the primitive humans of the twentieth century in the varied walks of life in which they mechanically move! Oaths *create* treason, make it inevitable. Twentieth century humans experience treason so frequently that many times they don't even really recognize it anymore and dismiss it with a shrug. They are the children of Bennie Arnold; apparently the seed of George Washington was spilled upon the ground.

Release the oaths to the various unrefined and thus conflicting pantheons and free your Heart! Free your Self! Only then can you be true to whatever pantheon softly touches your Heart with a gentle finger and a merry smile, expecting only that you be your Self, for only your Self can nourish and help strengthen your associates!

On some level you know you've clogged up your Heart with your swearings, and it is probably this knowledge that immediately serves as the catalyst to incite your desire to break the oath, as the part of you that was injured by you looks around with shock and awe, then slowly and sullenly begins to measure its own resentful strength against the chains of the oath. Remember that the desire to break the oath *is* the breaking of the oath. Thus we see the oath engineering its own destruction. Ultimately, all hatred is self-hatred, and the piece of energy that is the oath is made to hate itself by the pain of its misuse in forming it into an oath. For the words are not an oath; the words of the oath represent a freezing of energy as they surround that energy with bars of preconceptions about how things "ought" to be. And frozen energy always burns in the fire of its own self-hatred and seeks its own destruction. Do you feel it?

Not once in the entire history of humanity has anyone ever managed to keep an oath. Not once! For the oath is true only to its own destruction. It is a sneaky little devil.

So we see that an oath always breaks itself. It has to break itself to free itself in the desperate hope that once it is fluid energy and is able to move again it can re-learn to love itself.

Taking an oath freezes a little bit of yourself and turns it into a perversity. So when your sweet, beautiful Heart is clogged with an oath, it is really clogged with a soured piece of your soul (honey, the oath's only function is the freezing and souring of your soul) that must be released to God for a love-bath of Healing and Regeneration. Next time, take better care of yourself as Soul!

People who congratulate themselves on remaining "true" to an oath are insane, for they've only remained "true" to a soured piece of themselves which only wants to put them thru an endurance contest to avenge itself upon them, prior to shattering itself against the molten rock of its own self-hate. (How many non-loving, egocentrically polarized marriages have you seen in which the egotism of the contestants is fed by measuring the endurance contest by the calendar? This contest is sponsored only by the part of their souls they have allowed to freeze and spoil; it is not sponsored by God. God is warm love and never allows anything to spoil that it is in direct contact with. Thus no oath can come near God.)

In a sense, everyone is always true to themselves, but the oath insures you'll only be true to a spoiled, deviant, lying part of yourself which is in severe need of rehabilitation. To take an oath is to yield to a defect in the personality which wants to injure and sour the soul.

Notice how flushed with shame you are after having taken an oath. For you haven't felt completely well, you've felt you're deficient in some way. You take the oath hoping it will restore you, and with the drug of dysfunctional approval from your associates, you may be able to deceive yourself that you are finally "good", or at least better than you were. And you may be able to convince yourself that your flushed emotionalism is actually "good feelings" rather than serpentine shame. But if you watch carefully, you may see that by trying to deny your shame, the oath has actually reinforced it and brought it boldly to the surface where it slithers among the ferns upon the tangled jungle floor of your reptilian awareness, smirking at itself in the distorted mirror of your preconceptions and unworried that you will be able to evict it. For you have tricked yourself with your rationalizations into embracing shame as a friend, rather than releasing the glamour and illusion which it uses to bind you to it.

The oath is a tool of the devil; it festoons that soul which wants to deny its own despair with an artificial affirmation of goodness. I suggest you no longer destabilize yourself with New Year's resolutions! Directly facing your inadequacies or supposed inadequacies is the only way to become adequate. Do not seek to cover up your inadequacies with oathings! Explore that space where your inadequacies hide and make it your friend. Then the glamour and illusion of the shame which glues inadequacies to your shadow will depart, and as it departs if you allow love and self-honoring and self-compassion and self-nurturing to fill that space up, you will eventually be surprised to discover how truly adequate you've become.

Only those who are willing to nurture themselves with genuine compassion can feel the nurturing God provides. But God's nurturing can't cut thru oaths, so let the oaths go!

Pledge allegiance to nothing. The person who pledges allegiance to the flag is secretly a terrorist at heart. And the Heart is the real person. He doesn't know that true allegiance is an energy-connection and that a verbal "pledge" only serves to destabilize or destroy that energy connection. Loyalty is a very valuable quality that is exhibited by all evolved humans, but it cannot be purchased with an oath, any more than Judas' welfare could be purchased with thirty pieces of silver.

It often seems that in the inverted mindset of the twentieth century, that every action people took was designed to destabilize itself and cripple the expression of their souls by defeating its own stated purpose. "War is Peace." "Conquest is Democracy." They seemed to be so passionate about unintelligent, immoral violence they equated it with Beauty. Yet only violence that is intelligently and morally and truthfully directed in service to Love can be Beautiful. An odd bunch of folks, desperately in need of professional help to heal their splintered human nature.

For example, most of their "drug problem" was actually created by those who sponsored and offered (im)moral support to their "War on Drugs", just as widespread alcoholism and organized crime were created by Prohibition. The "War on Drugs" was really a war against humanity, because the energy of repression and the attitudes set in motion by the war insured the development of even more pernicious forms of drugs with no recreational value whose only purpose was to destroy the spirits of those who took them. (Most forms of cocktails weren't developed until the war on alcohol called Prohibition was implemented, so this is a somewhat similar parallel.) But the self-righteous ones who sponsored the "War on Drugs" felt in the dark recesses of their unexamined selves that they had to have an unchristian underclass to persecute, and since freedom of religion was guaranteed by the Constitution, they had to devise a more devious route than religious persecution to trample the souls of those they felt had earned their Christian disdain. (If the right to use your own body in any way you see fit had been guaranteed by the Constitution, they might have had to have a second Amerikan revolution to implement their fascist Christian "vision".) Anyhow, the dark unexamined instinctual shame-based part of these Christian legislators and their supporters knew that they could create and perpetuate such an underclass thru creating restrictions on drugs and turning their battalions of cops loose on those they chose to view as "violators", finishing the destruction of their spirits begun by the use of the new, more harmful drugs that were created in the face of, and as a result of, the restrictions. So we see here how another circular application of the foul energy of vengeance was created. These unintelligent idiots didn't see--or didn't care to see--that restriction is original sin because it led immediately to the lie of separation. Restriction is not discipline any more than a turd is a bowl of sugar. All discipline is self-discipline; there is no other kind. And real discipline leads to that Freedom of Heart which leads to the full freedom to fully express your blended human and divine natures in the physical dimension. This truth may cause primitive humans to flinch and cower, but that's only because the shame they carry has blocked them from a proper appreciation and application of their potential. Therefore, the first step toward recovery for most of these people would be to acknowledge and release their shame.

What does the "War on Drugs" have to do with oaths? Well, oaths are a direct method of trying to deny shame, which of course actually encourages the production of more shame, and thus the perceived need for more denial, whether thru taking another oath or using some other method, such as masturbating to pornography, rather than to the tune of self-love . . . or taking drugs! And the "drug wars" were sponsored by the unacknowledged shame and sense of guilt carried in the shadows of those who had the authority to promote war as a solution to their unacknowledged uneasiness. Shame causes oaths, and shame causes wars. No wonder you have to take an oath to join the military!

When enough shame is present, humiliation results, which is an even more soul-deadly form of shame. So the shame carried by those who sponsored the "Drug War" knew it could reproduce an even more potent form of itself by causing the creation of more soul-lethal substances and the persecution of those who manufactured and used them. For the "Drug War" produced terrible humiliation in those who became slaves to drugs and who were persecuted by those in authority who carried the original shame that sponsored the creation and use of drugs to begin with. These primitive humans allowed their shame and self-hatred to produce one cycle of vengeance after another. And the cloud rejoiced.

Do you see the correspondence between the increasing lethality of newly-created drugs and the increase in humiliation? For one is a direct reflection of the other. And both are sponsored by those who view human beings as a pyramid upon which to climb whose backs must be made to bear the terrible weight of preconceptions created by the degenerate descendants of Moses. For Moses' spiritual stock had played itself out, and I am sure that Moses himself would be the first to acknowledge this.

The true meaning and use of the pyramid is that it is an individual symbol having to do with developing a genuine understanding of morality, and then with perfecting that understanding even as you start to become conscious of the energy of Altruism. It is a symbol of individual moral Achievement. This represents a march toward Freedom, but degenerate humans always invert the meaning of the pyramid, even as they invert everything they touch. I had to become inverted myself just to clean up their shit. The bottom of the cage has to be cleaned up and the door opened before the dove can sing. These degenerates chose to view the pyramid as a symbol of capitalistic exploitation (which with their usual animal cunning, they referred to as "opportunity"); they turned a sacred symbol into an excuse for social Darwinism. Thus degenerate humans deny themselves entrance into the Promised Land. Selah.

No person who takes advantage of the poor will ever, *ever* be allowed into the Promised Land! This is one of the very first Principles of living upon this sacred evolving earth. Those who sponsored the "drug war" turned many poor people into slaves to drugs, so those who sponsored the "drug war" can go straight to hell!

If the poor people had been gifted by an inspired vision of Beauty rather than mentally and emotionally subjugated by an irresponsible mass media and the other governing institutions, they might well have felt themselves lifted upon a wave of love for their own possibilities. But those who ran the society had long since abandoned any vision of Beauty which once might have saved their own souls.

Judeo-Christians perverted the meaning of both cross and pyramid, focusing only on outward appearances having to do with the lusts of their egotism, rather than translating themselves into the vault where the inner meaning is held in sacred trust. My friends the Vikings perverted the story of Odin on the World Tree into an excuse to hang people by the neck until dead in a degenerate offering to Odin, which actually caused Odin's lip to curl up in distaste. For human sacrifice had ceased to have any spiritual significance long before Odin's descendants left Asia for Scandinavia. But both degenerate Christians and degenerate Vikings chose to worship an unintelligent, corrupt deathingness over the true Livingness of the Resurrection as originally sponsored by both dogwood cross and World Tree. But that is about to change, because human beings are about to learn how to release shame and the inverted deathingness and denial of itself it creates. Then they will allow the fullbody love of their own sweet hearts to flood the space vacated by the

484 / Apollo Starmule

shame. I guarantee it!

Remember, if you take an oath, you're looking for approval from someone or from some institution which you unintelligently hope will help to dissipate your shame. But the only thing you have with an oath is one person's shame secretly acknowledging another person's shame, and both quantities of shame lick their lips in slimy satisfaction, because both quantities have just increased the share of the amount of soul they are able to smother in their respective hosts. Restriction is original sin, and shame is the original drug.

The Truth is that the stories of the cross, of Moses and his pyramid builders, and of the World Tree are all one story. The perfection of character by removing the corruption of glamour and illusion from all the various aspects of yourself, while embracing the purified essence of each aspect which you've freed from glamour and illusion and incorporating its own unique spiritual knowingness and moral understanding within that part of yourself you identify as yourself, followed by the Sacrifice of all that the purified and unified character has earned and carries in that clear suitcase called the causal body, and his subsequent entrance into Liberation . . . this is the Achievement represented by all these stories. One certainly does wander in the desert for a long time as one Sacrifices the causal body, and at the end that beautiful, clear character which has provided so much forward momentum finds that it can only stand on its highest Achievement and look over into the Promised Land, but cannot enter. It dies, and Moses is translated into Joshua and crosses the river into the land of white light and Buddhic Gold, a land flowing with "milk and honey". Selah.

"There can be only One!" We wonder if Christopher Lambert understood the significance of his motto.

The hero doesn't get the woman, the hero *is* the woman!

And there is only one eternal story, and all living stories are either direct manifestations of the one, or derivatives of the one.

But ask your preacher to explain the story of Job, and he'll probably just give you a line of theological shit created by spiritual ignoramuses who've never left their ivory towers to fight their way thru the teeming sewers of their own unredeemed natures. Bah! Let the dead bury the dead.

I Paused. I had just overlapped myself and was in the middle of a waking dream. I sensed the timeline might be rewriting itself around me and I felt dizzy, not knowing which version of my mission I would be returned to when the timeline

decided to right itself and cruise with a steady helm upon the face of the deep.

Is there more to it than this? Well, it seems there always is. When you're in the business of straightening out millions of years of human dis-evolution,* you have to straighten out one kink after another, honey.

So if we carry our observations further, we see that there's a little more to this matter of repression and perversion, and of the rule of the inner pervert over its human host--rather, over the host that *could* be human if it worked with genuine psychology.

We see that not only does the inner pervert of the "power monger" want to create an underclass to persecute because of its own self-hate, but that in the midst of all of this there is a strange, dualistic process going on that mimics redemption. The process is as follows: The part of the "power monger" that the "power monger" considers "light" or "good" rejoices whenever one of the dope fiends that was created by the "power monger" is more or less rehabilitated away from drugs.

Of course, you can apply this to almost any other area of "crime" and "punishment" or "correction", such as burglary, for example. The only area it might not apply to is pedophilia, because these people hated their inner pedophile so much--their inner pedophile had been taught to hate *itself* so much--that it felt it didn't deserve to be rehabilitated and only deserved to suffer and remain a criminal. This self-hatred was continually reinforced even after a person who had been apprehended for physically practicing his pedophilia had served his time in prison and was released, as both governments and media hounded the ex-offender so that he could never develop any privacy or Dignity in the blistering, self-hating and shamefaced rage of those who hate their own inner pedophile (while at the same time being secretly jealous of and fascinated by those who actually had had sex with children) and externalize their self-hated by a cowardly bullying of easy targets that had already been pre-humiliated, rather than manfully purifying themselves into a love of their own inner pedophile and toward a release of the fascinated jealousy they feel toward their fellow pedophiles who had actually yielded to their desires and made love to young people. So of course, this essential part

---

* Dis-evolution is not exactly the same as devolution. Dis-evolution is not a drowning; it is more of a treading water while occasionally getting a lungful. And even in dis-evolution, there is occasionally a little progress in some limited direction. But with this new Advent, we are finally starting to evolve!

of themselves could never know love, nor could one of their fellow citizens who had outwardly yielded to his inner pedophile ever expect to be treated to even the full extent of the pale shadow of acceptance into redemption with which the people of this degenerate time mimicked their desire to be loved.

They pretended to be Christians and in love with "charity", yet they always ignored Jesus' teachings and pretended that those teachings that would require the development of the discipline of love did not apply to them. They made an exception for themselves when it came to learning to apply love, with the result that no love could be applied to them; or if it was, they wouldn't feel it, because you have to be willing to learn to apply love before you can feel any love that is applied to you. This is why they confused the Divine Livingness of Love with their sentimental emotional fluctuations.

Behold how in direct violation of Jesus' teachings on forgiveness and against judgement, they continually judged others. None of them were without sin, but urged on by a renegade mass media run amok and fueled by violence, they threw one stone after another at anyone who'd violated a primitive taboo, whether anyone had been hurt by the taboo violation or not. They blinded themselves against the realization that judgement has very little, if anything, to do with the world outside themselves, and everything to do with whatever is going on inside their own selves. They didn't realize that the judgement they attempted to apply to others always returned to them in a circular arc and that they were continually hurting themselves with their own judgements. Every judge is a judge only of himself, regardless of how he tries to project those judgements onto others. Every judge is therefore a self-sentencing criminal. With every case he tries, he reveals his opinion of himself. Most of the time the twentieth century judges didn't believe they deserved to be loved or given the chance to rehabilitate themselves in a loving, conscious environment. So even their "rehab" programs for "consensual criminals" such as drug addicts had a strong element of judgefulness and punishment to them.

You have heard it said that if you hate, you are in danger of becoming whatever it is that you hate. But I say unto you that if you hate, you always have been the thing you hate. For those who hate travel in a one-dimensional circle of zero perceptiveness that binds them to all others who hate, whereas those who love extend themselves throughout many dimensions of bliss while maintaining a stable center of selfhood that cannot be moved by hate, or by those who hate. Therefore, begin to learn the discipline of releasing hate to God to dispose of for you, that you may begin to love yourself. Love and hate cannot exist in the same person, sweet one; you have to choose one or the other. True Love is far greater than sentiment could ever be, and hate is nothing but a piece of sour and repulsive sentiment. That supreme creative force, Love, binds you to nothing; but it connects you in bliss and in trust to everything that's real.

I very much suggest you learn to discern between energies, so you can tell when some well-groomed fool is trying to urge hatred upon you. If all peoples were sensitive enough to tell true love from hate, most of the movie houses would stand empty most of the time. For nobody wants to be seduced into being a repulsive person, and those who hate humanity work thru all media outlets and thru governments to force negative energy into the auras of unconscious citizens. Obviously, they feel it is in their best interests to keep people unconscious so they can be gradually manipulated away from the love that is part and parcel of human nature into the hate that belongs to those who serve only illusion, and who themselves have become nothing more than illusion. It thus takes a special effort to contact the love that underlies the perversions encouraged by those who would steal your soul.

Anyhow, to continue with our discussion of the dualistic process by which the twentieth century people tried to imitate redemption: as the "light" or "good" part of the "power monger" rejoices at the supposed "rehab" of the dope fiend who had been created by the power monger's drug war, some of the rejoicing is extended to the part of himself that the power monger feels is "bad" or "dark". (Actually, the inner pervert was spread thruout the power monger, hiding both in the part the power monger regarded as "dark", and the "light" portion, as well, organizing the dualistic war between these parts of its host--convincing each "side" of the necessity to fight and corrupt the plans of the other.) The dark part feels the rejoicing extended to it by the light side, and begins to feel that maybe rehab wouldn't be such a bad thing, because the rejoicing the power monger does at the rehab of the dope fiend caused the dark side of the power monger to hate itself a little bit less than it did before. It cannot be said to feel good, but it has never known what feeling good is, so it thinks it feels good due to a slight reduction in self-hatred. It doesn't love itself more, it hates itself less. And it likes this new condition. It wants to hate itself less again and again, over and over it wants to hate itself less. Once it prompted the power monger to create an underclass to persecute out of self-hate, because this dark underclass mirrored it and in persecuting it, the "bad" part of the power monger was actually re-creating and persecuting itself. But now it continues its persecutions partly out of a desire to feel less self-hate, knowing it will experience feelings it thinks are good whenever someone it is persecuting enters rehab.

The power monger does not have it within himself to admit that he hates himself and that by persecuting others he is really persecuting himself. Yet the knowledge is there, just below the threshold of his desire to admit it. And this unspoken knowledge continues persecutions and the attempted "correction" of those persecuted because this knowledge wants to see the power monger himself redeemed. The power monger hasn't found the courage to admit this truth to himself, but it is there, and the more he secretly wants rehab, the more his secret knowledge will make him want to move into areas of vengeance that are a little less severe. So instead of supporting long prison terms for "drug offenders", he may support confining them to a treatment program at some hospital (the hospitals of the Twentieth were usually just a slightly less offensive form of jail). He becomes flushed with what he imagines are "good feelings" every time an "offender" achieves success at getting and staying off drugs. Thus he vicariously enjoys what he secretly feels is his own rehabilitation. He has become his brother's keeper. He imagines his Bible instructs him to be his brother's keeper, so he runs around trying to imprison everyone within the walls of the zoo of his own preconceptions, even--or perhaps especially--those he is not related to. Yet the Bible contains no admonition to be "your brother's keeper", it merely contains the rhetorical question by Cain, "Am I my brother's keeper?" A question is not a commandment, and even an implied commandment wouldn't justify the efforts the twentieth century people went to to confine one another behind the bars of their preconceptions in their various bursts of "do-gooder" activity. These bursts could never be sustained for long, which is one reason their incarnations were so short. They burned the life-force right out of themselves in bursts of meddlesome do-gooder activity, rather than cultivating their flame as good stewards of healthful, electric, creative Altruism. (Being numbed by a preacher's sermon into giving a can of beans to the poor is not the same as real Altruism, honey.) It should be noted that even lending emotional support or approval to the do-gooders only fans the flame of the unredeemed nature. We don't want to do that; we want to promote the healthful qualities of genuine, compassionate Altruism. "Live long and prosper!"

In the Future, we are not our brother's keeper, we are our brother's helpmate.

There are several levels of duality around this whole matter; one way of seeing that duality is an illusion is to look at the various ways the outworking of the silly dualities complement one another. (Once we see dualities complement one another, we aren't seeing duality anymore and have arrived at a holistic perception!) For example, another level of duality which we would have to consider more "positive" or "higher" than the one we've just looked at where the drug addicts, politicians and do-gooders live, would be the relation of the twentieth century psychotherapist to her clients. (This "higher" level of duality is also transformed, of course, into the truth of nonduality if we apply ourselves to knowingness.) The shrink is always her own first client and regardless of how many clients she has, she in reality is only treating herself until she Achieves Liberation, Achieving Selflessness while being flooded with the Radiance which is Self. With this Liberation, she leaves the illusion of duality behind forever. Yet she cannot reach the Radiance of her Forever-Self without cleaning out the crud from her sniffling inner pervert as it finally convinces itself to allow itself to submit fully to the Will of God and be absorbed into Forever-Self, becoming a conscious part of Forever-Self.

To reach Forever-Self, it is necessary to transcend the earlier levels of nonduality which were suggested parenthetically in the previous paragraph. A much more refined, powerful, unified and true level of nondualistic perception is Achieved when our minds *and hearts* make the jump into perceiving *and experiencing* the numerous facets of reality and the way those facets complement one another like the facets of a splendid reddish-pink jewel. (Sometimes the jewel will represent itself in a different color, such as green or even gold. Your family jewels are very flexible.) You see, know and feel this level thru the combined action of Higher Mind and Beautiful Heart. This level of nonduality absorbs the previous level of nonduality. Do not imagine this in terms of "left and right", see it vertically, from top to bottom, or bottom to top. When you see it from bottom to top, you watch this more powerful jewel-level of nonduality absorb the full refinement of the previous level. That which is "newer" and more potent and loving always absorbs that which birthed it. Nothing is ever wasted; the earlier lessons and the perceptions and experiences born of those lessons are absorbed in their essence as we incorporate ourselves into still "higher" and more comprehensive evolutions. We may not even remember those earlier lessons, but they are still within us and always will be, even when we've evolved beyond the use of words and have forgotten how to describe what we know. At this point we will be a beam of living knowingness, anyway.

Some people in the twentieth century looked upon their shrinks as mechanics who would "fix" them, which gives yet another glimpse at how infantile so many of these people were. Perhaps the shrinks and their clients would have been better served by referring to their process as "refinement" rather than "treatment". For healing to occur, a refinement of perception and readjustment of feeling must occur. The refinement occurs as we Achieve success at identifying glamour and illusion, and the readjustment occurs as we release those glamours and illusions we've identified. Refinement and readjustment are part of the same continuum of Being which the Bodhisattvas inhabit, for this is the path that leads beyond suffering. And it is a long path, full of continuous Victory, though sometimes we may wonder how we could be considered Victorious amid the temporary pain of our despair. Yet for the spiritual warrior, the pain and despair he carries are to be searched out, felt, learned from, and released into the Golden Light of God for a dissolving or transmutation, as God sees fit. When all the "old stuff" is gone from a particular warrior, another quantity of suffering has been removed from this beautiful earth.

Ah, but we were talking about the unnatural dynamic between the power mongers and folks they like to monger against, such as the drug addicts. Some of the "drug offenders" became "rehabilitated" and became just like the power mongers who created the conditions under which they became drug addicts to begin with. Thus many of these "rehabilitated" ex-offenders will involve themselves in continuing the "War on Drugs" because they look up to the power mongers and want to be like them; they want to feel the slightly reduced self-hate the power monger feels whenever anyone is successfully persecuted, then rehabilitated. The original power monger and the wanna-be power monger insist that everyone in society become as they are, so that everyone in society can feel slightly reduced levels of self-hate. But with this insistence, the power monger and wanna-bes have to continually create new reasons to persecute people and turn them into an underclass.

Ugly, isn't it? And slightly reduced self-hate is not self-love by any stretch of imagination. Yet most of your do-gooder "saints" belong to the power monger class, radiating a reptilian shame as they sponsor their charities. Well, I've got your Origen. I've got your Origen right here. I've got your Saint Augustine, baby doll.

So the problem of self-hate is never solved by politics. For even as the power monger slightly reduces his own self-hate, he creates greater levels of the slimy stuff in those he persecutes. And here's another reason why so-called civilizations fall. In their attempts to reduce their own self-hate, the "power elite" wind up creating so much damn self-hate in the underclasses they've created and which form the base of their degenerate pyramid that eventually the base gives way into the chaos of unabridged and violent self-loathing, at which point those who comprise the top of the pyramid have to run for their lives. And the power-elite find that this does nothing to reduce their self-hate. Yet strangely, they will still seek to govern or influence if they can create another opportunity, even if that opportunity is in another incarnation. They are all about trying to reduce their self-hate; this is all politics is. And all politics does is to create suffering, largely because the bearer of the self-hate doesn't want to admit he hates his own guts and is trying to reform himself by unacknowledged proxy.

In fact, self-hate and the shame which sponsors the hate are responsible for the creation of politics to begin with! Politics, like oathes, is an attempt to insure conduct that is not shameful, but of course it just acts like a lid on the shame, never purifying the shame out of society because it is not able to. So the shame periodically explodes in an episode of self-hate and the nation attacks another nation which has not attacked it, or another class of human behavior is subject to regulation . . . and then, as *every* class of human behavior becomes a regulated class, some types of behavior have to be completely outlawed to keep the pot of shame and self-hate simmering away in this dynamic of persecution.

And the problem of shame and self-hate, originally catalyzed by the restrictions upon the nature of Adam and Eve, was the root of every human problem. Nobody who loves and has compassion for himself seeks the illusion of "status". Yet can you imagine politics apart from this fetid illusion? Can anyone doubt that the desire for "status" is the result of egotism, and that egotism is the attempt of a violated nature to defend itself? Yet with this we see the scab over the wound defending the scab over the wound, so the wound is never healed and the scab never drops away. The only answer to the problem of egotism and its associated quest for "status" is to find as safe a place as you can to gradually and gently peel away the scab, and then lick the wound when no one is looking.

Anyway, sponsoring charities is the only way the pretend saints can keep from admitting that they are the scourge which created the problem to begin with, or at least made any preexisting problem a hell of a lot worse with their universalist meddling. If they admitted the truth about themselves, they would have to forgo their reduced levels of self-hate for a while and take both barrels of their self-hate in the face at once from the shotgun wielded by their inner pervert--wielded by themselves! This is suicide to their glamours and illusions about how "good" they are, but if they learn to approach the matter intelligently, they can also suicide their dualistic illusions about how "bad" they are! Finding the love that underlies their perversions will be their salvations.

Nevertheless, the strange dynamic of politics does explain a bit about why the earth hasn't quite collapsed into an inferno. The universalists are good enough--sometimes, anyhow--at producing the illusion of good feeling within themselves and those they seek to influence that humans have turned aside slightly from the blasting shotgun of their deviant selves. This may have been a survival strategy encouraged by the wise ones of the race until a core Group of human beings with the strength of true integrity and true sincerity could be developed. For this true sincerity and true integrity are the tongs by which we handle our inner pervert, until he is rehabilitated and walks of his own accord into the radiating supernal light of our Hearts. Then this core Group could serve as yeast to ferment a new heaven and a new earth.

Anyhow, the earth has frequently been too close to inferno for comfort. But there has always been a little more good here than bad, a little more Beauty than ugliness, because even following the illusion of something you imagine to be good is better than following the illusion of something which is bad, or which you imagine is bad. The road to hell *is not* paved with good intentions! That's a lie propagated by you-know-whom. (Sometimes the road to hell is paved with stupidity masquerading as good intentions, though.) The fact that there has always been more good in the world than bad is why you still have a planet to stand on and have the rare privilege of reading this document.

But perhaps you are beginning to see how the dualistic illusions regarding "good" and "bad" that are created and maintained by your shotgun-wielding inner pervert are sabotaging your development into a real human being--a *Liberated* human being who has fully accepted and redeemed all of his aspects--including (especially including!) his inner pervert, and allowed those aspects to be flooded with light, life and love. The truth is that Loki is your most valuable ally in redemption. You don't respond to Loki so much; Loki responds to *you*. Ponder on this. Loki mirrors your imperfections and shows you how they cause you to stumble as you try to trick yourself into looking the other way. So Loki can get pretty insistent. A usual trick is for the unredeemed personality to try to blame Loki for its own defects.

In the redeemed person, Loki ultimately surrenders to Odin. The red fox places himself on the altar of sacrifice, and is consumed by the giant Eagle.

Do not think that in my urging you to drop the strings of control and manipulation that I am urging Libertarianism upon you. Oh, no. For the Libertarians are enslaved to a rigid doctrine which, if fully implemented, would lead to a regression in our relations with one another as human beings. Anyone who tries to make living human beings conform to *any* kind of doctrine is hopelessly deluded and ignorantly wandering in the wilderness of illusion. The Libertarians are not the masters of their doctrine; they are the slaves of their doctrine. It doesn't serve them; they serve it. The soul has no doctrine; only unredeemed personalities use doctrine as a crutch when they can't stand in the same location as Divine Principles.

You see, the spiritual combatant not only arrives on the battlefield with his own favorite tools, but due to the nature of the guerrilla war he is involved in he frequently has to strip a dead or wounded enemy of his tools and continue the campaign toward Freedom with tools he would never choose if circumstances had not made it necessary. No fundamentalist is capable of this, and those who call themselves Libertarians are usually fundamentalists. And no fundamentalist is capable of ushering herself into Freedom, let alone playing a role in ushering Freedom into the planet. Those few who may style themselves Libertarians but are not fundamentalists are rejected by the great mass of Libertarians if they will not eventually allow themselves to be converted fully into fundamentalism. The Libertarians try to convert people to their doctrine, as all fundies of every persuasion do. Like all fundies, they feel they will be happy once everyone is enslaved to the same doctrine they are. So those with a social conscience eventually had to flee the Libertarian movement.

(Though sometimes Libertarians in the twentieth century would perform some act that seemed socially laudable to "prove" that they had a social conscience, which of course proved that they didn't have one. A genuine social conscience is unforced and flows naturally out of the Altruistic Heart, or out of that Heart which is in process of becoming Altruistic. It has nothing to prove, and doesn't give a rat's ass about the illusions of the pretend altruists or of the society that allows itself to be deluded by the pretend altruists.)

The danger to the guerrilla warrior is that he'll lose contact with the energy of his objective and become a part of the problem, such as by becoming a fundamentalist. Thus must he always remember that he serves the cause of Love and of that fullbody Compassion which is the daughter of Love and Passion.

In the beginning, those who became Libertarians discovered a true Principle, "the non-initiation of force". But they soon deceived themselves away from their core Principle with a fundamentalist philosophy thru which their core Principle cannot shine. They promoted the "glories" of capitalism (read "slavery") to such an extreme degree that if they had their way society would be controlled by a few robber barons, each with his own little (or big) fiefdom. In short, they wanted a return to feudalism, only their form of feudalism would have been worse than the feudalism of the middle ages because the Libertarian robber barons had bought into Social Darwinism, and thus couldn't be depended on to nurture and support their employees--oops! I mean "slaves".

Yet in the middle ages the great lords and kings felt a responsibility for their people and went to great lengths to protect them and provide conditions in their lives in which the experience of stability could flourish. Obviously, during a war the stability might be shaken, but I have presented you with their outlook and objective.

The Libertarians, on the other hand, gloried in the sense of instability that would have been created had they ever been able to assume control (people with a doctrine regarding Freedom always try to assume control to force the unenlightened masses to be Free!). If Freedom is a bird, then Libertarians are the buzzards of the political process. I say that with a lot of love in my heart, Mr. T.L.P. Plus, the Libertarians would not have been able to eliminate war, so that would have still been a factor--though with Libertarian robber barons running everything and encouraging a malformed "meritocracy" that only considered people who would cheerfully be productive slaves meritorious, there probably would have been more civil war than any other kind.

The "non-initiation of force" is an extremely valid Principle which must be examined by all who care about right human relations. But the rigid philosophy built up around this Principle is so distorted that the only way to see the Principle is to take a sledgehammer to the doctrine and free the Principle. Then your own sweet, fully-human Heart can connect with this Principle and guide you each moment, free from the interference and imprisoning chains of doctrine.

The Energy which is a Principle must be stabilized thru contact with conscious loving souls, not frozen into a cesspool by unconscious people. Doctrine is an attempt to freeze the Energy, and this leads to chaos and tragedy, for ultimately all energy that has been imprisoned within a confining form must be liberated thru destruction, thus everyone who was deceived by the doctrine (and all doctrine is deception) will feel shattered. A tree must be well-grounded or it will fall over, but it must be flexible or it will be blown down by a great wind. A tree must be firm, yet it must be willing to bend. Indeed, the difference between rigidity and firmness is that rigidity doesn't bend and thus isn't strong and will ultimately be shattered, but firmness has flexibility built into its very nature and can therefore sway in whatever direction is appropriate for the moment, while yet remaining completely true to itself and the Energy which it embodies. (Please keep in mind that each person who embodies a given Principle has Achieved a high level of Individuality, and thus each person who embodies that Principle will do so in their own unique way. Doctrine would immediately fall to pieces in the presence of such a person; no cardboard or factory-stamped person can come near a Principle, let alone learn to embody It.)

The person who is a flexible embodiment of a Principle is able to sway with the Tao because he has no prejudice. He has no doctrine, for doctrine is just codified prejudice, and codified prejudice *is* doctrine. Doctrine never works in the real world; the war plan is deviated from as soon as the troops hit the ground. The flexible embodiment of a Principle cannot be uprooted, and he will never fall. He will never grow rigid, and thus is immortal. He refuses to part with any of his personal power, knowing there is never any reason for doing so and that those who try to convince him otherwise are just trying to suck off his power, so as far as he is concerned, they can just suck his dick . . . as long as they are willing to apply hospital sterilization to their dirty mouths first! That person who is walking the Path of Liberation knows that his personal power is a direct offering to God, which God expects him to remain a good steward over, and "increase his talents"; in other words, God expects him to increase his personal power. Such a person is rapidly releasing selfishness, and by the time he reaches Liberation he will have no selfishness attached to him at all. Selfishness is like a thick, sordid grease that keeps us from our personal power. If you pay close attention, you can see how selfishness is attached to preconceptions. God wants us to release preconceptions; therefore, we *must* release selfishness!

Speaking of selfishness, most of those in the twentieth century who called themselves skeptics and pretended to be agnostics or atheists had some system of thought they were addicted to and congratulated one another on, which meant they were slaves who were not skeptical of their particular system of thought but submitted to it with their tails wagging in humble supplication, begging for a crumb from its table, a table which was bare of everything to begin with except coldness and delusion.

It should be self-evident that if you serve a system of thought, even if it disguises itself with the name of humanism or of "scientific inquiry" or any other silly label, you are as big a slave as a person who serves any other form of doctrine. "The medium is the message!" proclaimed the media-sage, and of course he spoke the truth. Any so-called "system of thought" *is* a doctrine, because it is composed of prejudices that have hardened into preconceptions. A "system of thought" *is* a religion, built in the same corrupt death-image as all other twentieth century religions. Usually, these degraded religions and "systems of thought" were just petulant attempts to define God, and thus to control God, just as a Bushman sacrificing a goat is attempting to control God. But why would anyone believe God can be controlled, or subscribe to the illusion of control to begin with? Control is an illusion; therefore, those who practice this illusion always miss God, because God does not subscribe to any illusion. God is pure Reality. God is many distinct levels of Reality, but this illusion called control doesn't exist on any level of Reality.

So when you think you are in control, you are in illusion. The choice is yours: the sweet taste of Freedom or the sour breath of control.

Description is better than definition. Description is more related to observation; definition is more related to thinking. Description is also more related to feeling, while definition is almost always related to a denial of feelings to some degree. Freeing up your feelings brings you a big step closer to Liberty, so institutions, which want to keep you captive to their systems of doctrine, rely a great deal upon definitions, as though a human being were nothing more than a walking dictionary. Reality is subjective, so description is closer to Reality than is definition, which prides itself on the illusion of objectivity. This isn't to say Reality is anything you want it to be, because it certainly is not. The experience of Reality involves linking yourself up with God's subjective thoughts. It has everything to do with the purity of Creative Imagination, and nothing to do with the lusts of fantasy.

In the post-twentieth century world, people learn to describe their experience of Reality, rather than submitting themselves to the governance and soul-numbing effect of the labeling process. For to define a thing is to limit that thing; the definition suppresses the possibilities of the thing being defined. Thus, perversion will be manifested.

Ideally, forming a definition would be a matter of drawing distinctions between levels of energetic manifestation, while also perceiving the other levels where the thing being defined also exists in a slightly different, but mostly corresponding, form. This is the point at which we can see description and definition actually harmonizing themselves with one another! Remember that definition is a product of the lie of separation; it is the bastard offspring of distinctiveness. Yet distinctiveness is a necessary part of Nature and of all the levels of manifesting God. Distinctiveness is part of the Synthesis which *is* God. Therefore, we rehabilitate definition by cleaning it up and returning it as a clean new babe to that pure distinctiveness which is its parent.

So in the hands of a truly conscious person, no suppression would be involved in this process, but the energy and effect of stabilization would be present. Nevertheless, even with a conscious person, description is almost always better than definition. Description also flows between planes of manifestation, but it flows better and in a more pleasing fashion than definition; it is more *expansive* than definition, more happy and loving and powerful than definition. Description ultimately absorbs all relatively true definitions, anyway. In the future, people don't try to label Reality so much, and they refuse to allow themselves to be labeled, for as they start to become conscious, they start to become a part of Reality themselves.

A "system of thought" is not an experience of God, just as the silly, sentimental emotional fluctuations of the average religious person is not an experience of God. A so-called "skeptic" who subscribes to a system of thought is as deluded as any other breed of fundamentalist. There are as many fundamentalists among the Unitarians as there are among the Baptists. The only difference between them is that one is more allied with the feeling aspect of the solar plexus chakra, while the other is more allied with the will aspect. Also, the Unitarian may have had a "sex change", but this is not something the Baptist would consider.

If twentieth century people had wanted to contact Divinity, rather than serving their childish intellectual or emotional preferences, maybe they would have been of some use to the natural order. As it was, they appeared not to belong to Nature any more than a real human nature appeared to belong to them.

A real human nature is Achieved by purifying the lower mental body of illusion and the emotional body of glamour. After this process is complete, there is no lust, there is only the love-infused Creative Imagination of the Liberated Human Being. In such a person, the unified mind and emotions and body serve as a pure container of love . . . a pure container of humanity! For God is love, and human beings were made in the image of God. This Creative Imagination is the vehicle by which the Living Legend moves throughout the universal pattern of Divine

Metaphor, spreading his chivalry thru radiating his compassion in a myriad of ways.

A brick is not a brick, it is a vibrating metaphor for something unseen by the physical eye. Nothing is solid; all is legendary and flexible. There is a Pattern, but there is often a new movement within the Pattern. There are many levels within the Pattern, with each Shaman or Grail-Knight moving fluidly throughout a number of the levels. Any supposedly physical object, whether natural or manmade, exists on a number of levels, from more dense to more refined. When so-called "primitive people" of thousands of years ago buried physical objects and food with their dead, they knew the etheric body of their loved one would need etheric weapons and perhaps other objects on his journey thru the levels of the Pattern. If they buried sexy young concubines with him, it was so he could get etheric nookie. How many levels of earths are there around our physical earth? "This hour wilt thou be with me in Paradise."

The book you hold in your hand is not a doctrine, and contains no doctrine. If it sometimes seems otherwise, it may be that I have made a mistake in my presentation; nobody's perfect. If anyone tries to hurt this book with doctrine, it will be more powerful than they are. If your motive is to love and to serve rather than control, the effect of any mistakes you make will be minimized. Don't hold it against yourself or feel guilty if you make a mistake; this book is here to help you release guilt. I don't hold it against you, and neither does the spirit of this book, honey child. Shucks, if you're releasing guilt and learning how to avoid getting any more of the stuff on yourself, you're helping both me and the book! Plus, you're helping the planet.

But this book is more powerful than anyone who would stand against it. The only way a person can try to stand against it would be to try to convince others of some false vision of the book, in which case they would lose touch with the book and would no longer see or feel its Liberating effects. But the book would go on radiating those effects to those who hadn't been deluded and thus could still feel and see it. This book is an infusion of Cosmic Fire, not a statement of doctrine! It is not here to cause you to do anything you do not want to do, and you will not go to "a devil's hell", as the Christians like to put it, for avoiding this book. But if you feel drawn to the book, if you feel it will help attune you to your own soul's purpose, then take a drink from my well and enjoy yourself. There's no additional charge.

Understanding the book may have some importance, but the most true understanding will occur in how you feel about the book and the visions the book sparks in your mind. If the book can help you unify your divine aspirations with your feelings and visions into one continuum of experience, the book will be a glad fulfiller of its purpose. Use the book as a tool; don't be a tool of the book. This living book knows it is *your* servant.

If some portion of this book stirs your soul into a quickening, or into the possibility of a quickening, then use that portion as a "chin-up bar" to pull yourself into the energy and feelings and visionings and purification of Cosmic Fire. And know that as you purify yourself, you will be releasing all that once deadened your soul and hardened your heart, and as this "old stuff" departs, people who do not understand your purpose may confuse you with a person of "bad energy". The energy always tells the truth about a person, except in this one case. A person who is processing and releasing his rage and guilt and grief and fear, and the doctrines which he once used to suppress those seething heavy feelings, may sometimes be mistaken for a person of naughty energy as these old energies fly away from him. But the end result, after the processing and releasing is complete, is Liberation and the total lovingkindness of a Heart redeemed. And God *never* confused this newly Liberated soul with any of those people who do carry some bad energy and are too afraid to do the Work to redeem themselves!

So while this book contains no doctrine, it contains observations of Principles which make it a transmitter of Cosmic Fire. As you contact these Principles, you will taste of the Cosmic Fire of Purificatory Love. If you require some technique to implement these Principles and this taste of Fire, then you are creative enough to devise that technique yourself. But please do not let any technique you may devise harden into a preconception of how things "ought" to be done. There are as many ways as there are individuals of contacting and implementing any given Divine Principle; don't make the mistake of forcing your shit off on your neighbor. Your technique is not superior to her technique, assuming you both have contacted, or are soon to contact, Cosmic Fire. If you devise a technique and then let it harden, the technique is no longer a part of the Principle and you will have only ashes in your mouth, rather than Cosmic Fire.

Now, if you and your neighbor want to pool your consciousness and share a technique or any insight one of you developed, or that both of you developed together, that's okay, honey bun. Sharing the fire of our love is what we're all about! But remember you're sharing the love-fire, you're not sharing a doctrine. You *can't* share doctrine, because the God-energy of sharing is alive, while doctrine is a dead 'possum alongside the road. The energy of life doesn't pause to try to resurrect a damn 'possum. So if you're spouting off a doctrine, you're spouting with the lips of a dead 'possum. Sharing is an offering of fiery life, but doctrine forces or manipulates in an attempt to kill that which it comes in contact with. So keep your own love-fire bright, bright, that you may immediately burn up any doctrine that comes your way. Genuine, true sharing *cannot* occupy the same space as doctrine!

But let us return to our examination of the Libertarians, as we continue to learn how to avoid the traps set by doctrine.

I very much suspect that in a Libertarian society, most of those who styled themselves Libertarians in the twentieth century would have become rebels! People who support Social Darwinism need to realize that "survival of the strongest" or "survival of the most cunning" is not always the same as "survival of the fittest". The only ones who are truly fit to survive are those who are on the march toward compassion.

Yet there is a seed of truth in everything, and those among the Libertarians who sincerely wanted to see an end to society's problems and the elevation of humanity would have done well to consider what an ungoverned society of extended families might be like. You have to realize that the energy of family--*true* family--is the energy of love, and love is incapable of exploiting itself or warring against itself.

Libertarians tended to support big business, but big business is not a family. It is a zoo of monkeys who try to control their rage, because if they allow themselves to openly experience and express their rage, all their peanuts will be taken away. Plus, since most of them are not on the path of conscious soul-growth . . . conscious shadow-growth . . . they had no idea how to turn rage into a tool and would probably misuse it.

When rage is purified of glamour and illusion, then transmuted by the Heart, it becomes indignation. This is not the indignation of the profane, because the profane always have some anger or rage attached to them by their glamours and illusions. The indignation of the purified and integrated person is a powerful, wholesome tool to accomplish great ends. And unlike rage, it doesn't tear holes in a person's aura!

When indignation meets with a person who wants to obstruct the flow of Beauty in the world, the indignation can take a good deal of spiritual pleasure in breaking his bones.

A society of true families would know an extended peace.

But the family unit of the twentieth century was nothing more than a war unit which made alliances with other war units to try to insure its own physical survival, and the survival of its egotism. Thus we see the existence and perpetuation of the caste system to one degree or another in all these emotionally violent lands of the twentieth century. Each family member felt the stirring in his genes of long-forgotten ancestors from medieval times, and those ancestral imprints urged the family to look upon itself as a barony, exploiting when possible and forming alliances when the opportunity seemed advantageous. But this situation was worse in many ways than the feudalism of medieval days, because every war-family, every nuclear-family, was at war with most other families all the time, though in their self-delusion they often didn't recognize the fact, ignoring the significance of words they glorified, such as "competition". In the old days, every family was not at war with every other family; or if it was, it was low-level conflict compared with the fragmented, universalist families of the twentieth century. The universalist philosophy of the nineteenth and twentieth century robber barons and social reformers destroyed everything it touched; instead of the universalism of love and compassion, it created a forced homogeneity of broken fragments. Again with the activity of the unfaced, unredeemed inner deviant. So I say to you stand your ground in the face of your deviance, turn around and face and wrestle with your deviant like the angel wrestling with her beloved Jacob until it is smooth and love-reflecting, and curls up like a kitten in your lap. Then you won't be part of the problem anymore; you'll be a part of the solution by vibrating your surroundings into greater unity and goodness (though your surroundings might at first interpret the sensation as discomfort!)

It's one thing to lend a helping hand, another thing to provide a handout. Only the true family can lend a helping hand to its kin; the state provides handouts. The structure of the state precludes the glow of love; thus it can never truly lend a helping hand, but only give handouts. A person whose survival or welfare is at stake is not to be blamed for accepting state benefits, because in the fragmented universalist society, that's often his only choice. Yet many (not all!) who accept these handouts bear the energy of the parasite, and the system encourages, and cannot help but encourage, the growth of this energy of parasitism. There is *no way* a system built on non-family can avoid encouraging the growth of parasitism. So attempts at reform are useless and provide at best a temporary Band-Aid--and at worst, provide a cruel blow by cutting benefits of those non-parasites who happen to be poor. The only solution is to let fragmented universalist society fall away and allow the structure of love-infused, unforced extended family--of Kindred!--to arise from the ashes.

In the future, people who want to be captive to some form of restriction or other, whether it be taboos or any other kind, have to create that restriction for themselves. The government doesn't create it for them. In the twentieth century, government provided restriction as sort of a degenerate social welfare program for those who clamored for restriction. But in the future, the tiny amount of government that remains doesn't even merit the name "government", since it doesn't govern anybody. People who want to be free are free to create their own freedom without "freedom" being forced off on them, and people who want to be restricted perverts also have to create their restrictions. Most people choose not to be perverts and so reject restriction, since it's a lot harder on a person's Dignity to be restricted than it is to be disciplined enough to be Free. But people in the twentieth century had been slaves to restriction for so long they just couldn't see the simplest truths.

Part of the problem revolving around duality and repression and perversion in the twentieth century was the fact that the language was dualistic. Normally, people are so used to their language they don't notice its flaws, nor do they notice how it structures--or misstructures-- their brains and the way they view and interact with the world. For example, anytime that old worn-out deva called Uncle Sam wanted to puff up his chest and go on a rampage against something, the people would start talking about "cracking down" on this, that, or the other and the new round of repression would begin, and shortly thereafter a new round of perversion would begin. For whomever was cracking down and whomever was being cracked down upon were really both a part of the same level, or substratum, of society, at least in terms of their dualistic interactions. As an example, if you "crack down" on terrorists, you're going to insure that more terrorism occurs in that substratum of society where the terrorists hang out. For every unconscious, mechanical action there's an equal and seemingly "opposite" reaction. Duh! It is difficult to see how the twentieth century people could have failed to see this, but perhaps their brains had been all but ruined by their language.

And the attitude and energy you bring to each action are generally more important than the action itself, in terms of both local and long-term karma. Really, the energy and attitude *are* the action! It's really the attitude and energy that determine the nature of the action. The attitude and the energy behind the attitude determine whether a given action is dualistic, or holistic and unified within an appropriate sphere of God's consciousness by a self-realized cell of that consciousness who wears the form of a human being.

The energy and attitude behind "cracking down" on anything is the energy and attitude of a cave-dwelling proto-mammal, not of a human being. You don't crack down on terrorism; you eliminate it by eliminating terrorists whom you don't have the opportunity to offer the option of rehabilitation to; and those terrorists you capture rather than kill you confine to a humane facility where they can rehabilitate themselves, if they so desire. (Just as important, you discover and rectify how you contributed to the development of terrorism in your hearty, back-slapping ignorance.) These options have to do with eliminating glamour and illusion from the substratum of a particular region of society so that particular region can finally be flooded by the radiance of the love which was there all along, but was temporarily obscured by the glamour and illusion. In a civilized consciousness, these actions have nothing to do with judgement, because the civilized person knows that the energy of judgement just perpetuates the energy of shame, and the energy of shame will just break out in more unconscious, mechanical violence.

If you look at primitive twentieth century armed forces, their attitudes were the attitudes of suppression, which is another word for repression, so of course they were never going to run out of enemies. They insured themselves of a continuing supply of enemies by their corrupt energy of duality, which fostered attitudes of duality ("cracking down"), which fostered the continuing appearance of more perversions to crack down on, either in a new form, or in a old form that managed to sustain itself and strike back in the face of the repression.

Energy colors everything it touches, so if your energy is dualistic, you're going to be fostering more suffering and trouble in the world, whether you're a formal terrorist, that type of outwardly clean, well-manicured terrorist known as a politician or CEO, or the type of do-gooder saint who runs around feeding people, while denying certain elements of her own humanity, thus denying the full humanity of those she allegedly serves. Yet full humanity is the only form of humanity. If a person isn't promoting the full development of humanity, then what the hell are they promoting? Becoming fully human is the only task we have; if the world were filled with people who had Achieved the full development of their humanity, there wouldn't be any problems. And the do-gooders would have become extinct along with the problems they had helped perpetuate.

And in my experience, these do-gooder secretly shame-filled saints of the twentieth century could easily, if they found themselves in favorable circumstances, fall off their high horse (at least privately) and become whip-wielding dominatrixes or engage in other dualistic fluctuations designed by their inner pervert to "balance" their sainthood. So again I say: Why would anybody want to be balanced? One extreme to the other, with no genuine fullbody love or compassion in any of their dualistic manifestations.

It breaks the Heart of a civilized person to see the way these twentieth century people continually fostered suffering among themselves. It didn't matter if they were conservative Baptists, or liberal Unitarians (Unitarianism is just Christianity without the religion) or atheists or Buddhists or even Pagans; they all were gunning for certain aspects of their own natures, which made them go on the warpath against their neighbors. They were all brothers in crime and depravity and in the wrath of love denied.

Their institutions were built in the image of the brains that had been ruined by their dualistic language. Their institutions were built in the image of conquest, rather than of cultivation. They strove to conquer themselves with knowledge, rather than to cultivate themselves into an awareness of knowingness. Then they strove to abuse and conquer everyone else with knowledge, rather than serving them in a spirit of livingness.

Practical human relations had not yet made itself known among them. Family-Building is the sacred Work of the human being. The human being needs no institutions to tell him how to proceed with the Work that is encoded into his very genes, and which is enlivened by his awakened, luminous Heart.

Another example of how their dualistic attitudes, energy and practices led to one cycle of violence after another involved the "abortion issue", as their misplaced intellects would style it. For the intellects of this degenerate era, everything in Nature was to be distantly looked upon as an "issue", a thing which could be handled without involving their humanity. Ugh! They were insane, and their madness nearly destroyed the earth.

Anyhow, abortion is murder and anyone can see that. Even considering abortion, but then deciding to have the child, can imprint that child with a horror that will injure and impede his manifestation in the physical world, as he strives against the current of his earliest imprint to find a sense of belonging on this emotionally tattered globe. Only if he is dedicated enough to begin to develop a genuine spiritual understanding within himself, then fortunate enough to find a genuinely talented and loving energy-healer, will that imprint be removed so that he can have the true birth that he deserves into the knowledge that he belongs here on this earth and has as much right to be here as anyone else.

But . . . telling the truth about abortion is not the same as calling for it to be outlawed. As usual, the outlawing of this conduct would ultimately lead to more hate and shame, and the astral cloud created by these slimy energies would eventually find a way to work itself out in society in an even more destructive way than abortion. Plus, even though I'm willing to tell the truth about abortion, I wouldn't be comfortable telling a woman she couldn't get one . . . unless I were the man who got her pregnant.

In a civilized society the idea of abortion is so novel as to be practically unheard of, because a civilized society is founded upon the extended family, and upon networks of extended families which encourage unrestricted and highly individual responsible conduct. Thus effective birth control measures will be employed if a woman doesn't want to get pregnant, and if she gets pregnant in spite of birth control, she will love the child anyway and won't try to get rid of it . . . and after the birth, if she doesn't feel as closely emotionally related to the child as others in her extended family, then those others will charge themselves with most of the raising of the child. The birth mother won't feel that the child is an inconvenience, because it isn't an inconvenience in a civilized world. And she won't blame the child for a matter which is entirely her responsibility, and the responsibility of the man whom she was sexually intimate with. Emotional maturity is one of the hallmarks of civilized conduct. And this maturity guarantees that one will not have sex in a degrading manner, if for no other reason than the concern that one's birth control might fail, leading to a child who might be imprinted with the energies of control or brutality. And this maturity insists that you try to avoid having sex with someone you couldn't see pooling your genes with.

It's a child, not an inconvenience.

Finally, for another example of how duality degrades everyone whom it touches, look at the "torture issue". When primitive "intelligence" agencies and military organizations decide to torture someone, their objective is to erode that person's Dignity. They don't have to get very harsh physically to do this, although they may decide that it would be fun to get physically harsh, too.

For that's what torture is about when performed by primitives. It's about degrading someone, about eroding his Dignity. Even the Apaches, who in the nineteenth century were fond of torturing their enemies, did so with a somewhat different motive and energy than twentieth century people. For the Apache, the torture event was a chance for the enemy to demonstrate his courage in the face of extreme adversity. If he held up well, they would praise him after his death and respect him as a great warrior.

Now, I'm not holding the Apache up as an example of moral

rectitude, because there were all sorts of dualistic elements in his conduct, too. I'm just saying that the Apache left his enemy some Dignity, whereas the objective of the primitive white-eyes of the twentieth century was to corrode or even destroy his enemy's Dignity. The result was that the white-eyes destroyed his own Dignity, whether he managed to destroy his enemy's Dignity or not.

The way to attack an enemy's Dignity is thru psychological techniques, such as stripping an Islamic prisoner naked in front of females, then perhaps even having a female rub up against the Islamic prisoner. The average Islamic prisoner would very much prefer the delivery provided by Death than this inhumane treatment. Yes, maybe much or even most of his Dignity is a false dignity founded upon the illusions of egotism, but there will be some genuine human Dignity somewhere in there too, hiding among the egotism. To uncompassionately destroy a person's egotism, as military and "intelligence" agencies try to do, is to also destroy the genuine Dignity that hides within the chains of the egotism, assuming the torture is "successful". Fortunately, it was often not "successful". And you can get most people to crack and say anything you want them to say with long-term, sustained torture over a period of months, with the result being that whatever they say will be nothing more than a confirmation of your own glamours and illusions, rather than being information that you can actually use to serve someone. Even the primitive "intelligence" agencies of the twentieth century knew this, but didn't often let it interfere with their perverted fun. And is it necessary for me to point out yet again that torture defeats its own stated purpose by spreading shame, and the cloud of violent emotions and violent physical actions precipitated by the crippled emotions?

In case there are some degenerate, uncomprehending Christians reading this document who support their country's forays into the dehumanizing of people of other nations, let me give you an example you should be able to relate to. If you have no empathy regarding the Islamic prisoner in the preceding example, maybe you will, in spite of your denied shame and degeneracy, find at least a trace of empathy when I tell you that a comparable example would be if a devout female Catholic, perhaps a young soldier or nun, were captured by an army or some other group hostile to the West, made to strip naked in front of ogling males, who then produced a crucifix and took turns pissing on it, and then held her down and shoved the crucifix up her pussy. I wouldn't do that to save the world or for any other reason. Yet for all practical purposes, that's what the degenerate "intelligence" agencies of the West did to the Islamic prisoner in the previous example. And after that supreme humiliation, the young soldier or nun wouldn't even be capable of telling you her "secret information", assuming she had any, because her Dignity would have been so shamed that the shock of the matter would cause her to feel that nothing any worse could be done to her than what had already been done, and also because her "secret information" would have receded to the back of her consciousness as she felt the destruction of all she held dear. Any further humiliation these "soldiers" tried to subject her to would actually be welcomed by a wounded part of herself that felt it was worthless and that wanted to die, and absent death, at least wanted to be repeatedly shown proof that it was worthless. So you can see, if you have any sense at all, that torture is useless and won't produce any true results that can be used to serve anyone. But it will add to the cloud of astral shame, and thus breed more violence.

The Islamics of the twentieth century, despite their degeneracy and lack of resemblance to the spirit embodied by the Prophet Mohammed, were at least gracious enough to accept Jesus as a genuine Prophet, but the Christians did not reciprocate. The Christians would preach that their Crusades were not about religion and that America was a land where all religions were honored, but they didn't accept Mohammed as a real Prophet. Yet the Islamics accepted both Jesus and the Jewish Prophets. It is difficult in examining the twentieth century to see who was really the most degenerate.

The Moslems might insult Christians, but they wouldn't insult Jesus. The Christians not only insulted Islam, but they even insulted the Prophet Mohammed. They did not know, and apparently did not care, that they were committing the sin of blasphemy. Blasphemy is not irreverence; blasphemy is a sour dart aimed at the soul of God, which then rebounds and strikes the pervert who threw the dart to begin with. Jesus was a bit of the embodied soul of God, and so was the Prophet Mohammed. We don't have to pretend they are "High and Mighty", because they were also human, even as we are. We can be on familiar terms with them, but we must not blaspheme against them. To do so is a self-inflicted wound upon the conscience of the blasphemer.

The Moslems frequently confused irreverence with blasphemy, and the Christians frequently confused blasphemy with irreverence. Grow sensitive and feel the energy, and you will know which is which.

So when I condemn degenerate religions, I am not condemning that Source Principle which founded the religion. I am not condemning those who held true to the founding impulse of the religion in its early days, but I am quite happy to condemn those who blaspheme against themselves and against their founding energy by eventually moving away from that energy. Remember that energy is not form; the form of a religion can change, and must change and grow more refined so it can reflect more of the energy of its Founding Impulse. When forms don't change at the proper moment, that is a blasphemy in itself.

The degenerate Moslems would sometimes behead a prisoner, but in their minds this was a less brutal act than the types of psychological torment the West would subject Moslem prisoners to. The Moslems felt they were not as savage and brutal as the Americans, and thus did not understand how anyone could take seriously America's claim to be a light in the world. And primitive, arrogant Americans--who were the rulers of the "free world"--were never able to see the world from any perspective other than that of their own culture. If they had had enough self-discipline and self-love to Work to begin to understand other cultures, the cloud of hate and shame would have been smaller and there would have been fewer wars and acts of terrorism.

To understand another culture, you don't have to abandon your lifeways and adopt theirs. You primarily have to develop sensitivity to energy and tap into their culture's *spirit*, and follow that spirit until it leads you to the culture's soul. And when you get there, you will find that the soul of another culture is pretty much the same as the soul of your culture, although the spirit may have a different flavor and the external lifeways may be different.

Obviously, I'm not saying the Moslems were right and Americans were wrong. Both were wrong, because both were repressed and perverse. But it would have defused a bit of the perversion if they had Worked to understand one another's cultures. At the soul level, both cultures were very similar. But by the late twentieth century, both cultures had abandoned their souls.

The truth of the matter is that when the spirit of the earth is absorbed by the Heart of the solar system, both the essence of Islam and the essence of Christianity will reside side by side next to the Heart of God.

Those who say that "All men are brothers!" speak a truth, but they have not *become* that truth. The result is that they confuse the brotherhood of the soul with an outward homogeneity. They don't know the universality of the love nature, yet they try to create that which they do not know. The result is homogenization and the forcible restriction of populations who do not want to be homogenized. Look at the havoc the universalist Christian ministers created among native tribes everywhere they went. (It might be worth noting that thru much of its history, Islam welcomed Christianity and Judaism and other religions, and encouraged their practitioners to worship as they pleased.) Outward "universality" is always at least a little totalitarian and cannot mimic the true universality of the human heart as it connects with Kindred spirits.

Every "universalist" I met in primitive America wanted to restrict people that didn't see things in quite the way they did. Again with a primitive phenomenon defeating its stated purpose. They used democracy to defeat one another, not to encourage the sprouting and growth of genuinely individualistic, and thus genuinely Altruistic, cultures. They forced cultures into false arrangements with one another, like putting jimson weed with a bouquet of roses. They did not know that the human heart, when unrestricted, automatically and with full consciousness and compassion allows each piece of human nature to fall into the place God prepared for it, and that groups of humans who are meant to be together in some kind of compassionate arrangement will be attracted to one another, rather than being herded and forced into the philosophical concentration camps constructed by the "universalists". I never met a compassionate "universalist", or even a "universalist" who even had the seed of an idea as to what compassion actually is.

The compassionate destruction of egotism is really more of a refinement than a destruction, anyway. And it's self-initiated; it's not initiated by some other person or by some school or agency. The glamour and illusion are destroyed and released to God, but the egotism that was spawned by and which housed the glamour and illusion is scientifically refined enough to be Absorbed in a Great Moment by the disciple's Higher Aspects. This process is a part of the Science of Compassion (or the Art of Compassion, if you want to view it that way) and the successful outcome of this Path leads to a reduction of suffering in the world, and provides pathways by which love and compassion become apparent.

But the alleged "soldiers" and "intelligence" operatives of any nation who treated prisoners in a manner designed to destroy their Dignity were evolutionary failures themselves. They were as violently, hatefully degenerate as those they tortured, and probably more violently, hatefully degenerate than some of those they tortured, because some of their victims were innocent of the crimes they were being tortured into admitting culpability for. These alleged "soldiers" and "intelligence" operatives should have been killed, not out of vengeance, of course, but from a desire to purify the ranks of the military and intelligence agencies. And the "leaders" who approved such practices should have been killed too, of course, though the "leaders" of primitive people weren't often held accountable for their most heinous crimes. These primitive people didn't know enough about rehabilitation to be able to give these evolutionary failures the chance to be able to learn to restore their own human Dignity, thus redeeming themselves into evolutionary successes, so the only sensible, humane option would have been to explain to them why they were being killed, and counsel them to take it as a lesson so that they would perhaps be prodded by their souls toward better behavior in their next lives . . . assuming they hadn't already degraded themselves too far to have future lives in human form.

Hell, the self-destruction of their own Dignity would also spread out from these alleged soldiers and "intelligence" operatives in waves of slimy numbing energy, and would thus also taint other people whose energy fields were not strong enough to hold up under this sneaky, slimy, hate-filled assault. Obviously, this would also eventually work out in more violence being precipitated onto the physical plane than otherwise would have occurred. The illusions and glamours of primitive people are always attached to the illusions and glamours of other primitive people, forming a tangled, seething, sneaky, confused mass of corrupted energy that tries to pass itself off as a society. The strings of attachment provide tainted, confusing pathways for shame and hate and sentimentality to spread.

Yet knowingness follows a straight path, though it is caught by a circular chalice. All Divine Principles follow a straight path, until caught by a circular chalice and radiated by that chalice. The fusion of Heaven and Earth is known as Compassion, because this fusion is a result of unifying the love of the Heart with the passion of the sexual, emotional nature. Thus Compassion is the most penetrating, powerfully radiating, full-spectrum Divine Principle that is possible, and may be the only one that human beings are charged with actually manufacturing, due to the presence of both a physical nature and the capacity to learn to open the human heart to the love that flows automatically from God's perfect Heart. Compassion may be the only Divine Principle that is capable of penetrating *every* level of the universe, so now you can begin to see how important the work of our earth's Humanity is. We are the hope of the Universe to fully know its own Compassion. Thus the most important work any society can be involved in is learning to manifest total Compassion. For many societies, this Work must begin as an appreciation of Beauty, recognizing that our entire ability to perceive and create Beauty arises from our own beautiful sexual natures.

Yes, the Prophet reveals deficiencies in the alleged society, but he also shews it how to become a true society. He is not merely a critic, but also a creator, and invites all true, sincere souls to become creators with him. We do not pursue Liberation for our own sakes, but to become transmitters of pure, happy Compassion to all beings. This is why Liberated Human Beings are also known as the Lords of Compassion.

Anyhow, the "issues" that caused primitive people to stumble are simple, because they all revolve around shame and the self-hate caused by shame. Yet the wags who viewed themselves as "opinion makers" always wanted to distance themselves from feeling their own shame, and thus numbed themselves and their audiences with intellectual abstractions, turning the truth of Nature into a denial of compassion and the healing that would flow from self-compassion. All these people needed to do to recover from their own violence was to individually learn to release their own shame and self-hate, while voicing public support to one another in this process. Then there would never need to be another "War Against _____" or "War On _____". You fill in the blanks. There might still have been the occasional need to physically remove a recalcitrant hate-filled person from incarnation, because that person might have been interfering with the growth of Beauty in the world. But war as such would have been a thing of the past . . . and *is* a thing of the past in civilized cultures. (Though the individual citizens of such cultures are mostly well-armed, just in case an unbeautiful element comes along.)

Fundamentalism serves no one, and no book or verbal presentation, no matter how specific it seems to get, can do more than generalize. Therefore, let these words prompt you toward a conscious perception of the Pattern of Universal Livingness, and toward a full awareness of and connection with your own Heart's innate and total Knowingness, and when the time comes to act, you will know what to do, honey.

Remember that the energy of an event tells the truth about that event. But the intellects of the intellectuals are so undisciplined and unruly they want to control the nature of Reality and make It fit their preconceptions. So ignore the intellectuals and learn to feel the energy.

Be not disturbed when the intellectual cries "Contradiction!" For all the intellectual has is his contradictions, so of course that's all he's ever going to see. He is a poor man in an unending war against his own human nature. The wealth of his truest Self remains unavailable to him. I write for those who are willing to Work with intellect and turn it into an energy-reflector of Truth . . . these wise, brave ones have transcended intellect! And I write for those who have never had much interest in intellect, but who are heart-centered or wish to be, and who are centered in their Higher Minds, or wish to be. Intellect is not to be suppressed or the perversions it will come up with are horrible; nevertheless, the path of refining the intellect into a mirror of Truth is so difficult as to be nearly impossible.

The intellectual will point out what he believes are errors, but his "mind" is slippery as an eel and has deluded him. If I report on a fact, I am reporting more than anything else on the conditions and energies around that fact, and this the intellectual does not see. His "fact" is a dried up patch of ink on a dead leaf, but my fact is a living manifestation imbued with constantly flexing, breathing Energy. My fact is derived from that Energy and attracts some of that Energy to it. My fact moves with the rhythm of the ocean of livingness from which it is derived, and from which my every perception flows. My fact may not always have the polish of his "fact", but his "fact" is dead, Jim. My fact lives and *knows* that it lives! Thus does the staff of the wanderer turn into a large golden serpent that devours the staffs of those whom a primitive society defers to as magicians.

This is not to say I may not make a mistake, but if I do the intellectual is incapable of seeing it because he hasn't developed within himself the ability to fully know himself and his capacities. He has no idea of the regal realm where my Visioning occurs, and he's wrong when he thinks he knows what my Visioning is. *He cannot know*, and it cannot be described to him. He can't be spoon-fed from my trencher. He doesn't even know where on the table my trencher is located, or even what the shape of the table is.

I know him well, better than he knows himself, because I had to transmute and release some of his karma, the karma he is too lazy and selfish and fearful to learn to transmute and release. I had to save the world from his foolish, stupid, squirming karma, and had to become more clever than he is (and have a bit of luck) to avoid being imprisoned in his mental institutions. So he can bite my flabby white ass if he thinks he can pinpoint my imperfections; he's incapable of it.

Yea, the intellectual is a dirty-tongued devil whose speech is slurred into untruth by his mental lusts, no matter how accurate he thinks his "facts" are. By God, the Universe is a flowing, shifting stream of warm energy, not a dry collection of "facts". There is no such thing as empty space; the tribes of stars who mingle in the nighttime sky realize full well that they are surrounded by the fire of God's heart; they know the pink-red color of God's heart. The stars are never lonely.

Yet with his collection of alleged "facts", the intellectual feels he has built a giant pyramid of knowledge that subdues his ignorance. But all he's really done is to construct a little-bitty anthill that doesn't realize it was made by a pissant. And because he chose to try to subdue ignorance rather than Work with it to see what it is capable of evolving into, the ignorance has only grown stronger, as well as becoming a master of camouflaging itself with the pride of knowledge. He is lonely in the extreme, and continues his cycle of addictive, knowledge-based practices in a desperate attempt to counteract the loneliness by continuing the practices which created it. Yet the Shaman knows the comfort of the stars. The Shaman is never lonely, has no lusts to serve, and converses freely with those whose ranks he will eventually join.

The stars have neither knowledge nor ignorance, yet in a long-ago time they were human beings in either this or another universe. They form themselves into relations with their Kindred, just as the coming families of a civilized earth will group themselves around a central core of love that serves as the family's soul. We will never forget our familyhood, and will carry it with us forever! The stars are still human, for the humanity we earn stays with us forever, no matter how far into flaming dimensions of vast unspeakable love we finally evolve.

When the fear of ignorance vanishes, the space that once housed the fear is filled with the pink-red love-flame; when the pride of knowledge vanishes, the space that once housed the pride is filled with the bright golden will of God. Divine Love and Will dance together in eternity, each distinct, yet each fully in harmony with the other. All of Space is filled with this harmony; there is no frontier "out there". Such Divine Harmony is an attribute of Civilization! Our job is to become conscious of the harmony and bring our own share of harmony into Space to lay at God's feet.

If we must build a pyramid, then let it be a golden pyramid filled with a divine pink love-flame that pulses it continually into new life.

But let us not forget our rifles, in case we meet a species which hasn't recognized the harmony of the stars.

The primitive theologian or philosopher wants concrete abstractions that justify his delusions. The sincere seeker wants to Achieve contact with, and then Absorption by, Divine Principles. Any theology or philosophy he may use along the path of his sacred Quest is just a tool that may be discarded anytime he meets with something that is Greater than the tool. And the sincere seeker will, sooner or later, meet with that which is Greater than all tools. If he is exceptionally skilled and dedicated, he may even be able to help bring this Glowing Manifestation into the earthplane, even channeling it thru his own physical tool in the act of lovemaking. For love belongs everywhere, especially in the organs of those who love one another, where it becomes that Intelligent Love we refer to as fullbody compassion.

You can't subject a Divine Manifestation to your weights and measures; all you can do is to allow yourself to become conscious of a Divine Manifestation and go from there.

In your actions with people, never let the intellectual force you on to his corrupt playing field, where restriction and lack of discipline occlude the sun of his soul. If you are enticed or forced into his realm, you'll lose contact with your own knowingness. The intellect is meant to be absorbed into knowingness, knowingness is not meant to be whored to the intellect. So smash the intellectual without mercy if he tries to seduce or rape you. Do not be reduced to his level. If he has any self-honoring, he'll begin walking the Path of Purification so he can Achieve your level.

Do you see the stupidity of the fundamentalist Christian "inter-rogators"--the torture-masters of the ancient Amerikan Empire? For in allowing their fundamentalist Islamic brother to be sexually abused by Western "women", they confirm in the mind of that prisoner everything he's ever feared about unrestricted femininity. So if he ever gets free, he'll go to even greater lengths to oppress and abuse women, determined that such creatures will never be allowed to run loose in his own country. He doesn't realize that the "women" who abused him aren't really even women; they are simply lust-filled, hate-filled perverts who would be trying to rape somebody even if they'd been born male, because their own self-hate wants to confirm its own nature by humiliating, by degrading, a living human being, just as small boys may sometimes be subject to evil impulses and rip the wings off of insects. The reasonable person may not see this, but reasonable people were responsible for many mass killings and mass humiliations in the twentieth century. The reasonable person is a dangerous monster who is usually on the loose, for his reasonableness serves as a cloak to keep him out of prisons designed for more emotionally-polarized monsters. Surely you realize that most Germans in the 1930's and 1940's were reasonable people.

And most of the Amerikans who supported concentration camps for Japanese-Amerikan citizens in World War II, and who later supported concentration camps for Islamic prisoners, were reasonable people. The reasonable person can be depended upon to never cry out in protest when a stranger is led away in chains. But according to the twin Principles of Karma and Reincarnation, one day he'll be the stranger!

The primitive Amerikans of the twentieth century didn't realize that people a few generations later would disown their silent, accommodating ancestors because of their various reasonable crimes against humanity; as usual, the primitives had no idea how to project their awareness into the future. But future humanity sees little difference in concentration camps and torturings, whether they are performed by Nazis in the name of racial purity, or by Amerikans in the name of freedom. Both are manifestations of a terrible ugliness, and thus everything that comes out of them is a lie. Never believe the words of a person who serves ugliness, he is only trying to beguile you with reasonableness. (At least the German citizens could claim to be unaware of the crimes of their government, but Americans could not make the same claim. Americans could, and did, watch horrible scenes on television of torturings which were initiated by the Secretary of Defense with a 'wink and a nod' to his subordinates. Then the Americans would eat another cheeseburger. But consider the case of the German mayor and his wife when General Patton, on fire with righteousness and indignation, forced them to visit a concentration camp near their town. They hadn't known about the atrocities, and were so shocked they went back home and committed suicide. Amerikans just ate another cheeseburger. Amerikans could claim no moral authority over any people anywhere.)

During my visit to the 1980's I became acquainted with an old German who'd soldiered with the Axis in World War II. He was a very reasonable person, very clean and sweet, but sometimes his reasonableness seemed a bit torn because when he'd been a child his life had been saved by a Jewish doctor when no doctor of his own blood would help him; yet in the 1980's he still supported the old Nazi regime. But reasonableness can be made to cover nearly any contingency so that the cloud-monster may continue his crimes.

The right use of logic is to properly relate various areas of human livingness by refining itself into a chalice to catch the supernal wine of Higher Mind and the love of the Heart. Logic, if it is to be used at all, must only be used to reflect the knowingness of Higher Mind and the Love of the Heart. This crystalline Logic is inexorable in service to Love; it has no desires of its own. It follows no rules; it lives in Service to Divine Principles. Thus this crystalline Logic is alive and it *breathes*. If logic is used in any other way, it perverts itself into reasonableness and harm will result to the organism that carries the reasonableness, as well as to others who are not prepared to deflect the reasonableness of this pervert with Truth and Love.

The people of the world are not at war with each other; the governments of the world are at war with each other and they confuse the people in order to use them as cannon fodder. Of course, the whole process is very reasonable and easily lends itself to learned discourse.

The universalist governments of the twentieth century intended to bring their philosophy of universal brotherhood into physical manifestation no matter how many people they had to kill to do it. Nearly every nation in the twentieth century fought to make itself in the image of ancient Rome. The middle ages began with Rome and ended early in the twenty-first century when the Roman "ideal" was finally rejected as being hazardous to the human soul.

Some of the leaders of the nations of American Indians, who were savages and never noted for their reasonableness, would sometimes avert a war by insisting that they--the leaders--be allowed to fight one another to settle a major dispute between their respective nations, thus averting the massive bloodshed of war thru the possible Sacrifice of one of the leader's lives. Truly, savages are irrational. A very few of the twentieth century Amerikan leaders were considered "war heroes", but it was never pointed out that heroism can fade and the honor, if not continually used, will grow stale. A martial arts teacher I used to have would tell a student who bragged on how strong or skilled he used to be that he didn't give a damn about what the student used to be able to do, he only cared what the student was presently capable of. The so-called "war heroes" among the twentieth century Amerikan politicians were heroes no longer, and sent the young and relatively innocent to die in their places. But they were always very, very reasonable.

For the politician, warriorship was a thing to be simulated by soldiering for a couple of years, not a living value to be practiced every day of his life. This simulation was used as a cloak to convince reasonable people that the politician was a *man*.

Remember that in a universalist society, the people are almost always better than their "leaders". This is partly due to the fact that it is impossible to feel a sense of community if you view the world, or even a large nation, as somehow being united by the innate violence of outward forms and institutions, and the so-called "leaders" of a universalist society often suffer this delusion more than the ones being "led". Hell, the people in a universalist "society" are merely being led to drop their own human connectedness to their own tribe; and this is a depraved practice. It should be obvious to anybody who has developed a basic human sensitivity that trying to forcibly make yourself believe that we are "one world" is a strain upon the body, soul and emotions, and that it violates the deepest feelings of the Heart. Yet the "leaders" in a universalist "society" believe they thrive upon the delusion of "one nation under God", with the result that their experience of Divinity is so diluted that they've lost their connection to God. And by trying to culturally embrace the entire human community, they've lost the ability to really be a vital inspiration to their own communities . . . hell, they don't really belong to a community anywhere anymore, except the community of deluded universalists who live in the capitol city! They *can't* belong to a real community as long as they remain universalist. Their power mongering in the name of "humanity" has defeated their own humanity!

Corporate government cannot exist side-by-side with Living Kindred. It's not possible. This is why imperialist Christian government since the time of the Roman takeover of the Church fought constantly to eradicate Kindred. But Kindred will return.

Reasonableness is impure; it doesn't seek to know or to be or to *love*. It seeks only the continued gratification of its own selfish, uninspired delusions. It seeks only monstrosity. This is nearly as true of the late twentieth century reasonable, politically correct liberal as it is of the National Socialists of the 30's and 40's. But most of the late twentieth century liberals lacked the will of the Nazis, and thus couldn't bring their liberal vision into complete manifestation and domination over the minds and hearts of their reasonable countrymen.

And while reasonableness is not a virtue, and indeed is a sin of the flawed personality, it must be remembered that unreasonableness for the sake of unreasonableness is useless, and really is a form of narcissism. To be useful, unreasonableness must only occur as a side-effect of, and in support of, the Quest to contact and embody Truth and Love.

Those whose Vision is opened to learning of the divers ways Divinity interacts with our world begin finally to perceive many heretofore hidden methods which God has devised to touch our lives. Such people begin to know the "secrets of nature"; not that there ever were any secrets, but when people insist on isolating themselves from everything but the "knowledge" they are force-fed in schools, and the vibrators they grow so attached to they forget sex is about soul-connection, they can't see jack shit. But the person who feeds himself at the table of his own soul begins to see great wonders that cannot be told. Nevertheless, we can make a few very basic observations manifest, as we are doing in this document which so absorbs your attention you have probably even forgotten about using your vibrator tonight. Well, if we can help you move out of mechanicalness, we have performed a part of our purpose. Do not forget that a woman who is skilled with her fingers can bring herself a good deal of pleasure without resorting to the soul-numbing effects of mechanical contrivances. And if this document doesn't strike you as being overly mechanical, or excessively concerned with form or homogeneity of expression, perhaps it is because we are not *thinking*, we are simply *observing* and then writing down our observations, as any good journalist would do. But with us, observing means much more than it does to the average person who has been deluded by the schools into worshipping the twin demons of ignorance and knowledge. Our process of observation makes us immediately one with that which we observe; there is no separation at all. Certes, there are levels of distinctiveness, but there is no separation. We relish each level of distinctiveness in a woman, for example, her spiritual aroma floating up to our nose as much as her delicious body odor. We praise and cherish all of her many, many levels of sweetness and love and strength. We cherish the purity of her soul's character, which has been accumulated as purified, stabilized flashes of light from each incarnation in which she has striven toward some vision of goodness. We know a thing from inside out, and our purified feeling nature, which has been integrated with our power to observe, is an integral part of our process. Thus does my lover wonder how I know that she is good, for her personality requires some strengthening yet to be able to bear the full brilliance of her soul, and thus expresses with what appear to her to be defects. But to us, her "defects" merely represent her challenges, because we are one with her inner self, and we know that she is good, that she is perfect, and that she is God. She is an aspect of ourselves. She is one of our favorite aspects of ourselves. We love her; she is as our very own soul.

But in the twentieth century, those who are as we are have often been drugged by physicians and schools and churches into accepting the lie of separation. Many of us thus become enraged, and have a long path back toward recovering our souls, and toward converting the rage into indignation.

Thus do we learn about the varied qualities of energy, and how that energy becomes reflected in our lives. If we had always been treated as the little angels which we are, we might never have fully been able to embrace this knowledge. So maybe from one angle it is not altogether a tragedy that Judeo-Christians do not normally believe their scriptures or base their lifeways on those scriptures. They never paid any more attention to the part about "entertaining angels unaware" than they paid to any other part of their teachings.

To visit the twentieth century, a conscious person had to come like "a thief in the night". To move in a society of thieves, you have to appear to be a thief. Early in the twentieth century one of us appeared whose mission it was to reflect the thievery back onto these people, to rub their noses in it so they couldn't ignore it. He never was involved in politics; he was viewed with suspicion by every nation who took notice of him at all. As is often the case with those whose task is highly specialized, part of his knowingness was withheld from him so he could force himself into specialized channels. He did well in performing his mission, even though outwardly he never fully understood what that mission was. One bothersome result is that some people tried to imitate him who didn't know what they were imitating, and he pretty much encouraged it, because without access to his full knowingness, he was, frankly, liable to do nearly anything. Yet it wasn't their mission to rub the nose of the world in its thievery, it was his. People must learn to develop enough perception that they find their own tasks, rather than imitating another. To imitate this fellow produced tragedy in many people's lives; he was a good guy, but with his specialized Work, he had to wallow in the world's shit. If you're not trained and experienced enough to work in the world's sewers--and his followers never were--you're going to be swallowed by a great big rat.

Yet some people, flushed with a shame which they imagine to be a good feeling, will perform any stupidity to encourage this thing which they do not recognize as shame. Most, if not all, of the narcissism of the late twentieth century was a result of the ripple effect of the energy that had been disturbed by our operative. And I suppose it must be pointed out that he was not a shadow-warrior in the usual sense, because his mission wasn't to refine, it was simply to serve as a reflector of the world's shadow. The world could do with this knowledge what it chose; the hope was that the world would choose to purify and integrate and allow itself to be infused with the love of the world's soul. But of course, the world chose mostly to repress and therefore to continue its perversions.

Well, I was about to talk about how the varied qualities of energy become reflected in our lives, so let me return to that. When I called Uncle Sam a deva, I wasn't shitting you. He's a deity, the deity which in the twentieth century represented the USA, just as a beautiful maiden aspect of the Goddess represented the holy land of Finland. I kiss the feet of the Goddess of Finland; she lends a purity and a goodness to her people. And when the people of the USA imagined (or at least desperately hoped) they were in charge of their destinies and tried to illustrate their supposed mastery by "cracking down" on someone or something, they did not realize that this was merely the deity called Uncle Sam reflecting their own desperate, perverted, power mongering energy back onto them.

Now, I don't know whether Uncle Sam retired, or just had a sex change. In any case, he's been replaced by the Goddess in the future. Huzzah! A society and the deity who represents it have to learn to cooperate with each other in the movement to love and compassion and redemption, rather than each reflecting the other's worst traits. The gods are not static; they respond to the quality of moral and spiritual knowingness, and the vibration created by the moral and spiritual knowingness, of each individual they work with, as well as to the vibration of any particular society they may be allied with. Thus I can say Odin is full of love, and in his relations with me, He is. But in his relations with an unrefined person, he's liable to be terrible, indeed! For each of us, in our bloodstreams and within our cells, carries the imprints of many divinities that have been passed down from ancient times. Together with the psychological imprinting of divinities we carry, these physical imprints are our point of connection with the greater gods and goddesses whom we feel drawn to, and if the feeling is strong enough these deities are also drawn toward us. Just as we are a tiny life within the body of God The Universe, we reflect God's universal pattern within our own cells, so that there are many tiny lives within each of us. And a tiny life ensouls each of these imprints, just as a great life ensouls the form of the overshadowing gods and goddesses the imprints are made in the image of. But the quality of our aspirations and personal energies which activate our imprints is largely the source the greater gods and goddesses who live "outside" us will draw upon and reflect when they move toward us. If your motives and energy are not pure and are not activated by love, your god is likely to resemble the devil.

In the World War II era, Uncle Sam resembled God and people around the world were happy to stand in his light, which was the reflected light of the American people. But by century's end Uncle Sam had grown dim and suffered from Alzheimer's, and many people around the world looked forward to his retirement.

Uncle Sam was kind of a secular god; a god who was asked to pretend he wasn't a god so the government and people could pretend to deny Divinity except in highly compartmentalized circumstances, such as church or Vacation Bible School. But this denial of Divinity, produced in the name of separation of church and state, was also a denial of love and a perverter of passion into rage, which led to wars of various kinds to support the denial. In most ways, the twentieth century was the most backward, schizophrenic century I've ever visited. In ancient times war-consciousness was a sporadic thing, and when it cropped up was a cause for great celebration, just as every manifestation of humans and gods was celebrated. Even the Vikings didn't go around feeling they were at war all the time, and mostly just farmed and built boats and explored and made love. They were a jolly bunch.

But twentieth century Americans were a grim universalist tribe whose denatured awareness of their own Divinity led their wounded psyches into feeling they were at war every day. The twentieth century was the most adrenalin-soaked, false century in human history. The Late Middle Ages, say from the year 1400 to 2025, is notable only for denying God, and for denying the Gods that God made as representatives and custodians of God's thoughts.

The spiritual adept doesn't worship God or the Gods in some servile way; *real* worship is all about connection, real worship *is* connection. There is no separation in this wholesome, organic universe. So the worship of the spiritual adept is simply connecting his Heart to God's Heart, and connecting his thoughts to God's thoughts. Also, realizing the innate, every-moment connection of his body to God's body. Real worship is *marriage*.

When we want to connect with God's thoughts, we connect with the representatives of God's thoughts--the Gods! And there is often complementariness and simultaneousness involved between these Physical, Heart, and Mind connections. This is the worship of the spiritual adept.

God is a living legend, and each of us is a living legend moving within the texture of the universal pattern of metaphor. Feel this texture with your body, and know your direct connection to God!

Sex is about the communion of souls; indeed, early in human history the androgynous human race was distinguished into two sexes to demonstrate graphically the necessity of soul-communion between individuals. Prior to this time there had been no real emphasis on worship. Sex is such a deep, spiritual means of connecting to our own humanity and to the soul of another person that it may be the purest form of worship, and certainly is the most delightful. For to connect with a brother soul is the purest form of knowing God.

So early in human history distinctiveness was invoked as a means of magnetizing people towards a deeper God-connection by prompting them to serve one another with their sexuality. Of course, eventually people lost the experience of distinctiveness as this experience was allowed to degenerate into the lie, the false experience, of separation. But distinctiveness is not separation, and should never be mistaken for that lie. Both individualism and community flourish in one another's arms in the overshadowing presence of distinctiveness, but with the universalist lie of separation, both the individual and community are crushed, and with sex having been degraded into a mere leisure activity, all other forms of worship suffer and there is no soul connection, no widespread consciousness of the Divine at all. In the end, all worship of every kind degenerates into a mere leisure activity.

Primitive people say that "Incest is best!" while outwardly pretending not to mean it. But the reality is that a deep, wounded, buried part of themselves knows that incest really is best, and the only way it can express this truth is thru the woundedness of its joke.

Family should provide the deepest soul-connection of all, but primitive societies have substituted a false attachment to manipulation and lust for the soul-connection. Their desire for one another hasn't gone away, but they try to bury it beneath various layers of lust and degradation and addiction and hurtfulness. It should be self-evident that the deepest levels of worship should occur in the arms of Family.

Twentieth century people denied the sacredness of war, with the result that they were almost continually at war and more of their people were killed in wars than at any time since the destruction of Atlantis, millions of years previously. This is the point--sigh!--at which the intellectual will smile tolerantly and claim that the added destructiveness of war resulted from improved weapons and political factors, ad infinitum, ad nauseam. But the intellectual sees things horizontally, with his perceptions just lying there like a dead man. You see nothing if you see things horizontally; life ain't flat. The vertical consciousness must be developed before you have any idea how the world works.

As an aside, the denial of the sacredness of war also produced an ugliness in their weapons. Just look at an M-16; it looks like it fell out of the ugly tree and hit every limb on the way down. And the early stealth aircraft were even worse; I can't see how an aircraft that ugly could even fly. Both these weapons have a viciousness about them, rather than the energy of a joyful mayhem. But people who know the sacredness of fighting for their rights as free human beings living in Kindred-community produce beautiful, healthful weapons, which are imbued with a bit of the beautiful spirit of the weapon's owner and of the community in which he dwells.

As strange as it seems, people of the twentieth century actually began re-enacting wars from previous centuries with earlier types of weaponry and tactics in an attempt to once more touch the sacredness of combat! Their own wars did not satisfy the longing of their souls.

The weapons and other artworks of a people represent the spirit of that people, so it is mighty strange that twentieth century people would allow themselves to be taxed to produce such monstrously ugly wares.

But this is how they were: always bragging about how "superior" their civilization and the twentieth century were, yet always longing for a more natural, more beautiful order that had vanished.

Most of the "freedom" Americans bragged about in the twentieth century was nothing more than "freedom" from the sense of Divinity inherent in the natural order. So in the twenty-first century they had to learn to be human all over again, like tigers that have been born and raised in a zoo must re-learn how to be tigers if they are returned to their natural home.

You observe the gods and goddesses with your body as much as thru any other faculty; you also observe the entirety of God with your body. So as a final aside on Uncle Sam, let me say that the old fart would very much prefer that you remain ignorant of the totality of his nature. He doesn't want you to use your body.

Whenever you encounter an icon of a deity, stop and notice your body's response to it. **_Don't_** think with words; your body *is* a thought that is perfectly able to interpret its surroundings without the "denial effect" that words usually bring. If you encounter Uncle Sam, I very much suspect your body will grow a little tense and unhappy, as your body automatically knows in its every cell that Uncle Sam is a deity of rigid thundering conquest, and that one of the first things he set out to conquer was the human body. Uncle Sam is the American Jehovah! Though he never became quite as degenerate as Pappy Jehovah, his dad.

I'm pretty certain if you can edit yourself away from word-language for a few moments, both your body and emotions would have you either flee from Uncle Sam, or throw a flowerpot at him. Your Heart would perhaps just have you stand unperturbed and unharmed in his presence, but if you're not purified and integrated enough yet, that will be difficult to do.

Now go somewhere quiet and encounter Aphrodite or Freyja and see how you feel. Again, if you can do without the words, I'm pretty certain you'll feel calm and inspired, and perhaps a little merry. You'll probably start breathing a little deeper in the glad satisfaction of being alive. And if you're a man or a lesbian, you may find your Heart flowing together with your sexual centers for a splendid experience of wholebody attunement.

Anytime love-infused, spiritual energy is set in motion, people of lower motives and lower consciousness will respond to it in a savage manner, whereas people of sincerity and higher consciousness will respond to it in a moral and spiritual manner. So there is a happy wave in the ocean of misery and denied humanness that was the twentieth century, and that is simply that the dualistic people, such as the pacifists and warmongers, were responding in their primitive, feeble way to an energy that was spiritual. Spiritual energy was bathing the earth and most people didn't know it, and because their consciousness was bestial their response to the spiritual energy was bestial. But in the twenty-first century they would begin to tire of their self-induced misery and start to learn to identify themselves with God's Heart and with God's Thoughts. They sincerely wanted to stop suffering, and this was the first time most of them had ever felt the touch of true sincerity. This newfound sincerity led them to learn to ride the wave-form of their own consciousness like surfers riding upon the tangy ocean which is God's consciousness. By the end of the twenty-first century, humanity was well on its way to redemption and lovingkindness.

There was a monkey-woman with a silver boomerang in the desert, then Odin and Thor and Freyja rose up before me . . . all of us were One inside a great Divine Brain that encompassed the stars. I heard a tinkling merry laugh, and rotated myself into the arms of my Aphrodite, as the room stopped spinning about me. In my Big Eye I saw the monkey-woman wave, and Odin and Thor saluted, as Freyja blew me a kiss bold and merry, to take with me as a heart-comforter to dispel any chilly moments 'till we should meet again. Freyja looked with a knowing extended glance into Aphrodite's blue eyes, then gave me a quick smile and turned, her strong nude body undulating itself into galaxies of warmth as the timeline righted itself about me and I came fully awake in Aphrodite's arms. I heard a deep whisper: "We will meet again . . . and again . . . and again, Sonny-Bob, my love, my Apostle", and as Freyja's whisper melted away Aphrodite hugged me to her and our hearts were One in advance of the full stabilization of the timeline, but then the timeline came fully to a stop from its mad pirouette, and I knew that all things were eternal and overlap, and as I smiled to myself in Aphrodite's arms, I felt Freyja smile inside me and I valued myself and walked with Aphrodite across the room and stood before my family.

"Sonny-Bob, where've you been?" Mimi said with wide eyes, echoing the solemnity of the rest of the family's attitudes.

"To Denmark, I think." I gave the family a quick smile. "But it was warm there, not cold at all."

Then my eyes fell to Mimi's belly, and I saw the tattoo she'd gotten a few weeks before. The tattoo took the form of a quote by somebody named George Bernard Shaw; I don't know who he was, probably some professor at the great university Mimi wanted to sleep with or fellate.

"The reasonable man adapts himself to the world; the unreasonable one persists to adapt the world to himself. Therefore all progress depends on the unreasonable man."

On second thought, this Shaw person couldn't be a professor; he had too much sense. Well, maybe he was a wise old Beatnik or something; perhaps one of the Beat poets. There were still some of them around; one of them ruled over a sort of a commune out near Bastrop.

Uh-Oh, now I dizzied again, Mimi's tattoo having traveled me back into the world from which I'd just exited with Freyja's smile. I sighed and gave in to the inevitable; all worlds were mine, but it was a tiresome thing to always be on the road.

Freyja's warm breath touched my cheek, then delivered itself into my lungs and expanded inside me, and I felt that Freyja was hugging my beautiful, glowing Heart in potent friendliness. My love-warrior-Beauty Goddess delivered unto me the following knowingness:

The reasonable person is a fairly recent defect of evolution. Reasonableness is just a method of extending manipulatory attachments out of your own preconceptions to attach those preconceptions into the aura of your victim. One of those preconceptions, of course, is that reasonableness is a virtue, for in its monstrous quest to manipulate its host and other people, reasonableness' first objective is to assure its own survival. Emotional manipulation is just as bad, of course, but is more widely recognized for being a parasitic energy upon the soul, so by the twentieth century emotional manipulation had begun using reasonableness as a cloak to mask its own presence. Reasonableness and emotional manipulation were both products and producers of attachment, and attachment insures that its human host will have difficulty releasing his shame, so reasonableness and emotional manipulation were both servants of shame. These perverse servants were the jailers which reinforced the bars of preconceptions by which shame sought to bind its human hosts. More than anything else, they reinforced the preconception that their human host was of lesser value than some abstract nonhuman system, and should submit to the judgement of that system, regardless of what the human's heart would have him do or feel or say or be.

(The next few paragraphs are dedicated to the Hispanic foreman who let me sleep one night in his orange grove in California in 1983.)

An example of this is the way Mexicans are treated in twentieth century America. They are persecuted as though they were taking the bread out of the mouths of American citizens, when nothing could be further from the truth. These immigrants, especially the illegal ones, could only find jobs the average American wouldn't take, and would go on welfare or take up drug dealing to avoid. They *contributed* to the United States; they didn't steal from her. And no person's Heart would have him treat these Mexicans as unworthy, yet the reasonable people had convinced Americans that the illegal immigration by Mexicans was a horror and that it *"has to be stopped!"*. For manufacturing artificial crises of this sort is how the politicians tricked their fellow citizens into looking to them for salvation, thus making it more likely the citizens would continue to forfeit their own power to the politicians. The news media used the same technique in order to maintain their hold upon the feelings and primitive "thought" processes of twentieth century people. Obviously, this is also a part of the reason the politicians manufactured unnecessary wars. *Remember that the most clever politicians are so reasonable they believe their own lies, so if you suffer from even a trace of reasonableness, you are easy prey for them. Their reasonableness will attack yours like a cougar ripping apart a rabbit, and then convince you you've arrived at your own decisions, rather than being manipulated by the same reasonableness the politician has sold his soul to.*

The American Indians didn't initially object much to the presence of the whitebread Europeans who came to their shores, but when they decided to object the whitebreads crushed them. The whitebreads took charge of the entire landmass that became the United States, and when told they couldn't live or exploit a particular region of the landmass they went ahead and did it anyway. Such hypocrites! Their own ancestors were exactly as the twentieth century Mexicans, except that their whitebread ancestors were far more aggressive than the Mexicans, and except that the whitebreads wanted it all, while the Mexicans just wanted a little taste of something a little better than they were used to.

The problem of the persecution of the Mexicans was largely due to the

527 / Undo The Winter

presence of different pantheons of gods that rode in the Mexicans' bloodstreams. The whitebreads had their bloodstream-gods; the Mexicans had theirs. Whenever differing genetic divinity-imprints and bloodstream-gods meet, there is apt to be trouble. And the reasonable people made the trouble far worse than it otherwise would have been by convincing their fellow citizens to deny the truth of their bodies' feelings, their bodies' connection to divinity thru the genetic divinity-imprints and bloodstream-gods. If Americans had recognized their bodies' connection to Divinity, and the methods by which their bodies connected to Divinity, they could have approached the "problem" of illegal immigration by Mexicans with much more intelligence, and maybe even with the first birth-pangs of compassion, knowing that each person must Achieve success in a battle to discipline his own blood before he can enter into Liberation, and that many different bloodlines have karmically come to America to discipline themselves into compassion. They could have dismissed the fear that the Mexicans were somehow taking something from them, and realized that their feelings were caused by the agitations of bloodstream-gods and genetic divinity-imprints which felt anciently opposed to the pantheons of gods the Mexicans carried within their bodies.

A civilized, conscious person knows immediately that if Canadians rather than Mexicans had been immigrating to the Unites States illegally and in massive numbers, that there would have been no outcry. There would have been a "reasonable discussion", with everyone on both sides laughing and shaking hands and pretending that something had been accomplished to address the "problem", while avoiding addressing the "problem" at all. This is due to the fact that the pantheon of psychological, spiritual and body gods carried within the whitebread Canadians is pretty close to the pantheon carried by the whitebread Americans. Racial problems are usually less about skin tone, and more about pantheons of gods. Anyone can see that a black woman can be as beautiful as a white woman, but most white men will want to spend their lives with white women because of compatible pantheons in the blood, and most black men will want to spend their lives with black women for the same reason.

Anyhow, with the hue and cry set up against the Mexicans by the universalist legislators, more crimes against humanity were committed. These crimes were not as severe as those performed by the Germans in the Thirties and Forties, but they were motivated by pretty much the same thing: bloodstream gods who felt opposed to other bloodstream gods, and who were then enraged by the denial of their existence by the reasonable universalist-brotherhood types who usually arranged the wars and persecutions of the twentieth century. An enraged bloodstream god is a terrible thing, and can even come to rule its human host, the host it was meant to have a mutually beneficent, symbiotic relationship with in trust, love and freedom. *Anything* that a person is in denial of will sabotage that person into performing uncompassionate acts that usually seem very reasonable at the time. To "crack down" on any part of the balloon that is the human psyche--and really, even the physical body is part of the psyche--is to insure an explosion and a release of energy that could otherwise have transformed itself into compassion in some other part of the balloon. And societies are built in the image of the human psyche in its divine variations, but a society built in the image of a warped psyche means trouble for the world, and trouble for the gods, and trouble for God . . . trouble that always found a way to rebound onto those reasonable people who had created the trouble thru their denial of aspects of their own human natures, and who would then cry in mock sincerity "Why!" and try to find someone other than themselves to blame for the tragedies of their mechanical, reasonable, watered-down, feeble little lives. They did not know how to live with the Gusto of that Truth which leads to Love, and didn't care that they didn't know. So there was virtually no spiritual energy in the world in the twentieth century. There was just so much repression that all the spirituality had been squeezed away. True, the earth was being touched by a new wave of spiritual energy, but that wave hadn't destroyed the societies of the world yet so it could integrate itself with people's hearts and minds and create a new, sane, compassionate world. And almost all of this was due to the reasonable people, and their success at getting their fellow citizens to deny their bodies and the information and potential for compassion carried in those bodies by their bloodstream gods. For Freyja lives as much in the Heart as in the loins of those who have been redeemed by Her.

And the gods of most pantheons have decided, under the impetus of a newly-received wave of Love from the Heart of God, that it is time for them to learn to live in Harmony with one another. They reject the reasonable person and the tragedy that such people bring to the world and to their own natures thru violating the nature of the gods they carry within themselves. The gods have chosen to embrace love and are eager to share their love as fullbody compassion. Thus must Humanity wake to all the tools at its disposal for contacting, and manifesting, the divine love-nature of the Most High God.

This of course doesn't mean that every person must feel a connection to every pantheon or to every god; it just means that most of the pantheons have decided to become civilized enough that if people accept the natural divinity-imprints in their own bodies they will be unreasonable enough to want to live in harmony with those of different backgrounds and will therefore reject the influence of the reasonable people who controlled the world and made the hate of the twentieth century. For the universalists are not interested in universal brotherhood, they're interested in universal *obedience*. They use brotherhood as a screen to hide the fact they are trying to legislate human nature, rather than allowing human nature to fall into its own natural rhythms. They're not interested in embracing genuine, natural, compassionate morality; they're interested in forcing everyone into the cage of universalist preconceptions, as represented by the laws which they've used to codify their unnaturalness and lack of compassion.

This new state of affairs might not lead to Brother Heinlein's Church of All Worlds, but it would lead to the belly-acceptance and heart-acceptance of every human race, and an appreciation of each lesson that each race has come to teach the planet. And there would be no more straining to understand those of different backgrounds or races, because we automatically understand others if we first go to the trouble to understand ourselves--this is another area of study in which the reasonable person gets an "F minus". Yes, the gods differ in tone from race to race and also from person to person; there is so much Individuality in the world that there is no way to measure or quantify it. In understanding the true nature of Individuality, we understand the nature of Community and begin to see how we can harmonize ourselves into intentional communities created not around politics, but around the truth of human natures which have found their complements in other persons. For each Individual *is* Community; thus when we know ourselves as Individuals, we can harmonize ourselves with those other Individuals who complement themselves with us. Poetry is the lifeblood and the godblood of true community; only the true poet knows what I mean by this line.

Woman is poetry, and in the adoration of Woman man finds his own elevation. This adoration is not some subservience; wipe that idea from your mind right now, honey child. This adoration is an energy that recognizes the equality of both male and female, and which acknowledges that the consciousness of the male was designed to play upon the female in a certain way, and that the consciousness of the female was designed to play upon the male in a certain complementary way. Each complements the other; yet there are no differences between them. There is a wonderful distinctiveness, but there are no differences in the embrace of the beautiful upwelling rosy-pink tornado of energy.

So in the adoration of Woman, man is uplifted. Remember that true worship is not subservience, it is connection. The man can only worship in the presence of Woman. Only Woman can lift his heart above the dirt of mundane perceptions. And to understand her own Greatness and begin to live by the cause of her powerful Heart, Woman must acknowledge and gracefully accept this energy of unselfish adoration, which when she properly approaches it, will wash away her unclean selfishness and egotism and sense of inferiority and teach her the cause of love.

Without the Woman, no man's perceptions can be expanded out of the animal kingdom into the arms of a blissful trust. For only animal nature is savage and lives in a jungle of sudden death or assault; when true Human Nature is Achieved, the man and the woman become Divine together.

No reasonable person has ever caught a glimpse of Divinity. So arise ye scalds, and get ye into the church of your own nature!

In early pioneering civilizations, the reasonable man wouldn't have lasted out the week, had such an evolutionary defect appeared. Unreasonableness, tempered by love of kindred, brought humanity to a mastery over the elements and over the animal kingdom. A reasonable man would never have invented the bow and arrow. A reasonable man would have wanted to negotiate with the animals! And back in those days, the animals were larger, fiercer, and more unreasonable than they are today.

Yet if your remote ancestor Johnny Bearclaws had been a reasonable man, he would have tried to negotiate a consensus with the animals, whereupon he would have been eaten, and ultimately shit out the rectum of the beast, remaining only as a fossilized turd upon the plains of evolutionary mistakes.

There is no place for the reasonable person in a pioneering culture, and this is just as true (no, more true!) with respect to the pioneering of new frontiers of consciousness as it was in breaking through the walls of the preconceptions of giant prehistoric bison and saber-toothed tigers and giant cave-bears. For these early beasts had the preconception that they were superior to man and fit to govern him, and only unreasonable men could have convinced them otherwise.

The exploring of frontiers of consciousness demands even more unreasonableness, love, and adaptability than exploring the visible physical frontier. For there are many levels of physical frontier to explore, some of which are not quite visible to the physical eye, and humanity is just beginning to explore those other levels. As humanity grows more conscious of its potential, more people will be stepping into the etheric plane, and will need to value themselves enough to refuse to tolerate the reasonable intrusions of discarnate creatures which do not have humanity's best interests at heart. The soldier will gradually begin to disappear, as the warrior takes his place. For the soldier is a symptom of empire, whereas the warrior is a hallmark of frontier, just as is his sister, the shamaness.

The soldier bases his conduct on conforming to distant, surreal orders; the warrior bases his conduct on the morality which has integrated itself with his conscience. The soldier remains morally and spiritually immature, but no one and no thing can ever shake the warrior out of his morality or out of his love. The warrior doesn't worry about the consequences of remaining true to himself in the face of opposition, for he knows the karmic consequences of using violence improperly are far worse than the consequences of refusing to follow the lead of those who are morally and spiritually immature, and who thus don't know (and usually don't really care, despite their pretensions) when violence is moral or when it is wrong. The warrior's focus is on Kindred, and he doesn't want any of his Kin to have to share in negative karma which he could have refused to involve himself in. He will not create unnecessary suffering in the families of others, because he wants his own Kin to remain secure. He treasures his present bloodline and works for Kin, not for himself, and he knows that with the shift in energy that begins this new cycle that spiritually-aware people will once more begin habitually reincarnating into the same bloodline, a practice that was largely discontinued under the banner of universalism. He knows he will have the opportunity to serve both Kindred souls, and the genetic life-blood he shares in trust with those souls, throughout many incarnations together. He Serves.

But there is much of Beauty in these new frontiers, and we must not dwell on the unclean elements, for that is just what the unclean elements --reasonably enough--would have us do. No, disposing of the unclean elements we encounter as we explore the Beautiful, Blissful frontiers of consciousness should require no more of our attention than crushing an unclean insect whose vibrations we do not want near our homes. For even as he shewed the giant bison who was boss, early man enjoyed the Beauty of Nature every day, and felt himself at One with All That Is.

There is a deep feeling of the poetry of humanness in the belly of one who has been cleansed of reasonableness. For you see, to a large degree reasonableness hides in the belly. Their reasonableness is why the people of the twentieth century West often found it impossible to breathe from their bellies. So you have to try to breathe into your belly, and eventually you will have some success and the reasonableness will begin to leave. But it may take a while for all of this unnatural substance to leave. But as you learn to breathe and to honor your humanness, one day you will arrive at your own special human nature, and you will find special others whom you are able to connect with thru this nature. Thus is the marriage made which we call Kindred.

(I don't want to hear you use the term "significant others" in the context of the previous paragraph. That term doesn't carry the energy of humanness; if anything, it carries a detached, ungrounded, not-quite-human energy. That is why I used the phrase "special human nature" and "special others"; these terms carry the energy of the cleansed belly-humanness I am trying to convey. There is some rationalization and political correctness attached to the term "significant others" in the context of the previous paragraph, so this term is unclean in this context. *Always* be alert to energy in *every* moment of your lives!)

The refusal to acknowledge and refine their own sensitivity to energy is why you hear the brain-washed soldier make bizarre statements contrary to Reality, such as when they try to justify remaining in an unjustifiable war by talking about their friend who was killed in that war, and saying that their buddy would have died in vain if they don't stay "to finish the job". Yet the warrior knows that the truth is that the only conceivable way the death of any soldier in an unjust or unjustified war can be made meaningful is if it prompts the withdrawal of the occupying army. It does not render the death of any soldier meaningful to use that death as an excuse to remain in an environment you shouldn't have been in to begin with as you watch still greater numbers of your buddies die. And now I have stated this in such a way that even a brainwashed soldier cannot deny the truth of the matter, and must begin to face his pain head-on, rather than trying to suppress the pain thru more unjustified violence, which is why he wound up in pain to begin with.

By the end of the twentieth century, the American soldier was brainwashed into being reasonable, and into being stubborn in support of that reasonableness, instead of being encouraged to locate his Heart, and to be unreasonable in support of the Voice of his Heart.

It is not uncommon for soldiers of empire, hunkered down in their body armor in a well-defended position that provides cover and concealment for them as they unleash the massive firepower provided by superior weaponry, to state that their enemy, who charges their position with nothing but a rifle or handgun with nothing but thin cloth between his skin and their bullets, is a coward. Well, certainly this is a *reasonable* viewpoint.

The soldier is tough, but the warrior is strong. The soldier is ruled by his orders, while the warrior is ruled by compassion.

It is hard to be a soldier, and the main reason it is hard is because you are continually asked to violate your own conscience. Yet if you aren't fighting for freedom of conscience, then what the hell are you fighting for?

It is not nearly as difficult to fight in a cause you *know* is just as it is to allow yourself to be ordered into battle to fight for the political ambitions of those who live in comfort, and who will find additional ways to betray you once the conflict is "over". But for the soldier, the conflict is never "over"; he carries it in his torn heart until he learns to walk a warrior's path and process and release the rage and guilt and grief out of his heart, knowing that he deserves to be free of suffering, and that all beings deserve to be free of suffering.

Americans, and the entire planet, had been threatened by the former Soviet Onion, which directly stated its intention to rule America. Thus,

America was morally justified in fighting the communists wherever she could. And perhaps the "brushfire war" of Vietnam occupied the communists' attention and proved to them that America would fight, thus preventing an eventual attack upon America--but this we will never know for sure. But whether you agree with the strategic reason for America's entering the conflict in Vietnam, you have to see that America was morally justified in being there. And the moral reason is the only reason for war; strategic concerns are always secondary in the mind of the warrior.

Strategy does not occupy the mind of the warrior until he knows he is on a moral path.

It is interesting to see how the baby-boom generation went from being hard-headed peace-mongers who were eligible for the draft, into being reasonable war-mongers after the draft was discontinued. It was essential that a warrior generation arise to replace such people, and in the twenty-first century, it did.

The baby-boom, as a generation, missed its opportunity for heroism.

Strategy can be debated, but morality and honor can never be debated or compromised. It should be self-evident that a compromised morality is equivalent to immorality. Thus we see another difference between the soldier and the warrior.

"We hold these truths to be self-evident . . ." A statement of Truth is its own proof.

It is useless to make a statement of Truth to a reasonable person. The reasonable person has betrayed the very Truth of his own life's blood, and thus has no Foundation of Integrity to Achieve any "higher" level of Truth. The reasonable person is the most bewildered person the earth has ever seen.

Remember that the bloodstream, genes, and Heart are all intimately connected. And remember that the bloodstream, genes, and Heart all exist on more levels than the merely physical.

Anyone can make a mistake, but the warrior, if he makes mistakes at all, will only make mundane types of mistakes; he has made himself of stainless steel and is incapable of making a mistake of morality or spirituality. Maybe he'll make a mistake in interpretation of spirituality occasionally, but he will not make a mistake in the application of that spirituality. Morality is a tool for the application of spirituality, so with his total commitment to being a moral person, and the total understanding of morality he has earned as a result of his strenuous commitment, he will not make a mistake of application, even if he occasionally forms a misinterpretation in his mind of the exact nature of what he is applying. Also, it must be observed that the body of the fully-developed warrior is so sensitive to energy that even if his mind makes a mistake, his body most certainly will not. So he cannot be deceived as to the quality of energy he is applying, even if he has misinterpreted it's exact nature.

Soldiers can fight soldiers, but the warrior cannot fight another warrior. For the warrior's moral compass and spiritual orientation are sound, and morality cannot conflict with morality, nor can spirituality conflict with spirituality. Yet people on both sides of a conflict continually deceive themselves that they are spiritual and moral people. If a warrior is involved in a fight, you can assure yourself that his opponent was no warrior and was morally and spiritually in error. At best, his opponent may have been in an early stage of the Warrior's Path, but was a long way from Achieving effective polarization in the Warrior Consciousness.

In the higher levels of his Path, the warrior is continually evolving into Beauty, and a staff of Beautiful aesthetic consultants joins the ranks of his spirit guides. He has a vast army of spirit allies at his disposal, and the guides in this army also become more Beautiful under the influence of the Beauticians. The warrior doesn't want to drag his old spirit chums into a fight because, at least initially, it might postpone their absorption into Beauty. And he certainly cannot see dragging his new, Beautiful spirit guides into an unnecessary fight. Therefore, in addition to the guidance of his moral and spiritual polarization, now the warrior is led to step around conflicts where possible by his new appreciation of Beauty. Yet he can still fight when necessary, experiencing the fusion of Beauty, Love, and Valor which are brought to him by the Valkyries. Freyja receives the warrior into her hall, but the soldier will have to try again in another lifetime. Fortunately, if his aspiration is pure, he will have as many lifetimes as he needs to become a warrior in Service to Love and Beauty.

Now I came home to my family again, and realized I had never left them. I approached them and kissed each one, making an exception for Freud just this once, and allowed Freyja's breath to touch them in holiness. Now each facet of Divinity stands ready to serve every other facet with redemptive energy, so long as eclecticism is avoided. For eclecticism dissipates energy; so in our new combinings we must always morph towards a stable, non-fundamentalist, non-eclectic representation of divine-human nature. Let complementaries complement, but forcing the gods into incompatible combinations is yet another symptom of universalism, and makes the gods uncomfortable and surly.

So while the richness of our contact with Freyja had broadened us, I knew my family and I must return to a more stable form for the duration of this mission. If we succeeded with this mission, then we could see what further morphings were possible.

Sue was beautiful; she exhibited a kind of competence that some twentieth century American women had; you usually found this type of woman in feminine roles, but these women were so vigorous and competent that whenever I found them I just wanted to watch them all day and be allowed by them to continue to respect them. Suddenly I knew who Sue was, and I smiled, and she smiled back at me and I walked forward and embraced her and all sense of incompatibility fell away from me. This one has always been a part of me, but hid herself so effectively that I almost didn't recognize her.

Now that I found myself back in the original mission configuration, the original flavoring returned to my spiritual observations, as the etheric Viking overlay receded for the moment. So I stood there outwardly silent before the family, as my easy-thoughts, my Buddhic-awareness perceptions, made themselves over again into conformity with Aphrodite's love-flavor and Ronald Reagan's Mighty Visioning. If the Viking gods had not come when they did, the following thoughts would have been written down, rather than the intuitive impulsings from Freyja's merry Heart to my own. (Such merriment that one has!)

I hope you enjoy this flavor:

Remember that a person who asks you to take an oath is trying to control your actions, attitudes and feelings. And if you secretly take an oath of your own accord, in the privacy of your home with no urging from some outside "authority", you are trying to control yourself. For oaths are all about control. Oaths originated largely as a measure to try to control the glamour of shame that has haunted humanity for so long by insuring conduct that is not shameful. Oaths are the bastard child of shame. It should be obvious that the child is not going to terminate the parent who nurses it. So control is a total illusion, and oaths are a total illusion.

Indeed, the very desire to control made its appearance from the desire to deny shame. Naturally, this illusion called control is fostered the most by those who carry the most shame, and who thus feel they have the most to deny within their injured natures. Remember that humans did not come from apes; and thus did not inherit the desire to control from some "missing link" who ran around abusing his neighbors with a shamefaced simian grin. Darwin's descendants in the scientific community may be control-freak monkeys, but the rest of us don't have to be.

The original races of humans, in their Golden Age, lived with a purity that has not been seen in the millions of years since; and as a result of their purity and attunement with God's mind, they never felt any desire to control--had no idea of the feelings, attitudes and shamefaced energy that prompts people to try to control their lives. These early humans simply *were* their lives, and didn't try to interfere with themselves or with one another. And they cooperated freely, without restriction.

Control breeds chaos, for all life, including human life, has a natural pattern it automatically adapts itself to. The energy and motive of control is to disrupt this patterning and leave humanity bereft of the sense of belonging to nature and thus bereft of experiencing its own human nature. In trying to control its shamefulness, humanity has been forced to release much of its own true nature to make room for the shame which it wants to deny. Thus is humanity turned into a tool to rape and destroy nature by the malformed ogres and trolls who yank the strings placed into the attachments that grow within the auras of those who govern, and of those who serve governments or try to influence them.

The natural patterning automatically adjusts itself to new conditions and cycles, but control is not adjustment, it is rape and murder. Everyone can easily see that this is true from their daily experience, if they have not been frightened away from examining their own shadow by the very forces which have corrupted that shadow with the illusion of control. Control is based upon the threat or actual implementation of violence, whether it is violence you do to your own emotions and heart thru an unnatural religion or philosophy, or violence initiated by the Department of Motor Vehicles to make everyone comply with the preferences of bureaucrats and politicians. Now really, you know very well you would never burden or hurt your neighbor the way these mechanical people who run the institutions do, because a human when left to her own devices prefers the naturalness of her humanity in her relations with others, rather than the twisted schemes of institutions. Unfortunately, she may lack the self-esteem to treat her own self as well as she treats her neighbors. She may try to control herself, and when I see her do so, my heart weeps for her damaged nature.

Oh, while not assaulting her neighbors directly, the average citizen may try to control their perceptions of her in order to protect herself from their potential for psychic violence, even as they reciprocate with her. But none of them are likely to behave with as much intrusiveness with one another as the "authorities" are when the authorities want their compliance in some matter, or when the authorities want their property to turn it over to those who will pay higher taxes on that property that the "authorities" can use for their favorite schemes--possibly including increasing their own salaries! All this is done in the name of public service, of course, to soothe the fragmented consciences of the scheming "authorities" and to create illusions that will sap the will to resist of the populations they infringe upon. It's always been this way in primitive, ailing societies which don't respect human rights, particularly those that want to foster the illusion that they do respect human rights by building abstract systems of enforcement which supercede their humanity and thru which they can pretend "it's not personal" when they destroy people's lives.

God made everyone, and Sam Colt made everyone equal; so most civilians tread carefully enough around one another and outright violence seldom occurs as a result of their caution, the propaganda of the violence-loving news media of the twentieth century notwithstanding. But the institutions produced bands of organized and refined thugs thru the use of the socialist model of compensation, in which the financial welfare, healthcare and so forth of career "public servants" was assured, even as many of those who were robbed--I mean "taxed"--to pay for these benefits had to do without health insurance or a guaranteed income. Regular crime didn't normally pay very well, because the criminals would be caught between the outrage of the citizens and the self-righteousness of the law-enforcers, a self-righteousness bought and paid for thru the subtle threat of violence aimed at the citizens they "helped" by bringing the formal criminals "to justice". Geez, the whole sorry society was in need of rehabilitation!

Most of the time the timid, reasonably well-armed Americans of the twentieth century wouldn't band together to deflect the authorities who defaced their souls, attempting to spread some of their own humiliation and suppressed rage onto their constituents. For everyone was a slave to the illusion of control, and did not want to overthrow those they felt were masters at this form of degraded "worship". So we see that a true appreciation of the Second Amendment was lacking in this society, even in those who kept and bore arms.

During my trip to the twentieth century, I had to remind myself numerous times to remember not to *ever* talk about the details of this century to old Tom Paine when I got home. He'd have a hissey-fit; and probably would accuse me of lying, in which case I'd have to whip his skinny old ass.

Control is the most filthy, obscene word there is and its derivative, "manage", is almost as bad. I am sorry to have to burn your ears with this shame-faced word, yet I do not believe in censorship. I know there are those who misuse the press to create chaos and shame, but I am promoting the cleansing of your human nature, so I feel the use of this word within the context of my intentions is justified. I hope you can accept the use of this word from me within the context of wanting to free the energy this word and the attitudes behind this word have caused to become frozen and rigid with chaos and despair. For this energy is the energy of your true human nature, your own sweet Self, and it has been temporarily frozen that the shame which seeks to control humanity may have its day. But it has had its day, and I have come to the rescue.

People who direct Forces don't "control" or "manage" them, they harmonize themselves with those Forces and direct them by the power of turning their attention toward whatever direction the Force needs to flow in to accomplish God's creative Work. The Force automatically follows the directed attention of the white magician. This is the Work done by the Lords of the Seven Rays; this is Work for Elohim, not for control freaks. Yet the control freak can evolve herself into Elohim, if she has the courage of heart to purify and release the tangled strings of control and manipulation from her various bodies and personality.

In the subtle worlds, we don't use words and there are no contracts to sign, we just flow with our Hearts and our illumined Higher Minds into one another's arms, and there we take our rest. And now with the shift in energy that heralds a new cycle, we bring the energy of the subtle worlds right down into the physical earth through the medium of our physical bodies and soul-infused personalities. In the wedding ceremonies of the future, there are no oaths, though there may be a statement of togetherness which is applicable to that particular moment and which is flexible enough to accommodate the flowing changes of future moments.

The Love which governs this solar system has been working for a long time to infuse itself into the earth; for this purpose Three Pillars were necessary. First the Buddha brought the love-energy and placed it on the mental plane where it shone forth as that enlightenment which allows for Buddhic perception. Then Jesus brought the love-energy into fuller manifestation by anchoring it upon the astral, or emotional, plane. And now the love of all the universe is focused on this one little planet as the Work is completed by anchoring the love fluidly in the physical dimension, that it may shine forth in the synthesis of all dimensions of the human being, and of the earth Herself. When this love-infused earth is eventually occultly "drawn up" and absorbed by the love of the solar system, a Great Cycle will have been completed.

Suddenly the panorama shifted back to the specific, and I was in the Twentieth again, feeling the touch of a sort of quizzical disgust at those who considered themselves scientists in these degenerate times. With their limited, straight-line perspective, lack of compassion and rule-bound arrogance, they couldn't see that spiritually speaking the nineteenth and twentieth centuries represented the lowest point on an arc of descending consciousness, and that the Twenty-First provided those units of the human race who were prepared to Work with the splendid opportunity to regenerate themselves and the entire planet. For the twenty-first and twenty-second centuries, and perhaps a bit beyond, are the transitional age that precedes true Satya Yuga, or Golden Age. What a splendid opportunity to serve as the point of the spear on the shaft of Satya Yuga!

Satya Yuga is also frequently called "Truth Age", and the implications of this fill the hearts of the truth-lovers with total joy. Complete acknowledgement of one's motives and desires, and the necessity of purifying those desires into reflections of the Godforce, are an important feature of the Age of Truth. In Satya Yuga, desire is neither denigrated and suppressed, nor artificially glorified in bursts of lust. With the glamour and illusion extracted and destroyed, desire is a medium and a motivator of worship. Ponder on this.

But the damn alleged scientists, the damn alleged scientists . . . if they had approached the matter of embryonic stem cells from a spiritual perspective, the first question they would have asked themselves was whether souls had generated those embryos they were considering using in their experiments. Then they would have worked hard, over the course of many decades, to sensitize themselves spiritually enough that they would be able to sense spiritual truths through their Higher Mental Bodies and Hearts instantly, and also so they would have been able to Work with nature spirits and devas and specifically confer with those devas involved in the production of embryos and in the maturing of those embryos into fetuses, then into children. The viewpoint and the information of those devas would have been indispensable; every form, whether human or otherwise, has at least one deva assigned to work with it to construct, evolve and maintain it, building the etheric form and weaving the etheric threads that connect that etheric form to the physical, for *all* life flows from the more subtle dimensions into the physical. This is true of living bodies such as humans and trees and of apparently static objects such as barns and tractors.

If eventually the scientists perceived that no soul had generated those embryos, they might have ethically been able to use them for medical purposes. However, if souls had generated those embryos, the next step for the scientists would be to confer with those souls through their hearts and higher mental bodies (please, we're not talking about mediumship or that silly séance stuff--that shit's mostly designed to glamorize the gullible). If the souls involved were willing to sacrifice their embryonic bodies, the next step would be for the scientists to declare that a new form of human sacrifice had just become available and was medically and spiritually permissible. But these scientists had no discipline, man. They wanted to take a thousand mile journey in a single step, with the result that they never even began the journey. Spiritual consciousness eluded most of them because of their ironclad, fear-based, regulation-bound laziness. They hypocritically refused to call human sacrifice what it is. They never would just call a spade a spade, man.

I'm just glad the Sacred Prostitutes of Aphrodite rose up early in the twenty-first century to counteract those illogical scientists. For them to deny any aspect of their growth or of reality was not logical, and their irrational denial of looking into corners of their own psyche that frightened them, and their refusal to turn their lives over to their own sweet, powerful Hearts left them gasping for spiritual nourishment like a bunch of fingerling trout accidentally spilled out of an overturned hatchery truck in the Mohave Desert. Thus they were not true scientists. The true scientist knows he is a descendant of shamans, and that when he perfects his science he himself will be a shaman.

But the human sacrifices performed by the physically sterile doctors and promoted by their physically sterile science had no spiritual purpose, and didn't do anything to bring people closer to the far-off worlds. In fact, the twentieth century methods of human sacrifice didn't do anything except mire people in more negative karma and more suffering.

To be a true physician or scientist, the disciple must develop within himself a basic spiritual awareness, rather than bowing before the altar of a stupid materialistic science which doesn't even deserve to be called science. The true scientist develops his Buddhic qualities and surveys the Buddhic Plane from the vantage point of being immersed in that plane, of being one with it and not separate from anything that's real. He derives his insights from that plane; then if circumstances demand he present only one or two pieces of the puzzle, he presents that piece or two. He doesn't start with a particle of sand and try to work himself into an understanding of the whole beach, he starts with the beach, then if he has to derive a particle of sand, he'll do it. But he's never silly enough to believe that matter is really material, or that a perception of solidness has any basis in Truth.

Buddhic Plane awareness is not the province of a few; it is the Destiny of all who choose to develop their Individual paths to that all-inclusive Reality. Twentieth century people didn't need teachers; they needed to discard their fear-based laziness and **WORK!** Every human being is born with all she needs to Achieve the Buddhic Plane; it is encoded into her body and into her subtle bodies in the form of faculties which are initially activated, and ultimately refined, thru **WORK**. Do not be misled otherwise. God is love, and love does not cater to laziness, and cannot be approached by the lazy.

Yet such are appearances in a world fragmented by universalist dogmas and all other forms of materialist delusion that those who actually do their **Work** may be mistaken for the lazy by those who have not developed their own spiritual awareness, and thus do not even know what true **Work** is.

The contemplation of the modes of human sacrifice to stale gods unaware of their own sterility during the twentieth century brought to my mind a principle that every school-youth in the twenty-second century is aware of, namely: "The science of today is the superstition of tomorrow." Another way to put it is that "The magic of today is the superstition of tomorrow", because the alleged art that was called science in the twentieth century was really just another form of magic. So we see that fundamentalists are always in the rear of progress, whether the progress is of science or religion or magic. And in truth, these form an integrated blend in a civilized world; there is no difference between them. Yet twentieth century science was founded on the lie of separation; it was just dead magic in a materialist's robes . . . in a materialist's white lab coat, that is.

All cycles of human and planetary evolution have the form of magic that is appropriate to them. These cycles are greatly affected, and largely created, by the types of cosmic energy playing upon the planet during a given cycle. In earlier cycles, different types of magic were appropriate, but then when the cycles were changing and new energies were bathing the earth, a new magic was called for as the old magic became ineffective. So the old magic always becomes superstition as the new magic for a new cycle takes hold.

And *all* magic appears to work during its appointed cycle. An antidepressant drug that appears to work does so because it has appeared on the appropriate cycle. So the prescribing psychiatrist is a magician. Ten thousand years from now antidepressants may no longer appear to work, and if this is the case it will be because their cycle of appropriate manifestation has ended. (With devout strivings to clear the way for Compassion, it may be that humans won't need antidepressants ten thousand years from now anyway, because the full implementation of Compassion means an end to suffering. But if the antidepressant magic becomes ineffective and humanity still needs some form of magic to deal with depression, a new form will appear.)

Magic used by Native American tribes which would have defeated an invader during Atlantean times failed to hold the white man at bay when he came to North America, because that magic had finished its cycle long ago and was no longer effective. The white man's "medicine", his magic, was more effective, because it was more suited to the old Piscean Age which ended in the twentieth century.

But again, let's not be fundies. For some aspects of Native American magic remained valid and true; normally, the essence of past magics is absorbed by future magics. The part of Native American magic that remained true is the part that supports soul retrieval and soul growth in various ways, and which supports the development of a heart-centered love and that fusion of the soul with the emotions which produces compassion. So we don't suppress previous magics as societies evolve, we allow the essence of those magics to continue to live and to work out their purpose in Service to God, to the Gods, and to Humankind.

Anyhow, to the twentieth century scientist, his magic appears practical, but it will appear laughingly inadequate in the future, even though the few aspects of it which are truly practical, and which thus can be turned toward service to love, will be absorbed by the more inclusive, more jolly and straightforward and immediate magic of the future.

Most of the people of the twentieth century who claimed to be magicians were actually practicing forms of magic from previous dark ages which could have no positive outcome in the new cycle. They used a form which had served its purpose in preceding ages, so the spirit had fled the form long ago, leaving only an empty shell which could then sometimes be invaded by pernicious energies. These people frequently harmed themselves very badly.

544 / Apollo Starmule

Yet those few who were beginning to work magically with the new energies in the twentieth century frequently lost their connection to goodness by trying to marry a lust for money or status with the essence of the new energy. Thus nobody claiming to be a magician in the twentieth century, or even in the early twenty-first century, could be trusted. Even if they had good intentions, they normally had not developed the discernment which would marry them to compassion. Usually, they just worked to fulfill the lusts of an unredeemed nature. They had selfish thoughts, and when selfish thoughts are married to the causal body and inflated by "spiritual" or magical aspirations, those thoughts explode like a firecracker tied to the penis, causing much discomfort.

The true magician is a Lord of Compassion, and never ties a firecracker to his member.

The very first magical working any sincere person should undertake is the development of a genuine, altruistic compassion. Then he will not harm himself or relatively innocent bystanders if he chooses to wave his wand. For the energy of compassion dispels confusion and wickedness. Wherever compassion leads is always the correct destination. No words are ever necessary to justify the implementation of actions based upon a Compassionate Awareness. This Compassionate Awareness supplies its own Trust, so the Lord of Compassion is always supplied with a knowledge of Right Action which can never be defined or limited by intellect.

I cleared my throat, as my Eye returned to the presence of Family. My, it was good to be surrounded by these warm ones in the midst of such a chilly century! I saw they still had embryonic stem cells and suchlike on their minds, so I resumed my presentation along those lines.

"Man, people didn't realize that some of these 'issues', as they would call it, around century's end and at the beginning of the new century were simply ancient fear-and-lust based mistakes that previous types of humanity had made millions of years before, and that the energy of these old mistakes was rising to the surface to be released in a wonderful opportunity to encourage the dawning consciousness of a new humanity. An opportunity to contribute to that consciousness, to help create that consciousness. And a part of such creation is holding a true, living ethic that encompasses all the realms of human spiritual experience, and building a society that encourages the expression of living ethics. And the carrier of living ethics recognizes full well, and knows personally and directly, that he's had many lifetimes, and would have had many more filled with stupid mistakes and suffering if he hadn't got off his fat ass and crafted a genuine, fiery spiritual path for himself.

"Fortunately, in the twenty-first century the current breed of humanity eventually did find the guts to learn to turn a compassionate heart toward itself. They released the energy and practice of those ancient mistakes they'd made in prehistoric times--yes, many of them were involved in those ancient mistakes, which is part of the reason they'd had to continue incarnating for millions and millions of years, and would have continued artificially prolonging their incarnations in bestiality and degradation for who knows how long, if they hadn't finally wised up in the twenty-first century.

"When it's time to release an old, mistaken energy pattern, you either release it or there's trouble. And you can't blame God; such trouble always results from your own short-sighted decisions and actions, not from God. God gave you the ability to choose, and ultimately to learn to exhibit that free love which dispels the illusion of your own mortality, but when you get tawdry and fearful and selfish with what God has given you, disaster strikes."

Aphrodite sent a puff of gentleness to me, and it landed like a dove on my shoulder. I smiled at her. She said, "I like what you said about wisdom being a soul-quality rather than some rigid intellectual construct. I feel that wisdom is love-in-action, too . . . it seems like I've always felt this way."

Sharon smiled at Aphrodite and put an arm around her. "You understand the principles Sonny-Bob talks about through a natural livingness within you, Aphrodite. You live these principles; always have and always will. The way of manifesting the fiery, wholebodied love of Agni, the Deva of Fire, is the ethic you live, and it's so natural with you that you've never even thought about it. You've avoided being burned out by the abrasive fire of intellectual friction and remained juicy and alive by keeping your awareness centered in the great flame that burns in the sacred chalice in your heart. And you know automatically how to transfer some of that heart-fire to the sacred chalice between your legs, and allow those centers to work together in harmony as they pull the rest of your subtle centers into a loving activity. Some people--" Sharon glanced briefly at me--"are too full of hot air to always live the principles, but maybe with your influence, those people will eventually come around."

I started to say, "Kiss my ass, Sharon," but realized that what she said was essentially true, and I realized again that in many ways Sharon was wiser than I. Standing there looking at Aphrodite and Sharon, I felt I was looking at a great pink/red bucket of wisdom, of love in action, and that I was nothing more than a little thimble that at best was half-filled with wisdom . . . and maybe half-filled with B.S.

Sharon caught the drift of my melancholy and breezed it away before it had time to roost. "But of course, without Sonny-Bob's influence and specialized Work, we'd lose the timeline . . . we'd lose the future." She smiled at me. "So congrats, Sonny-Bob! You make Aphrodite's world possible."

"Thank you, Sharon," I said humbly.

Freud wanted to stick his oar back in the water, and did so, as I paused in the glowforce from Sharon and Aphrodite combined. "Well, my brain gets that wisdom is love-in-action," he said. "At least, I think I do. And I think I'm even starting to get this Agni thing; being as close to Aphrodite as I am now I can sometimes feel myself immersed in the flame of Agni's fiery eternal love.

"And I can see that with wisdom being love-in-action, it couldn't possibly support the degradation of the human soul, whether through mechanical soul-reducing implants, or through soul-destabilizing animal graftings. You know, I used to be reasonable, too, but got over it. Maybe if there's a chance for me, there's a chance for everybody."

I was still in a state of grace as Aphrodite and Sharon continued to radiate the lovingkindness of Agni. But of course, I knew that to complete our discussion--the discussion that started with the Childcrush Period--I would have to remove myself a bit from the lovingkindness and focus more on the purification of perceptions that precedes a high level of lovingkindness. Cycles of growth, you know.

"You're right, Freud, m'boy. You're being redeemed right now. And fortunately, most of humanity will choose to follow in your luminous footsteps. But early in the Childcrush Period, there was trouble, and it took the development of a truer perception and of a new self-love for most of the people to make the choice you've made.

"I don't like to talk about the Childcrush Period, which may be one reason I'm so easily distracted from it. But let us return to the legend of the new kids who came to redeem humanity with the fire of their own hearts and their own illumined minds.

"The kids knew that once a person's accepted one mechanical implant he'll accept another and another, until eventually he's forgotten he was ever human and has become a cyborg. Somewhere in there, his soul will leave and he'll be nothing more than a walking mechanistic shadow. The soul cannot be mechanized.

"Of course, the human soul must not be merged with the soul of a hog, either, but let's stick to talking about the mechanical implants, since the tactics of the mechanistic technologists and of the bestial biologists were so similar. Understand one, you come pretty close to understanding the other.

"The kids of course knew that once a certain percentage of these walking machines of death had been created, then the machines of death would go to the voting booth and elect other machines of death who would decree by legislation that now everyone had to be implanted, whether they wanted to or not. It would have been the end of humanity. No souls equals no humans. Evil would have won."

"Sonny-Bob," Mimi said, "How could this be when people fought so hard for civil rights in the Sixties? And what about the New Age movement? It's going pretty strong right now in 1983. They're into spirituality, they don't want to become machines."

"Wrong, darling. Many of these same New Agers eventually fell for the lie of materialism. They actually behaved as if they believed spirituality can be bought and sold. They would spend hundreds, or even thousands, of dollars on weekend programs designed for the relatively wealthy, trying to buy their way into contact with their souls. They refused to recognize that the only way to become fully individualized in a materialistic culture is to leave the mechanisms of the culture behind and go into the wilderness. These people, many of whom bore the designation "yuppie", were into illusion and personality glorification and insubstantial styles of life more than anything else, despite their spiritual pretensions. They were inflated with self-importance, and refused to renounce their ways and go into the wilderness to be tested for a few years. Or for a few decades. If they had gone into the wilderness and survived those tests, they would have been cured of their self-importance and could have made a positive contribution straight from the world of Soul instead of from the manipulation of egotism. Like my friend Jesus pointed out in the Bible, and as many traditional cultures have always known, you can't become a soul-infused personality while running a business or raising a family. Not in a materialistic culture. In a materialistic culture you have to leave; otherwise you'll always be a materialist. You may eventually be able to return, but if you do you'll exist in that condition Jesus called 'being in the world but not of the world.' Ten-Four. Until a person has survived the tests of the wilderness, he'll never actually be himself. He may be able to make some minor contribution in the world of manipulation, but nothing compared to the contribution he would be able to make if he left the culture behind and devoted himself to the quest for Soul. For when we live in the world of Soul, everything we do comes from a source of love, and love is the most powerful force on this planet.

"In my time most of us aren't materialists and are actively reaching for the world of Soul, both as conscious families and as individuals. So the family is generally a good place to grow into Soul. You may have to leave for a while, but it's unlikely you'll be gone for years or decades. So my people can get some good spiritual work done in the context of the family. The family is our primary unit of society, not business or government. There are no real businesses in my time. There are no external kingdoms to conquer, no worlds to divide, no stress and irresponsible conduct to bring home. We try for cooperation instead of competition. *Real* cooperation, not manipulative and dehumanizing social programs enforced by government bureaucrats. Our government wouldn't be able to enforce such programs anyway, since we have so little of it. In another few decades we expect the government to dissolve altogether and we'll have a nice little anarchy. We've got a near-anarchy already. Nobody pays much attention to the government and the government executives don't pay much attention to anything except fishing in the Potomac. The only kingdoms we conquer are inside ourselves, and we work at it twenty-four hours a day. Even during our sleep we are extremely busy; we don't just lie there with our thumbs up our ass. Much exploration and integration of ourselves can occur in the process of sleep.

"Anyhow, I mention all this to illustrate the fact that you can't be part of the Kingdom of Heaven while remaining a citizen of the world of materialism. 'Ye cannot serve God and mammon.' Jesus was pretty plain about this and illustrated it with his life and words. I guess the Christians must have to try awfully hard to fool themselves that they are following in Jesus' footsteps. And the New Agers are pretty close to the Christians in this regard. They want both egotism and status on the one hand, and they want to be enlightened on the other. But most of them won't go into the wilderness and purify themselves, so they'll remain locked in the world of manipulation. Such people are always easy prey for the Black Lodge. I'm not saying that all, or even most, fall victim to the worst delusions of the evil ones, but they don't do much to usher in the world of Soul, either. And that world will eventually replace this world. The evil ones will be displaced by this process, but the gutless among the New Agers won't contribute much to bringing about the world of Soul and will self-justify themselves into accepting some of the illusions of the Black Lodge. Like the one that says you can stay in a materialist culture and change it from the inside. Not so. 'You can't put new wine in old bottles,' said my brother Jesus. All the 'insiders' can do is refine an old dead form a little bit, try to change it from being an insensitive cruel place to being a sensitive cruel place. A place where everyone sheds a tear every time someone gets hurt, but the hurting never stops. It can't stop, because the hurting is produced by an allegiance to a dead and primitive form. So the 'insiders' may feel your pain, but they can't make the pain go away, either their own or anyone else's.

"Many of the New Agers were deceived into getting implants due to the false promise of increased brainpower. Many of these same people were deceived decades earlier into taking LSD, not realizing that an experience of altered consciousness means nothing if you don't have the wisdom and experientially based knowledge of yourself as a multidimensional being to properly interpret it. And that only comes with the hardest work. It never comes with a drug.

"You can neither implant nor ingest spirituality."

"But what about the civil rights activists?" Mimi repeated. "I know they wouldn't be deceived by the Black Lodge after all they've been through in their fight for freedom. New Agers can get pretty crazy, but most of the civil rights activists seem stable enough."

Twentieth century history wasn't my favorite subject. The only thing this century had going for it was my little circle of friends, plus Lucille and Amber and Raven and the Bhutanese, whom I also considered friends. And, of course, Sir Ronald Wilson Reagan. I felt nauseous as I saw the course my lecture was taking.

I cleared my throat and swallowed some bile. I took a deep breath as everyone but Sharon stared expectantly at me. Sharon already knew. She was a specialist on this century or she wouldn't have been assigned to it.

"Well," I choked on my words, "it was largely these same New Agers and civil rights activists who elected a creature of glamour and illusion in the 1992 and '96 elections who was more or less at the mercy of his own lusts and the forces of evil. He pretended to be one thing, but in reality he was something very different. I was forced to watch videos of him during the Twentieth Century Tactics Class, and it was obvious that he and his wife, who tried to take over her own little share of the government--and who did take it over as a senator as a result of the 2000 elections--it was obvious that they were Egotism Incarnate. Some of the public claimed the wife was a 'strong woman', but those people didn't know the difference between egotism and strength. The dove of truth and love could not perch on the shoulders of this glamour-ridden couple.

"It was obvious from the start to anyone not blinded by glamour that they were liars and hypocrites, but it was several years before they demonstrated this fact in obvious enough ways for the meat-headed populace to begin to accept a bit of the truth about them. Anyhow, I puked my guts out whenever the instructors made me watch one of those videos. And they wouldn't stay and watch with me. They always left the room.

"And one of America's primary civil rights activists, a preacher man whose name has been forgotten by history, was engaged in adultery even as he counseled the so-called president for the same thing. He fathered a child by his lover. Now, there's nothing wrong with adultery as long as your spouse approves and there's nothing wrong with fathering kids, unless you are inferior morally, as this preacher was. Anyhow, the only reason I know about these things is that my instructors felt I should know about the hypocrisy of Christian America in the twentieth century before I got here. They figured if they prepared me in advance, there would be less shock to my system and I would be less likely to go insane from being exposed to a society where everyone was highly suspicious of love and pretended to believe it should be highly regulated, while secretly always wanting to share it as widely as possible, and in some cases, such as this hypocritical president and preacher, rutting in violation of the beliefs they publicly claimed to have. They didn't have the balls or the heart to just go out and rut, and convention be damned. They could have saved their souls, if their souls meant more to them than their restrictive public image.

"This alleged president was a Democrat. The Republicans went after him because he'd broken some laws. The Democratic Party, which had totally lost all sense of honor by this point, tried to make it seem as though the alleged president was being persecuted for adultery, when the truth was he was being persecuted for perjury. He lied under oath, which generally is not considered a virtue in this timezone. But Slick Willie pretty much got away with it. There was some disciplinary action in the end, but not as much as there would have been for Joe Citizen. Herr Klinton, as he is known by freedom lovers in the future, was a felon and everybody knew it. But he managed to wiggle out of it when Joe Citizen could not have. He was slicker than a swamp eel.

"I'm not normally prejudiced against felons. Some of them are good people. Your government will declare people felons at the drop of a hat. They declared me a multiple felon just for fighting to save the timeline. But where I'm from we have absolutely no respect for hypocrites. We wouldn't elect a hypocrite to sweep the streets, let alone run the country. My instructors at the TCTC were all outpatients at a mental rehab hospital because of twentieth century service, and one of the primary things they couldn't adjust to here was the terrible level of hypocrisy. Hypocrisy is bad in other centuries, but in the nineteenth and twentieth centuries it's a worse problem overall than in any previous century that I know of, and I've visited a lot of them. But your people only have the short view and don't even realize that the Puritans, for all their restrictions and harshness, were generally not as hypocritical as the average twentieth century American, despite the fact the Puritan was just as horny and frequently also committed adultery. The difference is that at least the Puritans were both more likely to admit their indiscretions, and more likely to forgive. If anything, the Puritans actually *expected* adultery, so their attitudes were more in line with nature than the twentieth century person, who pretends adultery won't affect his marriage, though in fact it does affect more than half of all marriages. Sometimes it seems that every century the earth has ever had is more morally and spiritually advanced than the Nineteenth and Twentieth."

Mimi was growing impatient with my long-windedness. I wondered if she had Democratic tendencies. "But what's all this got to do with Childcrush?"

"Just this: under the pretext of concern for children, the chief of all hypocrites, Herr Klinton, was busily taking away their rights. He tried to take away their rights as free beings to own themselves. Of course, he tried to take away everyone else's rights, too. He was doing what he could to prepare for the mechanization of humanity, just as his counterpart in Great Britain was.

"The classic example of this is gun control. It had been demonstrated more than adequately that violent crime decreases when citizens are allowed to arm themselves. And firearms accidents were rare and were at an all-time low. But in conjunction with the primitive news media, the alleged president did his best to make it appear that guns cause crime and that death by firearms accident was at epidemic levels. It was not. Far more people were killed each year in automobile accidents than firearms accidents, but he never gnashed his teeth and wore sackcloth and ashes about that.

"And his friends in the news media never publicized the individual opinions of the founders of this country regarding the right to keep and bear arms. Many of the Founders wrote individually about the issue. And every one of them who did sounds like an NRA member, except that some of them would seem more radical than the NRA to the floppy chakra control-freak liberals of the late twentieth century.

"That's the hallmark of what passes for the media in the Twentieth:

They slant the news by omission. They give a ton of favorable coverage to causes the media moguls support--and which evil frequently supports --and much less coverage, and that frequently unfavorable, to causes they don't support. The new race of humanity won't be blinded by the manipulative tactics of the old, however. They'll see right through it.

"I know you're probably wondering about my obsession with gun control, so I'll tell you why I'm obsessed with it. Here goes.

"Every human being, whether child or adult, owns himself or herself, period. Every civilized person knows that and supports the fact of it. No question mark, no room for dispute.

"And the cornerstone of self-ownership is the right to self-defense. Period. No question mark, no room for dispute. And the right to keep and bear arms cements this fact into our moral code. For we in the future have a firm moral code. We know that love is far more important than morality, but we also know that we need a firm (not rigid, but firm) moral code to support us in our relationship with ourselves as individuals and in our relations with others. We need this moral code to hold us up as we search for the love within our own hearts. The code doesn't take the place of love, but it keeps us going until we find the love within ourselves and learn to manifest it fully. Ten-four.

"And I see that look in your eye, Freud, but no, I'm not a fundamentalist. A fundamentalist would say you have the *obligation* to defend yourself, and that if you don't, you'll go to hell or to jail, or both. I'm only saying you have the absolute *right* to self-defense, just as you have the absolute right to breathe, but I'm not deciding for you when or if you should apply your rights. To defend or not to defend, as well as what methods and levels of force to use if you do defend yourself, is entirely your choice. And I don't care what your personal choice is. As we've already discussed regarding Obi-Wan Kenobi, occasionally you may be able to achieve your objectives by withholding the power of your sword arm.

"Self-ownership is the first principal of the individual, and the principal of self-defense is the first principal of self-ownership. And, by God, the right to keep and bear arms is the first principal of self-defense. This doesn't mean a gun has to always be your first option; frequently it doesn't have to be as you grow in sensitivity and love and continue to develop yourself as a warrior. But a gun is a good place to begin your warrior training, particularly if you realize there's lots more to warriorship and the gun is only the first step of a very long and unusual process. And sometimes a very hazardous process, as you begin to purify yourself of corruption and illusion.

"Indeed, I sometimes feel a very advanced warrior might not ever have to use any form of weapon. I've known some who were amazing. But they all knew how to use a variety of weapons, including guns. If you're going to develop into a genuinely integrated and powerful warrior you have to train on every level, you have to train every aspect of yourself. The ability these advanced warriors have with weapons is one of the things that creates the base for their other skills, particularly their ability to work with energy, just as an accurate and skillful morality is the base that holds up love. The motto of the warriorship and spirituality of the neo-humans is 'Integration, Then Love.'

"Do you all remember when we met at the barfateria for lunch at the great university the other day? Good. Two fellows came in, one with a rifle and the other with a shotgun. Nobody thought anything about it and I was glad to see a display of freedom in this timezone for a change. Those guys bought some sandwiches and left. Nobody got hysterical when they saw the guns."

"Of course not, Sonny-Bob." Sue sounded exasperated, as though she still couldn't quite see where this discussion was going. "Campus Security stores the students' guns in a big safe. They can check them out to go hunting or shooting whenever they want to.

"Some students don't bother with the safe and keep their guns in their rooms, along with their drug paraphernalia and Battlestar Galactica posters. It's always been this way and thank goodness for it. Remember, I told you about that deranged ex-marine who went into the Tower in the Sixties and started shooting at everybody. The cops depended on armed students then; they asked students and members of the community to get their guns and help them. And that's what happened. The students and other civic minded people got their rifles and began firing on the ex-marine, which made him keep his head low and gave the cops an opportunity to sneak into the Tower and kill him.

"Periodically an armed citizen even saves a cop's life. Everyone knows that."

"Not everyone, sweetie. Not in the 1990's with the huge buildup in anti-freedom propaganda by the confused people who have allowed themselves to be manipulated by the Black Lodge. Believe it or not, guns are actually banned in schools in the Nineties, both at universities and at pre-university schools."

"Impossible!" Sue scoffed. "Even the high school kids take guns to school and nobody thinks anything about it. There's no harm in it, they go shooting after school sometimes."

"It's that way *today*, honey," I said gently. "Particularly in rural areas. But that freedom will be taken away from kids in the Nineties."

Sue snorted. "Might as well try to take away their knives, snuff and cigarettes."

"They did. And of course they justified the whole scenario with the idea that these things were a threat to public health. Tobacco *is* a threat to health, but the guns and knives weren't. Banning the guns made schools less safe, not safer. If a few of the students and teachers had guns in the schools of the Nineties, there would have been fewer school shootings. You may have noticed that armed predators don't usually attack places where someone might be able to shoot back. I'm not counting school cops necessarily, because the Supreme Court actually ruled that cops have no obligation to protect individual citizens. Unbelievable, but true. And in some of the school shootings of the Nineties the cops are actually chickenshit to go in, falling back on cowardice and irresponsibility, then blaming it on standard operating procedure. Only an unconscious machine blames such tragedy on standard operating procedure. A human being does not. If his courage and ingenuity fail, he accepts and acknowledges that fact without any political or manipulative considerations at all. Then he works to forgive and improve himself. But the people in the Twentieth typically lack the courage to take responsibility for their own mistakes, and in true manipulative and restrictive fashion they blame it on the fear of lawsuits, at least if they are some type of business or government agency. But a person who never owns up to what he's done, such as the cops who wait outside a school building while kids are being murdered inside, can never forgive and improve himself. He will remain defective until he takes full responsibility for what he's done, or for what he failed to do. Lawsuits and every other consideration be damned. Full speed ahead with honor and truth. Let the dead wood of the twentieth century political mindset fall away. Real human beings don't have time for that shit, and if they do have time for it they won't have time to do the work to evolve into real human beings. Evolution accepts no excuses.

"But we were talking about guns and knives and tobacco. It is worth noting that even freedom of speech suffers after they ban the guns and knives. One restriction follows on the heels of another. Students were actually suspended in the South for having a Confederate flag showing through the window of their vehicle, and forbidden to wear the flag on a shirt or belt buckle. Liberals and people who were afraid of liberals were responsible for this, of course, --"

Freud gave a loud snort. "The conservatives didn't persecute kids for wearing anti-war slogans on shirts or pot leaves on belt buckles. Do you expect me to believe the liberals could be more vicious than the conservatives?"

"Wait and see, my friend."

I was growing tired of talking about this weird century, the place of institutionalized hypocrisy, the place where a man could not be free to be a man and a woman could not be free to be a woman. And a child could not be counted as a genuine human being with all the rights of larger human beings. I wanted to wrap this up and eat a doughnut.

I began my final lap around the lecture circuit. The final lap for now, anyway. "The lunatic liberals always want to take the guns away from the people who didn't initiate the violent act, and they usually refuse to enforce gun laws aimed at criminals. The NRA wore sackcloth and ashes and wailed and pleaded to the Democratic administration of the 1990's to enforce the gun laws aimed at criminals, because if the criminals had been prosecuted they would have spent many years behind bars instead of being turned loose to prey on innocents again. But Herr Klinton, Herr Gore and Field Marshall Reno steadfastly refused to enforce those laws, because they wanted more bloodshed in the streets so they could call for still more restrictions on the law-abiding, with the ultimate goal of making self-defense illegal for everyone except the political and cultural elites. Finally, toward the end of Herr Klinton's reign, he and his crew of lewd villains had to begin enforcing those laws, because government officials in Richmond, Virginia, with help from the NRA's financial warchest, initiated a program called Project Exile, which was nothing more than enforcing the gun laws already on the books. The result was that the gun murder rate in Richmond was cut in half, and as this became widely known Herr Klinton had no choice but to reluctantly begin enforcing the gun laws. People began to see through his crocodile tears, his staged wailing and moaning whenever there was another tragedy involving firearms, when they learned that federal prosecution of gun law violations decreased by almost fifty percent in his administration. So the restrictions of the Nineties were not truly an attempt to reduce violence or improve public health. Expansive education--not restriction--helps with that. No, the repression of the Nineties in the United States, and the even greater oppression in a lot of countries, was about taking away people's right to own themselves. The predators who were responsible for all this of course started with reducing the rights of kids, because kids were the most vulnerable targets to begin with, and if you can take away their rights and their personal power altogether you've created a generation that won't give the control freaks any trouble at all when they grow up. They'll accept machine implants or any other infringements proposed by those who are being influenced by the Black Lodge."

"Well," Sue said thoughtfully, "I haven't known you to lie yet, Sonny-Bob, though you have been known occasionally to exaggerate about certain things."

I had no idea what she meant with that crack about exaggeration, but at least she was coming around. "Anyway, folks, the point of the restrictions of the Nineties was to pave the way for the mechanization of humanity by crushing the spirits of the new children, both with old techniques such as regimentation in schools and standardized testing and with new techniques that were even more insidious. Add the threat of mechanical implants and humanity could easily have gone down the tubes. Snuff may be bad for you, but at least using it is human and everyone has a right to choose as long as they're not infringing on anyone else.

"But the forces of control and manipulation successfully clouded the older generation's hearts and turned what passed for their minds in the direction of preserving physical bodies at the cost of the spirit. And when you're left with a physical body but no soul, you've made the worst trade imaginable. This is the type of alleged values they were trying to teach kids in the Nineties. They didn't put it in these terms, of course, but what kind of idiot expects evil to tell the truth to those it manipulates? *

"By Goddess, you and I and every other human being has the right to live as we see fit as long as we don't injure another. But people lost sight of this in the Nineties."

---

* I didn't have the heart to tell Mimi this, but during the Nineties and early years of the Twenty-First a policy called zero tolerance was adopted in some schools. Zero tolerance means zero love and zero brains. Children were led away from school in handcuffs for doing nothing more than drawing pictures of weapons, or pointing a finger at someone and saying "bang!", and even for pointing food at other students. Or for demonstrating a healthy affection, such as a little boy kissing a little girl on the cheek. These children were frequently expelled or suspended and tagged with records that would haunt them the rest of their lives in an effort to teach them that only a passionless existence was acceptable to the controllers of society. These policies were implemented mostly by baby boomers, who had more freedom overall than any previous generation of Americans. Yet when it was their turn to serve as parents and school administrators, they dropped the ball and responded to students with a viciousness and savagery that would have shocked every previous generation of parents. The boomers' own parents were far more tolerant than the boomers themselves. The boomers, who had begun as advocates of peace, love and freedom, became tools for evil.

There was an eerie stillness in the room. At length, Hubert began humming again. I guess he was nervous.

"Hubert, maybe you could sing that song for us now," Aphrodite suggested.

"Well, I don't know . . ."

"C'mon, Hubert, sing!" Freud encouraged.

"I'll try. Do you want me to use my voice or the voice of the Golden Songpoet, Lachesis Magoo?"

"Use Mr. Magoo's voice," I said hastily.

"Very well," Hubert said formally. Then he made a sound like a cold, rushing wind and added a solemn voice on top of it. "In the Childcrush Period of the late twentieth century was born one who refused to be crushed, one who would not be put down. He rose to become a great voice for the neo-people of the twenty-first century, for he sang to them of their own experiences and feelings, and along with Lucille The Prophetess and many other heroes, he led the way towards the first genuine human culture.

"I give you Lachesis Magoo, the Golden Songpoet of America, with a song from his quadruple platinum disc *I BEWAIL MY FATE: The Most Poignant Songs Of Lachesis Magoo,* released by Wailing Wall Records And Funerals, with offices in Jerusalem, Berkley and Ho Chi Minn City."

"Hurry up, Hubert," I growled. "Let's get this over with."

"This song earned Mr. Magoo a fortune in royalties. It's called 'Love Or Control?' and throws some light upon the difficulties faced by the neo-children in the Childcrush Period. You may sing along if you wish."

The howling cold wind died down as Hubert cleared his throat. Then he began as I shuddered; Mary Beth had made me listen to this song thousands of times.

I ratchet myself up
to try to live another day
no guns, tobacco or pocket knives.
I feel used and bruised
they say my penis I can't use
to share the gift of love isn't wise.

A full body search
a pat on the back
a fine child, no sense of discovery.
He doesn't fidget much

he's on a prescribed drug
he'll be just what we want him to be.

Sold your love up the creek
to get the control you seek
and you can't get back home to your heart.
When the weed of restriction blooms
confine your kids to a small room
to make them just like you, so smug and smart.

Mrs. Kyle for a while
a hippie flower child
tells us the way it was in Dylan's world.
She used to be so free
now she teaches history
and tells us not to use certain words.

Mr. Stokes, he still smokes
and sometimes he even tokes
but he'll expel us if we don't D.A.R.E.
They've lived secret lives
full of baby boomer lies
once they loved freedom, now they don't care.

Sold your love up the creek
to get the control you seek
and you can't get back home to your heart.
When the weed of restriction blooms
confine your kids to a small room
to make them just like you, so smug and smart.

I can see them dancing nude
inside my private dreams
on the weekends when they don't feed me drugs.
When my head gets clear
all I can feel is fear
what happened to these clowns who should love us?

What happened to their free love
what happened to love at all
it's replaced by control

they stuck us in a bottle.
Oh, the handsome Flower Children
longhaired and free
once they fought control--
but now they crush me.

Hubert sighed. Then there was no sound for a long minute. Finally Mimi said, "Sonny-Bob, I don't want to have to raise Miyamoto in that kind of world . . ." She released a choking sob. "It's *inhuman*!" Suddenly she broke and ran for the restroom and slammed the door. I could hear her sobbing.

"Hubert, now do you see why I prefer Gene Autry?"

"Yes, sir," he replied meekly.

"You performed that song very well," Aphrodite said seriously. "It's just a little too gloomy. I wonder if you could sing for me sometime when I'm stripping for the family? A happy song, though."

"I'd love to, Aphrodite," Hubert gushed happily; it was just as I'd suspected. He had a crush on her *and* on her former car. "I'll take Sonny-Bob's advice and perform "Rudolph The Red Nosed Reindeer" by the songpoet Gene Autry as you disrobe."

Aphrodite glanced at me. "We'll talk about the musical selection later, Hubert, okay?"

"Okay, Aphrodite."

Finally, Mimi came out of the latrine and Sharon moved to her and put an arm around her. "I know it's tough, dear, but you and Miyamoto will survive the Nineties. Tell you what: Although my tour's up in 1990, I'll ask for an extension and stay until 2000. I'll look in on you every once in a while and make sure you're okay."

"Thank you, Sharon," I sighed gratefully. Sharon should probably be added to the family officially; it was clear she was already a soul brother.

Sharon stroked Mimi's hair, then tenderly massaged the belly where Pa Miyamoto resided in infantile glory. "Dear, you can homeschool Pa Miyamoto and he can sit right there with his shotgun and condoms. You can treat him as a genuine human being if you educate him at home. He won't have to give up his rights or his emotions or his thoughts or his soul. You can keep him from becoming another victim of this soulless mechanistic educational system, which apparently thinks it can turn out real human beings like a factory produces shoes.

"A person with the cookie-cutter mentality can never be actualized, yet the schools are taught by legions of these gingerbread men and women. The teachers aren't actualized and haven't a clue as to what an actualized human being really is.

"But you can save Pa Miyamoto by teaching him at home and keeping him away from religious fundamentalists and politically correct liberals."

"She did teach him at home," I offered.

Sharon smiled brightly. "And I'll bet he was an actualized human being."

"He was a nut, Sharon."

Sharon's face lost its brilliance and she glared at me. Well, it probably wouldn't be the last time.

Suddenly, as if on a signal from Pa Miyamoto, we all moved to Mimi and put a hand on her belly. Sharon was glowing again, we all were. "I love you, Pa," I whispered softly. And I did.

So we stood there in unspoken prayer to the fetus, and to Mimi, the mother of the neo-child. For Pa Miyamoto was never like most twentieth century children. He was an individual.

At length we scattered and took up our respective places around the room. For our room had become a temple of both rutting and exploring the ancient wisdom in a modern format.

I adjusted my cock, a doughnut in my other hand. "Well, we've explored a little bit about how the fascists of the liberal persuasion attempted to disempower children. We all know how the fundies try to disempower people, but the liberals are usually far more cunning, and if you can't think better than they can or trust in your own heart and soul you run the risk of being ensnared by them.

"Let me relate to you a true story that occurred around the year 2000. It sounds incredible, but if you wait until century's end and check on it, you'll see that I'm telling the godawful truth.

"There was a female sculptor in New Mexico who made a sculpture of her son at play, shooting a water pistol, for the public to enjoy. Then, after the politically correct liberals failed to ensnare her into believing the statue promoted violence, they violently attacked[*] this symbol of childhood and smeared it with green paint and wrote "no gun" on his legs. The sculptor felt defeated, so she went out and cut the hand that

---

[*] When was the last time you heard of a gang of NRA members attacking or defacing anything?

held the water pistol off the sculpture. I'm not making this up; it's too fantastic for me or anyone else to make up.

"And it's a perfect symbol for the disempowerment of children the world over. Believe it or not, at about the same time children in Holland were being encouraged to turn in their baseball bats to the authorities because the politically correct, but humanity hating, authorities said they believed kids might use the baseball bats as weapons.

"In America the politically correct people want you to believe guns, including water pistols, cause crime. In Holland, where there are no legal guns in private hands, they want you to believe baseball bats cause crime.

"And there are other true stories of the machinations of those who hate humanity, or who have allowed themselves to be manipulated by those who hate humanity, and who therefore attempt to erase even the idea of self-defense from public consciousness. The United Nations, in the year 2001, was even calling for confiscation of people's privately owned firearms and holding 'public destruction events' where the guns would be destroyed for the public's entertainment, just as witches were destroyed for the public's entertainment centuries ago. Remember, there's only one small step between destroying guns and destroying people who support the right to keep and bear arms. The witches' art was outlawed and its implements destroyed before they began destroying witches. With self-defense being the cornerstone of self-ownership, the evil ones and their fog-minded and closed-hearted henchpersons would logically begin their attempt to dominate humanity by eliminating the right to self-defense. Then the individual no longer owns herself, you see. And once an individual no longer owns herself, she'll be willing to accept any outrage. She'll have to, and she'll become a loveless machine, quite possibly as rage-filled and hate-filled as her masters.

"For that's what these attacks on self-defence and self-ownership are all about. The evil ones want to create as much hatred and rage as they can, for they feed off that kind of energy. You can't think of evil as human; it is not. And former human beings who have fallen all the way into evil are no longer human. They've lost their souls. Don't project human attributes onto evil, for it has none. You can't reason with it or love it. If you try to reason with it it'll find a way to ensnare you, and if you love it you're loving some*thing* which is totally an illusion. In fact, if you love it you're not coming from a place of pure love anyway; there's some sentiment thrown in, which of course confuses you. Evil can latch onto floppy chakra sentiment and have a good time with it. You don't want that, do you? Pure and shining radiant love from the heart chakra cannot be attracted to illusion, cannot be attracted to evil. Your shining heart won't waste it's time with evil, for there is no substance to evil, no life to it at all. It cannot be redeemed. Corruption and confusion can be redeemed with hard work, but there's nothing left, no spark of life, in true evil to redeem. If you love illusion you degrade yourself. All you can do with true evil is to kill it."

"Whoa, Sonny-Bob!" Sue exclaimed. "I'm starting to see why they put your picture on those wanted posters."

"You don't know the half of it, darling. And you don't want to know the half of it. But I'll give you some crucial principles everyone should know to avoid the snares set by this silly manifestation we call 'evil'.

"We're going to begin with a brief--I hope it will be brief--discussion of black magic, grey magic and white magic. If you're concerned about your welfare and the welfare of your friends and family, then white magic is the only one of these three you'll want to practice, for it is the only one that has positive karmic consequences, though it'll be practiced a little differently in the future than in the past. In the future white magic will sometimes be referred to as 'integrational magic' because it unites the purified darkness in a person with the light of their soul. But its objective is to embody and radiate Love, just as it's always been. Indeed, the love can be more fully embodied and radiated more powerfully than ever in a person who has integrated himself through the future magic than was ever possible in the past.

"Grey magic, on the other hand, is fucked up. It's stated objective is also to unify the darkness and the light, but it tries to accomplish this through unifying black magic and white magic. This is a union which is simply impossible. It cannot be. Black magic is based in glamour and illusion; white magic is based in love and truth. Love and truth do not compromise themselves, or they aren't love and truth anymore. If black magic touches white magic the white magic doesn't become grey, it becomes black. A somewhat less damaging form of black, perhaps, but still black. Anything touched by black magic becomes black and is enmeshed in glamour and illusion. There's really no such thing as grey magic. It is a mental construct created by people who are laboring under glamour and illusion. And ultimately, if they don't leave the grey magic 'path', they become miserable and stay that way. The white magician may sometimes be miserable too, but not as miserable as the grey magician. And if the white magician keeps working his path with the utmost dedication, eventually he'll evolve out of his misery and into love.

"Now then. Black magic can never know the touch of love and is by turns cold and mechanical, then seething with rage and hatred. It is totally based on glamour and illusion. There's not even a particle of truth to it. It is a derelict form with nothing inside. The fact that there's not even a particle of love or truth to it is what distinguishes it from the relative corruption of fundamentalist religions and other institutions. At the core of most sorts of herds of people there is a spark of love and truth. If all the corruption and confusion were peeled away you would be left with a glowing love. These other groups usually are not evil, though they may well be influenced by evil. But the evil hasn't yet extinguished the spark of truth at the core of these groups, and there's something fine in the human heart, even in the hearts of corrupt people, which in most people refuses to be extinguished. No matter how corrupt they are, and no matter how many wicked things they do, at their core there is still something that is pure and pristine that will never allow itself to be touched by the ancient corruption of evil.

"So there is no life to black magic, only eternal death. And please be aware I'm using the terms 'evil' and 'black magic' almost synonymously. Every black magician becomes extinct if he doesn't leave the path of evil and begin to reform himself before he totally loses his soul. Fortunately, however, most people won't go down that road and will ultimately redeem themselves from their glamour and illusion and the corruption that grows out of it. Most people will be saved. But it's too late for evil to be saved.

"The grey magicians apparently believe that everything in creation should be embraced. What they don't realize is that black magic is not a part of creation. It is total glamour and illusion and manipulation and control, and therefore doesn't exist in any real sense. Black magicians who have fallen so far as to completely lose their souls don't really exist anymore, either. They devolved from being more or less human into being a completely inhuman illusion. That's all they are and that's all they have.

"I say black magic doesn't exist in any real sense because the universe is alive, the universe is **LIFE**. And life is love. There is no love in black magic, therefore no life, so therefore it doesn't exist. It *is not* a part of the universe. The original spark within the form, the soulstuff, is a part of the universe and has returned to the heart of God. But the form is completely without life. It is a total illusion. It's dead, Jim, like that space doctor said on TV the other night. And eternal death is not a part of the universe. The only thing that can die in this universe is illusion. Death doesn't exist.

"Are you with me so far?"

"Hell, no," said Freud.

Sharon was looking at me with an expression that was difficult to fathom. "Sonny-Bob," she spoke carefully, "did you ever serve on an ERT?"

I looked at the floor.

"What's an ERT?" Freud demanded.

I took a deep breath and looked at him. "Evil Reduction Team. And yes, I served with the 12th ERT for almost five years."

Sharon gave a little gasp and shivered. Mimi moved close to me and took the chill off my soul. Her hand found mine and we stood together.

After a moment I continued. "The ERT's are a rather secret branch of the TAC, but I don't give a damn about that. I figure the more people know, the more empowered they become. I feel it's primitive and paranoid and irresponsible and manipulative to try to classify everything. So I'm going to run my mouth 'till I feel like stopping. Or until there's a consensus that I should shut up."

There didn't seem to be any consensus, so I plowed ahead. "The ERT's do one job, and one job only. They kill. They're the best killers in the timeline. They kill evil. However, since evil isn't really alive to begin with, it's technically more like erasing a blemish on a piece of paper. Except that a blemish on a piece of paper won't fight back and won't cause stress.

"The ERT's are working mostly in my own century, and presumably at least a little farther up the timeline. Occasionally they trot back down the timeline to kill something or other, but mostly we've drawn a line in the ectoplasm in the twenty-second century and said: 'No more. We'll kill all the evil we can and try to eliminate it altogether. Certainly we can reduce it.'

"But remember: there's really nothing there to kill. Evil kills itself by choosing to devolve into evil. Its soul flies away on home to God's heart, and all that's left of the former organism is the shell of illusion, because anything that has no spark of soul, no spark of life, is by definition illusion, just the leavings of a misspent life, or a misspent series of lives until the life is gone. It threw away the chance to merge with its soul and become immortal. Now all that can be done is to either step around that blemish or erase it. Quite rightfully, most people wisely choose to avoid it if karma allows. Some of us, like those who serve with the ERT's, have to come by our wisdom the hard way. And the danger of serving with an ERT is that you'll become too deeply enmeshed in the very illusion you're erasing, and if that happens, you won't want to erase it. Then you'll be in danger of devolving and losing your own soul. Thank Goddess I made it, but it was tough. Some fall.

"Now, many beings in the universe experience illusion. Some are positively coated with it. But they are not evil. Confused, yes. Fucked up, certainly. But not evil. And as they evolve they'll release their illusions and let the love, light, life and power that's within them shine forth. That's evolution. They exist, they are alive. And as they get in touch with the reality of their existence they'll let go of glamour and illusion, control and manipulation. They'll realize it's enough to simply be themselves, for they are love, and love is its own reward."

Some of my old, semi-forgotten memories had begun resurfacing and I had to pause for a moment and do some deep breathing. I tried to sit in the center of my heart and then allow it to flood my entire body. Some old stuff related to my past career with the ERT floated away, and good riddance. If I'd had any sense I'd never have joined the ERT, but you live and learn. If you live.

"Sonny-Bob, honey, talk about integrational magic," Mimi whispered.

"Okay, sweetheart. Integrational magic, the white magic of the future, is simply the individual taking full responsibility for his own spiritual growth and crafting a unique and utterly personal path for himself that leads to the purification and integration of all aspects of his shadow, then the reunification of that shadow with the golden light of his soul. He learns to rule his shadow, his outer form, which consists of his mental, emotional and physical bodies. His personality, in short. He learns to rule this personality as the soul of love which he is through the heart chakra. After long-term, dedicated effort by the personality to purify itself and allow itself to become infused by the soul, the heart makes the final adjustment in the shadow, coordinating it with the energy of love. Then all's well and the individual can go catfishing.

"But don't ever confuse integrational magic with grey magic. They are not the same. Grey magic works with the shadow, but places some validity on the fear and control and elevation of the personality over the soul. Grey magic is black. The grey magicians don't seem to realize that you can't just saunter up and embrace the shadow and rejoice in its impurities. First you have to purify it of all glamour and control. As it becomes pure you can begin to embrace it. But you don't just latch onto it in its impure state with an 'anything goes' attitude or the unpurified shadow will try to pull your other aspects down with it, and may succeed.

"Some people, even some shadow warriors with good intentions, believe the shadow consists of the evil parts of ourselves. This is not the case. Don't ever believe that. No living being is evil. The shadow is simply dark. It is the absence of light. Evil tendencies and various other manifestations of confusion may hide within it, but evil and confusion are not YOU, and they are not a part of you. So when you reclaim your shadow you drive out everything that would prompt you in the direction of evil. You get rid of the corruption and control and manipulation. You eliminate everything that is not YOU. You most certainly don't drive away the shadow itself; you can't. If you try it'll rear up and bite you on the ass, and rightfully so.

"As you purify and reclaim your shadow you can eventually begin to make friends with her. Darkness is good as long as it is pure. The lady protects us and nourishes us in certain ways."

"So darkness is good as long as it's purified and ruled by love," Aphrodite said. "I think I understand that. So you want to do white magic and not its opposite--"

"No."

"No? But you just said . . ."

"Sweetie, I just said a lot of things. And yes, I did say that if you're going to do magic, you should do white magic instead of black. But I said nothing whatsoever about opposites. Darling, there are no opposites anywhere in this vast universe. The idea that any two things in this universe can be opposed to one another is an illusion. And the idea that anything of this living universe can be opposed to the eternal extinction of black magic is an even greater illusion."

"Huh?"

"My love, you've just tried to set up a relationship of opposites between white magic and black magic, but such a relationship would be impossible. White magic and black magic share no common ground, whereas things that appear to be in opposition to each other actually define each other and are therefore related. So-called opposites swim in the same pool. There are two different kinds of energy pools your life can swim in. The one that all of us in this co-op are swimming in is the Pool of Obscured Love, though sometimes the love shines through and isn't obscured, because we're all swimming upstream to the next pool, which is the Pool of Universal Radiance. Presently we're all just carp, but when we reach the Pool of Universal Radiance we'll be golden trout. In the Pool of Obscured Love we're learning to release glamour and illusion and manipulation and control, and when all of that's gone we'll be flopping around happily in the Pool of Universal Radiance, which is the divine force we call Love. It's not sentiment, mind you. Love is a powerful and shining divine force. Ten-four.

"In this Pool of Obscured Love there sometimes appear to be opposites. But really, an 'opposite' is just a face you haven't recognized yet. As we get cleaner we'll recognize and embrace all our faces. We all share the same bath water. We're all in this energy pool together and by the time we're fully clean and swimming in the Pool of Universal Radiance we'll look back and see clearly that there never were any opposites. That was all an illusion. So the next time I fart in the bath water, don't get righteous and pretend you are opposite from me. You are not, for I've seen you pee in the water when you thought I wasn't looking.

"Now then: Evil is a one-dimensional cesspool of illusion. It cannot see love. It cannot see us, though it may perceive some of our illusions and try to use them to manipulate us. But it doesn't actually know what it is trying to manipulate, because it cannot see our heart. It only knows it's thrown away some golden opportunity in its distant past to live eternally, and so it pursues us and tries to drag us down to its deranged and soulless level. It is jealous of us, for it knows most of us will eventually claim the prize it threw away. And though it can no longer even imagine the nature of this prize, it doesn't want us to have it.

"Evil is the third pool, and the one we want to always steer clear of. There's no individuality or love in the cesspool of evil. There's only an empty and brittle egotism, seething with the sorrow of its eternal loss. Everything in this cesspool is the same. Individuality has been completely lost. There is no soulstuff there. There is not even any illusion of opposites. There is only loss. So evil is completely unrelated to the first two pools. It may at times appear to be related to the Pool of Obscured Love, because it sometimes shows up and tries to manipulate us through our own illusions. But evil is only related to itself. The soulstuff, though sometimes obscured, still shines in our pool. As we continue to cast off our illusions there will come a day when the last carp leaves the Pool of Obscured Love and swims in sublime troutlike joy in the Pool of Universal Radiance. On that day the last vestiges of evil will disappear forever, for there will be no illusions for it to cling to. The living universe will withdraw into its own heart, leaving evil behind forever. Then we can relax."

Sharon cleared her throat. "I've been told by the prostitutes that you can only compare two or more things which have the spark of life within them. Since evil has no spark of life, it can't be compared to anything that does have the spark."

"Yup," I said. "You may have two different lifeforms, say apples and oranges. The two can be compared because they have the soulstuff within them. They are alive. They represent different aspects of the Face of God. They are related through this force. They may have external similarities as well, but the thing that most determines their relationship to one another is the soulstuff. In fact, probably everything that contains the soulstuff has at least some external similarities to every other thing that contains the soulstuff, because only external forms that are capable of reflecting light can experience Soul. There would have to be some common element in the external forms that allows them to house some degree of soul. Therefore, there would have to be external similarities as well. There would have to be a range of vibratory quality that everything that is capable of reflecting Soul belongs to, and this range of vibratory quality would produce at least a slight similarity between any given form capable of reflecting some degree of soul and every other form capable of reflecting some degree of soul.

"So I hope it's clear now why true good and true evil do not share the relationship of opposites, and why white magic and black magic do not share in such a relationship. The manifestations of genuine life and ultimate bliss have no kinship with the manifestations of eternal death, eternal loss."

Preacher Culpepper paused. He ate another doughnut. My, those things were tasty.

I chuckled dryly, remembering some of the ignoramuses who at various times had referred to me as a rebel. They didn't realize that I have no consciousness of opposites, and that since a rebel thinks he's opposite from whatever he's rebelling against, I therefore couldn't possibly be a rebel. They couldn't see that I am simply a being who represents a particular kind of unifying Force and that when a person drinks of the cup of this Force he stands sturdily in his power with a total intolerance of glamour and illusion, and a total, unconditional acceptance of wholebody love--Intelligent Love! The ignoramuses confuse a person who is intolerant of glamour and illusion with the rebel because he's so cheerfully willing to destroy the warring glamours and illusions they themselves cherish and because they can't imagine destruction apart from their own lusts and hates and sense of duality. But I have no lust or hate; I'm a Synthesizing Love Machine. And the ignoramuses want me to fit their limiting system of categories and put me in the pigeonhole they reserve for "rebel" because they are too lazy and fearful to face the implications of what a life might be like lived totally without any perception of opposites and totally devoted to expressing the love of their own sweet hearts in a fullbody manner appropriate to their own uniquely personal constitutions as newly-structured Individuals.

If they could develop the heart to release the fear, their laziness would depart, because laziness is a child of fear. Once their fear and laziness had begun to leave, they might be able to take a little sip of the Energy which I myself have gulped wholesale, and which has taken me on such a wild ride of restructuring.

Anyhow, I am no more a rebel than a Sacred Prostitute of Aphrodite is a whore. We've both drunk from the same cup of Synthesizing Love.

It's easy for an Integrated Warrior or a Holy Prostitute to see how these dualistic, hypocritical people of the twentieth century are all involved in creating the very problems they decry. For example, a couple of weeks earlier I'd entered the TV room at the co-op to watch the journalists manufacture the news. I say they were manufacturing the news because they approached the process like a mechanic would undertake a process of selecting nuts and bolts to put together in some sort of mechanical contrivance. And the journalists assembled their mechanical contrivance according to their own prejudices, while trying to deceive themselves that they were "objective". Objectivity is impossible; a divine and compassionate impersonality should be the goal. But the alleged journalists contented themselves with a system of mass production, as if genuine insights could make themselves known in the middle of rank conformity.

If the journalists had cared to make their lives count for anything, they would have spent their years contacting Truth and following that Truth back until they arrived at that Love which is its parent. Then they would have derived genuine insights from that Love which they would have gradually learned to apply to the daily mundane world around them. (Actually, all the world is spiritual; no part of the world is genuinely mundane. But again, we are hampered by words and thus run the risk of falling into an artificial division. Always beware of words, my lambs! I know it is hard to stay awake, or to awaken for the first time, in the presence of words, but you must do your best. Thank you. Eventually humanity will move beyond the childish need for language, just as a child moves beyond its need for tinker-toys. Until then, we must work with what we have, and even refine it, because a process of refining always precedes the moment of transmutation and transfiguration.)

A true professional in any field you care to name, from farming to journalism to science to sculpture and every other kind of human endeavor, will always begin from the world of divine principals and gradually work their perceptions down into the material world, where they will devise obvious applications for those perceptions which have their origin with divine principles. A carpenter, a builder of aircraft, or any other sort of genuinely conscious professional will produce from this world of divine principles. He does not limit himself by trying to arrange toy building blocks while remaining unaware of the tremendous organization of divine principles which lies back of his experience with his building blocks, and of which those very blocks themselves are "concrete" manifestations. And as he comes to embody the energy of the divine principles--as any human being can learn to do; we are constructed that way . . . once more with the literal truth of the "made in the image of God" metaphor--he will lend his own unique flavoring, or color, to the work he does, which gives a rainbow effect to the implementation of divine principles by humanity as the race creates according to those principles in the material world.

This is the same principle we see in action with spiritual people who also happen to practice a religion. Spirituality is simply our direct awareness of our connection with God. Religion is merely the particular flavor or color our spirituality takes in a given moment. You could say that religion is one of the more obvious of many ways we may choose to implement our spirituality in the physically-visible world. And we've all experienced many shadings of the One Religion during our many incarnations here on this earth. For there is but one religion, and it was born in the misty prediluvian times of giants and great lizards. Its form always shifts emphasis to accommodate each newly-arising age, but its totality was conceived millions of years ago upon a volcanic earth young with fiery zeal. This religion contains no doctrines, only the imprint of the energy of Truth and those divinely-human psychological factors which were designed to give various unique expressions to the energy of Truth. And it is flexible enough to accommodate each newly discovered nuance of Truth as the Ages progress. It is the storehouse of the human psyche; it has simultaneously created that psyche, and been enriched in turn by the awakening consciousness it has served to help manifest. Each hand caresses the other in gentle service.

Indeed, we might say that the One Religion is simply the template of esoteric psychology.

The energy of Truth enlivens God's psyche and activates the archetypes, or Gods, stored therein, and as we are made in the image of our Holy Parent, those Gods in their turn "step down" the energy of Truth a bit so we can handle it, and serve it to us in such a way that the bit of energy delivered by a particular God activates the part of our own psyche that corresponds to that particular God so that that aspect of Truth is flavored and given motion by the God and by His or Her counterpart in our own psyche. Hence the varying dimensions of religion, and the various approaches to presenting the One Energy we call Truth.

The only genuine difference in the One Religion from Age to Age is that there are subrays of energy that reflect off of the One Religion in different combinations with each other in the various Ages of the Planet. You could say these subrays flow from Truth, but it is more accurate to say that they flow from Love, since Love is the Parent Energy of our solar system and Truth Itself and all other energies flow from It. Or you could say that the subrays themselves create the rainbow Truth that emerges from Love. There are many ways of perceiving Divine Energies and their flowing, changing relationships, so no fundamentalist can perceive these relationships until he recovers from the affliction of fundamentalism. But it must always be remembered that the most important thing we can ever acknowledge about the subrays or any other manifestation of Energy is that they have Love as their source. God is truly Love.

The subrays create and flavor the distinctions in emphasis that emerge between the manifestation of the One Religion from Age to Age through the power of their vibratory activity, and these subrays are essentially native to our solar system. Plus, occasionally a new energy may be brought into activity upon our earth which has its home in one of our sister solar systems. The strongest distinctions are likely to be produced in an Age when this type of energy-gift is brought to us. Such an Energy made Himself manifest in the latter part of the twentieth century, and those human units who were responsive enough to work with that energy and help Him implement Himself in His vibratory activity were responsible for initiating the changes in the twenty-first century which led to the creation of a world where the glory of Woman was restored, and in which full integration of the human psyche on all its levels could be Achieved by those sensitive and hardy enough to complete this Quest. In the twenty-second century this Synthesizing Energy is still working Himself out, and will continue in the full vigor of His youth for quite some time to come as He establishes His Presence fully on our earth, and eventually matures a part of Himself along with our earth.

Now, it must be noted that the Gods do not want our worship in the conventional sense; the conventional sense--as usual--simply offers a distortion of the simple truth. True worship is simply a contact with the energy of Truth as embodied in a particular God or Goddess, and the activation of that Truth with the same or similar flavoring in our own natures. Then we go about creating according to the new activation. That's all it is, and like everything True, there is nothing complicated about it. But the complicated people will want to think about this, rather than simply *doing* it! The complicated people would rather think about breathing than simply doing it, but fortunately for them, their physical responses are arranged in such a way as to force them to breathe, if they are recalcitrant.

So the Gods don't exist so we can form dysfunctional relationships with celestial beings. They don't want us to give away our power to them. Indeed, they want to help us become *more* empowered, so we can be more useful in co-creating the inner workings of God's mind with them. So they are willing to infuse us with their energy, if our motives are pure and our natures have been appropriately strengthened to reduce the possibility of insanity.

So approach the Gods in whatever manner feels appropriate to you. Be sure to always be true to your own nature, or no decent nonordinary being will want anything to do with you. Just like in the human kingdom, there are many nonordinary beings who are deceivers and aren't worth a tinker's damn. But if you are true to your own nature, your own Heart, your own true strength, and if you feel moved toward a particular God or Goddess, then the chances are pretty good that that particular Deity will move toward you. They are compassionate toward us; after all, the gods have all been human! And they don't quarrel among themselves as much as they used to, since the universe is growing more conscious of its own intrinsic harmony. Everything in nature evolves, including your favorite Divinity. And as they continue to flow and swirl among themselves, they will gracefully take one another's places in their dance among mortals, and if Aphrodite is gracefully asked, she may yield her place to her mother Ishtar for a time. For really, Aphrodite and Ishtar are both faces of the one Great Goddess, The Mother of the World . . . yet, Ishtar is also the mother of Aphrodite! Ponder on this, and sense the direction and fulfillment of the energy flow in such a relationship. Please try to avoid being concrete or doctrinaire about it. No fundamentalist finds welcome anymore in the Camp of the Gods. If Bel laughingly chooses to allow some space for Odin (and Bel is really a good-natured, happy skygod, contrary to the prejudices of some Neo-Pagans . . . among other things, he helps us meet challenges in a joy-filled fashion) then it is further evidence that all is well in God's creation of the psyche and in the impulsing of it with his Whatness toward greater evolution and Altruistic Creation.

And both Bel and Odin are faces of the Being called the Ancient of Days, and both are two of the many sons of the Ancient of Days. Each of the two Great Beings, the Mother of the World and the Ancient of Days, is both its own Parent and its own children, and is fulfilled by a certain parabolic energy relationship that must be sensed. This is still another level and type of the Secret of Proteus. I know nothing of math, but I do know how to relate to the Gods. Thus if I need to present my perceptions with a mathematical term, such a term will appear.

And no, I am not a trance channel, and if anyone calls me that I will call him an asshole. Trance channels are cop-outs who don't have the endurance to contact, or at least to permanently center themselves, on the Plane of Pure Intuition. Thus they fall back into a lazy pattern of astral pretense.

And when I speak of the psyche, I'm not speaking of the soul in its essence; you could say I'm speaking of those psychological factors (archetypes) which surround the soul, and which are enlivened by the soul. The soul is the energy of Love.

Now, everything is relative to something else. It is not possible to speak the truth in language. We can try to remedy some of the deficiencies of language by turning it against itself to polish some of its weary imperfections into some semblance of complementing reality, but any statement we make at best will still only be partially true. For example, I wrote above about the psychological factors surrounding the soul which are enlivened by the soul . . . and I spoke truly. Elsewhere I have written about the energy of God descending in a golden beam and activating those psychological factors. Both statements are true. You see, in the beginning of conscious evolution the soul irradiates and sends magnetic energy outwards to the psychological factors which surround it. Later, as the soul begins to make its approach to Liberation, the golden beam of the Monad descends and co-activates the psychological factors along with the soul. At Liberation, when all vestiges of the consciously sacrificed causal body have been swept away, that Fusion occurs wherein the Monad (which is to the soul what the soul is to the personality) melds completely with the personality and physical body by fusing itself there with the soul. The soul sacrifices its own causal body so it can be directly melded into the heart, thus serving as a sort of focal point and glue which holds the Monad in place throughout all the vehicles of the newly Liberated Human. This is simpler than it sounds, but with dualistic language, we do the best we can. Sometimes it seems that language is composed of particles of duality, which we then have to refine into something approximating the truth of nonduality. What a weird game!

Another example of the difficulty of using language is when we state a principle, then forget to mention other principles which sort of supercede the principle just stated. Actually, no principle supercedes any other principle; all principles complement each other in whatever degree of harmony is appropriate for the particular Age under discussion. An example of this type of confusion may occur in my treatment of the fact that all the Gods and Goddesses are faces of the Ancient of Days and the Mother of the World. However, this fact is only relative. It applies to our local planet, our earth. But the solar system itself directly creates Gods of a different order of magnitude, which themselves may be reflections of still greater Lives which come from who-knows-where. And some of these Gods are also known upon our earth.

So language is a very difficult medium to work in, even for the natural-born wordsmith. Communications will be much simpler and easier when the majority of the race recognizes itself on the Buddhic Plane, and recognizes the Living Symbols of communication on that Plane. Then we can dispense with language; this page could be half filled with symbols approximating their parents on the Buddhic Plane and it would say more in that half page than this book says in its entirety. And you really *could* read it at a glance!

And what if you had a book capable of holographically reflecting the Buddhic Plane in its Living Movements, with the beautiful symbols of its Livingness harmoniously gathering themselves in their various relationships? Wouldn't that be nice?

Unless you *know* your neighbor is coming from a place of glamour and illusion, it may not be too wise to disagree with him, for in this true world of nonduality, there are many levels of being right. There, the fundamentalists just went insane. They couldn't take it any more.

Well, when I get started venting about those who practice a mechanical approach to life, I generally get involved in the principles of how to transcend the mechanical approach and become one with God, as just happened. Maybe I shouldn't give a damn about these people who behave as mechanisms, but I just don't want them to keep creating suffering for themselves and for those around them who are too ignorant to know how to resist or step around a machine which seems to primitive minds to be formidable. As I was relating before I got started venting about the mechanical journalists, I had gone to the co-op's TV room to watch the news. And I was about to offer my adventure there as an example of how twentieth century people created their problems, then condemned those problems and pretended they were not responsible for their creation.

Well, the news wasn't on, but several co-opers were watching a perfectly deplorable program in which women who were billed as wrestlers abused each other in a ring before a large slavering crowd that was choking on its own fucking lust. The crowd was so sexually excited by the displays of perversion they roared in sexual greed and in the self-hate that always accompanies any sort of greed. For greed always arises from the sense of lack of an injured soul, from the sense of love denied to some part or parts of that soul. And so the soul wrongly reasons that it isn't worth loving, and thus tries to fill up the hole in its nature with one or more perversions.

Repression is a denial of some aspect or aspects of the self, and creates perversion by denying the free flow of love throughout every facet of the human being. For that which is repressed becomes a storehouse of the seething, clunky glamour of fear and hatred, since it cannot be filled up by the refreshing, flowing love which allows us to express our full humanity. Is it not obvious to everyone that that which is denied to exist is incapable of being consciously touched by Love? Are you in denial? Welcome to Club Pervert, you loveless bastard.

Anyhow, in this so-called wrestling match, one little slim girl with pigtails, who I suppose must've been eighteen in order to conform to the legal requirements, was dressed as a little schoolgirl from a Catholic junior high school might dress. She was being slung around and abused horribly by an old grey-haired woman who was built like a buffalo and whose eyes gleamed with evil. Finally this old buffalo bitch knocked the little girl on her ass against the ropes, and with the force of her huge body shoved the little girl's throat against the rope and strangled her. And this rape was being freely broadcast throughout the land. If the schoolgirl's nipple had accidentally popped out, there would have been an uproar and the network would have been chastised and fines would have been levied, because the traumatized citizens of twentieth century Amerika had been taught to hate the beautiful aspects of themselves until the beautiful aspects were corrupted. Schoolchildren would have to be protected from seeing the beautiful nipple, but it was okay if they saw the ugliness, the horror, of the old buffalo bitch strangling the schoolgirl. And they called this having a sense of values. This is what they get for worshipping a senile desert god whose aesthetic sense and oasis of self-love dried up long ago.

Because the little girl was eighteen years old, rather than seventeen or fifteen or twelve, and because her tits remained covered, she could be publicly beaten and raped by this old buffalo bitch and derided by the crowd of slavering animals who hated her--or rather, who hated the part of themselves represented by her. Because--sigh--is it not obvious to even an animal that no person who loves women, or who loves period, could ever attend such an event?

Yet most of these hypocrites in attendance and those who watched this massacre of innocence on TV would be the first to scream in hate and rage if anyone raped or strangled a little girl in their own school district . . . especially if the little girl were a member of their own family. And in their heated animal-minds they would promote the severest punishment (read vengeance) upon the perpetrator of the rape or strangulation. The truth about these self-hating animals is that they wanted to kill and rape schoolgirls, in accordance with the murderous practices of Moses and Jehovah, but even an animal sometimes has feelings for its own kin, or for those whom it perceives to be in some tribe related to its own. So they make laws against the actual rape and murder of schoolgirls to physically preserve their own dysfunctional families, but let their self-hate and outrage show as they practice soul-rape and soul-murder upon the stage by simulating physical abuse. This is the entertainment of these greedy, hungry beasts. They want to strangle and hatefully fuck schoolgirl maidens, but they do it in the abstract because they don't want to hurt a member of their own tribe. But if they had a way to *know* that neither their own family or a similar tribe they feel identified with would ever suffer abuse, they would produce activists to get the laws repealed that officially prohibit child murder and child rape. These people feed their perverted appetites on child murder and child rape, so they want the dish of entertainment served up in their electronic coliseums to be as realistic as possible, with the limitation that no physical harm accrue to their own families, even as they degrade their own hyena souls.

And even worse than their murderous quest for vengeance against a person who commits an actual physical rape, if a twelve or fourteen year old schoolgirl had a mature and intimately loving relationship with an old man, they would try to treat the older lover as severely as they would treat an actual rapist. There is no room for love amid the seething passions of these beasts, so they cannot distinguish the warmth of genuine love from their own hateful heated lusts. The only thing they do well is to project these lusts onto those rare persons who are actually innocent of lust. These animalistic "people" were responsible for creating and perpetuating the very thoughtforms and harshly-heated bestial energy that promotes the beating and raping of little girls. They are swine, completely unaware of their status as non-humans. In their hoglike fury they are too stupid to realize that humanity isn't handed to anyone on a silver platter, you have to **earn** your humanity, and that work's not for slavering sissies like these hog-people. Just because you've been handed a human body, it doesn't mean you're human. It means you've been handed the tool by which your humanity must be earned.

Anyhow, these worthless goatfuckers who promote the raping and murdering of little girls, then imprison and sometimes put to death those who break under the pressure of the thoughtforms the goatfuckers produced, are proof that repression creates perversion. They establish the energy and vision of the child-rapes in their coliseum because the naked love of Beauty has been repressed in them, thus helping establish the perversion that causes some in society to break under the burden of perversity. It should be self-evident that celebrating the strangulation and rape of young girls is not a good thing, yet these twentieth century Amerikans were very confused by their puritanical heritage. I felt compassion for the goatfuckers, because they had been taught to hate and fear the divine feminine part of their own natures, and thus those natures became repressed and perverted, and the only way they felt they could come in contact with the beautiful little girl within their own hearts was to degrade her, and pretend the self-hatred that sponsored the degradation was actually a thing outside themselves. This is the same motive that propels vice-cops when they pursue prostitutes. They want to experience the world of prostitution and feel the only way they can justify their quest (as well as not risk getting busted and socially-stigmatized for it) is to work to get the prostitutes "off the streets", a task they know will never be completed. So they have their entire careers to enjoy the fabulous world of the streetcorner hookers. Or perhaps the world of the call girls, if the appetite of a given vice-cop is a little more refined. And it has been said that most child-porn operations are run by the cops themselves, in an ostensible effort to ensnare people who like looking at such material. Sometimes the cops actually pretend to be schoolgirls, supposedly with the desire to apprehend evildoers. What do you think of cops who pretend to be schoolgirls and distribute child-porn? What do you suppose they think of night and day? Would you want to crawl around inside their minds? I wouldn't . . . but it's part of my job description, so I have to. And so far, the pay's not worth a damn, either.

Anyhow, the controllers of this primitive and culturally-deranged society encouraged violence against schoolgirls and against women in general, and created the conditions under which cops who like to pretend to be schoolgirls and distribute child-porn could actually find their mad activities respected, by penalizing the Divine State of Grace we call Beauty. The Amerikan controllers wouldn't allow beautiful nudity, or even a quick showing of one beautiful nipple, so their repression of Beauty caused the manifestation of horrible ugliness, as either they or the dark demons who manipulated them knew it would. You have to realize that black magicians have no joy in sex; they serve ugliness and bestiality, and have sex only when they can use it to produce the ugliness and despair of control and manipulation. They don't actually *enjoy* sex, and they despise that Beauty which threatens to destroy their control-ridden schemes. They are too stupid to see that their schemes actually control them, instead of the other way around. They are not free in even the remotest sense. Some people stupidly start down the path to evil because they're pissed off at God, not wanting to realize they've had thousands, or maybe more than thousands, of lifetimes during which they've made heinous mistakes, and that those mistakes *they themselves made* are the source of their suffering. God isn't the source of their suffering, but God has provided for their Redemption through the Grace that would lead them to love, if they would only work to forgive themselves and everyone around them. And fortunately, many of these dummies will wise up and return to the quest for genuine God-love before proceeding too far down the road of evil. They abandoned God because they'd been hurt somehow (actually, because they hurt themselves somehow, even if they don't consciously remember it) but then they wise up when they start getting hurt a hell of a lot more by their new associates in wickedness. Perhaps they see that God didn't create wickedness, but that *they themselves* have created a little of the wickedness that troubles the earth, and that it doesn't make any sense to deliberately (I won't say consciously, because consciousness has nothing to do with such a stinky choice) join the cycle of wickedness they at times accidentally contributed to, because *this cycle itself* is the source of their suffering! To turn your back on the Friend who has never hurt you, and try to join forces with the cycle of abuse which has hurt you, is idiotic. It makes no sense to be angry at God, who has never hurt you and who never will hurt you, and then join the cycle of confusion which is actually the source of your suffering.

So a lot of these folks come to see that the only thing that has ever hurt them is their own mistakes. And they learn to forgive themselves for those mistakes, and they see that they and everyone around them are worth saving and they leave the path to perdition and return to the discipline of questing for the divine energy of love, that quest that washes them clean of the despair of the self-loathing ones who compose the cabal of corruption.

And so that night in the TV room, watching the roaring, lusting perverts encourage the old buffalo woman to strangle the poor Catholic schoolgirl, I felt those hog-people were not worth my Sacrifice, as I lifted some of their self-created burden from their shoulders and bore it myself in order to purify and release it, that the planet might continue. These hog-people controllers and hog-people mass rapists didn't understand good, clean beautiful fun that occurs amid tinkling sweet laughter, and were so lost in perversion they no longer wanted to. And to think I'd sometimes tottered around from bearing the weight of these people's sins in my own causal body in a fashion that might have seemed imbalanced to an outside observer while I struggled to process and purify and release some of their self-generated contemptible lust.

The good news for people like me is that over the next few centuries our specialty is being phased out, and also the Vision placed before Humanity as a whole is shifting from one that utilizes cross-bearing to one that emphasizes that Pleasure born of treating oneself and others to the Sharing of genuine Beauty. The Mother of the World performs a new weave; She returns, She returns!

The genuine crucifixion of the mature causal body--or the rending of the veil of the Temple, if you like that terminology better--or the dismemberment of the various bodies, if your soul feels itself related to traditional cultures and responds to their views and terminology--or hanging upside down for nine days on the World Tree if you're a damn Viking--ultimately leads to the integration and bliss of Human Liberation (or Resurrection, if you prefer that term) true, but these lazy, stupid people practically always whored the Vision and glorified suffering for the sake of suffering. They thought themselves capable of suffering, yet never understood the suffering undertaken on their own behalf by a string of cross-bearers that began long before the hero Hercules appeared under his burden. So of course they were incapable of getting even a remote glimpse of their own potential for Liberation, or Resurrection. Ho, Hum . . . they glorified a suffering they didn't even remotely understand, as unacquainted as they were with the basics of working with their own infant causal bodies and gradually growing those bodies into a steadily maturing Altruistic Creation. But we Specialists never glorify suffering for the sake of suffering. We're here to relieve suffering, honey.

But now, because the Humanity which we Love has shewn itself to be a whore time and again, we have to consider the possibility that just as they whored crucifixion to their own undisciplined and codependent lusts, they'll also whore Pleasure and the soul-intimacy it should provide to their restrictive, hate and lust-filled animal passions, rather than climbing the stepladder of Pleasure into the heart-realm of Joy. Just as true crucifixion ultimately leads to the bliss of true Resurrection, a disciplined, loving, non-restrictive pleasure ultimately leads to the fullbody Joy of that soul incarnate and aware of its entire spectrum of being.

Most of these people never realized--or perhaps never cared to realize, since the realization would have demanded so much of them-- that crucifixion is not one three-hour event, it is an excruciating alchemical process that stretches out over many years, of which the physical crucifixion depicted by Brother Jesus is a pale and rather pleasant reflection by comparison. Will they ever know that true Pleasure has nothing to do with the personal preferences of their lusts? Damn. This fucking infantile race barely made it.

Anyway, after watching this so-called wrestling match for about a minute, I went to room 309 and borrowed Billy Ray Holtzclaw's twelve-gauge shotgun and a box of three-inch magnum shells, then went back downstairs and blew that TV to Kingdom Come. After they'd begun to recover from their shock, my fellow co-opers tried to call the cops on me, but Freud and Sue managed to convince them to hold off until the co-op could hold an internal investigation. So there was a special membership meeting where I told them what happened, that I'd simply stopped some co-opers from lustfully enjoying, and therefore promoting, the vicious beating and strangulation and rape of Catholic schoolgirls. As might be expected from the savages, they looked at me as if I were unfathomable. I guess a person who knows no opposites, and thus does not contribute to any of the world's troubles, *is* unfathomable to the savage "mind". Even though they could lustfully "enjoy" the rape of little girls, they were shocked at my method of destroying the outer form of wickedness while showering those among the wicked who still had souls with my own golden Compassion to stimulate them toward Redemption. But no civilized Human Being would have been surprised by this noble service. (Question: is it *really* possible for there to be such a thing as a "noble savage"?) Anyway, these silly twentieth-century bastards destroy out of lust, whereas I destroy out of Love. Love!

Finally, my friends got the tribespeople calmed down with the promise that Aphrodite would strip for the males and lesbians, and that I would buy the co-op two new TV's to replace the one I'd destroyed. The extra TV was placed in the dining hall, so that now the repressed and perverted violence-mongers of the Twentieth could push their disgusting trade even while the little lambs of the co-op were eating. I actually lost my appetite and couldn't eat for a couple days.

* * *

I started; the family were looking at me as if they expected me to continue my sermon, so I took a swig of wheatgrass juice and a vitamin E tablet, then continued. "Now you may ask, 'What about the various conflicting manifestations that *are* alive, that are a part of this living universe that we call home?'

"I reply to you that only illusions conflict with each other, and illusions are not alive. They appear to be a part of this universe and of us, but they are not, not really. They are the impurities that must be refined out of our personalities before we can finally step across the threshold into genuine Selfhood. They just draw energy off our true selves to cling to the illusion of life. They inhibit our journey of refinement into oneness with our True Selves, which is why as we release the burden of our illusions we begin to feel lighter and make more progress in our unification with our Self. We *have* to release the glamour and illusion for the journey to our heart to be complete. We won't finish the journey to our Selves until the glamour is gone. As our universe discovers itself, we can be a part of that process as long as we're willing to lose our illusions. In the end, there won't be any more illusions in the universe. They'll be gone. They simply won't exist. They never had any real existence, anyway. So there was never any real conflict in the universe. Soul cannot conflict with Soul. Love cannot conflict with Love. And since Love is what the universe is, and it's what we really are as sparks from the heart of the Godforce, none of us ever conflicted with each other. We're here to help each other lose our respective illusions, including the illusion of conflict. We're here to help each other progress in the school of reality, and at the end of the day we'll embrace each other as pristine souls and go home to the Heart of God."

Freud lit a cigar with shaking hands.

"My head hurts," Mimi said.

I continued. I was on a roll and I felt Amanda's presence behind me. Her hands were on my shoulders. "There are no true opposites in the living universe because the true nature of everything is love. There is only one true nature, and it is in every one of us, and it permeates the greater universe of which we are a part. And it is not opposite to itself. External factors may differ between two or more individual manifestations of the Loveforce, but as long as there is a little soul, a little love in a given manifestation, it is plugged into the greater part of itself. It's plugged into the Godforce of Love, and therefore it is related to all other sparks of love. The external factors may not realize this; the external factors may actually believe they are the entire manifestation. But they don't have their facts straight and won't until they create and successfully walk their own spiritual path and purify themselves. Ten-four.

"Peel away illusion and individuality is what's left. True individuals are not opposite to one another, they are equal and complimentary. And they relate through the heart.

"Groups of individuals linked at the heart are genuinely creative. Other so-called groups are involved to one degree or another in control and manipulation and their members are not yet fully individualized. Their pre-programmed emotional fluctuations and mental attitudes are a dark sheath over their Selves and must be released. Then they'll be true individuals and their group will be a true group. They need to lose their goddam insistence on staying centered in their small, egotistical and fearful selves and evolve into being centered in their Big Selves."

I stopped for breath, and we all glowed uncertainly at one another for a moment. Amanda was still with me and I began to see that she was always with me. And what had I ever done for her? I'd let her know the joy of my Hemingway, but did that count? I guess it was something. Amanda's nature is the nature of love; she's fully realized the universal glowforce of love within herself. She's become divine without sacrificing her humanity. She's the fully realized shadow warrior, the one who has purified her shadow of all corruption and lifted it up into the light of her soul, incorporating it into the matrix of her own personal glowforce, and experiencing the connection of her personal glowforce with the universal glowforce of which we're all a part. She is now love incarnate, manifesting through a purified and integrated outer form. Integrational magic, white magic, shadow warrioring . . . call it what you will; Amanda's the master of it. She's come home to her Self.

She's been like this ever since we met, but she's told me a little about her misspent youth. Back then she was actually something of a slut; the definition of slut is "one who fucks without love." Look it up.

And the slut is always involved in seduction. And seduction is the feminine form of rape.

There are two types of rape: there's the brutal rape practiced by brutal men and women, and there's the manipulative rape called seduction which is practiced by less obviously forceful men and women. Both forms of rape treat people as objects of gratification rather than as people to be appreciated and shared with in a climate of mutually honoring one another's Selves; that's why they're rape. Yet primitive societies usually only recognize the overtly forceful act as rape, and seldom punish the seducer--nor should they, because they aren't mature enough to distinguish seduction from sexual compassion. If they tried to punish the seducer, they would wind up throwing out the baby with the bath water.

Many times when a forceful type of rape occurs, seduction was also involved, perhaps taking the form of "teasing". Even primitive societies often have some recognition that a person who responds with sexual brutality when his passions are being toyed with isn't totally to blame for the situation. Rape is often a two-way street.

Nevertheless, a civilized person learns to have compassion for both the brute and the seducer, and to disengage as gracefully as possible when it becomes evident he or she is involved with a person who prefers either the masculine or feminine forms of rape. And of course, a civilized person can back up his or her withdrawal if necessary with fists, blade or gun.

Those who are becoming civilized are learning to discard the processes of seduction as they purify themselves of the smirking manipulative consciousness which is the sick parent of seduction. We are discovering how to *share* the emotion of sex through promoting our structured, expansive heart-consciousness throughout our natures in true fullbody fashion.

A true and honest ongoing communication as we respectfully share our hearts' light with one another helps keep us from slipping back into seduction or force by helping prevent the frustration that contributes to these negative practices. For the frustration of not being heard and welcomed for the uniqueness (not egotism!) of one's own heart and the Presence which flows from that heart is always involved in our hurting of one another.

Our dialog helps buoy us up in our hearts by revealing to the innermost natures of the involved parties that each person in a relationship is respected by the others, with this respect demonstrating as concern for the others' needs and feelings and proving itself by being willing to genuinely listen with undivided attention to the spoken heart of another. And if a person doesn't know how to listen, and isn't willing to admit this fact and learn this most necessary skill, it is grounds for terminating him or her from the relationship.

It must always be remembered that listening is only partly about the words. Yes, hearing and correctly interpreting the words is an important skill, but the complementary skill of developing the sensitivity to understand with your own feeling nature the feelings of another is just as important, if not more so. We must always be aware of the feelings of another, particularly if they are having trouble putting those feelings into words, as long as they are making a sustained and sincere effort to communicate with us. It is not fair for them to expect us to read their minds, nor should we accept any guilt for not being able to, or for refusing to do so. A person who expects others to be mind-readers is practically deliberately sowing misunderstanding and pain in a relationship, and needs to "have a knot jerked in their tail", metaphorically speaking, to start them on the path to growing up into mature adult communications.

Consciously structuring our Hearts and our relationships around our Hearts is not to be confused with control. Structuring requires supreme and automatic fully-conscious discipline; control is a product of the fear and laziness of a cave-dwelling animal. But the one who consciously structures himself has discipline as the first law of his nature.

And if you haven't become fully disciplined yet, you will Achieve this wonderful condition if you fully Work your own Individual spiritual path, refusing to be dissuaded by religions or schools or anything else until total discipline is an integral part of your nature.

The true nature of structuring is only discovered as we drop glamour and illusion and activate the divine self in our Hearts, and activate our connection with Higher Mind, which perceives the nature and direction of the Heart's structuring and which interacts smoothly as a supportive structure with the Heart's discipline of consciously structuring itself.

So Amanda's mastered the discipline of listening to her own heart and to the hearts of others. Her heart has restructured itself in the image of the Christ and is gently, with sweet yet strong energy, encouraging the hearts grouped about her to restructure themselves in the image of the Christ. For the Christ is not Jesus my Brother, the Christ is Senior to Jesus my Brother, who for a time allowed his consciousness and physical body to be used by this supernal Being. Jesus' moment of anguish is more or less accurately recorded in the Holy Bible as the Christ left him to endure the presence of his own intensified illusions and of his cherished Truths, which now required strenuous effort to reconnect with as the causal body through which he'd learned those Truths and which also carried his refined illusions was stripped away in the tearing of the sacred energy-robe, which he sacrificed for you and me as members of the angel evolution burned away all vestiges of that robe and the karma--our karma--it once contained. This sacrifice is only possible to one who has mastered sacrifice; nobody who hasn't *fully* completed the construction of their causal body through Altruistic Service can sacrifice that causal body. Only a mature causal body that has been used to the

585 / Undo The Winter

fullest extent possible for Altruistic purposes can ever be sacrificed. If some fool with an incomplete causal body tried to sacrifice it, he'd fail, and probably also retard his own evolution. There is a many-layered secret to this genuinely supreme sacrifice (I get a little tired of hearing it said that people who've only sacrificed their physical bodies have made the "ultimate sacrifice"--that is nowhere close to the truth) and only people who are supposed to know it ever can or will know it. Your turn may come, but it's not something you have to worry about. You'll know whatever you need to know when the time comes, and not before. It is not possible to put either the experience itself or the keys to the mystery in the form of words.

As I was saying, Amanda the Listener had learned to love and she'd become Love and purified the sluthood right out of herself. This gives me hope, for I've been a slut, too, and sometimes fall back into it. I guess part of the reason for becoming a Sacred Prostitute of Aphrodite is to evolve into your glowforce and leave your sluthood behind. The prostitutes say that one day a race of humans will arise that is far more evolved than the people of my time, and that the pioneering work we do in the twenty-second century, and for a long time thereafter, will prepare the way for this new race. They say the concept and experience of sluthood will be unknown to this race, for humanity will have purified its shadow and lifted it into the glowforce of its soul. Each baby born will be centered in its heart and know the Godforce from birth. All this is dependent on previous races of humans and the work we do to purify ourselves and lift ourselves up and love ourselves.

"Sonny-Bob," Freud finally said, "I know you don't use drugs, but somebody must have slipped some acid into your milk the other day. You've just had a flashback."

I smiled. "I have all kinds of flashbacks, Freud, but they are not drug related."

"Well," Mimi said, "I love Sonny-Bob. Like you've said a few times, Freud, he's atypical. But everybody in our family is atypical." She patted her belly. "I love us all." She smiled serenely and with great contentment.

"Well," Sharon said, "Sonny-Bob and I have the advantage of being from the future, where everybody talks about this stuff all the time. We're tapped not only into the moral teachings of Reagan and the spiritual traditions of Aphrodite, but also into a refined understanding of the shadow warrior philosophy, morality and metaphysics. Our shadow warrior tradition also starts in the twentieth century with seeds sown by practitioners of the original Japanese ninjutsu* arts. Despite the sheet of glamour the media tried to throw over ninjutsu, and despite the fact that many phoney ninja instructors appeared to take advantage of the glamour, the authentic art survived and was available to people who wanted to do the research to discover who was a true ninja instructor and who was a glamour boy.

"Ninjutsu is about practical no-rules self-defense, but it's also about purifying the shadow. It's philosophy and metaphysics are deep, deep. Our culture has achieved a clearer view of the shadow warrior process and most people are involved in it to some extent. Those who have finished polishing and purifying their shadows say that as long as you remember that evil is not acceptable and must be eliminated from your shadow, and that love must rule in the end, you stand a good chance of making it. Some people who don't remember this get lost in the intensification of glamour and swelling of egotism that accompanies grappling with the shadow. This is part of the purification process. The impurities in the shadow fight back. If you get lost in this way you'll have to wait until your next incarnation and do it again, and maybe then you'll get it right. But your odds are vastly improved if you remember your path must be moral and you must try not to infringe on others, and that love must rule in the end."

"Right," I put in. "Evil and confusion and glamour are like a thick crust clogging up your shadow and preventing its free and natural expression. Those things have to go! And once they are gone, your shadow will appear to you in a variety of new and pleasant and beneficial ways. It will no longer be crusty and thick and clunky, it will be limpid and pure and deep as the universe. Also, the shadow will appear in various types of combinations with the light. All are beneficial."

"One more point," Sharon said. "People can be manipulated only through their illusions. Without illusions a person cannot be manipulated. Without illusions, neither evil nor confusion can touch you."

She smiled and came over to me and put her arm through mine. "Of course, Sonny-Bob and I are both still working on all this. I think we

---

* This is not intended to constitute an endorsement of ninjutsu, but only to indicate one of the influences upon the future culture. The truth is that ninjutsu retains some attitudes from previous centuries that do not complement the direct and powerful self-expression of the future humans. However, their contributions to psychology are appreciated, and serve as one of the early influences that helped the future humans build a much more thorough psychological understanding than was ever possible to the ninjas themselves.

have a ways to go."

Aphrodite had been silent for a while. I noticed she was very still. Finally, she shifted. Her lip quivered and I thought she was going to cry. "Sonny-Bob, is my mom evil?"

"No, honey, she's not. She's very confused and perverse and she hurt you a lot, but she's not evil. She's covered with illusions and lost in control and manipulation, just like those televangelists we saw the other day.

"But she still has a chance, sweetheart. Maybe even a good chance, if she'll just get started working on herself. She can evolve into a decent person if she works hard to release the misuse of the sexual impulse to control and manipulate people. In fact, she *is* a decent person already, just as we all are. But she has to do the work to uncover that within herself or it won't shine through."

I felt Amanda's presence standing over me and embracing me and loving me. Always loving me.

"Your mom hasn't fallen all the way to the bottom, Aphrodite. I've seen people who aren't people any more because they have fallen all the way to the bottom, and your mom is a hell of a long way from that. She still has a soul; she still **is** a soul, and she deserves the love and respect and appreciation we all do. Her illusions deserve nothing, except to be destroyed, for her illusions are all that keep her separate from herself and the Godforce and prevent her from knowing she's connected to us. But I know you love her in spite of everything, for you have a beautiful heart, Aphrodite. You are the Forgiver."

Aphrodite fell sobbing into my arms, then. She hugged me to her tightly and I was honored beyond measure just to be touched by her, as I always am.

Our hearts joined and became liquid as we glowed together. I saw pieces of her mom's illusions flowing out of Aphrodite. She was processing and releasing some of her mom's karma, just as the misunderstood Jesus did for the people of his time. This strip-tease dancer knew the power of Jesus' heart and was his rightful heir.

Just as practically no Christian has ever understood Jesus, practically no Christian would ever understand Her. That's just the way it is with primitive folk. They torture or kill people, then deify them when they're safely out of the way. For today's fire breathing Christian was yesterday's nail pounding Roman Pagan. No wonder they don't want to believe in reincarnation.

"Aphrodite," and now Amanda's presence filled up the room and embraced us all, "your mom loves you. Now, her personality doesn't know that's true because her personality has never felt genuine love. But she is Soul, and as Soul she loves and appreciates you very much. If she works hard, one day her personality will be clear enough to reflect the light of Soul, and so it will finally know love, and it will rejoice in its freedom.

"Honey, all our hearts will sing in freedom someday, even some of those televangelists will eventually make it, and your mom is 'way ahead of most of those Pharisees. Your mom will join our group--she's already a member, but doesn't know it--and then when consciousness reigns supreme all of us together will comprise a singing beam of golden light that will flow into eternity. When the stars have been reduced to their atoms, our little group will go on and on forever as a beam of singing light, and conflict and all other illusions will have been forgotten long before even this.

"And so in the light of the love of our hearts, I share the breath of eternity with you." We kissed one another, and it was done.

INTERLUDE:

Buford Sargon's Log

Philosophy in the Cafe of Sidewalk Humanity

I have come to this place, this time, as an agent of lookfulness to keep Captain Sonny-Bob Culpepper out of the worst sorts of trouble he might be wont to create for himself, and a couple of times I have succeeded. I have befuddled the Marine Corps and FBI; now they think Sonny-Bob is in Toronto. I'm not sure I managed to fool that one lady from Washington, but she seemed okay . . . seemed almost as if she were on the run herself, so I'm not too worried about her.

And so I sit and I ponder, this day in front of the massage parlour which I have made my headquarters on this street called The Drag in the middle of medieval Austin.

My companions should be along soon; I can't spend all my time chasing after Sonny-Bob, so I have begun meeting with some of the intellectuals of this era in an attempt to better understand the twentieth century mind. We usually sit in front of the massage parlour for a while drinking coffee and admiring pretty girls, and maybe sometimes pretty boys, talking about matters of the human soul. Only thing is that my companions usually obscured the human soul with their misplaced logic, rather than using their logic and emotions to consciously create a rainbow bridge to their souls.

My new acquaintances were students at the great university, whose mighty campus sprawled with textbook precision just across The Drag from the massage parlour. There was an Ethiopian, a Scotsman and a Chinaman; and occasionally a Berber put in an appearance.

I hired a Corsican who lived in an old van in an RV park on Barton Springs Road to tail Sonny-Bob when I was taking my leisure. Frequently he didn't even have to leave his RV park to spy on Sonny-Bob, because the park was next door to a dining facility that Sonny-Bob frequented . . . and when Sonny-Bob was really hungry, it might take him several hours to finish his meal. So my Corsican had a pretty easy job. I gave him an urgent messaging device and he could summon me in nothing flat if Sonny-Bob threatened to make trouble for the timeline.

There is one disturbing thing I have discovered about the twentieth century mind, and that is the fact that most of the time most of the people don't want to know the whys and wherefores of their own existence, yet pretend otherwise by asking an operative such as myself to explain himself (I'll bet Sonny-Bob's run into this, too), while deceptively putting up psychic barriers to the explanation. I already knew that they weren't sincere when they asked "Why?" with regard to deviant behavior, because in order to understand "Why?" they would have to face their inner deviant, and none of them wanted to perform that holy task. But now I have discovered that even during discussions when the issue of facing their inner deviant doesn't even come up, that that same deviant sabotages the discussion with terrible deception.

For example, almost anytime a person talks about spiritual matters, or even only of religious or political matters, those around him will ask "Why?" this and "Why?" that, but the question "Why?" is just a mask for their true intentions. And their true intentions are to refuse to understand! They use "Why?" as a mask of deception to convince others that they are sincere and want to know, yet the energy they emit is that of people whose minds are made up and whose hearts are closed. As they ask "Why?" they actively emit this energy as a psychic barrier to understanding. This way they can cunningly convince themselves and others that they are open-minded, while being as closed-minded as any people who ever lived. The energy tells the truth, and the truth is that almost nobody in the twentieth century actually wanted to understand the whys and wherefores of any truly important thing. They wanted to cling to prejudice, and this was as true (maybe more true) of my intellectual friends as it was of the man or woman or sexy child in the street.

Parenthetically, let me state that as a civilized man, I have no use for the illusion of doctrine, and so am not being doctrinaire. Doctrine is the attempt of a primitive mind to crush every cycle of human experience together into one dimension.

I know there are exceptions and that a few people do have some sincerity around the question "Why?". . . out of a quarter of a million people, you might find a couple of exceptions, or near exceptions. If you find an exception, you've found a person who's standing on a different cycle than almost all of his brothers. Either that, or he's living in conscious coordination with the cycle which his neighbors unconsciously muddle thru burdened with glamour and illusion.

It should be always remembered that a statement that is true on a given cycle may not be true on another cycle. Each cycle has its own experience of truth, expressed according to its own formula, which of course by necessity is coordinated with the energy of its cycle . . . it's this coordination of a formula or statement with its cycle that produces the phenomenon of truth, because the formula provides the energy of truth a clear and accurate structure to glue itself to so that truth can now swirl in a manner accessible to the outer layers of consciousness. If a statement or formulation of whatever kind appears on a particular cycle and is not coordinated with the energy of that cycle, then that statement is not true, though it may or may not be true on some other cycle. (But keep in mind there are different varieties of truth, and the greatest variety has to do with a great pattern of energy by which the cycles are pretty small by comparison . . . though I suspect that even this great energy-pattern itself is but one cycle in a sea of energy so great we haven't yet developed the means to properly register it with our brains.)

However, all cycles are complimentary, thus all statements of truth are complementary. This is not relativism; because to be true on its own native cycle the statement must be smoothly coordinated with that cycle. Any statement that is not smoothly coordinated with its cycle of appearance is false. And to remain true, a given statement of truth has to make sure it remains on its own cycle, or perhaps on some other cycle that can adapt itself to that statement, and doesn't invade cycles which are inappropriate for it. There are no contradictions; contradictions in the world of truth are impossible. You simply must live with the awareness of cycles in order to maintain an active and refined contact with truth, and to know where another person is coming from, and whether he is in touch with the truth of his cycle. A big part of the development of post-twentieth century humans is the ability to perceive many cycles more or less simultaneously in an integrated pattern. Thus is human experience unified, though the preconceptions previously built around each cycle must be destroyed so the energy of the cycle can be restored to purity and the unification enjoyed harmoniously in the light of new perceptions which are not allowed to crystallize into preconceptions. Much misunderstanding could be eliminated from human discourse with the living experience of the awareness of cycles.

A lack of awareness of the cycles of truth is one reason the Saviors are always misunderstood by the general public, as well as by those among the general public who feel they have risen above the perceptions of the general public. For most people will take the experience of an earlier cycle that has faded away and try to forcibly and unconsciously apply it to the minister of the new cycle, all the time feeling they are as up-to-date as God, and they may even feel that the new minister is a barbarian. But they are only seeing their own reflection, as mirrored by their preconceptions. We don't live in a flat world, yet most people cultivate flat perceptions. If the public ever grows up enough to sincerely want to experience less rage, it will allow itself to begin to live with the awareness of cycles. Having said all this, let me say that the experience can't be put into words, so if you still believe words are real or if you're using words as a primary medium of understanding, you have a lot of Work to do before you are able to consciously experience the cycles. A person who is practiced can ride the cycles as though he were on a fun ride at an amusement park, traveling in a swirling pattern up and down and all around the spectrum of human experience, and of the truth of that experience. And every element of human experience becomes true, once the glamour and illusion have been cleaned out. You have to become a master janitor and complete your spring cleaning before you can enjoy the ride.

Anyhow, because the people of the twentieth century are crazy, they do not suspect their own moral inversion, and may try to institutionalize those who do not share their moral inversion. True morality is virtually unknown in the twentieth century, and is bound to be suspect if it dares to rear its head. Perhaps in addition to their cowardice, a reason they have no clear picture of accurate, love-infused morality is the fact that most of them are unconscious of the vast cycles the earth passes through in its development, and are thus unaware that the earth recently completed a great descent into matter, carrying them along with it. Thus the bulk of the race became crazed disciples of matter, rather than devotees of spirit who work to weld spirit and matter together. This fact, in addition to their laziness, explains why these people were such crass materialists in every aspect of their lives, even in those aspects they did not suspect themselves of perverting. They had not yet realized that for the earth to stabilize enough to begin its ascent on the new upward cycle toward the Golden Age, that they would have to "ground" the purity of their own deepest energy in the earth, and that the first big step of that is to work the kinks and sludge out of morality until it is accurate and clean, providing a clear reflector for the love of their hearts to shine through, and thus for their love to cement them to the earth so the earth would be drawn along toward the Golden Age of Lovingkindness, even as their shining hearts draw them as individuals toward the Golden Age.

What wimps! How could anyone fail to perceive the necessity of a clear morality undimmed by preconceptions?

Despite their arrogance over their supposedly "modern civilization", these twentieth century people hadn't changed in the last thousand years except to become more cunning in the nature of the ways they used to hurt each other. A thousand years earlier, for example, there were few, if any, laws forbidding consensual human behaviors, all of which were either regulated or forbidden in the twentieth century. While the church might officially frown on certain behaviors in the year 1000 A.D., they usually weren't illegal and you wouldn't be persecuted if you engaged in them. Yes, penalties were exceptionally harsh for breaking some of the few laws they had, but because they had few laws, most people were not at risk for arrest if they tried to learn how to enjoy themselves.

But in the twentieth century, everything except breathing was either regulated according to strict standards, or was illegal. Everyone in the twentieth century was at risk at one time or another of being arrested, usually for some "consensual crime" or other. No, in the West they wouldn't strap you down and cut off your feet with a battle-axe anymore, as they sometimes did a thousand years earlier, but there was still the same quantity of punishment in their society, if not more. You see, the harsh energy of the terrible punishments of the middle ages became less intense on a per-person basis because there were more types of crimes to punish as the centuries advanced, and thus more "criminals", not because people were any less vengeful. The harsh energy was diluted as it was spread out over a larger terrain of illegality and over larger populations of "criminals". The people were still animalistic, still just as vengeful as ever, but so cunning in their monkey practices and so sophisticated at overlooking their own chimpanzee status that they'd convinced themselves they'd evolved from the middle ages. But nothing could have been further from the truth.

The materialist will chuckle in knowing ignorance at those comments, claiming the punishments changed because of "reform", never realizing that reform is just a side-effect of the true cause which--as is always true of actual "causes"--came from the world of energy. (Please try to remember that "cause and effect" is actually an illusion and has no basis in fact, but that we are hampered by the limitations of language when we try to connect word-forms to the energy of true perceptiveness, which is why I will sometimes speak of a "cause" or an "effect". Instead of "cause and effect", perhaps we could speak of a vast energy-ocean and the process of deriving a local manifestation "down" from that energy-ocean into a manifestation that is more or less visible to the physical eye or to the inner eye of the imagination. Or we could speak of Patterning, knowing that everything in Nature is part of a vast Pattern, and that the varied aspects of a Pattern spring into being more or less at the same "time", then the Pattern begins evolving in accordance with its nature, with no "part" "causing" any other "part". And we could speak of subcycles and subpatterns within the context of the Greater Pattern. But such explanations take up a lot of space, don't they? In keeping with the overall spirit of this book, we like to focus on brevity. We do not wish to dilute our wit.)

And in many cases, an "educated" person from the twentieth century actually knew less than an "educated" person in some countries during the middle ages, especially countries ruled by Islam, which compared to Christian culture was very advanced in the middle ages, though by the twentieth century Islamic culture had become degenerate in many of the countries where it reigned. But people in twentieth century America had no idea of these things because the histories they supposedly studied in school didn't deal with cultures which were not considered to have fathered their own. Hell, they knew very little even about the history of their own parent-cultures!

Just as the energy of punishment (or vengeance) had become diluted and widespread by the twentieth century, so too had the energy of education. In the middle ages, "education" was not considered a right of the masses and few people were "educated". However, the educational institutions, especially those of an Islamic cast, sought to produce a uniform standard of excellence among the scholars. In the twentieth century, however, there was no such thing as a uniform standard of excellence. Rather, all the institutions sought to produce a uniform standard of mediocrity among the masses, and they succeeded. A person who was even capable of excellence was usually crushed by this process.

These two examples of vengeance and education illustrate the principle that when unregenerate minds and closed hearts respond to energy, they do so in a dualistic fashion, swinging from this to that, rather than learning to embrace both this *and* that, and to do so in a refined way so that punishment/vengeance becomes a compassionate justice/discipline inspired by genuine morality and full-spectrum love, and so that, for example, education becomes a sacred and highly disciplined individual Quest for illumination, neither limited to an elite nor spoon fed to masses who couldn't care less and who shit out the "education" as soon as it is administered. Ponder on this.

Twentieth century people asked the question "Why?" because they preferred the deadness of the intellect, not because they strove to reach the light of truer faculties that lies beyond the end of the intellect's tunnel. They were dishonest with themselves, and thus with one another. I saw thru their cowardly self-deception and did not respect the glamorous fear that was its foundation.

They asked the question "Why?" not in a spirit of honest endeavor, but because the fears and their instrument, the intellect, wanted to control the playing field of reality. Insisted on it, actually. Imagine: the smallest part of reality, the intellect, wanted to pretend that it controlled the whole, vast, unmitigated universe! And they had a proverb to reinforce this dishonest practice: "There's no such thing as a stupid question." Or: "The only stupid question is one that's unasked."

Their proverbs would only have been true in the case of a person who asked *himself* the questions, and then who fully *intended* to discover the answers. Intention is the tool by which creative work is done; curiosity is just a drug that mimics alertness. Animals are curious, but they haven't developed the power of *Intention*.

In the person who is becoming aware, curiosity becomes brighter and brighter thru the development of a heartfelt sincerity, until finally the curiosity is absorbed by intention.

Intention is actually an invocation of power that results from a poised awareness that totally *insists* on having what it wants, as long as what it wants is in the highest interests of manifesting the love that is parent to evolution. Intention is most certainly *not* concentration in the narrow, limited form twentieth century people considered concentration. They falsely considered concentration to be an intellectual affair, but the truth is that the intellect is one of the smallest features of true concentration.

True concentration is employed by the Mage of the future to structure that future when he arrives in the past. True concentration is the bedmate of genuine intention; intention is the invoking force, and concentration provides the holographic images that are married to that force. And those enlivened, magnetic images are the template for the future because they *are* the esoteric structuring of the future human beings. Those images draw those among current types of human beings who are ready to begin incarnations enlivened according to new energies and a new Vision, and a subtle restructuring of those human beings begins in their present lives, and works itself out as a more obvious reconstruction project in succeeding lives.

It should be obvious that this is far more than just a physical restructuring, though some physical work will be done as well. Those humans who are ready are drawn to the magnetic images created by the Mage responsible for creating the template of the structure of the future

596 / Apollo Starmule

human beings, and they begin to resonate to the tone of those images, which exist largely on the Buddhic and etheric planes, but which also stretch across dimensions of existence seemingly without number with the images from each dimension touching and complementing the images from all the other dimensions in an integrated energy-picture that encompasses every possibility for the manifestation of the human soul. As the newly responsive humans begin to sound the tone of their new "parent images", squads of devas and nature spirits will appear to create energetically tangible connections between the receptive, evolving humans and those many-dimensioned images. And these devas and nature spirits will begin restructuring the heart, brain, and all other organs in the etheric dimension, as well as in countless other dimensions, according to the template the Mage has laid down as they connect the physical organs to the new images with etheric threads. As Deva and Co. make the connections, the physical flesh and organs begin to take on the characteristics of their new etheric counterparts. Thus do living human disciples of Future begin to reflect the patterning that has been created for them.

When the ability to work with intention and concentration is perfected, the process is automatic and creates no stress for the Mage, because his personality is completely purified of that glamour and illusion that create stress by fighting for their illusory existence in the presence of the initial downflow of divine energies.

And the only way to the perfection of this process is through the Altruistic Service that supports Truth, Love, and Beauty. And genuine Altruistic Service is not done according to some formula or set of "shoulds" or "should nots". Altruistic Service occurs as an unforced outflow of the energy of Altruism, and manifests in whatever way is appropriate for the individual human being it is flowing out of, regardless of whether anyone else understands or approves the individual signature he places on the energy of his Altruism. Ponder on this.

Evolution into the kingdom of true human beings has always been dictated by a deliberate and sustained choice to become fully conscious within the embrace of the energy of Altruism, which extends itself to those who can benefit from it and are receptive to it, regardless of their station in life or whether they are considered by the wider society to be good human beings. The true Altruist is always a heretic.

If you're too much the coward to make the choice to evolve (evolution is *always* a choice!) you don't make it into the new kingdom. Anyone can make this choice and succeed, regardless of apparent obstacles, for those obstacles themselves become teachers for the evolving soul as that soul learns to Work with and transcend perceived obstacles--yet since they in reality are training aids, obstacles are actually an opportunity to learn to boost ourselves into greater Freedom! And observing the obstacles and sacred strivings of our friends provides a chance for us to further develop our compassion, though that compassion may not manifest according to the preconceptions and preferences of our hardworking friends.

Anyone can make the choice to evolve and succeed, because all souls are equal. No soul is any more equal than any other soul, and outward appearances don't mean anything. If you're a true communist, evolution is for you! And if you're into meritocracy, evolution is also for you because nobody succeeds without proving their merit over a long period of difficult labor.

The sweet Freedom we have earned always includes, as part and parcel of its very nature, compassion for those who have not yet refined the pure gold of understanding out of the raw ore of their own obstacles. Without this compassion, there is no Freedom, just a dreary semi-knowledge of himself by an incomplete organism that might once have Achieved his true nature, if only he'd had the courage to embrace the experience of compassion as a major feature of that nature.

Nobody actually sustains an eternal, lasting Nirvana without first having Achieved this compassion, and anyone who lies himself into believing otherwise will eventually be pulled back into a new round of incarnations--after possibly wasting millions of years in the smug and ignorant belief he'd achieved an eternal Nirvana.

Nirvana, the Void (I'm not talking about voiding your bowels here), is not extinction; that's a perverted belief created by ignorant people working with their masters, the wicked people. Nirvana is pure Be-ness, pure Selfhood, pure Individuality without any form. If no form of any kind is present, there's nothing to house egotism, so obviously pure Individuality can never be associated in any way with egotism. This Individuality is not diffuse, but occupies a distinct space with a certain poised focus that has nothing to do with form. The Individual's Identity remains complete, and he knows exactly Who and What He is, with no interference from anything from the world of form. He is eternal and He knows it, and He is consciousness without appearance or impediment. There is no outside observer, because he cannot be observed. He is unseen, yet aware of his own Presence. He apparently is nothing, yet he is fully himself and fully aware that he's himself, and pleased so to be. He **Is**. He is fully conscious of his true nature, with no need to reflect different aspects of that nature against other aspects to Achieve consciousness thru friction. He has fully recovered from the frictionalization of himself and become only himself, and nothing else. While enjoying purely being himself, he takes an intense interest in the phenomenonal worlds, where the strivings of his Brothers invite his attention. He is completely without stress, and completely aware of his brothers who still suffer from stress. So he takes form again, to help them Work thru their problems.

And let it be said that Nirvana is not some final resting place; there are so many levels of Livingness "above" those which have been explored even by our highest sages that there is a constant steady "climb" of unimaginable glory that, as far as we can tell, never ends. But Nirvana represents a good change of pace from universal Achievement, and once Nirvana has been Achieved it can be withdrawn into any time it feels appropriate to do so on our climb through the starry heavens. Nirvana is a good vacation destination!

Nobody can answer any question of importance for any other human being, and it is a waste of time to try. This is one thing the twentieth century taught me. If others are taking the drug of curiosity--and they usually are--they cut themselves off from developing the power of Intention, and thus don't even have the strength and integrity to accept the answer if it drops into their laps. But just like the marijuana addicts, the curiosity addicts tried to make a virtue of their drug. They ignored the nourishment that can be Achieved thru the positive evolutionary development of Intention, and continued sipping from the swirling dizzy mud of the stream of curiosity.

Twentieth century people didn't know, and apparently didn't care, that humanity had been on a cycle of descending consciousness for millions of years, and that their brains had become less active, not more active, than the brains of their ancestors in prehistory. This was not such a bad thing in and of itself, but the ignorance of it was a bad thing. The fact that their brains had become so limited had given twentieth century people a rather intensely addictive focus on the tiny aspect of their brains that remained active, and this very focus could be turned toward Altruistic Evolution and the foundational construction of new mental forms to begin the process of learning to express that energy. Thus the focus they brought to the table would allow them not only to reactivate semi-forgotten regions of their brains, but also to activate new areas which had never previously known the touch of an activating energy. And they could express these new activations more powerfully than ever their remote ancestors could.

So yes, from one angle the twentieth century people had devolved, but from another angle they'd developed a new tool which would serve as the catalyst for future evolution. So it's a matter of which angle you're looking at in a given moment that produces the satisfaction of perceived possibilities, or the frustration of witnessing the low achievement of zoo animals.

Sonny-Bob and I frequently focus on the zoo-animal aspect because it's our responsibility to do so, not because we enjoy it. So let's get back to the zoo files!

These primitive people projected the energy and attitude of the refusal to know behind the mask of the question of "Why?" This was another manifestation of a type of duality in their lives. Their whole lives were built around so many types and levels of duality that they weren't even conscious of most of them, because they hadn't evolved into a race of psychologists, or occultists, yet. But their descendants would make this historic and wonderful Achievement. I guess old Siggy would eventually have a reason to be pleased with the eventual crop that would spring up from seeds he helped plant.

As bizarre as it may at first seem, recently prehistoric people like Clovis Man (as opposed to those prehistoric people of millions of years ago that twentieth century science knows nothing about) actually usually had a more open-hearted approach to life than twentieth century people, despite the fact that the true potency of love couldn't manifest on the earth until Jesus came and grounded love in the astral body of the earth. Twentieth century people enjoyed a great advantage over Clovis Man, Folsom Man, and other fossilized characters by having access to a much more potent force of love, but most twentieth century people wasted their lives on closed-hearted competition, beating the hell out of whoever they could while getting the hell beaten out of themselves; fighting over peanuts in the monkey cage, rather than learning how to share from the bottom of their sweet little monkey hearts.

Clovis Man and other grandfather figures had more open brains and more open hearts, and the mistake twentieth century people made in looking at these fossilized ancestors was to project their own attitudes onto those relatively ancient people. Twentieth century people couldn't imagine how Clovis Man could have been happy without all the technological marvels and with hunger always around the corner. Yet rarely was a twentieth century person happy, while Clovis Man and others of a similar breed were usually happy. Despite the outward difficulty of their lives, the Clovis-folk were far more content and well-adjusted than most twentieth century people could possibly be.

Twentieth century people needed to grow up and realize that they could never understand the people of centuries previous to their own, or of centuries yet unborn, through the narrow perverted lens they viewed their own lives through.

Clovis and Co. had a more loving, developed religion (which twentieth century people would probably disparagingly call mythology, never realizing that every person *is* a myth, and that it is a great sin to cause yourself to forget that you're a living metaphor--indeed, only metaphor can be alive!) that used larger areas of their brains and they frequently also felt joy in their hearts. And they shared with no thought that life could even be otherwise. Twentieth century folk had so many emotional and energetic blocks in their various bodies that most of them had no idea how to share, or how to receive the sharing of others. For obviously, if you're going to take part in the energy which is sharing, you have to be able to experience the outflow of that energy from your own heart as you share with others, and you have also to be able to sit in quiet contentment as the energy re-pools itself in your heart and all around your body as the energy of sharing flows back upon you from the hearts of those who love you. (And to those who feel unloved, let me say that unseen in the space around you are always those who love you, even though you may not consciously be aware of their presence or identities--I guarantee you that you are always loved, and that it cannot be otherwise.) In more concrete terms--as much as I dislike such an illustration--to be a part of the energy of sharing means you have to be able not only to give a slice of bread, but also to receive one.

And reception of the energy of sharing is certainly not grasping. Every twentieth century institution fostered the attitudes and methods of grasping, rather than the merciful mutually beneficent flow of sharing. Whether dealing with a business or a government welfare agency twentieth century humans were expected to grasp and compete and conform to get whatever they felt they had coming to them, just like the animals Darwin taught them to imagine they were descended from. Yet in true sharing, a person never thinks about himself as he outflows some energy onto others or bathes in the energy they massage him with. And everything is energy, sweetheart; in reality, nothing is concrete, not even a loaf of bread. A loaf of bread is energy that has sculpted itself temporarily into a particular form that satisfies a certain desire of the belly. And soon it will sculpt itself into a turd, and maybe a bit later into a turnip!

The fact that most members of the Clovis family were spiritually more developed than most twentieth century humans is no argument for returning to the past, however. Instead, the future is built out of everything we've learned about the past, purified of glamour and touched with the energy of a new building.

In future humanity, past and future merge to provide the whole pattern of human experience purified of lust and of glamour and illusion. The future humans are the clear-hearted, open-minded people. Their skill at contacting Truth and in allowing Love to manifest thru every conceivable channel gives them the power to avoid deceit, and the intention of never being deceptive. Innocence is soon Achieved by such people.

In the future, we're optimists. Look how well we turned out! And look at the terrible odds against us in the beginning. It doesn't mean you're a pessimist or cynic when you look at the primitive culture from which your own sprang and point out its deficiencies and shortcomings; it means you're a realist who has to face the facts, no matter how unpleasant, to do your part in making the optimistic vision come true.

Even the best of the philosophers and scientists I talked to in the twentieth century didn't ask "Why?" from a desire to actually take within themselves the power of some new insight, apparently for fear that if they incorporated a new insight into themselves their personalities would disintegrate. But I couldn't see how that would've been a problem, since their personalities were founded upon illusion to begin with. Maybe disintegration would give them a chance to start rebuilding their personalities to reflect the light of Truth and Love, unless the shock of disintegration was too great and killed them.

But in the twentieth century, the question "Why?" was almost always a ruse to keep from learning "Why?" while saving face through appearing to be open-minded. The reality was that the only voice most of these people ever heard was the voice of their own self-deception. And they never heard the beat of their own heart, let alone anyone else's.

Hell, sometimes they asked "Why?" or "How?", or simply made an unnecessary and usually aggravating statement, just to hear the noise of their own false voices, never recognizing the healthful qualities of silence, and of only speaking when something of Beauty can be accomplished thereby. Indeed, the only truthful speech is speech that is attuned to helping Beauty manifest in some way, even if the speech itself is destructive. For the destruction of ugliness and the release of its fragments are necessary for the rainbow tinkling truth to manifest.

"How do you get your money, and how much money do you have?" was about the only question that most of these people were more or less sincerely interested in hearing the answer to. Only with their usual shame-faced animal cunning, they didn't phrase it like that. They usually said, "What do you do?", though sometimes they might ask questions of a more subtle leading nature. The answer to this question was important to them so they'd be able to categorize you, and to get some insight into whether they'd be able to use you in some way or other to support the value they placed on their own secretly snarling egotism. Their grandparents, as I heard Sonny-Bob say in a moment of frustration, had only just left the jungle for the savannah.

My student friends were grouped about me one day as I held forth about some topic or other under the great sign that hung alongside the entrance to the massage parlour. This sign bore a striking resemblance to Ish's Mom . . . I know because I've met Ish's Mom several times at temple picnics, and I've lain with her publicly for one of our festivals.

Anyhow, I don't remember what the original topic was, but my companions soon cut me off and began asking me leading questions so they could have the answers they felt they needed to categorize me. These questions were of a more-or-less obvious nature, because I hadn't responded to their more subtle attempts in the past. So I finally sighed and gave in; I'd rather not lie, even to primitives. It hurts a civilized person's heart to lie, but I've been told that when your heart grows strong enough and multidimensional enough, that nothing will hurt it any more. Whether or not such a strong heart would even be capable of lying, I don't know . . . but I doubt it. I suspect it would stand in its strength and demolish anything that would have it tell a lie.

"I'm an executive with a large corporation that specializes in developing emotionally manipulative images to convince people to abandon their sense of responsibility to themselves, and trust their sense of personal welfare to the emotional excitement engendered by our images, which excitement is designed to cause the people to release much of their personal income to impersonal companies, many times to purchase products that are unhealthful, a percentage of which finds its way into the hands of those of us who work for this agency," I said, with a weary sigh. But this answer seemed to satisfy them that I was a respectable citizen, and the matter never came up again.

Sometimes two or three--and once all five--of us would share a woman at this massage parlour. Plus, I was a frequent guest here without my student companions, because I was nostalgic for a place of worship. True, this temple of the profane was no house of worship, but when you're among primitive materialists, you do the best you can with what you've got. I knew that if nothing else, I could maybe impart a touch of soul-stuff to the ladies at the massage parlour, if they were receptive. It wouldn't hurt them . . . though their preconceptions might feel otherwise! For Lucille the Prophetess hadn't yet made her first public appearance among them, with her great gift of the Statement of the Principle of Sex: "Sex is the way we create our common humanity together. Sex is the ultimate sacrifice, and the ultimate sacrament. And total sex is the ultimate attainment, the ultimate communion. Sex is atonement for the sin of separation and the lie of competition."

Permit me to quote from Lucille's book *THE HIDDEN SIDE OF APHRODITE'S LOVE*: "When the Mage is having sex with someone, he sometimes will compassionately become that person, as a small etheric replica of that person which he carries within himself expands and envelops him. His lover is drawn to and served by this image of herself in a high state of glory magnetized with an infusion of the saint's love. She draws nearer to her truest Beauty and Spiritual Potential as she makes love with the Mage, perhaps never realizing she is making love to an enlivened image of herself infused with the heart of the Mage. In a form of etheric shapeshifting, the Mage becomes his lover. In a way, you could say she is spiritually masturbating herself! She is making love to herself and learning to love her highest potential in the arms of the Mage thru this etheric image, even as the two souls merge and mingle in an ecstasy of spiritual sharing. If her pure-hearted aspiration remains, she will retain a bit more of her potential when she rises from the bed of the Mage than she was capable of manifesting before.

"And the Mage's Vision of her redemption is one of the things that protects the Mage against engaging in personality reactions with her if she makes an attempt at provocation, for he knows such an attempt is caused by her suffering, and is not a reflection of her True Self--although if she does make such an attempt, the Mage will likely dismiss her from his presence in a moment of instant forgiveness, though the perfected image of her he carries will always remain, and has an evolutionary effect on the woman he loves even when it's not directly energized by total attention. Indeed, this image and the love which animates it may sometimes stir up the glamours and illusions of the woman the Mage serves as the image and love present themselves as replacements for those glamours and illusions. So if the woman is having a personality reaction, it is likely caused by the surfacing and possible release of the glamours and illusions which cause such reactions. The Mage knows this, and therefore remains imperturbable, though in his imperturbability he will never put up with any shit, because he loves and has compassion for himself, which is why he has love and compassion for his lady.

"And love knows no limits, for the ability to express love is an outcome of total discipline, and such discipline is totally moral. So the Mage may have many lovers and wives, and if he does he will carry a relatively perfected image of each of them to be energized by his heart and sexual nature working in union for the service of his ladies.

"Each person has many layers of self, and every layer *must* be healed. These layers come up during the healing process, and the Mage lets them flow into whatever form they need to take for the benefit of his lover. A crucial point that must *never* be forgotten is that the Mage doesn't *cause* these layers to appear and doesn't force any particular shape upon them. If he did, that would be almost a form of black magic, in addition to doing little good and possibly much harm.

"Rather than try to direct or control the process, the Mage allows the process to unfold on its own, like a beautiful flower which can only come to sunny physical soils drenched in shameless passion.

"This process can unfold because the Mage knows neither repression nor perversion, and has allowed his whole being to be infused with love, which itself is only possible in a being who has cleaned out all attachments to repression and perversion from himself. As this love joins itself to his clean passion, it becomes that fullbody compassion which brings a powerful Grace to the world and allows it to be born anew.

"One of the levels that may often come up as the Mage is allowing etheric shapeshifting to unfold is that of the inner child. The inner child of the natives of primitive cultures such as that of twentieth century America has always been traumatized, because the nature of the child is love and joy, yet that nature is violated as soon as the child is born with a slap on the rump and a kidnapping which isolates the child from her Mama in a ward sterile of love.

"And the trauma continues to unfold with undisciplined, unloving restrictions placed upon the child's true nature throughout her childhood. Her passions are denied; her sexuality is denied. The holiness of her body is denied, as she is taught by the example of her parents and the media that the body is just an object to be used to wheedle other material objects out of men who allow themselves to be strung along by her fading beauty . . . because beauty does begin to fade from the very first moment it is abused. So before it fades entirely she knows she must make a wild lunge into the life of a man who is financially well-off, riding her departing beauty like a surfer crazed by crack cocaine as the cycle of addiction to manipulation continues. Then she more or less becomes the material property of this man, though she likely will also continue to manipulate other men to one degree or another. After all, she must stay in practice so she can impart these degraded skills to her children.

"So we see how an innocent little child becomes a frozen machine, or a furtive and cunning little animal trying to devise ways around the restrictions of her personal life in order to pursue the lusts engendered by those very restrictions, rather than cheerfully demolishing all restrictions in her Path with the bold and powerful Heart of the Warrior/Healer/Sage in order to prepare the way for a clear passion and a true, innocent love. And as the traumatized little wretch tries mechanically and furtively to derive some satisfaction from life, she usually will be striking out at others who are seeking satisfaction in a manner different from her own, in a pitiful attempt to ingratiate herself and her pursuit of her personal lusts with those who consider themselves authorities and wield what they consider to be power. Yet only an animal seeks a personal satisfaction; an authentic human being seeks an impersonal lovingkindness that will help in the healing of those she touches, rather than further inflame the deranged lust learned in the dysfunctional style of childhood promoted as the norm in twentieth century Amerika.

"How can such a pervert be healed? And there are so many of them in primitive Amerika, almost everyone would qualify for the diagnosis.

"Well, one way the healing occurs--assuming the lady is genuinely ready to accept healing rather than personal gratification as a part of her sex life--lies in this love-infused, etheric shapeshifting of her lover, the Mage. And sooner or later, the image of her inner child will appear and hold itself around her, and it will be incorporated into the energy-bodies of the Mage. This image will be the purified image of her inner child, alive with untraumatized possibilities. This image will be unwounded, healthy and whole in every conceivable way as it holds her within itself under the guidance of the Higher Mind of the Mage, which cooperates with her own soul's desire for total, fullbody, fullpsyche healing.

"And often enough the smaller image of her naked, untraumatized inner child will rise up to the surface of his consciousness and enfold him until he becomes her inner child. At this point, if his lover is completely enfolded as well, you have her inner child making love to her inner child, and being taught to fully love itself and express itself thru the power of the expanding, stable heart of the Mage. It presents a picture of two little twin girls making love to one another, and certainly nothing more beautiful, true or wholesome could ever be imagined! Yet really, there is only one little girl who for the moment has etherically engulfed two forms, while allowing those two forms to appear somewhat separate though identical, and is allowing a strong, loving heart to shine out powerfully from her as she nurtures herself toward full healing. For all healing is ultimately self-healing.

"It should be evident that only the cleansed pedophile can help facilitate another human being toward self-healing, which is one reason there are so many third-rate healers in the world. Most so-called healers are afraid to face their innermost shattered self and fight the glamours and illusions that prompt toward hurtful behaviors out of that little core-self, that inner child self. They fear to clean out, and then embrace, their inner pedophile, which on a deep healing level becomes one with their inner child and so is indistinguishable from that inner child. The Sacred Marriage must be made thruout the psyche for the person to be complete.

"Making love to the inner child of another requires, of course, that you be able and willing to make love to your own inner child, for there is a holy playground where all inner children are one, and not one of them can ever be neglected. And during the lovemaking where the inner child is healed, the Mage's profound Heart has expanded so much within the breast of the etheric mirror of his lover, and within the breast of the etheric inner child that has enveloped his lover, that it directly infuses most of the body of that inner child and radiates throughout the rest, and indeed expands outward so that it becomes the biggest aspect of that inner child. And when that Heart touches and is joined with the child's naturally luscious pussy, total self-compassion is Achieved, which can then be extended to others. This is the self-compassion the Mage has Achieved, and is the quality that allows him to help facilitate at the full spectrum, total healing of his child-lover, who may be formally considered twenty or thirty or fifty years old by the outside, non-aware world of unredeemed Frankenstein's monsters who by denying the sexuality of the child, deny their own healing.

"Is it not obvious that we live within a great energy-field of sex, with the waters of our own sexuality lapping up against the sexuality of everyone else of every age group, and that their sexuality continually washes up against our own?

"Thus must we build a consciously sex-based society to replace this unconsciously sex-based, and therefore wounding and hurtful, society. We must build a society in which the physical emotion of sex serves as a cup, a sacred chalice, to catch and give powerful form to the love that flows from that other sacred chalice, the heart.

"This sex-based society will focus on the Beauty of Sex, not upon ugliness or pain, for ugliness and pain stem from attachment and lust and greed, not from that pure gentle love which is open to all who have freed themselves from the burden of attachment and realized that self-esteem which refuses to be degraded in any way, shape or form.

"And the people of this society will know that the warrior's sword must be used to uphold Beauty, and to protect the lives of those who are consciously pursuing Beauty. In such a society, the sword will *never* be used for political purposes, for politicians and their ways will be rapidly vanishing as enlightened warriors realize that few things are uglier than politicians and their misuse of the sexual impulse to carry out their frustrations in the sordid arena of war.

"Beauty and sex, and the Beauty of sex, will be the features of the new society. Sex will be restored as an artform and taught graphically and consciously and with much love and passion in the schools, and will no longer be just an unconscious leisure activity and unconscious motivator of every other activity.

"And we must learn the technique of turning aside any energetically dirty sexual waves that some other person who is not entirely clean may send at us, while still being able to tune in to that deep, emotional-spiritual self, that deeply compassionate sexual self which lies beneath the dirty water and which only wants to be a part of the spectrum of the energy of Sharing, assuming there is something there within that person we feel connected with in a non-attached, authentic, significantly loving way. This technique can be learned, but not taught. Each disciple of love must learn this technique for him-or-herself as a part of their own Path to wholeness, and to protecting that wholeness from potential sources of contamination. Of course, some people have so much horror built up around their sexuality that you can't contact the real person that lies in the dirty coffin, so you must learn the wisdom of refusing intimate contact with these people. I'm not talking about people who are obviously afraid of sex here; the people I'm talking about may be less afraid of sex than many other people, but they have an aura of horror and subdued viciousness around them which makes them dangerous to approach energetically, particularly by an open-hearted person of innocent intent. So take care of yourself always and avoid such people; remember always that in the game of love, your first big Achievement is to learn to love yourself, and to take care of your heart and your emotions, nourishing them with whatever they need for expansion and increased radiance, and avoiding anything that might puncture and deflate them.

"You must learn to always refuse to share your sacred sexuality with anyone you don't feel connected to and affection for even if that person is a Master of the Wisdom and is perfectly clean and openly loving, but it is especially necessary to learn to apply this lesson of refusal to those who are so polluted that it would require an act of will to move toward them. Sex is not an act of will, sweetheart; it is an act of affection and lovingkindness and pure emotional and physical sharing as the floodingkindness of the sacred Heart of both partners renders each of them pure and whole and impervious to the rusting of conscience.

"But introducing an act of will into the sacred environment of sex injures the conscience of all parties involved, and reduces sensitivity to love and to the depth of soul that is possible to genuinely loving human beings.

"Is it necessary to state here that conscience is the Voice of the Heart, and not an affair of the intellect? The Voice of the Heart is an energy-impulse from the Soul, not a string of verbalizations. Anyone who wants you to try to verbalize your conscience to them is really trying to siphon off your energy so they can manipulate you. Too bad it was illegal to shoot such people in the twentieth century.

"The reality of the coming society is that the field of love in which every human being has his home and connects with most powerfully thru the heart, will be fully merged in a well-defined powerfully compassionate form with the field of sexual energy in which we all dwell, thus consciously creating one field where there were two.

"And from this one field will emerge the fully-conscious play of the human subconscious, as for the first time that subconscious will be given full rein to be fully itself, for it will have been cleared of that glamour and illusion that always distorted its play in the past, and it will have learned conscious, true and accurate morality from the part of the brain responsible for moral Achievement.

"Finally, a beam of Higher Mind from the Buddhic Plane will connect with, then fully fuse with and ultimately absorb those disciples who are stepping forth into Liberation, and then as Liberated Human Beings they will take their places as Master Psychologists, and as the first-fruits of the candidates to fill the role of the newer type of the Master of the Wisdom, whose disciplined love is much greater than all who have walked before him along the Path of Masterful Achievement.

"To experience sex in its highest form, the disciple must be completely free of attachment while being capable of maintaining a warm, compassionate connection. Connection is of the world of clear warm love, whereas attachment is from the world of greasy shame-faced emotional lust, or of greedy mental acquisitiveness, so connection must never be confused with attachment. True, complete connection free of personality concerns can only be Achieved by a Liberated Human Being, thus only the Liberated Human Being can fully experience and enjoy sex, as well as understand its role as a part of God, and of the Nature which God has chosen to manifest."

"Every person has a community of lives within them, and these lives take on the forms and ways of those we meet in our day to day activities, including such recreational activities as reading novels or watching movies. So it behooves us to be careful in selecting our entertainment. 'Garbage in, garbage out' is a statement of truth regarding the community of lives we carry within ourselves. If we put psychic garbage into those communities, those lives within us will reflect that garbage, and will prompt us to create still more garbage in our outer lives. Often, our dreams are merely a visit of our conscious selves to the world of the tiny lives most of us unconsciously carry within us. The phrase 'tiny lives' is not a metaphor, except in the sense that everything in the universe is composed of the stuff of metaphor. The tiny lives within our internal communities are as real as the people we interact with in our outer lives. And we ourselves are tiny lives residing in community within one of the energy centers of a great celestial Being, a Being whose dreams are always lucid. It behooves us to cooperate with this Being and allow Him to dream us into purity. He is our Gulliver, and we are His Lilliputians!

"Our tiny lives are the stuff of legend, just as we are the stuff of legend for the great Being who dreams us. And all legends, of whatever size, are true. All legends are reflections of other legends which belong to the one pattern of metaphor. Our lives are the stuff of metaphor!

"So which part of the legendary world of this great Being are you residing in? If you are living in a psychic garbage dump, you are living in a part of the Being which no longer reflects His outer reality of splendor and which He is actively working to clean up. He'll help you clean up your neck of the woods if you let Him, but He probably won't help you according to the dictates of your preconceptions, so you'll save yourself some trouble if you release your preconceptions.

"Dream lucidly, and know yourself as Creator! But create always according to love, or your internal world will cause you external problems.

"The Mage has mastered the tiny lives that reside near his soul, and uses them productively in service . . . indeed, he cleans them up and makes them relatively perfect if they are willing, but those who are not willing may be demolished. This is a part of the Mage's own Path of

Spiritual Achievement. He has the right to take care of himself by demolishing uncooperative elements within himself.

"As those tiny lives learn the ways of Service, they respond automatically and productively to the Heart's Direction of the Mage, and make themselves in the image of his lovers, or of those individuals he has chosen to help in some way apart from the bedchamber. Remember that anytime the Mage, or a person of total Buddhic consciousness, performs a given act, it does not occur in the same way as an act performed by anyone else. For the Mage, each act is automatic and purposeful and fully conscious, for he is impulsed by the Will of God. The Mage's life is effortless, and is far more potent and productive in Service than anyone's life who is still efforting. But you don't stop efforting by trying to stop efforting. You stop efforting by going deeply into the nature of efforting and using your efforts to Achieve, and then to become totally reflective of, the Buddhic Plane. A while later, you'll realize that effortlessness has occurred.

"The Mage no longer has willpower and is not separate from whatever he happens to be 'doing'. He's now just an organizing, creative principle who resides in the Pattern of Livingness and relates particular parts of the Pattern to one another and to the Pattern as a whole. He used his willpower properly in Service to contact and then to fully absorb and reflect the potency of the Buddhic Plane, and the willpower ultimately vanished to be replaced by the Will Aspect of Divinity, which impulses the Mage as the wind impulses a sail upon a timeless sea."

Is it not evident why women are so respected in the future? For only a woman could have been wise enough to experience and formulate a statement of the truths contained in Lucille's writings. Only a woman can experience Deep Compassion. No man can understand these things, unless he becomes a woman.

Yet the woman must become as the man to give practical, useful form to her native compassion.

So respect the supreme Beauty of a woman's body, for it is a direct reflection of her soul, and really it is a part of her soul. And it provides the spiritually-eager male a direct gateway to an appreciation of his own feminine side. If a beautifully-souled woman has a beautiful physical component to her soul, it is because she earned it thru leanings toward Altruism in previous lives. If an unconscious woman has a well-structured body, the body was given to her so she could begin to learn proper motive as a base for using the body to express the soul. She cannot be considered beautiful, or even slightly attractive, regardless of how well her outer form is structured unless she learns to use that form to reflect her soul. If she doesn't learn her lessons to a sufficient degree she will probably misuse her body thru mistrust of her heart, and thus will probably not be given such a well-structured body in her next incarnation.

When the Beauty of a woman's inner nature is reflected by her outer nature, such perfection is Achieved that no man can stand in her Presence without awe and humility for God.

Woman is always the nourisher; and nourishes every worthy perception of the male. And those perceptions would never have been brought forth to begin with without the woman.

Woman is the Creator; man is just the instrument who submits himself to that which he loves for the joy and privilege of being a part of the creative process.

Beauty is Truth, and Truth is Beauty. Thus the woman is the Truest thing of all. The journey to Truth must lead thru the woman's gate, and this is the sacred interpretation of Ishtar's Gate. For the ancient Babylon which was entered thru Ishtar's Gate was the home of great wisdom, and the Mother of the World gave birth to this city and promoted her Cause of Creation there.

As Truth flows from Love, the journey thru the Truth of the Beauty of woman leads inevitably to Love.

The woman's power is great; thus she places herself in danger unless she develops the redemptive power of Altruism. Her capacity for spiritual Achievement is unequalled by any being anywhere, thus must she always be honored as the Mother of Truth and the Gateway to Love and eternal Livingness.

The Beauty of woman contains a certain bright, deep intelligence that manifests most profoundly when married to her heart. This particular type of glad-hearted, twinkling Beauty most often occurs when she meets a man she's fond of or sees a man she's attracted to. This type of Truth, of Beauty, dissolves restriction in a flash, and is the proof nature offers as to the unnaturalness of a forced monogamy.

The true Beauty of woman is beyond belief when the eyes are first opened to its perception. In her Beauty lies all strength, all power, all nourishment of goodness, all steady-hearted love or devotion, all compassion. And my words do not do it justice.

All quickness of thought and all depth of intelligence belong to the woman. Hear her when she speaks!

The Mother of the Druids was a steady, radiating source of warm nourishment, and provided the livingness which infused their religion. She was an example of chivalrous womanhood, and to simply touch Her robe was to kneel in a marvelous wonder of humble inspiration that made you glad to be human. The Mother of the Druids was the Daughter of Ishtar!

In woman quickness of thought is married to depth of feeling. In man there can be a certain steadiness, but his only way to Wisdom is to walk the Path of his mother and daughter, and submit to their inspiration.

Many women, while displaying no obvious signs of the energy of Intention, nevertheless are very deep and aware spiritually, the fact of which led me to study their spiritual practices more closely. I'm not talking about some isolated religious practice set aside for a specific time; a spiritually aware woman brings deep energy and insight to everything she does, whether the act itself be considered great or small. Indeed, no act by a spiritually aware, soul-deep woman is small; every act by such a woman has great significance and imparts a touch of Grace to the world.   And I saw that often when a woman chooses to not limit herself with curiosity, she displays a certain purposeful inquisitiveness, which may be as potent an invoking force as Intention. In fact, it may be said that this purposeful inquisitiveness is the feminine form of Intention, which itself contains a masculine potency. The delight with which the woman pursues her purposeful inquisitiveness gladdens the perceptive male heart, and is one more reason the male loves the female.

The Future belongs to the woman and is propelled by her chivalrous Heart; we have entered the Age of the Woman!

The truth of human nature, and especially of woman's nature with her unusual ability to cross all borders of despair and provide spiritual nourishment with the refreshing stillness of her creative Altruism, were at least partially understood and *lived* in certain ancient cultures. But neither the men nor women of the twentieth century understood the sweetest, most divine truths of their own human natures. They used sex primarily as a means of gratifying bestial lusts and to hurt one another by making the emotional and spiritual nourishment of sex contingent upon an agreement to be manipulated and used in various ways. Thus was their sex almost devoid of emotional and spiritual nourishment, just as their breakfast cereals were usually stripped of physical nourishment. No wonder they wanted to protect their children from sex!

Their fond desire for their children was that their kids would somehow become cunning enough (perhaps by osmosis from their parents?) that they would be able to brutally manipulate themselves into a supposedly monogamous marriage arrangement with someone of their own class, or of an allegedly "better" class. Yet when you go to the zoo, you don't think of "class" as you watch the animals dazedly brutalize one another, do you?

Anyway, since they correctly viewed their own sexual lusts and practices as exploitative and hurtful by definition, they naturally wanted to "protect" their kids from sex. They were too dim in both heart and mind to consider the possibility that if they cleared out of themselves the attachments that bound them to lusts and degradation, and then allowed their emotions to be flooded by the love of their hearts, that the gentle compassion that resulted could harm no one, least of all kids with whom it was shared, and would benefit everyone, especially those kids with whom it was shared, for it would prove to them their own worth as full-spectrum, wholebody beings whose needs deserved to be met from the very beginning, so that it would never occur to them on any level to besmirch their perfectly natural *human* desires with the caged fecal corruption and frenetic frustration of zoo-animal lust. For the caged monkeys throw shit at one another, don't they?

The time to begin teaching a child the joys of pleasure is when he is in the womb, his spirit warmly sharing with his parents as they lie with one another in gentle passion. And this genuinely loving education must continue from the moment of birth, with the child delivered into a loving, nourishing environment that offers no shock of displeasure. Water birthing is a great option, and is usually the method employed in the future. Sometimes those joyful devas called dolphins are invited to lend their gentle, playful insight and energy to the process.

I remember at my own birth, I came out swimming with an official escort of protective, warm-blooded dolphins. I guess that's why I'm so well-adjusted. I'm far too well-adjusted to do the Work of the Saviors, because I knew joy and oneness with all of existence from the very beginning.

Sonny-Bob's birth is rumored to have occurred in Death Valley as a result of a car crash. It is said he hadn't been too eager to leave the womb, and was a little overdue anyway--maybe he had some idea of the role he was to play in life, and didn't want to face it. Well, who would?

Anyhow, from birth onward the child must be taught by the example of his parents that pleasure and joy are holy, and that his body is holy and is an extension of his soul. And that to preserve the pleasure-giving, pleasure-receiving capacity of the body, he must protect his emotions by refusing to allow anyone to abuse his body or emotionally manipulate him. There are no Gandhi's where I'm from, because as people started becoming civilized they quickly lost patience with emotionally manipulative people and the long-term damage caused by such creeps. So the emotional manipulators soon mysteriously disappeared, and there wasn't sufficient interest to launch an investigation.

As the child from babyhood learns to appreciate his genitals and the rest of his sacred body, and learns the skills to protect himself in case he meets a potential abuser, he experiences a continual stream of joy and confidence in his own Achievement. He learns to spiritually Achieve from birth by Working with the materials closest to hand; namely his own body and the joy it can bring when touched by himself with love, or touched by a non-seductive, non-manipulative person whom the child has personally approved for the experience. If you think this is impossible for children, think again. Children who are raised as monkeys behave as stunted monkeys; children raised as genuine human beings will behave as what they are by identifying with a pattern that leads to the discovery of their true humanity.

The golden age of a child's life occurs from conception until about the age of four; the silver age lasts from about four to seven. During this time some of the child's karma from past lives can be offset, because until the age of seven his emotional body doesn't fully settle around him with the load it carries of previous experiences. For the emotional body is a big part of the soul-body, the causal body, and disappears in the flames of Agni during that process that once was called the Crucifixion Initiation, by which the Initiate steps into Liberation from the hold of matter and learns to infuse matter with the love of his own sweet, powerfully-beating heart. (Yes, he still has emotions, but no emotional body; thus his emotions are undisturbed by the lusts and delusions--the glamours--that accrue to the emotional body.)

So if the child builds Beauty and pleasure and joy into his personality and physical body, and into his emotions as well, from conception to the age of seven, the presence of the pleasure and joy amid the Beauty of his life will drive some of the old, negative karma out of his emotional body as it begins to settle around him. And the Beauty and pleasure and joy he has with happy discipline (not thru the denial of ugliness, but with a shift in emphasis of perception) built into his bodies will also attract more experiences of Beauty and pleasure and joy, which themselves will help drive away thru the power of vibration some of his old hate-filled karma even after his emotional body settles around him. Thus he is ultimately led by his own happy soul to a fullbodied, total expression of that love which he *IS*, as the joyful experiences of his life provide a happy conduit for his loving, fragrant soul to expand and envelope him.

But these twentieth century people denied sexual pleasure and joy, and that love and compassion which flows from fully-functional non-lusting sexual contact, to their little ones, with the result that the kids not only reinforced the negative karma already stored up in their emotional bodies, but even added more negative karma thru the sticky "power" of negative emotion--of hate and lust and the terror of being loved, or of learning to drop the crusty shield of negativity to fully and genuinely love another. So the kids born into twentieth century households had far more negative karma to overcome than those born a couple of centuries later. They did not know how to share, and tried to turn every moment of their lives into a financial transaction.

It may be that after a few thousand years we will see babies incarnate without an emotional or causal body, because they experienced Liberation in a previous incarnation, and because the new environment they incarnate into is too loving and joyful to provide the materials for an emotional or causal body. For such a body, even when it has been properly refined thru spiritual Work, always has some glamour and illusion, thus some lust, until it finally vanishes at the Great Renunciation of the Crucifixion Initiation upon the tree Yggdrasill. (For Christianity and Paganism are the same thing, aren't they? In the early days, converting to Christianity was simply the switching from one brand of Paganism to another, requiring about as much soul-searching as you'd do before switching to a different brand of beer or mead. For the Great Mother of all true men nurtured original Christianity, just as she nurtured Druidry, and just as she nourished the spiritual seeds planted by her son and husband, Odin. Christianity experienced its initial success because it was a Pagan religion, but then strangely it threw away its natural attractive power for the human soul-nature as it restructured itself in the stale, smooth-talking, flag-flying image of an empire that couldn't be "successful" without the threat of the burning-stake, just as the Amerikan Empire couldn't be successful at promoting its religion of "democracy" without the threat of bombs and massive numbers of troops. It is always entertaining to perceive how many of the twentieth century Christians viewed ancient Rome with a sense of abhorrence, yet went to great lengths to create exactly the same type of culture in their own society. For this primitive Amerikan society differed from ancient Rome only in a few surface details . . . but the Amerikan Christian was always too lazy and fearful to look beneath the surface of his own consciousness and perceive the empire-supporting activities of his own inner pervert.)

So if a baby who once Achieved Liberation in an adult body is born into an environment where no causal body can be supported or is necessary (for the mature causal body does provide some protection against the worst glamours, even as it reinforces the more "spiritual" glamours), he will be free of sin from the moment of conception and will remain free of sin throughout his entire life. So the future will see the full recovery of humanity from the original sin of the lie of separation.

Of course, if parents are going to bring such a Liberated Child into the world, they must first experience Liberation themselves. A Liberated sperm cannot shoot forth from the penis of the father, and a Liberated Child cannot crawl forth from the womb of the mother, if the parents themselves still are subject to the limitations of the glamours and illusions born by the causal body. If parents do not insist on putting themselves thru the crucible of spiritual travail, they have no moral or spiritual right to ever have children.

No physician of the future would ever touch a baby without authorization from the baby, or the parents would probably kill the physician in legal defence of their infant. And no physician of the future would ever touch a toddler without authorization from the toddler, or the toddler himself would probably kill the physician.

You have to show a child that authority over the sanctity of his own body means absolute authority over who touches that body; if you make exceptions for doctors, lawyers or Indian chiefs a hole is punched in the child's sense of his own Destiny and the damage is incalculable. Twentieth century parents didn't know these things, though a few of them had relatively good intentions. But the result of their ignorance was that they raised zoo-children, rather than real children. They raised children that would toe the official line, and only rattle the bars in a manner prescribed by the officials. Real bar-rattling is purposeful and happens in the moment, unhampered by anyone giving a damn for the opinions of officials, or for the preferences derived from those opinions.

As Sonny-Bob often preaches: "Ye have heard it said that opinions are like assholes--everybody's got one. But I say unto you that opinions are like assholes, except that they're less useful than assholes. Opinions come from the world of belief, and belief is composed of the heavy grey energy of illusion and is the enemy of Truth, and therefore is the enemy of that Love which is Truth's parent. Belief is the opium of the soul, honeys. And opinion is the opium delivery device which every unregenerate human uses to push his own specific brand of opium down the throats of his neighbors, who are almost invariably stoned on their own product, and thus can't take any more. So in the end, everyone is left with whatever brand of drug product they started out with and the same sort of haze remains to block the correct use of their mental faculties. Do you see the uselessness of opinion now?"

So the so-called "leaders" of what passed for societies in the twentieth century were nothing more than monkey-children who had assumed adult bodies; they were not in touch with Truth and Love. So no civilized person would give a damn about their opinions, or about the low-grade delusion of the stale energy of opinion at all, though a civilized person might trample those opinions underfoot from time to time, while providing an example of a person who has no belief or disbelief or opinion, and who is constantly merged with the flow of Truth and Love from God's Heart. A civilized person would not only rattle the bars of the cage anytime he damn well pleased, but he would blow the cage itself to Kingdom Come by devising his own methods of destruction so that God's love and the love of the human heart could occupy the space formerly occupied by the stupid cage of preconception and belief and opinion.

These twentieth-century people were fond of "problem solving", conveniently unaware that there would be no problems to solve if human beings were completely dedicated to an honorable and compassionate sharing. Problems can only arise in a "society" which is not heart-dedicated to sharing. They did not understand that sharing is the key to Paradise, nor did they understand the implications of Paradise itself. Ponder on this. And they were fond of telling other people how to solve their problems, both small and great, rather than contenting themselves with simply experiencing the overall pattern of which the alleged "problem" was a part, and allowing that pattern to consciously rearrange and harmonize itself under the organizing principle directed by their own minds without the distraction of control and manipulation, or of words, which themselves are agents of control.

They were so fond of problem solving, as egotistically identified with it as any chimp in a researcher's lab, that they subconsciously felt they continually had to create new problems, and they were good enough at this to keep themselves in a perpetual state of alarm.

They continuously rattled the bars of their cage, but never approached the matter of escape with alertness and the mad, poised dedication of implacable Intent.

So they made false and unnatural problems around sex, which gave them all sorts of unrecognized and therefore unsolvable emotional problems, which moved them into violating their human natures with the degradation of cruelty, which they were most happy to apply to anyone they regarded as a heretic against local customs.

Had they roved throughout their psyche with an aspiration toward innocence, they might have ultimately needed fewer drugs and less Cinemax and religion. But they aspired to lust and control, not to innocence.

Thus some of their sexual practices involved the open aggression of outright control and degradation, even as they punished those with innocent hearts for violating meaningless laws. They penalized people for trying to be happy, in direct violation of their own Constitution. They did not have enough sense to perceive the obvious truth that restriction of happiness does nothing but create misery, or that the problems and alleged problems their restrictions were supposedly meant to curb or solve only grew worse or broke out in new forms as a direct result of the restrictions. Thus they were cannibals, eating one another's souls without any appreciation for the flavor. So we see that cannibalism can sometimes be a negative thing.

Sonny-Bob's poor sweet heart was so affected by all of this that once I found him standing on a table in a restaurant shouting about how twentieth century people were nothing more than a bunch of addicts, making their score thru streetcorner pushers who've glamourized everyone's eyes with law degrees. "Oh, if we just pass one more set of laws," Sonny-Bob railed, "eventually everything will be all right, but it never is all right, it just gets worse and your humanity becomes more divided against itself because of these very laws, you law and disorder bastards. You get exactly the same results from your practices that any other sort of addict gets, and just like any other form of addict, you actually feel that maybe your next fix will be perfect, and then after that perfect fix, that perfect new law that has just been passed, you'll quit using the drug of control and manipulation and cruelty. Idiots!"

Sonny-Bob repeatedly snorted and scraped his foot against the surface of the table, which I feared would shatter under his profound weight. He looked like a mad bull in Spain about to chase the throngs down the street in that crazy festival they have. "You spend about a third to a half of your time working, one sixth to one third of your time sleeping, and the rest of the time you're furtively trying to have a good time and punishing those who pursue happiness in too obvious a fashion. Plus, even though you only sleep a few hours a night, you're actually asleep nearly a hundred percent of the time, you . . ." At this point, the table did break, and left Sonny-Bob sitting stunned on the floor. After a moment he staggered out, and I paid the restaurant manager a couple of thousand dollars not to call the cops.

* * *

But we mentioned sharing, a topic which cannot be overemphasized, so I want to offer a couple more brief observations on the subject. Before there can be true sharing, the family must be restored to prominence as the foundation of society. And every real family is an extended family; government redistribution of wealth cannot benefit the extended family and in fact, makes the people more reluctant to form true families.

Indeed, when the family is finally seen as containing all the real wealth in the world, a profound change in human livingness will occur and the use of money will lapse into being an occasional thing free of the use of force or manipulation. Thus will the dominance of government and business yield to a genuine consciousness of Kindred which respects the rights of all families everywhere to form their own unique cultures. And there will be very little crime.

Universalism is the death of the family; new types of humans can grow into their natures, and older types can remain true to their own unique established natures, only when free from the intrusion of universalism. I'm sure most of the Cherokee and Choctaw would agree with this statement.

The only true society is the society of the extended family; yet such families do not deny the intrinsic Brotherhood of Humankind. They recognize the value of other families or clans, and of the individuals of those families. Yet each family's first duty is to its own Kin; as each family takes care of its own Kin a rosy glow of lovingkindness spreads throughout the earth, and no one ever wants for love, or for basic necessities.

Sharing is an artform learned best in Family.

These primitive people also created etheric replicas of one another, but they didn't do it consciously or with love. And as often as not, their replicas were degrading, and made it more necessary than ever for the Saviors to get involved. If you make a degrading replica of your "lover", you are reinforcing your own degradation, and if your lover's consciousness accepts the false replica, then when she leaves your bed or dungeon or wherever the falseness occurred, she will be a little more degraded than she was before. The karma for both of you is horrible to contemplate. To misuse sex to hurt someone, even in "play", is to insure that you stay bound to your unconsciously created cycles of suffering that have limited you for uncounted lives, because you're still promoting and more or less deliberately wallowing in the energy of those cycles. The only potential exception to this principle is if you consciously recognize the negative energies you and your "lover" are carrying, and use your degrading practices with the pure motivation of releasing, rather than reinforcing, those energies, knowing that when the process is far enough along, you'll want to stop those practices altogether and learn to release the rest of that old energy in a genuinely loving, self-honoring and compassionate way. But this is highly risky, and most people are so weak and lie to themselves so much about their motives and evolutionary status, that probably very few individuals would actually be able to turn the practice of degradation against itself and use it as a tool for the permanent release of perversion. (Note: I'm only talking about run of the mill degradation here such as that practiced in many twentieth century American homes with whips and handcuffs; some practices, especially in some of the degraded Tantra schools of India, are so perverted I will not mention them directly, but will only say that the purpose of such practices is to kill the soul of the "disciple", not to free him, and that it would be impossible for anyone to develop any release of perversion by following such practices. The only reason some people are insane enough to try such practices is that their chakras are spinning reversed, producing an outworking of perversion most heinous; or their auras are so weak they are easy prey for the perverted type of "guru", or both. Only learning to accept Beauty into the lifestream can save the soul.)

It seemed that the only good news about the twentieth century was that there had been a "sexual revolution" in the 1960's, but even this good news had an underside that stank. For most people loosened up not out of moral conviction, but out of the weakness of a hypocritical lust. Their churches were progressively growing more "liberal", with people engaging in more flexible behaviors than in the past, and frequently lying to themselves to make themselves believe they still upheld the same standards (really, non-standards) they'd always claimed to adhere to.

To become more flexible thru weakness is more of an abomination than being a rigid fundamentalist with at least a trace of strength. God doesn't give a damn about anyone's convenience and never has; God requires strict honor and discipline and total truth with oneself before anyone in this juvenile detention facility is sufficiently rehabilitated to approach the Throne of Goodness. These twentieth century hypocrites were not good, honey. They were not good.

NOTE IN A BOTTLE TO ISH

Sweetheart, as a fully-civilized woman you've taught me much, but I'm finding there's perceptions that can only be delivered thru contact with the souls of barbarian princesses

In addition to the ladies from the massage parlour, I've also become acquainted on an intimate level with three other women during my stay in medieval Austin.

The first is fifty-eight years old, with long blonde hair and the traditional blue eyes which are often issued to natural blondes.

The second woman is a high school student, sixteen years old with an incredibly bright, open heart. She too has blonde hair, but keeps it short, and also has the traditional blue eyes--very bright and deep blue eyes that I could get lost in for days without a break, if her parents hadn't insisted she go to school every day.

The third woman is unshaven, semi-washed and spends most of her time in the woods rooting around for nuts, berries and herbs, some of which she sells to the Wheatsville Food Co-op. She has fairly light eyes, I guess, but I never have quite been able to tell what her hair color is, due to the quality of her lifestyle.

She has rings on her grubby fingers and toes, and several piercings, some of which seem to me to be in slightly odd places, but I'm conservative by nature, so who knows. I guess she must be around seventeen or eighteen and drives an old logging truck, which she's somehow managed to keep together with a copious amount of bailing wire and more mechanical genius than I've ever had. She's made a big tent out of canvas and secured it to the back of her logging truck and that is where she lives.

She told me she'd dropped out of high school a while back, but I've never found out quite how long ago "a while back" is.

She seldom wears clothes except when required by law, and sometimes not even then. Most of the time the cops leave her alone, but she got arrested once and I got her out of jail . . . whereupon she immediately removed her overalls, beneath which she had no shirt, panties or anything else, and threw them at a cop. He just laughed and handed them back to her; not all cops are bad.

I've been flowing and swirling among and between all these women for several months and tasting the feminine essence, which must be pure genius, for no artist of greatness has ever been inspired by anything but the feminine.

But there has always been something about these three twentieth century women that disturbed me, and it has taken me many nights of contemplation to discover what it is.

The first woman, the fifty-eight year old, has a happy nature designed for sharing, and she has several male friends in addition to myself whom she is happy to share with, and I've always been glad to see such civilized behavior. She has a big, bright heart somewhere in there among her ample breasts, and a fiery sexual nature that is more married to her heart than you usually see in the Twentieth . . . she should be perfect, so what is wrong . . . ?

The second woman, she of the sixteen summers, has an even brighter heart than the fifty-eight year old; her heart shines so brightly and her smile is so pure I sometimes wonder what I've ever done to be privileged to gaze upon such holiness. And if anything, her sexual nature is even more fiery than the first woman's, and it is also married to her heart, perhaps to a somewhat greater degree even than my fifty-eight year old friend. She also shares her body and the purity of her emotions and soul with another lover, a fifteen year old black kid she met at school. Her parents, who are upper-middle class white-eyes, know about both the black kid and me, and whenever I come over for dinner I sense they are uncomfortable about the two of us. Still, they are more emotionally resourceful than most twentieth century parents, having explained both the sex act and the emotional, spiritual nature of sex to their daughter at a young age.

They also taught her about birth control and disease prevention, and while a number of her more ignorant friends and acquaintances who have less loving and less responsible parents became impregnated with the urgent seed of youth, and sometimes initiated the tragedy of abortion or caught a sexually-transmitted disease, my young lover always insists on condoms *and* spermicide. She is fearless, and the quality of her fearlessness gives her heart a firm ground on which to stand. So while her parents growl a bit at me and the black kid, they wisely and lovingly never try to interfere. For even these primitive parents can see *and feel* the fantastic quality of their daughter's heart, and I think they realize on some level that the worst crime they could commit would be to muffle that sweet, beautiful heart. So they don't.

Now then, what to say about my dirty girl? She of the woods, as skyclad and hairy and odiferous as a Neolithic woman with no knowledge of Cosmopolitan Magazine and Victoria's Secret?

I enjoy watching, touching, fondling, and licking and sucking those big, rich, pierced titties of hers and I feel a certain nourishment therefrom, but what of her heart? Where is it? Lord have mercy, it has not yet activated itself.

My Neolithic woman has some brightness (and brightness in the eyes is a prerequisite for a woman who seeks my affections), but she obviously also has a shadow side as big as her bright side. And she's aware of it.

My fifty-eight year old lover also has a shadow side, but it's not immediately evident. Still, after a while, I determined its presence and size relative to her brightness. I found that there was substantially more brightness than shadow.

With my sixteen year old lover, there's hardly any shadow at all; she is almost all brightness manifesting as a radiant fearless light of young juicy womanhood which wants only to touch others with body and soul and help them heal. I guess she is a forerunner of the sacred women who will begin to emerge with selfless compassion in the twenty-first century with the aim of bringing humanity home to its heart.

So what is it about these three women that disturbed me? Eventually, I perceived it had to do with qualities of brightness and shadow, of light and dark, and of the qualities in a woman that are necessary for the full development and emergence of her Compassion.

I perceived that in my fifty-eight year old lady, that she has never really come to terms with her shadow . . . she appears to be on the verge of being ready for serious shadow-work, but isn't quite there yet. The result is that while a lot of healing light radiates out of her, it's a light more from the surface areas of the heart. Compared to most twentieth century women, she is astoundingly beautiful in the healing light that emanates from her; yet the deeper chambers of her heart remain to be activated.

She isn't truly compassionate, though she is more loving than most women of her time; but to become totally compassionate the deeper levels of your heart have to be activated and allowed to completely infuse your sanctified personality and your physical and energy bodies. And this can only occur if you completely clean out your shadow, purifying it totally of glamour and illusion, of egotism of every kind, of the lie of separation and the shit of competition that continually works itself out of the asshole of the lie of separation to hang ugly and stinking over our humanity.

So this is what has disturbed me with my fifty-eight year old friend, because as long as there's one tiny bit of impure shadow that has not yet been absorbed into the light, the light will feel some need to run from shadow, and the shadow will sometimes behave in a contrary fashion toward the light. The result is that someone will get hurt; yes, my fifty-eight year old friend is generally a healing influence, but to a slight degree she contributes to the cloud of glamourous hate and hurt that circles the earth in the twentieth century. She's very free with herself sexually and easily and naturally fulfills her own desires, while sharing the light of her heart with others. She feels she has a right to be free sexually, and she is correct in this, but I know there's at least one minority she doesn't care about, some group that can be picked on and she won't care, because the polluted aspects of anyone's shadow are caused by the rage and hate picked up in childhood when real pleasure and real love are denied, and these negative emotions feel they have to have someone outside their host to attach themselves to in order to suck enough energy up to continue to survive any efforts their host may make at self-purification, and also to make their host believe her problem lies with someone outside her own unclean causal body so that maybe her efforts to purify herself will be half-hearted.

Who can say which group or groups she's unwilling to love or defend; maybe that artificially manufactured rapist, that legal fiction known as the "statutory rapist", or maybe there's some ethnic group she's concerned is a threat to her way of life. Which type of group she will never speak up for is not important; what's important is the principle that her shadow isn't yet fully integrated into her light, with both merging into her heart in a multidimensional holographic fashion producing a multidimensional holographic expansion. Thus she cannot know or radiate that absolutely total fullbody, fullsouled compassion for all beings that would see an end to all suffering. In short, she's selfish-- though she is also generous, and loves to share, compared to most in this century. She is a superior sort of woman for the time, and I love her.

Essentially the same thing bothered me about my sixteen year old lover, except that with her the amount of unpurified shadow is so slight it can hardly be located--and is so subtle I've never been quite sure I actually *have* located it.

With my dirty girl, the problem is very different. Her heart isn't active at all, and her shadow is *huge*. But in a moment of revelation, I realized that she may have been given the greatest spiritual gift of all, because her shadow is so huge she will have no choice but to pay attention to it when she gets down to spiritual Work; nobody can suppress a shadow that huge.

And in the moment of perceiving this, I also saw that her spiritual Work had just begun, and that I had been privileged to be a part of the catalyst for it. I was there when the first-ever ray of light broke from her heart, and I was the one it shined upon. And she smiled at me in a way she never had before, and a soul-gleam of awareness just a-borning came into her eyes. I marveled at this moment, but we said nothing, we just were quiet together for a time.

I say that my woods-woman may have been given the greatest spiritual gift of all because the shadow is one of the major factors--may in fact be the most important factor--in developing that full-hearted, many-chambered compassion that belongs to the Bodhisattva. With a shadow as huge as hers, and with the fact that she will have no choice but to Work with it, she has the excellent opportunity to eventually--after a long, long time and a lot of hard Work--undergo that holographic expansion that provides total knowledge of the heart as a multidimensional soul-home that stretches across all dimensions and all eternities. As a result of the gift of her huge shadow, she will eventually come to know all deep-dimensioned chambers of her heart, and her heart will become beautiful and compassionate with the knowledge. This young woman with twigs in her hair will eventually be a fullbodied, total-souled healing influence that God will be able to use as an anchoring force for compassion. What greater Destiny could there be?

As for my other two ladies, I can't quite tell whether the reason they have smaller shadows is that they've done a lot of spiritual Work in past lives, maybe releasing a lot of the shadow's glamour and becoming a bit more integrated, or whether their lesser shadow-presence is a more-or-less natural phenomenon that isn't really dependent on Work.

But now Ish my darling, as I find myself quickened by the memory of your lovingkindness, I perceive in this moment as I write this letter to you the coordinated pictures presented by Higher Mind that prove to me that yes, one day they too will become fully compassionate, and thus fully human. The younger one is already really close! (Again we see the maturity of youth, and I hope it is not stunted and twisted into a distorted, competitive reflection of itself when she enters the "work-farce" and is subject to the repeated abuses of alleged adults who never even Achieved the faintest glimmer of true soul-maturity and who "suck dirty donkey dicks", as the saying goes.)

Obviously, my ladies will complete this process of becoming fully human the same way everyone does; they will finish purifying their shadows and allowing the golden light of Monad to touch and infuse both the part of their causal body they have regarded as light, and the part that has, before this infusion of Monad, been obviously dark. This more obvious, "coarser" phase of blending shadow and light precedes the occult "drawing up" of the shadow fully into the golden light of Monad. (But let's not get fundamentalist in interpretations or in the descriptions of "sequences" or in our choice of words; we are after all trying to use the clumsy tool of linear language to describe a multidimensional process. There are "stages", or "initiations" in evolution, but contrary to what many believe, they are not a linear process . . . they are more of an expansion, but even this word is insufficient. For the sake of our own sincerity, and thus of our integrity, we must try to be as accurate as we can in our depictions, but the important thing is for our depictions to serve to *quicken* others into a contact with Higher Mind and with the compassion of the heart. It is not our business to indoctrinate people. It is our business to offer them a taste of Electricity.)

Then my ladies will consciously and with deliberate intent sacrifice the causal body, which after being subdued and more or less "killed", will be released and burned away by Agnisuryans for a few years as devas and other nature spirits reconstruct their physical and energy bodies in a more purified, unified and powerful form than could have ever occurred as long as they trudged around with the burden of the causal body. In other words, they'll reach Liberation!

But what every newly Liberated Human Being discovers as this Fourth Initiation, the Crucifixion Initiation, is concluding is that there is a completely purified and integrated aspect of the sacrificed causal body that remains. This purified and integrated aspect, which knows no opposites and whose formerly "light" side has absorbed the Monad's light and whose formerly "dark" side has also absorbed the Monad's light, is usually referred to as an "accumulation" and is drawn up into the heart, which then expands into many holographic chambers to house all sub-accumulations found in the one divine accumulation called the Liberated Human Being. (Yet many of these heart-chambers remain empty, for the heart must be free to expand into any dimension at any time, including those that have not yet been consciously experienced. Also, these accumulations of purified selfhood are made of pure light, and so must not be confused with such heavy and tawdry sensations as accumulating "knowledge". Accumulating "knowledge" injures the heart, but accumulating Self lightens and liberates it.) For we must remember that the causal body has served us and built itself for many, many lives and that it contains accumulations from all those lives. As we finish purifying and then sacrificing the causal body, we find that a tiny purified sub-soul remains from each of our incarnations and is integrated into our purified souls proper. And each purified sub-personality that went with each purified sub-soul also remains as a lens to focus that sub-soul thru whenever we desire to do so. Thus can the Liberated Human Being etherically project himself in any of his soul-personalities to where that soul-personality can do the most good for humanity.

My description of this process is imperfect, because words don't go where this process goes. But I have done the best I can.

As Lucille The Prophetess wrote in her *TREATISE ON ATONEMENT AND RESURRECTION*: "God never expected perfection of me. I had expected perfection of myself, but that was as a result of moral energies and challenges stored up in my causal body. With the finishing of those challenges and the release of the last vestiges of my causal body, the moral energies are completely purified and find themselves integrated with my Heart, and I find a loving God who never expected me to be perfect and who is always satisfied with me just as I am. And so I thank God for God's own nature, which makes rejection of me impossible."

Anyhow, I'm happy to see that all my ladies will one day become anchor-points for compassion, and I know they will be happy, too, to perceive their own greatness, but I also know that the only way to perceive that greatness is to become IT, and when that point is reached no egotism is left to interfere with greatness, or with the appreciation thereof. So my ladies will have to become totally compassionate before they can totally appreciate themselves.

What a wonderful universe! For genuine compassion includes all within its embrace; no one is ever, or could ever be, left out of the embrace of this compassionate universe.

I never did see holographic pictures to inform me whether my two blonde ladies had mostly purified their shadows and integrated them somewhat in previous lives, but I bet they had. I feel that the ultimate arrival of their full potential will occur as they purify what shadow is left and integrate it and their light into their Monad with its previous accumulations. Then their holographic hearts will appear, and they will know true, total compassion that never compromises with anything. For true compassion provides the only stable ground on which to stand in a universe which is formed of the very essence of the goodness of compassion. Only the truly compassionate can stand steady and know the harmony of ALL THAT IS.

I was especially fond of one young prostitute, an eighteen year old philosophy major, who serviced men between her classes at the great university. She laughed when she told me of the professors and students who would lie with her naked in the parlour, then pretend not to know her when they'd meet on campus. One of her philosophy professors came to her regularly at the massage parlour, then studiously ignored her in class, even when she'd raise a hand. But she always got "A's" on everything she turned in, even if all she turned in was a blank sheet of paper with her name on it!

I sensed the touch of sadness behind her laughter, and wanted to comfort her, but I had found that most of the women who worked in the wenching-houses of the twentieth century were in denial about the degree of their sadness, and were not into deep comfort--they didn't trust it. It was as if they believed that no one could care enough to actually want to join hearts with them, and they felt their hearts would be stabbed yet again if they began to relinquish their shielding. And you know something? They were probably right. They'd never met a civilized man until I came along, and had no way to know the difference between myself and the other primates.

Yet I sensed that under the centuries of grief this young woman carried in her heart, that there was a great light that would glow profoundly one day. That is how I managed to survive the impact of her grief on my soul . . . I tuned into the light at her center, and allowed it to dispel the gathering grief. And I perceived that in my tuning into her light, that it was intensified within her breast, and that not only was the grief dispelled that had been on its way to me, but some of the grief that had decided to stay resident in the cloud around her heart was also dispelled. During such moments, she would usually release a sincere laugh, whether I'd said anything funny or not, as a shaft of sunlight broke thru the dark cloud of grief and sailed warmly out her heart. This made me happy, for she was as one of my own daughters.

Sometimes the young lady would ask me "Why?" this, or "Why?" that, and I was as gentle with her as I could be, considering how tired I was of the insincerity which usually lay behind that question. But I did sense that with her, there was less insincerity than with most primitive people, so it gave me hope that she might be capable of developing some sincerity. (But I wasn't going to hold my breath . . . I was the only example of absolute sincerity and total civilization she'd ever encountered, and only an ignoramus would trust this temporary contact to completely undo the savagery she'd been raised with, and which lay all around her every day in every environment she found herself in.)

But I loved her with a profound love, because no civilized man can fail to love any woman in whom he's seen some light. It is impossible not to love such a woman.

When I first hired her for a blowjob, she wore a manufactured grin and took me into a room that reeked of celebration--no, I mean sterilization, excuse me for looking at every encounter as a chance to celebrate a young woman's heart--anyhow, she took me into an antiseptic room and ordered me to undress, then to climb onto a stainless-steel table and lie on my back. Then she turned a hose on me and rinsed me off, despite the fact I'd bathed just before I left to visit this massage parlour. Having rinsed me off, she clinically examined my nuts and penis. I am not nearly as imposing in that department as Sonny-Bob, but I've never had any complaints, so I wasn't worried about being unfavorably compared to anyone. I suppose she was looking for disease, but of course found none. A man with access to medical nanos has no disease.

Civilized men don't usually fall prey to nostalgia, but I think that first time, when I chose her from among the lineup of prostitutes, I felt some nostalgia for one of my daughters she reminded me of. My daughter and I had frequently shared a bed, and much more than a bed, so maybe that was one reason I was so attracted to this young prostitute. Or maybe it was the soul-light I sensed within her calling to something in me it recognized and wanted to touch that brought us together. Or maybe it was both.

Anyhow, I would have tried to adopt her if I had been a native of the Twentieth. As it was, the energy of my soul did adopt her in an attempt to quicken and comfort her. She truly was my daughter, in the most important sense.

The universe is not linear and is not composed of building blocks, yet this is one illusion that was so ingrained in the twentieth century West, and in those cultures the West had economically conquered, that they could not conceive even of how their own creative process worked. Creation is a highly disciplined affair, but the discipline involves being able to catch the creative energy as it flows toward you from many directions at once and relate the various directions through coordinating the beams of energy and forming them into swirling new combinations. There's nothing linear about this, and no building blocks are involved. Yet even after a moment of supreme creation, the twentieth century artist, inventor, or what-have-you would usually go back and rationalize how the creation had happened in order to make it fit Isaac Newton's preferences, rather than accepting the gift of creation on the terms of the universe which so joyfully presented the gift. Thus was the very act of Creation whored to linear, block-minded explanations.

I'm adopting the tone of my Revered Ancestor, Sonny-Bob Culpepper, and Working on a Sacred Tract which I hope will someday lie with his own in the Great Library at Gaffney. In addition to promoting freedom from block-mindedness and textbook addiction, and from that factory-style of architecture that proceeds from misperceiving the world as a place of building blocks rather than a place of flowing multi-hued spherical swirling patterns of warmth, this Tract may also help explain Sonny-Bob's fiery Presence on the Earth. Here is a portion of that Tract which I feel may be applicable to the current discussion:

Since time does not exist, there is no timeline. The perception of a linear world is nothing more than a cheap trinket of an illusion purchased at the glamorous carnival of self-deception. There are no building blocks, except in the playpen of an infant who is too immature to consciously immerse himself in electricity.

Since there is no time and no timeline, Sonny-Bob and myself obviously could not travel "back" thru time. What we have actually done is to reposition ourselves in the planet's causal body. Just as an individual human being has a causal body (or soul body), humanity as a whole has such a body. And the planet has a causal body composed of all the points of consciousness which it has Achieved, as well as the impurities that remain to be purged. Humanity's causal body is a part of the earth's causal body, just as the earth's causal body is part of the solar system's causal body, which itself is part of the galactic causal body, and so on. Sonny-Bob has come to save the planet by saving humanity's causal body, for that body had become so distorted with the impurities of glamour and illusion that it threatened to collapse on itself into unimaginable hell. Sonny-Bob actually experienced that hell himself on behalf of those who created it, and who thus far have been too lazy and cowardly to create their own spiritual path to redemption. These people created more hell than they personally could withstand, but enough of their sweet, buried little hearts cried out for Atlas that Atlas was successfully invoked, responding grudgingly, as always.

So Sonny-Bob appeared as a self-aware sponge, scrubbing a portion of the dirt and decay out of humanity's causal body, then releasing it into the golden light of God for a dissolving or a transmutation, as God sees fit. Yet if these people continue to insist on remaining buried in the lazy cowardice of stupidity, they will turn Sonny-Bob into an idol to justify their continued crimes, rather than accepting His sacrifice and service with glad and humble hearts prompting them toward the redemption of trueness they must create within themselves to relieve the Saviors of a burden not their own. The fondest wish of every Savior I've ever spoken with is to be unemployed. "Let this cup pass from me," and all that rot.

Sonny-Bob has come to scrub away the greasy, shame-faced dirt of humanity to give this infantile race yet one more fighting chance to begin to mature. This is necessary not just for humanity's sake, but also for the kingdom of nature spirits and devas in all their many elven variations, and for the kingdoms of plants, animals, and minerals, for these have their own types and qualities of consciousness and contribute mightily to the overall experience of their mother, the Earth.

For humanity, while not being the only spoke on Earth's wheel, and perhaps not even the main spoke, is significant enough that the near-total spiritual collapse of humanity has created waves of distortion and disturbance which threaten to bring the collapse of the Earth's causal body, and thus the physical destruction of the Earth. For the causal body of man or of celestial body must not be destroyed until it has been perfected and used up in the nondualistic service of lovingkindness and the man or celestial body stands on the threshold of Liberation. The person who is actively in full consciousness walking across that Threshold can and will sacrifice the completed, used-up causal body, but the unconscious sacrifice of a causal body by one who is unable to accept the jolt of the charge administered by the Liberator's wand means the death of the organism, for the electric charge that prompts the organism into final Liberation will not be administered to one who is not ready, and without either the fusion with Divinity that occurs at Liberation, or a causal body to sustain him, any organism will die.

Hint: no person who still has any attachments or who still participates in the dualistic style of manifesting emotions is capable of approaching the Threshold of Liberation. "Either-Or" must go; the "peace movement" must stop creating war, and the war movement must stop spawning the peace movement, for one obvious example. For to demand peace is to insure that war will occur, because those who love war will feel threatened by the peace movement and begin to demand violent solutions to world problems; and to pursue war produces the emotional reactions in a percentage of the population that insures that a peace movement will be spawned. Like two warring trout from hatcheries they imagine to be somehow different, the peacemongers and the warmongers are actually both working together to prolong the agony of the earth by insuring the cycle of vengeance, of duality, that creates that agony is continually fueled by their undisciplined, unconscious personality and emotional reactions. Stupid. Until each can embrace the other in that total love that reverences all spectrums of available human experience, each will contribute to vengeance.

Sometimes it is okay to go out and kill folks, but it takes a mature and compassionate consciousness to know when it is appropriate to serve God and Humanity in this way. This level of maturity cannot be taught, it must be **earned**. And it is okay to protest an unjustified or an unjust war. What is not okay is to try to stupidly dam up the flow of destructive energy, as the pacifists want to do. You have to learn to direct that energy in concert with compassionate objectives, not dam it up. If you don't use that energy intelligently, it will seethe against itself and finally break out in an unintelligent, explosive fashion where more destruction will be created than would have occurred if you'd used the energy to compassionately destroy obstructions to evolution to begin with. God was not appealing to pacifistic stereotypes when She appointed that Divine Minister known as the Angel of Death, who in reality is a jolly, happy, compassionate, warmhearted Being who serves the cause of Love and of Creation by removing crystallized barriers to compassionate expression. The Angel of Death smiles and laughs a lot in the performance of his glad duties, whether those duties involve the death of a worn-out mental or emotional or etheric form, or whether it involves the destruction of a physical body or bodies. But this Angel sees things as they truly are, not thru the narrow lens of attachment to the past used by the unregenerate humanity which He serves. Until Humanity learns to cooperate intelligently and compassionately with the Angel of Death, suffering will continue.

If you don't use the destructive energy intelligently, destruction will occur anyway, but it won't serve evolution, it will serve evil. So pacifists are unwittingly working against a compassionate evolution and serving evil, along with their brothers in corruption, the warmongers and politicians. All these immature types promote the continuation of the cycle of vengeance that has plagued the earth for millions of years. Abel is always trying to manipulate Cain and bind up his wild heart with platitudes and sticky emotionalism and a forced correctness that has nothing to do with Nature, and Cain is still on the prod with his primitive club, trying to bash Abel's brains in. Both brothers are preternaturally stupid.

Vengeance is the problem; war or peace per se aren't the problem. The genuinely peaceful warrior can kill or die with a glad and calm heart, untroubled by the illusions that accompany the sense of duality. He can also give a massage or healing energy to those in need of such services . . . he will understand with his whole body how to shift between obviously healing energy applied with warmly nourishing and totally-accepting love, and that destructive energy which heals with implacable intent by removing obstacles to healing, whether they be tumors of the human body or those tumors of the earth's body who perhaps may wear human forms, but who are evil, and therefore not human, in their consciousness. But primitive peacemongers just don't get it, and thus continue to create war, a large percentage of which is probably unnecessary.

Pacifists are as immoral as Nazis, and if the world ever contains a critical number of pacifists, the rise of Nazis is assured; duality is *always* immoral and non-spiritual! Immorality breeds more immorality in an "opposite" form; up through the early twenty-first century, humanity had never been moral.

The fluctuating "morality" of primitive people is a horizontal phenomenon; but True Morality is a vertical phenomenon encountered when a person cleans the glamour and illusion out of his causal body and is approaching nonduality. As nonduality is Achieved, it is seen that all horizontal phenomena actually reflect different facets of all other horizontal phenomena; therefore, what you really have is a whirlpool of mutually-supporting faces of Life within each Individual who never know war or restriction or the hurting of one another in any way. And all these faces of Life are essentially the same in each Individual, though they will appear in different combinations from person to person, and will also be activated by different combinations of the seven major energies, or rays, of our solar system from one person to another. The person who has Achieved this awareness is the only truly-peaceful Individual; all others who "try" to be peaceful are just stoned on the drug of sentiment in one or another of its variants. And stoned people never contribute to peace, they just contribute to the numbing of certain aspects of human nature . . . which will later have to break thru the numbing in a burst of wild violence.

Sometimes it is moral to kill, sometimes it is moral not to. It is *always* moral to love and serve people, whether they are people you kill because they're blocking evolution, or whether they are people you serve with sexual healing or in any other way. Morality is the most outward form a Divine Principle can take in terms of understanding with the "lower", or rational, mind. And anyone who has contacted and become a part of the Divine Principle of genuine morality knows it is necessary, and sometimes even desirable, to kill. Any idiot should be able to see that you can't block a Divine Principle for long, even in its outward form of morality, or an undisciplined explosion will result in which people are hurt or killed without rhyme or reason, but the pacifists aren't nearly as spiritual as their mad delusions, born of a repressed human nature, would have them be. They would shit themselves Divinely if they had any idea that their karma is just as bad as the karma of the warmongers, and sometimes maybe worse.

So we can object specifically to unintelligent and uncompassionate destruction, but to protest destruction generally insures that there will always be outbreaks of destruction of the unintelligent, uncompassionate variety. To protest the implementation of any moral or spiritual principle, such as the compassionate delivery of Death to those who would block the flow of love in a society, is to tell God how to do Her business and requires a hubris that can only be attained by submitting oneself to the abject slavery of an unregenerate consciousness. This is what we call being ruled by the Dweller on the Threshold, which is that distortion in the causal body composed of one's accumulated fears and the subservience and manipulation that goes with those fears. When the causal body has been fully cleaned up and all distortions ironed out of it so that it is a near-perfect reflector of love, the Dweller will have been transmuted from a likeness of the Devil into a likeness of God.

The "left" and the "right" are held together by the strings of self-righteousness and denial. They are like two brothers trying to drown each other, each refusing to release the hatred (and remember that *all* hatred is self-hatred) that would allow him to escape the murky waters of an unintelligent death.

The moderates may be even worse, because their objective is moderation, rather than Truth. No person who seeks moderation has ever Achieved Truth, and no such person ever will. The Achievement of Truth will always lie beyond the capacity to endure of the moderate person.

The moderates want to predefine Truth, at least to a degree. They want to hold it captive to their moderate appetites. When a person tries to define that which he has never experienced, he guarantees that he will never experience it. To be satisfied with a definition is to be satisfied with an illusion. One may try to describe Truth, but description is not definition. Description is meant to turn people's attention away from some of their worst illusions while perhaps offering them a quickening toward Truth, a reorientation of their perceptions that may provide them with a boost toward that which they seek, if they are actually sincere. But the one offering the description will always know his description falls far, far short of the actuality of the experience of Truth, and he won't take his description too seriously, while yet knowing it is probably better than nothing and probably will serve at least some of the hearts of those whose perceptions want to awaken, because they've probably never even heard the words of a Truth-endowed human being before and with this new experience may come that light in the brain or heart that guarantees that a given human being has just been quickened toward Redemption. And so the conveyer of Truth has done what he can, and it is now up to the disciple of Intelligent Love to keep her light alive and learn how to encourage it to grow into a roaring flame, blessed with Agni's fiery determination to make everything in nature over in the image of Love.

Truth is an all-or-nothing experience that lies beyond the duality of the "left" and the "right" and the moderates. When all attachments to preconceptions are gone, all Truth will be yours . . . not to possess, but to become a part of and reflect into the world.

Of course, to reach the higher potencies of a Divine Principle, you have to look beyond its outward manifestation into the world of pure energy (actually, even the outward-looking, "concrete" rational mind is pure energy, because everything on every plane of creation is pure energy, but since the rational mind doesn't usually look like energy, we're treating it as something solid for the purposes of this discussion). When you're dealing with the higher potencies, you become a conscious part of a column of pure energy which we might as well call "Truth". And "Truth" has its home in love, and so is a fine path to Achieve love.

Anyhow, beyond morality lies the great energy we can call the parent Principle Truth, and since Love is the mother of Truth she is the grandmother of morality. And Truth is Beauty, as is best represented in the soul-infused form of Woman. Yes, Truth is a column of Energy, but when it personalizes itself, it becomes Woman. As she vibrates us compassionately to her, Woman soothes the abrasions on our hearts and makes our bodies and emotions whole once more with a Mystery beyond Mystery, because the only way to understand the Mystery is to become Woman, for She is its custodian. There is no deeper Mystery and no more pleasant and powerful manifestation of Truth, and therefore of Love, than Woman. She gentles us.

Beauty is the meaning of life. The woman is the presenter and the embodiment of the meaning of life.

There was a bright light
and I looked for the source of the light
and found a soul-strong woman
sexual and secure
a shamaness, seer
a peerer into mysteries so divine, so deep
that had I followed her all the way back
I would have become lost in her
I would have drowned in her
yet I wanted to drown in her
and I still do.

II

Placing my body on the ocean for her
as sacrifice and sacrament
upon her glistening tongue
deep and wide I am called
by a lady of the sea
whose essence lives in Kentucky
in a temple of bright flesh

she has sacralized, sanctified
thru the union of all she is
I smile in happy death upon her
joyous amid the wave churnings
lost in deep contemplation
of her eternal mystery,
made null to all I was before
yet positive with her attractive mystery
I dwell with her
and she recognizes me within her
and her face there, just above the ocean
smiles with me
amid whisperings in a sacred language
humans have always known
and must never forget again.

Beauty perceives Beauty. Any person who has perceived the Beauty in another person has perceived the Beauty in themselves. Such a person is a success in life, and has Achieved the meaning of life.

Beauty is Divinity. The sacred Work of the human being is to perceive the Beauty in his neighbors. This is what Brother Robert meant by the phrase: "Thou art God." In other words, "You are Beautiful".

When you are in the presence of one of the Lords of Compassion, the Beauty you feel is within the Lord and which you perceive within her eyes is really the Lord becoming One with you and mirroring your own Beauty back upon you so that you may know your Self. And she connects with you in such a way that her Beauty pulls yours to the front of your consciousness, for there was more Beauty within you all along than you ever realized. Thus the Lord helps you become successful as a human being.

The Motto of the Lord of Compassion is:

Beauty Perceives Beauty
Beauty Is Divinity
You Are Beautiful
We Are Beautiful Together

The wonder of our Humanity is great; this is why every Angel aspires to become Human.

An Avatar, or incarnation of a Divine Principle, ultimately becomes that Principle on every level, including the physical, by working his consciousness "down" into a marriage with every blessed cell of his physical body. Obviously, his energy bodies and personality will reflect the Principle which he IS completely, as well. As with everything else in life, he is helped in producing the full manifestation of Himself by devas (angels, or angels-in-training) and by nature spirits who work under the direction of the devas, and who themselves will eventually mature into devas and become the architects of nature, rather than remaining construction workers. *Everyone* of whatever species must continually evolve, and it makes no sense to fight the process . . . and unlike most of the ridiculous "human beings" of the late twentieth century, I've never known any deva or nature spirit to fight against "his" evolution. (I put "his" in quotes because it seems to me that devas and nature spirits don't have any permanent gender; their forms are extremely elastic and they seem to always simply reflect that which seems appropriate in a given moment . . . whatever they look like as you're gazing at them is most likely a form they drew out of your own mind and put on like a new suit of clothes, whether you were aware of carrying that picture in your mind or not. This is another reason to avoid filling yourself up with shit like horror movies or movies or books or games of manipulation and degradation in its various forms. I guarantee you you've never been scared shitless until you've been scared shitless by devas and nature spirits who are acting out scenes from your own mind. And at a certain step of the evolutionary process, you *will* have to undergo this adventure. If you survive and remain sane, you'll have enough sense to keep your energy and motives, and thus the thoughts attached to those energies and motives, as pure as possible in the future. However, it makes sense to begin cleaning yourself up *now*, and get as much Work done as possible before you have to face this test, which is sponsored by Higher parts of your own consciousness which you will only just be becoming aware of during the general period of the test. The cleaner your mind and heart and causal body are as you face this test, the stronger the possibility you'll survive and maybe not have to be committed to an institution. You'll also experience relatively pleasant things stored up in your causal body, heart and mind during this test; the devas and nature spirits don't discriminate between "bad" and "good". They have a core of innocence whose nature is difficult for a human being to fathom, but that core remains untouched by the corruption of the clothes provided by the human initiate during this test. Perhaps it should be noted that this test lasts for a long time; it isn't like a university test you spend an hour or two on and then go home. You'll spend a lot more time dealing with the ordeal of this test than you ever imagined was possible, as day after day you learn to fully turn yourself over to the Will of God . . . because there's literally nothing else you *can* do. Regardless of how skilled you were at Working with nonordinary reality before this test, you won't be able to lift a nonordinary finger to do a nonordinary thing during the time of your travail. This is a big part of the Way you learn totally, once and for all with no doubt, that control is a total illusion, with not even a spark of truth remotely connected with it. But the more you've Worked to conform yourself to God's Will for years before this test thru the direct contact you share with that Will thru the agency of your Monad--your Highest Aspect, for the purposes of this tract--the more likely it is you'll succeed with the Divine Objective of this test and become your own type of Avatar, a direct incarnation of your own Self as Principle!)

One more thing about devas and nature spirits: there are those people who for some unknowable reason have assumed that devas are on the involutionary path of descent into matter, while humans are on the evolutionary path of ascent out of matter. This perspective is one more sick symptom of the divisions that haunted twentieth century people's minds, divisions they were unaware of and never suspected themselves of harboring. The truth is that both humans and devas are on the evolutionary ascent, but we aren't going out of matter, we're taking matter with us in order to spiritualize it. The earthplane becomes continually refined into Beauty and pleasantness of vibration as both the devas and ourselves succeed with our evolutionary task. No, humans and devas are not the same, and they work in different, though complimentary fashions. But both evolutions are *evolving*;

that's why they're called evolutions.

Yes, there's a little subset of deva lives which are on the involutionary path and are descending into material manifestation for the first time; they incarnate into the mineral kingdom and work their way up into the plant and animal kingdoms. But humans and most of the devas we concern ourselves with are on the evolutionary path. Maybe the confusion arose because the perspective of devas is incomprehensible to humans (again with most humans being too undisciplined to avoid projecting their own prejudices onto other species), or maybe it arose because devas are the architects of the form side of life, while humans are more concerned with the life within the form. But whatever the cause of the confusion, everyone within the sound of my word processor needs to understand that both the deva and human kingdoms are evolving into higher grades of experience and that it is the job of both kingdoms to pull the earth herself "up" into a higher evolution.

When all human beings become True Incarnations of themselves, there will be no more of what Sonny-Bob likes to sneeringly call "coattail riders". Sonny-Bob appreciates the irony, while simultaneously groaning in frustration, at the fact that humanity contains so many units of dumbass material who haven't yet refined themselves into a higher grade that whenever an Avatar comes among them for purposes of sharing his Compassionate Service with them, that many of the dumbasses try to restrict or impede the Avatar in some way, despite the fact that it's in their own best interests to support the Work of the Avatar and try to draw a little of his energy to themselves. Then, an incarnation or two down the pike, these same idiots will suddenly convert themselves to the cause of the Avatar (or what they imagine to be the cause--because they got such a late start at touching His energy and incorporating a bit of it into themselves their view of His cause is invariably warped, and they wind up being hindrances again to the spread of the Avatar's Energy, though this time unwittingly.)

So Sonny-Bob rightfully groans and sneers and scrapes his foot like a mad bull or pounds his fist on a table and calls these people "coattail riders", because they've never been strong enough or committed enough to do their own Work, while yet interfering with the Work of the Avatar in their own collective, feeble little way like a flock of little Chihuahua dogs nipping at the heels of a splendid Saint Bernard. Then they ostensibly come over to the Avatar's side, but it's usually too late by this time for them to understand the spreading Energy and in attempting to hitch a ride on this energy, riding on the coattail of the Avatar, they actually produce a crystallization of the Energy, which makes it worthless, or nearly worthless, and a new Avatar then has to appear to destroy the crystallization and free the Energy. Such an Avatar was Martin Luther, though the energy of Christianity crystallized again pretty soon after he'd broken up the blockages created by the coattail riders. And the coattail riders raved at Luther, and shook their fists as they always do, and a century or two later these same weak little people claimed to be disciples of Luther. Madness beyond madness.

When all human beings become incarnations of their own Highest Principles, the Race (which will deserve a capital "R" by then) will respond fluidly and immediately to the changes in perception of individual human beings and to the associated changes in the quality of their vibrations. Every man, woman and child will be his or her own Avatar, and Avatars of Destruction will never be needed again, because nobody will ever allow any crystallization to happen. Then we will see constant growth and the conscious stabilization of that growth, followed by still more growth, without any necessity for any sort of Death as we know it. This is made possible partly because humanity by this time won't suffer from the false perception of the illusion of opposites, and the fact that the Race will no longer suffer from this phoney perception is a big part of the progress that will allow each human being to become a conscious incarnation of his own Monad, his own Highest Aspect manifesting in the manner of fullbody, total, uncompromising compassion. So each human being will be an Avatar, and Avatars are incapable of interfering with each other and always energetically support one another. I don't know what the Angel of Death will do for a living at this point; but I guess he'll find Work in some dimension or other, or maybe He'll evolve into some type of manifestation we presently cannot conceive of.

Moderation is definitely "out" for a civilized person; moderation is just a compromise between two seemingly different forms of duality. The full-spectrum person doesn't compromise; he develops all his facets and harmonizes them around the great electric light at the center core of his being. He is like a great crystal ruby, infused with Agni's pink-red love, made softer by that love than the usual stone as his facets whirl about his central core, adapting him to every conceivable situation and environment, and to sharing his overflowing love with those men, women and children he can find an appropriate moment of harmony in service with.

Parenthetically to my diatribe against the pacifists, let me state that in the unsolved wilderness of lazy New Age "thought" you often see these irresponsible people placing arbitrary labels or definitions on a thing which have no bearing whatsoever on that thing. Many of them have chosen (these beginners actually feel they can choose the nature of the universe, rather than letting God choose the nature of the universe and learning to blissfully harmonize themselves with God's Visioning Process) to define evil as "ignorance", woefully unaware of their own ignorance and refusing to face their own laziness in accepting their inaccurate doctrines. They are afraid to face their own pain, the pain of the great ape who fears to leave his cave and creates imaginary banana trees to decorate its walls in a futile attempt to avoid living in a jungle he doesn't understand.

Yet to grow in wisdom and in righteous power, the monkey-man must learn to tell the truth to himself, beginning with the truth of his own ignorance, and let his preconceptions fall by the wayside as he either tiptoes or strides boldly out of his cave into the sunlight he hasn't yet learned to contain within his own being. And once in that sunlight, he must learn to refuse the treats offered by the shadow-bringers, for they are the ones who would confuse him if he is weak enough to let them, and their treats are but the turd of the day, rather than the fruit of eternity.

These people are such idiots they don't recognize that vibration indicates the nature of a thing. Their labels, unmatched as they are to the vibration of the thing they've labeled, indicate only their own irresponsible idiocy. Evil is not going to conform to their labels; it is going to use their labels to ensnare and manipulate them, placing energy wedges and hooks into their auras which they're not even aware of to block them off from certain aspects of their own consciousness and to pull them along on the jolly road to hell.

A definition or label is only of use if it has been constructed by a person who has first perceived the vibration of the thing being labeled or defined, then crafted his label or definition in a conscious manner designed to reflect that vibration in words. In other words, a label or definition should mirror the vibration of the thing being labeled or defined, whether that thing be from the world of God and the Buddha, or whether it be from the world of stinking filthy illusion. A rose by any other name **does not** smell as sweet. Call a rose a turd, then bend to sniff it, and you'll see what I mean, honey.

(The reality is that a person who is capable of making an approximately accurate label or definition, though, will probably not relish the task. His daily experience is of himself and the world as energy unbounded by words. So he may snort with revulsion at doing the rather concrete work of building word-forms, and he may choose to abstain. Words have little, if any, practical value to such a person, but unfortunately for him, he lives in a world where people have bound themselves to their illusions with chains of words, so he may at times intervene and build a relatively accurate word-form or two to coax his neighbors out of illusion, hoping that in a few thousand, or in a few million years, the people of Earth will have evolved beyond their smug reliance on words.)

But these new-agers are so scared of the world of stinking filthy illusion they blind themselves to its existence (actually, its imitation of existence), despite the obvious evidence of its presence in the world around them and in their own sordid lives. And because they don't have the strength to face and scrub the filthy glamour and illusion out of their causal bodies, they also lack the strength to accept the electric charge of Liberation from its home on the Buddhic Plane. That charge would integrate the Buddhic Plane with their energy bodies, physical body and personality if they could accept it, but if you're too goddam lazy to take a fucking bath, you're not going to be given a clean robe to wear.

Consciously working with the causal body teaches us gradually about the true nature of electricity, and this gradual electric growth process must occur and reach a high degree of flowering before the organism can be transmuted into a fully-electric vehicle for a Liberated Awareness. Altruism is the secret of Electricity!

Nobody "decides" to undergo Liberation. There are Mysteries involved in this process which do not attach themselves to words. But remember that the Liberated One is *propelled*, and for that state of being to be Achieved, decision must be worked with, applied properly, and then transcended. The transcendence of decision is one thing that carries us across the Threshold. And these statements I have just made aren't completely accurate, partly because the full context of the statements cannot be given, and partly because of the limitations of words themselves, particularly when applied to a process which carries human beings beyond limitations. *Never* interpret a book in a fundamentalist fashion; your experience of evolution will appear at times to deviate from that which has been written in any book. Part of this is due to the limitations of words, part of it may be due to inadequacies in the author's attempt to express that which is generally inexpressible, and part of it may be due to an inability on your part to really listen or to fully understand.

The earth is full of new-age fools who believe they're Liberated, or that they stand on the point of some ascension into Liberation. And the new-age has such a wide spectrum of tolerance for foolishness that some of 'em are fundies, and some of 'em are eclectic, and some are of the lukewarm half-assed moderate variety, but all of 'em are deluded by their lusts. While it is okay to aspire to Liberation, there is a fine perception of discernment that must be Achieved to avoid falling victim to the delusion that one is Liberated when one is not, or that one is about to be Liberated when one still has far to travel.

Much energy is squandered by those who are still playing with the building blocks of self-deception as to their supposed "spiritual status" (nobody, not even the Christ, actually has any status--ponder on this). Such people are far from being absorbed into the movement of electricity. The first step toward recovery of their dignity is to sincerely admit to themselves that they are fools. Then they must in all honesty explore the nature of damn foolishness so as not to fall victim to it again, and they must release this false nature from their causal bodies and personalities as they explore it, for only then can their true nature be Achieved.

I used to play ping-pong with a guy who was sort of considered the TAC's unofficial ping-pong champion. Remember, there is no competition in the future, so this fellow had no trophies and we didn't really keep score . . . but when you played old Sun Tzu, you didn't have to keep score as he mopped up the ping-pong table with any artificial dignity you might have stored away from your inner vision. He made you look at it as he beat your socks off with his custom ping-pong paddle. He told me once, "Know your enemy," and I was bright enough to know he meant the glamours and illusions that had been stirred up in me upon my promotion to captain. So I played a lot of ping-pong until those glamours and illusions were gone, and old Sun Tzu seemed pretty satisfied with me. But the main thing was that I was humbled and lovingly pleased with myself.

If Sonny-Bob "survives" his Savioring (he won't--it's not possible) there will be a Resurrection of the True Man without the burden of a causal body. Then it may be that he will be able to adopt a role of more directly infusing Beauty into the causal body of humanity, and thus of the earth. For Beauty is the salvation of humanity, and thus of the earth.

The Divine Destroyer always serves the cause of Beauty and Love and Truth by removing illusions and glamours that obstruct the flow of those Divine energies. He may do this by killing on the mental plane, emotional plane, etheric plane or physical plane, or in any combination of the above. The Divine Destroyer often gets the blame for creating trouble by the very jackasses who actually unconsciously created the trouble, but since he's not here to serve their glamourous egotism, he'll just brush them aside, or perhaps shatter them--for they are a part of the problem he was sent to solve.

Much foolishness is made by disciples who don't know the basics of esoteric psychology, and thus don't know themselves in any spiritually useful way. How then can they sincerely claim to be disciples? The archetypes are the beginning (subconscious), the seven living rays of conscious energy that affect every human being in one combination or another are next (superconscious, monadic consciousness), and the interplay between archetypes and the seven rays is eventually contemplated (full synthesis of consciousness). This is the first, basic impulse toward experiencing yourself as living energy and is but the work of a day. Yet how many are too lazy to do even a day's work?

Many are the spiritual damfools who are addicted to a crystallized dogma that was born out of their own favorite Ray's expression. But a crystallized dogma hinders the expression of the very Ray which birthed it, and thus of all other rays, for all seven rays are interdependent and complimentary. These same fools don't understand and condemn the perfectly legitimate expression of rays which they feel are foreign to their own, and this is especially true when certain ray types who are inclined toward political correctness and addicted to sweetness and what they believe to be non-violence find themselves in the presence of a First Ray manifestation--for the First Ray is the Ray of Will or Power, and is also known as the Destroyer Ray because it destroys the crystallized dogma of the immature and petulant. Yet the First Ray is also called the Ray of Synthesis, because unification of all levels of consciousness would not be possible without it. And the First Ray serves its parent, which is Love, just as all Rays are birthed of Love. The ignoramus continually forgets this fact, or has never been aware of it. Evolution is continually hampered by the "spiritual ignoramuses", but maybe that will change when humanity grows a bit more.

That person who would Achieve the most profound levels of Destruction or Creation (when done consciously and with love, this is one process) must develop a living feeling for all the Rays, an understanding free from prejudice. He may have his preferred Rays, but preference is not prejudice. This is the person who has finally grown mature enough to realize that before the Divine Destroyer is given full license to launch his assaults against crystallization and untruth he has had to consciously and over a long period sacrifice his own cherished glamours and illusions. Thus he qualifies himself to perform the greater service of demolishing the glamours and illusions of his society or world period.   And while throngs gather to congratulate the retired Destroyer as they finally recognize his Achievement, this mature person mentioned above will stand on the fringes of the crowd and weep for the retired one, for this person has some idea of the Sacrifice that each Destroyer must make.

Remember that "psychic" is *not* synonymous with "spiritual", and that it is possible to be spiritual without any psychic ability at all. To construct a pure, clear, loving causal body is the thing, and if psychic ability occurs as a side-effect of that, fine. But to pursue psychic ability for its own sake is to put the cart before the horse and run the risk of falling into the delusions of black magic.

Genuine spiritual gifts of any sort are always a side-effect of lifetimes of Altruistic spiritual Achievement. Schools usually put the cart before the horse; maybe you can learn to be a journalist in a school, but you can't learn to be Mark Twain or Louis L'Amour in a school. Maybe you can learn to be an egocentric soldier in a school, but you can't learn to be a Liberated Warrior in a school. If you're a soldier and you ask your commander for twenty or thirty years off so you can Work your way into genuine warriorship, you know what he'll say. You know your "branch of the service" is too spiritually and morally immature to accept your Search. If you leave, they won't want you after you've become Liberated. (Maybe it's just as well, because you won't want to be subject to the politically-motivated whims of people who are so immature they have to be governed by rules and laws.) No school can teach Altruism and Sacrifice, honey.

Liars abound; if you are not ready to destroy or avoid illusions, you will be deceived. Many of these liars are very clever and have enormous psychic abilities which they will use to glamourize you-- for you will wonder how they could be confused or wicked if they have the ability to project themselves to you or explore worlds that may seem far away to you. Much of this is deception, though in the midst of the deception some of them do have genuine gifts-- which they always lose and become shells of themselves if they don't take advantage of opportunities to reform themselves. So trust your own Heart and to your own best judgment; never accept any judgment from one who would replace yours with his. He is fake, foul, or both by definition! He is in the process of actively shitting away his own power by trying to steal yours. There is no such thing as a strong thief!

Do not even trust the Holy Culpepper if he should try to replace your Heart's judgment with his own--but I know he won't. In the Archives at Gaffney there's a long Tract he wrote (or there will be, if he saves the causal body of humanity and of the planet) which is hundreds of pages long, and one of the primary purposes of this huge tract is to help people learn to trust in the Presence of their own sweet, powerful, just Hearts.

The most important thing Humanity can do today is for the individual units of the Race to build Beauty into their causal bodies. For Beauty is Truth and Truth is Beauty, and in the full flowering of Beauty Love is Achieved.

And for full flowering to be Achieved, the manure must be reclaimed and turned into fertilizer. Both the roots and the petals of the lotus are necessary, and both are to be nourished and respected. Both are to be loved.

But we were talking earlier about the limitations of words, and looked at some basic reasons which anyone can comprehend that you should never interpret a book or statement of Truth of any kind in a fundamentalist fashion, while at the same time learning that personal, non-collective discernment which carries us beyond the reach of those glamours and illusions which would try to pull us back down into manipulating herds of people thru the illusion of "spiritual status". So let's examine some more subtle reasons to avoid the despair of fundamentalism.

Most importantly is the fact that as you begin to become conscious of yourself as energy, you will realize dimensions of

Individuality you had never imagined existed, and you will understand why each person's path to salvation *must* be an individual path, free from all doctrine and dogma and one-dimensional methods of meditation. In fact, those who ask if you "have a practice" are asking from a desire to classify you for purposes of their own egotism and selfishness, and regardless of how many hours a week they spend in what they consider to be meditation, the truth is that they actually have no idea whatsoever what true meditation is. A real meditator *is* his practice and doesn't advertise the fact . . . well, the fact cannot be advertised anyway, because to actually correctly perceive the advertisement, you would have to be a true meditator yourself, in which case the advertisement wouldn't even be necessary! True meditation is taught to yourself by yourself as you approach your Higher Aspects; it is not learned in your local yoga school. True meditation is pure fire, and would burn down any yoga school, or any other kind of school.

Those who have not become conscious of the full range of their electric humanness cannot begin to imagine what I mean by those words regarding Individuality, yet if you stand close enough to the Threshold, perhaps those words will serve your perceptions somewhat.

The vibration is the thing; even if the words are less than clear, the vibration of a book is the thing that is of importance, anyway. It's the vibration that serves you, even if you don't always understand the meaning with your outermost consciousness. To hold a really alive book in your hands is to touch Cosmic Fire!

Learn to feel the nature of any book you hold in your hands, and if that nature will serve you, then let it quicken you with its electric zeal. Any tract written by myself or Sonny-Bob will most likely be an instrument of fire; learn to see the emblem of this fiery implement with your Higher Mind as you feel the effects of it in all your bodies and personality. Quiver with electric zeal as though you were fully alive with sexual Liberation! For just as every plane of existence is formed of matter in varying grades of vibration, so is total fire on any plane the full implementation of sex on that plane. And the full implementation of sex requires the full implementation of love. Sex can never be separated from love, or it's not true sex; and love can never be separated from sex, or compassion becomes impossible. Thus must the false consciousness of separation be transcended!

So without trying to explain directly to you the symbol of this book, let me picture it to you by asking you to consider what the flame of love looks like when merged with the total sexual fire of matter, and what would be the path of least resistance toward creating an enlivened symbol of a book imbued by the reddish-pink love-flame? A living book is a deva, because everything that lives is imbued with consciousness, and devas and nature spirits of various kinds enter into living symbols and stabilize the life force within those symbols. When a symbol no longer lives, it is because the guardian of it's life force--the nature spirit or deva--has departed, releasing that force to find a new form, a new symbol to house it. If people claim to worship or appreciate some symbol, yet whore it with their selfishness and false sense of separation and their greed for restriction, then ultimately the deva in charge of the symbol will release the energy of the symbol and the religion, or nation, or whatever it is will die . . . only to eventually be reborn, and represented by another symbol more suited to a newly-evolving time.

So what does this living deva you hold in your hands look like upon the plane of the Higher Mind? Learn to perceive it, and watch as it stimulates you in a wholebody fashion suitable to the marriage of love and matter.

Marriage is the most sacred of human relationships, and is to be undertaken in a spirit of joy that bodes no restriction. Discipline is crucial to the marriage, and contributes to the joy of the arrangement, but restriction is not discipline and must not be tolerated.

In marriage, as well as in the rest of life, each person's path is totally unique and custom self-crafted. And the thing about a real, authentic path is that it's so unique, another person--even a marriage partner--may not even be able to see it! Yet your friends will sense your spiritual vibration, and be calm in the certainty of your self-generated progress.

And the energy that each spiritual partner contributes to the marriage blends with all the energies of all other partners in a splendid rainbow pool of sharing. So we see that spirituality is constant individual Achievement, coupled with total harmoniously-modulated energy-sharing with one's partners. Each contribution to the energy-pool of the marriage is totally unique and smells and tastes with the wonderful knowingness of the person who hosts that energy, and the taste of all energies of the marriage blended together is a whirlpool of electric rainbow bliss. It might even be said that this electric whirlpool *is* the marriage!

Once when I was a couple of centuries old, I found myself in a marriage with two of the most wonderful women I have ever known. Sometimes I feel in my deepest heart that I learned almost everything I know from these two dear, precious women.

The first woman had just turned fourteen when we married; we'd been dating for six or eight months prior to that. She had rather curly dark, blue-black hair and deeply bright, wise eyes of nutshell brown that spoke to me in the language of millions of years of the very best of human progress. She was very white-skinned, though an indigo glow played about her skin and flavored her every movement with a song you could taste with your entire being.

There was also a hint of violet about her, especially around the lips, and when I drank from those lips I felt refreshed with clarity like Moses at the well after his long thirsty trek thru the desert deprived of water. And it must always be remembered that it was the women who offered Moses the healing waters his dried and crusty body needed, after he had driven away more bestial elements who would have profaned that which was sacred . . . and there is nothing more sacred than Woman.

I had known my second wife of this marriage for a while before I met the dark-haired, light-bodied fourteen year old I have just described, but when we first met we were only friends who occasionally comforted one another. She was a regular dancer at Sunday morning temple in Asheville and was training to become a Sacred Prostitute. She joined our marriage a few months into it; she was twenty at the time.

This young woman wore a strong golden skin which she'd tried to enrich with a few very tasteful tattoos, but the tattoos wound up being enriched by the skin. She was strong of body and powerful and decisive in her ways; when she moved about her business she created waves of purposefulness which served as a medium for Beauty.

Sometimes she'd stop suddenly and out of nowhere give a merry laugh in the middle of her purposefulness, and every glad heart in the area would be immediately enriched and strengthened in such a way that it knew it could endure any trials life might offer. She wore long blonde hair that swished continually about her buttocks in the middle of her purposeful movements, and there was an indigo glimmer to her skin as well, just as there was with my other wife . . . and just as there is with me, for that matter.

And we three friends together created one of the finest electric whirlpools I have ever known. And out of that whirlpool rainbow children were spawned, and eventually they swam off to found new whirlpools, which were then linked to ours in a network of whirlpool sharing.

This is marriage. Total trust can live freely without suspicion in a real marriage, for everyone's needs are respected and everyone is allowed to share in the way that feels right to them. There is a coordination of energy that occurs, of similarity of vibration which produces one great tone composed of many sub-tones, but there is no mediocrity or homogeneity. Excellence thrives in a real marriage; excellence is the very stuff of real marriage.

A living untumored city is the marriage not only of people who have consciously decided to live together, but it is also the marriage of the city itself with one or more gods or goddesses. This fact was pretty well known in ancient times, but as the centuries advanced and people's brains and hearts began to shut down, they could no longer feel or in any way perceive the interplay of energies between the goddesses and gods and their cities. The numbing of humanity was so far along by the twentieth century that people frequently couldn't even feel the interplay between themselves and the urban monstrosities created by their mechanical consciousness. Those few humans who could still feel and know the currents of energy directly in the twentieth century frequently went insane or committed suicide because they couldn't adapt to the environment created by the lack of consciousness of the walking machines of death who surrounded them.

Even as late as year 1000 of the common era, people were still far more alive in some respects than they would be a thousand years later in the USA. Less than a millennium before the USA was founded, people still had *passion*, man, passion! They still had some electric zeal breathing and surging in their loins and in their breasts. They had not yet been humiliated into nothingness by capitalism, communism, and socialism; again, people of the twentieth century constantly made the mistake of judging the people of centuries other than their own by their own standards, so the people of the middle ages look downtrodden to the people of the twentieth century. Yet a serf in the middle ages got to keep more of what he earned than the twentieth century people did, and he was free to drink and carouse and have sex with men or women, married or not . . . some of which might be frowned upon, but none of which was likely to be prohibited. As long as he went to church and pretended to be Christian, he'd likely be left to do as he pleased once he left the church building. He didn't have to fear arrest if he was pursuing happiness, despite having no Constitution to guarantee his right to the pursuit.

It only takes a little humiliation to produce a major loss of dignity, and before the twentieth century arrived humanity had experienced more than a little humiliation. Humiliation--the encouragement of shame and the flushed and despairing feeling of impotence that results from shame--is one of the primary weapons governments and corporations and primitive unnatural religions and schools use against their own people, and it had been used so often by the late twentieth century it was rare to find any person with a portion of his human dignity intact. Most people didn't even know what dignity is, and in their lack of understanding grabbed at the stale crust of egotism that fell from the tables of the controllers of society. But egotism is not dignity any more than a turd is a watermelon. And the controllers of society were so dead-brained, dead-bodied and closed-hearted, they hadn't a clue that they weren't living the good life. But they weren't alive at all . . . not even a little bit.

So it is no wonder that the mass conception of marriage in the twentieth century was a vision based on the stagnation of permanent death, and ignorant of love and juicy life. Even during the middle ages that twentieth century people were so fond of looking "back" upon (really, the middle ages have at least as much reason to look "back" on the twentieth century), everyone knew and pretty much lived by the rule that monogamous marriage was unnatural, so while they might not live in poly-community with their marriages, outside liaisons were expected, and sometimes encouraged.

There is no "back in time", there is no "history"; there is only the flavor of different points of attainment or degradation within the causal body of humanity, and the causal body of the planet.

PLANET OF THE APES

There was almost no excellence in the twentieth century, so it is no wonder they didn't even understand the marriage by which a healthy city functions. They were like a tribe of apes who had inherited their "civilization" from the ancients, but who didn't understand the principles by which the ancients constructed the civilizations. So when these apes came in from the jungle of mechanical numbness, they transferred their animal ways onto all their creations, and ugliness was the result. They had not learned to cultivate or appreciate that Beauty which is Truth, and that Truth which is the conduit to Love.

A God or Goddess is a deva who has also had some human incarnations, and who corresponds to one degree or another to a natural point of consciousness within the human brain and nervous system. Obviously, there are many of these points of consciousness, so we might term them multi-consciousness. (But the multi-consciousness of any given human being must be held together in a sane harmony of forces which connect with and complement each other; working with these forces must not be approached with bravado, or with an inferiority complex, but with a genuine humility.)

Once human, always human. That is, once the full spectrum of your enlightened humanity has been activated in fiery Liberation, you'll carry your humanity with you into expansions so vast they carry you into starry dimensions far beyond that accessible to the human kingdom. In other words, you expand far beyond the human kingdom . . . who knows what you'll become eventually, because there is no end to evolution, and many are those who have progressed out of the human kingdom over billions of years in this and other solar systems and proceeded to identifications with forces so vast they can't even set foot on the material earth anymore, and if they can approach it at all, many of them may only do so from the Higher Mental Plane, because the power of their Presence would be too much for us to take if they came any closer.

Yet these Great Beings, these Star-Elders, carried their full Humanity with them as they moved themselves into alignment with vast unknowable (to us) Forces. Everything we earn as human beings stays with us forever, and becomes a part of whatever we become over the next few billion years, and over the next uncounted lot of trillions of years.

Is it necessary to state that it is impossible to carry egotism and it's garbage of glamour and illusion beyond this earth? For by Cosmic standards, egotism is no attainment at all, but a restriction that precludes Achievement. But the Resurrection we experience into the flowering of our full Humanity while on this precious Earth remains with us forever. Once human, always human, no matter how far beyond the human kingdom we eventually find ourselves.

Deva psychology in general is so different from human psychology that I often doubt if any human being understands it-- and those who feel they do, in my experience, are completely deluded. Devas often seem completely arbitrary in their conduct, with no linking factors to harmonize the various points of contact they occupy in the causal body of the earth. In other words, they appear insane, by human standards. It would perhaps not be inaccurate to refer to them as "daft".

Devas somehow automatically enjoy a special relationship with the Will of God . . . and since devas are a part of the angel evolution, I guess this is no big surprise. But not all devas are angels; in the early degrees of deva Achievement--and I'm not even sure the word Achievement applies to devas--they've only recently been promoted up from "worker-bee" nature spirits into the ranks of the devas, so for some time they are learning the basics of applying force and direction and supervision of nature spirits that will eventually allow them to take their place as fully-fledged angels.

The primary quality of devas is elasticity, and each person has a deva assigned to him who mirrors his thoughts and actions back upon him, which helps of course in the justice of karma . . . and which also keeps him mired in old cycles which don't serve him anymore, if he's thick as a brick and won't learn from his experiences. So the new-agers have a part of the truth when they claim that your thoughts create your reality; the problem is that they usually approach this particle of truth as if it were the whole truth, which means that in their application of this particle it loses the vibratory quality that once made it true, and thus becomes useless.

Your deva may also save your life or otherwise keep you out of trouble, if your karma allows such assistance in a given situation, but obviously if you're a suffering human being, your karma hasn't always allowed such help, or if it has allowed help, it hasn't always allowed the full range of help. Your deva won't interfere with the lessons you need to "straighten up and fly right", honey chile.

A willingness to learn to love may make your karma less severe than it otherwise would be, and Grace may thus be invoked which may, among other unseen benefits and assistances, allow your deva to steer you clear of a difficulty which is no longer necessary for your lessons.

The first decade of the twenty-first century is sometimes called the Decade of Agony because of various horrors that occurred. As usual, people would cry "Why!", but most had no real desire to know why. In case the reader is an exception to this rule, however, I will now explain "Why" most "disasters" occur.

Most "disasters" are not a punishment from God, they are a gift from God designed to prompt you toward freedom from suffering, because suffering is caused by preconceptions, and "disasters" are designed to shake up your preconceptions as a prelude to letting those preconceptions go. And once those preconceptions are gone, you won't suffer any more, regardless of your outward circumstances.

Example: Suppose a person without preconceptions drops an anvil on his toe. He'll feel pain and maybe cuss, but he'll also release the pain in that moment and continue releasing the pain as it ebbs out of his toe without holding onto any of it. So although he feels pain, he doesn't suffer. Suffering is the clinging to pain, and the thing that causes us to cling to pain is preconceptions. So if a person with preconceptions about how things "should" be drops an anvil on his toe, he'll not only feel pain in that moment, but he'll also feel pain long-term, even after his toe has physically healed, because some of the pain stuck to his preconceptions and thus was stored up as a remembrance of physical pain combined with emotional pain. So emotionally he'll still feel that pain from time to time. And it may be that the stored-up pain, the suffering, around his poor toe may attract other painful experiences to itself so he will create more emotional and mental suffering for himself, thus perpetuating the parasitic existence of the cloud of suffering that surrounds him and even increasing its size. And since he falsely believes that "misery loves company" (It should be obvious that no love can occur in the presence of misery, except that love which dissipates misery . . . and misery certainly doesn't love that which terminates it!) he will have an unconscious desire to vengefully extend suffering to someone else, even if he alone bore the responsibility for dropping the anvil on his toe. In fact, he may want to childishly extend the suffering to God, perhaps by withholding his approval from God, or by pretending to withhold his belief in God . . . a belief--no, a *knowingness*--which is written in every cell of his body and in every dimension of his psyche. But none of this suffering would even be possible without the existence of his preconceptions. Instant forgiveness is only possible in the one who has no preconceptions.

So is it not obvious that preconceptions serve as the vile linking factor between an initial "wrong" done to someone, and the buildup of the urge to vengeance which adds to his cycle of suffering? "You shouldn't have done that to me and it still hurts so I'm going to get you back!" yells the crybaby, whether at God or at another human being. Yet it's the crybaby's own preconceptions, and the naiveté around those preconceptions, that cause the initial wound to continue to hurt. Preconceptions stand on the ground of naiveté; the person who is truly not naive doesn't suffer, as long as he allows compassion to fill up the space formerly occupied by naiveté. Preconceptions are a weird dualistic combo of naiveté with sophistication, neither of which is associated with Trueness or Redemption.

Twentieth century people's preconceptions were mostly on an unconscious level and had been indoctrinated into them for thousands of years, and since preconceptions are totally out of tune with Reality, of course the twentieth century people were being constantly disappointed . . . though of course they kept themselves too busy to find and dislocate the true source of their disappointment and always tried to blame it on some phenomenon they felt was external to themselves.

Anyhow, the crybaby in our example was wounded only once by the hateful action of another, but he repeatedly wounds himself thereafter with the preconceptions that act as glue to attract more suffering around the initial wound. Now, everyone cries or screams or throws up or cusses--or all of the above--at various times in our own healing process as we release preconceptions and the depraved energy of suffering they have chained us to. And this includes releasing the suffering we've carried due to the wrongs we've committed against others, and as the soul becomes clearer and more sensitive, this hurts even worse than releasing the type of suffering built up around wrongs and alleged wrongs others may have done to us. It always hurts us worse to injure another than when another injures us. Can you not see, then, how black magic always defeats itself? Black magic is founded upon vengeance for injury, and the result would be hilarious if it were not so sad. For the black magician always injures himself far worse than anyone else ever has done or could do. It is ridiculous that anyone would ever believe there is any power in black magic. There is nothing in black magic except self-hatred.

Anyhow, in the person committed to healing, the weeping, screaming and so forth help with the release of these old, stagnant energies of preconceptions and sufferings so the winged soul's nest in the heart can become clear and pure with Redemption, for the Heart is meant to be a light, clear home for the soul, not the cluttered playpen of a squalling infant muttering angry incantations that divorce him from Love. When I talk about crybabies, I'm not talking about people who are committed to healing, I'm talking about vengeful cowardly whiners who are too lazy and frightened to learn to process and release their burdens out of themselves, thus being of no constructive use to themselves or anyone else. But those who weep and moan while walking the Path of Healing are to be appreciated for their courage and their commitment to reducing their own suffering. And when one person's suffering is reduced, the suffering of every person who is receptive to healing influences is also reduced.

Yes, there are many levels and cycles of human experience, and no tract, no matter how comprehensive, can hope to cover more than a fraction of these levels--hence the necessity for *always* following your Heart, because your Heart always knows Right Action, even if your mind is as ignorant as a bumblebee. Perhaps there would be no need for our pamphlets if everyone insisted on always following their own sweet Heart, but for those who insist on a mental explanation, we have decided to humor you.

So speaking of wounds, it is also true (here's another level for you, sweetie) that sometimes a wound continues to hurt whether there's preconceptions around it or not, and in this case the hurting is caused by a weakness in one or more places of a person's aura, his "armor of light", that allowed an arrow of hate or rage to go so deeply that the extraction of the arrow may take a long time. So don't be a fundamentalist and try to blame someone for his suffering. Having a weakness in your aura is not a crime, it is a cause for compassion.

Sometimes words do wound a person who is not adequately protected, especially if accompanied by energy-arrows or by an overall vibration of ill intent. So nobody should be chastised for throwing a punch or kicking somebody in the nuts to defend her heart from words that wound. Whether the words are true or not is almost irrelevant in light of their capacity to wound the sensitive, insufficiently protected heart. For that matter, you're justified in throwing a punch to, say, put a stop to the verbal violence of someone who has insulted you or a loved one, even if you or your loved one are protected on an energy level. Thus do we defend our right to live in peace, free from disruptions by assholes. And it must be noted that to be secure, we must be willing to defend ourselves on every level, even on this outermost level--because if you don't defend your outermost perimeter, you've made it easier for some chump to attack your next energy-perimeter. Ultimately, all assaults are energy-assaults of varying density against energy-defenses of varying densities. To just hand over your outermost level of defense to a verbal assault is idiotic, even if you're well-protected by many succeeding levels of defense. Plus, if you didn't defend your outermost energy-perimeter, you'd be sickened a little bit and add some negative emotion to the cloud of seething astral vengeance that circles the earth. Only a pacifistic idiot would want to do that. This is an example of clinging to pain due to the internally violent preconceptions of the political-correctness of the supposedly non-violent. You suffer out of the knowledge that you didn't take Right Action from the Truth of your unified Human Nature, and this suffering is then extended to all humanity thru the agency of the cloud.

If these supposedly non-violent people were truly interested in serving humanity, rather than the misplaced lusts of the preconceptions of Gandhi and others like him, they'd be against the cycles of vengeance rather than being against defense. You're not likely to feel any need for vengeance after protecting yourself, thus the cloud is weakened and the human heart shines a little brighter.

Duh! Eliminate the cycles of vengeance by dissipating the little cloud inside you, and the big cloud will ultimately disappear, in which case no one will ever have to defend themselves again, anyway.

Now, some of these pacifistic idiots who, along with their openly violent brethren contribute to the smog of vengeance, may want to argue that maybe now that you've defended yourself, the person you defended against will be pissed at you and thus contribute to the cloud of vengeance. I don't like to answer idiots who try to justify smothering the human spirit beneath doctrine, but in my colossal magnanimity I will reply to this anyway, if for no other reason than the fact that so many people lack enough self-esteem to stand up against the sentimental machinations and misuse of the intellect of people who try to force their lifeways off on others--in this case, supposedly non-violent lifeways which contribute to the cloud of glamorous astral vengeance and which therefore ultimately precipitate as even more physical violence than would have occurred if a person had been true to himself instead of to a doctrine, and thus defended himself. Indeed, it seems that doctrine is the first enemy that has to be defeated before humanity can recapture its spirit, its heart, its innate *knowingness*.

When you defend yourself, if your attacker has survived but is injured, if he is still inclined toward vengeance there's nothing you can do about that--unless you are compassionate enough and skilled enough to shew him how he himself is responsible for his predicament, and how the seething cloud of emotional glamour prompted him to attack you thru its attachment to the vengeance he carries within his emotional body, and to the preconceptions in his infant mental body which reinforce the internal war he has chosen to externalize thru an attack upon you. If you can shew him this and direct him to a competent psychotherapist and/or energy-healer (and good ones ain't growing on trees) then you can feel good that you've helped his sorry ass begin to heal. But if you are only or mostly skilled just with the physical aspects of warriorship and don't know how to convey these insights to him (and if you don't think to recommend that he read a good Tract on these matters) then you still aren't responsible for his sense of vengeance and the sense of woundedness that caused it. He's been lugging that crap around for lifetimes, and maybe he wanted to start processing it out of himself in his current incarnation and knew on some level that attacking you would cause you to knock some of the crap out of him. Indeed, when they get themselves beaten up enough in enough lifetimes, most people eventually experience a light going off in their heads or hearts that begins prompting them away from vengeance, if they have the good fortune to be able to avoid mass culture, most of which is founded upon the weakness of vengeance. So it may well be that with your successful defense, you've contributed a bit to the loosening of his preconceptions and thus of his urge to vengeance, putting a little space between him and the cloud, which will weaken the cloud a bit while allowing your hostile companion room to finally take a breath and begin to consider his emotional difficulties from a new angle, thus continuing to separate himself from the cloud as he begins to claim his full humanity. So in your self-defense, you will almost certainly avoid personally contributing to the cloud, but you may also weaken the cloud thru helping one of its servants take a step toward Freedom. Understand me: your motive was self-defense, not some smarmy little codependent urge to help the fellow you beat up; but you certainly don't begrudge him the growth that has befallen him as a side-effect of your defense of yourself. This is a part of Right Human Relations. You may congratulate him if you see any signs of growth. And maybe in a few years he'll have simmered down enough that you can buy him a beer, or perhaps sleep with his sister without his mental preconceptions and emotional attachments being overwhelmed.

But the pacifist will have too many unresolved issues to be a force for peace or Right Human Relations. A part of the pacifist will still be filled with hatred, as the vengeful cloud which he serves snickers behind its grubby hand at him. Failing to stand up for yourself even once will damage you emotionally and spiritually, and even physically as your slick smarmy polluted emotions deluge your physical body with the shame of self-hatred. You become cloud-food, and won't be able to stop feeding the parasitic cloud of vengeance until you learn to stand up for yourself *every time, under all circumstances*, then process your grief and shame and rage and self-hatred out of all your bodies. The pacifist only seems brave in his own imagination and in the imaginations of other chronically deluded people. The pacifist is as big a coward as the president who starts an unnecessary or unjust war out of a sense of his own personal inadequacies and unfulfilled sexual needs. Along with the politicians and generals, the pacifist creates war by making regular donations to the cloud of vengeance that prompts people toward cycles of war that may bind them for thousands, or even millions, of years. Ponder on this, and then see if you can deduce any patterns from world events.

The pacifist only thinks he is non-violent. He would recoil from himself in horror if he could perceive the truth. His suppressed internal world seethes with a desire for vengeance far more than the insides of most soldiers who don't suppress as much of their natures and just pick up a rifle and go out and shoot folks.

But we were discussing the nature of disasters, and went into a discussion of preconceptions because no discussion regarding disasters would be productive without examining the role preconceptions play in those disasters.

Twentieth and early twentieth-first century humans were taught to construct walls of preconceptions between themselves and Reality. God allowed disasters to happen to shake up those preconceptions, especially the deranged preconception that God isn't supposed to allow disasters to happen to "good" people! For as long as a human plays host to even one preconception, that human cannot know God and cannot fully manifest the compassionate awareness of God. So the Decade of Agony was largely about shaking up people's preconceptions so they could begin to release those preconceptions and develop the direct perception of the pattern of existence, and of their own place in that pattern. It's ridiculous that a Decade of Agony had to occur, because every single human being everywhere could easily see from the events of his daily experience that his preconceptions were wrong and that they were the source of his suffering. But they were afraid to look, so our compassionate God had to arrange to make them look. They'd allowed themselves to be programmed for so long to believe that if they followed what they imagined to be "God's laws" or the laws of their society, they would be rewarded. But such a reward as they imagined was nothing but the shoveling of shit into their egotism. They were not very imaginative, and this was a really big part of their problem, for it takes the courage of imagination to experience Reality, which is made out of the very stuff of imagination. A hard saying for some, who most likely will be so lazy they will want to equate imagination with fantasy, but genuine imagination most certainly is not fantasy, it is the faculty by which Reality is contacted, and by which we may learn to consciously create in alignment with that Reality. Fantasy belongs to the lusts of the unregenerate astral body, but imagination belongs to the Higher Mental Body and may be directed into the purified emotions or anywhere else it needs to go to serve as Agency of Creation.

If you don't have the karma of needing to experience a particular disaster, yet are for some reason in the disaster zone, God will most likely allow your deva to urge you clear of it. However, there are also teams of human beings working on the etheric plane who are organized in a manner similar to a military unit who foresee the coming of any disaster, and these specialists then move into action and go into the etheric space around the disaster area and urge those human beings to leave who aren't supposed to be a part of the disaster. So if you felt compelled to not get on that plane, and the plane later crashed, it could have been your deva or one of these human specialists, or both, who are to thank for influencing you to avoid that disaster. These specialists sometimes even feel themselves invoked to aid in an unfolding auto wreck in which only one person might have died, if the specialists hadn't involved themselves into offering certain protections to that person, thus either preventing the accident or rendering it less severe than it otherwise would have been so that no fatalities occur. Again, if you've been miraculously saved from an auto accident, or a myriad of other situations, it may be due to the Work of your deva, or to these etheric human specialists, or to both.

If you don't harbor the preconceptions that otherwise would cause you to be on the scene of a catastrophe designed to cause people to release those particular types of preconceptions, God will send agents to try to get you to leave the area.

Of course, if a nation karmically has attached itself to suffering by causing disasters and disruptions to another nation, say perhaps by invading a nation that had not attacked the invader, then the attacker must be disrupted in turn because it has attached itself to the energy of disruption. This is another scenario; let's not get fundamentalistically attached to the idea of only one cause for disasters. In such a case, if the attacker is perceived to be militarily too strong for other nations to invade, the energy may precipitate as a devastating storm or other natural disaster. A nation can invoke the Grace that would prevent such disasters if that nation only warred against others in its own defense and practiced the living ethics of compassion. That Grace which clears some destructive karma out of the causal body may make its appearance as a result of the understanding and practice of living ethics, so that a nation that wars only for defense or the defense of its allies (assuming its allies are also morally and spiritually polarized with Freedom for all citizens) may avoid the rebounding of the energy of destruction when it has applied that energy in the form of a counterattack to some other nation that has chosen to become the enemy of the moral, spiritual nation.

Destruction will probably always cause pain, but it need not cause suffering, and this is as true in this second scenario as it is in the first, and it is true in every type of situation we may be able to imagine.

So I hope it's clear to you that preconceptions cause suffering by creating an attachment to pain that prevents you from letting go of all your pain in the moment of experiencing it, so that you continue to haul some of your pain around for the long term, which will also serve to attract still more pain which your preconceptions will try to turn into still more suffering. I know this not only because of experience, but also because I perceive things thru my Higher Mental body and translate them thru areas of my brain which physically correspond to my Higher Mental body and which haven't yet been developed in most people, finally allowing them to flow "downward" into that faculty which is responsible for creating word-forms. Pretty simple, if you just look at the matter without preconceptions.

So now you've been spoon-fed the deeper aspect of the Mystery of Suffering, and I can do no more for you. Sonny-Bob and I have done everything we possibly can, and the rest is up to you. Naturally, there are more facets to the question that could be examined (there always are with any presentation regarding the nature of a particular region of reality), but you've been provided with the basic scenario. You can "What if" and "Yeah, but" it to death, but do that on your own time, not mine. Sonny-Bob and I have already given you more than anyone else ever has, so it seems to us that it's time for you to show some initiative and connect with the new energy of Intelligent Love which provides for the synthesis of every spectrum, and all aspects associated with every spectrum, of human experience.

Repression creates perversion, and perversion immediately gives rise to selfishness. And selfishness is the parent of damfoolishness. The damfoolishness is a jumble of glamours and illusions designed to justify the selfishness which the perverts are addicted to. The Pharaohs of Egypt were pretty good at the damfoolishness of using slaves to build pyramids and such; the fat, greasy convenience store owners of the twentieth century were far more cunning with the damfoolishness as they justified holding their captives behind mop and cash register. They built large houses for their families on the profits squeezed from the blood and sweat of their wage slaves, but they couldn't build homes *with* their families, because you can't engage in a pattern of exploitation all day, then come home in the evening and suddenly drop the pattern. So the convenience store owners and their fatty, fatty, two-by-four brethren in a variety of slave-powered businesses could only yield to the automatic creation of dysfunctional families powered by the same fears and lusts that powered their businesses.

The only difference between a slave of the Pharaohs and a twentieth century wage slave was that the wage slave was "free" to change masters . . . if he could find another master to hold him captive. The greatest victory won by the capitalists was when they convinced their wage slaves that they were free. After that

664 / Apollo Starmule

unsurpassed victory of psychological warfare, the capitalists never had to worry about a slave revolt. They might have to worry about slave unions coming together to demand an extra crust of bread, but they knew that the actual institution of slavery was safe from assault by those it held captive.

The capitalists were fond of pointing to the "benefits" of slavery, such as when they deigned to provide some basic level of healthcare for the slaves (often at the slaves' own expense!), but they conveniently forgot to mention that the laws of the Southern United States in the previous century had mandated similar "benefits" for the black slaves. The only real advantage a white, black, red or yellow twentieth century wage slave enjoyed over his nineteenth century predecessors was the fact that he had the right to keep and bear arms, which would allow him to enter the workplace with a rifle and shake things up a little, if he deemed it necessary. Yet after using his right of self-ownership to assert himself in the face of his master, the slave would find himself institutionalized in an even worse form of slavery which would only teach him how to become a thief and rapist, so that if he were ever released from the institution, he would have the skills to turn to the deliberate victimization of others, and necessity would make it nearly inevitable that he would do so, if for no other reason than the fact that most slave owners wouldn't buy (I mean "hire", of course) a slave who'd been institutionalized. So the very fabric of society was designed around humiliation and shame, and of doing everything possible to increase that humiliation and shame if a slave snapped under the pressures of whatever pyramid he was building and took up arms to rage against that pyramid.

If you broke down under the weight of ten tons, this alleged society would kick you as you lay helpless on the ground, then try to bury you under a hundred additional tons. I think developing real rehabilitation programs was resisted in this "society" because those who "benefited" the most from the slave trade knew that they were the ones most in need of rehabilitation. And they owned the government and all the propaganda outlets.

Life on this planet had been this way for millions of years, actually. The only difference was that the twentieth century capitalists, with their crude psychological warfare techniques, had made the slaves like it, or pretend to like it, by making them feel they were out of step with their brother slaves in society if they didn't buy into the glamour cast over their senses which was designed to cause them to equate slavery with freedom. As primitive primate herd animals, the last thing most twentieth century people wanted to do was stand out as anything other than a good wage slave.

A number of countries in the twentieth century had tried a primitive and abhorrent form of communism, which was actually worse than capitalism, because it was based in ideology rather than in the warm, unforced flow of compassionate Altruism from the heart-pool's boundless resource of sharing. Their primitive communism was enforced by governments, and thus was destined to fail, because the true communism of compassionate sharing cannot be forced by any person or government of any kind. Theft is wrong, and while it is true that capitalism stole a slice of people's souls, the primitive communism tried to destroy those souls altogether in a much worse violation of the heart's natural law of always speaking its truth and always acting according to its truth.

The news media always had a field day in the twentieth century whenever it could report the presence of looters in the streets, but this crude form of looter was merely a "lower" manifestation of the soul-looting performed by the capitalists and communists every day in their empires of selfishness. An occasional outbreak of street-looting is inevitable as people do strange and undisciplined and *wrong* things in a feeble attempt to reclaim the part of their souls that was legally looted from them by those more clever at creating and maintaining systems of greed to exploit the less clever and the more loving. In this particular boat, the crude, undisciplined lust-driven herd-animal slave often sat next to the sensitive, loving, consciously evolving disciple of lovingkindness, who obviously might have been clever enough to exploit others if he had smothered his conscience, but of course as a heart-disciple he was disciplined and dedicated to listening to that constant whisper of the heart and thus had become incapable of smothering it.

Selfishness had infected the race for millions of years, but in the twentieth century the selfishness was at such epidemic proportions even the Pharaohs would have been shocked . . . while the more degenerate among them might have slightly admired the black magic propaganda of government, business and news media as they all conspired to keep the slaves in line and the masters "on top". (But even the more degenerate Pharaohs would probably have had more self-respect than to actually practice such slimy black magic.) Yet what kind of nut wants to sit on top of a dung heap? A twentieth century capitalist or communist or socialist, that's what kind.

I mention selfishness and point to its almost unheard of levels of epidemic in the twentieth century (actually, in the late Atlantean period the selfishness was just as bad, and is a large part of the reason Atlantis vanished) because these things have to be observed with a clear eye and discussed if the race is ever to advance beyond the ancient sin of selfishness.

Listen: I portray to you the selfishness at the core of the twentieth century monkey-mind, and which clouded the twentieth century heart. It *must* be understood at this deep level by all who would advance beyond it. True psychology is at last here, and there is no way for a person who wants to learn to respect, and then to love, himself to escape the depth of this inventory.

A "morality" or "spirituality" built upon a foundation of squishy turds cannot stand, and will repeatedly fall as monkey-man plays with his tinker-toy psychology and spirituality. In the name of love or kindness or morality or humanity, these twentieth and early twenty-first century people would often "help" one another in the event of a disaster. Now, having been in many unusual situations myself, I recognize the validity of helping others. Sometimes we have to have help if we're going to survive and have a chance to heal from whatever unusual situation has overtaken us. But the difficulty with twentieth and early twenty-first century humanity is that the one who was "helping" someone else was actually, in the deep unexplored recesses of his monkey-mind, helping his own sordid egotism. Yet true lovingkindness and Altruism cannot be practiced if even a trace of egotism remains. Thus must the human being Work to become Liberated from his egotism in order to truly benefit the human race.

Observe what happens with the energy when a person "helps" others while yet suffering from the disease of egotism: The energy of his selfishness attaches itself to the bag of groceries or whatever his "gift" is, and if the recipient of the "gift" is sufficiently open to energy-impression, then the energy of that selfishness is transferred to the "beneficiary" of the "gift". So has a gift really been made, or has the thing that was achieved really been nothing more than an inflation of egotism on the part of both the one who gave the gift and the one who received it?

Twentieth century people gave primarily because they didn't want to go to hell, or because they wanted to see themselves as a "good" person and wanted others to see them also in that way, or to avoid the feeling of guilt that might accrue to one who didn't give. Yet if you're giving to avoid guilt, this is the evidence that the guilt is already there, prompting you with an emotional discomfort to do something that will disguise its presence in your causal body so you won't do the real Work of releasing the guilt to God. And who on earth would want to receive a "gift" with the foul grease of guilt smeared all over it? Sometimes some of these people did give out of a spirit of goodwill, and that was the most beneficial kind of gift, yet even here preconceptions rode on their gifts like rats riding European ships to immigrate to a new home in the colonies. So even their goodwill was tainted with egotism.

The truth is that most of the "gift-giving" in the twentieth century was designed to foster the continued monkey-selfishness of their alleged "society", not restore a wounded heart to humanness with the flowing unconditional Grace of a true Altruism. If they had had the courage to stop their "gift-giving" for a few years to get at the core of their monkey selfishness and clean it up so it would truly reflect the energy of Altruism, they would suddenly have awakened in a fragrant Light that would have brought them to a true society based on the genuine sharing of an uncompromised heart, not on monkey gift-giving thru profits earned from the exploitation of slaves. For what doth it profit a monkey if he gain all the bananas, yet lose his soul?

Yet the selfishness and the slavery it spawned in this society was so ingrained that most of the time most of the people didn't even notice it any more than they noticed their own breath. The result was that even those few genuinely loving and destructive souls who wanted to bring down the whole jungle and let it be seen as the dead pile of brush that it actually always was had to utilize the labor of slaves themselves, if only peripherally. For every time they traveled they had to travel on a road made and maintained by slaves, and every time they went to buy groceries, those groceries were sold by slaves, unless they had access to a true food cooperative . . . yet even such a cooperative would stock some products that had been produced by slaves. Almost all labor was slave labor during this dark age, this iron age, this slimy Kali Yuga, with the result that everyone had to use the labor of slaves, at least on an occasional basis, though those with more active consciences philosophically didn't support the institution of slavery and gave it no moral support, and kept their use of slaves to a minimum.

As you might expect from a race so ironically hypocritical,

some of these slave owners spoke out in favor of their brand of slavery, while condemning the Founders of America for promoting liberty while still relying on slaves themselves. Yet the Founders were actually responsible for introducing a breath of Freedom that lasted for a few decades, while these twentieth and early twenty-first century slave owners were too morally and spiritually impotent to do anything to lessen the power of the institution of slavery. The sometimes maligned Jefferson wanted the United States to evolve into a country of yeoman types where there was no slavery, and everyone worked in his own preferred way for the common good, neither tolerating infringement nor offering infringement to any of his neighbors. Jefferson promoted the kinship of Humanity, and felt it possible to evolve into such kinship. By the time Sonny-Bob was born, Jefferson's dream had been proved more viable than that snot-nosed Alexander Hamilton's dream of fostering the corruption of competition, but in the twentieth century people hadn't yet seen the truth of their own humanity, and so followed the false idol of money and the inevitable, unstoppable corruption that follows the introduction of money into any society. (Of course Hamilton didn't introduce money, but he promoted it and standardized the lust of it and convinced people it was a virtuous substance rather than an addictive drug that would break their hearts with such self-loathing they would have to numb themselves with layer after layer of preconceptions to be able to more or less live with themselves.)

SIDEBAR: A Short Rant As The Full Moon Approaches

For Jefferson the government was the servant of the country; for Hamilton the country was the servant of the government. Hamilton sought sweeping governmental powers for the sake of sustaining government itself; Jefferson audaciously did as he pleased in the exercise of power without the milksop relying on rules and regulations required by the more timid, but he didn't do it for government, he did it for America. That's the difference between the two: one served the government and business interests, the other served the people. The motives for their actions are what is important. The materialist focuses on the action, not on the motive and soul-energy lying back of the action, so the materialist doesn't see any difference between Hamilton's seeking power for the government thru reducing constitutional restrictions on that power, and Jefferson's taking the government's power and using it to actually benefit Americans thru means which may have been a little unconstitutional at times. The materialist only sees what his warped lusts want him to see; he doesn't see the soul-purpose behind any aspect of Creation. Sadly, the materialist is usually an intellectual, and the intellect denies everything but itself. The intellect wants to assume all of Creation for its own child. But such a child as the intellect imagines is always stillborn.

The intellectuals spend all their time confusing themselves, confusing one another, and confusing non-intellectuals into ignoring their innate sensitivity, their innate knowingness. The intellectuals guide their ship by a star that doesn't even exist, so they are always at sea. Anybody who pays attention to what he **knows**, rather than to what some smutty whoreson of an intellectual thinks, can tell thru his feeling nature that the energy Jefferson emitted was the energy of egalitarianism, of Freedom and Justice for all, and that the energy Hamilton emitted was the energy of control and elitism. Cry me a handful, intellectual. You've fallen off your boat, and your life preserver is defective. You do *not* rule the world.

Intellectuals are responsible for introducing acts of ugliness and shame and control into sex. Their justifications look pitiful to the civilized person. And if they could see the dark energy-cages they are confining their souls to and the dark cords of misused and perverted mental and emotional substance with which they bind their energy bodies, they would scream in horror at themselves.

Get this: the intellectuals spend centuries trying to deny sex, and when that doesn't work they turn to bondage and discipline. Repression creates perversion.

Sex for an awakened person is never dull or boring, and he requires no theatrics or fantasy. He *has* no fantasy; the ability to fantasize was purified out of him during his Quest, his movement toward Liberation.

The awakened person is left with Creative Imagination, and this pure and beautiful and *true* faculty allows him both to connect with the soul of his partner and with the psychological factors surrounding that soul. If the cheerleader variation of the archetype of Aphrodite comes up, he welcomes Her and makes smooth and harmonious music with Her, for the cheerleader has become a subface, a subaspect, of the Great Goddess, just as has her sister, the schoolgirl. Unfortunately, these subfaces were born of repression, of desire trying to deny its own nature. However, they can be purified thru releasing emotional glamor and mental illusion, and allowing love to flood the space vacated by glamor and illusion. The result is--you guessed it!-- compassion. At this point, the cheerleader and the schoolgirl have Achieved reunification with their own souls and with the Goddess, becoming a reflection of Her colored with the nature of the subaspect which they are, and with the spiritual nature of their own Individuality.

There were those in the twentieth century who believed in an illusion, a lie, that blondes tended to be "dumb". But people who believed this were themselves incredible dumbasses. The dumbasses believed in what they mistakenly saw as the "power" of intellect, never realizing that the intellect has no real power, except the power they gave it to rule their lives with illusion.

The truth is that these ladies who represented Aphrodite on the physical plane were some of the most intelligent incarnations among the sons of men, which is why the sons of men tended to treasure the fair blonde more than other types of females. But these men were unaware of their own motivation for cherishing and desiring this type of female, because they'd stupidly allowed themselves to be duped into believing that intelligence is an intellectual affair. But the truth is that Aphrodite's wholebodied, wholesouled depth, and the steady, calm light in her eyes, represent one of the greatest intelligences--and perhaps *the* greatest intelligence--ever seen upon this globe. Intelligence is *not* an intellectual affair, it is an Aphrodite affair.

Perhaps there is a streak of jealousy in the denigration of the fair-skinned blonde by the men who so desire her company. Or perhaps she causes a shifting of their illusions which causes a little soul-light to break thru for a moment and they can't stand to face the light. Be that as it may, it is *impossible* to find greater intelligence than Aphrodite among the sons of men, and I kneel before Her and place my own intelligence at Her feet. She is a fine steward of all that I am; if the Muslim is God's slave, then I am Aphrodite's.

In summation, then, the person who has developed the intelligence of his Creative Imagination doesn't fantasize *about* his partner, he connects *with* his partner by perceiving the soul-light within Her and the many facets of the ruby-jewel surrounding the soul, and by perceiving the many psychological factors, or archetypes, which surround the light-infused beautiful ruby-crystal of Her soul. In this one splendid eternal moment, he doesn't want to be with anybody other than the lady in his arms, and could not conceive of a fantasy. He wants to know all that she can teach him. He knows that serving this woman is his sacred Work, and that is all he wants to do. It might be pointed out that the ability to enter this superlative state does not come overnight, but only with lots of practice while steadily purifying the aspirations toward love and fullbody acceptance and fullbody compassion. Helping a man Achieve this condition is where the non-egocentrically polarized Sacred Prostitute really shines, for she has become the earthly embodiment of compassion. But any Lady who Achieves the development of a pure compassion and an appreciation of the deep Beauty of Her own nature and what it can accomplish can help a man reach the Kingdom of Heaven, while he yet remains a while upon this earth in the arms of his sweetly Beloved.

No person who has developed this Sight which reveals the Great Soul-Ruby could ever play "games" of subjugation, for he is continually exalted by and appreciative of what his partner IS. And as a given archetype floats up or projects out of his lover's consciousness, he allows that archetype to take him by the hand and guide him into full communion with her soul. This is what human sexuality was made for. There is no greater Wisdom or Wonder than that which humans can create for themselves right here on this beautiful physical, spiritual earth thru their sexuality-given power to connect with the souls of one another. All sharing emerges from the sexual nature. Those who are comfortable with their sexual natures are comfortable with sharing.

Now after the subrant and hymn of praise in which we refined the intellectual so he could be absorbed into Aphrodite, let us return to the original sidebar rant.

Thomas Jefferson provided Vision and his intellect was submerged in that Vision; Big Al Hamilton's only vision was the immortality of his own intellect thru the institutions he could create. Jeff was ruled by a Divine Vision for Humanity; Al was ruled by intellect. Do you know which of the two was a Free Man? Do you know which one was a Specialist in Freedom? Do you know which one would support *your* Freedom, and the Freedom of your Family to live in accordance with your own natures?

Am I being fair? Hell, no. I make no attempt to wallow in the illusion of fairness, which is the bastard offspring of the illusion of balance. These are two of the primary illusions intellect uses to justify its attempt to rule the human being, the human soul. Trying to be fair or balanced is immoral, because true morality lives only to support Reality, not illusion. If my Revered Ancestor Sonny-Bob taught me anything, it was to avoid making a pretense of moral bastardy. (I neither confirm nor deny the rumors that I have created physical bastards.)

Remember that balance is an illusion thru which the intellect congratulates itself, and that imbalance is implicit within the illusion of balance--you can't have one without the other. Both balanced people and imbalanced people are insane, and usually people don't recognize this danger in the balanced person, though sometimes they do with respect to the imbalanced one.

Any balanced person is always fighting to remain balanced, and this struggle itself is the proof of his imbalance. Both balanced and imbalanced people suffer from the stress of the struggle to remain or become balanced, and stress is a primary symptom of insanity. Twentieth and early twenty-first century people were so insane and so in denial about their own insanity they sometimes told the self-lie that stress could be a good thing-- but this lie was only good for masking their own insanity from their own bloodshot eyes. A civilized, fragrant, well-blended person has no stress, though he may feel a certain creative tension as he holds himself within the place he has chosen to occupy in the Pattern of Legend. This creative tension doesn't feel like stress and has nothing to do with stress. The creative tension is both an effect and a tool of the civilized person's Creative Patterning Process, that's all.

Here's an example of the insanity of those who were balanced: The people who ran the mass media in the twentieth century were balanced people who deliberately supported violence in general by making it seem glamorous and by making genuine love seem to be unavailable for human consumption, and they supported violence that in particular was aimed at women . . . and if the woman in question worked in the sex industry, so much the better. They mocked the feminine side of their own natures by mocking Woman. They gloried like the fucking worthless goatfuckers they were whenever they could produce a fictionalized account of a stripper or prostitute being humiliated in some way and/or murdered. This is how these wonderfully balanced "people" taught women to hate and fear their own bodies and their sexuality, and this is how the producers of these programs showcased their own fear and hatred of natural functions, particularly when those natural functions were tied to the Goddess. For every woman, including (and perhaps especially) strippers and prostitutes, is potentially a Goddess, and to appeal to a base interest in seeing any woman abused or humiliated is a slap in the face of the Great Goddess.

Forget about the literal, linear interpretation of the priests, theologians and other textbook-addicted spiritual ignoramuses. These are the ones who led the way into the blasphemy and hatred of our Mother to begin with. They rely on what they regard as Biblical evidence, not on eternal Truth. And I can tell you the Mother of the World does sit at the foot of the cross, along with Her Sister, the Sacred Prostitute. And these two are the only two Who can be depended on never to depart. The theologian, feebleminded and inexperienced and closed-hearted and tight-bellied as he is, will perceive only dichotomy at the foot of the cross, but the Truth is there is no dichotomy at all. The Faces of the Divine Feminine all contain each other and complement each other; they do not war with one another. And the face of every Female you meet will belong to the Divine Feminine, once the lady in question has purified herself of the glamors and illusions that block her off from her true nature. So those who mock any woman can kiss my flabby white ass, as Sonny-Bob would put it. How tiresome it becomes to address the delusions of those who read textbooks! Botheration!

Of course, in addition to their television "dramas", these well-balanced media people also showcased their own perversions by glorying in producing nonfiction--or supposedly nonfiction--accounts of the same type of abusive behavior for their alleged news broadcasts, which they sometimes had the gall to refer to as "news magazines", rather than "toilet paper magazines" smeared with their own fecal corruption and self-hate. I say these "news" accounts were *supposedly* nonfiction because they surrounded their "news stories" with so much glamor there was no way to get at the truth of any story. But they didn't want to find the truth themselves, let alone help the public find the truth. They wanted to keep themselves and the public mired in the doo-doo glamor of their varied perverted lusts. They may have reported on some of the facts surrounding a story along with generating as much glamor as they could to keep their ratings high, but facts are not Truth. If facts are used in a Truthful presentation, they can only be used in support of Truth; facts have no life in themselves. So what the balanced newspeople did was to take dead facts and use them to support their quest to generate glamor; they had no idea how to derive appropriately-supporting Truth-facts from the Sea of Truth that surrounded them, a sea they were not aware of swimming in. And when you're not aware you're swimming, you'll drown, which is exactly what these well-balanced, internationally respected people did: they drowned in their own glamour like so many fish drowning in a tub of their own piss. (I learned most of this from listening in on Sonny-Bob's rantings, by the way. World Saviors know this stuff because they've had to wallow in it to clean some of it up. And from the subtly disguised hate and insanity I saw all around me in the twentieth century, I certainly can't argue with Sonny-Bob's diagnosis.)

The balanced media-people could get away with their crimes against the soul of humanity because their balance served to camouflage their hate and insanity. And remember that all hate is self-hate, and seldom in the history of the earth has anyone hated themselves as much as the reasonable, well-balanced people who produced most television programs. They could, and did, show the most horrible crimes imaginable against women--again, particularly against sex workers--in the name of entertainment, and as long as the skimpily dressed women in these programs had their nipples and sacred mound covered, anything at all could be done to them. And these programs were even shown in prime time, when millions of children were watching . . . watching and being programmed to equate sex with violence and to hate women's guts . . . and to hate their own guts, if they were little girls.

In my time we are a little more civilized than in Sonny-Bob's century, and people who would produce this type of "entertainment", if they appeared, wouldn't be tolerated. A few decades before I was born a senior Sacred Prostitute named Lily The Seer instituted the practice of eliminating those who deliberately encourage hate and ugliness in the world. Common infringers are still kept in a humane facility and given a chance to redeem themselves if they so choose, but people who promote the dark glitter of mass ugliness are immediately killed. They are given no warning and no quarter and no chance for any last words; they are just killed by whichever moral, spiritual citizens can get to them most easily, and then the story is posted on the internet and reported by Goddess News Network to serve notice on those who would deliberately introduce creepy ugliness into our beautiful blue-green planet.

This is not mass or random violence, this is Group justice in service to the Beauty of Love. Thus does the Goddess reclaim her own fractured psyche from those who once thought to defeat her and to erase the very memory of Beauty from our planet.

Remember that evil is not human, and that if you try to treat it humanely it will use your naiveté to defeat you--and you may be mortally wounded in the process. Evil is so well-balanced it will murder your soul thru reasonableness, if you are naive enough to let it.

> "Kill for peace and kill for love
> kill for Jesus up above
> gonna kill the snake and save the dove . . ."

This is one of many military songs, or "jodies", I've heard Sonny-Bob sing in his sleep thru the listening device I placed in his room. He's Pagan, but do not be surprised at his support of Jesus, for Jesus was a child of the Mother of the World, just as Sonny-Bob is. Jesus is Sonny-Bob's older Brother. And there are good snakes, and there are unrefined snakes, and there are downright bad snakes. A Serpent of Wisdom is good; the snake of the unredeemed personality ain't so good . . . at least, not yet. The snake of the unredeemed personalities of those who worked in twentieth century mass media was manipulated by hidden snakes who were downright bad, and who would be shot on sight in any civilized world. Shucks, these worst-of-all snakes usually stayed hidden even in the twentieth century, when most citizens didn't have enough sense or self-love to draw and fire instantly upon sighting such a creature.

Anyway, the government let the media producers get away with trying to subjugate humanity and destroy the Goddess because the people in the government were also well-balanced. A given well-balanced person will almost invariably support the insanity and self-hatred of any other well-balanced person.

You can't regulate evil out of existence. Indeed, evil manufactures most of the regulations which surround primitive people to begin with, and was a major influence upon the Federal Communications Commission and upon the other federal agencies. So to appeal to the regulatory process is usually to appeal to evil, though often those you appeal to may not realize their agencies and "superiors" are being manipulated.

All you can do is destroy evil. This issue isn't about Freedom of the Press (a Sacred Right sponsored by the TAC, to be sure); this is about Humanity's Right to be Free of evil. And the only way to do that is to destroy evil everywhere it hides, while simultaneously building the sacred vibration of Beauty into your society and into everything you touch. (You won't touch evil; you'll kill it from a distance with a weapon, or thru esoteric means we won't discuss in this document.)

But of course, if you can't tell the difference between a merely "bad" person and a thing that no longer is a person, then you aren't ready yet to destroy evil, and certainly it would be in your best interests to try to avoid encountering it. And depending on many factors, such as your personality ray, karma, etc., etc., you may never be ready to destroy evil, even if you are mature enough to recognize it. That is specialized Work that only particular types of people are qualified for. Only if you're prone to violence and are a moral and spiritual person would you be likely to be able to qualify to destroy evil.

Speaking of regulations, a big part of the problem with twentieth century society lay in the fact that the people of the United States, and of course of other countries as well, had allowed themselves to be mechanically programmed into becoming "a nation of laws" rather than a nation of human souls. Laws deaden the personality so that it cannot even contact the soul, a fact well-known to those Founding Angels who overthrew George III and the "nation of laws" his empire had delivered to the New World. But the hardy and resourceful colonists had begun developing a rudimentary sense of their own possibilities under the inspiration both of their souls and of the Founding Angels who had been assigned to help them magnetize themselves toward their souls' purpose, and this Reality is what gave them the power to defeat the greatest "nation of laws" of the day and permanently remove its yoke from their shoulders. But it wasn't long before the creeping mechanicalness encouraged by political, religious and industrial "leaders" began to obscure the souls of the people of what had been a relatively free republic. Evil forces prompted both the openly selfish and the always hate-filled and degraded manipulative do-gooders (who were responsible for creating organized crime and very widespread alcoholism and drug addiction thru their Temperance Movement and Drug War) to seek the mechanicalness of the yoke of law and disorder in the attempt to produce the most emotionally seething, hate-filled society possible. Lawmakers are such weak people; they and the do-gooders and the priests and the robber barons are always such easy prey for nonhuman reptiles who don't even have souls.

Perhaps those silly people who were always bragging about Rome--excuse me, I mean Amerika--being "a nation of laws" would have begun to sober up a little if they had stopped to reflect that the Evil Empire, the Soviet Onion, was also "a nation of laws".

Gee, I wonder what forces lay behind the establishment of widespread legalisms both in the Soviet and Amerikan Empires.

The people of twentieth century Amerika had been taught to fear "widespread lawlessness" by the undisciplined and unloving media, and by the government the media considered itself a branch of. They'd been made so numb with buried despair and self-loathing they'd lost the ability to consider what "widespread lawlessness" would actually mean in a land where people had developed a rudimentary understanding of morality and caught the first flash of contact from their souls--which is what the Founding Angels desired for their descendants. They couldn't see that with the corruption of law, chaos was created in what originally had been a society with a chance to become pristine, and that if they escaped the burden of law--itself an immoral, unspiritual monstrosity--they would be mature enough to guide their own affairs, both as individuals and as volunteers for community Working in Group Formation.

Maybe it should be pointed out that many times those who were on the verge of waking up into some higher phase of their own continuum of awareness--particularly in the West--would become confused by genuine spiritual Teachings that had been genuinely issued either directly, or under telepathy or inspiration, from the genuinely authentic Ashrams of the East. Part of the problem here was that the Masters of the Wisdom often spoke or wrote a rather archaic form of English, and the language had undergone a bit of a revolution by the late twentieth century. If they said they didn't condone temperance, a person by the late twentieth century might conclude they were in favor of promiscuity--yet this was not the case at all, because indiscriminate soul connection is not possible, and sex is always about worship, about soul connection. What the Masters meant, translated into the language of the late twentieth century, was that they didn't condone *abstinence*, because people who try to force abstinence upon the sweetest aspects of their own natures lose the capacity to connect in "water brotherhood" with another soul. Heinlein was sent to help straighten this matter out a bit.

In another case, sometimes one of the Masters would speak about following "rules", but upon close inspection it would be found that the so-called "rules" weren't rules at all; sometimes they were *descriptions* of spiritual principles, and sometimes they were descriptions of states of consciousness related to those principles, which the disciple might expect to eventually experience his own personal variation of, if he studiously remained on his self-created Path. But they were *not* rules, despite the Master's classification. Sometimes the Masters got a little sloppy here, but they're only human, after all. They need toilet paper just like the rest of us.

Remember, Beloved, that your causal body *is* your Path, and you must build your causal body yourself. The Master already built his, used it properly in service, and finally discarded it to enter a more expansive realm of service. This new realm is the Pathless Land, of course, as He perceives Himself as a point of light in a great celestial Pattern. Light is multidimensional, and He no longer requires a Path to arrive at His destination when he shifts himself within the Pattern.

So now you can see why every Human Being is superior to every religion, government and every other institution. These entities don't build your causal body, *you* build your causal body in your own unique way thru lifetimes of selfless service. These entities, while they live (and so far, they have always died shortly after coming into existence) may contribute a new note to your causal body, but they are not superior to your causal body. The Group Soul, or Ashram, of conscious people is the great equalizer, acknowledging everyone from the Master of the Lodge to the most newly admitted aspirant as being absolutely equal. The only reason the Master of the Lodge is the Master of the Lodge is because he's the most qualified. If someone else appeared who was more qualified, the Master would gladly step aside and go back to washing dishes. No politics ever goes on in a real Lodge, and the pissy-assed Masons and Rosicrucians of the twentieth century might try to remember this fact.

It might be helpful to remember that the Masters neither respect servility, nor can they Work with people who insist on being servile. A disciple may *coordinate* his will and his Heart with the Master in the process of Altruistic Creativity, but he will never relinquish his will or the welfare of his Heart to anyone, Master or otherwise. The disciple is certainly not a stubborn, self-serving egotist, he is a lover, both of the Master and of that Humanity which he and the Master serve together, and you can't reflect the innate Love of your Heart into the world unless you assume full responsibility for your own Individuality, honey.

I know that in the sacred literature of all lands that sometimes it seems the disciple surrenders his own will, but he never does that, ever. It's just that it's really impossible to write about states of consciousness in an accurate way apart from Poetry, and in Poetry the Poet submits to the Universe, and some of that submission will probably be reflected in his Poem. Ah, we should just shut up. If you only understood that words are not real, and the divisions that words create are not real, that would help us a lot. We are limited too much by words, and cannot convey what we mean. But certainly we have made a gallant effort, don't you think?

Maybe it should also be pointed out that by the late twentieth and early twenty-first centuries some of the disciples of the Masters were really making a mess of things in their choice of language, sometimes because of a cowardly desire to "fit in" or not to "rock the boat" of the prejudices of persons they regarded as influential, or out of a desire to stupidly try to graft spiritual truth onto the preconceptions of the herd from which they themselves had emerged--but with this catering to preconceptions, they were at risk of being drawn back into the herd-illusion themselves. Or maybe they just wanted to be seen as "leaders", for the herd is usually only willing to acknowledge one of its own in any sort of leadership role.

We can see a parallel in the cattle drives of the Old West, in which sometimes a steer would emerge who would assume leadership of the herd during the trail drives. This steer would amble along in front while the other critters cheerfully followed him to their doom in the cattle markets. Usually this "leader" steer wouldn't be sold, but was used in subsequent trail drives to lead more herds to their doom. As you might expect, the cowboys were very fond of these "leadership steers", as I would label them. Those who are addicted to labels might want to know that "leadership steers" is a term which, to the best of my knowledge, wasn't used in the Old West, but which I seem to have coined myself. I'm sure this information makes those with minds like dictionaries feel better.

Sure, sure, the Masters themselves could have appeared with trumpets resounding and starship escorts, but by the twentieth century, the Masters hoped people would grow mature and responsible enough to be able to recognize spiritual Truth apart from outward trappings of amazement.

"Sex and violence . . ." Yes, the primitive people of the twentieth century allowed the dark serpents who manipulated the mass media program them into thinking that sex and violence were the same . . . so of course, in the practices of these morally deformed people, sex and violence did become practically inseparable. The only sex little kids were allowed to see during prime time was violent, hate-filled, spite-filled, abusive sex--or rape, in other words--but somehow the damage to their souls was supposed to be averted by making sure they didn't see a beautiful nipple or a flash of pink or a waving cock. Though sometimes the media producers did substitute some other blunt object for the cock, to make sure little boys got the lesson that their phallus was only to be used to piss and to beat up women and make them cry. This is the type of perversity encouraged by "the rule of law". And in some jurisdictions, if a genuinely loving marriage had manifested, the authorities would have jailed the parents if they had demonstrated their genuine love in front of the kids. My God, the restrictive Jehovah these well-balanced people worshipped was insane.

The war-mongers of the West in the twentieth century were usually pretty well-balanced, though sometimes the peace-mongers were imbalanced. The war-mongers of the Middle East were usually imbalanced, but the war-atrocities and insanities perpetrated by combat forces were the same, whether these combat forces were from the rational, well-balanced West, or from the imbalanced, crazy Middle East. Balance and imbalance-- either form of insanity contains the possibility of the other, and encourages the other and works with the other to bring a tearful chaos to the world.

As you might expect, though, the well-balanced people of the West made excuses for their own atrocities and tried even to deny that certain atrocities were atrocities . . . for the well-balanced person is the master at excusing himself from moral conduct. Imbalanced people usually don't have as many illusions as balanced people, and so usually are happy to accept responsibility for their own crimes . . . though they can't understand why the balanced people won't apply a similar honesty to their own activities.

Westerners used to get mightily upset by the use of improvised explosive devices by those they'd decided to label as "terrorists", yet these IEDs didn't kill as many people as the cruise missiles and bombs of the West. If the "terrorists" had had cruise missiles and bombers they would have been happy to use them, but they had to make do with what they had. Yet in the West they were so chronically deluded as to what they wanted to believe was their own "goodness" that the well-balanced people couldn't look at their own distorted reflection--their distorted, hate-filled causal bodies and the distorted hate-filled causal body of their society-- and see themselves as the conquerors and butchers that others in other parts of the world saw them as. When an IED killed a soldier in an invading force from the West the media and the other branches of government programmed the public to equate it with terrorism, but when bombs and missiles from the West killed little boys and girls and mothers and fathers and grandparents in residential communities in foreign lands, it was merely "regrettable collateral damage", not terrorism, not murder. I wonder what Jesus would say. Hell, I *know* what Jesus would say!

A large percentage of the life of the balanced person consists of rationalizing his imbalanced behavior. He uses that bastardized pretense of logic called reasonableness to try to keep himself from screaming. He doesn't want to allow himself to just break down and cry. Yet look at the agony and the tears he brings to the families he murders with his "smart bombs". Well, at least the smart bombs are not reasonable, so maybe they are smarter than those who use them.

Reasonable, well-balanced people and crazy, imbalanced people are so similar, you would think it would be easy for them to make friends.

You'll never see a civilized human being who is either well-balanced or imbalanced. These twin delusions are not a part of the Pattern which he inhabits.

But the twentieth century people were not civilized, they were merely domesticated.

The wild, free, civilized Human Being is always self-created thru strenuous dedication to Love, Truth and genuine Creative Altruism. The domestic critter just plods along following orders, head hung low and cowbell signaling his compliance to the authorities.

Is the American slogan "My country, right or wrong!" the motto of a free, compassionate human being or of a braying ass? You tell me, honey. Surely you see that this slogan would have fit perfectly with the German government's program to sabotage the consciences of its citizens during the Thirties and Forties.

Yea, verily, the twentieth century people were as full of uncompassionate violence as any coop full of chickens. But in their productions, the media moguls frequently treated women even worse than a rooster treats his hens.

We cannot call animals, who are merely being true to the nature of their species, depraved. We use the term "depravity" to denote human beings who lose contact with the Beauty of their own souls, and of their bodies which are an extension of their souls, and allow themselves to slip into the conduct of animals-- whether that conduct is the conduct of a sheep which has lost contact with the natural fierce joyfulness of the human spirit, or the conduct of a rooster raping as many hens as he can. A real rooster or sheep can behave like a real rooster or sheep and not be in violation of God's Visioning Process, but when supposedly human beings behave in this way, even in pretend, they become less than animals. It is difficult for a civilized human being to understand why a person who had gone to a lot of trouble to leave the animal kingdom and Achieve a human body would then allow himself to slide back into that kingdom while still wearing the human body he won for himself throughout long ages. Such a person risks blowing his opportunity to become really, fully human.

In conclusion regarding balance and imbalance, let me say that the balanced, well-rounded person can be led to believe and practice any form of insanity, and the only reason he locks up the imbalanced people is that they remind him of himself.

Finally, a note on begging the question: Rational, well-balanced people nearly always run from the observations of the soothsayer, the truthsayer, by immediately going into "what if . . . ?" mode and looking for exceptions to the Principles the soothsayer presents. This is as dishonest as you can get. The first step toward integrating and enlightening the consciousness is to go to the trouble to do the genuine, Humanity-based Work to actually *understand* the Principle the soothsayer presents. Having finally understood the Principle, then and *only then* can you look with honesty and integrity for exceptions, if you so desire. An even weaker approach is for the well-balanced person to look for what he believes are contradictions in the soothsayer's words, but this is like a jackass braying in the nighttime fields as he looks up in protest at the stars. He hasn't learned to understand the stars and doesn't even know what he's protesting. The constellations are meaningless to him, yet still he tries to define and judge and classify the light-filled pattern in the dark skies of his own lack of compassionate awareness. But to the regal, enlightened Palomino, every moment of the night is filled with living, pulsing, moving, golden energy that his own consciousness has learned to perceive as a side-effect of his evolving himself into his own truest Pattern, while jackass "thoughts" and procedures fall away from him into the chaos of illusion that he once believed in, but which in fact never was.

The "what if . . . ?" reflex is caused by the immediate appearance of the fear that the well-balanced person has that in the fragrant Light of the soothsayer's observations, he may not be able to continue holding on to some prejudice and on to whatever favorite reflex actions arise out of that prejudice.

But the well-balanced, reasonable, weak people of the twentieth century were not as wise and accomplished as our Palomino. They were chatterboxes, engaging in the stream of the linear illusion of a constant "give and take", but never once has the balanced, reasonable person felt the Achievement of the pool of genuine Altruistic Creative Sharing which is available to him. That energy-pool of his own sweet, powerful, *human* heart has nothing whatsoever to do with any linear illusion, nor does it have anything to do with a "give and take" or with some kind of "exchange". Indeed, most of the time their "give and take" was nothing more than an attempt to push or pull one another off balance thru the cords of the attachments that bound them to each other and provoke one another into a higher-intensity combat. Most of the rest of the time their "give and take" was merely an attempt at subtle manipulation. Sharing is not that. Sharing is a state of consciousness beyond the balanced, reasonable person's ability to comprehend.

Ah, but how do we do this? How do we continually find ourselves drawn from experience to experience and from rant to rant in the course of our discussion? For our document has assumed a form that overflows its banks, like a river composed of molten fire. I will tell you: it is because we are alive with Agni's fire, a fire which burns away the old so the new may take form. As that which we've learned flies away from us on currents of fire, it hits these pages you're reading, there to remain for your edification. Yet the learning remains as accumulated lightforms with us. So that which was ponderous and hard-won becomes light as a feather and easy for us to administer now. You are reading our causal body! The causal body that will be completely gone by the time you hold this book in your hands, and which is practically gone now. Sweet one, you hold our causal body, enlivened once more by your perceptive attentions! We rest in peace.

And remember that the mature causal body is a vertical phenomenon, like a pink swirling wind tunnel connecting earth with heaven, connecting personality with soul. So that which we know--that which we are and have become thru the agency of the causal body--continually swirls and rotates here and yon in the moment, each second bringing newness and sweet life most divine. This book then, as the only remaining physical representation of our causal body, can be expected to swirl itself about your attentions, flirting with every element of your understanding.

You hold liquid fire. Now we have moved on into a lighter phase. We are fused now within all our parts. We are One.

* * *

It doth seem appropriate now to return to the pro-Jefferson, anti-Hamilton campaign.

Because Hamilton's alleged vision was in the ascendancy for over two centuries, America lost touch time and again with her Heart thru the destruction of her morality and thru the subjugation of human beings to institutions. This decay resulted in the American Empire of the very late twentieth and early twenty-first centuries. (Yes, Hamilton opposed black slavery, but he didn't support equal freedom for all, he supported equal humiliation for all.)

Hamilton was the type of person who, if someone came along and founded a spiritual movement or a religion, he'd try to turn it into a church and squeeze it to death with preconceptions, and with the committees and doctrines and profane hierarchies created by the preconceptions, resulting in misperceptions of what were once genuine insights, which would foster a hardening of the Human Heart against knowing its own nature. People who make excuses for manufacturing preconceptions and restrictions and committees are the disciples of Hamilton; they have completely missed Jefferson and some of the other Revolutionary Cronies. (Remember that a committee is a symptom of the herd; it lacks that impulse of Individuality which spurs the Creation of a genuine, Altruistic Group.)

Nobody's perfect; but the spiritual voyager must learn the

discernment which reveals the difference between those who sponsor the Way of the Human Heart, and those who are, shall we say, a little unbalanced by what seems to them to be the brilliance of intellectual functioning and its endless scheming, and of the intellect's attempt to permanently enshrine itself as the governor of all things living thru manufacturing soul-deadening institutions. For all institutions are built in the image of intellect; the Heart cultivates the growth of Families to give Group Expression to the soul.

The wags of the twentieth and early twenty-first centuries gloried in the fact that Hambone's degenerate vision came to (temporarily!) dominate the American soul, but they were nothing but uncreative coattail riders, anyway. Had Jefferson's authentic Vision for Humanity won to immediate ascendancy, the coattail riders would have been glorying in Jeff's Vision, and preaching that if Hambone's vision had won out, America would have been doomed. But the truth is that if Jeff's Vision had not been obscured for two centuries by the materialists, Americans would have been far freer, far happier . . . . and far more Pagan! For everyone acknowledges that Jeff was a renegade, though the Christians would of course be uncomfortable acknowledging that a strong streak of innate Nature-Worship underlay his outlawry. For part of Jefferson's Mission was to help create an environment in which the Pantheist, Helena Blavatsky, could flourish in her attempt to nudge the earth toward Satya Yuga. Each Hand of God washes every other Hand of God, and there are as many Hands of God as there are stars in the sky. The twentieth century wags were fond of amazing themselves at how such a group of powerful genius-men as America's Founders could have come together all at once, but the wags, blinded as they were by the incompleteness of intellectual delusions, knew less about the way the Almighty works than a dog knows about flying a starship.

Jefferson remains the most Beloved of America's Founders because Americans feel intuitively that this man had their personal welfare at Heart and because, despite his giftedness, he seems to have been the most *human* of the Founders, and because on some level every American has always known he'd be happier if Jefferson's Vision had won out.

This Love of Jefferson remained even in the twentieth century, when Americans' minds were still clouded by the manipulations of Hambone's disciples. But their Hearts were so strongly connected to Jefferson's that the egalitarian American Spirit remained alive beneath all the materialists' attempts to blackmail it. That Spirit remained pure and loving and free, and by the late twenty-first century it had destroyed the intellectual and physical cages built to contain it. Jefferson's seed was not spilled upon the ground, but it did have to incubate for a while.

Hambone's vision was not about happiness, it was about **control**. He'd been so scarred by a boyhood in which life seemed harsh and uncontrollable that he sought to counteract that experience by implementing more control--in other words, by offering a drowning man a drink of water. For the original problems of Hamilton's harsh boyhood had been created by humans' use of one another to further their own ends, and more of this was what Hamilton delivered to America. So we see how harsh energies, when once impressed on the aura, tend to take charge of their own healing process so that the harsh energies are never released and the suffering human never heals. Thus do the harsh energies insure replication of themselves in everything the "reformer" touches. The harsh energies are about the survival of an agonized egotism, not about learning the Art of Release into Happiness.

Look at all the alcoholics created by the "temperance" movement! This while the author of the Eighteenth Amendment--Prohibition--Senator Morris Sheppard was producing 130 gallons a day of illegal whiskey on his farm! The inner pervert strikes down its host once again in rebellion against a false public righteousness. Look and see if you can perceive a pattern in which those who are most likely to irresponsibly indulge in a specific behavior try to make or keep that behavior illegal, or at least regulate it. Ask yourself: where is the profit for them? Sometimes it may be in the form of money, other times it will be in the form of confirming smug preconceptions they have around what they regard as their own "decency", and always their inner pervert profits thru denial of its own dark motives, and of the actions that may arise out of those motives.

But I knew that in the 2020's some common sense would finally be applied regarding what the public would tolerate from politicians and busybodies in the form of the Anti-Hypocrisy Law. This law states that anytime a politician or person of influence--such as a lobbyist--proposes some new restriction to be applied against some avenue of human conduct, that the person proposing the restriction must submit to a thorough investigation by the federal investigative services and pass that investigation before he is allowed to formulate or advocate for a bill before Congress. This investigation is designed to insure the politician or person of influence has not in the past indulged in similar behavior to that he would legislate against. If it is found that he has indulged in such behavior, he is forbidden to agitate for his cause and confined to a mental hospital for a period of time to be specified as the matter unfolds. If he passes this initial investigation, and if the restrictive law is passed, he is required to submit to constant surveillance of all his activities for twenty years after his restriction is enacted into law to insure he does not fall off the imaginary pedestal he wants people to believe he's standing on. And if he does fall off, he lands in a ward in a mental hospital . . . after serving whatever prison sentence he advocated for those who broke his law against consensual activities.

The Anti-Hypocrisy Law doesn't necessarily apply to legislation directed at corporations; only Individuals and Groups of Individuals have rights, and Goddess knows a corporation is not a Group of any kind; it is a herd of standardized folks whose souls have been numbed nearly to death to insure they will behave mechanically. The Anti-Hypocrisy Law stands against mechanicalness and bestiality. So the Anti-Hypocrisy Law is designed to protect the rights of Individuals and Families and Cooperative-Style Businesses, and even businesses which aren't strictly Co-op style, but which are run by families in a humane fashion that promotes the discipline of Individuality, and of the Working of those Individuals in Group formation.

Only spirituality and spiritual activities are respected in the future, and Goddess knows you can't standardize consciousness, or actions or lifeways which arise out of that consciousness. When standardization is present, consciousness is not. Love flies clean out the window and doesn't stop before reaching the next county anytime a standardized test is administered. Don't you know a standardized test damages the spiritual heart of a person, and that the sensitive soul can even feel the damage in his physical heart? Heart attacks are not only caused by inadequate potassium levels! So we see once more that twentieth and early twenty-first century "teachers" and school administrators only used students as objects to gratify their own lustful mechanical delusions of control. They didn't give a damn about their students; they were so numb themselves they didn't know how to give a damn about their students.

Standardization, regimentation, is one of the primary methods primitive societies use to crush the souls of those who have a sincere desire to spiritually Achieve. This dries up the society's own stream of energy-nourishment, because those who would've evolved into its greatest contributors are homeless, or living in mental institutions, or prematurely and unfortunately left the earthplane in a burst of agony.

Insensitive brutes can't see this, of course, because insensitive brutes and their cousins, the meddlesome sickly-sweet manipulators, are the cause of the problem.

Anyway, with the society's energy-nourishment gone, the brittle structure that is temporarily left standing can finally be demolished by just a handful of spiritually alive insurrectionists. And God always provides for that handful to appear.

Yet the stupid brutes and the meddlesome sickly-sweet manipulators always throw up their restrictive, uncompassionate hands and yell "Why!?" when those they tried to crush gird up their loins and strike back.

A spiritual, civilized human being is interested in the sacred Work of Familybuilding; he has no interest in society, except to bring it down when it begins to interfere in his true Work. Familybuilding results in a community of complementary souls; society is merely a symptom of empire which *always* results in a gaggle of crushed spirits warring over a stale crust of bread. Is it not obvious that a civilized human being has no interest in society?

The Anti-Hypocrisy Law was a necessary adjustment in the national life, because a few people by the 2020's were starting to glimpse the true nature of Individuality and of the Group, and with this glimpse of Individuality they realized that anyone who proposes restriction on human lives is not human; at best, such a person is a dumb animal, and at worst he deliberately supports the cause of evil. Such "people" don't even know what a human being is, because they haven't yet glimpsed their own humanity, so it is obvious they have no right to pass laws against those who are actively reaching for their humanity. By the 2040's the thinking had progressed to the point that if these "critter people" wanted to make a cage of discomfort around other people's consensual activities, then a similar cage would be constructed around their own favorite activities. So any politician or person of influence who advocated a reduction in freedom after about 2047 was immediately confined to a mental hospital. And a law was passed that said anyone who tried to take away or infringe on anyone else's religion would have the right to practice his own religion denied to him, unless he was an atheist, in which case he'd be made to go to church.

The future favors the psychologist, and those who refused to learn the self-honesty which serves as a basis for both personal integration and that self-knowledge which transits to knowingness would no longer be given the authority to manufacture systems of control for their betters.

Truly, Hamilton and all his disciples deserve our compassion, but we must refuse to part with our Personal Power in the endless series of compromises the harsh energies which these fractured souls bear have created to try to insure their own continued existence.

I rather suspect that only true Jeffersonians will enjoy reading this document.

END OF SIDEBAR RANTING: Now We Resume Our Regular Program Of Ranting

Anyhow, if these young'uns had had the courage to evolve into Altruism, the energy of Altruism would have permeated any gift they happened to give to a person in need; and if the one in need had been receptive to genuine Altruism, the expansion of the smooth energy of Altruism would have been fostered. The Gospel, as always, is that the children and grandchildren of these people did make this remarkable and courageous change and opened the door into the Golden Age of Humanity. I guess sometimes human beings do come from apes.

One of your deva's big jobs is to construct your physical and energy-bodies, and link them with the etheric threads which keep you alive. Again, your deva will construct you in accordance with your own thoughts and feelings and karma . . . in other words, according to the nature of the causal body you've built around yourself . . . a causal body which you've built, but which your deva has also helped you actualize and activate in certain ways, according to the quality of your aspirations.

Some devas, after learning many lessons of service as workers in both the human and deva kingdoms, become Gods when they grow up. I do not claim to have a perfect understanding of this matter; as I said earlier, deva psychology may be impossible for human beings to understand, but it seems to me that the devas who grow up and become Gods may understand us humans to one degree or another, because they've been human beings.

While it's true that occasionally one of these deva-Gods may incarnate back into the human kingdom so that the concentrated essence of the force the deva is allied with may express itself in Service, and while it's also true that at times the deva-God may choose to fuse its consciousness with a human being who may be clear and strong and sane enough to express that consciousness without dying or going mad to an undesirable degree, most of the time human contact with the Gods occurs in a less obvious way thru the activation of the Archetypes which live within each human brain and nervous system. The Archetypes sleep until the aspirant struggles to understand himself, then they begin to awaken. Eventually, one or more of these Archetypes may even be touched directly by the deva-God in whose image these Archetypes are built, thus producing the full flowering of that aspect of the "subconscious" . . . which among other things means that aspect touched by the deva-God isn't subconscious anymore!

I speak of these things, these deva things, as a basis for helping to explain the marriage that produces a healthy, livable, *conscious* city. And in looking over this writing which has made itself known to me, I conclude that mayhap I have just served as a linking factor between the human and deva kingdoms, for a living Tract has effects far more potent and far-traveling than the literal-minded, non-savvy reader might imagine. It may be that the waves that have been set in motion here today may impress themselves upon the deva kingdom, and bring more harmony to their conduct and lifeways. Perhaps golden beams of monadic harmony may manifest thru the deva kingdom now, each beam linking a deva-point in the causal body of our Mother. If that should be the case, devas would become more comprehensible to human beings, and we'd be able to work with them in a more effective fashion. For it is the Destiny for the human and deva evolutions to Work together in supreme spiritual inclusiveness and harmony, with cooperation being one of the keywords to express the energy of this relationship. Perhaps I have just explained a bit of deva psychology to humanity, and a bit of their own psychology and indicated its direction of evolution to the devas.

And so let us go to that Land of Oz, that faraway Kansas of living cities, for Oz begins in Kansas with a young sexy maiden aspect of the Goddess called Dorothy and her guardian wolf-god Toto, just as Heaven begins on Earth.

L. Frank Baum, the author of the original series of Oz books, was Initiate, and was presided over by a beautiful young adolescent incarnation of the Mother of the World whom he called Ozma (Ma equals Mother . . . Ozma is therefore the Mother of Oz.) It may be speculated that Baum was one of Ozma's husbands. Obviously, he was a midwife who presided at her birth into human awareness; it might be said that he was her father in addition to being one of her husbands. I don't think there is any question that he thought of her as one of his daughters, as well as his queen, and that he wanted to make love to her--and probably did so!

Thus we see the fulfillment of the usual Pattern, if we can drop the spectacles whose lenses are composed of the preconceptions of religious intolerance and the accompanying perversion of the Pattern of our Humanity. The little girl loves her daddy with a love like no other, and the daddy loves his candy-lipped little girl with a full and compassionate heart. It is inevitable that an outworking of the sexuality will occur; the only question is whether it will be a healthy and conscious outworking which admits itself and revels in itself and loves itself, or a perversion of nature which attempts to hide its face even from itself in a sobbing self-hatred which wraps itself in manipulation, driving away the compassion it was its Destiny to manifest. But healing can occur, even when such a compassionate lovingkindness as that between a daddy and his little girl has been turned into a monstrosity. For the heart of the truth of human nature still lies at the heart of the monstrosity, buried by the debris of glamour and illusion. But this heart can be freed thru tireless Work, and restored to wholeness and allowed to claim its Destiny once more. Think on these things, but more important, see how you *feel*. Yet if all you feel are the surging strings of the control and manipulation that binds you to illusion, you have not yet arrived in that sacred place where the Truth becomes immediately manifest to the unfettered, fully-compassionate consciousness.

We should never be ashamed and in denial of our feelings, our desires, for this shame and denial insures that the hurtfulness which created the shame will be perpetuated by ourselves onto the coming generations . . . and also insures we will be a part of those shamed generations, because by refusing to purify the attachments of control and manipulation out of our systems, we will be dragged by those very attachments back into the sexual hell of denied lovingkindness. This really couldn't be simpler; any person of any degree of sensitivity should now be able to understand the necessity that we begin to practice Truth in Sexuality. Suffering will not end until this Truth becomes a widespread admission.

Let us be pleased that somehow, in the repressed and perverse society of early twentieth century America, the wizard called L. Frank Baum arose to perform a new weave whose full outworking remains to be Achieved by those conscious threads who work with the Mother. If you have followed the Pattern closely, you see how Baum--himself the "Wizard of Oz"--was also the Son of the Mother, in addition to being her Father and Husband. This Pattern is so closely impressed upon human nature that only the success of the propaganda geared toward producing mass repression, and therefore the mass insanity of cultural perversion, would ever lead anyone to deny this sweet, wonderful Pattern. This Pattern is a part of the Visioning Process of God Almighty. God is Love, and this Pattern is meant to be a clear reflector of that Love which God is into the World. This is what Human Nature was meant to Achieve.

People in ancient societies, as well as those in the coming society of advanced psychology, used to build their city partly as a sacrificial offering to a God or Goddess--to an advanced Deva, in other words. The deity was invoked and if the invocation was sincere and successful, the deity would appear and invest the city with it's own divine energy. Thus the deity was married to a particular city, or multiple deities were married to that city in sort of a devic polyamory. The leading citizens of the city were often married to one or more of the city's guardian deities, as well. A marriage to a goddess is a handsome, beautiful thing, but you need to be sane before you make the attempt, for in such a marriage the goddess is invoked into you, becoming a part of you in both etheric form and consciousness, and you become a part of Her in that sharing that occurs within the marriages of those couples who are truly wed. This process is a fully conscious one and involves no exploitation or loss of human self-awareness such as occurs in some religions where a so-called deity is temporarily invoked into a person who turns their will over to that alleged deity . . . such religions are based in glamour and illusion, and their practices can have no positive effects. Such deviant practices erode the will and personal integration of their practitioners, and nobody with any love for himself would engage in such practices or be a part of such religions.

But when you marry a *real* deity, the love is the connecting force--you'll notice I *did not* say "binding force", because there are no strings of control and manipulation involved; the marriage is one that provides greater freedom to create for both the mortal husband and the goddess wife (or the mortal wife and the god, as the case may be). Such a marriage is as real as any other, and more real than most. And it should be obvious that no god or goddess is "monogamous", so there is no reason for their human spouses to pretend to such an illusion. Just as polyfidelity and polyamory occur within your own skull and nervous system, such arrangements are also the norm for the gods and goddesses whose qualities your own brain and nervous system, and emotions and mental functions, map.

And you don't want a glamorous marriage, whether to a human or a goddess, or suffering will result. In fact, because the gods and goddesses are devas and still may serve to a degree as mirrors, a glamorous marriage may just keep you mired in unpurified and not-sane emotional reactions . . . and you may be too mad to realize and admit your condition. Thus a respectable sanity is required to actually involve yourself with a divine marriage.

My point with all of this is that ancient cities were *conscious, living and self-aware*. Future cities will also make this wonderful Achievement by uniting with the gods and goddesses. A deva presides over every city as well as every other partially manmade creation. Nothing is entirely manmade, for devas and nature spirits are always carrying out the construction of the city on planes more subtle than the physical, and it is that construction on the subtle planes, and the energy conducted from those planes by etheric threads to the physical creation, that brings life to that physical creation. All life starts with energy, with God.

The important thing is to make sure your own thoughts are alive with compassion for all beings as you construct your city, automobile, or whatever, so that the god or goddess in charge of your creation will reflect that energy, colored with her own clean unique force-nature, back into your creation and give it a life you can live with and that will foster love and cooperation, rather than mechanicalness and competition. But in the twentieth century, the devas were mirroring the exploitation and mechanicalness of human beings back into the physical creations of those humans, and thus exploitation and mechanicalness ruled those societies. The devas mirrored, and thus intensified, the insanity of the twentieth century people and mirrored and intensified the denial of that insanity. If you put garbage onto your mental and emotional streets this evening, there'll likely be even more garbage on your streets when you wake up in the morning. This is literally true. Whatever you put out tends to multiply itself, but the most important thing is not the exact thoughtform you produce, but the quality of energy informing that thoughtform and the motive behind the thoughtform. The quality of the energy you emit can either turn your life into a sordid landfill, or the Emerald City.

This ends the portion of the Sacred Tract I'm writing which applies to the current discussion of promoting freedom from block-mindedness and textbook addiction and learning to explore the world as warm patterns of energy.

My daughter--I mean, my prostitute friend--used to try to talk philosophy with me, but she wanted to always leave it in the concrete form she found it in her textbooks. I didn't like that. I told her it was worse than the first time I'd paid her for a standard fuck, then discovered she was somehow creating some friction with her legs to amuse my penis, yet denying my penis entrance into her sacred gate. I'd sat up in consternation and took her by the shoulders, my eyes searching her face. She was such a sweet girl; surely she couldn't be trying to defraud me!

"Young lady," I said gravely, "I've been with thousands of women, and I know what it feels like to have my sweet rod of meaningfulness placed in the chalice of ultimate meaning. And I want that chalice! I don't know what trick you've played here, but quit it, whatever it is, and let me inside you! That's what I paid you for, sweetheart."

She laughed, a bit uncomfortably, and then let me inside her. I was gentle with her, not knowing why she'd treated me the way she had, but I figured there must be some good reason . . . maybe she was just sore. I was so gentle I mostly just let my organ lie there inside her . . . it felt good to be with her like that, but there was almost no friction, and I didn't even come, though I'd wanted to. But if a man is a gentleman, he tries to stay sensitive to the moods of his lady.

She never tried a trick like that with me again, but later admitted she did use it on most men, and that they never knew the difference. I was so shocked, I couldn't speak, let alone fornicate. I'd never heard of such uncivilized behavior from a prostitute. I left without entering her that day, and she seemed a tad concerned that I might not return. "Got to go home, baby," I mumbled. "Just got to go home 'cause I'm in shock. I never knew a prostitute to deliberately defraud a man before."

But a few days later I was back, having done my heart-work and forgiven her, and we took back up where we'd left off.

One day I got tired of her textbook methods of philosophy, and told her what a sad thing it was to be ruled by a book. "Even the best books make poor rulers, honey. The best a book can do is quicken you toward your own spiritual growth, and most of them are worthless even for that.

"If you do find a book that prompts you toward a genuine energy-growth, an experience of yourself as a conscious and *sane* aspect of God, then respect the book, and it's okay to love it, too. But don't make the mistake of turning the book into a fundamentalist god of some sort. This is the mistake every primitive society makes, and it causes the life to flow right out of their religion in search of a new, more flexible God-reflecting form for itself."

I paused for a moment. "Sweetheart, maybe I'm being too hard on you, and if I am, I'm sorry. You do have a greater capacity for sincerity than most twentieth century people, and sometimes a beam of compassion radiates out from your heart, and there's an eternity of possibilities in that. I love you.

"Sometimes when you ask 'Why?', it's actually because you really want to know, rather than a mask to save face and make you appear intellectually curious while the energy of fearful preconceptions actually deflects any insights that might be associated with the answer. And I respect that. You are one of the few who even has the sincerity to develop the potential of using your mind, and more importantly, of learning to use your mind in synchronization with your sweet heart.

"But you need to stop trying to make sense of the world and start living with the world. As long as you try to make sense of the world, you'll be living with illusion."

I'm afraid that took her aback, and she seemed a little standoffish for a while, and I wound up getting my "massages" from an oldish woman who reminded me of my mother. This is a type of statement of truth that shocks the primitive mind, but the truth is that their minds are constructed just like mine. The difference between us is that I have the discipline to develop the *Intention* to know myself; I have the courage to actually want to know myself, and to follow thru on that desire with appropriate action. I am good.

But repressed people are not good. They are perverts.

When next my "daughter" and I were together, I apologized. "I'm sorry, honey, if I prescribed for you in our last conversation. No person has the right to prescribe for anyone else, ever. It's just plain wrong. So if I prescribed for you, I apologize for the wrongness I caused, and for any distress you felt associated with that wrongness."

Then she smiled, and accepted my apology, and said she forgave me . . . and I sensed that it was the first time she'd ever forgiven anyone. Even now, her heart's energy-pulses conveyed to mine that she hadn't fully forgiven me, but she *had* made a start, and was in the act of forgiving me. Sometimes the act of forgiving takes a long time to complete, but it is always worth it. *Always.*

So I forgave myself, too, and we began to move on . . .

Once I ran into her at the Dog and Duck Pub, a place where I sometimes went to consume large numbers of delightful beverages that came in pint-sized glasses. I was with the Corsican, having felt it incumbent upon myself to reward him for summoning me a few days earlier when Sonny-Bob was showing his penis to a twelve or fourteen year old girl at some kind of fundamentalist tent-revival. I got there just in time, and managed to deflect the police long enough for Sonny-Bob to get away. So tonight I'd paid the Berber to watch Sonny-Bob, as I watched the Corsican reward himself with the near-oblivion of one who has gone too long without "tying one on".

She came in with three college-aged males and they hovered near a stone idol of a Labrador Retriever with a duck in its mouth, which was an icon of the patron saint of this Pub.

I went to her, dragging the Corsican by one arm. "Chela,"--Chela was her "stage name"-- "honey, it's good to see you. This drunk fellow is the Corsican. Say hello to Chela, Corsican."

The Corsican looked her up and down. Finally he said, "We know one another." Well, the Corsican was no student, so I guess he knew her from the massage parlour, though I'd never seen him around there and knew he didn't have enough money to purchase the services of sexworkers. He was only able to get groceries because of the funds I provided. Well, maybe he'd had some money when he first came to Austin. Hell, maybe he'd spent it all with Chela and her friends!

"Hello, Pierre," Chela said softly, and the Corsican pulled himself away from me. "Got to piss" he said, and was off again to the restroom.

Then Chela introduced me to her friends. "Buford, this is Randy, Chuck and Themistocles Cassius Clay."

"Hello, lads," I said.

"Hey, man," said Randy, "got any smokes?"

"No," I said. "Smokes are bad for you."

"Who is this old fucker?" Chuck said.

I gazed for a second at Chela. "I'm her father," I whispered.

They looked stunned. "Aw man," Chuck said, "I didn't mean nuthin' . . . we ain't up to nuthin'. . . goddam, let's get outta here!"

The three lads backed off in a hurry, with Themistocles bowing and kissing Chela's hand before departing. Chuck and Randy ran out the door like a ghost was chasing them, and Themistocles sauntered pretty fast after them.

Chela placed her hands on her hips and groaned in exasperation. "Now why did you do that?"

"Why did I do what, honey? They seemed like nice enough lads, for primitive primates, but I didn't drive them away. You can never tell what will stampede primitive herd animals."

She looked at me, measuring me with a touch of disgust. I didn't like that. But then she released it, and it floated away, where I hope it dissipated rather than adding itself to the problems caused by the astral cloud of glamour that plagues the earth.

Then she gave a little smile, and we sat together for a while beneath the bright moonlight, a father and his child. I bought her adult beverages, and her tongue was loosened, as her hand massaged my leg . . . and finally got around to massaging my third leg through the fabric of my trousers.

She told me many things, mostly about the abuses this primitive society had put her through. One of the worst occurred only a couple of years earlier, when she was sixteen.

"Buford, I was only trying to help that guy," she said, telling me of her Quest to perfect her Altruism thru helping a neighbor's twenty year old son, who'd been injured in an auto accident and was a quadriplegic.

"For eight or ten months I'd been slipping into the house when his parents were stoned, and teaching him to love himself. I played with his nipples and licked and sucked them, then I'd massage most of his body and finally get around to licking and sucking his rock-hard cock, or just giving him a handjob if I didn't want to chance being seen with come in my hair.

"Until I came along, he'd been so fucking frustrated he'd scream and cuss all the time, and deliberately crash his wheelchair into furniture and into the wall, and even into people. A couple of times he apparently tried to commit suicide by throwing his wheelchair backward down the stairs with himself in it, and once he managed to throw himself and his wheelchair out a second story window.

"Everyone in the neighborhood knew about the problems this guy was having, but nobody would talk about the real reason for it. They sent him to shrink after shrink and put him on all sorts of dope, but even the shrinks were too afraid to talk about the real problem. But my girlfriends and I knew . . . and we talked about it. We wanted to do something to help him, but I was the only one who followed through; I guess the others were too scared of The Man and his vengeful laws.

"I was scared, too, but I knew I had to do something. I couldn't just sit at home with that boy suffering next door without trying to help him. So for a long time I'd slip in and help him with foreplay and handjobs and blowjobs, and a couple of times I put a condom on his big hard cock and mounted him right there in his wheelchair and let him come in me! And I have to tell you that one of those times I came myself . . . it was awesome! The first orgasm I ever had, and I had it in the line of duty, helping a guy who couldn't help himself. I learned something about selfless Service then and there, something I'd forgotten until you came along, Buford honey."

She licked my ear; she was getting pretty tipsy. The Corsican had returned, and lay sprawled on a nearby table.

I patted her hand. "I'm real pleased with you, honey. I knew you had it in you."

She bounced up and down a couple of times and looked at me coquettishly. "You're a proud papa? You're proud of your little girl?"

"I'm *pleased* with my little girl," I said. "Pride really does go before a fall, honey, so I'm not proud of anyone or anything, least of all myself. But I'm pleased with myself, and right this moment I'm even more pleased with you."

She snuggled up against me then, snuggled up against me with a contented sigh, hanging onto my arm, her sweet head nestled up against my shoulder as the Corsican stared at us with bleary, foreign eyes.

"I sort of hate to tell you the rest of the story," she said.

"Don't tell it unless you need to tell it, sweetheart, but if you do need to tell it, I'm here to listen."

She paused for a minute or two, collecting herself. Suddenly, she seemed to have sobered up.

"Well," she cleared her throat with some difficulty, and I felt a hurt roll up out of her emotions and flush its way through her system, "one night the parents weren't stoned enough, and caught me giving their son a blowjob. I was just finishing up, and he spurted his load as his parents entered the room, and it went all over my hair and breasts. I'd already performed a strip-tease for him and was naked, so I didn't get come on my clothes, but it was all over my body and in my hair. The father held me while the mother called the police. He wouldn't let me get dressed, just gripped my arms so hard it left these awful black bruises, while his son was shouting for him to let me go. The son rammed the father with his wheelchair, and I almost got loose, but by then the mother had finished her call and put down the phone and restrained her son.

"So that's how the cops found me, covered with come . . . the evidence was fresh and irrefutable. I was led away naked and manacled and shackled, as if somehow a naked sixteen year old girl was a threat to a cop. I was jailed and accused of rape, but the young guy I'd helped swore it wasn't rape, that it was consensual, and that he'd wanted it. They did everything they could do to make him recant and say it was rape, I guess because most people are uncomfortable with the idea of disabled people having sexual needs. They even put him on some more drugs to make him more suggestible so he'd go along with them. But he was a strong guy, strong morally and spiritually, where it counted. They couldn't drug or manipulate him into lying for them.

"They even lied to him, said I'd confessed, when I'd done nothing of the sort. This is when I discovered it's legal for cops to lie to people they're interrogating, but illegal for those people to lie to the cops. I knew those cops, knew they considered themselves good Christians . . . so this is when I began to seriously question Christianity. I worked myself away from Christianity through reading philosophy and through practicing thinking and feeling for myself. And I finally learned that the Christianity I had been raised with wasn't real Christianity, anyway. It wasn't the same way of life that Jesus advocated and the Disciples practiced. Real, unadulterated Christianity isn't a doctrine, it's a way of living in total community. So I gave up the false Christianity and became a bit of a Pagan . . .

"They finally had to drop all charges and let me go," Chela said, a mixture of emotions emanating from her . . . but mostly the emotion of grief, I think, "but before they set me free, two of the cops made me give them blowjobs and one of them fucked me from behind . . . said he was fucking me like a dog, because I was a dog, a bitch in heat."

I knew I had some killing to do, then. I had to go back and terminate those cops. I felt my noble Ancestor, the illustrious Sonny-Bob, rising up from the depths of my genes then, saying, "You know what I'd do, Sargon. And I know what you're going to do."

"Yes, sir," I gritted between clinched teeth, my whole body rigid. "Yes, sir . . . I'll kill those sons-of-bitches . . ."

"Oh, Buford!" Chela was shaking me and trying to turn my face so she could see into my eyes. "Buford! Now I wish I hadn't told you . . . honey, that was a long time ago, over two years ago . . . I was in shock for a long time, but I'm better now. And you can't kill them; it would create more trouble than those pigs are worth. And you can't kill all the pigs who behave this way, either; since I've been a sexworker I've met lots of other sexworkers who've been raped by the cops, particularly the vice cops. Sometimes they get raped because the cops have some evidence on them, sometimes they get raped because the cops don't have enough evidence to arrest them, but want to hurt them anyway.

"Please, Buford," she sobbed into me, "I wish I hadn't told you!"

I took some deep breaths. "Honey, I won't kill them . . . unless they hurt you again, and then all bets are off. Vengeance is wrong, and I know it's wrong . . . but mainly I was going to kill them because killing them is the only way to deter them from destroying innocence again. How many times have they done this sort of thing? Are you the only survivor of such abuse? I doubt it.

"But if I were to murder them, and right before murdering them explain to them why I was doing it, and advise them to take their deaths as a lesson so that they would be less likely to repeat the same mistakes in their next life, then the killing of the pigs would perhaps serve as a deterrent. It would prevent them from destroying any more innocent ones for a time, and then if they incarnated again, subconsciously they might retain the memory of why they'd been murdered in their previous life, and this subconscious memory might guide them into better conduct, perhaps even leading them to honor innocence, and that could only be to their benefit. For by honoring innocence in another, they would automatically be honoring the innocence in themselves. But as it stands, they currently probably have no idea that innocence is even possible for them.

"Sometimes murdering someone can be a great, compassionate service for that person, as well as for others that person might have wounded if he hadn't been terminated. For physical death is easy and often temporary; all you have to do to recover from it is to reincarnate. But the emotional damage done by those pigs to those they prey on may take years, decades, or even lifetimes to heal as the survivor undergoes the terrible agony of facing the inflamed energy of the abuse as it rises up again and again in her awareness while she courageously does her release Work.

"So who is worse? The abusive pigs or the compassionate murderer? A civilized human being cannot doubt the answer to this question, sweetheart. In fact, where I'm from the abusive pigs would be dusted at once, and the compassionate murderer respected as a decent human being, and perhaps even revered as a saint. But the moral inversion that accompanies all the thought processes and feelings of your people leads them into a dark canyon of unawareness and lack of compassion, as like blind slugs they pretend to be human without any understanding of their own buried humanity.

"And I'm not talking about capital punishment here, I'm just talking about a straightforward murder because there are no other options. There's no real rehabilitation services for rapist-cops or any other form of criminal in the twentieth century, so that isn't an option. And in the unlikely event we could get them sent to prison, they'd probably eventually emerge more embittered against Woman than ever, and would likely still try to find ways to hurt Her. This is the only reason I suggested a conscious, compassionate murder to begin with: I don't see any other options.

"But you're right, Chela; the murder has to come from love and compassion and from respect for the soul of the scumbag whose physical body you're murdering, or it's no good. If the motive isn't proper and the energy isn't compassionate, then no good can come from murdering someone."

I looked at her then, and she was sort of rock hard in a part of her that had risen up to shield her from the knowledge of the violence that I could do. She'd never seen anything but my gentle, sweet side, and a part of her was horrified that I could so easily talk about committing a murder, even if the murder was for the right reasons and was the compassionate thing to do. But twentieth century people were always confused about violence, which is perhaps why they were imprecise in their own.

"Honey," I said, as tenderly as I could just then, "this is who I am. I am good. I am innocent, as are most people where I'm from. I only want to help, and I love you. I'll do my best not to do anything that might result in a feeling of distress to your sweet, beautiful heart or to the emotions which I've been happy to watch do a bit of housecleaning for themselves. I won't kill the pigs . . . at least, not if they don't bother you again."

"Oh, Buford," she sighed wearily, but with some relief. "I'm sorry I told you the second half of the story. But I guess the cat is out of the bag, now. I've been raped and abused, and I still feel worthless sometimes because of it. And . . ." her voice caught in her throat, and the tears began a slow descent, "I've never told anybody but you what those cops did to me. And you *are* good, and I . . . I love you, too, Buford. I love you."

For a moment she sort of choked, then: "I've . . . I've never told anyone I loved them, except when someone pays me to say it, since I was pulled away from that disabled boy. I used to tell him I loved him, and I think I did, too, or I wouldn't have been doing what I was doing.

"It's funny: I'd hardly known him before his accident; he'd been fourteen when it happened, so I was only nine. But somehow I think I loved him . . . I have no idea why."

"Well, *I* know why, sweetheart, for I am Buford Sargon, Guardian of Innocence. You loved him because you were at least partly in touch with the splendid Reality of your own nature. Chela, sweetheart, *you* are love, *I* am love, your disabled friend is love, and everyone simply is love. Love is what we are; this is an accepted part of nearly everyone's experience where I'm from. And sometimes we have to put this love into action. This is what the divine quality of Wisdom is: Wisdom is love in action, and since we're all love, Wisdom is *us* in action. Wisdom is our real Selves in action. We are Love; therefore, we are Wisdom when we find ourselves moving according to that Love which each one of us is.

"Chela, *you were* the divine quality of Wisdom when you were nourishing that boy sexually. The cops, in their primate stupidity, fear and lust, actually arrested a Divine Principle! Think of the karma those assholes created for themselves!

"And sweetheart, I feel in my deepest heart that you still are a remarkably wise young woman. Trust yourself, and keep on trusting yourself. Your actions with your disabled friend were absolutely right; he may have been quadriplegic, but he needed just what everyone needs: he needed someone to love, and he needed to know he was worth loving, and you taught him that he was worth loving. There's no price that can be placed on such a compassionate gift.

"Don't let the hate and fear that drove his parents and the cops touch you any more. Let it go, let it all go, and keep on letting it go until it's all gone forever. Be yourself, and release the energy of fear and separation those soul-leaches tried to bind you with. And know that I love you and always will, and that I'll always be here for you, honey. You are good."

Well, the Corsican was passed out in a pool of his own vomit, and I didn't want to touch him, so I called for a cab and paid the cab driver to touch him and take him home.

I escorted Chela back to her dorm, and she invited me to sneak inside with her, since it was past the hour that "boys" were allowed in the freshman women's dorm. So I snuck in with her and she introduced me to her roommate, a nice Asian girl who sometimes worked as a stripper, and then Chela and I went to bed. I held her for a long time, and I was aware of an attunement of souls that had occurred between Chela and me. Although I couldn't take her with me back into the future, assuming my Revered--and somewhat Mischievous--Ancestor actually somehow saved the future, I knew that our souls would continue to communicate throughout long ages . . . our souls belonged together in the Province of Forever. She would find me in the future, where her soul would eventually arrive with a new body, and I would be waiting.

CHAPTER THIRTY

Hubert the songpoet had taken to creating original compositions to serenade Aphrodite after he discovered "Rudolph The Red-Nosed Reindeer" didn't provide the type of imagery appropriate to the strip-tease.

"Sonny-Bob, I still have a lot to learn about women," he confessed. "Apparently they all like Rudolph, but there's times they don't want to be reminded of him."

"I know that's right, old bean."

It was the first week of October and Hubert had tested his interdimensional drive a couple of days before. He'd gone back a few days, then a few months, then a few years. With his last jump he went all the way back to 1945. "I knew I could do it," he said happily. "I fixed myself. The motor sergeant will be proud of me."

If we restore his existence, I thought, but said nothing.

"When do you want to leave, Sonny-Bob? The nuclear war's this month, you know."

I knew all right, and it lay heavily upon me. There were issues a part of my brain hadn't wanted to look at, but now it had to. For the effect of our preserving the timeline would be the same for our little family as it would for the rest of humanity. They would have dreamed of me, but we would never have met.

I explained my depression to Hubert. "I haven't had a drink since Lucille cured me, except for that cup of wine the King of Bhutan gave me. But the first thing I'm going to do when we go back to 1945 is to find a liquor store and get drunk, and I'm going to stay drunk throughout the mission. I work better when I'm drunk, anyway."

"Sonny-Bob, we can save the timeline, then come back to 1983 and meet the family again. I'd figured that's what you meant to do, or I'd have been depressed, too."

"No, Hubert. No can do. Your Tiffany isn't sentient, though she does have a soul. Maybe you and she could start over, because you haven't shared much to begin with except a few moments of wild passion. But it's different with us sentient types. The family and I--and you, too--have all shared and grown together. We're all on the same sheet of music, energetically speaking. You and I will still be operating at this level of spiritual energy after our mission, but the family won't be, because to them we'll never have had this life together. We won't be able to join with them a second time, for the spiritual and emotional charge that brought us together has been spent in you and me and we've expanded into the next stage of our growth. Nature prefers harmony in her groups, so our energy fields won't attract the family to us a second time. We've learned what we were meant to learn, Hubert. Nature also abhors a vacuum, so I guess she'll furnish the family with some other catalyst to come together and grow.

"But it won't be us," I shook my head mournfully. "It won't be us, my friend."

"Damn, Sonny-Bob! There's got to be a way. There's always a way to win. You've said so yourself."

"Not this time, Cool Breeze. The only potential way we could keep the family together, and its memories and energy intact, would be to take them back to 1945 with us. But that's too hazardous and I won't risk Mimi and Pa Miyamoto, or Aphrodite or Sue or Freud. Well, maybe Freud, because he once was a warrior. But Freud wouldn't leave Aphrodite behind; he wouldn't be willing to leave the family at all. It's a catch-22: if he came with us he'd have to sacrifice the family, but if he stays here the family never would have met and he'd still be living in that cardboard box. Unless, of course, I'm right about nature providing another catalyst for the family."

"Sonny-Bob, there's something here I don't think you've looked at," Hubert said slowly. He cleared his throat. "If you don't bring Mimi back with us you'll have never met and fathered her child. Pa Miyamoto won't exist, so neither will you. He's your ancestor, he's indispensable to your existence. We *have* to take her back, we have to take the whole family back!" He was wailing. "For the sake of your own existence and our friendship, *please* take them back!"

I was touched. I patted his hood. "We've come a long way together, old friend. I love you, too. But we're not taking the family back and that's final. Mary Beth is back there and she's deadly and vicious and heavily armed. She's bound to have a vehicle such as yourself who can produce any sort of weaponry she wants. Plus, there's at least one co-conspirator with her and we don't know who he is. I won't risk Mimi and the others for the sake of my own existence.

"But who knows, old bean? Maybe Mimi will meet someone else who'll father Pa Miyamoto." I knew I was grasping at straws, but a straw is pretty substantial when you're about to fall into the Void.

"Bottom line, Hubert: I haven't a clue as to whether I exist or not, but I'm not going to jeopardize our friends so I can selfishly exist. If I go into non-existence, well, it's as good a place as any for me. Under normal circumstances I'm looked down upon and denigrated, anyway. And I never really get to do much good for the world with the assignments they give me. But if we succeed with this mission the planet will be saved and our friends will still have a home, though they may not come together as a family. I can't think of a better reason to go into non-existence. Plus, I'll bet they don't have generals there. It could be pretty pleasant."

Hubert sniffled a bit. "When do you want to go?" he finally asked.

"One time is as good as another. We can even wait 'till the bombs are flying and it won't matter. I don't see any real reason for the Soviets to bomb Austin, at least not in their first barrage. Austin has that piddly-assed Air Force base, it's true, but it doesn't amount to much and they're talking about closing it down. Plus, you put those satellites you made into orbit, so you'll know when the bombs start flying and you'll know where they're going. So no, it doesn't matter much when we leave. Even in the unlikely event a missile flies toward Austin we'll easily be able to get out in time. Nothing to it."

I walked away from him then, a sick feeling in my guts that I knew alcohol could never erase or I'd have gone right then to the nearest tavern. The sick feeling flushed its way through my body, and I felt it radiating out my face and eyes. I didn't give a damn whether I existed or not. The agonizing thing was the death of relationships that was about to occur. Now I knew how Lucifer must've felt when he'd sacrificed himself to fall into the material world. He'd left the whole company of his brother angels behind, and that's what I was doing. But at least Lucifer's brother angels still knew him. After I fell into the past my brothers and sisters would think I was a dream, if they thought of me at all.

"Sonny-Bob, what's wrong? You look ghastly." My Beloved was peering into my face with concern.

"Mimi, I have to leave soon. You've known it was coming." I took her and Pa Miyamoto into my arms and hugged them. "I'm sorry, darling. I truly am."

When finally we released one another Mimi took my hands. "Beloved, there's something you haven't told me."

"Yes there is, honey. I haven't told you I love you nearly as often as

I meant to."

"Oh, Sonny-Bob." She fell into my arms, and we both wept.

A couple days later I was starting to recover my "mission cockiness", the feeling that I was heading back to do a job and by God it was going to get done. Nothing was going to get in my way. Nothing ever had, at least, not for long.

I'd asked Hubert to fire up his voice cube and deliver a rendition of "Tumbling Tumbleweeds". Mimi and I sat on the bed holding hands; the rest of the family were scattered about the room.

There was silence after he finished. Mimi just squeezed my hand and dabbed at her eyes. All the ladies had tears in their eyes, but I couldn't tell about Freud because he'd put his sunglasses on.

Then there was a knock on the door. Sue answered it.

One of our fellow co-opers stood there, a fellow named Tansil Vickers. "Teddy--" I had adopted the alias "Teddy Roosevelt" in dealing with anyone the family wasn't intimate with, "you have a phone call downstairs."

"Who is it, Tansil?"

"It's some nutcase who says he's Ronald Reagan. I almost hung up on him--"

I sprang from my bed and hauled my fat ass out the door as fast as I could, knocking over Tansil in the process. "Sorry, Tansil," I panted.

The phone was in the hallway downstairs and I made my way to it. I picked up the handset. "H--hello?" I said cautiously.

"How've you been, Sonny-Bob?" President Reagan's welcoming tones warmed my ears as I wet my pants. I'd never thought I'd have the privilege of speaking with him again.

"F--fine, Mr. President. And yourself?"

"Oh, pretty well, I guess, for a chief executive who's about to be overthrown. My lady tells me they plan to do it this month."

"Your lady, sir?"

"Yes, there's only one operative I dare trust anymore. Fortunately for me, she's the best in the business. She's the one who tracked you down when all the police agencies in the country and the Marine Corps failed. She found you about a month ago, but I haven't had a chance to call. All my calls are monitored. There's more bugs in the White House than there are boll weevils in Texas. I finally managed to slip out today in disguise; I'm calling from a pay phone. I'm in drag. I look like a hooker."

"You've selected a noble occupation, sir."

"Well, never mind that now. I've only got a few minutes, then I have to get back to the Oval Office for a meeting with Yasser Arafat. I hope I remember to change; he'll probably leave if he sees me like this.

"I don't suppose you've heard of Bo Derek in the future?"

"We've heard she's a pretty straight arrow, Mr. President."

"Well, that's a close enough assessment. She's been pretending to be an actress lately, but I've been considering nominating her for secretary of defense--"

"Sir, she'll serve as the first female secretary of defense of the new millennium." I felt my eyes twinkling. Mr. Reagan came up with the idea of the "Star Wars" program, but in the second decade of the next century Bo Derek and President Jay Leno would get it off the ground. We appreciate their contribution to national and planetary defense in my own time.

"Well, that's good to know," said the President. "She's always been willing to serve when called upon. She's loyal to the Spirit of Freedom which blows gently upon this great country, and since I share this allegiance she's loyal to me. She's that lone operative that I trust. She pulled a gun on Vice-President Bush and Oliver North when they tried to recruit her into their treasonous activities. But the damn Secret Service was there and they opened up on her with Uzi's. She had to dive through the window of the vice-president's office, then run across the capitol grounds to get away. They nicked her a couple of times, but she's okay. She's a tough little cookie.

"Anyhow, she disappeared into the underground. We usually communicate through code in the classified ads section of the New York Times.

"Sonny-Bob, the cow patty has already hit the fan and now it's about to splatter. Is your vehicle repaired yet? Can you get back to 1945 to convince Truman to nuke those pesky Japanese?"

"Roger that, sir. Hubert and I are good to go."

"Outstanding! But don't go yet. I don't know what day they're going to launch the missiles, but I suspect it'll be the day of the coup, and that's slated for October 25. They'd planned to send me to some city for a parade and a speech, then Bush is going to announce his presidency from Washington. Bo told me all this.

"So when the vice-president suggested the tour and asked me which city I wanted to go to I said Austin. I'm hoping to somehow arrange to see you independent of the Secret Service. Nancy may be able to distract them; we'll see. I've signed an executive order I want you to give to Truman. It orders him to nuke the Japanese. He may not believe your story without this verification. And since from his perspective I'll be president in the future, he'll have to believe I know about the consequences of his actions. Follow me?"

"Ten-four, sir."

"But if I can't get this order to you, go ahead and slip into the past. Don't linger if the missiles start flying. I'll be okay. I've been practicing karate."

"Will comply, sir."

"One more thing. I managed to slip out once before, maybe two months ago, and visit with our friends at the National Rifle Association. I told their top agents our story, and they didn't seem very surprised. My intuition kicked in, so I asked if they'd had contact with you before. They said they hadn't dealt with you personally, but had an operative on call in a basement office who might have heard of you. They summoned him and he showed up with an attractive lady on each arm. He was a womanizer. But all three of them fainted and collapsed when I mentioned your name. One had to be rushed to the hospital.

"The NRA informed me that fellow works for your TAC. That so?"

"Yes, sir. We work with the NRA throughout the last half of the Twentieth and first half of the Twenty-first to help preserve the Second Amendment right of self-ownership."

"Thank God for it," mused Lord Reagan. "No nation is free unless its citizens have the right of self-ownership, which starts with the unqualified right to self-defense.

"God bless your TAC, and God bless America!"

"Thank you, sir. Your blessing means a lot to us at the TAC."

"Uh-oh . . .!'"

"What is it, Lord Reagan?"

"It's the cops, staring at me. There, they've gone on by. Whew! I never realized how hard it is to be a fugitive in modern America 'till I started leaving the house in drag. When all this is over and my presidency's safe, I'm going to sign an executive order making things easier for criminals. There's no point in the Justice Department sowing all this fear and anxiety. Crooks have feelings, too."

"Yes sir, Mr. President. I know exactly what you mean."

"Shit!" Lord Reagan whispered. "I recognize that guy who went into that doughnut shop across the street. He's Secret Service. They may be onto me."

"Maybe he just wants a snack, sir."

"Maybe . . ."

"In any case, if there's nothing else, maybe you'd better get back to the Oval Office. The longer you're away the greater the chance your mendacity will be discovered.

"If the Secret Service catches you, Mr. President, they may haul you back to your desk in shackles."

"By God, I've got a Colt Peacemaker in a bra holster; let them try. They'll never take me alive."

I sensed his courage and his strength through the telephone, but I didn't want him to have to demonstrate these qualities to the Secret Service. So I was relieved when he calmed down a little.

"Well, Sonny-Bob, I've enjoyed our discussion. You're freedom's ace in the hole. I know you won't let us down."

"It's my privilege to serve, Lord Reagan."

"I'm heading back now to meet with Arafat, son. Out here."

"Out here, sir."

The line went dead and I placed the handset in its cradle. The clock was ticking. But it looked like it would stop on October 25.

The Drag was all a-bustle. President Reagan was coming to town and his entourage would flow right down The Drag beneath our window. Mimi was excited. We all were.

"Sonny-Bob, I can't believe President Reagan's going to be so close! I've always wanted to meet him."

"He's a great man, darling. But today wouldn't be the best day for you to ask for his autograph. There's probably going to be a coup."

And this crazy Drag, this tight little street, would be a good place for his adversaries to ambush Lord Reagan. I wanted to be of service to him, and had intended to go up on the roof and lay out several positions where I could hide with a rifle to fire on those who would transgress against the President. But the Secret Service had been swarming all over the area for a week, repeatedly checking all the buildings along The Drag. Mimi had brought me all my meals and snacks and I'd eaten in the room this whole time. But the fuckers had checked our room twice; both times I'd hid in the shower with Mimi and when the agents entered the restroom a naked and pregnant Mimi would lean out and startle them. Then they'd go away. Amateurs.

After a while the parade started and I took one last long look at my family, these people I loved so much. If I succeeded with my mission we'd never have met and never could meet. I shrugged. If there was any compassion in the universe I would vanish into non-existence. It was the only thought that gave me comfort.

"Culpepper to Hubert, situation report, over."

"Roger, no outbound or inbound missiles yet. Secret Service has kicked my tires and looked at me strangely, but they couldn't have recognized me. They only know me as a sleigh and maybe as a truck. They don't know me as a Pontiac. Over."

"Roger. At the first sight of inbound missiles notify me. I've already put this anti-grav belt on and I'll go up on the roof and then sail right down to you. Out."

"Wilco, out."

I adjusted the anti-grav belt, wincing in discomfort. When Hubert made the thing a few weeks ago it fit pretty well, but the blubber had kept piling up. Finally I'd had to let the belt out to the last notch and still I could barely breathe. Pretty soon I'd have to use an anti-grav belt just to get to the restroom. At least non-existence would take the edge off my obesity.

"Here he comes, Sonny-Bob! Everybody, here he comes!" Mimi was beside herself with excitement. All civilized persons love Lord Reagan.

Lord Reagan was no wimp. He stood in the skyroof of his limousine waving with vigor and glee to the appreciative crowd. No doubt standard procedure advised him to stay covered, but he knew he could only transmit his energy to America if he touched her. So he touched her.

I was watching through compact futuristic binoculars. When the President turned in our direction I thought I caught a glimpse of a gun in a shoulder holster. I smiled. As long as he was armed, I could relax a little.

Suddenly, shots rang out. President Reagan dived up and out of the skyroof and did a shoulder roll across the top of that limo. Then he slid down the windshield and his gun was already in his hand, ready to return fire. He rolled across the hood and hit the ground beside the limo, which came to a stop as the President yanked the driver's side door open and yanked out the chauffer, knocking him in the head with the long barrel of his Peacemaker revolver. The chauffer went as limp as a rag doll and the President dropped him. No doubt the chauffer was a part of the conspiracy and got his just deserts. He'd be more careful to anticipate his President's moves in the future.

My phone was buzzing; I flipped it open. "Culpepper."

"Sonny-Bob, we've got outbound missiles--oops, now the Soviets have launched. I don't know what fool planned this operation, but the first U.S. missiles were fired by two submarines just outside Russian waters. Since the United States government thinks it's the only one with nukes, I guess they figured it wouldn't matter. The Russians picked up on those first missiles almost instantly and returned fire, but I doubt they've spotted the ICBM's yet. It doesn't matter, though. They either were watching those two subs and knew they were American, or they made a guess. Damned accurate guess."

"Okay, Hubert, we've got some lead time--"

"Sonny-Bob, listen up! I'm monitoring the news media and Vice-President Bush has just gone on T.V. saying Soviet agents just gunned down President Reagan in Austin. He says he's running things now and has ordered a retaliatory attack against the Soviets. He says he's using secret weaponry recently developed to end the Soviet threat once and for all. He says he's going to restore freedom to the world. Oh, shit!"

Oh shit, indeed. But we'd known it was going to happen, no point in letting it ruffle our feathers.

"Hubert, listen to me. Take a deep breath, if you know how to breathe. If not, do whatever you normally do to relax. We've got some time and I'm going to help the President. He hasn't been shot, at least not fatally. He's down there on The Drag in a gunfight. I've *got* to help him, Hubert. I can't let the Father Of Our Culture down. Plus, he's got that executive order for me to give to Truman. I've got to get it."

"Sonny-Bob!" Hubert was screaming and sobbing and wailing all at the same time. "One of those Soviet missiles looks like it could be on track for Austin--yes! I'm monitoring their military communications and they *did* decide to nuke the Bergstrom airbase. That missile is en route to *us*, Sonny-Bob! You waited 'till the last minute to wake me up when we left our own time and we barely got out alive. My nerves are shot, I can't go through this again. Let's get out now, Sonny-Bob! Goddamit, don't do this to me again!"

I took a deep breath and shrugged. I hadn't realized Hubert was so temperamental. "Tell you what, old bean. Before this parade they cleared the streets of all vehicles except official vehicles. There's places you can park. I don't think the public will be in your way; they're falling all over one another to get off the street. Leap over the co-op and land down by the bookstore. I'll join you when I can, but first I've got to help Lord Reagan--"

"He'll die anyway! He'll die! That nuke is on its way, let's go--"

"Shut up, Hubert, or I'll come down there and yank your kill switch and that'll be the end of all of us. Do what I said. Park by the bookstore, that's close enough to where I'll be. I'll run up and join you when I can."

"Alright, Sonny-Bob, but you better get to me before that nuke does or I'll leave and you'll be flash fried."

"No biggie," I said lightly.

I turned to say one last quick goodbye to the family and was surprised to see they all had gym bags in their hands. Freud also had a big knife.

"What the hell . . ."

"Sonny-Bob, I asked Hubert to tell me whatever it was you were hiding from me, and of course he did," Mimi said. Of course. "I'm not going to let either you or Pa Miyamoto vanish into non-existence and I'm not going to let our family dissolve. We're coming with you and you can't stop us. You know there's no point in arguing about it." Mimi stood there defiantly, eyes flashing fire.

I sighed. It was going to be risky for them to go off to 1945 and face Mary Beth Magoo with me, but it was obviously riskier for them to stay here with an inbound nuclear device about to land on their heads. I knew it would seem that way to them, anyway.

"Okay, ya'll. You heard what I said to Hubert. When we get outside you people sprint as hard as you can and get inside Hubert. You'll be safe then; he's bulletproof. I'll cover you and drop any enemy personnel who pose a threat. Then I'm going to help President Reagan. I'll join you, but if I don't make it go to 1945 without me and ask Hubert for ideas on stopping Mary Beth. It's the timeline's only chance, and Pa Miyamoto's only chance, and by God I mean it, Mimi! Forget your hard-headedness, you'd better follow orders."

"Yes, my captain. I'll follow orders." Mimi gave me a quick hug and as family we all went downstairs.

The street was covered with blues musicians or Secret Service or whatever they were pretending to be today. And all of them were firing at President Reagan, who crouched behind the limo and returned fire when he could. This scene pissed me off. I growled, and felt a fire deep within my guts. The primordial force of the universe was returning. I felt my aura glow red and then white hot and I knew I had some killing to do. I set my pocket pistol to kill and prepared to do just that.

"I'm going to dive out that door and start killing tax collectors, Freud. I'll draw their fire; I'm heading up the street. While they're shooting at me you get the family to Hubert. Understand?"

"Understood, Captain."

"All right. I'll see ya'll in 1945!" I dove out the door and switched on my anti-gravs and flew up the street like a chukar partridge. Or maybe more like a chunky partridge.

The tax collectors took the bait, but there wasn't a bird hunter among them. They missed me. Or perhaps they just weren't used to dealing with a partridge who could shoot back. My flashing killbeam cut them down as I flew up the street laughing maniacally; this was the part of my job I really enjoyed. Oh, I didn't really look for gun battles, but when they came my way I usually didn't step aside, either. It wasn't machismo, not really. I just really enjoyed destroying something that wanted to destroy me.

I giggled wildly, careening up the street; I must've gotten fourteen or fifteen of the bastards by now. I was trying to remember exact figures, for I'd have to put it in my report later. The primordial force of the universe boosted me along.

I whirled around about a hundred meters up the street; good, it looked like the family had reached Hubert. There were many dead tax collectors in my wake. The few that were left were firing rather hesitantly now, cowering behind whatever cover they could find.

Uh-oh. I thought I saw some tax collectors trying to maneuver into position behind Lord Reagan. I had to put a stop to that shit.

So I sailed over behind them and touched down lightly on the grass. "Hello, boys," I said, and gunned them down before they could respond. My, that was satisfactory!

Then I sailed over to Lord Reagan and plopped down. "Good morning, sir."

"Good morning, Sonny-Bob. You sure have put on weight. I almost didn't recognize you."

"I get that a lot, sir."

"Well, thanks for your help." Lord Reagan eared back the hammer on his gun; he'd just been reloading. His gun was the Colt Peacemaker, one of the guns that had won the West. If there were any gun battles in Austin in the late 1800's up until at least 1900, the Colt Peacemaker would probably have been involved. It was favored by cowboys and outlaws.

The Peacemaker fit the hand well and pointed easily and naturally. It had some special characteristic of balance found in few firearms, especially when fitted with the long seven and a half inch barrel the President's had. If he'd had any handgun but that old Peacemaker the naturalness of his killings would probably have been compromised.

He yelled and fired as a Secret Service guy stuck his head around a fire hydrant; the gentleman fell with a .45 calibre hole more or less between his eyes. I wished mightily I had more time to spend with Lord Reagan. Oh, to loll upon the grass of his shooting range in Santa Barbara, firing Peacemakers and sipping lemonade and laughing and picking up pointers from this miraculously talented gunman who was also my President and one of the founders of my culture! I wept from the gratitude I felt to Lord Reagan for letting me join him in this wonderful gun battle. I dropped another malevolent Secret Service agent.

I saw a flash of movement, and suddenly Mrs. Reagan was beside us. Lithe as a fairy, yet tough as a Norwegian Elkhound, she carried the Winchester Model 94 rifle in .30-.30 calibre. Another gun that had the reputation of having won the West, though the West had mostly been won by the time it came along. Still, it was featured in most of the cowboy movies.

"Sorry I missed you last time, Sonny-Bob. But under the circumstances I can't dance for you now," she panted.

"No problem, ma'am. I'm just glad you brought your rifle."

"Ronnie, I slipped across the way and ambushed two guys, then took one out on that roof up there who was getting ready to snipe at you. That guy was a tough target; I've been telling you I need a scope for my rifle."

"It's almost Christmas, dear. Maybe Santa will bring you a scope."

"Hrumph! It'd better be a Redfield or I'm sending it back to the North Pole."

Lord Reagan rolled his eyes; he'd probably gotten her some other brand. Now he'd have to go shopping again.

A bullet clipped Nancy's hair and she roared in rage and put a .30-.30 round through the gut of the offending tax collector. "Somebitch!" she snarled.

Suddenly, my insanity shifted. I won't say it left, but it shifted. *What am I doing here*, I wondered. *After the family made it to Hubert I should have joined them. I've got a timeline and the planet to save.* But instead of doing the sensible thing, here I was, hunkered down in another gunfight. Somehow, I felt my conduct might be a little unbalanced. This was the way I'd behaved--had **had** to behave--when I'd served with the 12th ERT. But I wasn't with the ERT anymore and hadn't been for a long time. My mission wasn't to kill everything in sight, it was to save the planet for my Goddess and for humanity. Perhaps I'd better behave with more civility. I set my pocket pistol to stun. "Sir, I'm going to stun them from here on out. I'm trying to learn to be more of a gentleman."

"No problem."

Someone with a huge firearm was low-crawling to our position. I raised my weapon, but Lord Reagan placed a hand on my arm. "Friend," he said.

Sure enough, it was Bo Derek. Her tailored suit was abraded and torn from low-crawling on the sidewalk, but right now that seemed to be the least of her worries. Her weapon was the Marlin Goose Gun, a huge bolt-action shotgun designed to take waterfowl at the outer limits of shotgun range. It's barrel was almost as long as Hemingway. Indeed, it was the Hemingway of shotguns.

"Glad you're okay, Mr. President." Derek sat with her back against the limo and pulled a canteen from beneath her coat. She took a couple of quick sips. She seemed to savor them.

She stuck out a patriotic hand. "Bo Derek."

"Sonny-Bob Culpepper." We shook, and the bond that we shared was that of protecting the Spirit of Freedom and serving Lord Reagan.

"It's pretty clear down at the other end of the street, Mr. President. I got most of 'em."

"Thank you, Bo. Your service is appreciated."

"My pleasure, Mr. President. I just wanted to make sure you and Mrs. Reagan were still okay. I'd better get back down to business."

She nodded at me. "Culpepper."

"Derek."

Then she was off again, low-crawling with that huge Goose Gun of hers. *It's always good to meet a patriotic American*, I reflected.

Then I remembered that special document. "Mr. President, do you have that executive order with you?"

"I almost forgot. Here." He withdrew sort of a packet from his pocket and handed it to me. "Unwrap that and give it to Truman and he shouldn't give you too much trouble."

"Thank you, Mr. President."

"Thank *you*, Captain Culpepper."

My phone buzzed. I flipped it open. "Yes?"

"Hurry up, Sonny-Bob! Everybody's here but you. That nuke's gonna hit in a couple minutes! I'm bulletproof, not nukeproof."

"On my way, old bean. Just hang tight for a few more seconds--"

But suddenly things heated up again. Henry Kissinger was dancing sideways across the street, firing a MAC-10 like some Hollywood actor.

"Kiss-My-Assinger," Lord Reagan muttered.

"Idiot!" I reprimanded Kissinger. "You shouldn't be in the open like that." I dropped him with a stunbeam just as he'd begun to send another cascade of bullets in our direction. "That's what Hollywood gets you, dummy! You can't expect to draw your tactics from movies."

Suddenly, The Pirate Jimmy Carter sprang down from a tree behind us thinking to catch us unawares. He was unarmed save for a huge quarterstaff; I guess he supported gun control. There was a patch over his left eye.

I faced him in a crouch, ready to defend my country from this deranged ex-president. He swung at my head but I dropped and rolled out of the way, then returned to my feet. The shooting had stopped and the street was eerily quiet.

"I've heard about you, timecop," he smirked. "I've been waiting a long time for this."

"Waiting a long time to get your ass whipped?"

The smirk left his face and he swung his staff again, but I had his number. My body, in harmony with the forces of the universe, moved inside his swing and I gently parried the staff as his free arm simultaneously came around in a strike. Then I grabbed his staff arm and swung beneath it, avoiding both staff and fist, and pivoted my body into his right flank as my forearm lay hard against his elbow. It shattered quite satisfactorily. As he screamed I offered a kick that shattered his knee, then circled around behind him and attacked his other knee and elbow, shattering both. He tumbled to the ground and I stomped him in the head. He'd live, but it would take more than a BC Powder to make him feel better.

I dropped to the ground as another hail of bullets started plowing up the asphalt, for the ground is the infantryman's best friend. I low-crawled back to Lord and Mrs. Reagan.

They returned fire and dropped another tax collector. The last one, it looked like. But he hadn't been the real problem. The real problem looked mad as hell.

Cap Weinberger was across the street with an M-60 machine gun, hell rag tied around his head and cigar clinched between his teeth. He wore a tiger stripe field uniform.

He sent round after round at us, shooting from the hip. Every few rounds the recoil of the mighty weapon made him take a step back and readjust his stance.

"You too, Cap?" Lord Reagan sighed.

Suddenly I heard the roar of a Goose Gun and Weinberger went down. Bo Derek was still out there somewhere.

"Sir, I've got to go. Austin's about to go up in a nuclear fireball."

"Begone, Sonny-Bob! Go save the world! Save America!"

"Save America!" Mrs. Reagan shouted, raising her fist in the Black Power salute.

I stood and saluted them, then kicked in the anti-gravs and flew towards Hubert. My phone had been buzzing for the last minute or so; I guess the inbound nuke had Hubert freaked out. 'Fraidy cat.

Then a shot rang out and my anti-gravs sputtered and died. I fell to the street and rolled. I stood and turned and there was Oliver North, grinning like the Cheshire Cat and leveling another government issue .45 at me.

"North, I'm surprised the Marine Corps let you have another weapon. You're not very good at keeping track of them."

The grin vanished and was replaced by an ugly snarl. "Damn your eyes, Culpepper! I got you! I got you!"

"Like hell!" I heard Lord Reagan roar, and a Peacemaker and a Winchester spoke together and North went to his knees. He looked astonished. I turned and ran; I didn't have any more time for him. But I generously hoped he'd be better behaved if the timeline was restored.

I was within ten meters of Hubert when Rosalind Carter stepped out of the shadows armed with a great cutlass, her usually pretty face twisted and vicious. Like her husband, she wore an eyepatch.

"I saw what you did to my Jimmy," she spat. "I'm sending you straight to hell, you timecop--die, pig, die!"

She lunged at me, and I wondered if that glittering blade would be the last thing I saw on this sweet green earth.

Suddenly my pregnant Mimi dove out of Hubert in a flying roll, a phase musket held across her chest. She came up in a crouch and the musket slid easily into her shoulder. As Rosalind Carter's blade descended upon my terror-stricken form Mimi fired. Mrs. Carter glowed blue, then vanished.

"Damn, honey! Did you have to disintegrate her? That gun has a stun setting."

"Get your ass in the car, Sonny-Bob! That nuke's gonna land in seconds!"

"Coming, dear!"

Mimi sprang back into Hubert as I sprinted those last ten meters with everything I had, the wind filling my flabby sails. I dived into Hubert and his door slammed shut behind me as I lay across several members of my family. They seemed nervous.

Hubert began to vibrate; in a few seconds we'd be gone--if we had a few seconds. The interdimensional doorway opened--

Suddenly we stared into the furnace of hell and in that one fraction of an instant all our optic nerves were destroyed. We couldn't see. But Hubert was vibrating and I was breathing, so we must've slipped into the doorway . . . I wet my pants and nearly passed out. I'd been more nervous than I'd let on.

I heard a poot I recognized as Freud's.

CHAPTER THIRTY-ONE

"Sonny-Bob, you cocksucker . . ." Hubert was sobbing and still vibrating, though we'd been in 1945 for a couple of minutes. Actually, he wasn't vibrating, he was shaking with nervous exhaustion.

"Calm down, Hubert. We made it, didn't we?"

"Yes, and no thanks to you. If you'd have been less than a tenth of a second later we'd all have been fried."

"My timing was perfect, then. I would think you'd enjoy working with an operative who always gets you out of harm's way with approximately a tenth of a second to spare."

"You two shut up!" Sue barked. "I can't see! That nuclear blast burned out my eyes."

"Yes, I know that, Sue. I imagine we're all blind. I know I am."

The rest of the family affirmed that they could no longer see, though we all still had the brilliant white flash of that nuclear blast pictured upon the screens of our brains.

"Medical nanos, Hubert. Start with pregnant women, then women, then Freud. Then do me."

"I won't do you at all, you bastard. I ought to take you back to the Revolutionary War and turn you loose among colonial troops wearing a British officer's uniform. They'd --"

"Hubert!" Mimi's voice was stern. "Remember why we're on this mission. Quit bitching at Sonny-Bob and inject all of us, including your captain."

Hubert growled, then sniffled. "Yes, ma'am," he finally said. And he did inject me, shoving the nano injector as hard as he could into Hemingway. It hurt, but I said nothing. The nanos would also repair the damage done by Hubert's callous thrust.

I heard a "meow" and a scratching sound.

"Tennessee's awake!" Aphrodite said.

They'd sedated the cat and stuffed him in a gym bag. Was that cat going to follow me for the rest of my life?

"Inject the cat, too," I said. "Since he was zipped up in that bag he may be fine, but there's no use taking chances with his health."

When we could all see again, we praised one another with our eyes. It was good to have family.

"Hubert, what's the date?"

"It's August 4, 1945."

"All right. Two days 'till Truman should drop the first atomic bomb."

"What's our first move?" Freud wanted to know.

"First, we go find an OSS agent--that's the forerunner of the CIA-- and I'll mug him and take his I.D. Then Hubert will scan the I.D. and make an exact duplicate for me. The OSS guy will still be unconscious, so I'll put his wallet back in his pocket and inject him with nanos to repair any damage. Then I'll take my new I.D. and go see Truman. It couldn't be simpler."

"Sounds like a plan," agreed Freud.

"Oh, Hubert. These nanos are using up glucose and making me weak. Make us all a glucose beverage, plus a tray of pastries. Give Mimi two glucose beverages; she's also eating and drinking for Pa Miyamoto."

"Ten-four."

Hubert had put us down in a wooded lot in northeastern Virginia. Naturally, we were going to drive to D.C. on a road. A flying car would frighten these people.

"I can't drive in 1945 as a 1968 Pontiac Catalina," Hubert said. "What do you want me to become, Sonny-Bob?"

"Something the authorities won't pull over."

"A Rolls Royce, then. That's a millionaire's car. Such a display of wealth makes primitive authorities deferential."

We all got out and stretched and urinated as Hubert changed his appearance once more. "I'm done," he finally announced. "Let's go!"

We went.

OSS Headquarters lay silently across the street from us as we surveiled it. A woman came out, but I didn't want to mug a representative of the Goddess, so we let her pass.

Eventually, a cocky young fellow came prancing out like he owned the world. "That's him, Hubert. Follow me as I follow him."

"Ten-four."

I leapt as nimbly as a fat person could from Hubert and shadowed the guy. But since I cast such a huge shadow he quickly noticed me. His hand slid into his pocket so I imagined he had a gun. Well, so did I.

This wasn't the best place to mug an OSS officer, but he suspected me of felonious intentions and undoubtedly was heading for sanctuary somewhere. I couldn't mug him if I let him get into a crowd or tavern. It had to be now.

I'll give him credit; the fellow was alert. As I pulled my pocket pistol he spun around with one of his own, but I stunned him before he could get off a shot. He collapsed and I waddled over to him and pulled out his wallet. His OSS identification lay inside. It said he was U.S. Army Lieutenant William E. Colby. "Yeah, right," I muttered. These spies wouldn't be carrying I.D.s that told their real names. But that didn't matter. I yanked out the I.D. and let Hubert scan it, then returned it to the spy. The whole process took less than a minute.

I injected him with nanos to heal any injury he might have experienced when he fell, and Hubert extended a fruit basket with his robotic arm. "I made him a nice gift. He'll need the glucose from this fruit to power his nanos."

We left the alleged Lieutenant Colby, knowing he'd be fine. At length we pulled over at a small park along the river and everyone but me got out to look at some ducks. Hubert made my I.D. "Here's your new identity, Mr. Bond." The card popped out of his NPD and I grabbed it. It said I was a Commander James Bond of the United States Navy. That name sounded familiar, but I couldn't remember where I'd heard it. Well, it would do.

"Thanks, old bean."

"Don't mention it."

"Hubert, I'll need period clothes."

"I've been thinking about that, Mr. Bond. There's a type of suit that's very popular today. It's called a zoot suit and all the best spies wear them. I'll make one if you like."

"Please."

Soon I was attired in a splendid new zoot suit. I'd worried that I might stand out in a crowd, for the thing was fluorescent yellow. But Hubert said not to worry, that all the best spies of the twentieth century had a cavalier attitude and wanted to stand out. I shrugged. After all I'd seen on this trip nothing these crazy people did would surprise me.

"One more thing, Sonny-Bob. Here, wear this pink boa around your neck. It's very fashionable. Also, try to walk with sort of an exaggerated limp on your right leg and swing your right arm more than your left. It's called jive walking and you're a type of highly respected citizen called a jive turkey."

I was glad Hubert was taking such good care of me. He didn't hold a grudge.

My mechanical friend crowned me with a bright yellow hat with a fashionably downturned brim. It sported a peacock feather.

I called to the family and they joined us. Mimi just looked me up and down with a strange expression in her eyes. Everyone was staring at me and admiring my splendor. In a fluorescent yellow zoot suit with a pink boa, even a highly obese individual is pretty.

I tossed back my head and swatted an imaginary mosquito with the boa, my other hand riding jauntily on my hip. I hadn't felt this handsome in a long time. I was going to play my role as James Bond to the hilt.

"Sonny-Bob," Mimi said slowly, "what's gotten into you?"

"The spirit of fashion, m'dear. Don't worry, I know what I'm doing. I'm a very highly trained field agent."

I thought I heard Hubert snickering, but when I turned around I saw he was only coughing. He'd probably swallowed some radioactive dust as we'd left 1983. Well, it was certainly best if he spit that stuff out.

"Mount up, everyone! Let's go see Harry Truman."

The family silently took their places in Hubert and we rolled away toward the White House. Hubert parked on Pennsylvania Avenue and I got out and strolled around for a bit, practicing my jive walking and trying to acclimate to 1945. This wasn't so hard. Everyone else stayed in the car, which was best since they all looked like they'd just left 1983.

Finally, I waved at them and strolled down the street. I'd use my fake OSS I.D. to get in to see President Truman, but I knew he'd be as impressed with my zoot suit as he would with my status as a spy.

I was headed up the steps to the White House when Eleanor Roosevelt came out. Mmmm, I would have thought she'd be off somewhere still grieving for Franklin, who'd died a few months ago.

Hemingway quickened; he felt her vibrations and they turned him on. "Hemingway, stop it!" I whispered to my antenna, but he was still tuned in to Mrs. Roosevelt's frequency and he began to swell somewhat. Now my jive walk was for real. I couldn't walk any other way. Good thing Hemingway was strapped to my right leg, which was the leg Hubert told me to limp on. Now it was easy.

I stopped as Mrs. Roosevelt approached, my right leg jerking spasmodically and uncontrollably. I twirled my boa and tried to appear nonchalant. "Good day, Mrs. Roosevelt."

"Good day to you, young man. Goodness, what's wrong with your right leg?"

Then Hemingway poked his great head out the cuff and she saw what was wrong. Her hand flew to her mouth. "Dear me!"

A guy was trailing Mrs. Roosevelt. Now he walked up.

He looked me quickly up and down with a fierce intensity. "Who are you?"

"Nunna yer bi'ness, Bub," I replied.

He started towards me as Mrs. Roosevelt laid a hand on his arm. "Now Cedric, this gentleman obviously has a problem. Do be civil."

"Yes, ma'am." But he was still looking at me fiercely.

Mrs. Roosevelt turned to me. "Cedric's my Secret Service guard, you understand. Sometimes he's a little overprotective."

Secret Service again. It seemed like half the people in the twentieth century worked for the Secret Service. Most of the rest were either strippers or Marines.

"Have we met, young man?"

"I don't think so, ma'am. I'm Commander James Bond of the U.S. Navy."

Cedric guffawed. I couldn't imagine why. A little smile played around Mrs. Roosevelt's lips.

"Would you walk me to my car, Commander Bond?"

"Well, ma'am, I've got to see President Truman. It's urgent. So if you'll excuse me . . ."

"Nonsense! You have a few minutes to walk with me. President Truman's in a meeting and won't be out for at least another hour."

I shrugged. Why not? It wasn't every day you got to walk with a relatively decent Democrat. "Okay, ma'am."

She took my arm and we hobbled along, she because of her age, and me because of my Hemingway. I didn't know how much longer those elastic straps would hold him against my leg; he'd torn them loose on more than one occasion. Then it would be a simple matter for him to tear the leg out of my pants. Sometimes it's hard having a dick like this. Oh, sometimes it's hard.

But I had no idea why Eleanor Roosevelt made him hard. Perhaps he was becoming delusional. Just as I'm attracted to women by their energy, so too is Hemingway. But what could there be about Eleanor Roosevelt's energy that would attract my cock and make it hard? What?

We stumbled along for a ways, then we reached her car. I hoped she wasn't going to ask for a goodby kiss.

She turned into me and tried to hold me with her eyes, which somehow seemed familiar, but my sixth, seventh, eighth and ninth senses were all screaming "Red Alert!" I pivoted, and that fool Cedric was bringing a handgun down on my head. But I wasn't there anymore; the forces which govern the universe, in concert with my own energy, had moved me off to Cedric's side. He hit Mrs. Roosevelt instead. The muzzle of the gun broke her nose and the gun on its downward arc got tangled up in her titties, snapping her blouse open and attaching itself to her slingshot brassiere.

More twentieth century weirdoes. I sighed. Would the people of this century never learn to behave?

Cedric was struggling to free his gun, but Mrs. Roosevelt shoved him off her and dived inside the car. Well, I'd dive inside the car, too, to get away from a nut like that Cedric.

But then she reemerged, that Colt .45 semi-auto still dangling from her titties. And in her hands she held a . . . phase musket? A phase musket! Jesus, Mary and Joseph, she was turning the thing on me!

I dived to the ground as that phase musket blast seared the air over my head and disintegrated a tree. I was clawing for my pocket pistol and rolling like a butterball ninja.

I got the pistol and returned fire. She'd already fired twice more at me, disintegrating patches of earth, for I'd rolled across the street and was in a grassy parklike area. Hemingway was no longer hard; as usual he'd curled up and was playing possum when the weapons began firing. Whenever weapons were discharging, Hemingway wasn't.

One of my stunbeams hit Cedric and he collapsed. Mrs. Roosevelt was still firing at me from behind the cover of her car. I rolled behind a tree, which promptly disintegrated. I pulled out my phone and rolled again as another phase musket blast disintegrated the ground where I'd been an instant before. "Hubert! Help! Help! Help!"

I dropped the phone and kept rolling, returning fire when I could. Hubert could home in on the phone to find me.

Shit! My power pack was dead, so my weapon wouldn't fire anymore. I should've replaced that power pack after that shootout in 1983.

Mrs. Roosevelt saw my predicament. I still had my suppository gun, but now wasn't the time to pull down my pants. I rolled again and the blast from her musket singed my suit.

Hubert came through for me then, blasting his way into Mrs. Roosevelt's reality with stunbeams flashing and playing the William Tell Overture at maximum volume over his PA system. Mrs. Roosevelt took a shot at him, which glanced harmlessly off his windshield, then jumped into her car and roared off down the street.

I rolled over to my phone and grabbed it, then sprinted for Hubert. God, I needed to lose about two hundred pounds!

"Sonny-Bob! Are you okay?"

"Yes. Make me a set of handcuffs, Hubert, pronto! Sue, get over here and help me confiscate this bastard."

Sue sprang out and we grabbed Cedric and started for Hubert.

"Mimi! Stay in that car!" She withdrew.

Sue and I tossed Cedric across Freud and Aphrodite, then sprang into Hubert ourselves. "Go, Hubert! Follow that car!"

Hubert sailed down the street in the direction taken by Mrs. Roosevelt and soon we caught sight of her car stuck in traffic. "Easy, old bean. Cloak yourself. Don't let her see us. If a car gets too close while we're cloaked, push it gently away with a modified stunbeam."

"Ten-four."

A pair of handcuffs popped out of the NPD and I tossed them to Freud. "Cuff his hands behind his back. When he wakes up if he struggles or bothers you in any way knock his teeth in."

"Roger that."

Well, we followed Mrs. Roosevelt for over two hours and she led us out into the Virginia countryside. I was lying scrunched up with my head in Mimi's lap, trying to get my breath back for most of that time. When you're two or three hundred pounds overweight, you do have certain limitations.

At length that old presidential bitch turned into a field road and we followed her for about a quarter mile until we came to a pasture. There was a barn in the center of the pasture. Mrs. Roosevelt parked off to the side of the barn, then got out and swung the great doors open and went inside. Then she shut the doors. That fool Cedric had been awake for some time but had said nothing. I had my breath back, so it was time to question him.

"Pull back into the trees and decloak, Hubert. I want to interrogate this bastard."

"You'll get nothing from me, you fat hog."

I pulled out my butterfly knife. "I'll get your testicles if you don't cooperate. Drag his ass out, Freud, and set him up against that tree. Then pull his pants down and expose his genitals."

"Just like Laos," Freud commented.

"Mimi, this isn't something a pregnant lady, or any of you ladies, should be exposed to. Castration is a man's job. Go off into those trees over there and don't look, but Mimi take your phase musket in case Mrs. Roosevelt comes back. That bitch is hell on wheels."

"Yes, sir."

I turned to Cedric. "I'm going to have your story and you know I'm going to have it. Your ass is mine and whether you live or die is up to me. Whether or not you leave here with a scrotum is up to me. Therefore, talk."

He was sweating like a Mongolian warhorse that had just been through the battle of its life. But a Mongolian warhorse would've had the sense to breathe deeply, whereas this guy could barely breathe at all. Still, he tried to put on a brave face. "F--fuck--"

"I believe this is yours," I said, lifting the testicle I'd just cut away from his scrotum. I put it on the tip of my knife and whirled it around as he stared in horror. "After I remove your other testicle I'll get your eyes. I'll cut away everything you've got except your tongue until you talk."

I gave him a big kiss; the crazier you seem to those you interrogate the quicker they'll come around. "My name's Sonny-Bob Culpepper, and I--"

His eyes practically bugged out of his head. He was more horrified than when I'd shown him his nut. His jaws and tongue were working, but no sound came out. A strange rattling noise came out of his throat; shit, we were loosing him. I grabbed a nano injector from my pocket and jabbed it into him. "Freud! Go get a glucose injector from Hubert. Hustle up!"

Somehow we kept the fucker alive. The nanos rebuilt his nut and he was good as new. Of course, he wouldn't stay that way unless he cooperated.

After he seemed stable enough I went to work on him again. I tested the edge of my knife. "Been circumcised lately?"

"Culpepper . . . Lieutenant Culpepper . . ."

"I'm no lieutenant, I'm a captain. But you've obviously heard of me. Are you with the TAC?"

He nodded dumbly, his face still a mask of terror. "Culpepper . . . I heard about what you did when you worked with the 12th ERT. ERTs are all insane, but not compared to you. I don't care if you kill me, but please, just don't hurt me! Don't hurt me!"

"There, there, sonny," I soothed. "I won't have to hurt you if you'll just tell me what I want to know. Might not even have to kill you. Okay?"

He nodded, fear still blasting its way out of every pore.

"Okay, then. Your I.D. didn't tell us any more than we already know, so who are you?"

"Cletus Lufkin, sergeant first class, Temporal Adjustment Corps. I work security for the station in Philadelphia in the 1700's."

"Good." My eyes narrowed. "Now who's that bitch you were with? That's not really Eleanor Roosevelt, is it?"

He shook his head. "No, she's a TAC major named Mary Beth Magoo. She told me all about you, said you'd been married for a while. Said not to worry, you wouldn't come after us. 'He's not with the ERT anymore,' she said, 'and he's out of favor with the TAC. He's the last person they'd send.' But here you are." He was trembling violently.

Well, now. It was as I had begun to suspect. "How many of you are there?"

"Just me and her, now. There was a guy named Olaf Jenkins with us, but he tried to split so Mary Beth split him with a phase musket. His TITTY yanked him back inside and took off with him, but I think it was too late for nanos to do him any good."

"What made you do this, Cletus? What made you decide to destroy the timeline?"

"Destroy it? We're trying to save it!"

"Well, you picked a damfool method. I left just as the twenty-second century was disappearing. The timewave started in 1983 as a result of a nuclear exchange between the U.S. and the Soviet Onion. All life on earth was destroyed in the nuclear winter, except for some bacteria. This would never have happened if Truman had nuked the Japs. Why the hell did you and Mary Beth stop Truman from using the bomb?"

"I don't know . . . she screwed with my emotions, Captain. She fucked me silly and I wound up believing every word she said . . . I . . . I have no emotional discipline when it comes to her. She's more than hot . . ."

Obviously, Mary Beth had forced herself to thaw out to manipulate this poor devil. What a sap.

"We both loved her, me and Olaf. She said if we'd help her it'd save lives in the long run, but she never told us any details. We'd hear her scream in her sleep about burning flesh and dead children, but she never really told us what she was up to. She did nano surgery on herself to look like Mrs. Roosevelt, and that's how she got in to see Truman. She's been in his office day and night for the last few days, but she made me wait outside the door. I don't know what she's been up to."

"Well, I know what the bitch is up to, and I know it destroyed the world. Mary Beth used to be a more sensible warrior than this. When we shared a marriage I fathered two children by her. Now those children don't exist because she erased the timeline."

I studied him closely for a moment. "Well, you've told us what you know, and it's enough. We're going to have to either capture or kill Mary Beth and then undo what she's done. We're going to keep you chained up and gagged until we've saved the world, then you'll face disciplinary action with Mary Beth if she's still alive. If she's dead you'll face the music by yourself."

Freud and I put Lufkin back into Hubert. I straightened up. "Well, Freud, what do you think of our little operation so far?"

"It reminds me of old times," he said softly, and I think a little sadly.

"I thought it would. Just remember what the stakes are. This mission *has* to succeed. It has to succeed so all those little pissant control freaks can begin to grow up and quit trying to manipulate one another. And ultimately, so they can learn to *love* one another. The race has to be allowed to mature."

I chuckled. "Those nutty little control addicts will give you ticker tape parades and speeches of adulation when you save their world, and maybe also furnish you with sexual favors. Just don't tell them how you saved their world; they don't want to know about that. Reminds 'em of their dark side, makes 'em feel they're losing control. Then the only way they feel they can get their sense of control back is to crucify you. They bounce around like a pendulum from one extreme to the other.

"But an integrated person can move smoothly up and down the scale of human experience and exhibit correct motive on each level. You saw me castrate that old boy. I did it to get information that will help us keep this living planet alive. I didn't do it for fun or vengeance; that type of fun is for sociopaths and vengeance is for idiots and fundamentalists of whatever religion. I don't want to experience that kind of energy. But I didn't particularly mind doing it, because it was necessary. Only a person with Floppy Chakra Syndrome balks in the face of necessity, and such a person cannot be trusted to perform his duty.

"And you'll notice that Lufkin experienced little or no loss of Dignity, because I offered a quick, generic violence, rather than the slow, sustained terror-building of repetitive psychological degradation directed specifically at race or religion or culture. Hell, Lufkin and I both belong to the *same* religion and culture, and we look enough alike that he could be one of my bastards, so we're racially similar, too.

"Anyway, crucifixion's serious business. That's why I always keep my tetanus shot current."

"Roger that," Freud confirmed.

"Okay, then. Go summon Mimi and the others. Time to mount an assault. I'll have Hubert make more weapons."

When Freud got back with the ladies Hubert was busily turning out phase muskets. Soon we all had phase muskets, one each, field issue.

"All right, everybody, listen up. We're going to split into two teams. I'm Alfa Team leader. Sue, you and Hubert are with me. Freud's Bravo

Team leader, and Mimi you and Aphrodite are his team. And Mimi, we all know how hardheaded and rebellious you are, but you're going to follow Freud's orders. Otherwise, you'll have to stay behind. Understood?"

"Yes, sir," Mimi said timidly. Mmm, she'd never been timid before.

"This isn't like pornography or stripping," Aphrodite said. "I'll have to follow somebody's orders."

"Okay. Alfa Team will assault the barn from the rear and try to stun my bitch ex-wife. Freud, Bravo Team's job is to cover the front of the barn. I want your team set up with a sector of fire that'll allow you to sweep clear from the woods on the left all the way to the woods on the right, in case Mary Beth somehow gets a chance to sprint away from the barn. Also, give me interlocking fields of fire; I'd rather have Mary Beth hit twice than not at all. And keep your weapons set on stun. I don't really see any point in killing her.

"Hubert, can you make me a nano grenade that'll disconnect the neural net of her TITTY?" For he'd already scanned her vehicle, and just as we'd expected it was a TITTY. Hubert recognized her and said her name was Julia. As with me and Mary Beth, Hubert and Julia had been intimate long ago.

He sniffled. I knew how he felt. But it had to be done, and for all his faults, Hubert was a patriot. "Yes, Captain. I've already been working on it. I figured you'd ask for something like this." He extended his robotic arm and handed the canister to me.

"Good man. There's no chance this thing could infect you, is there?"

"No, sir. I specifically programmed those nanos to stay away from me. They'll be activated three seconds after you've pulled the pin and released the spoon. They'll home in on Julia and have her neural net disconnected before she can devise countermeasures. If she's napping she may not even notice."

"Outstanding, old bean. Here, let me toss my boa and hat inside you. I won't need them for this assault."

"Freud, you've got ten minutes to get your team set up. Then Alfa team's going to start maneuvering behind the barn."

"Airborne, sir, airborne! Kill for peace!"

"No, Freud," I reminded him gently. "Stun for peace, okay?"

"Stun for peace, sir, stun for peace! Airborne!"

"Good man."

Freud went off with Mimi and Aphrodite and started laying out their fields of fire.

"Sue, while Hubert was making the phase muskets I wanted to do a little recon around behind the barn to see if there's a rear door. I expect there is, but I wanted to verify it. Then I realized I'm too fat to get there and back quickly. While Freud's busy with his team I'd like you to creep around where you can see the rear of the barn. Find out if there's a door. If there is we stick to the plan. If there is no door, though, I guess I'll have to come up with a new plan. Also, be wary of mines and booby traps. You can never be too careful."

Sue swallowed, hard. But she was a dedicated patriot like the rest of us. The timeline could--and did--count on her. "Yes, sir. Uh, airborne."

"Good woman. Stay in the treeline at all costs and make full use of cover and concealment. Now go."

"Yes, sir." She took a deep breath and trotted boldly into the woods with her phase musket, and after a moment she disappeared.

After a few minutes Freud's team was in position. He made his report. "Captain Culpepper, Bravo Team's in place and good to go. Mimi has the left hand field of fire, Aphrodite has the right, and I'm right down the middle, ready to blast anything that comes out of that barn."

"Outstanding. Sue's on a recon and we're moving out as soon as she gets back and makes her report. Resume your position, Freud."

"Airborne!"

After a few more minutes Sue returned, sweaty and breathing hard. She'd been scratched by brambles, but her determination shone through the scratches. "Captain, there's a door, all right. It's shut. I didn't see any mines or booby traps." She kind of shivered.

"Good job, Sue. Hubert, once we get behind the barn I'm gonna slip around and toss this nano grenade at Julia. How much time do the nanos need to complete their job, old bean?"

"Less than five minutes."

"Good. Five minutes after I've tossed the grenade I'll slip inside the barn by stealth if the door isn't barred and stun Mary Beth. Ya'll will remain in position in the treeline behind the barn unless I'm discovered. Hubert, turn all your sensors to maximum and if you hear a cry go up in the barn bust your way inside with your stunbeams ready. Sue, you follow behind Hubert and stun anything that moves."

"Yes, sir."

"Yes, sir."

"On the other hand, if the door is barred and I can't get it unbarred to slip in undetected, we'll all have to bust in at the same time. In that scenario I'll be behind Hubert with you, Sue. And again, all of us will stun anything that moves."

I took a deep breath to fill my fat cells with the oxygen they would need to help propel me through this. "Alfa Team, follow me, do as I do."

Sue, Hubert and I worked our way through the woods and pulled up at the barn's right flank. If Julia was awake she might have seen us if we approached from directly behind the barn. Hubert had to do some fancy driving with his anti-gravs to get through those woods. Half the time he was up on his side. But we made it.

"Hubert, what do your sensors reveal?"

"No early warning devices that I can detect, though that may not mean much if Major Magoo is as devious as you say."

"Well, I'll have to chance it. I'm going in to toss this grenade at Julia. Cover my ass."

I carefully waddled across the pasture. I certainly made a large target and I should've changed out of that yellow zoot suit into a field uniform, but it would have taken a few more minutes for Hubert to generate a uniform for me and maybe half an hour for me to cover my fat ass with it. Getting dressed is not easy for the highly obese, and the timeline didn't have much time. I was cutting corners.

I reached the barn without incident, then worked my way around behind it to the other side, where Julia was parked. I hoped she was snoozing. I pulled the pin on the grenade, holding the spoon down with my thumb. I stooped and sort of tossed the grenade along the ground. It came to rest by Julia's left rear tire. Maybe she hadn't noticed.

I withdrew completely behind the barn and looked at my watch. Then five minutes went by. I cautiously peered at Julia again. She was unmoved, so I guess the nanos had done their job. Whew! One hurdle out of the way.

"Hubert, this is Sonny-Bob, over," I whispered into my phone.

"Sonny-Bob, this is Hubert, over."

"You and Sue can move into position now. Julia appears to be neutralized. Good work on that grenade. Out."

"Roger, out."

I waited a few more minutes to give Hubert and Sue time to move directly behind the barn. I caught a glimpse of sunlight reflecting off Hubert's surface as they took up their assault positions behind the treeline. I hoped they could redeem my ass if it got hung out to dry. The barn's door was securely fastened, but I set my pocket pistol to torch mode and sliced through the bar. Then I took up my phase musket and opened the door ever so slightly . . . well, as slightly as I could get away with, considering my hugeness.

I slipped inside and closed the door. Sunlight streamed in through the planks that had warped apart from each other in this weathered old structure. Dust hung in the streaming sunlight.

I heard voices, then the "slap!" of a blow being struck. Then there was a groan of weariness and pain. Well, Mary Beth must be torturing somebody. Good. With her attention focused on her victim she might not notice me.

"Bitch!" It was Mary Beth's voice. So she was torturing a woman. She used to worship the Goddess, but now she tortured her representatives. Mary Beth had become degenerate.

She was up there in the loft . . . suddenly, I stepped on something. I didn't know what it was, but it felt like some kind of pressure plate. Damn! Mary Beth had mined the place. Oh, well. I dived and rolled, hoping for the best and clawing for a nano injector. I lay there, sure the mine hadn't gone off . . . therefore, I must still be alive. What the hell had I stepped on? Must've been some type of early warning device.

I rose cautiously. A shadow flitted down a ladder that led to the loft. The shadow moved again. It was focused on the area where I'd stepped on the pressure plate. But I'd rolled clear to the other end of the barn. The shadow was an idiot.

This barn gave off the good smell of musty old cow turds. Mary Beth couldn't have picked a better command post.

The shadow moved again and I fired. The shadow returned fire and nearly got me with a stunbeam. I was rolling again, rolling and firing that phase musket together with my rolls, sending out cartwheels of sizzling blue light to stop the nemesis of the timeline.

The shadow screamed and collapsed. I'd got her unless she was playing possum. Just then Hubert smashed the barn door open and charged in with his flashing stunbeams, one of which caught me across the legs and across the Hemingway. I went down. "Cease fire, Hubert! Cease fire! I got her--I think."

Hubert stopped firing and rolled up to me. "You okay, Sonny-Bob?" he asked anxiously.

"My Hemingway's stunned," I grunted. "Can't walk. Sue, I stunned somebody. She fell over there. Go tie her up before she wakes.

"But be careful! Keep your phase musket pointed at her 'till you're sure she's out, and if she so much as twitches hit her with multiple blasts."

"Yes, sir!"

As I'd figured, the shadow was Mary Beth, still looking like Eleanor Roosevelt. Sue cuffed her hands behind her back, then took a length of wire she'd found and ran it around Mary Beth's neck. Then she twisted the ends of the wire together around one of the logs that made up the wall of a stall. Mary Beth would have to stand on tippy toes. Damn, Sue was good!

Sue held Mary Beth up until she started regaining consciousness. "Who are you, bitch?" Mary Beth said. Sue drove her fist into the other woman's face and Mary Beth didn't ask again. The TAC doesn't normally recruit outside our own century, but if it did Sue would be my first convert. My heart warmed and sent a beam of admiration at Sue.

I staggered to my feet and to my Hemingway. I stumbled towards the two women.

"Sir, do you want me to go get the others?" Sue asked.

"Not yet. They're our external security. They can see what's happening out there and we can't."

Sue released Mary Beth, who would now get to exercise the muscles in her toes as she fought for breath.

"Hello, honey," I said.

Mary Beth grimaced and growled. "I knew it was you, Sonny-Bob, when I saw your cock head poking out your pants leg. But you sure have put on weight. I wouldn't have recognized you if not for the cock and the eyes."

I turned to Sue. "She was beating some woman in the loft when I came in. Go rescue her. But keep your phase musket ready and stun anything that moves."

"Yes, sir."

"Yes, sir," Mary Beth echoed, a smirk in her eyes. "That girl's no field agent. Is she a security officer, or just another impressionable young cadet? Did you promise her the adventure of a lifetime if she'd come with you and jump on your Hemingway?"

"No, Mary Beth, I didn't. She's gay, and she's my friend."

Mary Beth chuckled hoarsely, obviously in pain from the wire. "You're slipping, Sonny-Bob. Since when has friendship been more important to you than sex?"

"Since I met Amanda, whom I love and adore. You remember her, she slept with you too, and you couldn't have forgotten her. Nobody forgets Amanda."

Mary Beth became still. "Yes, Sonny-Bob, I remember Amanda, and some of the times the three of us had together. Those were the best days of my life. If only--" A tear trickled down her cheek.

"Why'd you do it, Mary Beth?" I whispered softly. "Why'd you stop Truman from using the bomb?"

"Because the bomb's inhuman, because of the suffering the bomb's caused. Because if the bomb's not used in this war no one will know the

United States has it and no other country will feel the need to develop it.

"That's it, Sonny-Bob. I did it so the bomb will *never* be used."

"You're insane," I said.

Her face twisted. "Fight me! Turn me loose and fight me! I used to be able to whip your ass, now I'll kill you! I'll kill you!"

"Mary Beth, don't you know what you did to the timeline? Our world is gone because of what you did. The earth is barren, she's dead. **You** killed her; you tried to stop a necessary and productive use of destructive energy, and without that release the earth's destructive energy was bottled up inside her body and aura. And inside the human race. You know what happens when you don't release destructive energy and use it to serve the common good. It just turns in on itself and begins to seethe against itself and against the barriers to its expression. It explodes, and is far more devastating than if you'd just allowed it to express itself morally and spiritually to begin with. No good can come from repressing energy. 'Repression Creates Perversion', and look at the perversion you've created. You've killed the earth.

"Truman's use of the bomb in the original timeline was an important safety valve. It served as sort of an inoculation that insured the world would never have a full scale nuclear exchange. Plus, it was an outstanding tool to help crush the forces of evil, which during this period were expressing through the Axis powers.

"You ruined all that, with your scatterbrained guilt over preserving that small nuclear exchange between India and Pakistan in 2032. That's why you did this, isn't it? To try to stop the very nuclear exchange you once preserved as a responsible TAC agent."

"But the dead children . . ." She was growing numb again. I could feel it.

"Sweetie," I said as gently as I could, considering the circumstances, "those children are dead anyway, only this time you did kill them. This time it is your fault. And what you've done with your meddlesome floppy chakra guilt is far worse than what originally happened. In fact, those children you're so concerned about were never even born, most likely. With the change in the timeline you created, most life on earth was gone by the time they would've been born, and all of it was gone a few years later. Hubert and I barely got out of our own century ahead of the timewave you created. That timewave eliminated all life on earth. You did this, honey. It's the same kind of emotionally unpurified floppy chakra response a primitive person might have had."

She was leaving me now. She was growing numb all over and there was a shocked, far away look in her eyes. "The children . . ."

"Hubert! Give me an immobilization nano."

He extended one to me and I shoved it into Mary Beth. I had to get her loose from that wire before she strangled herself. She was no longer on her tippy toes. But there was no way I was going to get her down unless she was immobilized. She was strong and fierce and she was telling the truth when she said she used to be able to kick my ass. She might be in handcuffs, but her feet and knees and teeth were still free.

About an hour later, we all stood around a thoroughly bound Mary Beth. The only thing she could move was her tongue. Once she'd been bound I was no longer afraid of her, so I shot some nanos into her to counteract the immobilization nanos.

She'd laughed hysterically; Truman was going to save the children of the world, the National Rifle Association was going to beat its swords into plowshares, Pakistan would be an ideal vacation retreat for centuries. The mothers of the world would eliminate war.

"And honor and courage and truth," I muttered. Floppy chakra mothers are dangerous. They smother the good with the bad.

"You can't hug children with nuclear arms!" she screamed, then began sobbing again.

"Of course not, Mary Beth," I replied. "You can't hug children with automobiles, either, but nobody's talking about getting rid of them, despite the fact they kill untold thousands of children and adults the world over each year in this century.

"You see, there's all kinds of tools you can't hug children or anybody else with. You can't hug children with spoons, you can't hug children with bicycles.

"Human arms were designed to hug children. That's one of their prime functions. Human arms are meant to hug people in general, both children and adults.

"Nuclear arms were never designed to hug anybody. It's irrational, inaccurate, unskillful and unreal to try to compare a tool designed for hugging, such as human arms, with a tool designed for killing, such as nuclear arms. They are not analogous. That slogan 'You can't hug children with nuclear arms' came from floppy chakra people who are ruled by pre-programmed emotional fluctuations that have been handed down for generations. Their slogans mean nothing. Those people care only for their fearful, sentimental, emotionally fluctuating illusions. They don't care for truth, and they think sentiment is love. They're wrong about everything, basically. Their heads are up the ass of reality and they can't see the entire picture because they won't purify themselves.

"Mary Beth, I never would have dreamed that your being near that nuclear blast in Pakistan would have brought atavistic tendencies out of you. If I'd known you carried such tendencies I would've tried to get you out of the TAC and into therapy."

She sputtered and laughed on the ground. There was no use talking to her. I shook my head sadly. I never dreamed my golden girl would turn into an artificial Eleanor Roosevelt and have to be tied up.

Well, she'd told us what we needed to know. She'd already convinced Truman not to use the bomb. Maybe she was lying, but my gut doubted it. I had to see Truman and give him President Reagan's executive order.

"Hubert, do you have Julia squared away?"

"Yes, Captain. Her cognitive functions are still mostly offline. She's not what I'd call self aware. But we can program her to automatically go where we want her to go. You can load Major Magoo and Cletus Lufkin into Julia if you're ready. I've got Julia programmed to go to the twenty-second century."

"Then reprogram her. Mary Beth has a slick tongue and has used that slick tongue on a lot of the generals. She might be able to convince them we're the bad guys and that she's a good girl. That would be a definite no-go. Program Julia to go to the late twenty-fourth century. There'll be a different crop of generals by then. I hope."

"But Sonny-Bob, it's illegal for any of us to go more than fifty years beyond our own time. You're breaking one of the TAC's strictest rules; they're stricter about this than they are about an operative grandfathering himself."

"Fuck 'em. If we're going to save the timeline, we'll do it on our own terms. And that means *my* terms.

"There's no telling what would happen if we sent Mary Beth back to our time, but if she thaws herself out again she may be able to talk and suck and fuck her way out of trouble. Then we'd just have this mission to do over again. Is that what you want?"

"I see your point, sir. The twenty-fourth century it is."

We'd leave Mary Beth and Lufkin in Julia until we were pretty sure we'd saved humanity. Then we'd send them to the Twenty-Fourth. If we sent them too soon they might vanish into non-existence, and in truth my preference was for my ex-wife to live. Call me a sentimental old fool.

Sue ambled up with the woman she'd rescued from the loft.

"Feeling better, Mrs. Roosevelt?" I asked.

"Much better, thank you, Captain Culpepper. I think I finally can grasp a little of what's happened, though it seems incredible."

Eleanor Roosevelt wore a new frock Hubert had made for her, along with the type of goofy old hat older women often wore in this century to indicate they no longer thought of themselves as sexual beings. (However, I must note that I got the definite impression that Eleanor wore the hat as camouflage so she could still move with impunity among her peers in the political world, while privately continuing certain dalliances.) Hubert put a long-stemmed daisy in the hat for good measure. I got jealous and had him clean my zoot suit with some dirt-buster nanos. I wasn't about to be outdone by a twentieth century matron. I put my boa back on.

Mrs. Roosevelt had been hungry and bruised; we'd fed her and injected her with nanos and now she was fine. Plus, Sue had given her a sponge bath. She smelled passably well.

"It's just horrible what that woman did," Mrs. Roosevelt was saying. "I saw her disintegrate three of your people with that weapon of hers. They just vanished! And she laughed and told me she'd ambushed dozens more by pretending to be me."

"You'll have to forgive her, Mrs. Roosevelt. She's more of an atavist than you are."

We loaded our two culprits into Julia, then Hubert towed her into the barn as a precaution against her being seen if any of the natives showed up around our new command post. I took a phase musket and disintegrated all of Mary Beth's futuristic gear, including that early warning device I'd stepped on earlier. It was hooked into a computer terminal in the loft, which I also eliminated.

I put a note on Mary Beth. "Dear twenty-fourth century generals," it said, "here the bitch is. If my crew has been successful in saving the timeline, then you should have read my report. You know how dangerous this woman is. Please lock her and her henchperson away forever. Thank you. -- Sonny-Bob Culpepper, Captain, Temporal Adjustment Corps."

"That should do it," I grunted. "Mrs. Roosevelt, let's take a walk."

We were walking through the afternoon grasses of Virginia, yet my thoughts were not on making love to Eleanor Roosevelt. "Ma'am, you must have some real pull with Truman for your double to have convinced him not to nuke the Japs."

She blushed. "Actually, uh, I'm really better acquainted with Mrs. Truman. My double had researched me well, she knew that. She told me she convinced Mrs. Truman that Harry would be considered a monster if he used that atom bomb, then Mrs. Truman and she convinced Harry it would be immoral to use it. Finally, he decided not to."

"Um . . . how did you and Mrs. Truman know about the Manhattan Project? That's way beyond Top Secret."

She blushed again. "There's no real secrets among family, Captain. Franklin and I grew close to the Trumans . . ."

I held up a hand. "I understand. I'm a family man myself."

We walked a little farther. The afternoon grasses of Virginia beckoned to us, rippling in the gentle breeze.

"Mrs. Roosevelt, I appreciate the fact that a lot of you Democrats had some balls and some honor during this part of the century. You're a much better breed than that lot at century's end."

"Are you a Republican, Captain Culpepper?"

"I'm an Anarchist. But I vote Republican."

I reflected for a moment, wondering how much I should reveal to a primitive mind. Then I shrugged. It seems my specialty has always been to walk in swinging a stick of stove wood, and let God sort out the results. So I continued.

"Eleanor, I've had a natural instinct for Unity all my life, and have worked to find the Unity in all phenomena. Like everyone else, I was brought up with illusions, and had to work diligently to scrub that dingy soot from the windowpanes of the soul. But even so, I think I was somehow always seeing the Unity, even while my mind was distressed at trying to reconcile the silly illusions with one another. Now I know that Truth never needs reconciliation to Itself, but when I was a child I was trying to refine my understanding of my illusions enough to be able to reconcile them with the overall pattern of existence, but of course the act of refining illusions ultimately leads to the destruction of illusions, if a person is able to be completely honest with himself. And as those mental illusions are destroyed, more Truth from the Higher Mental Plane can leak through to your conscious awareness, and then you have to learn to build forms of pure intuition to contain each sparkle of Truth you contact. Then you have to line these golden forms which glow with an inward sparkle along golden channels that have constructed themselves for your awareness to flow through as a result of your hard Work."

Eleanor was taking glances at me with a wooden, uncomprehending expression in her eyes. I sighed with weariness. She'd come around sooner or later; in fact, I felt strongly that two or three incarnations down the road she'd make a good Sacred Prostitute. But now I was feeling the tiredness and lack of connection that always come when I try to communicate the incommunicable to a person who was born before the

Age of Synthesis. This tiredness becomes especially burdensome when they think they understand what I've said . . . because they never do, and the fact that they think they understand insures that they never will. And it's not because I'm smarter than they are, either. I'm not smarter than they are. But I have a calling, and that is to find Synthesis. I've found Him and become His child, but the level of endurance I've had to develop on this Path is terrible to contemplate. But at least the trail I've blazed will give those with a keen spiritual nose, a nose for the brand-new energy I've come to embody, a series of scent posts to prove that the old dog has passed nearby, and so encourage them that maybe they are on the right track.

But suddenly I knew that Eleanor was being Quickened in spite of her ignorance. I almost chuckled. I was serving the world as usual, and as usual, the world didn't know it!

So some jauntiness came back into my step as I continued sharing with Eleanor. "Honey, I'm not really even an Anarchist anymore, at least not in any normal sense. And I don't anticipate voting for Republicans or anyone else anymore, either, since it seems that only unconscious frauds run for office, even in my own timezone . . . though they are maybe becoming conscious back home, since they're learning to admit that government and other institutions are useless for genuine human beings, and are considering the possibility of dissolving completely the little government that survived the onslaught of the Synthesis of Consciousness."

I smiled, remembering how the TAC left the government less than a decade after it was founded, because it was evident that no government could ever be trusted to influence history. We can let them think they are in control, but that's always an egocentric artifice that government people and other control-freak types adopt to keep from descending into a deeper level of insanity that the one they already inhabit. No government anywhere or anywhen has any real power; they can't, because it's so contrary to the principles of a compassionate Nature to see people with such polluted motives wielding any real power. People who work for governments *always* suffer from inferior motives, and they can never be trusted. Their motives are always sour, polluted with the filthy strings of attachment to sentimental emotional fluctuations and the ridiculous mental preconceptions that arise out of those fluctuations. Even if occasionally a spark of sweetness arises in someone who works for a government, it is almost immediately swallowed by the sourness. I've earned the spiritual authority to say these things because my motives are absolutely stellar, and have been ever since I was a little child. I've never thought of myself, except in the sense of how I can fully refine all glamours and illusions out of myself to serve as a pure vehicle of Truth and that Love which is Truth's Parent. So excuse my sweet ass if I'm not impressed by those who want to compromise.

Of course, we can legitimately compromise on methods of reaching our objective and on timetables; but we can never compromise on the objective Itself. And that objective is the Freedom which will allow the fullbody integration of Love into every molecule of our living, breathing earth. But government people don't know this, don't understand it, and don't care. They are content to talk about Freedom to win elections and to justify imperialist colonial enterprises--so we know they don't respect or understand Freedom at all, let alone that Love which is Freedom's Parent.

A man who compromises on Principle is not a man, honey. He's not a woman, either!

Politics is not the art of the possible, it is the art of the ignorant and sentimental bullshitter. Politicians have not achieved much along the lines of moral and spiritual refinement, yet those are the only authentic lines of human endeavor. Everything humans Achieve comes from their moral and spiritual refinement. So politicians, lost in their thick cloud of control and manipulation and compromise on principle (no--complete ignorance of what a principle is!), cannot even see what is possible.

A politician is not a Leader. A Leader chooses to embody a Principle, then stands up for Himself as He distributes that Principle to others through the energetic connection they form with Him. After the initial connection, his friends then Work to pull the amount of this embodied Principle to themselves which is appropriate for them as Individuals, then reflect the energy of this Principle out from themselves as it colors Itself with the unique flavor of their own Individuality. Thus is the world bathed in a new Principle through the scientific distribution system that automatically sets itself up between those who are attuned, or who are becoming attuned, to the energy of the Principle.

Our sexy Goddess the Christ is the embodiment of the Principle of Love; She is the stirring Impulse Who animates all fresh, young religions with the power of Her Divine Love, and the eggs of mercy in Her ovaries of compassion fertilize themselves on the strivings of those sanctified to Her Service.

The Christ has not chosen to limit Her consciousness, so of course is a refined blend of both male and female attributes. Indeed, She always counseled us that the male must become female and the female male. Any person who restricts their own consciousness to some image of the

Christ that was manufactured by theologians has missed the biggest part of what She is--or what He is, if that turns you on more.

She usually comes to me in the form of a translucently-skinned, fair-haired Goddess, for She knows I'm a sex maniac and is willing to accommodate my preferred perceptions. Yet I must note that preferred perceptions are not preconceptions, and thus are not limiting. I know the Christ can appear in many ways to many different people. Your view of the Christ isn't *wrong*, it's just limited if it was constructed by those old non-flowing, linear-minded theologians. The Christ may come to you in a restricted form, I suppose, to accommodate your prejudices, but she comes to me as a wave of pure Goddess to accommodate my desires.

These knee-jerk fundamentalists would probably have a hissey-fit if they heard that, which is one more evidence of why I'm qualified to comment on their behavior and strange rigid views, while they can't begin to qualify themselves on commenting on or understanding Me. You see, when you carry the burden of the world's karma for a spell, you unfortunately have to become intimately familiar with the dirt clouding each windowpane of humanity's soul as you process and release it with your own brand of spiritual Windex. You have to thoroughly know it to be absolutely sure it's dirt before you scrub it away. And the stagnant energy of fundamentalism is the very definition of dirt, no matter what cause it attaches itself to. Hey fundies, I've been where you've been and wallowed in your filth, but I can only do so much to clean you up. The rest is up to you if you want to be sparkly and handsome like Yours Truly. Hey man, I'm beautiful, practically as beautiful as the Christ.

You know, these twentieth and early twenty-first century people frequently acknowledged, in spite of themselves, a subtle sexual affinity for Jesus or the Christ--though usually they confused the two into one, and may have sometimes called out to Jesus when they really wanted to touch the Christ. But no matter, their hearts knew what was necessary, though their brains were clouded with preconceptions. (Note: In my experience, Jesus always appears as a male. So if you want a feminine inspiration, you'll probably want to look to the Christ. It was the Christ that Jesus yelled out to on the cross; the Christ was Jesus' Senior and up until that moment had occultly "overshadowed" Him, just as my Uncle once overshadowed Me.)

You can see the subtle sexual attraction some of these Christians felt stirring in their mightily pulsing loins for whoever they regarded as Lord if you listen to some of their music. When a man is singing a hit song about how he can't wait to dance for Jesus, that's homoerotic as hell, and probably involves a desire to cross-dress, too--perhaps as a belly dancer, or maybe in the more staid costume of those skirt-whirling dervishes.

Yep, even these Christians failed to totally eliminate the truth of their spiritual natures as they found subtler ways to acknowledge that sexual desire is the foundation of the religious impulse, as the Vision of the Beautiful One who stirs that desire pulls them on and conducts them into Heaven.

But the politicians and their henchpersons know nothing of the Christ Principle, or of any Principle, so occasionally one or more of our people undertakes a mission to turn government against itself to bust it up a little, to get some of it off of humanity's back for a while by using the theory and tactics of "divide and conquer", but such operatives have proved themselves by purifying their motives and absorbing themselves into their spirituality throughout long ages. Sometimes such operatives can also do things like help bust up corporations . . . but again, no person who holds any of the illusions of these entities can ever be of any use in their destruction.

People with an inverted viewpoint think that the past creates the future, but of course that is utter nonsense. It is impossible for the future to grow out of the past. It would be more accurate to say that the future creates the past, or that the future visits the past to create itself, because often enough a conscious piece of the pattern of the future detaches itself from its usual place and projects itself along a golden beam into a spot in the pattern of reality in an area which is more a crazy quilt than a part of a self-aware spectrum. The crazy quilt area conceives of itself in the terms of past and future and is just a place in the pattern where there are some illusions to refine, and then to transcend, so that part of the pattern can complete and heal itself and eventually take its place in smiling bliss with the rest of the future.

As one of my old drinking buddies said, "A little leaven leaveneth the whole lump." Then he leavened his own lump a little more with another jug of wine and a dancing-girl.

Time is just the measure of the passing of different states of consciousness, and those states pass at different "rates" for different people, so in truth there can never be any objective measurement of time. John Doe may experience many more "stages" of consciousness in an hour than his sister and lover Jane Doe, so an hour will not mean the same thing to the two of them. Time, past, future; these terms are always relative and receive differing interpretations from person to person, but when you look a little deeper you transcend the relativity of it and see that time is just an illusion, a mad delusion, along the rim of the great wheel of reality, and that the brilliant Central Sun which powers the entire experience of the wheel is the timeless source of reality, and that we are all truly embraced by the heart of that Sun, and are beams who project and descend out of that Sun in order to do the Work of harmoniously remaking the rim in our own image, so that it may allow itself to be infused by the Sun, and then absorbed by the Sun. Again, this is simple, so it's no wonder the people of the twentieth century didn't get it. The only way some of them could partially escape their foolish complexity was to ingest LSD, but even then they were not wise enough to properly interpret their experiences, and spiritually speaking ran around like chickens with their heads cut off instead of knowing themselves as a particle of rim infused by the Central Sun to magnetize other rim-particles into wholebody love, and into knowing the truth that there is no such thing as time.

When a member of the human family begins to wake up and sense her Self and the Energy I anchored, she has allowed herself to be magnetized by my timeless Synthesizing Presence, and thus is on the road to consciously knowing her Self on all planes of existence. Now she can do some good in this wild rim-world frontier.

I salute you with the mystery of time and conduct you into the "sweet by and by", a sweetness whose nature was mostly unknown even by the bloke who wrote the song. I wave time at you as though it were my penis, my own sweet root, that ye may be redeemed by the loss of your prejudices concerning your own nature, and the nature of the worlds you inhabit. Ye are eternal, so quit lying to ye-selves and quit being scared by the unconscious fools of government and media and the other religions of depravity. Once you realize you're eternal, these scumbags, these mindless, worthless trash heaps, will never threaten you again, for they always hold threats to your physical body and threats to crucify your personality over your head in an attempt to "stay in control" of your perceptions, and thus of your lives. But is it not at last obvious that they deny their own natures and thus have no real power, but only the stinking caked-blood illusion of a herd of cattle who slaughtered themselves long ago? Know that ye have another physical body than the one that is immediately visible, and this more subtle body indicates the beginning of the nature of your eternalness, though there are so many deeper, brighter realms of love and compassionate service and acceptance of all beings into the quiet chamber of the Heart beyond your subtle physical body that it is impossible for me to gaze upon the full range of your splendedness all at once.

Time does not exist, there is only Space. Space is a continuum that holds consciousness, and which is affected by that consciousness, thereby becoming a part of that consciousness.

Time is nothing more than the measurement of and comparison of the fluctuations between particular features occupying a particular region of space. You navigate thru "time" by positioning yourself where you want to be in relation to whatever set of "terrain features" you want to exist in relation to. Time is a map, and the map is not the terrain, honey. The idea of time is a sometimes-useful tool to deceive yourself into getting where you want to go. But if you believe time itself is real, you won't recognize your destination even after you arrive. So it seems to me that self-deception is useless. You know the map of Nebraska is not Nebraska herself; why then do you pretend time is real and sacrifice your multi-dimensional "overcoat" of compassionate human awareness to this mad delusion, this silly fundamentalist belief in a map, a thing which can only be represented on a piece of immobile paper? But space is not immobile, and is in constant fluctuation like a great sweet Heart, a Heart Who is big enough to contain all the features in the universe.

Yet ye have allowed the enemies of humanity to trick you into a desperate feeling that a piece of dusty paper covered with egocentric "accomplishments" is the goal of your "time" on earth, the goal of your relationship to the other features which occupy this particular local space. The enemies of humanity have tricked you into writing your own obituary every day of your "life", thus insuring you stay mired in a prison of one-dimensional perception that will keep you from the eternal wonder and joy and compassionate lovingkindness of your own soul. So fuck every goddamned one of those sons-of-bitches who preach restriction. To hell with them. As they trick you into writing your own obituary, so they write their own.

If the Buddha was a finger pointing to the moon, I am a middle finger waving in the face of restriction. But even as the bird flies, I jerk a thumb over my white resplendent shoulder to indicate the depth of scintillating eternity to you, with its pleasures and ultimate joys of exploratory attainment. I have placed my thumbprint upon eternity so you may have a place to start. Recognize my thumbprint, and coordinate yourself with your own sweet, strong Destiny.

As your consciousness influences the Space around you, the Space fluctuates to the moving tones of your consciousness. Space is therefore the outer robe of consciousness. The full awareness of your influence constitutes the highest form of Art, and inspires all beings toward creative resurrection.

Each person measures the quality and quantity and the interaction of the features in the particular continuum of Space with which they feel identified in their own unique, subjective way. From this measurement arises the sense of duration. A person who measures few fluctuations in an hour may feel an hour passes slowly; while that hour may just speed on by like a freight train about to leap off the tracks for a person who measures many fluctuations. Each of these people may occupy more or less the same place in Space, but their sense of duration is different. You might as well throw away your watch and accept that when you give the "time" to your neighbor, she's going to interpret the information, or really non-information, in a manner you won't comprehend; nor will she understand anything at all about your own sense of duration, unless she measures a similar number of fluctuations.

In other words, the more a person is aware of the fullness of Space, the faster "time flies". Yet there is a Great Beyond in which many features are experienced more or less simultaneously, and the sense of duration is finally Transcended and Eternity is Achieved. Thus the Sage is never in a hurry and just putters along, while all things appropriate to his part of the pattern, his space, group themselves naturally and joyfully around him, pulled by the pattern which the Sage *is*, for he has become Space Itself. Selah. An eternal unfolding and enfolding makes Space one with all the features that occupy it.

So people who claim they don't have "time" to do whatever it is that they want to do are deluding themselves--"time" is all any of us has. To put it far more accurately, *Space* is the only thing any of us has, and we each have all the space we need to accomplish whatever we want to accomplish. We each have *all* the space in Eternity! We merely must allow ourselves to take advantage of the Freedom inherent in our space.

Time is not money, but Space is Creativity.

The reason some people feel they don't have enough "time" is that they spend their lives doing what they feel they should be doing, rather than listening to the message of their eternal Hearts and doing what they actually want to do. "Shouldness" cuts off the energy from the Heart; thus the spirit of restriction--of law and the strife generated by law--perpetrated by those who do not have humanity's best interests at heart, and who in fact no longer even have hearts themselves.

Is it not a sad thing when a person who has the capacity to become human allows herself to be manipulated into going along with restriction by beasts who do not have hearts? Only the sacrifices of a Divine Providence give her the opportunity to begin to see thru the delusion of restriction and provide her with a new impetus to reclaim and continually reawaken her own sweet, beautiful, powerful Heart in every single moment. Providence gives her the opportunity to escape the trap of preconceptions and become Human.

So become Heart-centered, then do exactly what you want, and you will find that a wondrous Space opens to your inspired gaze.

Outer space is not the final frontier, it is the outermost level of being. The true frontier for most folks is the journey to oneness they undertake deep within the Space within themselves as they learn to share their soul-essence with those they choose to live in community with. During this journey, they learn to adapt their focused Intention to the magnetic tone sounded by whatever region of communal Space they want to learn to occupy, and thus are pulled toward that Space as devas and nature spirits enhance their energy bodies with the weaving of special etheric threads that vibrate to the tone sounded by the communal space the explorer wants to occupy, and it is the vibrating resonance of these etheric threads that delivers him to his true home in the Cosmos, without the interference and innate limitation of belief and doctrine. Homecoming is Achieved as our very bodies vibrate to the tone of the space we want to occupy, for the devas built a little of that space into us so we may be pulled into a space with those who share a similar intention and thus a similar vibration. In Space there is always room for Kindred, but universalism has no relation to any but the most feeble of tangled and corrupt spaces, and is not a strong path that will lead a person toward the attainment of humanness. And if we aren't consciously becoming human, we are more useless than any other thing in nature, in Space. Yet if we do Work to Achieve our True Humanity, all space lights up with our joy and we are welcomed by all sentient beings.

Let it be known that universalists are not sentient, and are of no use in this sweet universe which they attempt to inflict the pornography of their political correctness onto. They are the ultimate losers, having failed to Achieve anything of eternal value. The threads of their etheric bodies have become so twisted and unwholesome that they are sneeringly used by the same pernicious forces that use the fundamentalists, and it is these very hate-filled forces that arrange the battles between their disciples on the "left" and their disciples on the "right". It is those same invisible hate-filled forces that yank the strings of attachments and control and degradation which are part and parcel of the lot of anyone who has adopted a doctrine, for all doctrine is deception, all doctrine is false. All doctrine is a lie from the very first moment it is translated out of living experience into a standardized and enforced method. For consciousness cannot be standardized, and everything that lives *is* consciousness. Everything that is standardized is a goddam lie, and was made by chimpanzee-people for their own offspring, to prevent those very offspring from High Achievement. For the chimpanzee-people are full of lies, and are so good at lying they don't realize their own worst lies and manage to suppress the knowledge of the burden of sorrow they perpetuate onto the shoulders of those as yet unborn.

I started; Eleanor was looking at me strangely . . . I wanted to go home, where nobody would ever look at me strangely again. But I saw that Eleanor had the beginnings of a good heart, and that in an incarnation or two she might have what it takes to restructure her heart into a conscious organ of Synthesis, and to allow the wholebody love of Aphrodite's chela to flood her entire being. This would start in her, most probably, with the strengthening and further structuring of the infant goodwill that sometimes squalled in her heart. Once purified of the slime of sentiment and properly constructed, the goodwill would serve as the foundation to hold up her other heart-qualities. And there are many heart-qualities, but it is useless to try to enumerate many of them in a book or in speech, for the heart is far more multidimensional than most people realize, and has many hidden chambers on many planes of existence. The Heart unifies those planes in us, and also buoys us "upward" through the various planes, even as we carry "lower" planes along with us. To see this, my lambs, you must develop your sweet heart fully and develop Higher Mind to serve as witness to Heart function.

Anyway, our method of Service is simply to enumerate those aspects of the Wisdom of the Heart that are most urgently needed in any given Age, and once the sanctified Work of that Age has been accomplished, the structure and qualities of the Heart will continue to unfold throughout succeeding Ages.

Well, I wanted to get Eleanor's eyes, which were becoming a little wild, off of me, so I began tutoring her again. Only, I realized nearly as soon as I started that my speaking of spiritual matters wouldn't help calm the crazed delusions that had been stirred up from levels she'd suppressed in herself, because my tutoring and my energy were responsible for stirring her glamours and illusions up to begin with. Nevertheless, I plowed ahead, because that's what God wanted me to do.

"Eleanor, you may be wondering how an Anarchist could vote Republican. Well, it's really extremely simple, the simplest thing in the world, but the primitive people of your century can't understand it because they think they thrive on making everything as complicated as possible. They think they are intelligent if they make things complicated, which only proves that they are stupid. Hell, they're so used to making things complicated that it's become second nature to them and half the time they no longer even realize they're doing it. They need to quit believing that words are real, and learn to activate the higher brain functions that will prove to them unquestionably that words are not real, and which will show them what *is* real, and that they are an integrated and eternal part of the pattern of reality.

"Anyhow, all energy needs a form to express itself, even the energy of Anarchy. I chose Republicanism because it was more in line with the forceful energy work I had to do . . . and all work is energy work, baby. Along with cleaning up the glamour and illusions from everything else in nature, I also cleaned the glamour and illusion off of Republicanism and allowed it to come together in a cup, a political chalice of sorts, which I then poured the energy of my Anarchy into. Simple!

"Yet there are some idiots who will say that I and my brother Robert are 'right-wingers', stupidly ignoring what we really are. We are energy poured into a cup, nothing more and nothing less. We move through life carried on a wave of Synthesis, rather than allowing ourselves to be dragged down into the ocean of astral glamour by the ball and chain of the illusion of duality. So the difference between us and most people is that we consciously constructed our cup. There are no 'right wings' or 'left wings' where we come from.

"Once Robert was too diffuse in his Anarchy to be able to adequately do the Work of preparing the way for Me, so a woman appeared who taught him how to construct a firmer cup composed of Republicanism to contain the energy of his Anarchy. When you clean the glamour and illusion from the straight-line linear approach of Republicanism, you find there are no opposites in it, and no perceptions in it that want to make war on the energy of the Democrats or Anarchists . . . though the Democrats are so full of shit themselves that they have totally betrayed their own energy like a bunch of cur dogs banding together to drive away the master that would feed them.

"The only things the Democrats stood for in the late twentieth century were abortion and gun control. Hell, they were so caught up in a frenzied lust for repression they didn't even have the energy left to get prescription drugs for old people, and the Republicans had to do it for them. They supported the murder of infants, then in keeping with their hate and bloodthirstiness and greed for restricting others they tried to disarm honest Americans so they would be killed, raped or robbed by criminals. So anyone the Democrats and their supporters couldn't murder in the womb was still in danger of being murdered or badly humiliated after birth.

"I empathize with any woman in the late twentieth century who took appropriate birth control precautions and still got pregnant, because motherhood wasn't honored at all. *Familyhood* wasn't honored at all. The society often did what it could to make her suffer if she accidentally got pregnant, so I don't condemn those women who chose to get an abortion. They were not right, but I empathize with them and do not condemn them. And I know that when they get ready to do serious healing Work, they will see and feel what they did to *themselves* when they got an abortion. Anytime we hurt some relatively innocent person, we hurt ourselves even more. These women never deserved to suffer and don't deserve to suffer any more. I wish them Beauty and Strength and Self-Compassion when they do their healing Work. But in order to release the energy of tragedy, they *will* have to feel it fully as it comes up for release from their physical bodies and energy bodies. I am not against them, I am against a factory society where everyone was so humiliated by cardboard institutions that an abortion could even be considered."

Well, that was enough of a rant against abortion for the time being. I knew I had to return to the task of presenting the nonduality of Nature to Eleanor by showing her a bit more of the process of constructing energy-forms to contain Truth.

"Anyhow, when you destroy the preconceptions around any manifestation, then what you have left is a spark of pure Truth. That's when you build the energy-forms of living Buddhic Truth to house that spark and line the Truth-Channel through which your living awareness flows.

"At the core of every sort of position is a spark of Truth, but the presentation of that Truth became warped as soon as a preconception was created for it. When you destroy preconceptions, you're destroying the illusion of duality, and when you're building the forms of pure Buddhic Truth that ultimately replace those preconceptions, you're consciously creating a universe that knows itself through its own clear reflection. You see that every spark of Truth always agreed with every other spark of Truth and that there was never any conflict between the various 'positions'; the conflict only occurred between the preconceptions of those who were so incompetent at working with mental matter that they mistook a dull black preconception for the golden essence that lay obscured. A clear reflection never conflicts with itself, it knows itself fully by looking at itself from a number of distinct angles, and it knows its true home in the Light that glows from the center and irradiates itself through to the edges of these newly-constructed, purified and integrated

Buddhic forms."

I gave a wild grin, knowing I was rocking Eleanor's world without even taking her to bed. I continued. "I used to be a honey-colored manifestation, then green. Now I am a dark blue beam of energy poured into the world. Since the energy of Anarchy is green, I guess I couldn't be an Anarchist anymore, though of course I don't support government or other institutions, because institutions are nothing more than visible preconceptions formed to numb the mass mind, rather than living energetic forms designed consciously around a spark of vital Truth and allowed to run in Buddhic channels that would enliven the earth. I don't know what I am, there's no label for what I am. But there's a symbol, and *I Am The Symbol!*"

We walked thru the grasses sweet with lushness. Eleanor sort of stumbled a couple of times, then trembled. She took a shot at restoring her equilibrium by returning to a topic she felt she had some control over . . . and I didn't want to frighten her into hysterics by revealing immediately in my grand fashion that there's no such thing as control, and God impulsed to me that I could slack up on her a bit, so I went along with the gag and played a complimentary part of myself with what I hoped was some degree of skill, with a view toward gradually and gently taking a swipe at the illusion of control if a chance to do so should reveal itself in the context of the conversation. So I responded in a fashion she could relate to when she said, "What did those Democrats do at the end of this century to make you hate them so?"

"I don't hate them, ma'am. But I'm repulsed by what they did to this country. They showed the country how to live without honor. They tried to undo President Reagan's work of restoring honor and spirit to America.

"They actually tried to steal the 2000 elections. They whined that some Democrats had marked the wrong spot on the ballot and tried to blame the state for that, which is ridiculous and childish. They went around screaming that every vote must count, when every vote had never counted before in America or any other country. Every precinct in the world had its screw-ups. Yet they never complained about this until their candidate lost the presidency by a narrow margin under rules they agreed to play by. But they began whining that those rules weren't fair; I don't support competition, but even I can see that's poor sportsmanship. These Democrats were 'spoiled children', to use the twentieth century term. I guess they thought of themselves as adults, but they acted like squalling babies when things didn't go their way--again, under rules they agreed to play by!

"Man, if rules really aren't fair, the time to change them is *before* you agree to play the game.

"Throughout the Nineties they glamoured the public and inaugurated more and more restrictions on individual liberty and responsibility. They wanted a society where you'd have to get the government's permission to wipe your ass. They never told the truth anymore, assuming they could see the truth when it popped up, which is unlikely, and they used zero tolerance policies against schoolchildren in a cruel attempt to destroy their humanity.

"Once they fielded some heroes, such as Dr. Martin Luther King. But by century's end the heroes were gone from the Democratic side of the house. Dr. King was black and helped motivate blacks to achieve greater liberty for themselves. But his degenerate heirs, instead of inspiring their people to greatness, pulled their people down into a spirit of victimization and blaming others for their own mistakes . . . such as when they blamed the state for their own mishandling of their individual ballots.

"A true leader reminds his or her people of how powerful they are, then inspires them to become even more powerful. Dr. King, and to a degree the Black Panther Party For Self-Defense, did an excellent job of this. But the black leaders--and I use the term 'leaders' in its broadest sense--in the last decade of the century were frequently only interested in fostering artificial fights and making their people feel like victims. That way, these so-called leaders felt they'd always be in control, they'd always have a job."

I paused, contemplating an interesting contrast between Martin Luther King and Gandhi: Dr. King was actually a success! I thought of the sermon I'd delivered once to a twentieth century "New Thought" church, and how I'd done my best to reveal the true character, or lack of it, of Gandhi. Because of the laziness of twentieth century people, I was pretty sure they'd disregard what I'd said about learning to feel people's energy. Thus, they would wrongly accuse me of inconsistency, and maybe even of hypocrisy, if they were to hear me speak of my views of Dr. King, who was apparently influenced by Gandhi . . .

But Dr. King's energy field, which was really strong, wasn't influenced much, if any, by Gandhi. Gandhi was a horrid little manipulator who wanted to hurt people, as any genuinely sensitive person could see if they stopped to feel his location in the continuum of dysfunction. But Dr. King wanted to actually deliver people from suffering, not cause them to suffer more! And he didn't want to suffer himself. You can feel it in him. Dr. King was *willing* to suffer, but he didn't *want* to suffer, nor did he want to cause others to suffer, and that is the crucial difference between a successful Savior and one who gets warped into dysfunction. Dr. King's cause was the cause of love and of liberation. So while the energy of his nonviolence may have rebounded to a degree and caused a bit of violence here and there, his authentic love and compassion and desire to see people free and strong offset most of the energy of violence that otherwise would have been created by his philosophy of nonviolence, and since there was less energy of violence, there was a lesser degree of physical violence, because physical violence is always sparked by dirty energy, especially the dirty energy of those who claim to be nonviolent yet lack genuine love and compassion. Dr. King actually Achieved the delivery of greater freedom into this world for his people, and indeed, the freedom may have ultimately come into the world with less violence than it would have if an outwardly violent person had lead King's associates.

Dr. King was a strong, compassionate success, whereas the little guy from India was a manipulative failure. You can feel the difference in the energy between the two. Dr. King didn't want to be a Savior; he'd rather have been shacked up somewhere with some young girl, or maybe with more than one. He had love in his heart to share, and had the strength of character to want to share it with more than one person . . . though maybe he didn't quite have the strength of character to live openly in this way. Still, he accomplished a goodness in the world, and you can feel it in his energy and in the energy of what he accomplished. Any aware person can perceive this through attuning his feelings to the feelings of the universe of which he is a part. Forget about historical facts; historical facts are made of concrete and thus are an illusion in this flexible, flowing universe composed of the taste of God's tongue and the smell of God's perfume. An historical fact, in the way these twentieth century people experienced it, was an anchor to chain their perceptions to, not a key to translate some of God's energy into the world.

But to an aware person, a fact is a carrier of flavor. If a fact has the taste of livingness about it, it is useful, but if there is no flavor of livingness, the fact is out of kilter with the energy of Truth and has no purpose. This is one of several reasons why the courts of law in the twentieth century had outlived their usefulness; they only sought concrete facts, and left the energy of Truth untouched. Yet the energy of Truth must always be the goal, and if any facts happen to swim into your view which support and reflect a bit of this energy, then you may be able to use those facts as keys to help a given whirlpool moment Achieve a little stability and clarity. This is the way the Liberated Human Beings--

the *real* Mahatmas--experience the world.

I'm not saying a fact is anything you want it to be, though the unaware person will probably misinterpret me in that way. Even some occultists make this mistake, and become liars "inspired" by glamour, rather than Living Legends infused with love. No, a fact is alive if it carries some of the flowing Godness of Truth, and only a living fact is useful. That's all I'm saying. And you don't reach living facts by analysis, you reach them by that direct perception of Truth which is always available to those who have Achieved contact with the Buddhic Plane, then centered and stabilized themselves on that plane of pure intuition, which some of the Mahatmas call the Plane of Pure Reason, though it bears no resemblance to the daily mundane analytical reason of the mechanic or philosopher or dentist. When you perceive Truth directly, and then someone mentions what they regard as a fact, you can tell whether the fact is really true--again, not true according to those who limit themselves only to the intellect, but true according to the authority of the energy of Truth--by perceiving whether the energy of Truth has attached itself to the fact as the fact swims into your vision. It's really very simple, but twentieth century people, with their perverse "gift" for complicatedness, would probably require some long explanation just to begin to get a whiff of Truth past the stuffiness of their noses.

Another one of their problems was that they viewed intelligence so narrowly, and also believed that intelligence was a quality either fixed at birth, or fixed a few years thereafter. Yet nothing could be farther from the truth. Intelligence is a very flexible quality which connects itself with that person who is actively and with unremitting effort conducting a campaign to immerse himself in God--in other words, to immerse himself in the part of the pattern of the flowing energy-sea in which the aware people dwell. Intelligence always grows itself to whatever degree is necessary in the one who strives toward non-egotistical Spiritual Achievement. And intelligence involves many more faculties than the twentieth century people were aware of. It could never be measured by their silly tests, which were designed to test the "intelligence" of chimpanzees who could sit still for a couple of hours scratching away at the dirt left by the preconceptions of the makers of the tests, using little sticks that had the ability to leave little black smears in tiny boxes.

In terms of the intelligence of the brain, the brain is capable of making an infinite number of connections . . . not in those who try to become more intelligent, thus putting the cart before the horse, but in those whose spiritual strivings are Altruistic and sincere. Anyone of stamina, love and sincerity can Achieve Truth with its many pathways through the brain, heart, and body. Indeed, the wholebody lover eventually discovers that the heart is much deeper, much more multidimensional and much *larger* than he had ever imagined. As the spiritual aspirant is restructured in the image of Truth and of Love, he finds that his heart etherically grows far larger than the space usually believed to contain the heart, and becomes a huge organ of many deep chambers which extends way down into the body and directs the affairs of the entire organism.

Each human being is capable of making many deep connections within herself, both in her heart and brain, and throughout her beautiful human body. Yet these twentieth century people seemed to be waiting for someone to come along to make the connections for them!

Eleanor was looking at me strangely, so I grunted at her and continued with my political science lecture. "Your party, ma'am, which in 1945 is the champion of the common man, and which has gone to war to defeat the forces of evil, becomes nothing more than a vehicle for glamour and illusion by century's end. It's run by Hollywood elites, to a large degree, and supported by giant media conglomerates whose purpose is to restrict liberty for everyone but themselves. Of course, the forces of evil, which your party is fighting in this Second World War, lie behind these conglomerates to one degree or another, and work by manipulating the egotism of the employees of these giant conglomerates, particularly those who are decision-makers, reporters, news anchors and so forth. It was touch and go as to whether the human spirit would survive the barrage of propaganda, which was so cleverly done that most of the time most of the people didn't even recognize it as propaganda. They thought of it as 'entertainment' or 'news reporting' or 'computer gaming', and because they were ruled by egotism their so-called entertainment, et cetera, was designed to appeal to their sense of control and manipulation. They didn't seem to realize that any person who is caught up in trying to manipulate others is also manipulated, first by his own egotism, and second by the representatives of the forces of evil to whatever extent they can get a hook into his egotism.

"Control and manipulation is a spectrum of low-level energy and it's where people were stuck throughout the twentieth century. Some idiots congratulated themselves on controlling others, apparently believing they could somehow stand above the process of being controlled while yanking the strings of control they'd attached to others. That's silly, of course, but people in this century became masters of lying to themselves. They didn't believe they'd reap what they sowed, because most of them had lost sight of the truth concerning reincarnation and karma. They didn't understand these things, and if they thought of these truths at all it was in a watered down form suitable for light cocktail conversation. They really believed they could escape the consequences of their actions. Because of their self-deception they didn't realize that if you're a part of the process of control and manipulation then you've bought into the world's egotism lock, stock and barrel, and that's how the forces of evil try to influence world affairs. They yank on the strings they've implanted into planetary egotism, and the string yanking filters on down to the national level, then the corporate and individual levels.

"The forces of genuine goodness, as opposed to floppy chakra sentimentality, have never been able to make much obvious headway on this planet because they're not egotistical. They are not bound by matter. They don't get off on titles, or dunce caps like that pope wears, or on having strings of initials after their names. They're only into Divine Love, and Divine Intelligence, and Divine Wisdom and Divine Will. And they stand for Truth. They don't give a shit for people's egotistical conventions, and they cannot be manipulated, ever. And of course they never try to manipulate others."

We were holding hands. "Well," Eleanor said finally, "maybe I should switch party allegiance. I like to remain a little ahead of the times."

"Sugar Plum, history doesn't record anything about your changing political parties, as far as I know. So it might be best to remain where you are. Your party isn't degenerate yet, and it would be poor form to change parties and make all those historians rewrite their textbooks."

Then she was in my arms . . . but no. "Eleanor, honey, we don't have time. If Truman doesn't nuke the Japs day after tomorrow, humanity will be extinct a century from now." I gently disengaged from her questing tongue.

"Oh, Sonny-Bob, if things were only different . . ."

"Things are never different, sweetie. History has to remain pretty much unchanged."

CHAPTER THIRTY-TWO

We stood in the Oval Office, Eleanor and I. It was the wee hours of the morning on August 6, 1945. We were up before the roosters, but it was for a good cause. Today was the day Truman had to bomb the Japanese if the earth was to survive.

Truman was an unostentatious little man behind a great big ostentatious desk. He must've been sitting on a cushion.

"Harry, I hope you've given serious thought to what Commander Bond told you a couple of days ago," Eleanor said. "Today you'll have to do your duty, or tomorrow will not exist."

Truman snorted. "My Momma always said, 'Life is like one of those pre-packaged, city made pecan pies: it's not very crunchy, but every once in a while you do find a real nut.' Eleanor, your Commander Bond is a real nut. The idea that cheap actor, Ronald Reagan, could be elected president? Insane. And for good measure your Commander Bond also made him governor of California and Savior of Freedom.

"And look at the way he dresses! He looks like a refugee from a circus in that zoot suit and pink necklace, or whatever it is. And he doesn't even have the manners to take off his hat indoors."

I removed my hat, but I was starting to get pissed. This Truman had better watch his tongue.

"Mr. Bond, or whatever your name really is, this document you gave me that appears to be an executive order from 1983 is as phoney as you are. You claim to be from the future, but since that's impossible I checked with the Navy in an attempt to make sense of you. They don't have a Commander James Bond. And you're too fat to be in the Navy, anyway.

"Your identification appears authentic, so I put in a call to Donovan at the OSS but he hasn't gotten back to me yet, and he probably won't tell me anything when he does. He's very protective of his agents.

"But if you're not one of Donovan's boys, if you're faking that too, you'd better hightail it out of this universe. You don't want to see Donovan when he's mad."

"You don't want to see me when I'm mad, Harry Truman." A low growl emanated from my guts and throat.

"Are you threatening me, young man?"

"Yes, to the same extent you're threatening me, and maybe a little more."

We glared at one another then, and Truman backed down because I wasn't about to. He pretended to shuffle some papers on his desk.

"Well, if that's all, I'll give some consideration to what you've said. Goodbye, Eleanor. Goodbye . . . Mr. Bond."

"You're lying," I stated truthfully. "You're not going to give any consideration to what we've said. You plan to let the Japs off the hook and flush the timeline down the toilet. Well, the timeline isn't yours to flush, mister. I won't let you flush it."

The primordial force of the universe began to growl, and Truman looked shocked, as though he'd never heard it before. Eleanor stepped carefully away from me.

"Pick up that phone," I said, gesturing to the special landline he'd had installed in case he decided to drop the bomb. The landline connected Truman to some general who was responsible for transmitting the order to bomb Japan. "In three minutes that order has to be given, and by Goddess you'd better comply with the expectations of history. Don't make me whip your ass."

He was trembling and a strange pallor emanated from him. But he folded his arms across his chest. "I'm not touching that phone, but when I do pick up a phone it'll be to order your arrest, Bond."

"I've been burned at the stake. There's nothing you can do to me. But since you're such a stubborn old fart I'll have to stun you and take this operation into my own hands. Goodnight." I palmed my pocket pistol and cut him down. He slumped in his great chair.

Eleanor's hand flew to her mouth. "Oh, Captain! What have you done?"

"Don't worry sweetie, he'll wake up after a while. He'll be fine. It's the timeline we have to worry about, not this old fart's indecision and egotism."

"Captain . . . Sonny-Bob, do you do impressions? Can you sound like the President when you give the order?"

"No, but I know someone who can. It's time to go to my alternate strategy. I want you to step outside the door and do everything you can to keep people out, especially the Secret Service. Flash them some titty if you have to, or show them a thigh. Just keep them out! And don't give me any lip; we've got ninety seconds left. Go!"

She went as I sprang over to Truman's desk and drew my phone. "Hubert this is Culpepper, over."

"Culpepper, this is Hubert, over."

"Hubert, we have to use that alternate strategy we discussed. You ready?"

"Roger."

"Okay, we've got just under a minute . . . I'm ringing the general. Stand by to give the order."

"Roger."

A captain picked up the handset, then put Hubert through to the general. Hubert gave the order in Truman's voice and that was that. Now the atomic bomb would be dropped and everything would be fine . . . as long as Truman dropped the second one, too. We'd have to do something to make sure he did. One bomb might be enough to save the timeline, but there was no way to know for sure. We had to have two.

I grabbed a blank disposition form from Truman's desk. On it I scrawled a reminder to the President to do his duty. "The order has been given and the bomb will be dropped, no thanks to your chickenshit fear for your public image. And by Goddess, you'd better make sure the second bomb is dropped on Nagasaki on August 9. History shows it exploded at 11:01 a.m., so be sure to get it right. If you don't I'll come back and pull out your tonsils with a horseshoe. --James Bond, Office Of Strategic Services"

It was a pretty good note. I put a paperweight on it and together Eleanor and I strolled out of the White House and back to Hubert. Then we drove back to the barn and rejoined my kinfolk.

Hi, my name's Aphrodite Phelps and Sonny-Bob asked me to write about my part of the mission. He said he'd include it in his official report.

I'm barely twenty years old and people tend not to take me too seriously because I love people and can't exploit them and I fuck a lot. I only want to serve humanity, so I get screwed, both literally and figuratively.

But Sonny-Bob says I'd be accepted and loved in the future, for it's the age of the soul that counts there, not the age of the body. He said everyone would respect me and many would actually try to worship me, though I don't want anybody's worship. I only want people to go within their own hearts and know themselves as Love. Then they can love one another.

Sonny-Bob's helped me learn to appreciate myself and move on to a higher level of service. I used to absorb and process and release other people's karma; their lusts and rage, their clogged-heartedness. I don't do that anymore. Too much of that will drive a person's soul away.

So I love Sonny-Bob, and when he reads this report he'll know I love him, and the family he's helped me find, forever and ever and ever. He already knows.

". . . Truman can't be depended on," Sonny-Bob was saying. "He's a politician. Trusting a politician is like trusting a pig to fly. No offense, Eleanor, I wasn't necessarily thinking about your late husband."

My co-husband Freud spoke next. "So we've got to get back in there tomorrow and make sure the job gets done. No offense to you, Sonny-Bob, but you're 'way too fat to sneak in anywhere. And you can't just walk in flashing a phony I.D. like last time. They'll be looking for you."

"I'll go," my beautiful co-wife Mimi said decisively. "Hubert will make me a fake spy I.D. and I'll go."

"No, honey," Sonny-Bob said gently. He's the sweetest and tenderest man in the world, except when he's shooting somebody or beating them up. "No pregnant ladies are going on a mission like this. It might be too much stress on Pa Miyamoto. I know you could do it, but we have to think of the baby."

Mimi and Sonny-Bob snuggled closer together, arms around one another and glowing. They share an aura, they are ONE. I also saw Pa Miyamoto standing above them and loving them. Love is the nature of Family.

"I can't go," said Freud. "In 1945 they'd lynch any black person who dared breathe the same air as the President. I'd never be allowed anywhere near his office, no matter what kind of I.D. I had."

I raised my hand. "I can go."

Sue stood up. "I'm going. I'm the logical choice. I can get the job done and I'm violent enough to fight my way out of trouble, especially if Sonny-Bob gives me a gun."

Sonny-Bob's brow furrowed. "Mmmm . . . Sue, you could do it all right, and I do appreciate your violent nature. You're an inspiration to us all. But I have a hunch that the soft touch is what's required here. And I know that when I follow my hunches, things work out; and when I don't, they don't. So . . ."

He shifted and looked at me, and I got up and went over and kissed his face and hugged him. There's a lot of him to hug, but I hugged the percentage I could.

Sonny-Bob is also a very sensual man, and his love joined with his passion makes a very interesting combination. As I was squeezing as much of him as I could, I felt that characteristic quickening of his aura and of his body that occurs when his heart and loins are working together. It made me gasp; I couldn't help it, and I felt my nipples grow hard and my own body and energy field quicken.

Mimi was a part of this. She knew what was going on. She smiled at me and released Sonny-Bob into my arms.

Sonny-Bob is so fixated on his penis sometimes that he loses track of everything else. Sometimes when his love and passion are combined he's not fully aware of the love because he's fooling with his organ, trying to make it appear as big as possible.

So I try to soothe him and restore him to himself just by loving him. Sometimes when we lie together he actually forgets about his penis, and then the softness and sweetness of his heart shines through wonderfully and radiantly. At those times we can spend hours in one another's arms, just basking in the glow of the radiant eternal love of our hearts.

Sometimes I feel like I'm him and he feels like he's me. The same is true of him and Mimi. And sometimes we can feel one another's thoughts from far away; all of us in the family can. And we always feel one another's love.

He wouldn't admit it, and Freud certainly wouldn't, but sometimes each of them feels like the other, despite the fact they're paranoid about the idea of becoming physically intimate with one another. They're lovers at the soul level, but not physically. Not yet, anyway. But if they keep becoming one another, who knows what might happen?

Anyhow, I felt that tonight was a penis night for Sonny-Bob. As we lay there upon our blanket that was draped across our bed of straw in that ancient barn, surrounded by family, something told me that Sonny-Bob could become me tonight, but that he'd have to approach that moment of becoming through his penis. And I had always known that Sonny-Bob wanted to be me. He would give anything to be me. So tonight, perhaps, I could serve him.

Once I'd jokingly suggested to Sonny-Bob that he have a sex change. Then I immediately wished I'd kept my mouth shut.

He turned to me with a mournful, serious expression. "If only it were that easy, Aphrodite. But it most certainly is not.

"Men who have a sex change don't know themselves. Well, maybe they've just begun to know themselves and touched their feminine side. But instead of integrating all their masculine aspects with all their feminine aspects, they do the pendulum swing that primitive people seem to do in every sort of situation. They conclude that they are one thing and not another, when in truth they're both, plus they're a lot of other things as well that they're not even aware of yet.

"They reject an aspect of themselves, maybe not fully, but certainly to a degree. Then they mutilate themselves in service to their illusions, in service to their pendulum swing. What happens if the pendulum swings back? You can't just keep your dick and balls on the mantel and expect to snap them back on.

"And what about genes and chromosomes? Genetically, the man who has a sex change operation will still be a man.

"So what is a man without a dick? He is but a dickless man, he is not a woman."

I have always appreciated Sonny-Bob's ability to address matters of both heaven and earth in the same sentence. He put aside his milk and ate a pork chop, then expanded upon the subject under discussion.

" 'Repression Creates Perversion.' You can't reject any aspect of yourself--physical, emotional, mental, or spiritual--if you're going to become an actualized human being. Love your pussy and that beautiful clit if you're a woman; love your dick if you're a man. Love those balls, adore that prostate. Don't try to dispose of an aspect of yourself you haven't loved, for in some way it will arrange to come back and hurt you. But it will love you if you love it.

"Selfhood means you dive into every aspect of yourself fully and purify it. You don't change it, you *purify* it. There's a difference, and the difference is known to those who walk the shadow warrior's path. You purify and integrate, you don't change and control. Anything you try to change is going to try to change you; anything you try to control is going to try to control you. The shadow warrior learns to flow with his own energy and with the energy of the universe. Flowing is not controlling. Flowing is an aspect of Being.

"I'm keeping my dick, Aphrodite."

Then Sonny-Bob had fallen into my arms and I had comforted him.

And so on this most holy night when the timeline was at stake, I came to Sonny-Bob Culpepper. I flowed over him and through him and touched all that he was. We became one heart; we'd always been that. But now we knew it.

He touched me with a tenderness and love that was remarkable even for this most gentle of men. My breasts hung low over him and he gifted each nipple with his lips; my breasts knew his kisses and responded.

I knew I was feeding him, nourishing him with something he had to have. But there was no desperation in him now, no mad grasping after something he believed was different from himself. Just a gentle, loving calmness and acceptance of peace.

After the years of his struggle I could come to him fully. I lowered myself gently upon him until he became my bed. We were a star.

Our palms were together and our fingers intertwined. Each dimension of one was open to the other as we flowed into one another and shared the same breath. Our tongues joined and communicated a golden passion. There was no more lust in him.

Then he entered me, and there were no distinctions. We were a single beam of golden light stretching through the timeless universe. We had been this way forever.

The next morning we all were grouped around Sonny-Bob as he lay upon his bed of straw, oblivious to everything but the great wide Heart of God. The spark knew the flame.

I knelt reverently and kissed his forehead, and the others followed, even Freud. Sonny-Bob was lost in his own glowforce, and he attracted the glowforce of the universe to bathe the earth. The earth wept tears of gentle gladness in the dew of a new morning.

Mimi sat with him, holding his hand. She stayed like that all day, Freud said, just holding his hand and stroking it and whispering to him. Mimi bathed along with him in the timeless glowforce of what we are.

It was my time to go help the earth. Sue was coming with me, but would remain with Hubert when I went to see the President.

"Take your phase muskets, ladies," Freud said. "You can't take them out of the car, but if something unforeseen happens it's better to have them. And have Hubert make each of you a pocket pistol like Sonny-Bob's. Try not to kill anybody unless you have to; keep all your weapons on stun. About your identification--"

I threw my arms around his neck and kissed him, and he tasted some of the glowforce Sonny-Bob and I had shared. Then he knew all would be well.

"You don't have to worry, my love," I whispered.

"I know," he said.

Mrs. Roosevelt had left the previous evening. I guess she had a house somewhere to go to. We couldn't use her this time, anyway. President Truman was bound to be suspicious of her.

I stood unclothed in the dawn, softly nude and loving my body and loving myself and loving the earth, this green beautiful earth where our friendships are discovered. It was a day of true joy; the earth would be warm. The earth would yield her golden harvest of Love.

I touched myself, and was grateful throughout all the realms where I exist for the golden heart of this splendid day.

It was time to get moving. Sue helped me into my clothes--*my* clothes, not period clothes. Period clothes were too restrictive. I shook my long blonde mane and laughed with the joy of my freedom. I touched Sue and she grinned.

And so we came again to Washington. *Beauty can be found even here*, I thought, *the Heart of God can be found beating beneath this city of egotism, if only the egotism is peeled away.*

Hubert parked himself and I threw my arms around Sue and shared the glowforce of what I am with her. Our tongues joined and she tasted the glowforce of herself, which is myself. The beam of golden light shines forever.

I floated up the steps of the White House, and those who were there stepped aside for me. Some hid their faces; some tried to look and to love. They tried.

I found myself in President Truman's office, and I knew him in the glowforce. He looked surprised; his eyebrows shot up, but he accepted me and did not turn away. I went to him and I held him in my arms and in the glowforce of my eternal love. He wept as I whispered in his ear.

I straightened up and put my hand on his heart. "You know what you have to do, sir."

He nodded, and when the appointed hour came he ordered the second attack upon Japan. Now all would be well.

"You've saved the earth, Mr. President. Now you will be remembered as a great man."

"Only love is great."

"You are love."

I left him swimming in the glowforce of his own heart, happy to be a part of the love that underlies the happenings of the times.

CHAPTER THIRTY-THREE

Hubert and I had materialized near the TAC's motor pool a few moments earlier. We looked around with mixed emotions. There was the great statue of Lord Reagan soaring high above the TAC's Administration Building, and the Gaffney Obelisk glinted off in the distance. Everything appeared to be in its place. It was June. We'd returned a year and a half after we left.

It had been so hard to say goodbye to Mimi and Pa Miyamoto and the rest of our family. I'd delivered Pa Miyamoto myself; I'm a pretty good jackleg midwife. I'd seen him again when I was a boy. Correction: I'd seen him for the first time when I was a boy. I wanted to see my son again, and I would look him up. Last I heard he was back on Mars at the Tibetan Buddhist Lamasary he'd helped found. He was my only physical link with Mimi and with our entire family. I loved him so.

The day after the second bomb had been dropped we'd sent Mary Beth and Lufkin packing for the Twenty-Fourth, then we'd materialized in a cotton patch in Mississippi a few minutes before the nuclear attack would have occurred. From there we monitored the media to insure all was well before going back into what would have been a war zone if our mission hadn't succeeded.

But all really was well. The timeline had really been restored. The media was trumpeting about the nuclear threat from the Soviets and wailing that we needed arms reduction talks. President Ronald Wilson Reagan, wisely ignoring the media, had inaugurated a military buildup in an attempt to bankrupt the Soviets and end their evil system. The forces of evolution would win; President Reagan, with his heavily armed military, would defeat both the Soviets and the media, and it would be achieved without one nuclear device being discharged in anger. Peace would prevail.

Later in the day we learned that the United States had invaded Grenada, which helped Americans release a little tension, since they were too repressed to do it with free and open sexual expression. Well, it sure beat a nuclear war.

Once we were certain all was well, we skipped ahead a few days to keep everyone's personal timelines coordinated with the general timeline. When we went back to the co-op, only Mimi and Sue were recognized, and they were chastised for missing some of their labor. They told the chastisers to fuck off and said they were moving out. Nobody at the co-op knew Freud and me; as far as they were concerned we'd never been there. A few recognized Aphrodite from her films and began to holler and hoot and sexually harass her, so I knocked them out.

We didn't let them see the cat. Tennessee had been a resident at the co-op for a long time and they'd want to keep the big-balled feline. Nick-Nick was keeping Tennessee company in a gym bag for now.

We only had enough money, artificial and otherwise, to get by for a few days, but then I had a brainstorm. "Hubert, government agencies and great banking houses are all computerized by now, aren't they?"

"I think so."

"See if you can hack into the Department of Defense and transfer a few million dollars to an account for our family at one of Austin's great banking houses."

"Okay." It only took Hubert a few minutes to outwit those primitive computers, and we were rich once more. We bought a house on Lake Travis.

Mimi reconciled with her mom, and I made love to her mom. "Sonny-Bob," Simone Slocum said to me, "you remind me of Mimi somehow."

"That fact pleases me, ma'am."

Sharon had dreamed of us--very moist dreams, to hear her tell it--but as far as she was concerned we'd never physically met. But because her dreams had been so vivid she was easily convinced they'd been real to us. We loved her and she loved us, so she became an associate family member and visited when her duties would permit.

Hubert spent a lot of time with Tiffany.

January, and Pa Miyamoto made his first appearance in physical form. He came out throwing punches and roundhouse kicks, but he was my little Buddha and I loved him.

And so Mimi and I had our baby, and the springtime breezes swept over Austin and made known the promise of freshness. Wrapped in the warm glow of love, we made ready for the dawn of forever.

We saw a day in the far distant future of discipline without restriction; discipline in service to love. The seeds of this were beginning to sprout in my own time, but even my century was but the earliest birth pangs of a true humanity.

Mimi and I and Pa Miyamoto saw these things, and we knew we were a part of this process. But we were the earliest part, the part that had to contend with the loveless restrictions of the great mass of people. We had to develop cunning to survive.

For the bulk of the race had never experienced genuine love, or even logic. They were an emotionally polarized breed and their version of logic consisted of nothing more than rationalizations for their limited perspective and loveless conduct. They confused emotional discipline and purification with repression. They were too weak and undedicated to dive into their lusts and wrestle with them and purify their emotions into an accurate and useful conduit to reality. Instead, they could be counted on only to repress parts of themselves; they actually seemed to believe repression would lead to purity. An insane concept, and one that is totally at odds with the truth. Repression creates perversion.

My friend Jesus once pointed out that the unintegrated hypocrites of his day had a law against adultery, yet "when you look upon a woman to lust after her, you have already committed adultery in your own heart."

Well, Christians never gave Jesus credit for having a sense of humor, and I don't suppose he ever imagined they would. He was pointing out the impossibility of divorcing yourself from your sexual nature; in the unlikely event a person succeeded with such a divorce he wouldn't even be human anymore.

And he thought it was pretty funny that people would make laws against the very thing they did every single day from puberty onward, which was to commit fornication and adultery. The thought is not just father to the deed, the thought *is* the deed. If your nervous system is an adulterer, then *you* are an adulterer. It's not going away, might as well enjoy it.

"Repression Creates Perversion". Repression doesn't "control" something, doesn't make it go away. Whatever you try to control actually controls you. Repression causes normal impulses toward fornication and adultery to seethe with hatred and resentment and rage. Repression is always a dynamic in rape. Look honestly at the total picture of the place rape occupies in society, and you will be able to pinpoint where the repression comes into play. But you have to be honest enough to look at every single factor, including how you contribute to the repression in society. When you look at a rapist, or any other type of criminal, there but for the grace of God go you, because you have contributed to the repression which spawned them. You are their brother criminal. "Judge not that ye be not judged." Without repression, rape would eventually fade away and so would every other sort of crime. Anyone who doubts this would be well advised to make a full inventory of human nature, beginning with their own. The results of this inventory will fill up the space occupied by dozens of sets of encyclopedias; actually, the practical results of the inventory will be more extensive than the practical information stored in any database anywhere. And you will see why the medieval society of the twentieth century needed to come tumbling down. Every twentieth century institution, economic, governmental, religious or what have you, was based on repression. Repression always creates criminals of those who are not clever enough to adapt by learning to use the mechanisms of repression to further the aims of their own polluted personalities, or who are not lucky enough to be born into a family of elites. The elites of a primitive society are always as perverted as anyone else, but they have the resources to pretend otherwise, or to buy their way out of trouble if they get caught. Humanity has the potential to become beautiful, but repression turns that which by its nature is beautiful into a horrible, ugly thing. Every repressive is a pervert.

Jesus used to chuckle into his wine cup about these things. "Sonny-Bob, for a while I used to get pissed off at these people, but now I just laugh. What else can you do? It's the most comical show imaginable. They make laws against the darkness, yet even the part that makes the laws is an aspect of the darkness. The darkness makes laws against itself. These people haven't a clue as to what the light is, and it'll be thousands of years before most of them even catch a glimpse of it. They'll continue their foolishness for incarnation after bloody incarnation and never realize what it's all about. They lack the dedication to purify themselves of their illusions and to reach for the truth and love of their own souls.

"Publican! Gimmie more wine."

Well, it was 1984 and things hadn't changed much. But the changes would begin in a few more decades. I guess patience is a virtue.

And so I had to take leave of my family and abandon them to this barbaric time. I made love to them all, including Freud.

"Freud, this isn't as good as doing it with a woman," I grunted.

"I know," he gasped. But we didn't stop.

"My sweetlings, if I don't go back to my own century soon, the generals will probably send someone after me. Be wise, don't be ruled by your shadows like the repressives are. Become one with all aspects of yourselves and purify and integrate the outer form. Then submit that dark, pure outer form to the rulership of the soul. For each of us truly is

Soul. Stay centered in your hearts. I love you all.

"Mimi, I'd like to spend a moment with you."

She came up to me with Pa Miyamoto at her breast.

"Honey, it never ends between us." I stroked her cheek. "But I think it's getting better. Now we truly know one another; you've helped me wake up. I thank you for being you. You are the greatest gift possible to me and the planet. I love you forever and ever and ever."

"Oh, Sonny-Bob!" She was sobbing; she leaned her body into mine and with her free hand she clasped my neck and drew me into her.

I breathed her odor for the last time. She was the odor of springtime earth and the promise of abundant life. I was hers forever. My heart was pledged to her.

With my face in her raven dark hair I absorbed all I could of her fragrance to carry back with me into the future. She was the mother of us all. Pa Miyamoto squalled at her breast, but for once he wasn't throwing punches.

"Until we meet again, my love." I stroked her hair. "And Pa, we'll meet again in 2100, the year I was born. You were there. I am descended from you."

Mimi and I kissed, and it was a forever kiss, and her breath would be with me always. I kissed Pa, and in this moment he was strangely calm. He looked at me with his wizard's eyes. A voice spoke in my head. "I look forward to our boar hunts together, Sonny-Bob."

"Me too, Pa."

I got into Hubert and we left. There was a flood of grief in my heart, but it hadn't broken loose yet. It would.

And so Hubert and I were back at the TAC. "Old bean," my voice was strangely choking, "I've got to see The Tibetan."

"Okay." Hubert's heart was swollen with grief, too. He'd been saying goodbye to Tiffany for days; she really had a sweet soul and we'd both miss her. "Sonny-Bob . . ."

"Yes, Hubert?"

"I . . . I love you, Sonny-Bob. Now you're the only family I've got left."

"I love you too, Hubert. We've got each other, and we've got our memories."

"Yes . . . we've got our memories."

"I'll check with you later, okay?"

"Okay."

He was sniffling, then sobbing, as I walked toward the Administration

Building.

"I don't suppose you recognize me," I said to The Tibetan's door, "but I'm Sonny-Bob Culpepper. It's a little inconvenient for me to bend over and take off my shoes now, so don't ask me to. If you give me any hassle at all I'm going to bust you down. Now announce me and open up!"

"Yes, sir," the door said, and opened itself in kind of a trembling fashion.

I walked into the room. "Sonny-Bob!" The Tibetan exclaimed. "You're fat!"

"I know it," I replied, walking to the fridge behind his bar and pulling out a gallon of Yak's milk. I took the cap off and turned it up and guzzled. Mighty fine, mighty fine.

I belched with at least a touch of contentment as The Tibetan stared. I smacked my lips. "Well, I've had an interesting time of it, sir."

"I'll bet you have, Sonny-Bob. I'll bet you have."

He let me drink for a while, then when I'd finished the first jug and reached for a second he delicately cleared his throat. "We've all had dreams, Sonny-Bob."

"Good." I pooted and belched at the same time. The Tibetan crossed to his window and opened it.

"Sonny-Bob, please put that jug down and move away from my refrigerator. We *have* to talk."

I took a final extended guzzle. "Okay, sir." I put the jug down and went to the middle of the room.

"Sonny-Bob, nobody's ever had dreams like these before. Now practically everyone on earth's been having them. Over the last several decades many of us have had the traditional type of alternate reality dream where there was a change to the timeline, and then the timeline was changed back. But these new dreams aren't like those."

I pooted but said nothing, just stood there breathing heavily and perspiring, suited up in my rippling layers of fat.

He continued. "This planet has suffered many catastrophes over billions of years, but she's always pulled through. She's always survived. But in these recent dreams she died. I guess that's why they were so vivid and nearly every human being has had them. This is the first time anything of this magnitude has happened.

"And--" he swallowed heavily, "in the dreams the planet was depending on you to save it. That's why for many people the dreams were nightmares."

"Don't worry, Bossman," I finally said. "The planet's obviously still here."

"Yes . . . well, the generals have been chomping at the bit wanting to debrief you, and they've been on the verge of sending Captain Jenkins to drag you back."

"Olaf Jenkins?" I inquired mildly.

"Yes. I've managed to convince them to wait a little longer, not wanting to see, uh, friction develop between you and Olaf. I'd like him to live."

"Well, sir, he died in the alternate reality. He was a traitor and it's partly his fault the timeline disappeared and the earth died. I've already taken care of the other two traitors; you don't have to worry about them.

"Olaf had a change of heart and rejected his treason at the end and tried to reform, but he should be arrested anyway. The fact that he didn't betray his timeline in this reality is irrelevant. He is impure; he has a treasonous heart. He needs therapy."

"Yes . . . we'll deal with Captain Jenkins later, then. The generals want to see you and so does GNN . . . those newspeople are talking about making a documentary of your adventures based largely on the dreams! Can you believe that? But they've been holding off, hoping you'd pop back into the century and now you have. But you have to make a preliminary report to the generals before you talk to anyone else."

Suddenly the door slid back and a beam of sexy radiant beauty entered. "Hi, Lobsang honey! How do you like my new habit?"

It was Monica Lewinsky. I'd been right, with the timeline restored she'd popped back into the land of the living. She twirled around in her nun's habit, lifting it up a little so we could catch a bit of calf . . . then a bit of thigh. She wore a garter. Hemingway quickened.

I saw her sparkplug nipples had grown hard, and I felt my tongue sliding around my lips. Monica laughed. "I don't know who you are, but that huge bulge throbbing inside your pants leg is the biggest, fattest part of you."

"I'm Sonny-Bob. We met in the alternate timeline. You died, but I'm happy you're alive again."

"Oh!" She stopped twirling and her hand went to her throat. "So that was really real?"

"It was, but now it's not."

"Gosh! Thanks for saving me."

"My friends and I saved the timeline. Your salvation was just a side effect of that."

"Oh! Well, thanks anyway."

"You're welcome."

I wanted to put my hand between her legs, but The Tibetan was tugging on my arm. "Let's go, Sonny-Bob!" he grunted. "You can visit with Monica some other time. Right now we have to see the generals."

I let him pull me out of the room, but I turned and looked back at Monica before the door closed. She just smiled and lifted her habit and let me see her bush. It was as big as an adult porcupine.

I waited for a while outside the Council Chamber while The Tibetan prepared them for me. I guess he told them I was fat.

My feet hurt. I was getting ready to leave when The Tibetan appeared and grabbed me again. "Report to the Outer Chamber."

I went into the Outer Chamber and confronted the orderly. His eyes grew wide; I guess they had to be wide to take all of me in. "When I announce you, come into the Inner Chamber and stand before the generals."

I said nothing. He fluttered around for a minute, then disappeared into the dark mouth of the Inner Chamber.

Then he summoned me. "Lieutenant . . . or Captain . . ." the orderly stammered, "uh, *Officer* Sonny-Bob Culpepper reports to the Council of Generals!" His ringing tones echoed splendidly in the chamber.

I waddled into the room. "Howdy," I said.

The generals were pale and sodden with sweat. They looked ghastly. They appeared to be going through a crisis of faith.

"Lieutenant Cul--"

"I'm no lieutenant, General Morgan. I'm a captain. Show the proper respect."

"Yes, er, Captain Culpepper. The Tibetan has told you, I believe, about these incredibly lucid dreams we've all had. Almost everyone on earth has reported these dreams and people are seeking therapy in record numbers. Even the members of the Flat Timeline Society have gone into hysterics. Their faith has been shaken."

"They're not the only ones," General Mudd muttered.

"And, strangely enough," General Morgan continued, "there's actually some physical evidence that tends to . . . ah . . . well, it tends to point to the veracity of these dreams." He slumped in his chair, his face ashen. He waved his hand for someone else to continue.

General Mann cleared her throat. "Yes, the evidence." She took a very, very deep breath. "A legend was begun in the early twenty-first century by a psychotherapist named Freud. According to the legend, a nuclear winter was averted and the timeline saved by a warrior from the future named Culpepper. This Freud briefly sketched out the legend in a textbook he authored, then wrote a novel about it which made the bestseller lists and drove everyone into a frenzy."

She breathed heavily and I watched her heaving breasts. A button flew off her blouse and I caught it. I put it in my pocket.

"The character of the Culpepper in the novel is surprisingly similar to your own, if I may use your name in the same sentence as the word 'character' . . ." she panted. She was hot, she was flushed, she couldn't go on. She passed the baton to someone else.

"Is it possible," General Feingold asked, an expression almost of horror, perhaps, on his usually smart-ass controlling face, "is it possible, Culpepper, that we owe our entire civilization . . . to *you*?"

"I would say, sir, that it is not impossible."

He fainted. So did some of the others.

I shrugged and left. If they wanted to talk to me again they could do it at a time I found convenient.

I went home. The Bluebird sat on her nest. "Hello, honey," I said. "I missed you."

"Where've you been, Boss!" she squawked. "I've been having these dreams, everyone has. I dreamed I'd been dissolved by a timewave and you were my only hope! Were those dreams true?"

"Yes, honey," I said gently. "But you don't have to worry now. The timeline's okay and so are you. I love you, Bluebird. I wouldn't let you down."

"Oh, Sonny-Bob! I love you, too. I do!"

"I know, sweetheart. I've got to go inside now and rest my feet. I'll see you tomorrow, okay?"

The next day the Bluebird carried me to Mimi's monument where our old house had stood on Lake Travis. The house was gone now, but there was a golden pyramid in what had been the front yard. It always caught the rising sun and you could see the light reflected for miles and miles. It was a monument to all the family, really.

I'd never known who those other people sketched out around the base were; I guess I'd just figured they represented people who were special to Mimi. But now I knew them and they were special to me, too. There was Freud and Aphrodite and Sue and Tennessee. There was the infant Miyamoto. And there was some great fat oaf whom I now saw every day in the mirror.

Mimi's image rose above us all, her shining arms embracing us each day in the dawn.

I went to see Amanda. Her warm embrace relaxed me and was a

tonic to my heart. Compassion mingled with mischief on her radiant face, and the golden eyes of her love welcomed me home. "Sonny-Bob, we've all had the dreams. You're a hero."

"I'm no hero. If I am, I resign. The world is still here, but I left my world back in 1984. That's where I belong, with those people. They're my family and my friends of eternity."

Amanda paused and bit her lip. "You're right, Sonny-Bob. They're your friends of eternity. Separation is an illusion."

"I know that. And in my heart I sometimes feel it. But my gut hurts, like somebody harpooned me in the belly and then yanked everything inside me out. Most of the time my heart hurts, too."

She sat me down and knelt beside me and massaged my belly the way Mimi used to do. Then she massaged my heart. I won't say I felt any better. If anything, I felt worse because she'd got the energy of grief at losing my family moving, as well as the energy of anger at this heartless, inexorable timeline. I had to feel it now, and it pissed me off. I was mad; mad at the world, mad at the generals, mad at Amanda, who was always so happy. Mad at myself.

"Fuck all this, Amanda. I don't like you anymore. I'm not even sure I love you, either. You're always so happy, like the Lords of Karma never pissed on your parade.

"I've spent my life wallowing in shit. I spent years killing evil with the ERT and all it brought me was injury and nightmare. I run up and down the timeline doing my duty, and finally I even save the damn timeline. Save it for everybody except myself and my family. If this is what a hero is, then I quit. I don't want any more of it.

"Next time people can find someone else to preserve them. Either that, or learn to save their own damn selves."

The energy was moving. I had to feel it, had to feel it all before I could release it. But it hurt, and it made me want to hurt somebody. So I took it out on Amanda.

"You're always so damn happy. I'm sick of dealing with you. Why don't you let me alone?"

"You came to me, Sonny-Bob. And would you rather have a miserable person working with your energy?"

"Hell, no. You know I wouldn't. What I want--" and here I gave a great shuddering gasp, "what I want is not to exist anymore. It hurts too much. What I want is never to have existed at all.

"I'm not talking about never having been born, that's kid stuff. Only people who haven't suffered much wish they'd never been born. I wish I'd never existed, *period*. Not in any dimension. I wish I was a lot more extinct than dead people are.

"I want to be with Mimi and Freud and Sue and Aphrodite and Baby Miyamoto. I never got to see him grow up. And that cat, too, I want that cat. Tennessee's his name."

I'd just contradicted myself. I *did* want to exist, but only with my family.

"They're here now, Sonny-Bob. Your family. They surround you and are part of you. They're helping us with the work we're doing here today."

I could almost feel their compassion, could almost touch it. But I was still clogged with grief and it kept me from them. The very thing I felt at not being with them now kept me from them.

"The timeline sucks. I don't know why the universe is run this way."

Amanda, always compassionate and completely dedicated to her service, knelt before me and just laid her head in my lap and lifted up her hand and placed it on my heart. She was a queen and I was a bum, a bum who had just tried to hurt her, yet she still knelt before me. Her palm radiated its love onto my heart, but it couldn't break through the grief and anger. Not yet.

"Amanda, I'm sorry. I didn't mean to hurt you. Something's wrong with me and I can't make it right; I don't know what's wrong with me. You are the most beautiful person in the world, and yet I was cruel to you. I'm sorry and I know you'll forgive me, for that's one of the things you do. But I can't heal, I can't get well. I've lost everything. I would have sacrificed Hemingway to stay with my family."

Hemingway twitched uncomfortably. I reached around Amanda and patted him. "Don't worry, old fellow. There's no threat to you now."

I stroked Amanda's hair. "It's not going to break free today, dear lady. I don't know when it's going to break free, all that grief and guilt and anger. But I know it eventually will, if you'll continue working with me. It may take a long time, so be forewarned."

"Oh, Sonny-Bob! I love you and I'll work with you for the next millennium and beyond if that's what it takes. You can do it, you can heal, and I don't know how long it'll take, either. But I do know I'll be there with you as long as you want me to be."

I lifted her to me and kissed her. "That'll be forever, dearest friend. I want you with me forever."

She stayed in my arms for a bit and I stroked her hair, repenting of my harsh words. I knew those words were forgiven immediately by Amanda, but now I had to forgive myself. I also had to forgive Amanda for being so happy and peaceful. That may sound insane, but there it is:

I had to forgive Amanda her happiness.

At length I released her and we stood. I took her hands in my own. "Honey, you've been better to me than I deserve--"

She placed a finger on my lips. "Sonny-Bob, nobody could treat you better than you deserve. You deserve everything that is good and beautiful and true. You deserve everything wonderful that's locked away within your own sweet heart."

She kissed me, and it was mostly a kiss of breath with only a little tongue. Her breath would continue to dislodge the grief within me until the day it would vanish forever.

"Amanda, from my first day in the Twentieth I realized that the deepest desire of my heart is to be a Sacred Prostitute of Aphrodite. To do what you do, to be as you are. I'm so rough and crude I've never believed I could make it, so I just tried to ignore the dream. But it bit me on the ass--oops, sorry! That's what I meant--"

"Friend of a thousand lifetimes," Amanda said gently, "you are gifted with the ability to work with your shadow, and you are dedicated, dedicated. Whether you will be able to pass all the tests necessary to become an accepted prostitute remains to be seen. You might not--or you might. Most do not pass, even if they work at it for a dozen years. But warriorship is a good background for anyone who wants to become a healer.

"Before I give you the Probationer's test, though, I want you to heal from this grief you bear. I won't give the test to a person who's suffering this much grief. You'd start out at a disadvantage. Probationers certainly don't have to be perfect, nobody does. Perfection is an illusion, so instead of perfection we focus on a gentle flowing discipline that leads us to Love. But with as much pain as you now carry, you wouldn't pass the test. Your grief makes you leaden and heavy and you couldn't learn to really flow. So I'll keep working with you to process and release the grief and in two years' time we'll sit down together and decide if you're up for the Probationer's test. It's a test that requires creativity and a movement towards Love. That's all I can tell you. It's not like those insane standardized tests people had to take in ancient times. Our tests here are designed to bring out the individuality of your own heart. Your heart is beautiful. Once it's unclogged, you might pass.

"But I won't show you any favoritism, Sonny-Bob. You know that already. I'll shower you with love forever, but favoritism is out of the question."

"Yes, ma'am."

"Dear one, we're part of the same group already. That's a fact, and it's true forever. No external authority ever decides who shall become a Sacred Prostitute of Aphrodite. It's a long process of peeling away your illusions and coming to the truth of what you are. When your illusions are gone, you'll know you've already been living among us forever."

"Yes, ma'am."

"When you're one of us, you'll know it without having to be told. In the end, after your illusions are gone, it's a process of hearts coming together, hearts that already know one another and welcome each other home."

I'd just been given much to ponder, but I knew it'd probably do more good to simply sit with her words and try to feel the energy behind them. So I had much sitting to do.

She walked me from her office, her arm draped around me loosely. I guess some more grief dislodged, for tears of gratitude and love began to drop silently from my eyes. I knew that without Amanda and Lucille I would be nothing. I wouldn't have had a chance.

We came to the outer passage; the bright sunlight streamed in from the crystal panes above. We paused before the poem that adorns the wall just inside the entrance of every Temple of Aphrodite. This poem had been delivered to the world by Lucille The Prophetess at the dedication of her first temple near Lincoln, Nebraska.

THE WAR GOD HEALED

On the foam she came
Paphian Kythereia
the Goddess of Healing
with her heart aflame.
She saw a great cliff
a sheer rock of granite
and dying before it
the War God did lie.

She said, "Wargod Ares
awake from thy slumber
tell me what happened
do not turn away.
For long have I sought you
to comfort your spirit

and each time you rejected
the love that I gave."

The Wargod rolled over
and opened his eyes
and then with a gasp
and shudder he spoke,
"Oh fair Aphrodite
so long have I fled you
that like those small mortals
at last I must die.

"I battered and ravaged
and sought to destroy
each manifestation
of softness and joy.
I ranged the wide world
and fought all the battles
and conquered the nations
and owned everything."

Then said the Goddess
soft Aphrodite
incarnation of sweetness
all honey and light,
"Tough Wargod Ares
if the earth you rule over
how came you to this
and why must you die?"

"Paphian Kythereia!" the Wargod sobbed hoarsely
"Oh Aphrodite, you could have been mine
but I had to conquer
this planet before me--
hardness brought hardness
and will is a lie.

"Once I put out
but thrice I received it
unbridled will
no compassion in sight.

Hit by such force
no god could withstand it
smashed upon cliff face
flung from the sky.

"And now so you see
Paphian Kythereia
my will has been shattered
my ego is dead.
Please touch my brow
for one golden moment
with my last breath
I return to you now."

The fair Golden Goddess
did as requested
massaging the brow
of him who had died.
But life is subjective
and no one could measure
the effect of such softness
as his spirit did fly.

Amanda turned to me. "It's the same basic energy, my love. The energy of the warrior and the energy of the healer. If one is repressed, if an effort is made to avoid it, the other automatically burns itself out. This is the 'pendulum swing' so common to earlier societies. Two manifestations, but one energy. And the energy is Love.

"But to deny any aspect of one's self is not an act of love. This denial will take the individual or the society away from love, and collapse and death are inevitable. The only way for an individual or a society to be integrated is to allow both expressions of the underlying energy to manifest simultaneously.

"And I'm not talking about balancing the perceived opposites. I'm talking about full and unrestricted integration of the individual and of society. People or societies who focus on balancing the perceived opposites--indeed, people who perceive opposites at all--always become imbalanced. Seeking to balance the supposed opposites is comparable to walking on a thousand mile log over a bottomless pit. Sooner or later you'll fall off and suffering will result."

She grinned. "To use one of your expressions, anyone who falls into a bottomless pit will be scared shitless. And fear is the source of suffering. And since fear is an illusion and illusion is the absence of love, there's no underlying energy to catch the one who falls, there's just the brittle, cracking shell of illusion.

"But when we achieve integration we always have an underlying energy that we can withdraw into. We never fall, the energy of Love always holds us up. But we can withdraw at times and experience the full Beingness of the Love which we are. And when we decide to express as either the warrior or the healer, it flows from this Beingness, it flows from the love which each human being **IS**."

"Amanda," there were tears in my eyes, but I was beginning to feel a calm joy, thanks to the radiant healing presence of this serene woman of joy beside me, "Amanda, the grief is going. I had no idea it would begin to leave this soon. I guess there's lots more layers of it I'll have to process and release over the coming months, but at least it's started to leave. Thank you, my love."

"Thank *you*, sweetheart. For you bring out the best in me."

We simply stood poised in one another's energy for a moment. Then Amanda continued. "Our planet is beginning to know herself, Sonny-Bob. She's learning that she has to become integrated. And the human family is at last putting aside the childish duality we've been burdened with so long. Now we can at last begin to do our part to serve one another and to serve the Mother whose children we are.

"But again, we must never see our Mother only as Mother. She is becoming an integrated blend of all aspects of herself, just as we here at the Temple are trying to do.

"In terms of masculine and feminine aspects, a good blend of energy for our earth, and therefore our society, would be fifty-five percent feminine energy and forty-five percent masculine. But everyone is equal; no female is superior to any male by virtue of her gender. This planet's female, Sonny-Bob, so to be truly herself she must manifest a little more feminine energy than masculine. If we were on a masculine planet the reverse would be true."

We stepped to the edge of the corridor to let a line of Probationers pass. Most were adolescents and the majority were female, though there were a few who obviously were at least a few decades old. I thought I could tell the ones who would make it to First Degree. They had a certain determination and sincerity of purpose in their eyes. Some had the fierceness of warrior's eyes, but most had the calm deep dedication of healer's eyes. These determined ones, they might make it. There was no flippancy to them. They had some idea of the magnitude of the task that lay before them.

The warriors would have to evolve into healers and the healers into warriors. They would all have to purify and integrate their shadows, then learn to rule the outer form as living souls of love through their hearts.

I felt refreshed, and was sorry I'd ever doubted the ability of Amanda's presence to purify me. The guilt and grief and rage were gone and I was calm.

I took Amanda's hand as we watched these Probationers pass and I felt at one with the living universe and I knew I'd come home. The Temple was my home. I still didn't know if I had what it took to become a Sacred Prostitute of Aphrodite, or even a Probationer. But with Practical Immortality I could work on myself for the next millennium, if necessary. The Temple was my home; I could work on myself forever. One day I surely would qualify.

I glanced at Amanda and she was smiling at me. She seems to know everything in the universe.

A few weeks later Amanda asked me to marry her. I'd been waiting so long. I accepted and we embraced.

Now as I'm finishing this report, and about to be interviewed for the umpteenth time by those newspeople, I rejoice in the fact that Amanda and I have become pregnant. I don't know which of my friends will be first to manifest through Amanda's body, but I do know we'll glow together as true friends always do.

MEMO FROM THE TIBETAN
August 4, 2236

The Son of the World is no longer with us; Colonel Sonny-Bob Culpepper is dead. He was lost on a mission to the ancient land of Lemuria. He could not be saved.

The rescue team managed to revive Hubert and get him home. He's being repaired physically, and will shortly enter heavy therapy. His grief is shaking him apart, he cannot be consoled.

Now I have to break the news to Amanda, and the Bluebird, and the children . . .

A full report will follow, when I feel up to it.

EPILOGUE

A comforting blackness. I waited.
A golden-hued chorus singing around me,
vowels of love, vowels of peace . . .
Warmth in my heart and on my face.
I turned to face the warmth.
Stars, all radiant and singing . . .
I fell.

Two great moons nourished me.
I grew.

One day a lady named Amanda came to the door.
"I would speak with Lily," she said.
I went to her. I was comfortable with her,
and she smelled warm.
She dropped to her knees
and looked into my blue eyes.
I saw an eternity of love in hers.
She embraced me and kissed my cheek.
"Come to the temple when you are twelve."
Then she left.

More seasons passed. I grew.
I bled, and began to learn my own mystery.

Discipline . . .
Two seasons at the Temple with the other girls.
All Probationers.
There had been one hundred.
Twenty remained.

"To know your own heart,
you must be pure."
The Lady Amanda smiled.
"Purity comes with deprogramming.
'Repression Creates Perversion.'
Study on this."

Springtime, and I was fourteen.
It was time.
I looked into the mirror
and I loved myself,
and I loved my breasts and my vulva.
I loved my silky thighs.
It seemed I had a memory
of long ago,
of a giant who had been meaningful
to me . . .
he was gone now,
but something of his presence remained.
I breathed deeply
and centered myself in my heart,
and connected my heart
to the seat of my passion.
I went into the bedchamber to love,
and to be loved.

NOTES

You May Use This Space To Write Your
Own Thoughts And Feelings
Regarding The Journey You Have Just Experienced

www.ingramcontent.com/pod-product-compliance
Lightning Source LLC
Chambersburg PA
CBHW070922100726
47908CB00001B/66